SUSAN LEWIS

Wildfire

arrow books

Published by Arrow Books 2007

2 4 6 8 10 9 7 5 3

First published in Great Britain in 1997 by William Heinemann
First published in paperback in 1997 by Mandarin Paperbacks
Arrow Books
Random House, 20 Vauxhall Bridge Road,
London SW1V 2SA

www.rbooks.co.uk

Addresses for companies within The Random House Group Limited
can be found at:
www.randomhouse.co.uk/offices.htm

The Random House Group Limited Reg. No. 954009

A CIP catalogue record for this book
is available from the British Library

ISBN 9780099517795

The Random House Group Limited supports The Forest Stewardship Council (FSC), the leading international forest certification organisation. All our titles that are printed on Greenpeace approved FSC certified paper carry the FSC logo. Our paper procurement policy can be found at:
www.rbooks.co.uk/environment

Printed and bound in Great Britain by
CPI Cox & Wyman, Reading, RG1 8EX

To Gary

Acknowledgements

I must first and foremost thank all the staff at Ngala Game Reserve in the Kruger National Park, most particularly Ian Boyd, for the fun, excitement and invaluable help I received during one of the most fascinating and enjoyable trips I have made for research. My love and thanks also go to Glenn A. Baker and Mark Leonard for their unique Australian humour which gave such inspiration to the story. I should also like to thank Karen Lane for her wonderful introduction to South Africa and for the lovely time we had touring the wine regions and exploring Table Mountain.

I extend more love and thanks to Kay and Ted Stern who helped me so much with the Los Angeles part of the story; also to Jo Conner and Rose Fleury who helped me with background research. I also acknowledge and thank Sondra Krakower who gave me the benefit of her expert advice regarding Galina's mental instability.

My thanks also go to Stephen Kelly of De Beers for his guidance through the world of diamond dealing; to the management of La Mamounia Hotel in Marrakesh; to those who assisted me at the Hotel Grand Chalet in Gstaad and to Gerrie Pitt at the Four Seasons Hotel in Los Angeles.

'You will be like a shadow. They're going to see you, but they won't know who you are. You're going to follow them and carry out the instructions I give you. You'll begin by providing me with a detailed dossier on the woman. I want to know everything there is to know about her, no matter how trivial it might seem to you. Someone over in London has already been to work, the results are there, in that file. It's pretty straightforward, but I want more. The woman and three others will be flying out of London at the end of the week. You're going to leave New York tomorrow and be at the woman's destination when she gets there. The arrangements are made, you can collect your ticket at the airport.'

Randy Theakston's sharp grey eyes remained on the man who had spoken, even though he had stopped. He was a small man with a large face and a gaze that was as impenetrable as the bodyguard that flanked him. The millionaire philanthropist, as Theo Straussen liked to be known, had made use of her investigator's services several times in the past. The only difference now was that her assignment was taking her beyond the shores of the United States.

Randy was excited by the prospect, though nothing in her demeanour showed that. She was well schooled in the art of taciturnity, a must for someone in her profession. Her hair was grey, like her eyes, her middle-aged face blended easily in a crowd and her manner was as unimposing as her height. The only feature about Randy Theakston that might possibly get her noticed was the expensive cut of her otherwise unremarkable pants suit.

'Where is the woman heading?' she asked when Straussen showed no inclination to continue.

Straussen's lichen-green eyes narrowed, giving Randy the impression he was laughing. 'Some place in Africa,' he answered. 'The details will be with your ticket.' He took a fat Cuban cigar from the corner of his mouth and rested it on the ashtray in front of him. 'Oliver Maguire's movements over the next couple of weeks are taken care of,' he said. 'Right now he's here in New York, so you don't need to concern yourself there. Besides, I know all there is to know about Maguire. What I need is the low-down on her.'

Randy nodded, then, as though asking how much luggage she should take, she said, 'Will I need to carry a gun?'

Straussen's full-lipped mouth curved in a grandfatherly smile. 'It shouldn't be necessary,' he answered, 'but we'll see you have one anyway.'

'OK,' Randy said, putting down her pencil. 'Then there remains only one question – the woman's name.'

Straussen picked up his cigar and waited for one of his henchmen to strike a match, 'Her name', he said, 'is Edwardes. Rhiannon Edwardes. She's a journalist,' he went on, palming away a cloud of smoke, 'so don't get too close, 'cos the last thing we want is her getting wind of the fact she's being watched. Just observe and report back is all you do for now. Any more than that, I'll let you know.'

Chapter 1

'This is sensational,' Lizzy murmured.

Her eyes were shining in a way they hadn't for some time now, her arms were resting on the side of the jeep, while her short, curly blonde hair danced in the breeze. 'It's even better than I imagined,' she said. 'I mean, I don't think I've ever been anywhere that's made me feel quite so ...' She was shaking her head, searching for the right words, until her dark-blue eyes began to sparkle and lifting the brim of Rhiannon's safari hat, she whispered an outrageous account of how she was feeling through the mane of Rhiannon's fiery red hair. As they laughed, the open-topped landrover bounced over a jagged hole in the track, bumping their heads together.

Still laughing, Rhiannon straightened her hat and using the back of the seat in front to prop up her feet, she turned to survey the endless tangle of African bush, while thinking of how she too, now Lizzy came to mention it, was experiencing some particularly exhilarating surges of sexual abandonment. There was a very definite potency to the primitiveness of their surroundings, an hypnotic perfume to the wild aniseed and dry earth that curried the air. The setting sun inflamed the honeyed shades of the distant horizon, turning the forest of spiked, skeletal branches black against the sky; the primeval call of the wild was like an erotic chant on the senses.

'You sure it's not the proximity to old Androcles there that's getting to you?' Rhiannon whispered, nodding towards Andy Morrison the chief-ranger and joint-owner of Perlatonga Game Reserve whose land they were currently exploring.

'Who?' Lizzy blinked ingenuously, then smiled warmly to herself as she recalled the unmistakable throb of passion in Andy's voice when he had spoken about the lions earlier. As if he wasn't gorgeous enough with his ranger's sun-bronzed body, his sun-bleached hair and those positively indecent blue eyes! But when one added to that the seriousness he attached to his work, his deep and genuine love of the animals and the intense emotion that darkened his eyes and tensed his body when he spoke of them, he was, at least as far as Lizzy was concerned, the embodiment of every wicked fantasy she'd ever had - and some she was just getting acquainted with.

Lizzy's eyes slid over to Rhiannon's and the two of them grinned as, tossing her glorious hair back over her shoulder, Rhiannon gave a sigh of utter contentment.

'Zebra crossing,' Hugh quipped from the raised seat behind them as a zebra sprang out of the bushes and dashed across the path.

Everyone groaned with laughter as Andy slowed the jeep so they could try capturing the swiftly disappearing animal with their expensive cameras before it was obliterated completely by the prickly dry foliage and dwindling light.

'So come on then, Andy,' Hugh challenged, swinging the video camera down from his shoulder to rest it on the seat between Jack, the sound guy, and himself, 'you can tell *us*. Are they white with black stripes or black with white stripes?'

Andy grinned. 'You got me there, mate,' he answered, easing the jeep forward again.

'Are you managing to get much?' Rhiannon asked,

holding her hat in place as she turned to where Hugh was once again shouldering the video camera and training the lens on just about anything that moved. 'Surely it's too bumpy to get anything worthwhile.'

'Cinema verité,' Hugh grinned through his dense, silver-streaked beard.

Twisting round further so she could see Jack, Rhiannon winked, then turned quickly back as Andy brought the jeep to a standstill again. Elmore, the tracker, had got down from his seat on the bonnet and was standing in front of the vehicle, listening, sniffing the air and squinting through the twilight. He disappeared for a few minutes, leaving everyone waiting silently in the jeep, until returning from the thickening shadows he muttered something to Andy, then loped around to the back of the vehicle and sprang up behind Hugh and Jack.

'Looks like we got ourselves a couple of lionesses,' Andy explained, his Australian accent as mischievous and – at least to Lizzy's mind – as sensuous as his cobalt-blue eyes. 'So, you recall what I told you when we started out?' he went on. 'No standing up, no sudden movements or noises and for God's sake don't even think about getting out of the landie. They might look like great big cuddly old pussy-cats to you, but to them you look like tonight's barbie.'

Melanie, the teenage-spotted man-eater, as Lizzy had dubbed her, who was sitting beside Andy on the front seat, laughed a touch too loudly at Andy's attempt at humour, causing Rhiannon to smother a laugh of her own as Lizzy glared at the girl. Looks like an interesting night ahead, Rhiannon was remarking wryly to herself.

'Do you give the animals names?' Melanie asked as Andy put the jeep back into gear.

'Officially no,' Andy answered. 'We'll go in quietly,' he continued, inching slowly forward. 'If it's the beauties I think it is then you folks could be in for something of a treat.'

'Aren't you going to cock your rifle, Andy?' Melanie asked, managing to deep-throat the last few words as she leaned forward to where the Bruno .375 was clamped across the base of the lowered windscreen. As her fingers performed a blatant caress of the barrel, Andy allowed his eyes to linger a moment on the small, cone-shaped breasts beneath the clinging nylon of her polo-neck. Behind them Lizzy bristled and turned to Rhiannon, who was already grinning.

'I'm going to fucking kill her,' Lizzy muttered. 'No, I mean it,' she said when Rhiannon started to laugh. 'I've had just about all I can take of that little tramp with her teapot tits and sebaceous gland disorder ...'

'Sssh, she'll hear you,' Rhiannon warned, her brown eyes dancing.

'I couldn't give a flying fuck what she can hear,' Lizzy grumbled, grudgingly keeping her voice low, while turning to gaze at the shrubs and trees as the landrover moved from the track and began to plough steadily through the orange light of the bush.

Fifty or so metres in, after a muted exchange with Elmore, Andy slowed to a halt and peered through the almost impenetrable density of thorny acacias and mopane trees. 'There she is,' he murmured, pointing straight ahead.

Five pairs of intense, eager eyes followed the direction of his arm, straining to see through the knotted limbs of the bushveld.

'Oh my God,' Rhiannon breathed, lowering her feet to the floor as she caught the movement of a huge sandy-coloured beast where it lay panting in the long grass some ten or twelve feet away.

'Can you see it?' Lizzy whispered excitedly. 'Where? Where is she?'

'Right through there,' Rhiannon answered, pointing.

'There,' Hugh repeated, taking Lizzy's head between his hands and facing her in the right direction. 'Do you see her?'

'Holy Mary, Mother of God,' Lizzy chanted in disbelief. '*That* is a lion.'

'Lioness,' Melanie corrected her, keeping her eyes straight ahead and a trembling hand on Andy's muscular forearm.

'Didn't you say there were two?' Rhiannon asked softly, after smothering a laugh at the way Lizzy's hand made a chopping motion behind Melanie's neck.

'Reckon there're more than that,' Andy responded, starting up the engine and reversing back a little. 'We're going to circle round to the other side; should be able to get a better view from there.'

Rhiannon glanced back over her shoulder to check that Hugh had the camera running, then signalled to Jack to put a mike on Lizzy to record her reactions.

A few minutes later they were in the clearing, watching in total thrall as a dozen or more lion cubs of varying size and age frolicked and tumbled in the grass under the watchful eyes of five magnificent, though rather sleepy-looking, lionesses. It was hard to get a grip on the reality of being so close – close enough to hear their laboured breath and smell the sour stench of their bodies.

Rhiannon and Lizzy laughed softly as a lioness batted one of her annoying offspring with a giant paw, somersaulting him back into the midst of his siblings, where he picked himself up, shook himself down, then bounced back into the attack on his mother.

'It's the Perlatonga Pride,' Andy told them, his voice husky with emotion.

'Where's the male?' Lizzy asked.

'There are three males,' he answered. 'They won't be far away. Probably sleeping off their banquet. Look.' He pointed away to the left where the twisted bones of a stripped, bloodied carcass were just visible in the fading light. 'See the horns?' he said. 'It would have taken all five of these girls to bring that old buffalo down. There are more bones over there, seems like they've had themselves a regular feast.'

'Is it true that the lionesses do the hunting?' Lizzy wondered.

'For the pride, yes,' Andy replied. 'If the males aren't part of a pride, they hunt for themselves. Look up.'

Everyone tilted their heads towards the crimson sky.

'Vultures,' Rhiannon murmured.

Melanie shivered and wriggled in closer to Andy, dropping her hand to his thigh.

Andy either didn't, or pretended not to notice as he turned to watch Hugh train his lens on the speckled heavens, capturing the ominous circling of the avine predators.

'Uh, oh, seems like we're on the move,' Lizzy murmured as first one, then two more lionesses rose slowly to their feet.

As Andy turned, a smile of almost paternal indulgence curved his lips. 'Think you'll find they're telling us that the show's over,' he said. 'The girls are tired, they're going to find somewhere a bit more private to rest up.'

As the lionesses ambled away into the sanctuary of the darkening bush the cubs trotted along after them, getting under their feet and pouncing on each other as they rolled in the dust. It was hard to believe that these playful little creatures would one day become the most dominant and ferocious beasts of the wild.

It was a while after the last one had disappeared into the shadows before Andy restarted the landrover. As he did so Elmore spoke to him from the back and turning to look in the direction Elmore was pointing Andy started to laugh.

'Come on little fellow,' he said, as a bewildered, bleary-eyed little cub spilled out into the clearing. 'You're going to get left behind.'

'Oh God, he's so cute!' Lizzy laughed as the cub cocked his head inquisitively in their direction. 'How old would he be?'

'Around twelve weeks,' Andy answered.

'Oh, he's coming over,' Melanie squealed, making a dive across Andy's lap to hold her hands out to the cub.

Tipping her swiftly back into her seat, Andy turned to check that none of the others had been tempted to do the same.

'Surely a little thing like that won't do me any harm,' Melanie pouted.

'Probably not,' Andy conceded. 'But what do you reckon to his mother?'

'She's not here, is she?'

'Just sit tight,' he told her. 'And nobody move.'

They didn't have long to wait before the lioness returned in search of her cub, who was by now trying to jump up on the landrover. As she stalked imperiously towards them, Rhiannon saw Andy's body tense, though in the soft evening light his face showed none of the unease she could feel thudding in her own heart.

'Hello old girl,' he murmured softly. 'How are you doing now, mm?'

Rhiannon and the others watched, spellbound, as the lioness approached, her mean yellow eyes fixed on Andy's, the power emanating from the movements of her magnificent body seeming almost palpable in the dampening night air.

By the time she reached the jeep not a soul inside it was breathing. Her eyes were still on Andy. She was so close now he could feel her odorous breath warming his face. Her jaws were parted, the deadly incisors gleaming yellow and stained with blood.

It seemed like an eternity that she stood there, gazing into Andy's eyes, her tail twitching randomly over her back, her mighty chest heaving as she panted.

'Is she going to attack?' Melanie wailed.

Rhiannon and Lizzy tensed. Jack swore under his breath. Hugh kept the camera running, praying he wasn't about to record a sight he never wanted to see.

'No, she's not going to attack, are you, mate?' Andy said soothingly. Rhiannon half-expected him to reach out and stroke the lioness's neck, but so far he hadn't made a single move, not even for the gun.

Then a deep, gutteral sound rumbled softly in the lioness's throat as her golden eyes narrowed and she sank slowly back on her haunches.

Rhiannon felt Lizzy's fingers burying into her leg.

Melanie whimpered and recoiled deep into the far corner of the seat.

Andy was very still. It was as though the entire bush was pausing, waiting for the lioness to spring. Her eyes were piercing, her jaw was open, revealing the great predator's teeth. The only movement was from the cub as he frolicked around her giant paws.

Then suddenly the ground started to shake as a deafening, thunderous noise rumbled through the earth, seeming to echo right into the very depths of the jeep, filling the soggy warmth of the air with a sound as compelling as it was terrifying.

Lizzy turned wide, disbelieving eyes to Rhiannon. 'Was that what I think it was?' she murmured as the stentorian roar ebbed into the wittering chafe of bugs and bats and awakening night birds.

'You mean, dad?' Rhiannon whispered, smiling as she nodded for Lizzy to watch the lioness again. 'I think so.'

When Lizzy turned back it was to find the lioness once more on her feet, her topaz eyes blinking at Andy, the cub dangling from her whiskery jaws.

'The old man's calling,' Andy reminded her, still looking very much as though he was about to touch her.

The lioness stood her ground, seemingly oblivious to the struggling offspring in her mouth. Then, with no warning, she lifted a paw on to the door of the jeep. Her giant claws were only inches from Andy's heart, the size of it, the sheer deadliness of it was turning everyone's blood cold. The jeep listed under her weight, then with one final blink she turned round and padded off into the darkness, the cub still swinging from her teeth.

'Don't tell me,' Rhiannon murmured as the others let go a collective breath of relief, 'you once removed a thorn from her foot.'

Andy laughed. 'Not quite,' he answered. 'But I do know her. She's the lady I was telling you about earlier. The one who got caught in a poacher's trap and almost died. She was preggers at the time, so I guess you could say we didn't only save her, we saved the youngsters too.'

Lizzy's eyes widened in disbelief. 'Do you mean she was showing you one of the cubs you saved?' she said.

Andy shrugged and started up the jeep. 'Could be,' he answered. 'Impossible to say for sure.'

Rhiannon and Lizzy looked at each other.

'Please don't tell me you don't have a name for her,' Rhiannon said opening up her notebook, 'because I won't believe it.'

Andy grinned. 'Sorry to disappoint you,' he answered, turning to look over his shoulder as he reversed back to the track.

'You nurse a fully grown lioness back to health and you don't give her a name?' Rhiannon protested. 'No, I'm sorry, I'm not buying it. You treated her like she was a pet, you weren't even afraid of her ...'

'Oh, I'm afraid of her all right,' he insisted. 'She's as likely to kill me with affection as she is to rip out my heart in hunger. And her name's Sheila. As in, brace yourself, Sheila, which was what we recommended she do when we removed the trap from her shoulder. 'Course she was drugged at the time, but it seemed kind of appropriate.'

Laughing, Rhiannon leaned back in her seat and turned to Lizzy.

'Isn't he just divine?' Lizzy mouthed.

'Mmm,' Rhiannon yawned, stretching her arms above her head and turning her face to the night sky. The sight that greeted her took her breath clean away. 'Oh my God, will you look at that!' she marvelled, gazing up at the Milky Way. The stars were so thickly clustered together that in places they appeared like jewel-studded clouds, smudged and glittering and almost obliterating the night sky. 'Can we get a shot of it, Hugh? Will it come out?'

'We can give it a go,' he answered, heaving the camera back on to his shoulder. 'Can we hold it a minute, Andy?'

'God, this place is so romantic, isn't it?' Lizzy sighed, leaning her head back on Rhiannon's shoulder as they stared up at the sky together and waited for the land-rover to move on. 'I'll bet you're thinking about Oliver,' she smiled.

Rhiannon nodded. 'Yes,' she answered, feeling her heart go out to Lizzy for despite her undoubted attraction to Andy there was no question whom Lizzy would be thinking about.

A few minutes later the hiss and crackle of static broke into the silence and as Andy spoke into the radio Elmore climbed back on to his perch at the front of the jeep.

'What now?' Rhiannon asked Andy as they started to drive on.

'Now?' he answered. 'We start heading back to camp. Could be we'll see a couple of leopards, maybe even a cheetah, on the way. You probably just heard Gary on the radio with a rhino sighting, cow and calf, over by the Oppiedam. We could go that route, see if we can catch a glimpse.'

'Sounds good to me,' Rhiannon responded, stifling a yawn as she followed the beam of Elmore's spotlight into the trees.

This particular film-trip was one they'd all been looking forward to ever since it was first mooted, several weeks ago now, as it was the first time in months that the *Check It Out* team had assigned themselves something as pleasurable, not to mention benign, to check out as a holiday destination. Normally they were involved in considerably more complex and often sensational investigations and as their programme was transmitted on both terrestrial and satellite TV, they tried to give it as international a flavour as possible. On the whole this seemed to be working, for the audience rating was rising all the time and the ever-increasing mail bag showed that they had captured the imagination of audiences around the world with the diversity of subjects they covered. Subjects which ranged from a behind-the-scenes look at experiments with new drugs; to an hilarious half- hour on a Singapore student who was attempting to make the *Guiness Book of Records* by having sex with three hundred men in ten hours; to an in-depth report on the manipulators of the world's money markets and the resulting crises in a nation's economy.

Having made its début as an independent production company some fourteen months ago, *Check It Out* had already more than doubled its number of staff and there was talk now of running the programme for ten months of the year instead of the seven they were currently contracted for. As a director of the company and the show's executive producer Rhiannon Edwardes was effectively the head of their expanding team, but there were two people to whom, in theory at least, she was answerable, though if they called her more than once in a couple of months she would jokingly consider herself harassed.

Sally and Morgan Simpson, both of whom were ex-BBC producers, had taken their redundancy pay-offs from Auntie around two years before and used it to set up *Check It Out* Productions. The initial idea had been for Morgan to run the company with Rhiannon, their senior researcher from BBC days, as the main producer and

Sally, who was somewhat jaded by television after more than twenty years in the Beeb's current affairs department, as a fill-in producer if and when she was needed. It didn't take long, however, for the Simpsons to realize that handing the whole operation over to Rhiannon was probably the best, if not the only, route to go if the company was going to succeed, for Rhiannon had a freshness to her approach that had long since withered on the Simpsons' vine, and her enthusiasm for the newly conceived programme as well as her somewhat unorthodox ideas when it came to staffing, were all just a bit too much for diehards like the Simpsons to take on board. So with the minimum of fuss, the Simpsons had promoted Rhiannon to executive producer, made her a company director with equal shares, appointed themselves consultants, then taken off for an early retirement in the West Indies.

To have had it all handed to her on a plate that way was a dream come true for Rhiannon who had always hoped that one day, probably far into the future, she might be running her own company. But here she was, not even in her thirties yet and already at the helm of one of the year's most talked-about programmes, with a happy, hard-working team of journalists and technicians who were the envy of their peers from whom Rhiannon received a constant stream of CVs, videos and letters all but pleading for jobs. Experience had shown Rhiannon that with the right team, in other words the right blend of personalities, there was much to be gained from handing over the programme's reins to a researcher, a cameraman, a production assistant or a presenter in order to enhance their knowledge and appreciation of programme making, as well as to allow them the satisfaction of taking control of their own projects. This meant that it wasn't unheard of for Rhiannon to assume the role of research assistant, camera assistant or even office co-ordinator, though on this particular trip she was the producer while Lizzy, who thanks to the show had become a household name, assumed her normal role of presenter.

Melanie's role needed some work in the defining, for she had only joined the team a couple of months ago when, a bit like Paddington, she'd turned up in London with a note from the Simpsons – her parents – asking Rhiannon to give her a job and do what she could to see that their wayward eldest didn't get into too many scrapes. Rhiannon had been less than thrilled, but seeing that she hadn't much choice, she'd collected the girl from the airport, installed her in the Simpsons' London flat and put her on staff. Since when, Melanie had done precious little to ingratiate herself with anyone, least of all Rhiannon, had shown next to no interest in the programme and despite her generous salary was constantly borrowing from the rest of the team.

It was just after nine o'clock when the landrover finally pulled into the clearing at the edge of the camp. The other half-dozen jeeps that had driven the Reserve's other guests into the bush had already returned and early evening drinks were being served around the campfire.

'Mmm, dinner smells good,' Andy commented as the delicious aroma of freshly barbecueing impala drifted towards them.

Elmore, his gleaming ebony skin almost lost in the darkness, hopped down from his seat and opened the door for Melanie to get out, while a couple of willowy blonde assistants emerged from the reception area to take Andy's gun and help Hugh and Jack with their equipment. Rhiannon was on the point of gathering up her own things when she noticed Elmore's dazzlingly white smile as he gazed down at Melanie, who was staring up at him with such blatant allure that Rhiannon's mouth fell open in amazement. When, she wondered, had Melanie switched her sights from Andy to Elmore?

She turned to Lizzy who was zipping her camera back into her bag. 'What's the routine now?' Lizzy was asking, glancing up at Andy.

Taking the keys from the ignition, Andy turned round and resting his arms on the back of the seat he started to grin. Rhiannon watched in the half-light as his gorgeous blue eyes twinkled mischievously into Lizzy's.

'How does a quick shower followed by a screaming orgasm grab you?' he drawled.

Rhiannon choked as Lizzy's eyes dilated.

'It's a cocktail,' Hugh informed them, tucking the camera under his arm and winking at Andy as he hopped down from the back of the jeep.

'Oh,' Lizzy responded, starting to grin. 'What a disappointment.'

Andy laughed. 'Maybe we'll see how many you can handle in a night.'

As he climbed out of the landrover, Lizzy turned to Rhiannon. 'You might have to fly me home on a stretcher,' she warned.

Laughing, Rhiannon hooked her bag over her shoulder and reached out to take the hand of one of the camp's security guards who was waiting to help her down. Jack and Hugh were already in the covered reception with the blondes and Melanie was wandering off into the night with Elmore. She turned to where Lizzy was being helped down from the jeep by Andy and found herself starting to smile. They'd only flown in from Johannesburg that afternoon, so it certainly didn't seem to be taking long for the fabled aphrodisiac of the bush to start working its magic. In Lizzy's case, however, Rhiannon was only too aware of how fragile the euphoria was, for it was only distance and novelty that was encouraging Lizzy to shed her inhibitions as recklessly as she was. Not that Rhiannon had any intention of bringing her back to earth, for the last thing Rhiannon wanted was to be the voice of caution when she hadn't seen Lizzy this excited since the accident that had shattered her life.

'Ben'll show you to your chalet, Rhiannon,' Andy told her as they joined Hugh and Jack in reception.

'I take it you're Ben,' Rhiannon said, looking up at the security guard's beautiful African face.

'Yes ma'am,' he grinned.

To her surprise Rhiannon felt herself starting to blush and treated Hugh to a swift kick on the shin as he gave her a playful nudge.

'I'll take Lizzy,' Andy said, talking to the blondes. 'You can take the guys. Now listen up, everyone,' he continued, 'you've got half an hour to clean up, then the guards will be back to collect you to bring you across for dinner. Don't venture out of the chalets on your own. The camp's bigger than you think and we don't want anyone getting lost. More importantly, when you finally retire for the night you'll be shown back to your chalets and if you come out after that you do so in peril of your life. I'm not joking about this, the animals frequently roam the camp at night and you and your seasoned flesh will make a tasty meal for a *penthera pardus* or two.'

'A what?' Lizzy asked.

'A leopard,' he translated. 'Or a lion. Or a cheetah. There are plenty of them out there, so be warned. We've never had an accident at Perlatonga yet, so we don't want one of you guys to be the first. OK?'

As the others went off in vaguely the same direction, each being led by their appointed guide, Lizzy stood for a moment with Andy as he watched Rhiannon disappear along a tree-shadowed pathway with Ben. She was curious to see if he would comment on Rhiannon's stunning figure, but then they both laughed as Hugh's voice rang out of the darkness telling Rhiannon to treat the boy gently.

Slinging Lizzy's bag over his shoulder, Andy started along a narrow twisting path towards her chalet. 'You'll get to meet my brother, Doug, when you come over for dinner,' he told her, holding a branch out of the way for her to pass. 'He arrived a couple of hours ago from Jo'burg.'

'Is he older or younger than you?' Lizzy enquired, ducking away from a giant moth and raking her fingers through her curls to make sure it hadn't landed.

'Older. We've got two more brothers back home in Oz. They'll be taking over from the old man on the farm. It doesn't need four of us, so Doug and I decided to set up here. We've both got a passion for animals and since the old man met Carlita, his second wife, on safari here in the Kruger he developed a kind of fondness for the place. So Doug and I didn't have too much trouble persuading him to put up the moolah to get us started.'

'You're lucky to have such a wealthy father,' Lizzy commented, stepping into the light of the little veranda at the front of her thatch-roofed chalet and turning to face him.

His eyebrows went up as he nodded, but it was clear that his thoughts were a long way from his father as he gazed lazily into her eyes. Then his mouth curved in a half-smile as he lowered his eyes to her lips.

'Yeah, I guess you could say that,' he said, leaning an arm on the wooden post beside him while continuing to gaze shamelessly at her mouth and thinking about exactly where he would like those unbelievably sensuous lips to be.

'I'd say it makes you and your brother something of a catch,' she said, knowing what effect she was having on him and feeling the deliciously slow burn of response between her legs.

'Yeah, I reckon it does,' he agreed. 'Me, anyhow. Doug's already kind of spoken for.'

Lizzy nodded thoughtfully. 'Well,' she smiled, 'I think I'd better go and prepare myself for a screaming orgasm.'

'Just one?' he queried, raising an eyebrow.

Looking brazenly into his eyes, she pressed a finger lightly to his lips, then floated off into her chalet.

Chuckling to himself Andy started back through the camp, knowing full well that he was on for tonight. Not for nothing had game rangers been dubbed the sex gods of the bush by a Cape Town journalist, though it wasn't often that the sport came with the kind of chassis Lizzy Fortnum could boast. As readily available, sure, but they were rarely, if ever, under fifty and never did they have the kind of lips that gave such eastern promise to a blow job.

Looking up as he passed Rhiannon's chalet, he saw her at one of the windows pulling closed the shutters. Hidden by the darkness, he paused for a moment to watch her. She wasn't, at least by his standards, what could be described as a beauty, she had too many freckles for that and her features, on the whole, were pretty shambolic; eyes too small, nose too big, mouth kind of sloppy ... But boy, did she have a body! What he couldn't imagine doing with sheilas like that. And all that flaming red hair that could only mean a real, honest-to-goodness golden doughnut between those gorgeous long legs of hers. But Rhiannon Edwardes, tempting as she was, was strictly off-limits. Which was something he'd better remind Doug about, since one thing neither of them ever did was cut in on another bloke's dance, especially not a mate's. And Oliver Maguire, the international diamond dealer and Straussen-backed magnate, was not only a mate, he was also crazy bang in love with Rhiannon Edwardes.

Chapter 2

By the time Ben, the security guard, returned to take Rhiannon over to dinner she had showered and changed into a simple, round-necked, sleeveless black dress, low-heeled black pumps and the gold necklace and bracelet that Oliver had given her on their one-month anniversary. As she followed Ben towards the flickering gaslights on the tables around the campfire, nodding politely to the other guests as she passed, she was sorely wishing that Oliver were there now. The whole place exuded such a heady feeling of romance that it just didn't feel right to be here without him. Still, only eight more days and they'd be together again, she comforted herself as she sat down at the table allocated to the crew, her mouth watering at the delicious aroma wafting over from the barbecue.

Being the first to arrive at table, she helped herself to a bite-sized quiche from the hors d'oeuvre tray, then taking out her notebook, slid the candle a little closer and began to jot down a couple of questions she wanted to ask Andy tonight before she lost him to Lizzy. They were only planning to be on the Reserve for a couple of days and if everyone was going to prove as distracted as she feared, it was up to her to make sure they went away with enough material to make a programme. She arched a humorous eyebrow as she attempted to second-guess what Lizzy might put into her commentary, as the normal documentary conventions had been abandoned by *Check It Out* from day one. Meaning that if the African bush made you want to tear off your clothes and roll around in wild, sexual abandon with the nearest ranger, then that would be exactly what Lizzy would say.

Looking up as Melanie pulled out a chair to sit down Rhiannon met the girl's persistent antagonism with an amiable smile. 'Hi,' she said, noticing a radiant Elmore hovering beside Melanie and fleetingly wondering what the Simpsons would say were they ever to find out that their precious daughter had seduced the strapping young son of a Zulu chief. At least, if Elmore's grin was anything to go by, Melanie had. To look at Melanie you'd think she'd just got her face stuck in the plughole.

'Hi,' Melanie responded, slumping moodily into the chair and bunching her hands between her knees. From the way she was dressed she was obviously undergoing some kind of fashion transition between grunge and Fifties, for beneath her mandarin-collared short-sleeved shirt her bra cups were like ice-cream cones and the femininity of her flouncy net-petticoated skirt was thuggishly challenged by Dr Marten boots and a pair of steel-studded wristbands.

'Ah, you're already here,' Lizzy exclaimed, coming up behind Rhiannon and planting a kiss on her cheek. 'Mmm, you smell good.'

'And you look good,' Rhiannon replied, watching her sit down.

'Thank you.' Lizzy's smile was lovely as the gloss on her lips shimmered in the candlelight and her blue eyes shone with laughter. 'Did you call the office?' she asked.

'Oh my God, I forgot!' Rhiannon gasped, clapping a hand to her mouth. Then frowning she said, 'Was I supposed to?'

Laughing, Lizzy pulled in her chair. 'Not unless you particularly wanted to,' she answered. 'Didn't the others take off for Paris today?'

'To look into this French Gestapo thing,' Rhiannon nodded. 'Yes, of course they did.'

'Which means that only Jolene will be in the office and he'll have gone home hours ago,' Lizzy told her, 'so you can relax.'

'Thank you,' Rhiannon said graciously. 'Now, what's happened to the boys? Ah, here they are. Hugh, did you bring your guitar? I thought you might give us a few songs after dinner.'

'Depends how many screaming orgasms they've got lined up for me,' he responded. 'Either of you tried one yet?'

'I was just about to take orders,' Andy replied, joining them. 'But before I do let me introduce my brother, Doug, the other half of Perlatonga.'

As they looked up, both Rhiannon and Lizzy started to laugh with surprise.

'You didn't mention you were twins,' Lizzy said, throwing a quick look at Andy as she shook hands with Doug, who was every bit as tall and good-looking as his brother. 'Hi, I'm Lizzy,' she told him. 'And this is Rhiannon, our producer. Hugh, our cameraman. Jack our sound recordist. And over there is Melanie our ...'

'Trainee,' Rhiannon supplied, taking Doug's hand and smiling warmly into his eyes. As he looked back, to her surprise, she felt herself starting to colour, but fortunately the moment was swallowed into noisy introductions to Hugh and Jack, who sounded very much as though they had already made a start on the beers in their chalets.

'OK, Elmore, screaming orgasms all round,' Andy said, rubbing his hands together as he sat down at the head of the table between Lizzy and Hugh. Doug raised an arm to beckon for a waitress, then took a place at the other end of the table between Jack and Melanie. Rhiannon was in the middle with an empty chair opposite. The general noise level was starting to increase now as someone raised the volume on the CD player and a few couples from other tables began to jive under the trees.

'I was wondering,' Rhiannon said to Andy, dragging her eyes from Hugh who was leaning back in his chair and whispering to the blonde who'd escorted him to his chalet earlier. Never, in the seven years she'd known Hugh had he ever been unfaithful to his wife, but from the look on the girl's face and the unmistakable gleam in Hugh's eye Rhiannon strongly doubted she'd be able to say the same tomorrow. The power of African nights!

'You were wondering,' Andy prompted.

'Uh, yes. I was wondering about the safari suite,' she said, collecting her thoughts. 'If it's free I think we should get some shots.'

Andy glanced at Doug and both men grinned. 'Sure,' Andy responded. 'But you'll have to get in quick. It's booked out from tomorrow night and I don't think the guest we've got arriving will take too kindly to being interrupted by a TV crew. He kind of values his privacy.'

'Oh?' Lizzy remarked, intrigued. 'Who is he? Somebody famous?'

'Like I said, he values his privacy,' Andy told her, giving her a quick wink. 'But sure, you can do it when we get back from the game drive in the morning. He shouldn't be arriving until around midday.'

'What time do we start out in the morning?' Jack wondered.

'You'll get a call at five. We'll hit the dirt at five thirty. Breakfast is whenever we get back, which should be around nine or ten.'

'Will you be coming with us tomorrow, Doug?' Rhiannon asked, turning to him.

'Not in the morning,' he answered. 'Maybe on the afternoon drive.' He looked past her to where Elmore was approaching with a tray of cocktails.

'You call that a screaming orgasm!' Lizzy protested

when she saw the innocuous-looking cocktail in a white-wine-sized glass and not an umbrella or firework in sight.

'Don't be fooled by appearances,' Andy warned.

'What's in it?' Rhiannon asked, taking one from the tray.

'Trade secret,' he answered. 'But the base is tequila.'

Feeling Doug's eyes on her, Rhiannon turned to him and smiled. He smiled back and raised his glass.

'Welcome to Perlatonga,' he said, addressing them all. 'I hope it's going to live up to your expectations.'

Rhiannon allowed her eyes to linger on his face for a moment, thinking that his looks were marginally less obvious than Andy's making him, at least in her eyes, rather more attractive.

'I hear you met Sheila and her cubs this afternoon,' he said, bringing his eyes back to Rhiannon.

Rhiannon smiled. 'We certainly did,' she confirmed. 'It was quite an experience. You could almost believe she was tame.'

He nodded in agreement. 'Where was she?' he asked, looking at Andy.

'Out by the creek,' Andy answered, 'with the rest of the pride.' He started to grin. 'Sheila's the second great love of my brother's life,' he told everyone. 'He was the one who found her snarled up in the trap. He was the one who raised the alarm, and stroked her while we freed her. And, here's the big one, it was Doug here she allowed to pick up her cubs right after she gave birth. Never heard of anything like it before, but Doug and Sheila, well there's a special bond between those two.'

Lizzy looked at Doug, obviously impressed. 'And his first great love?' she asked.

Andy's eyes danced the challenge as he looked at his brother. Laughing, Doug shook his head and sat back for the waitress to put a plate of freshly barbecued impala in front of him.

'His first great love,' Andy declared, 'lives in Jo'burg. And a right merry dance she leads him too. Isn't that right, mate?'

Doug's eyebrows arched as he treated his brother to a meaningful look. 'Who's for impala?' he said, turning to Lizzy.

'Me, I'm starving,' Melanie piped up, thrusting her plate at Doug in a sudden burst of animation at the prospect of food. 'Oh great, jacket potatoes!' she cried, as a generous bowlful was placed on the table. 'Can I have a beer? You can keep those orgasm things. You like beer, don't you Jack? Let's have some beer.'

Andy's eyes met Rhiannon's, whose expression was half-apologetic, half-resigned, then signalling to a waitress he said, 'Bring us a couple of beers and a couple of bottles of Nederberg. One white, one red.' Then turning to Lizzy he added, 'Another orgasm for the lady?'

'I think I'll save myself for later,' she responded, her skirt falling open as she leaned back in her chair and crossed her legs. Andy's eyes dropped to the silky smoothness of her thighs, lingering there for a while before he raised them back to her face.

'Do you want to tell me what your programme's about?' Doug invited, as he took Rhiannon's plate to serve her. 'Andy mentioned something about a half-hour on South Africa, is that right?'

Rhiannon nodded. 'Stop, that's enough for me,' she said, as he piled meat on to her plate. 'Yes, we're here to check out the New South Africa, as everyone's calling it these days. So we'll be off to Durban and Cape Town after this.'

'You ever been to Cape Town?' Andy asked.

'I have,' Hugh answered, raising a hand as he downed the remains of his first cocktail. 'It's the first time for the rest of them.'

'Then they're in for a treat, wouldn't you say?' Andy replied. 'Cape Town's a real jewel. Not a patch on

Perlatonga, of course, but ...'

'Is that where Table Mountain is?' Melanie interrupted, her mouth bulging with food as she spooned a third jacket potato on to her plate.

Andy looked at her, clearly wondering if she was serious. Realizing she was he said, 'Yep, that's where Table Mountain is. Where're you folks going to be staying?'

'At the Bay Hotel,' Rhiannon answered. 'Do you know it?'

'Sure, we know it, it's where we usually stay when we're in Cape Town,' Andy answered. 'It's pretty pricey, but one of the best. How long are you planning to be there?'

'Five days.'

He nodded. 'We got a few people we can put you in touch with down there,' he said. 'Are you staying in Jo'burg at all?'

Rhiannon was about to answer when she noticed Doug nod for Andy to look over his shoulder. Following the direction of their eyes she saw they were looking at a rather elegant though extremely sombre-looking older woman, who was getting up from a nearby table where she had evidently dined alone.

'Who is she?' Rhiannon asked, as the woman was escorted back to her chalet.

'Her name's Randy Theakston,' Andy answered. 'She arrived yesterday from New York. A last minute booking. Hasn't spoken to anyone since she got here, not even on the game drives, so I'm told.'

'Really?' Rhiannon commented. 'Maybe she's just shy.'

Andy shrugged. 'Who knows. She definitely likes to keep herself to herself though, wouldn't even accept an invitation from the party over there to join them for dinner tonight.'

Rhiannon pulled down the corners of her mouth. 'I

guess she values her privacy,' she said.

'Or yours,' Doug chipped in. 'She was asking one of the girls about you earlier.'

'About me in particular, or about the programme?' Rhiannon said, sounding surprised.

'Both, I think. But then a lot of the guests have been asking what the camera's all about, so I don't suppose that makes her any different.'

'Why don't we invite her to join our jeep tomorrow, if she's on her own?' Lizzy suggested.

Rhiannon shrugged. 'We could,' she said, 'as long as she doesn't see it as an invasion of her space.'

'She can always say no,' Lizzy reminded her, smiling as Andy's hand found hers under the table.

Rhiannon nodded thoughtfully, then dismissing the woman from her mind she turned her attention to Doug to ask his advice about which animals they should focus in on for the best entertainment value. As they talked, Lizzy and Andy got up to join the other dancers beside the campfire, while Hugh and Jack fell into conversation with a couple of Canadians at the next table.

It was almost midnight by the time Rhiannon wandered on to the dance floor to say good-night to Lizzy, while Hugh slipped discreetly away with the blonde he'd been romancing for the past half-hour.

'Bed? Sounds like a good idea to me,' Lizzy quipped, then laughed as Andy whispered something in her ear before going off to talk to the other rangers. 'You'd just die if you could hear some of the things he says,' she smiled, linking arms with Rhiannon.

'Pure Aussie?' Rhiannon grinned.

Lizzy's eyes twinkled. 'Pure Aussie,' she confirmed. 'And I love it.'

'Do you think you're going to make the early start in the morning?' Rhiannon laughed.

'Do I have a choice?'

'No,' Rhiannon smiled sweetly.

'Then I guess I'll make it,' Lizzy grinned. 'But tell me this, if Oliver were here would you be so keen to make the early start?'

'Probably not,' Rhiannon said, 'but he's not and I'm the boss so you're just going to have to suffer it.'

'You're all heart,' Lizzy said silkily as Andy came back and slipped an arm about her waist.

'Are you ready to go?' he whispered, kissing her neck.

'Yes, I'm ready,' she said, winking at Rhiannon.

A few minutes later Andy was opening the door to Lizzy's chalet and standing aside for her to walk in ahead of him. As she stepped into the room she could see, in the soft glow of a bedside lamp, that someone had been in to turn back the bed and lower the fine white gauze of the mosquito net. Dropping her bag on an armchair, she looked up and caught her tousled reflection in the mirror. Then hearing the door close, she smiled as Andy's reflection appeared beside her own.

Neither of them spoke as they moved into an embrace, their mouths joining, their hips pressing against each other's, their hunger audible in the groans that murmured from their lips. His tongue was hard and demanding as he pushed it into her mouth and tightening his grip on her buttocks he brought her roughly against his erection, letting her know how ready he was for her.

Lizzy's head fell back and gazing into his incredible blue eyes she began to unbutton his shirt. He leaned forward to kiss her again, catching the hem of her skirt in his hands and lifting it to her waist.

'Oh, yes,' he breathed as he realized she was wearing nothing underneath. He moved his hand between her legs, pushing his fingers into the moistness. As they entered her she gasped and fell against him.

'You are one sexy lady, do you know that?' he said gruffly, brushing his lips against hers. 'Take it off,' he whispered, tugging at the skirt. 'Take it all off.'

Obediently she stepped away and removed the two items of clothing she was wearing.

'Beautiful,' he said, gazing at her. 'Just beautiful.'

Her breasts were small, but the nipples were prominent and hard and as he stooped to take one in his mouth her fingers twisted his hair savagely. She so badly wanted him inside her, but she could wait, for this feeling of being naked while he was dressed was blowing her mind.

Dropping to his knees, he slid his thumbs into her pubic hair and opened her wide. 'Wow,' he breathed, 'that's some joy stick you got there.'

Trying not to think of Rhiannon, Lizzy looked down at him as he flicked his tongue against her clitoris.

'Feel good?' he asked as the laughter died in her eyes and without waiting for an answer he drew it deep into his mouth, massaging it harshly with his tongue.

Minutes later as the first throbbings of orgasm began to pulse through her he rose to his feet, unbuckling his belt and kicking off his shoes. She pushed his shirt down over his arms, kissing him and stooping with him as he lowered his trousers. Then gripping his penis hard in her hand she felt his moan of ecstasy vibrate in her throat.

'You know, you got the sexiest mouth I ever saw,' he told her, kissing it and sucking it. 'I've wanted to put my cock in it from the minute I saw it.'

'Then why don't you?' she offered.

His eyes instantly darkened with lust and scooping her up in his arms he carried her to the bed. She pulled back the mosquito net and he laid her down on the cool cotton sheets, her head near the foot of the bed, her feet on the pillows as he knelt between her legs.

The overhead fan turned lazily above them as he sat back on his heels and she raised herself up to cup his balls in her hands. Then moistening her lips with her tongue she took him very slowly, very tightly into her mouth.

'Jesus Christ,' he muttered, his fingers digging into her shoulders as she began to move her head back and forth. 'Don't stop,' he groaned, taking her nipples between his fingers as she slid her hands round to his buttocks.

'Get up on your knees,' he told her a few minutes later.

Still holding him with her mouth she did as he said, positioning herself on all fours and feeling him move even deeper into her mouth as he leaned forward to stroke her buttocks.

'Keep going, don't stop,' he said. 'Just open your legs. Nice and wide. That's it.'

His penis was as solid in her mouth as the ache of desire between her legs. She was longing for him to enter her, but this felt so good, so brazen and unbelievably erotic. She slid her mouth right back to the tip of his penis then drew him in again. As his hands stroked her body it was as though she could feel herself merging with his lust, as though he was somehow blurring her senses with the sheer power of his need. She could feel him all over her; in her mouth, on her face, on her breasts, her back, her buttocks; she could feel him pushing inside her, thrusting his thighs against hers, gripping her waist and penetrating her deeply. Yet he was there in her mouth. But she could feel him behind her, knew that he was inside her, pushing himself deeper and deeper inside her.

In a daze she stopped and turned to see Doug kneeling behind her and as Andy's fingers tightened on her nipples Doug cupped her face in his hand, leaning over her and kissing her, sucking her lips between his, then pushing her back to his brother's penis. She took it in her mouth, moaning softly as Doug began to pump in and out of her, sliding his hands to the front of her and rubbing her. The sensations rising in her body were indescribable as both penises pushed into her with slow, rhythmic movements carrying her towards an orgasm such as she'd never known in her life.

They took her in every position, moving her between them, kissing her, stroking her, loving her and taking her through the night in a daze of unsurpassable pleasure. Through their gentle moans of desire and cries of fulfilment she could hear the distant roar of lions and haunting wail of hyenas – it was as though they were caught in an endless primeval ritual that bathed the senses in unendurable pleasure. As their bodies writhed beneath the canopy of white gauze, the ceiling fan stirred the thick, humid air. She had never known her body capable of such exquisite response, had never known it was possible for two men to share her and make her feel like the most beautiful, most sensuous woman alive.

When finally she slept she lay with her head on Andy's shoulder, her hip partially covering his, her hand on his chest. Doug got up quietly from the bed, walked over to where he had left his clothes, dressed quickly, then picking up his gun turned to look down at his brother. Andy was watching him and the two of them exchanged a knowing smile as Andy stroked the tousled blonde head on his shoulder, kissed it, then rolling her gently to one side, got up to leave too.

The sun was just beginning to rise as Rhiannon wound her way through the trees to where the guests were gathering for breakfast. Everyone was decked out in khaki shorts and shirts with a variety of hats and sun-visors and professional-looking cameras dangling about their necks. As they milled around the lounge with cups of tea and coffee, nibbling on small wedges of cake and puffing early-morning cigarettes, they were firing endless questions at the rangers whose patience and know-ledge appeared as infinite as the charm of their surroundings.

'Coffee?' Hugh offered, holding up a pot as Rhiannon joined their group.

'Please,' she answered, checking her bag to make sure she had everything. 'No sugar. Any sign of Melanie?' she added, looking up at Lizzy and finding, to her amazement, that Lizzy's eyes were far from the bleary, bloodshot ones she'd been expecting.

'She's just popped to the loo,' Lizzy answered, grinning at Rhiannon's response to her appearance. 'Sleep well, did you?' she asked breezily, taking the cup Hugh was holding out and passing it to Rhiannon.

'Not bad,' Rhiannon replied, taking the cup. 'How about you?'

With a brief, expressive lift of her eyebrows, Lizzy turned to Jack to ask if he wanted to mike her up before they left.

'How much tape did we use yesterday?' Rhiannon said, tearing her eyes from Lizzy and turning to Hugh.

'Thirty, forty minutes,' he answered, stifling a yawn. 'I've put a couple of ninety minuters in for this morning. Did you manage to get a shower, by the way? I didn't seem to have any water.'

'No, me neither,' Lizzy complained as Melanie rejoined them. 'At least only a dribble.'

'Apparently an elephant pulled the pipe out of the ground in the night,' Melanie informed them, picking up her coffee. 'They'll have it fixed by the time we come back, or so that woman over there just said.'

Rhiannon looked to where Melanie was pointing and saw Randy Theakston standing alone just outside the kitchens, apparently engrossed in setting up her camera. Beside her on the table was a smart-looking pith helmet and an expensive pair of binoculars. Her face was stern with concentration, though Rhiannon got the impression that her expression was probably always that way. When she'd finished with her camera she hooked it around her neck, then stood with a hand on her hip looking at no one, speaking to no one and presumably waiting to be told what to do next.

'Are we going to ask her to join us?' Rhiannon said, noticing that Lizzy was watching her too.

Lizzy shrugged. 'If you like. Do you want me to go and ask?'

'No, you go Melanie,' Rhiannon replied. 'And pack that yawning in will you Hugh, you're getting me at it.'

'Morning folks. How are you all this morning?' It was Jim, one of the other rangers.

'Pretty good, thanks,' Rhiannon answered.

'Hear the lions in the night?' he asked. 'There were several of them about the camp in the early hours.'

For no particular reason Rhiannon glanced at Hugh and almost burst out laughing when she saw his face turn white. Obviously someone hadn't obeyed the camp rules last night. 'Think I'll go and start loading the gear,' he said, banging his saucer with the cup as he put it down.

As he walked off across the grass with Jack and the ranger, Rhiannon turned to Lizzy, seizing their few minutes of privacy. 'So, come on, what happened last night?' she said. 'Was he good?'

Lizzy grinned widely.

'Lizzy! Don't keep me in suspense. You look fantastic, by the way, so whatever he did he must have done it right.'

Lizzy's blue eyes were dancing with laughter. 'I'll tell you this much,' she said, 'it was a first for me.'

'No!' Rhiannon gasped, impressed and intrigued. 'Why, what did he do?'

'You mean they,' Lizzy corrected smoothly. 'What did *they* do?'

Rhiannon's eyes instantly dilated. 'You mean ...? How many were there for God's sake?'

Lizzy laughed and picked up a piece of cake. 'Only the two,' she said casually. 'Andy and Doug.'

Rhiannon's mouth fell open as she struggled to disguise her dismay. Lizzy might think she was strong enough to handle this, but Rhiannon wasn't convinced. Nevertheless, she wasn't going to be the one to dull the light in Lizzy's eyes, so smothering her concern with a genuine cry of amazement she said, 'You're not serious! Both of them? What was it like, for God's sake?'

Lizzy shrugged. 'I guess you could say it just about blew my mind,' she responded airily.

Rhiannon was shaking her head. 'And how do you feel this morning? As if I need to ask. But what did you say when you woke up? Didn't you feel, well, *embarrassed*?'

'Embarrassed!' Lizzy scoffed. 'I felt seriously fucking amazing, is what I felt. Besides, they weren't there when I woke up, either of them.'

Rhiannon frowned, not sure what to make of that, though instinctively not liking it. Then bringing her eyes back to Lizzy's she started to laugh again. 'I don't believe you,' she said. 'There am I lying abed all on my ownsome absolutely *dying* for it while you've got the two most gorgeous men in the camp all to your greedy little self.'

'I know,' Lizzy sighed. 'But there are some things a girl just can't share.'

Laughing, Rhiannon put down her cup. 'Come on,' she said, 'looks like everyone's on the move. And try to take that grin off your face, will you, we don't want to frighten the animals. What happened to Melanie?' she went on, looking around. 'Did she ask that woman to join us?'

'Looks like it,' Lizzy said, nodding towards the reception, where Melanie and Randy Theakston were chatting with Andy and another ranger.

'Morning ladies,' Andy smiled as they approached. 'You both slept well I trust?'

'I did,' Rhiannon answered chirpily, earning herself a quick nudge from Lizzy. 'How about you?'

'Never better,' he answered, looking only at

Rhiannon. 'Let me introduce you,' he went on. 'This is Randy Theakston. Randy Theakston, Rhiannon Edwardes, producer of the *Check It Out* programme.'

'Hi, nice to meet you,' Rhiannon smiled, holding out her hand.

'Likewise,' Randy responded coolly, barely touching her fingers to Rhiannon's.

Rhiannon's eyebrows rose. 'Uh, this is Lizzy Fortnum,' she said, turning to Lizzy. 'Our presenter.'

'Hi,' Lizzy said, tearing her eyes briefly from Andy who still hadn't looked at her.

'You ready to get going?' he said, tossing his keys in the air as Randy and Lizzy shook hands.

'Do I have to have this thing under my feet?' Melanie complained, kicking the hamper as she climbed into the jeep.

Had it not been for Andy's curtness, Lizzy would have offered to swap places so that she would be sitting in the front. As it was, she decided not to. 'Just shut up and be grateful you're here,' she snapped at Melanie.

'Hop in then, ladies,' Andy said.

Rhiannon sat between Lizzy and Randy, neither of whom was much more communicative than the other, though Randy's aloofness, as Rhiannon made further polite attempts at conversation, was so pronounced it was almost offensive. In the end Rhiannon gave up and turned to absorb the passing scenery. As they bumped along the track heading out into the bush, she tried not to worry about Lizzy. Not that Lizzy would welcome being worried about, for Lizzy liked to think she was perfectly able to take care of herself. And she probably was, it was simply that Rhiannon couldn't bear for her to be hurt any more than she already had been, and the signs so far this morning were not looking good.

Some twenty minutes later they were parked at the edge of a track gazing out over endless rolling acres of bushveld, a glorious dawn turning the sky gold as a herd of impala roamed the plains before them.

'I can't believe I ate one for dinner last night,' Rhiannon wailed guiltily.

'They're not in short supply,' Andy grinned, by way of comfort. 'You see that fella through there,' he went on, 'the one standing slightly to the left between the trees? That's the buck. He's the guy who mates the whole herd.'

Hugh pulled the camera from his eye. 'The whole herd?' he echoed.

'That's right, mate,' Andy grinned. 'He's a busy bloke.'

'Then when I die I want to come back as him,' Hugh declared.

As everyone laughed, Rhiannon glanced at Randy – not even the glimmer of a smile touched her lips.

'Now there's an unusual sight,' Andy said, pointing. 'A female impala with horns. It's a freak of nature, 'cos you never normally see females with horns.'

'You never met my wife,' Jack muttered, twiddling the controls on his sound-mixer.

As they all laughed again the radio burst into life telling them of an elephant sighting at Crossreach. 'A lone bull,' said the voice. 'And he's not in a good mood.'

'Oh, how exciting,' Randy commented, causing Rhiannon to blink in surprise.

Andy lifted the radio. 'Message received,' he said. 'We're not far so we'll go take a look. Have you heard from base since we've been out, mate?'

Before the other ranger could respond base came through. 'Morning Andy,' she said. 'We're here.'

'G'day Jen. Any sign of Doug yet this morning?' he said, steering the landrover back on to the track and making towards Crossreach.

'Not yet,' came the reply.

'Then give him a message when he shows,' Andy said. 'Tell him our guest for the Safari Suite's arriving earlier than expected, meaning we'll be returning around nine thirty so the crew can get some shots before he checks in. Doug should be out there at the landing strip to meet him around eleven, tell him.'

'Will do. I've got a telephone message here for Rhiannon,' she said. 'It's from ... Oliver? He says to tell her he called.'

Andy glanced back over his shoulder. 'Message received and appreciated,' he smiled when he saw Rhiannon's face. 'Over and out.'

Randy shifted in her seat, tucked her short silvery hair behind her ears, then began to focus her camera on something way in the distance.

'Is he still in New York?' Lizzy asked.

'No, he was getting the red-eye back to London last night,' Rhiannon answered. Then after a pause, 'This is going to be the longest we've been apart since we met.'

'How long ago was that?' Randy asked, still looking away across the plains.

Lizzy's eyebrows rose as she and Rhiannon exchanged glances. 'Three, almost four months ago,' Rhiannon replied.

'He's American?' Randy said, capping her lens. 'You mentioned New York,' she explained when Rhiannon frowned.

'No, he's English,' Rhiannon answered. 'He mainly works out of New York though.'

Randy sniffed, then turned her grey eyes back to the semi-distance.

The look on Lizzy's face as she turned back to Rhiannon was vintage Lizzy – it was a look that spoke volumes.

It was several minutes later, whilst making a slow descent into a ravine and holding on to their hats as the jeep tilted from side to side, that Rhiannon said, 'Are you married, Randy?'

Randy turned her handsome face to profile. 'I was

once,' she responded. 'We divorced several years ago.'

'Do you have any children?' Lizzy ventured.

'No.'

Rhiannon grabbed for the rail on the seat-back in front as the landrover bounced up over a rock.

'Sorry about that, folks,' Andy said, glancing over his shoulder. 'Everyone OK? No damage?'

'No damage,' Hugh confirmed from the back.

'How about you, Lizzy? You surviving all this bumping around?'

Lizzy's eyes widened slightly at what she assumed to be a concern for the tenderness of her nether regions after the night they had spent together. Then catching him watching her in the rear-view mirror she smiled as he winked and the memory of everything they had done coasted a reassuring warmth all the way through her. Idly she wondered if Doug would join them again that night and found herself hoping not – after all, one could have too much of a good thing.

A while later, after failing to find the elephant, they stopped at a deserted waterhole and as Andy and Elmore began to unpack the hamper, Rhiannon and Lizzy wandered down the bank, discussing the commentary they would overlay on what they had shot so far that morning.

'Hey, watch out, you two,' Andy shouted over from the jeep as they neared the water's edge, 'there are crocs in them there waters so don't get too close.'

Rhiannon and Lizzy instantly stepped back and to their surprise almost knocked Randy Theakston over.

'I'm sorry,' Rhiannon said, 'I didn't realize you were there.'

'It was my fault,' Randy told her. 'I came up rather quietly.'

Rhiannon looked from her to Lizzy and back again, not sure what to say.

'Uh, how long are you staying at Perlatonga, Randy?'

Lizzy said, filling the silence.

'I leave the day after tomorrow,' Randy answered.

'For where?'

Randy's eyes travelled searchingly across the water. 'Cape Town,' she said.

'Same as us,' Rhiannon smiled.

'You ladies going to have some coffee?' Andy called out.

Randy turned and hooking her camera over her shoulder began to stride back up over the bank.

'Great company,' Rhiannon said, as they started slowly after her. 'I'm so glad we asked her to join us.'

'We must get her address,' Lizzy responded, her eyes fixed on Andy as he came strolling towards them with two cups of coffee. 'Thanks,' she said, smiling up at him as he passed her a cup.

'You're welcome,' he said, handing the other cup to Rhiannon. 'Sorry about the elephant,' he went on, 'but there are plenty around here so don't despair.'

'I won't,' Rhiannon assured him. 'What do you think the chances are of us sighting a cheetah?'

'Slim,' he replied. 'More likely to be at night.'

Rhiannon nodded, then catching the look on Lizzy's face said, 'Uh, I think I'll just go and talk to the boys, there are a few things I need to check with them, if you'll excuse me.'

'Sure,' Andy said, turning to walk back to the jeep with her.

'Hey,' Lizzy said, putting a hand on his arm to stop him.

As he turned to look down at her Lizzy felt herself start to colour. 'Are you trying to avoid me?' she challenged softly.

Though he laughed his eyes seemed oddly cold. 'Why would I do that?' he said.

She shrugged. 'I don't know. It's just the impression I'm getting.'

He looked at her for some time, then taking a breath, he dug his hands into his pockets and gazed out at the veld.

'Aren't you going to say something?' she prompted, hating herself for how pathetic she was sounding.

'What do you want me to say?'

Her face tightened. 'Why don't you try whatever's going through your mind right now?' she suggested.

As he brought his eyes back to hers she could feel her heart starting to pound. 'To tell you the truth,' he said, 'I don't think you'd want to hear it.'

Lizzy's throat was dry. 'Why don't you try me?' she said tightly.

His eyebrows went up. 'As I recall I did that last night,' he quipped, and giving her a quick pat on the bottom he turned and shouting for Elmore strode back towards the jeep.

Lizzy watched him go, so stunned that for the moment she couldn't even feel angry. Then suddenly her heart rose into her throat and her eyes closed as her mind started to replay scenes from the night before. It had all felt so right, so beautiful even, when the three of them had been making love; now it felt, correction *she* felt, sordid and ashamed; like an ageing groupie who'd just been slung from the back of a moving van. Or, more accurately, the lonely, frustrated widow who hadn't made love since her husband had died and now she had, was sorely wishing she hadn't.

For the first time in months she felt tears stinging her eyes. 'Bastard!' she seethed, turning her back on the jeep. 'How dare he do this to me?' But of course he didn't know what he'd done, had no idea how badly he had just crushed what little confidence she had. How could he when she hid her pain so well? Besides, she'd behaved like a whore so what more could she expect than to be treated like one?

Despite her anger she felt suddenly exhausted and

putting a hand to her head took a deep, steadying breath. Now wasn't the time to start thinking about Richard; if she did she'd lose it altogether. She had to think about Andy and how she was going to get through the next few hours without letting him see how much he had hurt her. Hearing him laugh she felt her whole body tense with fury, but there was nothing she could do to get back at him – they had a film to shoot and flattening the game ranger's ego wasn't exactly going to bring out the best in him, was it? So, disguising the ache in her heart with her sunniest smile, she turned back to the jeep, where everyone was sharing a joke as they climbed on board.

'Thanks for the coffee,' she said when she came face to face with Andy and extending her arm to one side she tipped her cup upside down, pouring the contents on the ground.

'You're welcome,' he said, arching an eyebrow as she tossed the cup into the hamper.

'What was all that about?' Rhiannon whispered as Lizzy clambered in beside her. 'What's going on?'

'What do you think?' Lizzy answered with a bitter little laugh. 'I've served my purpose and now I've been dumped.'

Rhiannon frowned. 'What do you mean, dumped?'

'What I said, dumped,' Lizzy responded, gazing airily out at the bush. 'You know what dumped means. Remember Phillip?'

Rhiannon's eyes hardened for an instant, but realizing that Lizzy had to be feeling pretty hurt to have made a remark like that she glanced over at Andy and felt her jaw tighten. She never had been able to stomach men who screwed a woman one night then, having got what they wanted, made her feel like a tramp in the morning.

'I think a couple of up-the-nose shots are in order,' she murmured to Lizzy, referring to the revenge tactic of taking unflattering shots of those they deemed to be deserving cases.

Lizzy nodded but Rhiannon could see that her heart wasn't in it, which could only mean that she was even more hurt than Rhiannon had feared. God, life could be such a bitch at times; this was the first time since Richard had died that Lizzy had felt ready, able even, to test the waters with another man and it had to turn out like this!

But, Rhiannon thought admiringly as they travelled back towards the camp, she really had to hand it to Lizzy for the way she was dealing with it. Her running commentary as they spotted giraffes and gnus, wart-hogs and hyenas, buffalo and hippos and even a civet, was as lively and witty as ever, and the dialogue between her and Andy when he stopped to point the animals out and respond to her questions was totally lacking in ire. The moment Rhiannon loved best, however, was when Andy, with an ubiquitous wickedness twinkling in his eyes, told Lizzy that baboons were the only animals known to have sex for pleasure.

Lizzy didn't even flinch as she turned her wonderfully expressive eyes to camera – and somehow, without knowing anything about programme making, Andy knew that a close-up of him was going to find itself in there somewhere.

Chapter 3

It was just after nine when they arrived back at camp and made straight for the breakfast tables where a hungry crowd was gathering around steaming hot plates of eggs and bacon. Skirting the mêlée, Andy went to sit with the other rangers, clicking his fingers at a waitress who rushed in with a pot of hot coffee and an order pad.

Turning her eyes away from the little display of despotism, Rhiannon ladled a generous helping of scrambled egg on to her plate, waited for Lizzy to do the same, then led the way to a corner table where they could be more private.

'So what did he say to you back there?' Rhiannon asked, tossing her hair over one shoulder and picking up the salt.

'Oh, I don't know,' Lizzy said dismissively, 'let's not talk about it, eh?'

Rhiannon looked at her for a moment, then popping a forkful of eggs into her mouth she started to chew. It wasn't like Lizzy not to want to discuss something, but pressing her probably wasn't the best way to go right now. 'OK,' she said. 'But if you want to put that bastard in his place then it's fine by me. This isn't the only game reserve in the Kruger Park and ...'

'No, let's just leave it,' Lizzy interrupted. 'I behaved like a slut and now I'm being treated like one. End of story. I'll survive.'

'Oh, for heaven's sake!' Rhiannon cried. 'You were three consenting adults and I don't see you treating him like he's ...'

'Rhian, leave it! We're both old enough and wise enough to know that men never suffer for acts of ...' She hunted around for a word and settled on: 'baboonism, so there's no point in either of us getting worked up over it. Like I said, I'll survive.' A moment or two later she started to smile. 'There's still Doug to confront yet,' she said, the smile instantly fading as she pushed her plate away. 'Shit, I feel such a fool. Anyway, end of subject. I'm going to get more coffee. Want some?'

'No,' Rhiannon answered, shaking her head as she took another mouthful of food, 'but I'll finish up your eggs if you don't want them. And Liz,' she added as Lizzy got up from the table, 'there's nothing to feel foolish about.'

Lizzy smiled and returning a couple of minutes later with a fresh cup of coffee she said, 'By the way, did you know that Elmore has invited Melanie to go and meet his old man?'

Rhiannon's fork hit her plate. 'The Zulu chief?' she cried.

'None other,' Lizzy confirmed. 'She told me this morning before we left.'

Rhiannon looked over to where Melanie was sitting with Hugh and Jack, her face bulging with food. 'Did she and Elmore spend the night together last night?' she asked.

Lizzy shrugged. 'No idea.'

'Oh God, what am I going to tell her parents?' Rhiannon muttered. 'I mean, how do you tell someone their nineteen-year-old daughter's upped and joined a Zulu tribe? Oh Christ, it's all going to be my fault. Twenty-four hours in Africa and she's ...'

'Rhiannon!' Lizzy laughed. 'He's only asked her if she wants to meet his father, not if she wants to become the next Zulu chief's great wife. And look at it this way, if she does join up it'll make a pretty entertaining programme.'

Rhiannon's eyes lit up. 'Wouldn't it!' she cried. 'How do you think we can talk her into it?'

'Why don't we just leave her here?' Lizzy suggested.

Rhiannon laughed. 'Not such a bad idea,' she remarked, downing the last of her coffee. 'Come on, we'd better get those shots of the Safari Suite before Howard Hughes or whoever he is arrives. Hugh! Jack! Ready to roll?' she called out to them.

'Right there,' Hugh responded, stubbing out his cigarette.

'Andy!' Rhiannon shouted. 'Ready when you are.'

'What do we need him for?' Lizzy objected. 'I thought we were just doing general stuff?'

Rhiannon looked at her, a pained expression coming over her face. 'Kill me for it later,' she said, 'but I asked him if he'd mind being interviewed while lying on the bed. Well, we need him to talk about the suite,' she added as Lizzy's eyes narrowed.

'But lying on the bed?'

'Why not? I mean, he *is* gorgeous, Lizzy, and a few shots of the two of you lying on a bed is a guaranteed turn-on. Of TV sets,' she added. 'Think of it as exploitation.'

'I am,' Lizzy responded meaningfully.

'Then think of England,' Rhiannon persevered.

'I bet Judith Chalmers never had to put up with this,' Lizzy grumbled, getting up from the table.

'I bet Judith Chalmers never had a ménage-à-trois with twins either,' Rhiannon responded. 'Sorry!' she cried. 'Sorry! It just slipped out. I swear I'll never mention it again.'

Laughing despite herself, Lizzy picked up her notes and hooking her bag over her shoulder followed Rhiannon and the others across the camp to the exclusive area of the Safari Suite.

From the outside, at least at first glance, it wasn't unlike the other chalets, with its beautifully thatched roof, wide wooden terrace and mosquito-netted windows, though of course it was on a much grander scale and secluded from the rest of the camp by its own shady garden and a bamboo fence. It was also, they discovered when they went inside, quite stupendously luxurious with its wonderful high ceilings, polished wooden floors and perfect mix of African artefacts and European antiques. In the sitting- room the huge sliding windows that occupied the whole of one wall opened out on to a private sun deck and swimming pool, beyond which tempting grassy trails led into the shrubs and trees of the bush. And the bedroom, which opened off the sitting-room, was so breathtakingly romantic, with its copious folds of muslin draping over the satin covers of the hand-carved bed and caught like petticoats at the windows, that it could have been part of a movie set.

'Isn't it lovely?' Lizzy murmured, trailing a hand across the foot of the bed as she walked to the window.

Rhiannon watched her through the misty bands of sunlight, knowing she was thinking of Richard. 'Yes it is,' she said softly, looking around at the ethnic paintings on the walls. 'What do you think?' she said, taking a pith helmet from a chest and putting it on.

Lizzy turned round and smiled. 'Very Karen von Blixen,' she said, pushing open the window.

The dreamy warble of turtle-doves accompanied by squawks and whistles and chirrups of a hundred more exotic birds drifted in from the trees, all but drowning the sound of Hugh and Jack and Andy talking and moving furniture about in the next room.

'It's so peaceful,' Lizzy sighed, stepping out on to the balcony. 'I know we're in the wrong country,' she added, gazing down at the garden, 'but it reminds me of all those wonderful scenes in *Out of Africa*, doesn't it you? I could almost believe that Robert Redford was about to fly overhead and entertain us with all those crazy aerobatics.'

'Mmm,' Rhiannon smiled, glancing over at the door as Andy walked into the room.

'Great pad for a spot of parallel parking, eh?' he grinned, rubbing his hands together.

Lizzy winced, then turning round she leaned against the wooden balustrade and looked back into the room. Her heart contracted at the disappointment and hurt his indifference had inflicted and she wished desperately that she didn't mind so much.

Andy looked from her to Rhiannon and back again, his smile starting to falter under their silence. 'It's a great favourite with honeymooners,' he said lamely.

Several seconds ticked by.

He drew a copy of the Reserve's brochure and tariff list from his pocket. 'In pounds sterling this suite'll set you back around a thousand a night,' he told them.

'How much?' Jack cried, coming into the room behind him.

'The equivalent of a sound man's daily rate,' Rhiannon informed him. 'Now, before you philistines completely annihilate the romance, let's get this in the can, shall we?'

Once again, as they started to shoot, Rhiannon found herself marvelling at Lizzy's ability to mask her feelings. As they lay there, she and Andy, side by side on the enormous muslin-covered bed, hands behind their heads, gazing up at the ceiling as, completely dead-pan, they went through an hilarious yet informative interview, Rhiannon could only feel surprise and dismay that things had turned out the way they had between them when, for the camera at least, they seemed made in heaven.

'OK,' Rhiannon said, when the interview came to a natural end. 'I just want a few cutaways and a reference to this mystery guest who's checking in later and then we'll be through.'

'What do you want me to say?' Lizzy asked.

Rhiannon thought. 'Just something about the fact that we can't find out who he is ... I know, we'll cut to some footage of Redford doing those aerobatic stunts you mentioned just now, and you can say that you're sure it's going to be someone famous. OK?'

'Got it,' Lizzy replied, getting up from the bed.

Twenty minutes later they were back in the open-air lounge sipping cold drinks and discussing who did and didn't have the energy to go for a walk with Elmore as their guide.

'What exactly are we going to see if we go, Elmore?' Rhiannon asked, perching on the arm of an easy-chair and resting her elbow on Lizzy's shoulder.

'I can tell you about the plants and the trees,' he answered. 'And the birds. Probably we see lots of insects like the dung beetle or the golden orb spider ...' He shrugged. 'Who know what we see.'

'He knows the bush better than most of us know our back gardens,' Andy told them, sinking into a chair opposite Lizzy's. 'And he'll show you things you'll never see anywhere else in the world. But be warned,' he added, glancing at his watch, 'if you go you'll be out there at least a couple of hours and the mercury's already pushing thirty-seven.'

'Funny how this dry heat is more bearable than the humidity we get at home, isn't it?' Lizzy remarked to Rhiannon.

'Mmm,' Rhiannon responded, looking across the camp to where a jeep had just pulled up in front of the reception.

'I vote we do the walk tomorrow,' Hugh said, pouring more iced lemonade into his glass.

'I'll go with that,' Jack yawned. 'I'm just about all in. What time did you say we were out again this afternoon?'

'We meet here at four,' Andy answered, yawning too. 'Depart at four thirty. They'll be serving lunch at one for those of you who can face it.'

'After that enormous breakfast?' Rhiannon groaned. 'No thanks.'

'Seems like the majority are in favour of a siesta then,' Andy said, putting his glass down and turning in his chair to where his brother was walking across the camp with another man, who was also dressed in full-length khaki trousers and an open-necked olive-green shirt. His long, dark-blond hair was swept straight back from his face and the sun-glasses that shielded his eyes appeared as expensive as the gold watch on his wrist. He moved with the easy grace of a man who knew his way around, as though he had been here many times before.

'Ah, here's Doug,' Andy said. 'And our mystery guest. So it looks like you're going to get to meet him after all.'

As the two men approached, Rhiannon, who hadn't actually taken her eyes off them since they'd got out of the jeep, found her smile becoming wider and wider until in the end she rolled her eyes and began shaking her head as she laughed. 'I don't believe this,' she said. 'I just don't believe it.'

'Don't you?' Lizzy responded, getting to her feet along with everyone else as Doug and the new guest entered the lounge.

'G'day folks,' Doug greeted them and laughing he stood aside as Rhiannon flew past him and flung her arms around Oliver's neck.

'Hi,' he murmured, kissing her lingeringly on the mouth, then gazing down at her.

'What are you doing here?' she said, smiling at the humour in his deep brown eyes.

'I missed you,' he told her with a wink.

Laughing she reached up to sweep the hair out of his eyes. 'I missed you too,' she said softly.

'Well, I guess the rest of you don't need any introductions either,' Doug grinned, going to pour a couple of drinks for him and Oliver.

'How are you doing there, Oliver?' Andy said, shaking Oliver warmly by the hand and slapping him on the shoulder. 'Good to see you again, mate.'

'It's good to be here,' Oliver responded, his other arm still around Rhiannon's waist as he took the glass Doug was handing him.

'Hi, Oliver,' Lizzy said coolly, kissing him on the cheek.

'Lizzy,' he said. 'Hugh. Jack. Melanie.'

He turned to Rhiannon who was still looking slightly bemused and laughing he said, 'So how's it all been going?'

'Pretty good,' Hugh answered. 'But I sure am glad you've turned up. She's been hell.'

'A right tartar,' Jack grunted in agreement.

'Isn't that something you have with fish?' Hugh quipped.

Oliver and Rhiannon were laughing. 'And what about you, Lizzy?' he said. 'Are you having a good time?'

Lizzy flushed, wondering if Doug had told him what had happened the night before. 'It's an experience I wouldn't have missed for the world,' she replied, forcing herself to smile.

Oliver nodded and kissing Rhiannon briefly on the forehead, said, 'If I'm interrupting I can always catch up with you later.'

'No, you're not interrupting,' Rhiannon assured him. 'In fact your timing is perfect; we've just voted in favour of a siesta before the next game drive.'

As his eyebrows went up Rhiannon laughed and looked over at Lizzy, wondering why she was behaving so oddly. Then she remembered that this was the first time Lizzy had seen Doug since last night, and Doug, just like Andy, was carrying on as though Lizzy wasn't even there. He and the other men started bantering with each other and making everyone laugh, as they treated Oliver to outrageously exaggerated accounts of the dangers they had faced on the last two drives.

As Lizzy watched them she was trying, not for the first time, to work out why she felt such an antipathy towards Oliver when he had never been anything but warm and friendly towards her and, as far as she could tell, open and honest with Rhiannon. With his dark-blond hair, clear brown eyes and ready smile, he looked exactly what he was, an ex-public schoolboy who radiated as much privilege as he did charm. At thirty-two he was three years older than Rhiannon and had, until recently, lived almost exclusively in New York where he'd received his training, and all his major breaks, as a diamond dealer. Since meeting Rhiannon he had started building up his business in London so they could spend more time together and so far everything was working like a dream. So much so, in fact, that Lizzy couldn't help wondering if that was what was giving her the problem – that it was all just too easy, just too perfect – and she was just too jealous.

As he caught her eye and smiled, Lizzy felt her insides tighten and finding herself unable to smile back she stooped to retrieve her bag. 'Well, I think I'll leave you all to it,' she said, putting her sun-glasses on before anyone noticed the tears that had suddenly welled in her eyes. 'I'll see you back here at four.'

Doug and Andy watched her go, then exchanging quick glances turned back as Jack said, 'Yeah, I think I'll hit the sack for an hour too. Good to see you, Oliver.'

'Yeah, good to see you,' Hugh echoed. 'Catch you later.'

'Sure,' Oliver replied, hitting their palms as they passed.

'The suite's ready,' Doug informed them as Rhiannon

wrapped her arms around Oliver again. 'I guess you know the way by now. I'll get someone to move Rhiannon's things over later.'

As Andy and Doug strolled off across the camp with Melanie and Elmore, Rhiannon gazed up into Oliver's eyes. 'I can't believe you've done this,' she smiled. 'You've come all this way just to be with me?'

He shrugged. 'Well, I might have a meeting or two in Johannesburg,' he confessed. Then kissing her softly on the mouth he added, 'But I scheduled them so I could get to spend some time with you here. What do you think of it?' he added, sweeping his eyes around the camp.

'I think it's one of the most romantic places I've ever been,' she answered honestly. 'It's got a kind of magic about it. It seems to do things to people. I mean everyone, just everyone, is falling in love or doing things they might not normally do.'

'And you?' he said, lifting her hair in his hands. 'Are you falling in love?'

'Oh, I think so,' she whispered.

As his mouth came down on hers she clung to him tightly. Despite his continual assurances and demonstrations of love, there were still moments when the damage of her past made her feel insecure and almost afraid to believe her own instincts.

'I need a shave,' he grimaced, lifting his head to look down at her.

She smiled. 'And I need a shower.'

Laughing, he turned her in the direction of the Safari Suite. 'Have you seen it yet?' he asked as they started towards it.

'Yes. We shot an interview there an hour ago,' she told him. 'It's wonderful. But what I want to know is how come you know it.'

'I told you before, I've stayed here a few times after meetings in Jo'burg or Durban,' he answered. 'I've brought clients here too.'

'Just clients?' she teased.

'Just clients,' he responded with a humorous arch of his eyebrows.

As they reached the threshold she turned to look at him again. He was right, he did need a shave and as beautiful as his eyes were they looked tired.

'It's a long flight from New York,' he reminded her when she remarked on it. 'And it turned out to be a pretty gruelling schedule while I was there.'

'How did it go?' she asked as they walked in through the door.

He took a deep breath and let it out slowly. 'Not bad,' he answered. 'But I think I'll have to go back again pretty soon. God, will you just look at this place?' he murmured, putting an arm around her shoulders and resting his head on hers.

'It's everything you said it would be and more,' Rhiannon smiled as they gazed across the sitting-room and out of the vast picture windows to the private pool and tangled mass of trees beyond.

'You sure you don't mind me turning up like this?' he said, as they walked over to the windows. 'I'm not cramping your style or anything?'

'What do you think?' she laughed.

Stopping to lean against a wooden pillar on the terrace, he stood her in front of him and gazed long into her eyes. 'Love you,' he whispered.

'Love you too,' she said.

Smiling, he tilted her face up to his and kissed her gently on the mouth. 'Didn't you say something about needing a shower just now?' he asked, lowering his fingers to her shirt buttons and starting to unfasten them.

'Mmm,' she replied.

'God, you smell good,' he told her, stooping to kiss her neck as he slipped her shirt down over her shoulders. Then dropping her shirt to the floor, he reached behind her to unfasten her bra while seeking her mouth with his.

'Mmm,' he groaned, his voice reverberating gently through her as he peeled her bra away and cupped her heavy breasts in his hands.

A sharp, stinging desire was pulsing between her legs as he bit gently on her lips and massaged her breasts, teasing her hard, aching nipples with his fingers. The feel of the warm breeze on her back, the hypnotic chant of the birds and idle chafing of the bush seemed to heighten the sensuousness of his touch, as though he were filling her with new, exquisite pleasures.

'Stand back, let me look at you,' he whispered.

Obediently she stepped back and watched the tension increase in his face as he swept her hair over her shoulders to reveal the full beauty of her breasts with their powdery coating of freckles and succulent red nipples. Her fingers sank into the glossy thickness of his hair as he lowered his head and drew first one, then the other nipple deep into his mouth, circling them with his tongue and sucking them hard.

Then resting his hands on her hips, he stood looking down into her eyes until finally, as his mouth closed over hers, he took her hand and placed it over the bulge in his trousers.

'There's a shower right there,' he told her gruffly, his breath catching as she squeezed him hard. Turning her so she could see the shower beside the pool, he put his lips to her ear and whispered, 'Take off the rest of your clothes, I'll go and find some soap.'

A few minutes later they were both naked beneath the cascading luke-warm water, gently soaping each other's bodies as they drew each other slowly towards the point when neither would be able to hold back any more.

It was when finally he laid her down on the tiles beside the pool and covered her body with his own that Randy Theakston slipped silently back through the trees, the film in her camera starting automatically to rewind.

*

Even before she blinked her eyes open, Lizzy knew that someone else was in the room. Or maybe someone had been there and it was the sound of them leaving that had woken her; she couldn't as yet be sure. She lay very still on the bed, sunlight streaming across her body as she listened to the incessant buzz of insect life and felt the cooling draft of the ceiling fan brush lightly over her skin. She could hear the steady drip of a tap coming from the bathroom and the distant sounds of the camp carrying on the afternoon breeze.

Allowing her eyes to flicker open she gazed up at the fluttering mosquito net that had been ruched above the bed, then raising herself on her elbows she looked around the chalet. Nothing, as far as she could tell, had been moved, but someone had been there, of that she was certain.

Swinging her feet to the floor she sat on the edge of the bed, conscious of something not being quite right, but for the moment unable to locate it. It was nothing, she felt sure, to do with her phantom visitor, it was something that had yet to surface in her sleep-shadowed mind. Then, as though someone had suddenly ripped back a veil, it was there. Her head fell forward as she hugged herself and struggled to hold back the familiar ache of despair. But the realities of her life, past and present, were already raining down on her in randomly brutal blows. Richard was dead. Oliver had turned up. Andy had rejected her. She was a desperate, frustrated woman who had allowed herself to be used like a tramp. She wanted Richard. Her life meant nothing without him. Why had God done this to her? Why had Andy been so cruel? Why did Oliver have to come into their lives?

Taking deep, steadying breaths she forced her head up and tried to slow her thoughts. It was always bad in the first few minutes of waking, she just needed a little time to collect herself.

Closing her eyes tightly, she dug her nails into the bed. Though she despised herself for it she knew how jealous she was of Rhiannon's relationship with Oliver. She deeply resented Oliver for being the one Rhiannon turned to now, when for the past two years, ever since Richard had been killed in a car crash, she and Rhiannon had been inseparable. They had come to count on each other, had always been there for each other, sharing the highs and lows of life, building the programme and watching their fame and fortunes grow. Then, three months ago, they had been at De Beers making a programme on the exclusive world of diamond dealing, when the elevator doors had opened and Oliver Maguire had walked into their lives, sweeping Rhiannon right off her feet and usurping Lizzy's place as Rhiannon's best friend.

Pulling herself up from the bed, Lizzy wrapped herself in a towel and walked over to the mirror. Her hair was still damp from the shower and sticking to her head. Finding a comb she began to drag it through her curls, though the heaviness in her heart seemed to be spreading to her limbs. There were times when everything felt so much of an effort that she wondered why she even bothered. Two years and she still missed Richard so much, felt so unbearably lost without him, that it might only have happened yesterday.

Fixing her eyes on her reflection, she tried forcing herself to smile even though grief was tightening her throat. How many times had friends told her that she must get out more, start building a new life and trying with other men. Despite her loathing of such facile advice she had, on a few occasions, made herself accept the dates that had been set up for her. From the outset each one had been a disaster. It was like suddenly finding herself in a foreign land where she knew neither the language nor the customs, where the people around her had no time or interest in her difficulties and every attempt she made to adjust seemed only to intensify the longing to go back. But it couldn't go on that way, she had to let go of the past and somehow make herself believe that it was possible to go on living without him.

Hearing a noise outside on the veranda, she turned towards the french windows, her hand instinctively moving to the knot in the towel. Sunlight was pooling on the mesh-covered panes making it impossible for her to see out, but noticing that one of the doors was slightly ajar she tiptoed forward, aware now of a peculiarly rhythmic creaking sound.

She drew back sharply as a shadow crossed the doorway. Though her heart was thudding she realized she was more curious than afraid and stepping quietly up to the windows she pressed herself into the folds of the curtains and peered out.

From where she was standing she could see the old wooden chair still swaying on it rockers. The creaking had stopped now and the shadow had moved from the doorway, but she was certain someone was still there. She allowed several seconds to tick by, then lifted the flimsy gauze curtain and looked out at the sleepy, sun-drenched afternoon.

Andy was standing at the edge of the veranda, his back turned to the chalet as he quietly smoked a cigarette. Lizzy's heart instantly contracted and she was on the point of drawing back into the shadows when, seeming to sense she was there, he turned round.

'You're awake,' he said, meeting her eyes through the window.

'So it would seem,' she responded, pulling the door open and folding her arms as she leaned against the frame.

A few seconds passed before either of them spoke again.

'Is there something I can do for you?' she enquired.

Pursing his lips at one corner, he looked away

through the trees, appearing to contemplate his answer. 'Look,' he said, finally turning back to her, 'we both know this isn't going anywhere between us, but I don't want to fall out with you and it seems to me that we're heading that way.'

Lizzy merely looked at him, aware of a distant anger rising inside her.

He glanced away again, digging his hands into his trouser pockets. 'I reckon', he said, avoiding her eyes, 'that I owe you an apology for this morning. When I said that you wouldn't want to know what I was thinking, what I meant was ... Well, what I meant was that you wouldn't want to hear ...'

'Don't bother to lie,' Lizzy cut in.

His eyes widened in surprise as he brought them back to hers. Then suddenly his face was drawn with anger. 'What the fuck is it with you?' he demanded. 'I'm trying to tell you ...'

'What is it with me?' she laughed in disbelief.

'Yes, you! You had your fun last night, you got what you came here for, so what the fuck's all this about?'

Lizzy started to speak, but he cut her off.

'You're all the same, you women who come here expecting to get laid. Well, you got yourself laid, didn't you? So what's the problem? More than you expected, was it? Better than you expected? Or is it that you want more? There are plenty of other guys about the camp, I'm sure they'd be only too willing to oblige ... But me, don't expect me to carry on playing your game like I was some kind of fuckwit who doesn't know his prick from his principles because I don't have time for all that shit.'

Lizzy's eyes were wide with shock, her heart was racing, but despite the hurt and anger she felt the fight start to drain out of her. He wasn't worth it. He simply wasn't worth the effort of getting herself all worked up over when in reality he couldn't matter less. 'Please, just go away and leave me alone,' she said quietly.

As she turned back inside, not even bothering to close the door, she could hear his footsteps on the veranda and sinking down on the edge of the bed she buried her face in her hands. 'Richard,' she whispered brokenly as the tears trickled through her fingers. 'Oh God, Richard.'

'Lizzy?'

Starting, she turned to see Andy standing at the door. 'I thought you'd gone,' she said through her teeth.

'I'm sorry,' he said gruffly.

Lowering her eyes she began slowly to shake her head. 'It doesn't matter,' she told him, wiping the back of her hand over her cheek.

He stood there, looking as awkward as a teenager. 'Do you think we could start this again?' he said finally.

Her voice was scratchy and faint as she said, 'Is there any point?'

Several more seconds ticked by until drawing a hand nervously over his chin he said, 'I know this is going to sound crazy, but ... Well, you know a guy gets tired of being a "sex god", of serving up the screaming orgasms and laying it on for the punters. But it seemed that was what you wanted and I've got to admit that in your case it was no hardship. I mean, the punters don't often come like you, in fact most of the time you wish they hadn't come at all ...'

When he stopped Lizzy turned to look at him.

'Oh hell, I'm no good at this sort of thing,' he said impatiently. 'What I'm saying is that I don't see any point in either of us pretending.'

'Pretending?' she repeated.

He took a breath, then suddenly realizing he didn't know what he wanted to say he turned his eyes to the ceiling. 'How the fuck did I get myself into this?' he muttered.

'No one's forcing you to stay,' she reminded him.

'No, that's right,' he said. 'Just like no one forced you to turn a three last night. *Fuck,*' he seethed, screwing up his eyes. 'Nothing I say is coming out right.'

'Then what are you trying to say?'

Bringing his eyes back to hers he grimaced, then taking another breath he started again. 'What I'm trying to say', he said, 'is that in a lot of ways I'm glad we did what we did last night, but I don't want to do it again.'

'Meaning you think I do?' she responded tightly. 'Well, for your information, it's the first time in my life I've ever turned a three, as you so charmingly put it, and while I won't deny I enjoyed it I have absolutely no intention of repeating it. Perhaps you could pass that on to your brother.'

'Sure, I'll tell him,' he said. 'And what about me, or do I get the elbow too? Now that you've got what you wanted? Or do you reckon you can bring yourself to stretch it out until you leave?'

Sliding a hand into her hair, Lizzy shook her head, trying to clear it. 'Excuse me,' she said, 'either I'm being a bit slow here or you're about as consistent as God. I thought you were telling me that we weren't going anywhere, or more to the point, that you didn't want to sleep with me again?'

'Sure I want to sleep with you, I just don't want to share you with my brother again and I don't want either of us to pretend that there's a future in this when we both know there isn't.'

Lizzy turned away, totally at a loss. 'Can you remind me', she said eventually, 'at what point I told you I thought there was a future for us, because it seems to be escaping me right now.'

'Women always think there's a future,' he replied.

Giving herself a moment to resist the urge to bounce his ego off the walls she said, 'You mean that you seriously believe I am considering giving up my home, my career, my family, my friends, not to mention my country, to come and shack up with you here, in the depths of Africa ...' She stopped as to her amazement she realized his eyes were dancing with laughter.

'Well, will you?' he said.

'Will I what?'

'Come and live with me here?'

The shock was so great that her mouth simply fell open.

'No rush. Think it over,' he said and turning on his heel he walked out of the room.

Doug was on the point of taking a beer from the fridge when his hand suddenly stopped in mid-air and he turned back to look at his brother, not at all sure he had heard right. 'Are you serious?' he said, letting the fridge door swing closed. 'You asked her to come and live here? What did she say, for Christ's sake?'

Andy shrugged. 'I didn't give her time to answer. Just told her to think it over and left.'

Doug was still gaping at him. 'What are you going to do if she says yes?' he said.

'What do you mean, what am I going to do? What do you think I'm going to do?'

'I don't know, mate, that's why I'm asking.'

Andy nodded towards the refrigerator, reminding Doug about the beers. Still looking at him Doug reached inside, took out a couple of cans and tossed one over.

'You're serious about this, aren't you?' he said finally. 'You want her to come.'

Andy shrugged and tilted the beer to his mouth.

Doug was shaking his head, still not quite believing this. 'You've only known the woman twenty-four hours,' he said. 'Christ, Andy, she's just another punter. She let both of us poke her last night and she'd let us again tonight ...'

'Forget it,' Andy cut across him. 'It's not going to happen again.'

Doug blinked. 'I don't get this,' he said, combing his fingers through his hair. 'Are you telling me you've fallen for the woman? Is that what you're saying?'

'It might be.'

'But how, for Christ's sake? When did it happen? I mean you couldn't have felt that way last night.' He waited, expecting Andy to respond. 'Maybe you did feel that way last night,' he prompted.

'Maybe I did,' Andy replied.

Again Doug was shaking his head. 'No, you wouldn't have let me in on the act if you ...'

'Why don't we try to forget you were ever in on the act,' Andy interrupted. 'I know we've shared a lot of women over the years, but this time it was a mistake. Just like Leandra was a mistake.'

Doug's face instantly hardened. 'That was a long time ago, mate,' he said.

'That's right, and I've never mentioned it again 'til now,' Andy reminded him. 'That's the way I want it with Lizzy – if she decides to come.'

Doug was right on the point of telling him what a bloody jackass he was making of himself when instinct told him to let it ride for the moment. He took a long pull of his beer, watching his brother all the while. 'What happened?' he said finally. 'I mean, when did you decide all this, because the last I recall you were going over there to tell her you didn't much appreciate her remark about baboons or something. What was that, by the way?'

Andy laughed. 'I'd forgotten about that,' he said. 'I thought she was going to do a hatchet job on us because of the way I treated her this morning, *that's* why I went over there.' He laughed again. 'Can you believe it?' he said. 'I go over there to tell her I'm sorry if I insulted her and not only do I end up insulting her again, I realize half-way through that ...'

'Yes?' Doug encouraged.

'Well, that I'm in this a bit deeper than I knew.'

Using a mannerism that was typical to them both,

Doug pursed his mouth at the corner and narrowed his eyes. 'And you seriously think you're going to talk a woman as sophisticated as that into staying here, in the back of beyond, with you?' he said bluntly.

Andy merely looked at him.

'Jesus, Andy!' he cried, slamming his beer on the table. 'No woman in her right mind's going to give up a life like she's got to come and play Jane to your Tarzan, especially not a woman like her.'

Andy's only response was to get up and walk slowly over to the window. They were in the kitchen of the sprawling thatch-roofed bungalow the brothers shared at the edge of the camp and as Andy turned to look around at the somewhat primitive facilities, he had to concede that perhaps his brother had a point. But Lizzy Fortnum didn't strike him as the kind of woman who got turned on by kitchens and even if she were he had the money to get her any damned kitchen she wanted.

Frowning down at his beer, he turned his mind back again to those few minutes he had been at her chalet this afternoon. He certainly hadn't gone over there with the intention of asking her to come and live with him – shit, as a firmly anchored bachelor that had been the last thing on his mind! No, if the truth be known he'd gone over there with the intention of making another score between the posts. Of course, he hadn't been expecting her to give in right away, not after the way he'd given her the brush-off this morning, but he'd been pretty certain he could win her round – after all, his maxim of treat 'em mean, keep 'em keen had never let him down before. But something had changed course somewhere and he still wasn't sure he knew where. What he did know, however, was that if he'd sounded as much of a jerk as he now feared he had, he wouldn't mind going out and shooting himself in the head right now. On the other hand, if she said she wouldn't mind coming here to live with him ... Shit, what *was* he going to do if she said yes?

But no, Doug was right, a woman like her wouldn't even consider the idea, was probably married anyway, or living with someone else and just out for a bit on the side, the same as most of the sheilas who came out here. He used them, they used him and everyone was happy. Except Lizzy Fortnum wasn't happy, anyone could see that – at least he could and he didn't consider himself the sort of bloke who generally picked up on that sort of thing.

'Tell you what,' Doug said, lifting his feet on to the table and crossing his ankles, 'spend the night with her tonight, alone, the two of you, then see how you feel in the morning. You'll have probably worked it through your system by then.'

Grinning, Andy took another mouthful of beer and walking back to the table mirrored his brother's position. 'Can't you do better with the advice than that?' he challenged.

'No, I don't reckon I can,' Doug replied after a moment's deliberation. 'In fact, I'd go as far as to say that if you seriously believe she'll come here to live then you're a couple of shingles short, mate.'

Laughing, Andy swung his feet back to the floor. 'A thousand rands says she accepts my offer,' he said, pitching his empty can into the bin.

Doug spluttered with shock. 'You're on, mate,' he said. 'And another thousand says you don't get her in the sack ag—'

'Excuse me,' Lizzy interrupted, knocking on the door as she pushed it open. 'I hope I haven't chosen a bad time,' she said, looking from Doug's stunned expression to Andy's vaguely embarrassed one.

'No, no, not at all,' Doug assured her. 'Come on in. What can we do for you?'

'Well, actually,' she said, desperately wishing she didn't feel so awkward confronting them both together like this, 'I've just come to ...' She turned to Andy and smiled. 'I've come to say thank you for the flowers,' she said. 'I found them on the veranda after you'd gone. They're lovely.'

Doug's eyes almost burst from his head as he turned to his brother. 'Flowers?' he mouthed.

Ignoring him, Andy said, 'I'm glad you liked them.' Then to Doug he said, 'Isn't there something you need to be getting on with?'

'No,' Doug answered.

'I'm pretty sure there is,' Andy insisted.

'No, honest, mate, I'm free,' Doug assured him.

Rolling his eyes, Andy looked at Lizzy and saw she was laughing. 'Doug, get the hell out of here, will you?' he said, keeping his eyes on Lizzy's.

'Oh, you want me to go,' Doug cried. 'Well, you just had to say, mate.'

When the door had closed behind him Lizzy turned back to Andy. They were standing either side of the table and it was debatable which of them looked the most self-concious until, quite spontaneously, they started to laugh.

'I'm not going to ask if you meant what you said,' Lizzy told him, 'because I'm not sure I want to know. I just wanted to tell you that ...' She stopped and felt her cheeks burn with colour as her courage suddenly failed her. 'I loved the flowers,' she finished quietly.

Walking around the table Andy pulled her into his arms and kissed her gently on the mouth. 'Shall we start again?' he whispered, wondering if she could feel the way his heart was thudding.

'Yes,' she nodded. 'Let's do that.'

Chapter 4

The attack happened with no warning. One minute they were watching the zebras grazing, laughing quietly as they created outlandish reasons for the stripes, the next the entire herd was in flight and a lioness was thundering from the brush, every muscle in her body rippling as she sprang with deadly grace on to a young stallion's back. Its hindquarters buckled, scudding across the earth, as the lethal claws ripped into its flesh. The rest of the herd vanished into the trees and the young stallion, not seeming to understand its plight, tried to struggle to its feet and follow. But the lioness's weight was too much and baring her teeth she sank them savagely into its neck. The zebra bleated, terror glazing its eyes, the hopeless instinct for survival prolonging its fight as its flesh was torn apart and bloodied teeth gouged right through to its bones. Dust billowed around them as their bodies thumped into the earth. The stallion struggled on, straining its neck upwards, flailing its hooves, its petrified eyes rolling in their sockets as the lioness's talons scored the blood from its veins and the great jaws clamped like a vice around its throat.

The awful snap of the spinal cord brought an abrupt end to the fray and the dying zebra slumped helplessly on to its side, gore oozing from its wounds as its lifeblood pumped over the coarse black-and-white hide.

The lioness stood over her prey, barely panting from

the effort it had taken to kill, as her tail systematically swiped at the flies on her back and dark, ruby blood dripped from her open mouth. The fervid panic of bird life, the settling dust, the circling vultures, the ambient terror, the dying heart beating beneath her all lent a painful pathos to the primeval savagery of the kill. The air, already turning black with flies, was stained by the bitter stench of her breath as she raised her head and growled deep in her throat. Then sinking on to her haunches, she buried her muzzle in the ragged hole she had gouged in the zebra's throat. The zebra's eyes were closed, but there was a last flicker of life as the flesh was dragged from its skull and its torn and quivering body finally yielded to death.

Knowing this was no longer a wise place to be, for the males were likely to descend at any moment, Andy started up the jeep and backed discreetly away. It wasn't the first time he had witnessed a kill, and it was unlikely to be the last, but no matter how many times he saw it he knew he would never cease to be affected by it. Beside him, Lizzy, who had taken over Melanie's place in the front, sat quietly in her seat, a hand bunched at her mouth as she gazed sightlessly ahead.

In the seat behind, Rhiannon turned to Oliver. His face was sombre as he pulled her head on to his shoulder. From the silence in the jeep Rhiannon guessed that the others had experienced the same horror she had, for the zebra's terror and pain had shown a facet of bush life none of them had given much thought to before, and its pitiful impotence in the face of such power was so moving that she could almost feel her own skin being torn from her bones by those merciless jaws.

Jack and Hugh sat mutely in the rear seat, the sound and camera equipment lying motionlessly in their laps. They had captured the kill, now they needed time to assimilate their thoughts and try somehow to absorb the mind-numbing shock of how close they had come to the brutal reality of nature.

In the end it was Hugh who broke the silence. 'What happened to the American woman?' he said.

Andy glanced at his watch. 'She'll be on her way back to Jo'burg by now,' he answered.

Oliver frowned and looked at Rhiannon.

'She came on a drive with us this morning,' she explained.

'I thought she was leaving at the same time as us,' Lizzy remarked.

Andy shrugged. 'She was, but something came up, she said, that meant she had to leave right away,' and circling an arm around Lizzy he pulled her head on to his shoulder.

Rhiannon glanced up at Oliver and they both smiled. Neither of them had any idea what had happened between Andy and Lizzy during the early part of the afternoon, but obviously something had and, for Rhiannon at least, it was a relief to see that they had put the awkwardness of the morning behind them. She just hoped that Lizzy wasn't going to get too involved, for her loneliness since Richard's death and recent almost panicked determination to get over it, had made her extremely vulnerable and perhaps not as circumspect as she might otherwise be.

But really it was absurd to be worrying about the depth of their involvement when they'd barely known each other five minutes and when even Lizzy, as starved of romance as she was, wouldn't be crazy enough to throw herself into a relationship with the first man she'd slept with since Richard – especially not a man whose accessibility had even more problems than his *savoire-faire*.

'OK?' Oliver said as she made herself more comfortable.

'Mmm, fine,' she answered, her thoughts returning to the disturbing vision of the kill. She wondered how it must feel in those seconds before the lion struck, when the belief in escape was paramount to survival, but when death was inevitable. She shivered. Of all the ways to die she couldn't imagine one more horrible than being mauled by a wild animal.

Then quite suddenly she was laughing as, with typically untimely wit, Hugh called out, 'So what's on the menu tonight then, Andy?'

Outside, the darkness was alive with the needle sharp buzz of insect life, the falsetto howl of hyenas, the warbling croak of frogs, the bellow of bull elephants, the snarl and scream of killer cats, the high-pitched whine of bats. All around them nature was fretting and fidgeting, while the exotic scent of the bush drifted in through the woven silk mesh at the windows. Oliver rolled on to his back, his fingers splayed over the taut flesh of Rhiannon's buttocks, holding their bodies together.

'I love you,' he whispered, reaching up to squeeze her breasts together.

Looking down at him she started to smile, her soft, pliant mouth glistening in the half-light, her coppery hair tumbling over her shoulders in a wild unruly mass. He was big and solid inside her, filling her with the promise of an as yet unleashed passion as his thumbs teased her nipples and swelling tremors of lust eddied between them.

Suddenly there was a loud knock on the door and as his face tightened with annoyance Rhiannon's eyes closed in exasperation.

'Oliver! Are you there, mate?' Doug shouted. 'Phone for you.'

'Oh no,' Rhiannon protested.

'Tell them I'll call back,' Oliver shouted, grabbing her waist as she made to pull away.

'They're saying it's urgent,' Doug told him.

'I'll call back,' Oliver shouted, driving himself hard

and fast into Rhiannon and watching her breasts bounce over her ribs. 'Shit, I'm going to come,' he whispered.

'What'll I do if ... ?' Doug started.

'Doug, this isn't a good time,' Rhiannon interrupted breathlessly.

Oliver started to grin, but his face suddenly contorted. 'Jesus Christ,' he gasped as she clamped her muscles around him, squeezing him painfully tight. 'How do you do that? Oh, fuck, Rhiannon,' he cried, thrashing around beneath her.

'Let it go,' she whispered. 'Just let it go.'

'Oh yes,' he cried, his back arching as the seed began to gush out of him. 'Keep doing that,' he panted, as she clenched his hardness again and again and rotated her hips wildly. *'Oh, Christ yes!'* he gasped, digging his fingers hard into her flesh as the thrust of his climax exploded.

Finally, as she felt the tension begin to drain from his body, Rhiannon eased the pressure of her muscles and looking down at his strained, exhausted face she could feel love spreading heat into every part of her.

'I love you,' he murmured, his body giving a delayed shudder in the receding force of his climax.

'Do you?' she smiled.

He smiled too as he sank a hand into her hair and rested his palm on her cheek. 'Yes, I do,' he told her. 'And you didn't come.'

'I wanted to watch you.'

He laughed softly and brought her other hand to his mouth. 'Then it's my turn to watch you,' he said.

'Hadn't you better go and find out who was on the phone?' she said as he eased her on to her back.

'This is more important.'

'But Doug said it was urgent ...'

'Sssh,' he said, kissing her again, 'whatever it is, it can wait.'

*

Randy Theakston was at the Carlton Hotel in down town Johannesburg. She had just got off the phone with Theo Straussen, and was now waiting for further instructions to come via the fax machine she'd set up on the desk. So far her assignment had been simple; Edwardes was an easy subject to observe and the photographs Straussen had requested were already on their way to New York. Even the shots of Edwardes and Maguire by the pool had been easy to come by, though whether they were the kind of thing Straussen wanted Randy had yet to find out.

She was sitting in an armchair, studying a street map of Cape Town which she already knew to be her next destination, when the fax finally came through. It was a single page, which she tore off the machine, scanned quickly, then sat down to read more thoroughly. She was surprised by what she was being asked to do and not a little perplexed. But if this was what Straussen wanted, then this was what Straussen would get – and his reasons for wanting it weren't something Randy was about to waste her time speculating on.

'Are you asleep?' Lizzy whispered into the darkness.

Andy turned his head and kissed her briefly on the nose. 'No,' he answered.

'What time is it?'

Raising his wrist into the paling rays of moonlight slanting in through the shutters he said, 'Nearly half four.'

Lizzy smiled sleepily and curling in closer to him listened for a while to nature's pandemonium outside. 'Have you slept at all?' she asked.

'No.'

'What were you thinking about?'

'A lot of things,' he answered, smiling as her stomach gave a protracted growl of hunger. 'That's what hapens when you skip dinner,' he told her.

'Are you hungry?' she said, turning to look at him.

'A bit.'

'Shall we go and find a kitchen to raid?'

Laughing, he pulled her on top of him and squeezed her tightly. 'Sounds like a good idea to me,' he said.

But neither of them made a move to get up and as she settled back down against him, her cheek resting on the hard, comfortable plain of his chest, her throat tightened with the almost forgotten joy of what it was like to feel a man's arms around her.

'What was that?' she whispered as a frantic screeching momentarily drowned the other sounds.

'Baboons,' he answered.

There was a moment's silence before they both started to laugh. Then rearranging their positions, they lay facing each other, legs entwined, fingers idling stroking each other's arms. His tanned, rugged features were softened by the first glimmers of dawn seeping into the room, his eyes showed no trace of their sleepless night.

She'd wondered if telling him about Richard would change the way he felt about her, for it would be obvious that she still loved her husband and maybe Andy would see that as a threat. But, as his dark-blue eyes moved across her face, following the trail of his fingers, she could feel herself starting to relax and turning her mouth to his palm she kissed it and hugged it to her cheek.

A long time passed as they continued to gaze into each other's eyes, barely aware of the stirring sounds of daybreak, the rhythmic hum of the fan or the fine gauze of the net that fluttered gently around them. Uppermost in both their minds was the fact that in a few hours she would be leaving.

At last his mouth covered hers, caressing her lips gently with his own as he eased her body in closer and began very slowly, very tenderly, to make love to her.

When it was over they lay in each other's arms listening to the steadying beat of their hearts and the inescapable tick of the clock.

'I can't stay, Andy, you know that, don't you?' she said finally.

He started to speak, swallowed, then said, 'Yes, I know that.'

She looked down at the dark hair curling on his chest and combed it lightly with her fingers. 'Did you mean it when you asked me?' she said.

He shrugged.

She smiled. 'Does that mean you don't know?'

'It means that right now I'm afraid of saying the wrong thing.'

'Why not just say what's in your mind?' she suggested.

'No, I don't want to do that.'

They were quiet again then, as, not for the first time, she tried to imagine what life would be like here, in the depths of the bush and so very far from London. But no matter how idyllic and romantic it seemed, in her heart she knew that she was no more cut out for this kind of life than Andy was for the city. Besides, what did she really know about him, apart from the fact that, though he would probably rather die than ever admit it, he was as lonely and starved of affection as she was?

'Have you ever been in love? she asked.

He thought about it for a moment. 'I guess there have been a couple of times when I've come close,' he answered.

Resisting the temptation to ask about those women she said, 'What would you have done if I'd said I wanted to stay?'

His face tensed, then seeming to relax again he said, 'To tell you the truth I didn't expect you to say yes.'

'But you asked anyway?'

He shrugged.

'Why?'

'Search me. No one was more surprised than me

when I said it.'

'Except me,' she laughed.

When there was no answering laugh she realized that she was in danger of allowing a pathetic search for reassurance to become a twisting knife in his pride. 'I'm really glad this happened between us,' she said, reaching up to stroke his face. 'It's, well, it's made me feel whole again and ...'

'Always happy to oblige,' he replied, looking at his watch. 'That's what we're here for, to keep the customers happy.'

'Andy don't! It meant more than that, to both of us ...'

'There were three of us, remember?'

'Oh, for God's sake! You're just being childish now,' she cried, pulling away from him.

He let her go and lay moodily on his back, his hands behind his head as he stared up at the ceiling. Beside him Lizzy circled her legs with her arms and rested her chin on her knees.

Long minutes ticked by as the air simmered with their antagonism and the distant commotion of the camp coming to life carried on the early morning breeze.

'Shit, there's no point to this,' he suddenly growled and throwing back the net he got abruptly up from the bed and reached for his shorts.

Lizzy turned to look at him, watching him as he hoiked the shorts angrily up over his legs.

'Andy, I don't see why ...'

'Don't say any more,' he snapped, cutting her off. 'We've gone as far as we're going so let's not drag it out, eh?'

'And let's not finish it like this,' she cried.

He continued dressing, his whole body radiating anger as he zipped up his fly and buckled his belt. As he reached for his gun, Lizzy got up and walked around the bed towards him. 'Why are you so angry?' she said.

'Angry?' he replied scathingly. 'Who's angry? I've just

made a right fool of myself ...'

'How?' she cried. 'Because you asked me to stay?'

'No, because I actually believed you might,' he yelled and yanking open the door he stormed off furiously into the rosy hues of dawn.

Lizzy stood where she was, watching the fly screen click gently into place. Though she was smarting she understood why he'd behaved the way he had, for a man as eligible as he was obviously wasn't used to being turned down – and, for the moment anyway, it appeared that the ignominy was too much for his male ego to handle. The most incredible part of it, though, to him as well as to her it seemed, was that he had actually thought she might accept his offer. Well, she had to confess that she *had* considered it, but only fleetingly and even then only as a flight of fancy.

'I mean,' she said to Rhiannon when they met up for breakfast later, 'do I strike you as a zoo-keeper's wife?'

'It's hardly a zoo,' Rhiannon laughed. 'But if you're asking me if I see you as a game-ranger's wife then frankly the answer's no. However, were I given a little more time to get used to the idea ...' She put her head thoughtfully to one side, successfully concealing the relief she was feeling that Lizzy wasn't about to do something crazy, which people in grief were often known to do. 'No, I still don't see you as a ranger's gal,' she said.

'Oh, yes, more coffee for me,' Lizzy said as a waiter started to hover. 'And more toast?' Turning back to Rhiannon, she popped the final morsel of the last slice into her mouth and wiping her hands on a napkin said, 'Amazing though, isn't it? I mean, that he actually asked me in the first place. I can still hardly believe it.'

'I have to confess I'm having a little difficulty myself,' Rhiannon responded flicking her hair back over her shoulder as she poured more tea into her cup. 'Not that I'm doubting your charms, you understand ...'

Laughing Lizzy said, 'But I've barely known him

forty-eight hours and I haven't exactly gone out of my way to promote myself as the perfect Waltzing Matilda in that time, have I? Or maybe I did,' she added, frowning. 'Anyway, like I said, he ended up walking out on me this morning and I haven't seen him since. Where's Oliver, by the way?'

'Gone to make a phone call,' Rhiannon answered. 'And don't look round now but Andy is heading in this direction.'

Lizzy was startled by how strongly her heart reacted. 'Does he still look angry?' she whispered.

'Can't tell,' Rhiannon answered. 'He's still too far away. There's something of the caveman about him, though. I reckon he might be about to drag you off into the bush by the hair ...'

'Don't mock! And for God's sake don't let on that I've mentioned any of this.'

Rhiannon gave her a pained expression. 'Would I?' she said. Then raising her eyes above Lizzy's shoulder she gave a beaming smile of welcome and said, 'Good morning, Andy. How are you? Still feeling a bit of a prat after Lizzy jilted you, are you?'

Lizzy stared at her in horror.

'Oh, I see, more of a dick.' Rhiannon nodded sympathetically, earning herself a swift kick under the table.

'I almost believed you then,' Lizzy laughed. 'Is he on his way over or not?'

'Why don't you turn round and find out?'

Lizzy glared at her, then very tentatively started to turn her head and almost leapt out of her skin as she came face to face with a rhino. 'Jesus Christ!' she choked as Hugh dropped the stuffed head in her lap. 'Take it away!' she cried, jumping to her feet and knocking it to the floor. 'Where did you get it, for heaven's sake?'

'A present from Andy and Doug,' Hugh answered, retrieving it. 'Jack's got a hippo.'

'Does it have to join us for breakfast?' Rhiannon

protested.

'No. We've already had ours. I've just popped across to pass on the message that we'll be flying out half an hour earlier than scheduled. In other words fifteen minutes from now.'

Lizzy's heart turned over as she brought her eyes back to Rhiannon's. 'I'd better go and find Andy,' she said, throwing her napkin on to the table.

'He's already up at the air strip,' Hugh told her. 'Saw him leaving a couple of minutes ago.'

'Shit!' Lizzy muttered, turning to Rhiannon again as Hugh walked away.

'Maybe there'll be a chance for a quick word before you get on the plane,' Rhiannon suggested lamely.

Lizzy was about to respond when her eyes suddenly shot to Rhiannon's and the mutinous expression Rhiannon knew only too well started to tighten her face. 'No, to hell with it,' she said harshly, pulling her chair back to the table. 'He knows where to find me so why the hell should I ...' Her voice suddenly broke and as her eyes filled with tears she slammed a fist on the table. 'For Christ's sake, what's the matter with me?' she cried angrily. 'Anyone would think I gave a damn! Oh God, this is pathetic! What the hell am I crying for? It doesn't matter, none of it matters. I'll never see him again – Christ, I don't even know the man so why am I ... !'

'Lizzy! Stop giving yourself such a hard time,' Rhiannon interrupted. 'You like the man, part of you has fallen for him, there's nothing to be ashamed of in that and it's perfectly natural ...'

'No, it's not perfectly natural,' Lizzy seethed. 'I've only known him for two days ...'

'So what?'

'I don't want to stay here, that's what,' Lizzy responded tightly.

'No one's saying you have to.'

'It's just not me to live in a place like this. Is it? I mean, *is it?*'

'No,' Rhiannon laughed, 'it's not.'

'So why can't *he* see that?'

'He probably can, but that doesn't mean ...'

'I mean, I can't help it if I'm not cut out to be ...'

'Rhiannon!'

They both looked up to see Oliver coming towards them, his handsome face drawn with concern.

'Lizzy, I'm sorry to interrupt,' he apologized, 'but I have to speak to Rhiannon.'

'Go ahead, don't mind me,' Lizzy responded curtly.

'Darling, what is it?' Rhiannon said, getting instantly to her feet. 'Did you get through to New York?'

'Uh, no, not yet,' he answered distractedly, drawing her out of earshot. 'Listen, darling ...' He sighed almost angrily. 'You're not going to believe this, but my credit cards have gone.'

Rhiannon looked at him, her face draining. 'Again?' she said incredulously. 'But that's the second time in a month.'

'You don't have to tell me,' he muttered.

'Are you sure you haven't just mislaid them?' she said.

'Positive. They were in my briefcase.'

'But who on earth would take them here?'

'God knows,' he responded. 'But they've gone, that's for sure.'

'Have you told Andy or Doug?'

'Not yet. I was hoping you were going to tell me you had them in your bag.'

'Oh God,' she groaned, absently watching Lizzy as she walked back to her chalet. 'It has to be one of the other guests or, God forbid, one of the staff.' Her eyes suddenly came up to his as a dreadful suspicion took root in her mind. 'Oliver, you don't think it's me, do you?' she said.

Despite his concern he couldn't help smiling. 'No, of course I don't, he answered. 'And considering I was in New York the last time it happened and *you* were the one who bailed me out ...' He looked at her with a rueful expression. 'I'm afraid you might have to do the same here,' he told her.

'Well that's not a problem,' she responded. 'What is, though, is who's actually taken them.'

He sighed heavily. 'The guys are going to feel pretty bad about this,' he said, glancing at his watch. 'Anyway, we don't have a lot of time. I'll go and talk to Doug and try to get through to New York while I'm there. The receptionist is waiting for us to settle up.'

'OK, I'll go see to it,' she said. 'And you'd better ring London to report the theft of the cards.'

'Rhiannon,' he said, catching her by the hand as she made to walk away. 'I'll pay you back.'

'I know,' she smiled, responding to the look in his eyes. 'But it doesn't matter.'

'It does,' he told her and giving her a brief kiss on the mouth, he started back across the camp.

Doug was on the phone when Oliver reached the office so picking up another line Oliver tried his office in London.

'Hi, it's me,' he said when his secretary's sleepy cockney voice came down the line. 'Did you receive the confirmation yet?'

'What?' she said.

'Naomi, wake up,' he told her. 'It's me, Oliver. Did you hear from Glenrow in Sydney?'

'*Oh yeah!*' she cried, coming suddenly to life. 'The diamond. God, you'll never guess what happened. It was really weird. I got this call to say there was going to be a problem getting the diamond to Jo'burg on time, so naturally I got straight on the phone to tell you. But before I even had a chance to dial the same bloke called back and said that everything was OK, it would be there on schedule.'

Oliver was frowning. 'Who was it?' he said. 'Did he leave his name?'

'No, I don't think so. I don't remember it, anyway. All's I remember was thinking, holy shit, Oliver's going to go demented when he hears this. But like I said, no panic now, the diamond'll be there bang on schedule.'

The pounding in Oliver's chest didn't lessen. 'Are you sure?' he said.

'That's what the bloke said,' she replied. 'Said he was sorry if he caused any undue alarm, but he got his shipments mixed up and there was no delay with ours at all. I told him I was glad to hear it, because we've had enough problems these last couple of months without him and his sodding delays. Well, I didn't actually say that, I just thought it, but it's true, isn't it? We've had a lot of really annoying things happen to us lately. It's like we've got some sort of jinx on us.'

'Yeah, OK, Nayms,' Oliver interrupted. 'Any other messages?'

'No, that was it. Are you still coming back at the weekend?'

'That's the plan,' he answered and after giving her a few calls to make and letters to get under way he rang off.

'Everything OK?' Doug asked, finishing his own call.

Oliver looked up. 'Yeah,' he answered, forcing a smile. 'Yeah, everything's fine.'

'You sure,' Doug persisted, "cos I got to tell you, mate, you look like you're about to throw up.'

Again Oliver attempted a smile. 'Yeah, sure,' he replied. 'It was just some mix-up with a deal I've got going, a pretty big deal, actually, and I thought for a minute something was going wrong.'

Doug looked at him. 'But it's not?' he said.

'No,' Oliver answered.

Doug nodded. 'Did you manage to get hold of

Straussen?' he said, picking up a pile of booking forms. 'He sounded pretty stressed last night.'

'You know, what I'd like to know', Oliver replied, 'is how the old bastard knew where to find me.'

Doug glanced up from the booking sheets. 'Why? You trying to hide from him?' he asked.

'Not exactly,' Oliver laughed, 'I just wish he'd give me a bit of space on occasions.'

Doug's eyebrows went up as he started towards the door. 'He made a pretty big investment in you, Oliver,' he reminded him, 'so you can't blame the guy for keeping tabs, now can you?'

'A little trust here and there wouldn't go amiss,' Oliver responded. Then, smiling, he clapped Doug on the back. 'It's been really great seeing you,' he said as they walked out into the sunshine. 'Really great.'

'It's been great seeing you too,' Doug replied, spotting Rhiannon over at reception, her golden hair glinting in the sunlight as she talked to Melanie while Hugh and Jack helped Elmore and a couple of trackers load the luggage and camera equipment on to a landrover. 'Pardon the pun,' he said, digging his hands into the pockets of his shorts, 'but you got yourself a real gem there.'

Oliver smiled. 'I certainly think so,' he said as Rhiannon spotted Lizzy struggling with a suitcase and shouted for one of the men to go and help. Then turning to Doug, his eyes dancing with humour, he said, 'Weren't getting any ideas there, were you?'

Doug's sun-weathered face broke into a grin. 'Does Dolly Parton sleep on her back?' he responded. 'By the way,' he went on as they started to stroll across the grass, 'did you know, Andy's gone and got himself hooked on the blonde? He even asked her to stay.'

'No kidding,' Oliver said, looking across to where Lizzy was climbing into the jeep. 'Seems like she turned him down, though.'

'Are you surprised? She doesn't even know the bloke, except in the carnal sense.'

Oliver's smile was sardonic. 'Still, I thought she might have given it a shot,' he said. 'She's been pretty lonely since her husband died – lonely enough to try it on with me a couple of times.'

Doug's eyebrows went up. 'You ever give it a test drive?' he asked.

'No.'

'Well, take it from me it handles pretty well,' Doug told him. 'Does Rhiannon know about her coming on to you?' he added after a pause.

'What do you think?' Oliver answered.

Sighing and laughing, Doug said, 'Well, Andy's going to be a tough one to be around for the next few days, now he's been given the old heave-ho. Not something he's used to. Heck, he's never asked a woman to live with him before, not as far as I know, anyway. It's usually them asking him.'

'Where is he?' Oliver asked.

'Up at the airstrip dealing with the punters who came in on the early flight.'

Oliver nodded, starting to smile as Rhiannon came towards them. 'Everything OK?' he said as she slipped into the circle of his arm and walked with them towards the jeep.

'Seems to be,' she answered. 'Did you get through to New York?'

'Still a bit early to try,' he replied, seeming almost deliberately to be avoiding Doug's eyes.

'So where is it from here?' Doug asked as they arrived at the jeep.

'Johannesburg tonight,' Rhiannon answered. 'Durban tomorrow and Cape Town until the weekend.'

'Well, have a great time,' Doug smiled, holding out his hand to Oliver. 'Keep in touch, mate. And if there's anything else we can do,' he said to Rhiannon as she kissed him on both cheeks, 'any more information you need for your programme, just let us know.'

They arrived at the airstrip a few minutes later to find the plane revving up ready for take-off. The guests it had flown in were already being ferried across to the camp, murmuring or gasping in awe as the jeeps paused alongside a couple of spotted hyenas lying watchfully in the grass at the edge of the runway.

'I take it Andy didn't come back to the camp?' Rhiannon whispered to Lizzy.

Lizzy shook her head. 'Not as far as I'm aware.'

Rhiannon looked over to where Andy was now, talking to the pilot, his thick fair hair blowing about in the wind. 'What are you going to do?' she said.

'God knows,' Lizzy responded. 'I don't want it to end like this, but I don't know what to say to him.'

'He'll probably have calmed down by now,' Rhiannon said comfortingly as the jeep came to a halt beside the plane.

To Lizzy's relief Andy was smiling as he turned towards them, then laughing at something the pilot shouted down to him, he came across to help transfer the luggage.

At last, after tossing the bags up to Hugh and Jack and going through the manly ritual of slapping backs and shaking hands as they said their goodbyes, he turned to where Lizzy was standing. Her heart twisted when she saw the laughter die in his eyes, but forcing herself to keep smiling she started towards him.

'Andy, I ...' she began.

'They're waiting,' he interrupted, holding her away as she leaned forward to kiss him.

'Will you just listen to me!' she cried, shouting to make herself heard above the roar of the engines.

Digging a hand in his pocket he pulled out a scrap of paper. 'Here,' he said, pushing the note into her hand.

Lizzy looked down at it flapping about in the wind.

Then screwing it up she lifted her eyes back to his face. 'Andy, this has meant a great deal to me,' she told him.

'They're waiting to go,' he repeated, turning his back on her and waving to the others who were watching out of the windows.

Lizzy looked at him, wanting to say and do a hundred different things; but realizing it was hopeless she turned away and started to mount the steps. She had almost reached the top when she felt his hand take hold of hers.

'This is the closest,' he said, the paleness of his face reflecting the effort it was costing him to admit it.

Their eyes remained on each other's for some time as she realized that he was telling her this was the closest he had come to falling in love. Her voice was barely more than a whisper as she said, 'I'm sorry.'

His mouth pursed at one corner, then swallowing hard he glanced out across the plains for a moment, before turning abruptly back to his jeep.

It wasn't until the plane was taxiing along the runway that Lizzy realized she was still clutching the scrap of paper he had given her. Unravelling it she looked down at it and felt a quick surge of emotion in her heart as she read what he had written. 'I'm a guy who's no good with words,' he said, 'but I think you know how I feel.'

'What is it?' Rhiannon asked, laughing because Lizzy was.

Lizzy showed her, rolling her eyes in a vain attempt to play down how much Andy's feelings were affecting her.

Rhiannon's eyes were dancing as though she were about to start teasing, which indeed she was until suddenly the warmth began to trickle from her smile and a curious unease started to steal through her veins. She couldn't imagine where it had come from, for there was certainly nothing sinister about those few short words nor about the man who had written them. Yet there was no mistaking the fact that a cold shiver had gone down her spine at the prospect of Lizzy ever returning to Perlatonga.

Still managing a smile, she handed the note back, then turned to look past Oliver out of the window. The concern was so fragmented and elusive that it was impossible to explain it logically and never having experienced this kind of intuition before she was as baffled as she was unnerved by it. They had spent a wonderful three days at Perlatonga, her memories, she knew, would only be happy ones, so why on earth should the idea of any of them returning cause her to shudder? Except, of course, she would be devastated if Lizzy left London which, she thought wryly to herself, wasn't only disgustingly selfish, but also totally irrelevant, for the loss she would feel were Lizzy to go didn't connect at all with the oddness of the feeling she was experiencing regarding the game reserve.

Deciding in the end to put it down to the quirk of a tired mind, she closed her eyes and allowed her thoughts to merge with the drone of the engines. She was just drifting off to sleep when she suddenly remembered Oliver's stolen credit cards and found herself wondering if it was mere bad luck that they had been stolen twice in the same month, or if it was in some way related to the recent theft of his BMW and discovery of some kind of fraud at his bank. Only a fool wouldn't tie the events together, but it was horrible to think that Oliver was being targeted in some way, especially when the credit cards had, on both occasions, either disappeared or been tampered with at the very point it would cause him the most embarrassment.

'Did you remember to cancel the cards?' she asked, sliding her hand into his.

'Oh hell!' he muttered, closing his eyes in exasperation. 'I knew there was something. I didn't mention it to Doug either, I got caught up on the phone and it went clean out of my mind.'

'We'll do it when we get to Johannesburg then,' she said, snuggling in more comfortably and deciding that to worry about anything now was simply a waste of time and effort.

And she was right, at that time it would have been, for no amount of concern could have prepared her for the traumatic events that were already beginning to take shape in a place and in a way that was a very long way from her control.

Chapter 5

The Santa Ana winds were blowing – gusting short, trecherous bursts of warm air through the Malibu Canyon; nature's fuel to an arsonist's flame. Huge tracts of the countryside were still, three years on, scarred by the horror of the fires that had blazed out of control for over fourteen days and caused so much fear and heart-break and destruction. So too had the floods that had raged terrifyingly through the county, devastating homes and lives and dreams. And then there was the earthquake, that dreadful, never-to-be-forgotten morning when freeways, skyscrapers, parks, hotels, million-dollar homes and entire families had literally been shaken loose from the earth's surface.

The Romanov estate had, by some miracle, managed to escape California's plague of disasters. It sat there on the bluff, intact and apparently invulnerable, twenty-two acres of prime Malibu real estate. Through the dense oaks and Monterey pines that overhung the impenetrable boundary walls one could snatch an occasional glimpse of the sprawling gardens, but the main house that was a vast, white, colonnaded villa, with two grey-domed towers amongst its myriad russet roofs, and high-topped feathery palms standing like sentinels around the secluded forecourt, was well protected from idle sightseers and over-zealous lenses. With its thick, perfectly smooth walls, enticing floribunda arches, hidden courtyards and stairwells and magnificent view of the Pacific, it was a splendid and glittering testimony to the two brothers who, more than fifty years ago, had arrived in New York along with many thousands of others fleeing the genocidal regimes in Europe, and had gone on to create one of America's leading publishing empires.

The Romanov headquarters were still in New York, a giant obelisk of industry and power on 54th and 5th that controlled half the newspapers in the land, as well as scores of glossy and specialist magazines that catered for every imaginable taste or craze or political bent. But though the seat of power remained on the East Coast, where the Romanovs had an equally luxurious but totally different kind of estate, the main family home had, for the past twenty years, been in Malibu.

Maxim Aleksandr Romanov had inherited the major shareholding in Romanov Enterprises some ten years before at the age of thirty. Having graduated summa cum laude from Harvard Business School just prior to his twenty-fourth birthday, he had spent the next six years working his way up through the ranks of the family business until his grandfather's death had catapulted him from the lowly position of vice-president, futures and holdings, to Chief Executive, Romanov Enterprises International. Max had been ready for his new role, both his grandfather and his great-uncle had been grooming him for it since he was old enough to remember, and the steadily increasing price of the stock, as well as the numerous acquisitions and takeovers of the past ten years, had proved just how worthy an heir Max was. Romanov shares had multiplied at least tenfold in value against an economic backdrop that had often been far from favourable – and Max's wife, Carolyn, had produced a son and heir to continue the Romanov dynasty.

The architectural style of the family house, as well as

the inconsistent nature of the many Romanov publications, had both added considerable fuel over the years to the speculation regarding the Romanovs' roots – not more so than now, for in this climate of political correctness it was quite simply obligatory for everyone to be labelled according to their birth. Meaning that in the past two years alone, Max had been described variously as Russian-American, Italian-American, Polish-American, Hungarian-American and even, on one startling occasion, native-American. He never attempted either to confirm or deny his origins, for he had been raised by his grandfather who'd delighted in keeping the world guessing and who had adhered until the day he died to his own personal maxim of 'tell 'em nothing, they'll make it up anyway'.

And make it up they surely did, especially over these past two years, when Max had heard himself described as anything from 'a billionaire publishing magnate whose royal lineage was most evident in the disdain of the Slavic looks he had inherited from Czar Nicholas II', to 'a coke-snorting procurer of innocent young girls whose virtue was auctioned off to the highest bidder during riotous and depraved weekend parties at the Romanov estate'. He had also read about the harem of naked women who comprised his household staff, always at hand to satisfy his every whim and those of his guests; and of his connections to a number of the world's more dubious, not to mention criminal, organizations. Something else he had learned about himself was that he was the bastard son of a Hungarian whore who had escaped the country during the '56 revolution by using what talents she had to procure a safe passage to the West from the Russian invaders.

There was, of course, an element of truth to every story. He was indeed a publishing magnate, though not quite a billionaire; his dark and finely chiselled features were most definitely Slavic, for both his parents were

Russian – though neither, as far as he was aware, could boast a single drop of blue blood in their veins. He had, on countless occasions, taken cocaine and several of the parties he and his wife had thrown at the Romanov estate had, it was true, well and truly pushed the envelope. The naked women were not on his household staff, though they were, albeit indirectly, on his payroll. And his mother had been a whore to the Russian army which was how she had managed to make her escape through Hungary nine months before Max was born. Her desperate bid to flee the terror of the NKVD meant that all Max knew about his father was that he was an officer of the Red Army. He also knew that both he and his mother owed their lives to the exiled Countess Katerina Casimir, who had received his mother in London, nursed her through her difficult pregnancy then sent her and her infant son on to New York where Max's grandfather and great-uncle had long ago given up hope of ever seeing their family again.

Countess Katerina's deeds of kindness, coming from a woman who was as aristocratic and Catholic as the peasant Romanov brothers from the Arbat were Jewish and – in their impassioned youth, Bolshevik – were acts that no member of the Romanov family would ever forget. Over the years a strong bond had formed between the two families as they, along with many others throughout Europe and the States, committed themselves to helping their fellow countrymen escape the continuing nightmare of communism and start new lives in the West. Though the older generation were all dead now and the reign of terror had finally collapsed, the Countess's granddaughter, Galina Casimir, and Max Romanov, continued to do what they could as an exhausted and crippled Motherland limped, bewildered and afraid, from the ashes of one of history's most heinous regimes.

The fact that Max was rich and powerful and

remained obdurately silent over the private details of his life would, ordinarily, have been exciting enough for the press, but the fact that a little less than one year ago he had been at the centre of the notorious Murder to Mishap trial was what kept the press hounds hard on his tail these days. No one, it seemed, could discover why the New York District Attorney who was prosecuting the case had suddenly accepted that Carolyn Romanov's death had been an accident, when Max Romanov was known to have confessed to the killing on the very night it had happened. Hell, the gun had had his prints all over it and police investigations had uncovered no other presence in the house, so it was obvious he had killed his wife. And right up to the fifth week of the preliminary hearings the DA had refuted Romanov's claim that the shooting had been an accident. A murder had been committed and it was the District Attorney's job, on behalf of the people, to see that justice was done. But then, just five weeks into the preliminaries, the DA's office had suddenly announced that it was now satisfied that the killing had indeed been an accident and all charges were being dropped. What new evidence had come to light to disprove foul play no one had ever been able to find out. What a great many wanted to know, however, was whom Romanov had succeeded in paying off, or who the victims of some kind of political blackmail were who had enough power to get this case dismissed.

As for the libellous insinuations that Carolyn hadn't been the first to meet her death at Max Romanov's hands – or at least at the hands of those Max employed – these were something he chose to ignore. As were the slanderous labels of 'Porn King' or 'Baron of the Bimbos' or 'Sex-Slayer of the Innocent'. Since three of the several dozen magazines published by Romanov were categorized as adult, it was only to be expected that a certain amount of feminist spleen would be vented in his direction – particularly since his wife had met such a violent end. And the thousands upon thousands of sexual deviants who had written to him as a result of the brief though explicit public airing of his own sexual preferences, as well as the salacious details of what actually went on at the Romanov estate – well, Max could only hope that writing about it was working it through their systems. If not, he had shipped the whole lot over to the nation's good pal, Oprah, who would no doubt find something more useful to do with the letters than he would.

Smiling to himself as he read Oprah's eloquently penned thank-you note, Max absently reached out to wipe the egg from his three-year-old son's chin. Aleksandr howled in protest and continued to howl until he realized his father was watching him, when his cheeky little face broke instantly into a grin.

'You should tell him off, Daddy,' Marina, Max's eight-year-old daughter, informed him. 'He's a naughty boy. You're a naughty boy, Aleks. You shouldn't scream like that.'

Aleks looked at his father, whose heavy black brows were lowered in an attempt to look ominous. 'Aaaarrrr!' Aleks roared, pretending to be a monster.

'You're not funny, Aleks,' Marina told him, with a precocious flare of her nostrils. 'He's not funny, is he, Daddy?'

'No, he's not funny,' Max assured her, eyeing his son purposefully.

'Weee*bang*!' Aleks cried, landing his egg neatly on the pristine white collar of Marina's new dress.

Max braced himself as Marina's face turned red with rage, then dropping the letter he was holding, he scooped her on to his lap as her temper suddenly deflated and she burst into tears.

'Sssh, there, there,' he comforted her, bouncing her up and down on his knee and stroking her long dark hair. 'It's nothing to cry about.'

'But he's ruined my dress, Daddy,' she sobbed, 'and

it's my best dress.'

'It'll wash off, honey,' Max soothed, knowing that all Marina's dresses fell into the category of 'best'.

'I don't want to wash it off. I want it to be new. I hate you!' she cried savagely, trying to kick her brother.

'Hey there,' Max said, swinging her legs out of the way. 'Aleks, say sorry to your sister.'

'Sowwy,' Aleks said, not looking in the least bit contrite.

'Smack him, Daddy,' Marina demanded.

'What about ... I tickle you instead,' Max responded, tickling her sides and making her laugh.

'No, Daddy,' she giggled. 'No, I don't like it. *Daddy*!'

'Me too, Daddy,' Aleks shouted, climbing swiftly on to the seat of his chair and launching himself bodily into the affray.

'Ow, he hurt me,' Marina complained, as Aleks landed on Max's shoulders and inadvertently trod on his sister's head.

Laughing, Max tumbled Aleks down from his shoulders and grabbing them one under each arm, ran out of the open patio windows towards the giant fountain at the centre of the courtyard, where he threatened to dump them if they didn't make friends immediately.

Shrieking with laughter and clinging to him as if their lives depended on it, they promised they were friends, that they would never, ever argue again and that they loved each other more than anyone else in the world.

'Daddy?' Aleks said, as Max carried them back into the breakfast room.

'Yes?'

'I want to wee.'

Even as Max looked down at the darkening stain on Aleks's shorts he could feel the damp warmth spreading over his arm. 'Marina, quick, honey,' he said, setting them both on the ground, 'run and get Aleks's potty.'

'I don't know where it is,' she protested.

'Then go ask Mrs Clay. Quickly now.'

'What about my dress, Daddy?' she said. 'What are we going to do about my dress?'

'Marina! Go do as you're told!' he said sharply.

Immediately Marina's bottom lip started to tremble and closing his eyes in exasperation Max hugged her to him. 'I'm sorry, darling,' he said, 'I didn't mean to shout. Don't cry now. Come on, there's nothing to cry about.'

'I want my mommy!' Marina wailed. 'Nobody loves me. I want my mommy!'

'Sssh,' Max murmured, kissing her hair and thinking of his own mother rather than have to deal with any unwanted images of Carolyn.

'Mommy!' Marina sobbed.

'Mommy!' Aleks joined in.

'Hey, come on now,' Max said, kneeling in front of them and trying to comfort them. 'It's going to be all right ...'

'You don't love me!' Marina said accusingly. 'You love Aleks.'

'I love you both, honey,' Max said gently.

'Can I help at all, sir?'

Max looked up to find Mrs Clay, the children's Scottish nanny, coming into the room. 'Ah,' he said with a grimace of relief. 'Aleks flicked egg on Marina's dress and ...'

'And it's my best dress,' Marina cut in heatedly, 'and now he's made it all horrible and I'll never be able to wear it again.'

'Oh, now, let me see there,' Mrs Clay said, peering down her nose at the collar. 'Looks like a job for Mary Poppins to me.'

Marina's eyes grew round. 'Mary Poppins!' she gasped. 'Can you do magic, Mrs Clay?'

'After a fashion, dear,' Mrs Clay responded, 'after a fashion. And what about you, young man?' she went on, turning to Aleks. 'Shall we get you cleaned up too while we're at it?'

'I told Daddy I did wees,' he informed her proudly, reaching up to take her hand.

'Did you now?' she remarked drolly.

'Yes, I did,' he said earnestly. Then cheerfully added, 'Daddy didn't do wees.'

Mrs Clay's sharp green eyes moved to Max as she chuckled. 'Well there's a mercy,' she remarked. 'Now, are you going to give Daddy a hug before we go off?'

Smiling, Max kissed and hugged them and was about to return to his perusal of the morning mail when a buzzer sounded in the hall announcing someone's arrival at the gates. A moment later Leo, the butler, came into the room.

'Mr Remmick and Mr Zamoyski are on their way up the drive,' he said stiffly.

'Thank you, Leo,' Max replied. Maurice Remmick and Ellis Zamoyski weren't anyone with whom he needed to stand on ceremony – in fact, as his right-hand men and possibly most trusted friends, they would be astounded if Max were even to consider taking himself off upstairs to shower, shave and dress on their account.

'All that's missing is the chunks of gold, the pot belly and a couple of bikinied broads,' Zamoyski joked as he and Remmick strode into the breakfast room to find Max in a black towelling robe, his bare feet propped up on an empty chair and an untidy stack of mail spilling over his plate.

Max raised an eyebrow. 'Did you have breakfast yet?' he said. 'Coffee? I'll get fresh sent in.'

'Where're the kids?' Maurice asked, noticing the debris around the table.

'Upstairs changing,' Max answered, slapping Ellis's hand away as he made a grab for Max's coffee.

'Mrs Clay working out, is she?' Ellis asked.

'So far so good. And yes, I still intend to take care of the kids myself as much as I can; yes, I know I need help, which is why I let you talk me into Mrs Clay; and no, I haven't seen the papers this morning.'

Maurice grinned. 'That predictable, huh?' he said. 'We'll have to do something about sharpening up our act. I think you should look at the papers though, Max.'

'The ones that count I look at,' Max responded, tearing open another letter. 'The ones you're talking about, I don't look at.'

'Today I think you should,' Maurice persisted. 'There's a lot of speculation ...'

'There's always speculation, Maurice, but there'll never be another trial. It's history. So let's change the subject, why don't we?'

'Don't you care what they're saying about you?'

'No.'

'Don't you care what's happening to the stock?'

'Get real, Maurice.'

'You're not as rich as you think you are, Max.'

'Correction. I'm as rich as I *know* I am.'

'The word from New York is you're losing your grip, Max,' Ellis warned. 'The forecast for this year is way down ...'

'Save it, Ellis,' Max interrupted. 'You're not telling me anything I don't already know and everything's in hand. So, tell me something I need to know.'

Zamoyski glanced at Remmick, his pale, feathery lashes dropping over his blue eyes as he waited for Remmick to hand over the report they'd both read before coming here. It had arrived on Remmick's E-mail overnight, backing up the photographs that had been wired over from Johannesburg earlier in the day. It was a fact of life that nothing was ever as straightforward as it was expected to be, so neither Remmick nor Zamoyski had expressed much surprise when they had discovered that complications were arising in an area where there ought to have been none. Both were interested to see, however, what Max would make of it.

Waiting for Leo to set down a pot of steaming fresh

coffee, Maurice slanted his eyes in Max's direction. Maurice was a good-looking man with a full head of silvery white hair and a per-manent tan. He was Max's senior by five years, had worked for the Romanovs for over twenty years and was godfather to both Max's kids. His wife, Deon, was godmother. Next to Max's children and Galina Casimir, the Remmicks were probably closer to Max than anyone, but even after all the years of knowing him Maurice was aware that there were facets of Max's extremely complex character that remained as much of a mystery to him now as what had happened on that fateful night Max's wife had got herself shot. Of course Maurice knew the story Max had given, and was perfectly aware of why the DA had dropped the charge, though whether the truth had been told was another matter altogether, for the only people present in the New York house that night had been Max and his wife.

It had been a rocky marriage right from the start, but a man in Max's position didn't get a New York society princess pregnant and walk out on his responsibilities – at least not when the princess's father was State Senator Harry Strominscki. The enforced union of the Romanov and Strominscki families had been the cause of the only major falling out Maurice had ever witnessed between Max and his beloved grandfather. The old guy had been so god-damned mad he had threatened to cut Max off and force him to change his name. Of course, no one ever really took the threat seriously; after all, Carolyn Strominscki could hardly be considered an unsuitable match, and it was well known that the old man's life revolved around his grandson. But Mikhail Romanov had never made any secret of the fact that he wanted Max to marry the old Countess's granddaughter, Galina Casimir, and the fact that Max had screwed up had been a crushing blow from which the old man had never quite recovered. What he'd have to say now about the way

Max's marriage had reached such an abrupt conclusion nine years down the line was anyone's guess, but it was Maurice's that the old man, unlike the rest of the world, would never, even for a moment, have countenanced the possibility that his grandson was guilty.

However, those less smitten by Max knew that not only was his guilt a possibility, it was a very definite probability, since Carolyn's hysterical and frequently public threats to reveal things about her husband that would make 'any decent-minded person sick to their stomach', as well as regularly declaring that she was going to divorce him and deny him the right to his children, provided him at the very least with a plausible motive for effecting an early introduction to her Maker. But if he had pulled the trigger, and there didn't seem much doubt that he had, then he'd sure as hell gotten away with it. And though Deon was of the opinion that no one who loved his kids the way Max did could ever harm anyone, Maurice, though he never for a moment doubted Max's devotion to his kids, wasn't quite so naive as his wife.

As the door closed behind Leo, Maurice reached out for the coffee pot and began to pour. 'We've got some news on Rhiannon Edwardes,' he said to Max.

Max frowned and looked up from the letter he was reading. 'Who?' he said.

Maurice reached down to his briefcase and pulling out a brown envelope passed it over. 'The British TV producer,' he explained. 'Rhiannon Edwardes.'

Max nodded as he remembered and pushing aside the rest of his mail he emptied the envelope on to the table. 'I take it this is her?' he remarked, picking up a set of ten by eights and flipping quickly through the first three or four.

'That's her,' Maurice confirmed.

Max's expression was unreadable as he slowed down his perusal and reached out for his coffee. He made no comment until he reached a naked shot of Rhiannon in some kind of outdoor shower with a man. 'What the hell is this?' he demanded, throwing the photograph on the table. 'And how did you manage to come by these shots? I don't recall asking for any.'

'She's under investigation,' Ellis told him.

Max frowned. 'Police?' he said.

'Private.'

'Do we know why?' Max asked.

'Not yet. But we do know there's a PI following her around South Africa and that said PI, who took these shots, is in Theo Straussen's pay.'

Max's eyebrows went up. 'Theo Straussen,' he repeated, looking down at the nude photograph again. 'What's Straussen's problem that he's having her checked out?' he said.

'We're still working on that,' Ellis answered.

Max eyed him for a moment, then pursing his lips he tossed the photograph back on the table and picked up the two-page report. 'I'll call Theo myself,' he said, scanning the document. 'So, did we learn anything new about her?' he asked.

'Not really,' Maurice answered. 'Everything's the way we heard it. Mother fourteen years dead. Father remarried, living in a suburb of Bristol, England. No love relationships to speak of after Phillip Chambers until this guy here. His name's Oliver Maguire. He's a Brit, a diamond dealer, and there, I believe, we have our connection to the Straussens.'

Max's face darkened and it was a while before he spoke again. 'Do we know if Galina's tried contacting Rhiannon yet?' he asked.

'There's nothing to say she has,' Ellis answered.

'But she will,' Max added, almost to himself. He looked at his watch: just after ten o'clock. 'What time's the meeting this morning?' he asked.

'Eleven,' Maurice answered.

'Then I guess I'd better go make myself decent,' Max said, getting to his feet. The photographs of Rhiannon were still on the table in front of him and pausing for a moment he looked down at them again. Once again it was impossible to tell what he was thinking, but even if Maurice or Ellis was inclined to ask, which neither was, the abrupt sound of Max's mobile phone would have cut them off. Reaching across the table, Maurice flicked it open and answered it.

'Sure, Maribeth, he's right here,' he said. 'I'll pass you over.'

On hearing Maribeth's name Max's eyes narrowed as a quick spasm of impatience tightened his mouth. 'Maribeth,' he said into the receiver. 'What news?'

'I'm fine, Max,' she replied. 'How are you?'

'Very droll,' he responded.

'I take it Galina didn't get there yet?' she said.

'Not yet.'

'Then she'll be on her way. I thought I'd better ring and warn you. I've managed to pull it off. She's going to be the face for the Conspiracy cosmetics range from here into the new millennium.'

'So who do I congratulate,' he said, 'you or Galina?'

'I guess both of us,' Maribeth chuckled. 'But Galina more than me.'

Max's smile was wry. 'OK, I'll remember that when she gets here.' He paused. 'So you think this is going to work out?' he said.

'You know I do. OK, it's a risk, but not a big one and I need her, Max. Yes, I know, there are plenty of beautiful women out there, but Galina's got something special. Well, you of all people know that, but providing we keep a close eye on her I can't see how any of us can fail here.'

'If it works,' Max muttered, 'it could be the answer to all our prayers. But I got to tell you, Maribeth, I'm amazed you got it past Harman. I take it you did tell him about the risks, because if you didn't, there's no deal going ...'

'I told him,' Maribeth cut in. 'And providing you're prepared to handle the security, he's happy to have her on board. Hell, Max, the man knows a winner when he sees one and ...'

'OK, spare me the rest,' he interrupted. 'You got my commitment to security. How much are you paying her?'

Maribeth paused. 'The publicity's gonna say five, but I couldn't get Harman past two,' she confessed.

'Reassure me that the missing noun is million,' he said.

Maribeth laughed. 'I guess that's her arriving now,' she said, as the sound of the door buzzer echoed down the line.

'I guess you could be right,' Max replied. 'When are you making the announcement?'

'We've called a press conference for Friday at noon.' Again Maribeth hesitated. 'Do you plan on being there?'

'I'll let you know.' As Max clicked off the phone Leo came laboriously into the room to announce that Miss Galina Casimir was on her way up the drive.

Both Maurice and Ellis were looking at Max. 'She got the contract,' Maurice stated.

'She got it,' Max confirmed.

'Holy shit,' Ellis murmured in astonishment. 'I never thought they'd go for it.'

'I have to be honest, nor did I,' Max responded. 'But try acting surprised – and pleased – when she breaks the news, huh?'

Hearing a car pull up outside he pushed the photographs of Rhiannon across the table towards Maurice, who quickly whisked them into his briefcase. Then hearing Galina's footsteps running across the hall Max turned to greet her.

'Max!' she cried, bursting into the room. 'Oh, darling,' she laughed, when he feigned surprise at seeing her, 'don't pretend you didn't know I was coming; Leo's bound to have told you. And don't pretend either that you haven't heard already, I know Maribeth will have called you ... But isn't it marvellous! Isn't it just wonderful? Are you happy for me, darling? I'm so excited! They chose *me*! Out of all the thousands they looked at, they chose me! And you'll never guess how much the contract's worth ... *Five million* dollars, Max, and that's just for starters ...'

'Come here,' he laughed, pulling her into his arms.

Her dazzling lavender-blue eyes were bright with an almost childlike happiness as they gazed laughingly up into his and as he swung her round, his hard, powerful body seeming to engulf her slender limbs and the tousled blackness of his hair making her own white-blonde crop shine like a halo by comparison, Ellis and Maurice got awkwardly to their feet, ready to offer their own congratulations.

As she turned to them Maurice felt as though something inside him were unravelling. She was the most gorgeous creature he had ever laid eyes on and even after all this time of knowing her there were still occasions when the sheer radiance of her could erase all coherent thought from his mind. Her features were as fresh as a New England spring, her almond-shaped eyes were many shades of blue and fringed with thick, glossy dark lashes and brows; her skin was a natural bronze and satiny smooth; her cheeks were moulded by the perfect sculpture of their bones; her nose was long and straight, the nostrils flaring their aristocratic lineage and her flawless red lips masked a smile that was even more luminous than the dazzling blonde hair that feathered around her face.

'Is Max cross?' she said, embracing Maurice, then turning to Ellis.

'Mad as hell,' Ellis told her, having to peel his tongue from the roof of his mouth to speak. Even the smell of her was enough to turn his bones to jelly and dressed the way she was, in white lycra shorts and white leotard that was cut high over her hip bones and revealed the dark shadow of her nipples and immaculate shape of her long, tanned legs, it was almost enough to make him forget who she was.

Galina laughed and turned back to Max. 'Is it true?' she said, taking his hands. 'Are you mad?'

His charcoal-black eyes were watching her closely and showing only humour. 'Real mad,' he confirmed.

She laughed again and raised her mouth to his. 'Show me,' she challenged.

Kissing her with lips that were parted and tender, though quickly pulled away, he held her at arm's length. 'Did you talk to the lawyers yet?' he asked.

'Oh Max,' she groaned. 'I've only just found out. I wanted to tell you first, not a stuffy old lawyer. OK, OK, I'll call them,' she said, seeing the look on his face. 'But can't we celebrate first? I'm going to be famous, Max. I mean, big-time famous. Conspiracy cosmetics are going to sell all over the world ... Call Leo, tell him to bring champagne and let's take it to bed.'

'I've got people arriving in less than an hour,' he told her, laughter darkening his eyes as Maurice and Ellis seemed almost to collapse at the very idea that he could even consider turning her down.

'Oh Max,' she pouted, moving in closer to him. 'Can't they wait? This is so special to me and I know you're getting hard just thinking about me ...'

Her words shocked Maurice and Ellis, who both turned away as she reached inside Max's robe and started to fondle him. For a while he let her, looking down into her eyes, then gently removing her hand he turned her round and pointed her towards the door. 'Go speak to Leo,' he said, 'I'll join you in a few minutes.'

As the door closed behind her, Ellis let go of his breath and flopped back down in his chair. 'I gotta have me some coffee,' he said, reaching for the pot.

The corners of Max's mouth compressed in a smile as Maurice said, 'Are you going to announce the wedding on Friday too? Get the whole thing over in one go?'

Max inhaled deeply, then scratching his fingers over the stubble on his chin he shook his head. 'No,' he answered. 'In fact I'm going to put the wedding plans on hold for a while.'

'How's she going to take that?' Ellis asked. 'I thought she was pretty keen to get hitched as soon ...' He trailed off, shrugging, as Max's stony gaze came to rest on him. 'OK, it's none of my business,' he said, colouring.

Max's face relaxed. 'I'll handle it,' he said. Then turning to Maurice he changed the subject. 'I want to know how serious Rhiannon Edwardes's relationship is with Maguire, how long it's been going, where it's heading, exactly what his connection is with the Straussens, and get someone to check the whereabouts of this Phillip Chambers guy who dumped her four years ago.'

'Five,' Maurice corrected.

'OK, five,' Max responded, holding out his hand for the photographs of Rhiannon. The nude one was the first to slide out of the envelope and staring down at it he was once again struck by how alluring it was, considering she hadn't known it was being taken, even though she appeared to be looking right into the lens. 'Where is she now?' he said.

'Cape Town,' Maurice answered. 'Maguire's in Johannesburg.'

Max lifted his head.

'He's due to join her later today,' Maurice replied to the unspoken question. 'According to Straussen's PI, Maguire's just paid something in the region of fifty big ones for a cabochon-cut champagne diamond, so I guess that tells us where the relationship's heading.'

Max looked impressed, then sliding the photographs back into the envelope he said, 'Stall the meeting for half an hour and get me Theo Straussen on the line now.'

As Ellis keyed the Straussen name into his organizer Maurice was tempted to remind Max that Galina was waiting, but didn't, since he knew that it was unlikely Max had forgotten. Maurice couldn't help wondering if Galina had, though, as squeals of childish laughter had started ringing through the house a few minutes ago, signalling the fact that she had been waylaid by Aleks and Marina. Which, Maurice knew, would be no hardship for Galina, since she was as besotted with Max's kids as they were with her. And no one who knew about Galina's and Max's relationship had ever doubted, even when Carolyn was alive, what a great stepmother Galina would make were Max ever able to gain custody of his children in a divorce. Of course, there was no problem about custody now and since Galina had been a part of Max's life long before his marriage even, their wedding, when finally it was announced, shouldn't come as too much of a surprise to the world.

When at last Max ended his conversation with Theo Straussen in New York both Maurice and Ellis were looking at him expectantly. Max's dark eyes were distant and unfocused as he ruminated on what he had just learned. 'The PI's a woman,' he said distractedly.

'Working for Straussen,' Ellis responded.

'Indirectly, yes,' Max confirmed.

'And Maguire's connection to Straussen?' Maurice prompted.

Max's eyes pulled focus as they came to rest on Maurice's face. 'Is a connection', he answered with a grim yet interested smile, 'that Oliver Maguire is going to be very sorry he ever made – if he isn't already.' His eyebrows went up as he lifted a photograph of Oliver and Rhiannon from the pile and stared at it hard. 'The guy's got to be crazy if he thinks he can get away with what he's trying to pull off,' he murmured. 'Either that or he values that woman more than he values his own life.'

Maurice and Ellis exchanged glances.

'Where did you say they were now?' Max asked.

'In a couple of hours they'll both be in Cape Town,' Maurice answered.

Max nodded and tossing the photographs back on the table he started out of the room. 'Keep up with Straussen's PI,' he said. 'This could be important.'

'To whom?' Ellis ventured.

When Max turned round his eyes were narrowed with surprise. 'To Galina, of course,' he replied, 'and whether or not we allow her to renew her association with a woman who, it appears, is about to be presented with a fifty-thousand-dollar diamond.' He pondered this for a moment, then said, 'A proposal at sunset on Table Mountain?'

Ellis and Maurice started to laugh. 'We'll let you know,' Maurice responded and picking up the phone, he began to punch out a number in Cape Town.

Chapter 6

'I take it that was Oliver,' Lizzy said, lifting her feet on to the empty chair beside her and tilting her face towards the sun as Rhiannon zipped the telephone back into her belt-bag.

'It was,' Rhiannon confirmed. 'He's just got off the plane.'

'How sweet of him to let you know,' Lizzy remarked.

Rhiannon looked at her.

Lizzy's eyes were closed, her T-shirt was sliding off one shoulder, her flimsy white skirt was gaping open to expose her evenly tanned legs to the sun. 'So do we take it that filming is now cancelled for the rest of the day?' she enquired silkily.

Rhiannon waited for Lizzy's eyes to open. When they didn't she moved her gaze to Jack, then to Hugh, both of whom were obviously wishing themselves elsewhere.

The four of them were sitting in the partial shade of a two-hundred-year-old oak at one of the magnificent wine estates of Franschhoek, eighty kilometres inland from Cape Town. The circular white-linen-draped table before them was cluttered with the remains of their lunch. A leaf floated from an overhead branch and settled on the table in front of Rhiannon. She looked at it, then at the dazzlingly white Cape Dutch house across the lawn where the vineyard's proprietors lived and where later they would buy some of the most deliciously oaky wines she had ever tasted. Everything here was so perfect, the unblemished blue of the sky, the reds and purples and pinks and yellows of rare flowers, the welcome of their hosts, the food they had eaten ...

'Well, is it?' Lizzy prompted, pushing her fingers into her hair while keeping her face turned to the sun.

'No,' Rhiannon answered shortly.

'Any news on Melanie?' Hugh ventured after a pause that was growing more explosive by the second.

'She arrived back in Antigua last night,' Rhiannon answered.

'Is she coming back again?' Jack said, helping himself to more wine.

Nobody answered and a few more minutes ticked by as Rhiannon sat with her fingers resting idly on the stem of her glass, while Lizzy sealed her simmering resentment with a benign little smile.

'So, Rhiannon, how many bottles are you going to buy?' Hugh asked, emptying the blanc fumé into her glass.

'I'm not sure yet,' Rhiannon said, taking the bottle from him and looking at the label.

'Why don't you call Oliver?' Lizzy suggested. 'He'll tell you how many you should buy.'

Rhiannon looked at Hugh. Beneath his khaki cap his wiry black hair was plastered to his head and beads of sweat glistened at the frizzy roots of his beard. The dark lenses of his sun-glasses were masking his eyes, but Rhiannon had no trouble sensing his discomfort. Giving him an almost imperceptible nod, she then smiled at Jack and downed the last of her wine as they got up from the table.

'It's not going to work, Lizzy,' she said, as Hugh and Jack ambled through the tables that were spread across the rich, spongy lawn.

Lizzy smirked. 'Saint Rhiannon the Super Cool isn't

going to get riled, is that it?' she remarked.

'Fuck you,' Rhiannon said.

Lizzy's eyebrows tilted.

'Why don't you just get it off your chest, Lizzy, then perhaps we can all get on with what we came here for.'

'Oh, you mean the rest of us have a role to play here?' Lizzy responded archly. 'I thought all this was just an excuse for you and Oliver to romance your way round South Africa.'

Rhiannon's lips were paling with anger. 'I didn't know he was going to show up and you know it,' she retorted.

'Do I?' Lizzy said.

'Yes, you do. And maybe you'd like to tell me exactly why I should put up with your childish behaviour when it's not my damned fault that Andy hasn't called you since we left Perlatonga. Nor is it Oliver's.'

'My childish behaviour, as you call it,' Lizzy responded through her teeth, 'has nothing to do with Andy not calling. It has to do with the fact that *you* are financing Oliver's trip and *you* can't see what a bloody fool he's taking you for.'

Rhiannon was very close to exploding, but taking a breath she forced herself to remain calm. 'His credit cards were stolen,' she said with exaggerated patience, 'so how the hell else is he supposed to get around?'

'Most people manage to get replacement cards the next day,' Lizzy replied. 'So why hasn't he?'

'Maybe he has. Maybe they're there at the hotel in Cape Town waiting for him,' Rhiannon said tightly. 'Have you thought of that?'

Lizzy turned to look at her. 'Are they?' she challenged.

'As a matter of fact, yes, they are.'

Lizzy's eyes bored into hers.

Rhiannon didn't even flinch.

'Has he ever paid you back all the other money he's

borrowed?' Lizzy asked bluntly.

'Just what the hell is this?' Rhiannon cried, throwing out her hands.

'Has he?' Lizzy pressed.

'Yes, he has.'

'All of it?'

'Every last penny if you must know.'

Still Lizzy's eyes wouldn't let go.

'You don't believe me, do you?' Rhiannon said, looking both shocked and confused.

'If you tell me it's true then I believe you,' Lizzy said with no warmth in her voice.

'Why would I lie about it?' Rhiannon demanded heatedly. 'Especially to you. I mean, if Oliver were borrowing money from me and not paying it back, don't you think my own alarm bells would be ringing by now? And if they were who else would I confide in but you?'

Lizzy's eyes remained flat and hostile until finally Rhiannon put her head to one side and treated her to a wide, ingenuous grin that was designed to take the salt from both their tempers.

'OK,' Lizzy said with a sigh. 'I'm sorry. I guess it's just that ...' She stopped and pulled her bottom lip between her teeth. 'I'm getting cynical in my old age, I suppose. And you're right, I'm royally pissed off that Andy hasn't called since we left the reserve. I really thought he might have by now.'

'So, why don't you call him?'

Lizzy's mouth tightened. 'I tried, the night before last,' she confessed. 'He wasn't there.'

'But you left a message?' Rhiannon prompted.

'Yes, I left a message,' Lizzy confirmed. 'And I wish to God I hadn't now, because he hasn't fucking well called back, the bastard. Whereas Oliver Maguire manages to call to tell you he's just got off a fucking plane. Which just goes to show that if someone wants to speak to you they will and no matter how many excuses you can think up as to why someone doesn't call the fact still remains that if they really wanted to they would. And why the hell I should be getting so worked up over this God only knows, when I only knew the man for two days and when I'll probably never see him again anyway, which is absolutely fine by me.'

Rhiannon's eyes were brimming with laughter. 'Sounds like it,' she commented.

Lizzy threw her a look, then, not wanting to laugh, turned away.

'So let me get this straight,' Rhiannon said, attempting to reason things out. 'Andy hasn't called you so that makes Oliver some sort of con man or crook? Is that right?'

Lizzy rolled her eyes and pushing her tongue into her cheek started to grin. 'I was genuinely worried that he hadn't paid you back,' she said.

'But he has.'

'OK.'

Rhiannon waited. Lizzy looked at her, pursed the corner of her mouth and looked away. 'There's more,' Rhiannon said, 'so you might as well finish it.'

Lizzy nodded. 'All right,' she said. 'It's the way things keep disappearing around that man ... Credit cards, BMWs, whole apartments full of furniture ... It's not normal. I mean, the guy's either a closet magician or ...'

'Or?'

Lizzy's eyes were dense. 'Or somebody's got it in for him,' she said frankly.

Several seconds elapsed as Rhiannon stared into Lizzy's face, quietly assimilating her thoughts. 'I have to admit that the same thought has crossed my mind,' she said finally.

'So, have you discussed it with him?'

'Yes and no,' Rhiannon answered, her stomach clenching with nerves. 'I mean, I know he's worried by it ...'

'How worried? Has he told the police?'

'About his flat being burgled and the BMW, yes. I'm not sure about the credit cards though.'

'Mmm,' Lizzy grunted. 'What about Oliver? Does he think there might be someone behind it all?'

Rhiannon shrugged. 'If he does he isn't telling me.'

Lizzy looked at her in surprise. 'That sounds like you think he's holding back on you? Do you?'

Rhiannon shook her head. 'It's hard to say,' she replied, gazing thoughtfully out at the garden. 'I suppose what I really think is that he's got an idea who might be doing it, but until he can prove it he doesn't want to say anything to anyone.'

Lizzy picked up the bottle of cabernet sauvignon, poured the last dribble into her glass and drank it.

Rhiannon turned to look at her, her tanned freckled face suddenly seeming very unsure. 'You really do think he's a crook, don't you?' she said. 'Your instincts are telling you that he's into something, or he's done something ...'

'Hold on, hold on,' Lizzy said, putting up her hands, 'don't let's start getting things out of proportion here. If all anyone's doing to harass him is nick a few credit cards, turn over his apartment and relocate his car then ...' Her eyes moved back to Rhiannon's. 'I was going to say that it can't be very serious, but on second thoughts if it were happening to me I'd be scared shitless.'

'So prettily put,' Rhiannon murmured, but there was little humour in her eyes as she considered what Lizzy was saying. 'You're right,' she said in the end, 'we could be making mountains out of molehills.'

Lizzy shrugged. 'We could be,' she said. 'And that woman walking towards us might not be a fascist pig.'

Rhiannon looked up to see the Afrikaans woman they'd earlier overheard telling her husband that if the black people who'd just come in were shown to a table anywhere near theirs she was leaving.

Rhiannon's and Lizzy's cold, shaming eyes escorted the woman, who was immaculately dressed in a pale-blue Chanel suit and matching shoes, until she disappeared down the steps into the car-park.

'So, what do we have on the agenda this afternoon?' Lizzy said, picking up her bag and taking out a compact.

'Only the vineyards,' Rhiannon answered, pulling a rolled-up copy of the schedule out of her belt-bag to read it. 'This one and some GVs as we drive back.'

'What about the interview in Stellenbosch?'

'They cancelled.'

Lizzy grinned. 'So you do get to see Oliver sooner rather than later,' she said teasingly.

'Not my doing,' Rhiannon countered. 'And since we're back on the subject I might as well tell you that I did something totally and wildly insane last night.'

'Well?' Lizzy prompted as Rhiannon's brown eyes started to dance.

'I asked him to marry me,' Rhiannon declared.

Lizzy's eyes dilated with shock. 'You did what?' she cried, half laughing, half stunned.

'I asked him to marry me,' Rhiannon repeated, her eyes shining with laughter.

Lizzy waited. 'So, what did he say?' she prompted.

'What do you think he said?' Rhiannon cried.

'Well I guess, by the look of you, it has to be yes,' Lizzy replied. 'Jesus Christ, why didn't you tell me before?'

'Because you've been in such a shitty mood all day, that's why,' Rhiannon retorted.

'But what on earth made you ask him? I mean ... Well, there's no reason why you shouldn't ... But, hell, Rhiannon, you didn't even tell me you were planning it.'

'I wasn't planning it,' Rhiannon responded. 'It just came out. We were talking on the phone and ... God, I can hardly remember what I said now. I think it was something highly original like: "Shall we get married?"'

'And he said?'

Rhiannon laughed and felt her heart falter and swell as she remembered. 'At first there was just dead silence at the other end,' she said, 'during which I died several times. Then he said ... "Darling, I thought you'd never ask."'

Lizzy was laughing and shaking her head and showing nothing of the misgivings she was feeling inside. 'Rhiannon, I've really got to hand it to you,' she said. 'Not: "Oliver, what the fuck is going on around here, are you involved in something shady or aren't you?" but: "Oliver, will you marry me?"'

Rhiannon's eyes narrowed as she pulled a face. 'I wish you didn't have such a down on him,' she said. 'He's really fond of you, you know, and if I am going to marry him then it's going to be really important to me that you two get along.'

'Which we will,' Lizzy promised getting to her feet. 'Just find out what's going on, is all I ask. And do it before you tie the knot, not after. OK?'

'I'd better do it right away then,' Rhiannon said, bunching her hair on top of her head and clipping it into place.

Lizzy stopped and let her eyes travel back to Rhiannon. 'Are you telling me you've already set a date?' she said.

Rhiannon laughed. 'Not exactly,' she answered. 'But as neither of us wants much fuss we thought we'd go for the first available slot at Chelsea Register Office.'

'Bloody hell,' Lizzy murmured, 'you really aren't wasting any time, are you?' Quite suddenly her face came alive. 'You're pregnant!' she cried.

'Wrong,' Rhiannon laughed. 'Just in love.'

Lizzy grimaced. 'Then I guess we'd better get these shots in the can and get you back to him as fast as we can, hadn't we?' she said, struggling to suppress a sudden and irrational longing for Andy, as the dread of losing Rhiannon began to bind itself tightly round her heart.

It was only when they joined up with Hugh and Jack in the cool, shadowy chamber of the wine cellar that she realized with a shock that the longing had been for Andy, not for Richard.

The roar of the Atlantic hurling huge crashing waves over the shore was coming through the open french windows as Randy Theakston let herself quietly into the room. Pausing, she looked around, her hands unconsciously clenching with nerves. At the far end of the elegant split-level hotel room that overlooked the white sandy beach of Cape Town's Camps Bay the curtains fluttered in the breeze, as dazzling sunlight pooled over the peach and pastel-green furnishings of the room.

Through the wall beside her she could hear the fast jets of water telling her that Oliver Maguire was in the shower. She knew it was him because she had watched him check in a few minutes ago, before following him up in the lift. According to reception, Rhiannon and the others were out filming and wouldn't be back for at least another couple of hours.

Moving stealthily forward, Randy's harsh grey eyes hunted around for the briefcase. It was almost sure to be locked if the diamond was inside, but Straussen had provided her with the combination, so all she had to do now was hope it was right.

Her heart contracted as she spotted the briefcase on a chair beside the TV and starting towards it she felt her hands beginning to perspire at the idea of touching it. Suddenly realizing that she'd stopped listening for the shower she froze her hand in mid-air and checked. It was still going. She had to be quick now if she was going to get that diamond out of the case and ... She stopped abruptly, almost gasping as the sudden shrill of the phone electrified her nerves. Sprinting quickly down the steps that divided the room, she ducked in behind the cabinet that contained the mini-bar. The ringing stopped and a surge of relief set her heart beating again as she heard Oliver's voice in the bathroom.

Perspiring badly now, she ran back to the briefcase, spun the locks, bungled it, spun them again, then flicked the clasps and pushed the lid open. She rummaged around, digging in amongst the papers, casting aside velvet bags and rolls, boxes and tissue paper. Hearing the telephone go down in the bathroom her heart gave a jolt of panic and she was about to slam the case shut when she noticed a leather pocket stitched to the upper lining. Digging her fingers inside, she pulled out a small leather box. Bingo!

Getting to her feet, she let the briefcase lid drop, rapidly spun the locks and turned to the luggage rack where Rhiannon's open suitcase was dripping underwear and dresses and jeans. Finding a small beaded evening bag, Randy was about to pick it up when the handle on the bathroom door started to turn. Her eyes rooted to it in horror. Her heart stopped beating and the corners of the leather box dug painfully into her palm. The bathroom was between her and the door, there was no way of getting out without being seen.

She waited. Her mind was turning numb, her instincts were failing. She had to get away before Maguire saw her. The door was partly open, it seemed he'd turned back for something. Now was her chance. Seizing the beaded purse she tore open the zip, stuffed the box inside, then ran swiftly and silently to the door. As it clicked shut behind her Oliver came out of the bathroom, towelling his hair.

It was around seven in the evening when Oliver discovered the diamond was missing. Rhiannon had already gone downstairs, leaving him to wrap up on the phone while she joined the others for cocktails by the pool. When he finished his call he went to his briefcase to consult a fax from an associate in Hong Kong and the instant he lifted the lid he knew that someone had been there.

His fingers went immediately to the pouch where he'd hidden the diamond. The shock of finding it gone came as such a blow that his breath stopped dead in his lungs. His face turned ashen, his heart began galloping dangerously fast. Taking a breath he pushed his fingers into his hair; he was starting to shake; his skin was breaking out in a nervous sweat. The diamond was worth over fifty thousand dollars and for the moment at least, it was uninsured.

It was several minutes before his mind began to surmount the shock. He had to think this through, had to try and work out what could have happened before he started calling in security, or the police. He picked up the phone, intending to get Rhiannon back to the room, but half-way through dialling he cut himself off, his blood turning to ice in his veins.

He didn't want to believe that Rhiannon had taken the ring, but she was the only one who'd been in the room with him since he'd checked in. Except she hadn't known the diamond was there. At least, he hadn't told her.

Feeling a wave of nausea sweep through him he buried his head in his hands. It was hard to make himself accept that Rhiannon would trick or deceive him the way his suspicions were suggesting, but he had to face the possibility that she might have. This could all be some kind of foul and brilliantly stage-managed conspiracy aimed to discredit and humiliate him in a way that ... His breath caught on the fear of it, even as his mind recoiled from the idea that Rhiannon would do this.

But never underestimate Straussen, he thought grimly

to himself as he got to his feet and wondered how in the hell he should handle this now. He was sure that by removing the diamond they had set some kind of trap for him, though for the life of him he couldn't fathom what the trap might be.

'What did she say?' Hugh cried, his greasy hands pausing in mid-air as he looked at Jack, then Lizzy, then Oliver. 'Did she just say what I thought she said?' he demanded.

Rhiannon was laughing. 'I'm serious,' she told him. 'That's our schedule for tomorrow.'

'She's gone insane,' Hugh declared, cracking open a langoustine and rapping Jack's knuckles as he tried to steal the delicious-looking flesh.

'Do you want me to run through it again?' Rhiannon offered, pulling in her chair as someone tried to squeeze past.

'I don't know that I'm ready for it,' Hugh grumbled, winkling a couple of mussels from their shells and popping them in his mouth. 'I mean, I was about to get seriously stuck into this wine, weren't you, mate?'

'I'm already there,' Jack answered, waving the empty bottle of Nederberg at the waiter.

They were at Quay Four, a lively Waterfront restaurant, where the heavy beat of live rock from the bar downstairs vibrated the floorboards and a tangy sea breeze wafted in through the wide- open windows. The clatter of cutlery and crockery, coupled with the general rowdiness of the place and the occasional ship's whistle blasting through the harbour, meant that they were having to shout to make themselves heard above the din.

'Have you tried that calamare steak?' Lizzy drooled. 'It's heaven. Hugh, that's the third langoustine you've had and I haven't had any.'

'Try the lobster,' Rhiannon recommended, dipping

her fingers into the lemon bowl in front of her and drying them on her napkin. 'Don't you want any more?' she said to Oliver who was leaning back in his chair and clearly only half listening to what was being said.

Shaking his head he picked up his wineglass and drained it.

Rhiannon watched him, wishing she was sitting next to him rather than opposite so that she could let him know how fed-up she was becoming with his moodiness. OK, they should have gone out alone tonight if they were supposed to be celebrating the fact they'd decided to get married, but there were only two more days left in Cape Town and this wasn't a holiday!

She looked at him again and a sudden bolt of unease twisted through her heart. Please God he wasn't regretting saying he would marry her? She dismissed the thought quickly, refusing to give in to the damnable lack of self-confidence that always seemed to be lurking somewhere in the corners of her mind. Then her heart relaxed as, catching her eye, he winked and reached across the table for her hand.

'OK, Rhiannon,' Hugh said, covering a burp with his napkin as he sat back in his chair. 'I think I'm pissed enough to handle it now. What was tomorrow's schedule again?'

Tearing her eyes from Oliver's Rhiannon picked up an oyster and dousing it with shallot vinegar said, 'OK, tomorrow.' Tossing the oyster back she swallowed it whole, then wiping her hands in her napkin she began. 'We're interviewing the minister for culture at seven at the Mount Nelson. After that it's Kirstenboch to see some of the world's rarest and most beautiful flowers. Someone from the tourist office will meet us there and stay with us as we go on to a couple of craft and flea markets and the Houses of Parliament which, I am assured, are quite stunningly Corinthian. If there's time before lunch we'll take a boat ride over to Ellis Island where Mandela was held prisoner, if not we'll do it straight after. They know we're coming so there shouldn't be any problem and it's a great opportunity to turn the cameras back on the mainland and get some shots of Table Mountain.

'When we come back we'll do some GVs and VOX POPS of tourists around the Waterfront. A couple of local celebrities will be joining us – a wine merchant, a TV presenter, a rock singer and a Penthouse Pet no less – then we'll get the cable car up to the top of Table Mountain to take a look at the view and the dassie and ...'

'The what?' Jack interrupted.

'Dassie. Rock rabbits. And hopefully we'll be blessed with a sunset. Oh, that reminds me,' she said, going to her bag for her notebook, 'I need to find out what time the sun actually sets tomorrow. Have you got everything so far?'

'You mean there's more?' Hugh gasped, horrified.

'Just some early evening atmos around the Waterfront again,' she answered, rummaging for a pencil. 'Oh, and there's one other thing I forgot to mention: if there's time ...'

'I don't believe this,' Hugh cried.

'If there's time,' Rhiannon repeated, looking down at her hand to see what the small square object was, 'we'll go back to the Mount Nelson,' she went on, turning the box over curiously, 'to film Cape Town society at tea. The day after tomorrow, by the way, we'll be driving along the peninsula to the Cape of Good Hope and coming back via Simonstown and the beach where penguins take priority over humans and a ...' Her voice was slowly losing momentum as she let go of her bag and using both hands carefully prised open the leather box.

The instant she saw the diamond her heart stopped beating. Her eyes flew to Oliver. Strangely, there was no expression on his face. She looked at the ring again and suddenly there was so much chaos in her mind that she barely knew what she was thinking. Dimly she was aware of the others murmuring in amazement and awe as tiny sparks of light seemed almost to animate the ring.

'Oliver,' she murmured, glancing at him as she gently lifted the ring from its velvet crease. 'I – it's ...' She started to laugh. 'Oh God, I'm shaking.'

'Just put it on, will you,' Lizzy demanded.

Rhiannon looked at Oliver again and wondered why he wasn't smiling. Then suddenly it was as though she could read what he was thinking and as his shock and confusion settled around her heart she felt her insides turning cold. She couldn't get a complete picture on this yet, but what she was having no problem discerning was that he'd had no more idea that there was a ring in her bag than she had. Yet the ring was something to do with him, at least she presumed it was ...

Putting a hand to her head she felt herself turn hot as she heard Lizzy say, 'Would someone mind explaining what's going on here, because I'm kind of lost.'

'It would appear,' Oliver responded, summoning a smile to mask the edge in his voice, 'that Rhiannon doesn't like her engagement ring.'

Rhiannon looked at him.

'Either that,' Oliver said, taking the ring and sliding it on to her third finger, 'or the shock of finding it has just been too great for her.'

Rhiannon smiled weakly and stared at him as his eyes bored into hers. Then suddenly he started to smile. Rhiannon blinked and tried to stop her mind reeling. What on earth was going on? One minute he'd looked as appalled as if she'd stolen it, the next he was laughing and joking as though he'd planned the whole thing.

'Shall we go?' he suggested.

'Yes,' she responded, finding her voice at last. 'Yes, I think we should.'

*

'What I want to know is how the hell it got into your bag,' Oliver demanded, following Rhiannon into their room and slamming the door behind him.

'I told you, I don't know,' Rhiannon cried. 'You saw what happened. I put my hand in the bag ...'

'It's OK,' he interrupted, putting a hand up for her to stop. 'I was just thinking aloud. I know you didn't put it there ...' He raised his eyes to hers and gave a surprisingly sardonic smile. 'Your face when you saw it more than proved that,' he told her, 'but I have to tell you it was a pretty big shock to me too.'

'So where did it come from?' she said, aware of the diamond weighing heavily on her finger, but not quite wanting to look at it. 'I mean it is yours, isn't it?'

His eyes narrowed. 'No, darling, it's yours,' he reminded her.

'You know what I mean,' she said, lifting her hand to look at it. 'God, Oliver, it's so beautiful,' she whispered.

Taking her fingers he looked down at the exquisite champagne-coloured stone, watching the ephemeral pinpoints of light sparkle and glimmer with each tiny movement.

'If I'm reading this correctly,' she said, raising her eyes to his, 'then the general thinking is that someone broke into the room, took the diamond from your briefcase and put it in my bag?'

Oliver looked at her.

'Well *is* that what you're thinking?' she pressed.

'I don't know,' he sighed. 'Yes, I suppose it is. I mean how else can it have got there if neither of us put it there? What are you doing?' he asked as she reached for the phone.

'Calling security,' she answered. 'If someone's been in this room we ought at least to report it. Hello? Yes, can you connect me with security please.' Turning back to Oliver she said, 'I don't understand why you didn't report it the instant you realized it was gone. I mean, I don't know what it's worth, but ...'

'A little over fifty thousand dollars,' he said, taking the phone from her and hanging up. 'There's no point getting them involved,' he told her. 'It'll only confuse things even further.'

Rhiannon was gaping at him. 'Are you serious?' she breathed, tearing her eyes from his and looking down at the ring. 'My God, I think I'm going to faint. A fifty-thousand-dollar ring disappears from your briefcase and you don't tell anyone?' Suddenly her eyes were back on his. 'Oliver,' she said quietly, her insides starting to churn, 'please tell me it's not stolen.'

He laughed. 'No, it's not stolen,' he assured her. 'But it is illegally in this country.'

Rhiannon blinked. Then deciding this was all starting to get wildly out of hand she said, 'Would you mind pouring me a drink?'

'Scotch?' he said, walking down the steps to the mini-bar.

'Brandy,' she answered. 'What do you mean the ring isn't legally in the country?' she said.

'I haven't paid any duty on it,' he answered. 'I will when we get to England, but I don't want to go through the hassle or the expense of paying it twice.'

'You'd have to do that?' she said.

'Possibly.'

'So how did it get here?'

'A contact of mine brought it in from Australia a couple of days ago,' he answered, bringing their drinks back up the steps and sitting on one of the candy-striped sofas.

As Rhiannon looked at him she could feel a distant yet unsettling sense of foreboding starting to grow inside her. She waited for him to look at her, then going to sit on the edge of the coffee table in front of him she said, 'Let's try to fill in some missing spaces, shall we?'

His eyes came up to hers and he smiled faintly. Then

draining his glass, he set it down on the floor beside him and linked his fingers beneath his chin. 'I've told you about Theo Straussen,' he said. 'Who he is and what he means to me.'

Though his voice and demeanour were relaxed, Rhiannon noticed that his eyes were piercingly intent as he waited for her to respond. 'Yes,' she said quietly. 'He's your mentor. The man who got you started, who gave you all the contacts.'

He nodded. Then taking a deep breath he said, 'I've been trying for a while now to break away from him. To go solo, become an independent.'

Rhiannon frowned. 'But I thought you were already that,' she said.

He shook his head. 'No. Most of what I do is still done for Straussen. I've been working on ways of wrapping it up for months, but I'm tied to him in a way that's almost impossible to get out of, that could very possibly ruin me if I try.'

Rhiannon's eyes were wide. 'But you're trying anyway,' she said softly.

He nodded. 'I have to,' he said. 'For the sake of my own sanity, I have to.'

'I don't understand,' Rhiannon protested. 'I thought you two were as close as father and son.'

His smile was bitter. 'Not quite,' he responded. Then putting a hand to his head as though to press back the anger, he said, 'It's true, Theo Straussen is my mentor, he set me up in New York and he's opened doors for me that would never have been opened if I hadn't had his backing. So, it's thanks to him that I'm where I am today. I owe practically everything to Theo Straussen, the man who moves in all the right circles, contributes to all the right charities, supports his local synagogue ... You name it, he does it, but none of it changes what he is underneath.'

'Which is?'

Oliver's smile was grim. 'A gangster,' he replied.

'You mean, like in the Mafia?' Rhiannon breathed incredulously.

Oliver nodded and pressed his fingers into the sockets of his eyes. 'I mean, he's not with the Mob,' he said, 'he's Jewish, but the Jews, they've got their own kind of mafia and Theo Straussen's right up there with the big guys.' He sighed and let his gaze move to the middle distance. 'I'm not going to try telling you I didn't know what I was getting into when it all started, because I did. I knew exactly who Straussen was and what kind of an organization he ran. But he held the keys to a world I badly wanted into.' He glanced at Rhiannon. 'Diamonds, not crime,' he explained. 'So someone I vaguely knew set it up for us to meet, Straussen invited me out to his house a couple of times and then, just when I thought he was getting tired of me, he made me an offer I couldn't refuse.' His laugh was dry and mirthless. 'Boy, what an offer. I couldn't lose. He was giving me everything I ever dreamed of and in return all I had to do was keep my nose clean. He needed kosher businesses and the idea, as he saw it, of a well-connected, fancy-talking Englishman running the diamond dealership was one that strongly appealed to him. So we struck up a deal that, at least on the face of it, looked like it couldn't fail. And it hasn't failed. The dealership's doing better than it's ever done and Straussen pretty much leaves me alone to run things. But there's never any question that I'm his man and that's not something I'm finding so easy to live with any more. The trouble is, like with all these things, they're a damn sight easier to get into than they are to get out of. I suppose I should consider myself lucky it's happening this way round, because if it was him trying to get rid of me ...' His eyes came up to Rhiannon's. 'There's no point going into that,' he said. 'The point is, Straussen's sussed the fact that I'm trying to break loose and he's letting me know that it doesn't fit in with him.'

'You mean the burglary at your apartment, the car, the credit cards ...'

'Are just small-time irritations,' he said, 'to remind me he's there. And the ring turning up in your bag – my guess is it was done to make me suspect you and start driving a wedge between us.'

She took a moment to digest that. 'But why on earth would he do that?' she said.

'Probably because I haven't asked his permission to date you,' Oliver answered bitingly. 'Mr Straussen doesn't like his people making independent decisions, he likes to be consulted – on everything. But the hell am I going to consult him about something like this. Everything I have, everything I own, has come courtesy of Theo Straussen, but my god-damned wife doesn't come courtesy of him, no matter what he might like to tell himself. I've just got to raise enough money to buy myself out of the deal and set up on my own. It's not going to be easy, but the alternative, the way Straussen's got it planned, is unthinkable.'

Rhiannon's eyes closed as she took her time absorbing what he had told her. Then opening them again she looked at him in the dwindling light. Dropping to her knees in front of him, she rested her elbows on his thighs and took his hands in hers. He looked back at her and her throat tightened with emotion as she watched confidence and uncertainty eclipsing each other in his eyes. 'What should we expect next?' she whispered.

He shook his head. 'I've no idea.'

'But you think it's going to get worse.'

He nodded. 'Yes, it'll get worse. Unless I decide to go on dancing to his tune.' His smile was grim as he watched his fingers linking hers. 'I don't really care for myself,' he said, smoothing a finger over her cheek. 'It's you I care about. You and our future and being able to share everything I have with you, everything I've worked for, everything that means something to me ... I want it to be ours. I want to put Straussen and New York behind us, so that we can move forward together, make a good life together.'

As his voice faltered Rhiannon put her arms around him and held him. His arms tightened around her and she couldn't help wondering how much he was holding back in order not to frighten her any more than he already had.

Chapter 7

Hey, Galina! What do you think?'

Lifting her head from the padded neck-rest of the make-up chair and peering through the bustling horde of beauticians, Galina looked across the room to where Verena, the costumier, was holding up a specially designed creation from Ralph Lauren.

'Wow, it's fantastic,' Galina cried. 'Has Maribeth seen it? She's going to love it. It's exactly right. Oh God, no more,' she protested as Mimi, the chief beautician, pressed her head rudely back on to the neck-rest and struck a meaningful pose with a pointed brush.

'Let's have the tray of blues back over here,' Mimi called to one of her assistants. 'And did anyone get hold of Peggy Wilson yet?'

'She's on her way up,' Verena answered, tucking the dress back inside its plastic covering and hanging it on a closet door as her assistant showed her the matching pumps. 'Maribeth's with her.'

'Can I have some coffee?' Galina wailed.

'No toxins. Get her some water, someone,' Mimi responded.

'I want coffee,' Galina insisted, knowing full well she wouldn't get it. 'Where's Cornelius? Has anyone seen Cornelius? He should have been here ages ago.'

'He's downstairs romancing the PR guys,' Verena answered.

'And we won't be ready to tackle your hair for at least another hour,' Mimi added.

'How long!' Galina cried, sitting bolt upright and narrowly missing a prod in the eye.

'Relax. Just kidding,' Mimi smiled sweetly, pressing her firmly back in position.

'Ouch! What's going on down there?' Galina demanded, craning round Mimi to get a look at her legs.

'Got to pluck out those stray hairs,' Sandy, the depilation artist, told her.

'I thought she was wearing flesh tights,' Verena said, turning from the spare make-up mirror where she was spraying her face with Evian. 'I've got her a dozen pairs of Dior flesh tights. What am I supposed to do with all those tights if you're making her legs up for no tights?'

'All right, keep your tights on,' Sandy retorted. 'She can wear tights. We just don't want any stray hairs poking through, do we?'

'You think someone's going to notice one lousy blonde hair poking through a pair of tights?' Verena cried.

'What's it to you if they do?' Sandy responded haughtily. 'Leg hair isn't your territory.'

'Ladies, ladies,' Mimi interrupted, muttering the reprimand through the slender wooden stem of a lip-brush which was clamped between her teeth.

'Do you think Maribeth's going to approve of this colour?' the manicurist wondered, tilting her head to one side as she pondered the pale mauve polish she was brushing on to Galina's immaculately fitted and shaped nails.

Crooking her fingers back, Galina strained her eyes downwards to take a look. 'She'll love it,' she said confidently. 'It's a perfect match.'

The manicurist beamed, for the painstaking efforts she'd gone to mixing the colours herself – using Conspiracy polishes, naturally – to get a match on the

Conspiracy trademark mauve was second only to the trouble she'd had getting the Brazilian prosthetics girl to allow her to fit the nails herself.

As the bedlam continued to ebb and flow around her with PR executives, product managers, stylists, beauticians and heaven only knew who else swarming in and out, Galina allowed her mind to wander out of the spacious suite at the Four Seasons Hotel to the grand ballroom downstairs, which was very likely even more hectic than the suite. When she'd called in on her way up none of the publicists or technicians or engineers or myriad assistants had even noticed she was there they were so busy supervising the construction of the presentation stand or the placement on each chair of a Conspiracy towelling robe and lace purses containing free samples of the new range of beauty products. It amused her to imagine what kind of pitch they might have built themselves to by now as the hour of the press call drew alarmingly closer and the reports that were finding their way into the make-up suite gleefully exaggerated the last-minute panic and disasters.

Sighing contentedly and moving on through her imagination as if she was hunting through TV channels, Galina tried, not for the first time, to get some kind of picture on what her life was going to be like from midday today when Primaire USA announced to the world that she was to become the face to launch their Conspiracy range into the twenty-first century. To her it was incredible, inconceivable even, to think that she was going to achieve the kind of fame that Max and Maribeth Courtini had spent the past five days trying to prepare her for. Until now her only real recognition had come from being a regular visitor to the Romanovs' Malibu mansion, particularly since Carolyn's death, when she had been dubbed the beautiful and mysterious woman with whom Max Romanov might or might not be having an affair. Apart from that, there had been preciously few spaces cleared in the limelight for her – just a couple of modelling jobs back in the eighties, a small part in an afternoon soap and one night-club appearance in Venice that had got her name in the papers for the vicious attack she had suffered on her way back home.

She had no need to work, for Max's grandfather had taken care of her in his will. The old man had supported her and her grandmother, the Countess Katerina, for as long as Galina could remember, which was how Galina had come to attend the smart English boarding-school in Gloucestershire, England. It was also how her grandmother had afforded the spacious, fully-staffed town house in London's Mayfair and the expensive Harley Street doctors she had needed in her final years. In fact, Mikhail Romanov's generosity was such that Galina had often wondered if the old man had been secretly in love with the Russian Countess. Max didn't think so, but then Max wouldn't.

'OK, a nice O with those lips,' Mimi said, snapping Galina back to the present as she clicked her fingers for someone to wheel forward the lipstick tray.

'It's not going to be mauve, is it?' Galina grimaced.

'Mauvish,' Mimi answered. 'Let's keep the noise down in here, shall we?' she shouted. 'Now sit still, there's a darling, the boss is watching.'

Galina's eyes flew open as she turned to see the head of Primaire's West Coast Operations, Maribeth Courtini, standing over her with Peggy Wilson, Senior Vice-President, Public Relations. 'Maribeth!' Galina cried, starting to get up. 'How long have you been standing there?' She gave a quick sigh of exasperation as Mimi shoved her back in her seat. 'She's a tyrant,' she complained. 'She won't let me move and I'm going to scream if she doesn't get her hand from around my throat.'

'Be quiet,' Mimi snapped.

Maribeth laughed, aware that Mimi and Galina had struck up an instant rapport from the moment they'd met which appeared to be founded in some kind of humorous antagonism. 'How are you feeling?' she asked Galina.

'Abused,' Galina responded with a menacing glare at Mimi. 'And nervous and excited and furious with Max that he's gone off to New York.'

Maribeth smiled. Her expertly hennaed chin-length bob was as unshakeable as her celebrated calm and her own carefully and liberally applied make-up erased several years from the fifty-three she had so far totalled. 'You remember Peggy, I'm sure,' she said, turning to the anxious-faced woman beside her with a honey-blonde earphone hairdo and an exquisitely tailored Donna Karan suit.

'Of course I remember,' Galina smiled. 'How are you Peggy? How are things downstairs?'

Peggy's kohl-rimmed eyes flooded with purpose. 'We'll get there,' she answered, with cheer-leading fervour. 'But the important thing now is that you feel free to share with us any zero hour anxieties you may be experiencing. I want you to know that we will all be there for you, Galina. We're pulling together for you to make this work because you're a very special person and we all love you and want you to succeed and I just know that you're going to make the whole world believe in Conspiracy ...'

'Oooooooh,' Mimi trilled, making ready to descend with her lip-brush.

'Peggy, I'm sure you'd appreciate some time alone to go over your presentation one more time,' Maribeth suggested, her hazel eyes twinkling with laughter.

'Oh hell, here comes Sweeney Todd,' Mimi warned as Cornelius, Galina's hairdresser, sauntered in. 'We're not ready for you yet, cutey-pie.'

Cornelius's pinched little nostrils flared as he pressed a finger to his cheek, saying, 'The woman is a Venus and you take three hours to make her look like a Venus?'

'Get him out of here before I do something I'll enjoy,' Mimi muttered to no one in particular. 'Galina, I know it's hard not to think of a blow job when your lips are like that, but try not to dribble, honey. It's not polite.'

Laughing, Maribeth turned to watch Peggy walk stiffly out of the room. 'Bad news, I'm afraid,' she said turning back. 'Susan Posner's turned up.'

'The Poisoner!' Verena cried from where she was lying on the bed, flexing her upper arms. 'Who invited *her*?'

'She's covering for the *Enquirer*,' Maribeth answered, looking down at Galina. 'I just wanted to remind you of what we talked about yesterday,' she said. 'Peggy and her team will be there to field questions you don't want to answer. With Susan Posner in the audience we now know that situation is likely to arise.' Behind her the door had opened and an enormous bouquet of white roses was swaying dangerously into the room. 'Is that you behind those flowers, Krystal?' Maribeth asked, searching for her secretary.

'No, it's me, Ula,' Max's personal assistant panted. 'Someone take these, please. I'm experiencing death by a thousand cuts here. God-damn men, why don't they use Teleflora like the rest of the civilized world? Galina, how are you doing, sweetheart? Max sends his love, he also sends these roses and says to tell you he'll be at Primaire in New York to watch the video link-up. He'll call you right after, he says. Any chance of some coffee anyone?'

'Mimi's banned it,' Galina told her through circular lips. 'But if you can find any I'd love one. Who's that massaging my feet? It feels wonderful. Are my nails dry yet, I've got an itch.'

'Where?' the manicurist demanded, pinning Galina's hands to the arms of the chair. 'I'll scratch it for you.'

'In my ear,' Galina answered.

'Use a cotton bud,' Mimi said, handing her one. 'Verena, did you show Maribeth the dress yet?'

'I saw it last night,' Maribeth told her. 'It's perfect. Is that mauve on Galina's eyes a tad dark, Mimi ... No, no, of course it isn't,' she corrected herself as Mimi turned dangerously affronted eyes upon her. 'It must be the light.' She looked at her watch. 'You've got another forty-five minutes in here,' she said.

'Cornelius!' Mimi snapped. 'Stop hovering that way, you look like you're trying to hold in a fart. You can have her in ten minutes, now beat it.'

'Did I see The Poisoner downstairs?' Ula said, coming out of the bathroom where she and a couple of others had deposited the roses.

'You did,' Maribeth confirmed.

'What's she doing here so early?' Ula demanded, leaning her gangly frame towards a spare mirror. 'What's she doing here at all? She's not a health and beauty hack.'

'She's doing a piece for the *Enquirer*,' Maribeth told her, 'and she's here early in the hope of catching a quick five minutes with me, so I'm told.'

Ula snorted. 'She can't seriously think you're going to give her anything on Max. I mean, I take it that's what she's after. Send her back to the nut-cruncher over in Burbank.'

'The what?' Galina said.

'Nut-cruncher. Shrink,' Ula elucidated, selecting a fuscia-pink nail polish from the manicurist's tray and testing it out. 'They say she's been seeing a shrink.'

'So? Doesn't everyone?' Mimi said, standing back to admire her handiwork.

'Not any more. It's passé. Cornelius, do you think you could do something with my hair?' Ula groaned, running the unpolished fingernails of her left hand through the neglected thatch of black hair that framed her lovely Irish face. 'Shall we try red? I kind of like red. Did you see that movie with Kim Basinger, or was it Sharon Stone? She had red hair. It looked sensational ...'

'OK, we'll give it another shot when you're dressed,'

Mimi pronounced, tissuing off Galina's lipstick and raising her voice to make herself heard over the fitness tape someone had just slotted into the video. 'Turn it down!' she yelled, sliding her brushes back into the felt roll. 'OK, Cornelius, she's all yours. Robyn, you got the camera over there? We need some shots for our records.'

'Any sign of any other arrivals?' Maribeth called over to the couple of assistants who were standing at the window keeping vigil on the forecourt below.

'A few,' one of them called back. 'No one recognizable yet.'

'Did you invite the women from your club?' Galina asked Maribeth, wincing as Cornelius peeled off her protective headband and began brutally scrunching her hair.

'Water,' he shouted. 'Someone bring water.'

His assistant leapt to the deed, thrusting a spray into Cornelius's outstretched hand.

'They'll all be here,' Maribeth said confidently.

'The Poisoner's after your club, isn't she?' Ula said, settling down to finish polishing her nails. 'Didn't I read somewhere that she's suing you for age discrimination?'

'She's trying,' Maribeth confirmed, watching Galina's reflection in the mirror as Cornelius went about his work. Galina's dazzlingly white-blonde hair was so short that, unless Maribeth had been watching this herself, she'd never have believed that it could call for such skill to style it.

'Does she want to become a member?' Mimi asked. 'Is that her problem? How old is she? She's got to be over thirty.'

'She's twenty-eight,' Maribeth said. 'And yes, she wants to become a member.' Sighing she added, 'I guess I'd better go see what she wants. Make sure, all of you, that Galina gets ten minutes' quiet before we get started. I'll be back to see you then, honey,' she said, smiling at

Galina in the mirror.

'Bring Peggy,' Galina said mischievously. 'I want to hear her last-minute advice.'

'Don't tease her,' Maribeth chided. 'It's not easy doing these press calls, as you're about to find out. Sée you all later,' and leaving the scent of Giorgio Red behind her she departed.

Being an expert at his craft it wasn't long before Cornelius was finished, and spinning Galina round in her chair so she was facing into the room he cried, 'Da-da!'

Ula, who was in the middle of telling everyone about a new cellulite treatment she'd recently read about, stopped and let her mouth drop open as the others gasped or murmured or simply stared in mute admiration.

'Will you just look at her?' Ula murmured. 'Galina, honey, you look like a god-damned angel. You look so gorgeous I – Hell, I don't know what to say. I feel like I could cry.'

Galina arched an eyebrow.

'No, I'm serious,' Ula said. 'I feel humbled and deeply moved to be in the presence of such divine beauty ... What was that for?' she cried, as a hand towel hit her in the face. 'I mean it. You look sensational.'

'Can I get out of this chair now?' Galina said, struggling up. 'God, I'm so stiff, I feel like I've been here a week.'

'Let's take a look at your back and shoulders,' Mimi said, coming forward and untying the pink gown Galina was wearing. 'Here,' she said, throwing the gown at one of her assistants, 'put that in with the rest of the laundry and someone bring me a touch-up stick.'

'You mean she's got a blemish!' Ula cried ecstatically.

'One day,' Mimi sighed, feeling every one of her hundred and thirty pounds as she gazed at Galina's perfect long-legged figure and beautifully burnished skin in the pure white silk and lace body from Anne Klein, 'I am going to look like that.'

'In your dreams,' Cornelius said waspishly.

Mimi eyed him nastily, then dabbing around Galina's shoulders with the touch-up stick, she said, 'OK, everyone out. Verena, be back in ten minutes to dress her. Cornelius and the rest of you in fifteen for finals. Ula, I take it you're staying?'

'You bet.'

'OK. If either of you needs anything you can get it for yourselves. No, seriously, I'll post someone outside to satisfy your legal-substance cravings, but no more than one coffee for you, Galina, and make it decaff.'

'It's like having a nanny,' Ula grumbled as the door closed behind Mimi. 'Is she always like that?'

Galina laughed. 'I imagine so. I've only known her four days, remember?' Sitting back in the make-up chair she pulled her long legs up to her chest and circled them with her arms. 'So, tell me, you spoke to Max this morning? What did he say? Is he still angry?'

Ula's small red mouth moved thoughtfully to one side as she pondered the question. 'No,' she said, sitting in another make-up chair and propping her legs on the arm of Galina's. 'I don't think so. He didn't sound it, anyway.'

'Not that you'd tell me if he did,' Galina grinned, her luminous blue eyes glittering the challenge.

Ula's answering grin made Galina laugh. 'He's furious, Ula, and we both know it,' she said.

'He's concerned,' Ula corrected. 'You know how much he hates publicity and he's worried about how you're going to handle it.'

Galina turned to look at herself in the mirror. 'What does he think, that I'm going to start talking about *him* the minute the cameras roll?'

'You know what I mean,' Ula said.

Galina appeared not to be listening as she eyed herself curiously in the mirror. 'I wonder what it's going to be like being famous,' she said.

'Conspiracy's gonna put you up there with the biggest,' Ula assured her.

Galina continued to look at the mirror, though it was evident from her expression that her mind was elsewhere. 'I wish Max were here,' she said bleakly. 'I hate him for going off last night like that.'

'He had things to do in New York,' Ula said tactfully.

Galina's dark, crescent-shaped eyebrows went up as her eyes focused on Ula's in the mirror. 'We both know that's not true,' she said.

Ula nodded. 'It is true. There are always things for him to do in New York.'

'OK,' Galina conceded, 'but they could have waited. He's gone to punish me for accepting this contract ...'

'Rubbish,' Ula interrupted. 'He's trying to protect you.'

'Like I need protecting?'

Ula looked at her with steady, uncompromising eyes.

'OK,' Galina shrugged, 'so maybe I do, but whose fault is that?'

'It's no one's fault,' Ula answered. 'Things are just the way they are, that's all. And Max doesn't want you to begin your career with Conspiracy surrounded by all the adverse publicity you'd get if the two of you were to go public on your relationship now.'

'So he's not using it as an excuse to get out of marrying me?' Galina said.

Ula's surprise showed. 'Is that what you think?' she said.

Galina's head went to one side as she considered the question. 'No, I don't suppose so,' she sighed. 'But there again I don't know what I do think. I mean, sometimes I'm not even sure if I want to marry him.' Her eyes slanted towards Ula's.

Ula was shaking her head and grinning. 'Not working,' she said. 'Even if I told Max what you just said it wouldn't change his mind on anything. You know what he's like.'

Galina pulled a face. 'Don't I just,' she muttered, resting her chin on her knees.

She was quiet for a while, lost in her thoughts as she pondered her unusual and extremely volatile relationship with the man she loved above anyone else in the world and who almost totally dominated her life. 'I still think he should have been here for me today,' she grumbled, evidently debating whether or not to let him off the hook. 'Except it's typical of him to go into hiding the minute the spotlight's turned on.'

'Wouldn't you if you were in his position and they said the kind of things about you that they say about him?'

'Max doesn't care what anyone says about him,' Galina scoffed.

Ula frowned. 'Why do you think that?'

'Because it's true. Max doesn't care about anyone or anything, except his kids, of course.'

'And you.'

'And me. He wants to protect us all because he cares about us, but he doesn't care for himself. He's not afraid of anyone or what they say about him. Nothing ever gets to Max. He's invincible, or hadn't you noticed?'

'Not especially,' Ula responded, knowing very well what was really going on here, for it was Galina's way to attack Max when she was feeling insecure or nervous or afraid, as she surely must be now.

'He should have stayed,' Galina snapped. 'I don't care what they say about me so why should he?'

'There's not only you,' Ula reminded her. 'There's Primaire and the entire Conspiracy campaign. They're spending millions, as well you know, so to kick off with the kind of publicity a public confirmation of your relationship with Max would generate wouldn't be particularly wise.'

'Stop being so reasonable,' Galina retorted. 'I just want to hate him for five minutes, OK?'

'Then call him up and tell him,' Ula suggested.

'Where's the phone?'

Digging into her belt-bag, Ula produced the mobile and handed it over. 'Press 3 for his direct number,' she said.

It rang several times before Galina glanced at her watch and felt her stomach tighten with nerves as she realized he had probably already left to go and watch the video link-up at Primaire's New York headquarters.

'Max Romanov.' His voice came so suddenly down the line that it made her jump.

'Hello, darling,' she smiled, turning away from Ula. 'It's me. I just called to tell you I hate you. Ula thought I should.'

'Is Ula there with you?' he said.

'Yes.'

'Then put her on.'

Rolling her eyes, Galina passed the phone over to Ula.

'Max?' Ula said.

'How's she doing?' Max asked.

'Fine. Just fine,' Ula answered. 'But nothing's happened yet. The press are only just arriving and she's not even dressed ...'

Galina reached out and grabbed the phone. 'I could have told you that myself, Max,' she said tightly. 'Why do you always have to ask someone else how I am? What do you think, that I lie to you or something? I'm nervous, OK? I'm as nervous as hell and I wish you were here and you damned well should be here. You didn't have to go out front with me, you could have waited somewhere behind the scenes ...'

'Galina, don't let's go into all that again,' he interrupted. 'I'll be back tomorrow night, we can talk things through then.'

'It'll be too late then. Everything will already have

happened then.'

'Put Ula back on.'

'No. Talk to *me*. I'm not a child, Max, nor am I a half-wit. I know what's going on and I understand why you're concerned and I love you for being concerned, but I need you here. God knows you deprive me of everything else, so you could at least do me the favour of being here when I'm going into something so big.'

From the silence at the other end Galina knew she'd gone too far. Her heart was thumping as she waited for him to speak, while inside she was debating whether she should teach him a lesson for this. 'I don't think you've got any idea how important it is to me knowing you're near,' she told him miserably.

'I do know, honey,' he said, surprising her with the gentleness of his tone when she'd thought she'd made him angry. 'It's important for me too. It won't happen again. Next time I'll be there for you.'

'Do you promise?'

'I promise.'

'Do you love me?'

'You know I do.'

'Say it.'

'I love you.'

'I love you too. And I'm sorry I'm being such a brat. I'll make it up to you when you get back.'

'You're darned right you will,' he said, making her laugh.

'Do you want to speak to Ula?' she offered.

'No. I'll wait to hear from you as soon as the show is over.'

'OK.'

'Good luck, darling. You'll be terrific, I know.'

'Yeah. Speak to you later.' As she clicked the phone off and passed it back to Ula she was about to say something when Verena walked in the door. 'Can you give us a few more seconds?' Galina said.

'Sure. But we're cutting it fine,' Verena responded, looking at her watch.

'A few seconds, no more,' Galina promised.

'I'm all agog,' Ula remarked when Verena had gone. 'What is it?'

'My old school friend, Rhiannon Edwardes,' Galina answered, sending Ula's eyebrows skywards. 'I saw some photos of her in Max's study a few days ago. Don't look like that, they were on the desk, I wasn't snooping. Is he having her checked out because of what I did to her or because of what she represents?'

'Jesus,' Ula muttered, 'you sure as hell pick your moments, Galina. What did you do to her?'

'Nothing much. Well, I suppose it was at the time, but it's years ago now and ...'

'What did you do?' Ula prompted.

'I ran off with the man she was about to marry.'

Ula's eyes widened. 'Nothing much, she says. Who was he?'

'A nobody. I can't even remember his name now. Peter something or other, I think. Or was it Phillip? I don't know, it doesn't matter. I just want to know what Max thinks of Rhiannon. Do you think he trusts her?'

Ula shook her head as though something inside it had got jammed. 'Trusts her?' she repeated. 'Where did that suddenly come from? And why should it be an issue?'

'Trust is always an issue with Max,' Galina responded. 'So what do you think? Will he let me write to her?'

'I'm afraid you're gonna have to ask him that question,' Ula answered, looking up as Verena came back into the room.

'If he does, do you think she'll come see me?' Galina said, getting to her feet.

Ula looked at her, trying to keep the disbelief from her face. 'Well let's put it this way,' she said, 'would you, if someone had run off with the man you were about to marry?'

'I told you, that was years ago,' Galina laughed. 'She's met someone else now and she probably can't remember the other guy's name either.'

'I'll put money on it she can,' Ula commented.

'OK, everyone,' Mimi boomed, crashing open the door and marching in like a general at the head of an army. 'How are we all doing? Galina, let me look at you? Someone get the Queen, her hair needs touching up. Maribeth! Maribeth? You were right there a moment ago ...'

'I'm here,' Maribeth said, coming in through the door with Peggy Wilson.

'We're going for the frosted pink?' Mimi said. 'Is that what we finalized?'

'Yes, the frosted pink,' Maribeth confirmed. 'Mauve lips are going to make her look like she's got a heart condition. In fact, try mixing the pink with the pearlized white.'

'In that dress?' Mimi cried. 'She'll look like a skier at a garden party. But it's a good idea. It might work. I'll try it.'

'Have you read Louisa Hay's book?' Peggy was asking Galina as Verena helped her into the immaculately tailored white silk dress with an over-the-knee pleated skirt and two deep-cut Vs at the front and back. It was stunning in its simplicity and couldn't have been better for Galina with her white-blonde hair and lovely golden skin.

'Whose?' Galina asked.

'Louisa Hay. She is full of such excellent advice and I must tell ... No, no, she says not to use the word must... I feel it incumbent upon me, Galina, to suggest that you turn to the mirror and look at your beautiful face and tell yourself that you love yourself. I did it this morning to help me overcome my nerves at making the presentation today and it works. I'm telling you, it really works.'

'Well that's good, Peggy,' Galina remarked smoothly.

'I mean, someone's got to love you I guess, so it seems like you've let the rest of us off the hook.'

The whole room plunged into silence as everyone stared at Galina in disbelief. It had been an unforgivably cruel thing to say when everyone knew that Peggy only ever wanted to make people feel good, even if she did take it a bit far at times. And for Galina to have hurt her now, only minutes before Peggy was about to go on and introduce Galina to the world, was as shocking as it was confusing.

Peggy's face was ashen as she tried nervously to laugh the insult off. Ula stepped forward as though to offer comfort, then fell back as Mimi looked at Maribeth and Maribeth looked at Galina.

Galina's eyes were wide with astonishment as she gazed nervously about the room. Then reaching out to Peggy she said, 'I'm sorry, Peggy. I'm truly sorry. I didn't mean it to come out that way. It was supposed to be a joke ... Oh God,' she groaned looking helplessly at Ula. 'Tell her, it was supposed to be a joke.'

'It's OK, honey,' Peggy assured her, patting her hand. 'I know it was a joke. It's what you British call irony, isn't it? And I know we Californians don't always understand it. I promise you, there's no offence taken.'

Galina looked at her, wanting desperately to cry for the stupidity that had suddenly come over her and spurred an insensitivity that had, she knew instinctively, put a whole new slant on the way the rest of the team now viewed her.

'Call Max,' she said to Ula, her voice trembling with emotion. 'I need to speak to him.'

Seconds later the phone was in her hand and she was sitting on the toilet lid with the bathroom door between her and the newly erupted bedlam outside. 'Max?' she whispered.

'Yes honey, I'm here. What is it?'

'Where are you?'

'I'm in the street on my way over to Primaire. Why? What's up, Galina? Did something happen?'

'I just insulted someone, Max. I mean, I was insufferably rude to her and I think everyone hates me now.'

'Galina! Pull yourself together. Everyone doesn't hate you, so stop exaggerating. Did you apologize to whoever it was?'

'Yes, I apologized.'

'Then what's the big deal?'

'You should be here, Max. I told you I couldn't do it without you.'

'Well it looks like you're gonna have to,' he said coldly.

'I can't. We'll have to call the whole thing off. Postpone it until you get back.'

'You get yourself in there and do what Maribeth tells you,' he said harshly. 'Do you hear me, Galina?

'Yes, I hear you. I can't do it, Max.'

'Then we're through, Galina. You don't go in there and show your face for those cameras, we're through.'

'You don't mean that, Max.'

He was silent, allowing the roar of New York traffic to swell down the line.

'You don't mean it, Max,' she repeated.

'I mean it, Galina. I've just about had it with you and the way you're trying to manipulate my life. Now either you get out there and give it your best shot, or we're through.'

'OK. I'm going in, Max,' she said, and smiling she clicked off the line and walked back into the room.

Chapter 8

As Max was shown into the conference suite at Primaire's New York headquarters Lanny Harman, the company's charismatic and flamboyant chairman, discreetly broke away from a group of young executives and came over to greet him. The vast plate-glass windows, with their enviable views of the Hudson and Hoboken, were in the process of being blanked out by electronically rolling shutters and the split-screen video-monitor that claimed an entire fifteen by twelve wall space was currently relaying a shot of the crowded ballroom over in Beverly Hills.

'Max. It's good to see you,' Harman said in a low, amiable voice as he shook Max by the hand. 'Sorry you couldn't make lunch today, I'd have enjoyed the opportunity for a chat.' There was no rebuke in his tone, merely the resonance of a regret that he'd been unable to lure Max downtown to his favourite restaurant.

'I just flew in last night,' Max replied by way of an explanation. His sharp eyes were scanning the room, checking out who was there.

'Do you want to be introduced, or do you want to play it low?' Harman said, ushering him further into the room.

'Let's keep it low,' Max said, with a brief smile that somehow got lost in irony.

'Did you talk to Maribeth this afternoon?' Lanny

asked, signalling to a secretary to bring them coffee. 'Looks like things are going pretty well their end. She's a beautiful girl, Max.'

Max raised an eyebrow, seeming to find the fact that the compliment was meant for him vaguely amusing. 'Yeah, she's beautiful,' he acknowledged, taking the coffee that was being offered him. 'I got the product projection data,' he went on, taking a sip. 'It's impressive. A targeted thirty-three per cent return after tax on a twenty-million-dollar outlay in a forecast period of five years is *very* impressive – if you can pull it off.'

'With your girl on board I believe we can,' Lanny smiled.

Inwardly Max winced. 'Galina,' he said affably. 'Let's call her Galina. And beautiful as she is, you've got to have some confidence in your product to be putting that much behind it.'

'I'll have the lab reports on your desk by the end of the day,' Lanny said. 'Conspiracy's gonna be a winner. You've got to have seen the way the stock's jumped this past couple of weeks since the market got wind of the launch.'

'A thirteen per cent increase,' Max remarked. 'Not bad. Lucky I bought in when I did.'

The others were all starting to take their seats as the press corps over in LA sought out theirs and peered critically or indifferently into their vanity purses of free samples.

'We've got three people making the presentation today,' Lanny explained, as he and Max found themselves a couple of chairs slightly apart from the rest of the room. 'Peggy Wilson, Vice- President, PR; Jimmy Han, Senior Lab Technician and Maribeth. Jimmy Han's not gonna have much to say – his end is scientific and today's not about science. It's about Galina. Everyone knows by now that the Conspiracy range is due to hit the stores by the first of next month. Today they're going to find out that Galina will be fronting the campaign – that it's her face they're gonna see every time they open a magazine, switch on their TV or drive their cars down the highway. Peggy Wilson's assistants are all on hand to field questions put direct to Galina. When she's had a bit more training and knows more about the range we're hoping she'll be able to handle the questions herself.'

Max said nothing.

'Beauty with brains are what today's women are all about,' Lanny went on, 'and definitely what Conspiracy's about.'

'You mean you rub in your night cream and wake up smart in the morning?' Max enquired, deadpan.

Lanny's pale-grey eyes slanted him a look, then chuckling good-naturedly, he said, 'I guess I should leave the sales pitch to those who know what they're doing. Did you see the guest list?'

'Yeah, I saw it,' Max answered. 'More stars than an African night sky.' He frowned, wondering why, when he'd never been to Africa, he should have used that analogy. Then remembering the photographs of Galina's friend, he instinctively glanced at his watch, even though his meeting with Theo Straussen wasn't until the next day.

'That's Maribeth's doing,' Lanny said. 'She knows everyone and getting 'em all out for a press call like this is gonna give us a launch that'll make Canaveral look like they're hiking a kite. I don't know how you're gonna handle it after today, Max, but when your girl's through with this press call there won't be a paparazzo out there in La-La land, or anywhere else come to that, who's not gonna be on her tail.'

'We'll handle it,' Max assured him.

Lanny's eyes returned to the screen as a general murmur crept around the New York conference room, while over in Los Angeles the audience of stars and press began to applaud. Galina, in a stunningly simple white silk dress and a discreet but fabulously expensive diamond and pearl necklace on hire from a Hollywood jeweller, was being led to the presentation stand where the entire Conspiracy range was artistically and invitingly displayed. As she moved alongside it, taking the position she had rehearsed to create the arresting vision that was soon to become a nation-wide sensation, Lanny felt a stab of pure joy descend from his heart to his cheque-book – he had rarely seen a woman more beautiful than the one the camera was closing in on now.

Unable to stop himself, he cast a quick glance at the man who held Galina Casimir and all that blinding beauty in the palm of his hand. This was the first time Harman had come into such close contact with the head of Romanov Enterprises and he'd been aware, from the moment he'd shaken Max's hand, that he was in the presence of an exceptionally astute and intelligent man. That hadn't come as much of a surprise, for Harman had heard how like his grandfather Max was, but even old Mikhail hadn't had the intensity or control his grandson seemed to exude. It was almost, Harman thought, as though the man were capable of transferring the very power that drove him into those around him, forcing them to carry the burden too. Harman blinked at the thought. He had always, albeit from a distance, nurtured a healthy respect for Max Romanov, but after just these few minutes in his company, and of course after seeing Galina, Harman had to confess that his respect was beginning to border on awe. That was until he recalled what Maribeth had told him, when an almost painful sympathy slid through him.

What was Romanov thinking now, Lanny wondered as Max stared up at the incredible woman on the screen. But Max's dark, impassive face was giving nothing away as he listened to Peggy Wilson welcoming the glittering array of guests, mentioning some of the more socially prominent and famous by name, before finally turning to introduce Galina.

As Galina accepted her applause, scores of flashlights exploded, capturing the beguiling loveliness of her smile, recording for tomorrow's front pages the unusual quality of her beauty and the dazzling radiance of her person. To watch the way she moved, altering her expression for the cameras, holding her face to the Californian sunlight streaming in through the windows, touching her fingertips to the diamonds at her throat, it was impossible to believe that she had never done this before. Even harder to credit was the fact that she hadn't been snapped up by another cosmetic house, a casting agent, a movie producer or any other main-stream entrepreneur a long time ago. But Harman knew the reason, and his heart gave a quick, unsteady beat as he inwardly prayed he'd made the right decision here, for if those security people Romanov had hired didn't do their job, the exclusive image of the Conspiracy range was going to end up right down the pan, along with too many million dollars to think about. On the other hand, if they did foul up and a scandal did break, there just wasn't any telling what dividends that amount of publicity might pay. And hell, he wouldn't be where he was today if he hadn't taken a risk or two, and that girl was so goddamned beautiful it hurt your eyes to look at her.

Turning back to the screen he saw that the camera angle had now widened to include Peggy, Maribeth and Jimmy Han. Galina was listening attentively as Han delivered his brief and lay-person-friendly oration on why the Conspiracy range in general and age-eliminator serum in particular was about to set new standards in the scientific and technologically advanced world of cosmetics.

'I'd like to know', one beauty writer interrupted, 'why, if you're targeting the older woman with Conspiracy, which pricing alone suggests you must be, why you are using someone as young as Galina to promote it? Or has she already been using the age-eliminator serum?'

Everyone laughed as the vision-mixer in LA punched up the feed of a second camera to show who'd asked the question.

'How old did she look before she started using it?' someone shouted from the back, sparking another round of laughter.

'How long has she been using it?' someone else wanted to know.

To everyone's surprise Galina stepped forward. Fortunately, being as stunning as she was, all eyes were focused on her so no one saw the panicked look that suddenly afflicted Maribeth's face, nor Peggy's instinctive though quickly arrested gesture to block.

'Beauty', Galina said, in her charming, upper-class English accent, 'is not about looking young. Beauty is about looking good.'

There was no more than a split-second's silence before the whole room broke into spontaneous applause. Maribeth's mouth fell open and Peggy's sharp intake of breath brought a steadying hand to her chest. Of course, everyone knew that women the world over would pay a king's ransom for the serum that would make them look younger, but a statement like the one Galina had just made was quite staggeringly brilliant in its profound marketability. In fact it was such an outstandingly commercial slogan that every writer in the house was busily scribbling it on to their pads as though it were a line Galina had been handed by the marketing executives of Primaire, rather than a priceless aphorism she had just come up with herself.

The executives in the New York conference suite were applauding too, their murmurs of approval interspersed with the wondering of who, in the LA office, had come up with such a shit-hot winner of a slogan.

Lanny Harman looked at Max, who returned the look

with a single raise of an eyebrow.

After that Galina very wisely made no attempt to upstage her moment of glory, she merely listened, again attentively, to Peggy's eloquent and effusively delivered exhortation on how very thrilled everyone at Primaire was that Galina was joining the Conspiracy – ha, ha! – to help women everywhere realize their own beauty potential and get in touch with their own inner-Galinas and learn the fundamental importance of loving themselves.

'Together, Conspiracy and Galina will help us to do that,' she cried, with an almost evangelical fervour. 'And now, before I invite you to take part in our open forum, I would like to ask you all to join me in showing our sincere appreciation to Galina for coming here today and helping us to see how a healthy and radiant soul is not only our link to the Universe, but is also a key player in the conspiracy of attainable beauty.'

Max turned to Harman in profound astonishment.

Harman shifted uncomfortably in his chair. 'The woman has been known to get a tad carried away at times,' he explained.

Max's dark eyes were alive with humour, though he refrained from comment as the LA audience broke into yet more applause and Harman breathed a sigh of relief as he'd been half expecting a prayer.

The next ten minutes or more were taken up with a quick-fire question-and-answer session on whether or not it was true Galina's contract was for five million dollars; what exactly her schedule would be and when it would begin; what she had done to date – was she famous in England; was it true she was descended from a Russian countess; did she plan on staying in the US; how did she like the States; and a hundred more inconsequential but necessary questions to help build her celebrity profile. Each and every question was answered by Peggy and her team with the occasional comment from Maribeth and much laughter and amused interest from Galina.

It wasn't until Maribeth was making moves to start ushering Galina out of the room that Susan Posner, the journalist who had first penned the Murder to Mishap line, and who had made it her mission in life to uncover what had really happened the night Carolyn Romanov died, finally rose to her feet. 'I was wondering, Galina,' she called out, her distinctively high-pitched voice cutting a swathe through all the others, 'what Max Romanov feels about your imminent rise to stardom? And why he isn't here today?'

Beside him Lanny Harman felt Max tense.

As Galina drew breath to answer Maribeth stepped quickly in front of her. 'Thank you once again, everyone, for coming,' she smiled, giving Peggy the chance to get Galina out quick. 'It has been a great pleasure seeing you all ...'

'Is it true, Galina,' Susan Posner shouted, her attractive, almost childishly pretty face an unnerving contrast to the vitriol that flowed so fluidly from her pen, 'that you and Romanov are lovers and have been since before his wife was murdered?'

Harman's head swivelled towards Max as a murmur of shock and excitement started to buzz about the Los Angeles ballroom. 'Just get her out of there,' Harman seethed under his breath as he turned back to the screen, though he was secretly delighted at what was happening for the added publicity it would bring.

'And is it true,' Posner went on, 'that you were at the Romanovs' mansion in upstate New York the night Carolyn Romanov died?'

Peggy and her team were all but manhandling Galina out of the room, but it was clear from the way Galina was trying to shake them off that she wanted to respond. And short of lifting her bodily from the ground there was nothing Peggy or Maribeth could do to stop her.

'Ms Posner,' Galina said, smiling sweetly, then blinking and laughing as the cameras started to flash. 'I'm sorry,' Galina said, putting a hand up to shield her eyes, 'I can't quite see you now, but I'm sure you can hear me. Max Romanov, like all my good and close friends, is extremely pleased and supportive of my contract with Primaire. He isn't here today for the same reason none of my other friends are here, they all have busy lives of their own. As for your questions about a romantic involvement between Max and myself and my whereabouts on the night his wife so tragically died – both these issues have been dealt with thoroughly and exhaustively in the past by the courts and by the few members of the press who experienced some curiosity about me and my friendship with the Romanovs at the time of the investigation and trial. Therefore, could I respectfully suggest, Ms Posner, that you make a visit to the local library, or perhaps surf your Internet, to get the information that for some unimaginable reason you appear not to have.'

Her impeccable English accent, coupled with her inherently aristocratic bearing and devastating politeness, added such weight to the putdown that, had it been delivered to anyone else, Harman might almost have felt sorry for them.

But Posner wasn't so easily beaten off. 'Where were you the night Carolyn Romanov died, Galina?' she persisted with brazen audacity.

Despite the audible murmurings of disapproval Galina's lovely face showed only a curious kind of pity. 'I'll tell you what,' she said with a note of gentle indulgence, 'I'll let you find that out for yourself. It won't be hard, but if you'd like to call Peggy here when this press call is over she'll give you some advice on how to get started.'

'Maybe you can tell me, Galina,' Posner continued, undeterred, 'as such a "good and close" friend of Max Romanov's, why he never returns my calls?'

Galina's eyebrows rose in amazement. 'He doesn't?'

she said. 'I can't imagine why,' and as everyone laughed and applauded she stalked gracefully out of the room.

Though Max wasn't laughing Harman could see the humour in his eyes and shaking his head to convey how royally impressed he was, Harman said, 'I really don't think we're going to have any problems. Not after that. She's a natural.'

'I'll tell her you said that,' Max smiled, getting to his feet.

'Is there anything we can get you before you leave?' Harman offered, keen to get to know this man better.

'Thanks,' Max said, taking a card from his inside pocket and handing it to Harman. 'If you could just have someone call my driver and tell him to meet me at the corner of 7th and Bleeker right away.'

'Sure,' Harman replied, hiding his disappointment and passing the card to a secretary who had overheard Max's instructions.

'Thank you for letting me be here, Lanny,' Max said, starting towards the door. 'I really do appreciate it.'

'Any time,' Lanny assured him.

Max nodded. Then with half-mocking, half-humorous eyes, he said, 'Tell me, this age-eliminator cream. Does it really work?'

'Why, sure it works,' Lanny cried. 'All the research proves it.'

Max seemed thoughtful for a moment, then bringing his eyes back to Harman's he smiled again. 'Sounds like you really do have a winner on your hands then,' he said, raising a single eyebrow. 'With or without Galina.'

Harman's smile wavered, then, as the full meaning of Max's words hit him the blood drained from his face. 'What are you saying, Max?' he said, as the elevator doors opened and Max stepped inside.

'Just that you can't fail,' Max responded.

Harman stood where he was gazing blankly at the elevator doors long after Max had gone, the veins in his temples throbbing, Max's words resounding. *With or without Galina. With or without Galina.* Surely to God Romanov wasn't planning to pull her now, right after they'd announced to the world that she was going to be the face for the future. No, he wouldn't. It had just been one of those throw-away remarks a person makes sometimes. But Romanov didn't strike him as the kind of guy who tossed out remarks like that without their having a live fuse attached. Galina was committed though, she'd signed the contract and if Romanov did anything to try to pull her now he'd have a law suit slapped on him faster than he could think. Except why would he pull her when she'd done so god-damned well for her first time out? She'd even handled The Poisoner like she was some kind of tea stain on the Queen's best frock.

Jesus Christ, god-damnit, Harman seethed inwardly as he turned back to the conference suite. He'd known from the moment Maribeth had reminded him exactly who Galina Casimir was that they were sticking their necks out on this one, for the girl's association with Romanov was more than a double-edged sword: it was a twenty-million-dollar gamble with nothing on the black. But it was one he'd been prepared to take, not only because the benefits, if they came, were guaranteed to outweigh the risks, but because, contrary to what The Poisoner believed, Lanny Harman knew for a fact that Galina Casimir had been nowhere near New York the night Carolyn Romanov was murdered. If there had been any ambiguity about that then Harman would have vetoed the very suggestion of Galina before it had a chance to hit his desk. As it was, he'd still had a hard time with it, for according to Maribeth, Galina wasn't without her problems. Still, show him someone who wasn't these days, and it wasn't like she was crazy or anything, just a bit unpredictable. However, Romanov had personally underwritten the contract, was doing what it took to keep her on the straight and narrow, and when Harman put that together with her beauty, her charm and the allusions to her romance with Romanov, whose mystique was a hundred times more powerful than any marketing package Harman had ever heard of, he pretty much reckoned Primaire stock was headed straight through the ozone. Except maybe he'd got it wrong. Maybe with Romanov the risks were just too great.

With or without Galina.

Taking a handkerchief from his pocket Harman wiped it round his neck and dabbed the sweat from his brow. Then, suddenly realizing what he was doing and fancying he could hear Romanov laughing, he flung the handkerchief in the bin and forced himself to take a dozen deep, centralizing breaths, before quietly letting himself back into the conference room. If Max Romanov was going to start pulling the strings around here then he, Lanny Harman, had better get himself prepared.

'Hello, darling,' Galina said into the phone.

'Hi, honey,' Max smiled, pushing the button to close the screen between himself and his chauffeur while scrolling quickly through the day's performing stocks on his computer.

'So, how did I do?' she asked.

'You know how you did.'

'I want to hear it from you.'

'I was proud of you, Galina.'

He could hear the pleasure in her voice as she said, 'I was scared half to death. Did it show?'

'Not a bit. I was particularly impressed with the way you handled Posner. The guys in New York are celebrating.'

'They're drinking champagne here too.'

'You going to join them?'

'Maybe.' She paused. 'I wish you were here.'

'I will be, soon.'

'I'm afraid, Max.'

'I know.'

'I don't want to do this any more. I want out, Max. Please. Can we get me out of it now?'

'No, Galina. Too many people have got too much on the line for you to pull out now.'

'That means you've bought shares in Primaire,' she said sulkily.

'Sure I did. I've got faith in you.'

Galina looked round as the door to the make-up suite's second room opened and Ula put her head in. Waving her in, Galina said, 'I deserve a reward for this, Max.'

'You just said you're weren't going through with it.'

'I said I didn't want to, not that I wasn't going to.'

Putting a hand over the receiver, Galina whispered to Ula, 'He'll ask to speak to you in a minute, but you won't tell him, will you? Please, promise me, you won't tell him what I did.'

'I swear,' Ula said.

'Max, are you still there, darling?'

'I'm here,' he answered distractedly.

'Thank you for the flowers. I forgot to say thank you for the flowers. Ula brought them this morning. I'll sleep on them tonight and hold them and think of you. Their thorns will remind me of the way you make me feel.'

'Put Ula on, honey.'

Holding the phone out to Ula, Galina turned to look at herself in the mirror, affecting a concentrated oblivion to what they were saying.

'Max, hi,' Ula said. 'I take it you were watching.'

'I was. What did she do after that you just promised not to tell?'

'Nothing,' Ula answered truthfully.

Max laughed, realizing that Galina had deliberately baited him. Then after tapping a few commands into his computer he said, 'She handled herself well. Better than I expected.'

'Peggy's very proud of her,' Ula responded, knowing it would make Max laugh, which it did.

'Did you find your inner-Galina yet?' he said.

'Still looking. The Remmicks are hosting a dinner to celebrate tonight.'

'Who's going to be there?'

'Maurice and Deon, Ellis, Mrs Clay, Marina and Aleks and me.'

'You and Ellis got yourselves sorted yet?' Max said.

'Mind your own business.'

'You are my business, both of you and it's time one of you backed down and said sorry.'

'Tell him that. What are you doing this evening?'

'Catching up. Has Galina said anything to you about wanting to back out?'

Ula's eyes flew to Galina. 'No. Why? Did she to you?'

'Yes.'

'Christ! Serious?'

'I don't think so.'

'What do you want her to do?'

'I want her to see it through, Ula.'

'Yes, yes, of course,' Ula said hurriedly. 'I just didn't know whether you ...' Realizing she couldn't go any further while Galina was sitting there she said, 'She really is sad you're not here.'

Meeting Ula's eyes in the mirror Galina smiled. 'Tell him I love him,' she said.

'She says to tell you ...'

'I heard. Tell her I love her too. Do you need to speak to me in private?'

'Yes.'

'OK. I'll be at the apartment in about ten minutes. I'll be there for the rest of the evening. Call me when you can.'

'Do you want to go back to Galina?'

'No. Tell her what I said and to be sure she calls me before she goes to sleep.'

'Will do.' Putting the phone on the glass-topped dresser in front of Galina, Ula stood behind her and began to massage her shoulders. The dress and diamonds had been taken off her a few minutes ago, but the make-up was still intact. 'How are you feeling?' she said, watching Galina's face in the mirror.

Galina shrugged. 'Kind of buzzy, I suppose. And a bit like it all happened to someone else. Peggy's a scream, isn't she? I think she's forgiven me for what I said earlier.'

'Of course she has. She knows you didn't mean it.'

Galina bowed her head and moaned softly as Ula increased the pressure of her fingers.

'Max said to tell you he loves you,' Ula said.

'Did he?' Galina smiled dreamily. 'Could you go and ask Mimi to come and take my make-up off?'

'Sure.' Kissing her gently on the top of the head, Ula walked over to the door. 'Did you come in your own car this morning or did they send one for you?' she asked, turning back.

'I came in my own.'

'OK. So you've got transport out to Maurice's. I'll go on ahead and meet you there. Unless you want me to wait. The freeway'll be pretty jammed up by now ...'

'No, you go on, there's no need to wait.'

After the door had closed behind Ula, Galina tiptoed over to it, listened for a moment, then pulled it open to check that no one was there. The small hallway between the two bedrooms of the suite was empty, the sound of voices in the other room was muffled enough for her to know instantly if the door opened.

Moving quickly back to the phone, Galina picked it up and dialled. Someone answered on the fourth ring.

'Hi, it's me, Galina,' she said.

'This is a surprise.'

'Can you fix it for tonight?' she said.

'Sure. But I thought you promised Max.'

'I did, but he's in New York. He won't know. It can be quick.'

'OK. But you're going to be famous now, are you sure you still want to do this?'

'I'm sure,' she whispered, swinging round as the door to the other room opened. 'Yeah, it's really good to talk to you too,' she said, smiling up at Mimi. 'See you then,' and she rang off.

The following morning Max was in his office on East 54th by six thirty. Apart from security there was no one else around, so he was able to spend an uninterrupted hour going through the papers and sipping the bitter coffee that Hans, the chief security guard, had brewed up for him. Galina had made a couple of front pages, though the *New York Times* and *New Yorker* had positioned her on inside pages with no more than the customary captions announcing her contract with Primaire. It was too early yet to know how the Los Angeles press had handled the story, but he was gratified to see that here on the East Coast there had been no mention of him at all.

Turning to the financial pages, he made a quick study of the world's fluctuating economies and the share prices that interested him, then picking up the phone he spoke first to London, then to Bonn, while checking through the data on the computer screen in front of him and preparing an E-mail for Ed Sherwin, Romanov's president. At seven o'clock he left the office and jogged over to the gym on 58th. After a strenuous hour's work-out he returned to the office to find fresh coffee and croissants on his desk, put there by Lauren, his secretary. The day was off to its customary start, Theo Straussen was due in half an hour so he had time now to go over the latest reports from South Africa.

On the scale of things he had to deal with, Rhiannon Edwardes's movements, motives and morals were trivial issues, but flicking through the updated photographs and faxed information, Max found himself surprisingly intrigued by the minutiae of someone else's life – someone who, for the moment at least, was so far removed from his own. There was every chance she would stay that way, for the very nature of what she did precluded her from ever being welcomed in his house. However, Galina was currently entertaining the idea of re-establishing contact with her old friend, so, before vetoing the suggestion out of hand, Max had decided to have the woman checked out. His guess was he'd draw a blind on it anyway, as he loathed journalists on principle and a journalist who was carrying the kind of grudge against Galina that this one might be would be a dangerous guest to have around.

Picking up his coffee, he gazed thoughtfully down at an enlargement of Rhiannon's unusual freckled face with its small, sparkling brown eyes, extravagant mouth and all that amazing red hair. But he was no longer thinking about her, he was thinking about Galina and the fact she hadn't called last night. In fact, it must have been some party they'd had over at Maurice's because neither Ula nor the kids had called either. He glanced at his watch. It was still too early to get on the phone so with a grimace at his concern he refocused his eyes on Rhiannon Edwardes.

'Max?' Lauren's voice came over the intercom.

'Yeah?' he responded.

'They just called from downstairs to say Theo Straussen arrived. He knows he's early, but I told them to send him up anyway. Shall I have him wait?'

'No. Send him right in,' Max answered, tapping out the code to check on his E-Mail. 'No calls or faxes from LA yet this morning?' he said.

'No. It's not even six a.m. over there.'

Going back to the file in front of him, Max quickly scanned the rest of the photographs and detailed report.

No nude shots this time, he noticed, almost laughing as he felt the disappointment. The fact that she had no idea she was being watched caused him no pangs of conscience, for as far as he was concerned those who snooped on others, as she in her profession did, were fair game themselves. Still, there was no evidence so far to suggest that she was carrying any sort of a grudge against Galina for the way Galina had taken off with the bridegroom-to-be a few years ago, in fact looking at her here, on the terrace of some Cape Town hotel, flirting with her diamond dealer boyfriend, she looked about as happy and in love as happy and in love could get. But Max knew better than to take anything at face value; he wanted to hear what Theo Straussen had to say about Oliver Maguire before he came to a decision on whether or not to close the door on Rhiannon Edwardes.

A few minutes later Lauren showed in three dark-suited men, the shortest and oldest of whom was Theo Straussen.

Max rose to his feet. Straussen's sharp green eyes seemed almost to hook into him as he walked round his desk. It was the first time the two men had met, though Max knew that his grandfather had harboured a not inconsiderable respect for Straussen, whose influence and reputation was the subject of as much conjecture and ill-informed opinion as Max's own. But, as Max knew only too well, there was no smoke without fire and he had little doubt that a good number of Straussen's morals would be found smouldering in the ashes come Judgement Day.

'Come in,' Max said, shaking the old man's hand.

Straussen's piercing eyes were boldly assessing and flecked with humour. 'I knew your grandfather,' he told Max. 'A good man. A wise man.'

'Thank you,' Max said, waving Straussen to a chair. 'Can I get you something? Coffee?'

'No,' Straussen responded, sitting down and holding

a pair of leather gloves between his gnarled old hands. 'I'm a busy man so let's come right to the point. You want to know about Oliver Maguire?'

Max regarded him steadily.

Straussen chuckled. 'You're thinking, you don't get anything for nothing in this life, and it could be you're right. But what you get here today, you get for free. I just ask one thing, that whatever problem you might have with what I'm gonna tell you, whatever your personal feelings might be, you keep them to yourself. OK?'

Max nodded and looped an arm over the back of his chair.

Twenty minutes later, as the door closed behind Straussen and his henchmen, Max walked back to his desk and opening the top drawer took out the photographs of Rhiannon and her boyfriend. The first time Max had spoken to Straussen on the subject of Maguire, Straussen had told him about a contract he and Maguire had. This time Straussen had told Max the details of that contract and Max had to concede that the old man had a right to be feeling as aggrieved as he was, when Maguire was showing every sign of breaking the terms of their agreement. Straussen's method of dealing with that certainly wouldn't be Max's, but then it wasn't Max's style to sit in judgement of another man's methods. Leafing through the photographs, Max stopped when he came to a clear shot of Maguire and looked down at his face. It was beyond Max how any man could enter into the kind of deal Maguire had entered into with Straussen, even if it did look like he had everything to gain. But if Maguire thought he was going to get out of it by doing what he appeared to be doing, then the man had to be clean out of his mind.

'Max,' Lauren said over the speaker, 'it's Ula on the line. She says it's urgent.'

'Put her on,' Max barked. 'Ula?' he said, snatching up the receiver. 'What's up?'

'It's Galina,' Ula said breathlessly.

'Where is she?'

'We've been out all night looking for her. She never showed up at Maurice's. I left her at the hotel. She said she was going to drive herself over. Everything had gone so well ... I never dreamt she'd take off ... Max, I'm sorry ... Maurice and Ellis are still out there looking.'

'I take it they've tried all the regular places?' Max said tightly.

'Yeah. There's no sign of her.'

'Who was the last to see her?'

'Mimi, the make-up lady. She said Galina was on the phone to someone just before she left, but she doesn't know who.'

'She didn't hear any names?'

'Not that she can remember. Galina's taken the phone with her, so we've got no way of tracing the call either. We've tried everywhere, Max. The hospitals, the airport, the railroad stations ... It doesn't look like she went back to her apartment at any time and there's no sign of her car ...' She broke off, turning away from the receiver as she spoke to someone else in the room. Within seconds she was back on the line. 'It's OK,' she gasped. 'Maurice just came in. They found her.'

'Max.' It was Maurice. 'She's OK. A bit shook up, but she's OK.'

'Where did you find her?' Max said hoarsely.

'She turned up at her apartment just a few minutes ago. She's a bit bruised, got a couple of cuts, but nothing serious.'

'Thank God for that,' Max sighed. He was quiet for a moment, his face drawn tightly as he thought. 'You've got no idea where she went, or who she was with?' he said.

'No,' Maurice answered.

'But someone's fixing this up for her?'

'It pretty much looks that way,' Maurice agreed.

'OK,' Max said. 'I'll call her at the apartment. Check out what happened at the hotel, why no one was on her tail when she left, then fire whoever's responsible.'

'Ellis is already on it,' Maurice told him. 'Deon's over at the apartment sitting with her until you get back.'

'Then tell Deon to sit tight, because I won't be back until I said I would. Now I want to talk to you about a meeting I just had with Theo Straussen. It might not be anything we need get involved in, but on the other hand, it might.'

Chapter 9

It was one of those days. From the minute Lizzy had got out of bed, in a mood that was as filthy as the weather outside, everything had gone wrong. She'd stubbed her toe on the bathroom door, burnt her hand on the kettle, spilt coffee down a clean top and then promptly locked herself out in the rain while dumping the rubbish. Fortunately the downstairs bathroom window was fractionally ajar so she'd managed to clamber through, but not without banging her face on the bathroom taps and smashing a brand-new bottle of Clinique toner. By the time the postman arrived with a fistful of bills and not a line of solace for the barbed edges of her temper she was about ready to scream.

Now it appeared that every lunatic driver in London was surfing the Cromwell Road heading towards Knightsbridge. Cars were coming at her from all directions, overtaking, harassing, threatening, honking, swerving off at the last minute and managing to wind her up to the point where the pains in her head were starting to feel like daggers. In fact her temper was so foul that the violence she felt towards the executive asshole in a Ford Granada who cut straight in front of her at the lights, leaving her on red as he sailed blithely on ahead, was murderous.

She sat there at the junction with Queensgate, steaming with outrage, her fingers drumming the wheel, her stress level soaring towards the point where she was either going to ram her precious Beetle into someone or start foaming at the mouth. To make matters worse, her wipers were smearing greasy rain all over the windscreen. But what the hell, she might just as well go blindfold into the affray – everyone else seemed to be.

The lights changed, the way ahead was blocked and nothing moved. Lizzy's hands tightened on the wheel, her teeth started to grind and encroaching insanity brought a wild and dangerous gleam to her eyes. Realizing how close she was to losing it, she forced herself to let go of the wheel, to take a few deep, relaxing breaths and even to attempt a smile at the guy in the next car. His apparent alarm was a momentary antidote and letting go of a tired laugh she closed her eyes and tried very hard to persuade herself that none of it mattered.

But of course it did. Everything mattered, though raging against God and the rest of the world wasn't going to change anything. She was a widow, she was on her own, she had no one to make bad days better or to turn sour moods to laughter. She hated the loneliness; she despised the self-pity; she loathed the way she got so obsessive about things when she'd never been like it before. She was turning into a nasty old woman, blaming the rest of the world for taking her happiness away, then kicking her in the teeth with Andy.

Sighing, she pressed her fingers to her eyes as though to push back the tears. Actually, it was the time of the month that was making her like this.

The lights changed to green and pulling slowly forward she reached over to her bag and began rummaging around for a cigarette. She'd been in a great mood since they'd got back from South Africa – well, let's not push it, Lizzy, she told herself. She'd been in a generally OK mood since their return a fortnight ago. There'd been a lot to do with the editing of the programme, the writing of the commentary and the setting up of new projects. It was true the evenings were lonely, but she usually managed to stretch out the day by working late or getting Jolene or one of the others to go for a drink with her before they rushed off to whatever else they were doing. Rhiannon was never free these days, all her spare time was taken up with Oliver, house-hunting and planning their wedding. In fact they were going to book the register office this morning so Rhiannon would be late in, she'd told Lizzy on the phone the night before. She'd been in a rush so she hadn't noticed how down Lizzy was sounding, but she never did lately. In the old days, before Oliver, Rhiannon would have detected her mood instantly, no matter how tight for time she was, nor how hard Lizzy tried to conceal it – but in the old days Lizzy had never had to, for they'd always had time for each other and always discussed everything that was going on in their lives.

So, what did she want, she asked herself sharply, that Rhiannon gave up Oliver for her? She winced as a sharp pain stabbed at her head. Of course she didn't want that. She wanted them to get married, she wanted them to be happy and she wanted ...

'Oh, fuck *off*!' she seethed as someone hooted her for changing lanes. She was starting to boil again, she could feel it building up inside as if she was about to go nuclear. And so what if she did? Who the hell cared? No one, that's who. She didn't matter to anyone. No one gave a flying fuck about her, so maybe one of these assholes would like to do her the favour of smashing her right into the next world, the way they had Richard.

Calm down! she told herself forcefully. *Just calm down*.

But she couldn't. If Andy would return her calls, if he would write her a god-damned letter in reply to the *two* she'd sent him – just in case he hadn't got the first – then this wouldn't be happening. She'd have herself and her PMT under control and she'd be ... ? Yes? What? What would she be? Happy? Who was she trying to kid? The man lived at the bottom end of the world, in the back end of beyond, she'd only known him for two days and here she was trying to make herself believe that he was the root of all her misery.

Well he was! Damn him to hell!

Of course he wouldn't be if she were to meet someone else. Someone more suitable who at least lived in England, even in Europe. Actually the United States would do, just not the African bush. And besides, she was only fixating on him because he was the first since Richard and because he'd made her feel special by asking her to go and live with him.

And she, like the pathetic, screwed-up, desperate forty-year-old she was, had actually believed he meant it.

Tossing the presents she had for her nephews out of her bag and on to the seat, she started to dig about for a cigarette again. Finding the packet at last she opened it up, felt around inside, then glancing down saw that it was empty.

'I don't believe this!' she raged, flinging the packet on the floor. 'Why are You doing this to me, God? You could have magicked one lousy cigarette into that packet. It wouldn't have hurt You. What is it, have You got it in for me or something?'

The tears were very close again now and the pain in her head and in her stomach was increasing all the time. Her periods never used to be like this. It was only since she'd started getting older, started moving towards the change ...

'Oh God, I can't stand it,' she cried, squeezing the wheel so hard her nails started to bend. 'What about kids? I don't have any kids.' She felt suddenly panicked. Her blood was running hot. Her head was pounding. Her breath was short, her hands were clammy. This couldn't be happening. She was going to have a nervous breakdown, right outside Harvey Nichols.

The lights went to red. She jammed on her brakes and the joker behind jammed his fist on his horn. The noise cut through her head like a chain-saw. She looked in the mirror. The man was apoplectic, but so was she. This was it! She was going to kill him. She was going back there and she was going to smash her fist right in his ugly fat face.

Flinging off her seat belt, she threw open her car door and stormed through the rain towards him. As she drew closer she could see his eyes, bulging with shock. Reaching his car, she tore open the door and jammed a gun right into his cheek.

'You fucking bastard!' she seethed, the wind and rain whipping about her head. 'Don't you beep your fucking horn at me like that. Those lights were red. We stop at red lights. Do you hear me? *We stop at red lights.*'

'Yes, yes,' the man gasped, his face chalk white with terror. 'Don't shoot. Please, don't shoot. I've got a wife and three children.'

Lizzy blinked.

'Please. I beg you. Don't shoot,' he sobbed.

Lizzy looked down at her hand and seeing the gun she felt her heart stop beating. 'Oh my God,' she murmured. 'Oh Jesus Christ.' She looked at the man. 'It's just a water pistol,' she said. 'For my nephew. Look.'

She squeezed the trigger and the man almost passed out.

Then suddenly someone was grabbing her from behind, manhandling her to the floor and rolling her on the tarmac as the water pistol was wrenched from her fist.

To her amazement, when she was finally able to look up, she saw a crowd of people standing over her, their faces stark and hostile against a backdrop of dense grey cloud. Then turning her head to one side she started to sob uncontrollably, for this wasn't a nightmare, she wasn't going to wake up any minute and find Richard or

Andy lying in the bed next to her. It was all, every excruciating minute of this miserable, hateful and humiliatingly lonely day, totally and inescapably real.

'Hi,' Rhiannon said, coming in through the door of *Check It Out*'s cluttered offices just off Oxford Street and dropping a batch of second mail on Jolene's desk. 'Everything under control?'

'As always,' Jolene responded, gazing pensively at the computer screen in front of him. He was a man today. Tomorrow he would quite possibly be a woman. Whichever, it didn't matter, he/she was a first-class office manager, an absolute genius with the computer and a veritable mine of hot gossip – though how he managed to acquire it no one could quite bring themselves to ask. He/she was ravishingly good-looking, whether male or female, with the kind of legs most women would die for, a splendidly naked head when male, the most striking of blondes when female and, again if female, a wardrobe that would make even Dame Edna's look dowdy.

'So,' he grinned, finishing off what he was doing and spinning round in his chair as Rhiannon hung up her coat. 'When's the big day?' The lipstick and rouge on his smooth West Indian face had evidently just been touched up and his diamond drop ear-rings glittered winsomely in the overhead lights.

Rhiannon's smile was widening as she looked round at the others, most of whom had stopped what they were doing to hear her reply. Carrie, Martin, Neil, Rohan, Lily and Reece were the researchers, production associates and producers who, together with Jolene, Lizzy and Rhiannon made up the *Check It Out* team. There were also, of course, the camera crews, editors, dubbing mixers and occasional directors, but they were employed on a freelance basis, whereas the production team were permanent fixtures.

'Where's Lizzy?' Rhiannon asked, glancing up at the imitation Big Ben that played an old ITN theme tune on the hour, and which, along with the forecast schedules, new and old graphics, programme posters, fake clapperboards and headline reviews, adorned the freshly painted office walls.

'Wouldn't we all like to know?' Jolene answered, crooking his wrist as he crossed his legs. 'I've had calls coming in left right and centre for her this morning and she hasn't even rung in to say she's going to be late.'

'Come on, Rhiannon!' Lily prompted, putting down the phone. 'When's the wedding?'

'Yeah, come on,' Carrie said, tucking her frizzy hair behind one ear. 'Stop keeping us in suspense.'

Rhiannon was laughing. 'OK,' she said, feeling and looking as though she might just burst with joy. 'It's on the thirty-first.'

'Of this month!' Rohan cried. 'Are you serious?'

Rhiannon nodded.

'That's only three weeks,' Martin told her.

'Oh my!' Jolene wailed. 'How am I going to find anything to wear in that time?'

'Who said you were invited?' Reece reminded him.

'Of course he is. You all are,' Rhiannon laughed, peeling off her French-workman-style cap and shaking out her red hair. 'It's at eleven in the morning, so you'll all be able to get back to work after lunch.'

'She's so generous,' Reece commented, looking at the others. 'Where is it? Chelsea?'

'Yep. And no, I'm not wearing white. I might go for cream, I'm not sure. But it won't be anything frilly or fancy. We'll be having lunch at the Ritz.'

'Wow,' Lily beamed. 'I've never been to the Ritz.'

'What about a honeymoon?' Neil asked.

'You'll have to ask Oliver,' Rhiannon told him, throwing a grin over her shoulder as she sailed breezily into her office. 'Have you tried Lizzy's mobile, Jo?' she asked, dropping her bag on the floor and sinking into the sumptuous leather chair behind her desk.

'Does Sharon Stone shave the pubes?' he responded, batting his eyelids. 'It's switched off.'

Rhiannon frowned. 'Then where is she?' she said. 'I told her the meeting was at eleven and it's already quarter past. By the way, did you get those tapes over to editing last night, Reece?'

'Yeah. I dropped them off around nine. Tony reckons he'll be finished by the end of today.'

'Great. So, what else is new? Have we got the ratings in for last week yet?'

'They're right there,' Jolene answered, nodding towards the stack of mail in front of Rhiannon. 'Number nine,' he added, which for their kind of programme was an excellent position.

'Are Hugh and Jack free to do the Scotland story?' she asked, starting to sift through the paperwork while the others returned to their computers and telephones.

'Hugh yes, I'm still waiting to hear back from Jack,' Jolene replied, the bangles on his wrists jangling as he smoothed a hand over the shining dome of his head. 'Frances from Ready Edit called wanting to know if we'd mind swapping with some LWT programme that's up against transmission. I told her it was OK, but it means we've got a through-the-night session on Thursday.'

'Whose programme is it?' Rhiannon asked, switching on her computer.

'Lizzy's. It's the South African one.'

'OK. Have you told Lizzy about the change yet?'

'I will when she gets here,' Jolene responded, slipping on the discreet little headset he used for answering the phone. '*Check Out* a good morning,' he greeted the caller cheerily, making Rhiannon smile. 'Yes, she sure is. Carrie, it's for you,' he called across the office.

The usual busyness ensued for the next ten minutes or so while Rhiannon made an heroic effort, considering how euphoric she was feeling, to get herself in tune with the day and return the couple of urgent calls that were waiting for her. Then, deciding that the monthly planning meeting, which was something she tried very hard not to hold unless everyone was present, would just have to go ahead without Lizzy, she shouted out for everyone to start winding up their phone calls ready to begin.

'I've just got to make one more call,' Rohan said, as the others started wandering into Rhiannon's office and sinking into the two-seater Habitat sofas that were scattered around.

'OK,' Rhiannon answered, starting to laugh as she noticed the pile of *Bride* magazines someone had left on the corner of her desk. 'Oh God, Jo,' she suddenly said. 'I almost forgot. Oliver's secretary wants to know if you can do a turn at some function she's organizing on Saturday. I don't know the details, I'm afraid. Can you call her?'

'Bit late notice,' Jolene answered, preening nevertheless, for his Diana Ross and Tina Turner impersonations were becoming quite *de rigeur* for parties about town these days. 'Isn't it a good morning? *Check It Out*,' he gushed into the tiny button of his mouthpiece as he took another incoming call and blithely ignored the depressing drizzle trickling down the condensated windows.

'Rohan, how are you doing out there?' Rhiannon called.

'Two minutes,' he shouted back.

'Do you want me to give Lizzy's mobile another try?' Carrie offered.

Rhiannon nodded absently as she made a quick flip through one of the bridal magazines. 'Yeah. Try her home too, while you're at it,' she said, as Carrie lifted the receiver on her desk. 'I'm just popping to the loo,' she added, getting to her feet, 'then no more delays, we're going to get started.'

'Yes, madam, I've written it down,' Jolene was saying as Rhiannon went past him. 'Spicer. Sharon Spicer. And you want Lizzy Fortnum to call. Are you sure I can't say what it's about? No, OK. Of course I'll make sure she gets the message. Thank you for your call. May all your moments be magic and all your facelifts fuck-ups,' he added after disconnecting the line and smiling sweetly at Rhiannon who had stopped on her way out.

'Who was that for Lizzy?' she said, looking down at Jolene's notebook.

'A frenzied-sounding personage by the name of Sharon Spicer,' he responded fruitily.

Rhiannon pulled a face. 'Why does that name ring a bell?' she said.

Jolene shrugged, then his eyebrows went up as Rhiannon started to grin.

'I know who she is,' she said and turning away, she continued on to the loo.

Jolene watched her, while tapping the keys of his switchboard to take another call. '*Check It Out*. Jolene speaking. I'm happy to take your call. How may I help you?'

The planning meeting, which stretched through the lunch-hour and well into the afternoon, was, as usual, an hilarious though extremely productive affair. Its purpose was to air new ideas, schedule the following month's transmissions and shoot dates, reschedule where necessary and cover any other business that was relevant. Among the many subjects mooted for future programmes that day were an exposé of female flashers; an undercover assignment for Carrie and Reece who were investigating an MP frame-up syndicate; a trip to Los Angeles to check out what fads were in store for summer; and a celebration of fifty years of the transistor.

'I'd like to know if anyone has any objection to me fronting the transistor programme, if we do it,' Neil asked, blushing slightly for he was *Check It Out*'s newest recruit and hadn't yet had any experience in front of camera.

'None at all,' Rhiannon answered enthusiastically. 'In fact I think it's a great idea since we're only going to give it a fifteen-minute slot. It'll be good practice. What did we propose for the other half?' she added, hunting through her notes.

'At the moment we've got female flashers down for a fifteen minuter,' Lily answered. 'I think Lizzy should front that. She'll be brilliant.'

Rhiannon laughed. 'She'll probably get us taken off the air, but yes, I agree she should do it. If we put the two together then we'd better make the flashers the second half as it'll probably be a pretty impossible act to follow. So Neil, when you're putting the transistor programme together bear in mind that you might need an out that links us somehow into female flashers.'

'I can think of plenty,' Jolene called out from where he was sitting at his desk.

'I know I'm going to regret this,' Rhiannon muttered looking round at the others. 'In fact, no, I'm not going to ask. You two get together after the meeting. Just keep it at least half-way decent, OK? How far are you with this French gestapo programme, Rohan? The one about *Les Renseignements Generaux*?'

'Yeah, we're doing pretty well,' he answered. 'I've got a couple of days' more shooting next week in Marseilles, then we're done. So no problem about meeting the TX date.'

'Good. I'd like to see some of what you've shot so far though,' she said. 'And you've been keeping in touch with the lawyers, I take it?'

'And Special Branch,' Rohan assured her.

'They're putting him through a witness protection programme when it's all over,' Jolene quipped.

'They might need to,' Rhiannon said darkly. 'Anyway, I think that about winds us up for today.

Oliver's coming over later and you're all invited to the Groucho for a glass of champagne, if you're free.'

'Well, wouldn't you just know, it's himself right here on the line,' Jolene said, sucking in his cheeks. 'Shall I put him through, mein Führer?'

'Tell him she's changed her mind,' Reece shouted back.

'Tell him I'm free,' Lily added.

'Join the queue, sweetie,' Jolene responded archly as, laughing, Rhiannon picked up her phone.

'Hello, darling,' she said, turning her back on the rest of the office. 'Everything OK?'

'Everything's OK,' he confirmed. 'And you?'

'Perfect.'

'I've got some good news,' he said.

Rhiannon sat up straight, hardly daring to hope that he was about to tell her the very thing she most wanted to hear. 'We've got it,' she whispered. 'They accepted the offer?'

'They did,' he answered, the smile audible in his voice. 'The agent just called. We should be able to move in right after we get back from honeymoon.'

'Oh, Oliver!' she cried, stamping her feet up and down in excitement. 'I love you, I love you, I love you.'

Laughing, he said, 'I'll be asking for proof later. In the meantime, Calvin and Polly have invited us to dinner at their place tonight. Do you want to go?'

'But I've just invited everyone for a drink at the Groucho,' she said. 'I thought that's what we'd arranged.'

'We did. And there's no conflict. Calvin and Polly aren't expecting us until nine. They said to bring Lizzy along too, if she'd like to come.'

'Oh God,' Rhiannon murmured, clapping a hand to her mouth as a pang of guilt hit her heart – she'd completely forgotten about Lizzy and the fact that she hadn't shown up all day.

'Something the matter?' he said.

'I don't know,' Rhiannon answered, feeling a very belated concern start to creep over her. 'No one's seen Lizzy all day and it's not like her to ...' She broke off as with immaculate timing Lizzy strolled nonchalantly into the office and started laughingly to deal with the barrage of questions that assaulted her.

'She's just arrived,' Rhiannon said quietly, watching the noisy reception that Lizzy was receiving.

'You sound worried,' Oliver remarked. 'Is she OK?'

'I think so,' Rhiannon answered. 'She looks OK. I just wonder where she's been.'

'Well once you've found out, do what you can to get her to come along tonight,' Oliver said. 'She's been a bit of a recluse since we got back from Africa. Is she still upset about Andy, do you know?'

'I don't think so,' Rhiannon replied. 'If she were, she'd be sure to tell me and she hasn't said anything.'

'So you don't want me to get in touch and find out what's going on at his end?'

'No. It's best not to interfere.'

'OK. I'll leave it to you to call Calvin and Polly to let them know if Lizzy's coming, shall I?'

'Yeah, sure.' Then suddenly brightening again as she remembered the wonderful mews house in Holland Park, she said, 'Have you got the photographs of the house so we can show off tonight?'

'Yes,' he laughed.

Rhiannon waited as putting a hand over the receiver he spoke briefly to his secretary, then came back on the line saying, 'What about your father? Have you thought any more about inviting him to the wedding?'

Rhiannon sighed. 'I haven't come to a decision yet,' she said. 'I mean, I want to, at least I suppose I ought to, but I can't without inviting the airhead too.'

'Is she really so bad?'

'She's insufferable. And the feeling's mutual, I can

assure you,' Rhiannon said hotly. Then laughing she said, 'Oh, who cares about them. The important thing is that you're there.'

'Oh, I'll be there,' he laughed. 'In fact I wouldn't miss it for the world. But there is one little snag, I'm afraid. I have to go over to New York the week after next.'

A sudden chill descended over Rhiannon's heart. 'Will you be seeing Straussen?' she asked.

'Probably. But I don't want you to think about it, OK? I'll handle it.'

'How long will you be gone?'

'I'm not sure yet. But I'll be back in plenty of time for the wedding.'

'You'd better be,' she said. 'Anyway, I have to go. I want to find out what Lizzy's been up to.'

'OK. I'll come and pick you up around six. Oh, by the way, did you see that piece in today's *Express* about your old friend Galina Casimir landing herself some multi-million-dollar cosmetic deal?'

'Yes, as a matter of fact I did,' Rhiannon replied, surprised that she'd forgotten about it until now. 'Quite a coup, eh?'

'A coup indeed. Makes you wonder how much Max Romanov had to do with it.'

'Max Romanov? Why would he have anything ...? Oh yes, of course, there was something about him and Galina in the papers at the time of the trial, wasn't there? Is she still seeing him then?'

'God knows,' Oliver laughed. 'I just seem to recall reading something about them somewhere along the line. Anyway, time to go. See you at six.'

'Lizzy!' Rhiannon called, replacing the receiver and getting up from her desk. 'Lizzy, are you all right? Where have you been all day?'

'Where have I been?' Lizzy cried theatrically. 'Where haven't I been, more like. But first things first. Did you book the wedding?'

'Yes,' Rhiannon laughed. 'We booked the wedding. It's on the thirty-first of this month, so make sure you're free. Now, where have you been?'

'Charing Cross Hospital, Chelsea Police Station, you name it, I've been there.'

Rhiannon's face dropped. 'Why? What happened? Are you all right?'

'I'm fine,' Lizzy chuckled. 'There was just this incident outside Harvey Nichols this morning ... Oh hell, it's a long and boring story, just suffice it to say that it managed to keep me tied up for most of the day and every time I tried to get to a phone it either wasn't working or it had been vandalized and the battery on my mobile is down. So in the end, when they finally decided to let me go, I thought the best thing to do was just come straight here. *Et, voilà,* here I am.'

Rhiannon was staring at her suspiciously. 'What kind of an incident?' she said.

'Just a traffic incident. Someone got knocked to the ground and they had to be carted off to hospital and then the police got involved – oh, I don't know. It was all pretty chaotic, you know how these things are.'

'But you weren't hurt?'

'No. Look at me, I'm absolutely fine,' Lizzy grinned, holding out her arms and doing a quick spin. 'Just bored stiff with all that red tape and dying for a glass of the sparkly stuff. I take it we are all off somewhere to celebrate.'

'We are,' Rhiannon grinned, linking her arm through Lizzy's and walking her into her office. 'Then we're invited to Calvin and Polly's for dinner. And guess what? You know the house I told you about in Holland Park? The mews house? Well Oliver just called and we've got it.'

'No!' Lizzy gasped. 'That's fantastic news. When do I get to see it?'

'Oliver's got some photographs. There's a chance

we'll be able to move in as soon as we get back from honeymoon.'

'Oh God, I'm so happy for you,' Lizzy smiled. 'Everything's working out just the way it should. You deserve this, Rhian, you really do. Which reminds me, did you see the piece in the *Express* ... ?'

'About Galina Casimir?' Rhiannon chuckled. 'Yes, I did.'

'Bitch,' Lizzy remarked.

Rhiannon's eyebrows went up. 'It's all in the past now,' she said. 'And actually, considering the way things have turned out, I guess you could say she did me a favour.'

'A favour!' Lizzy cried. 'You were six days away from marrying that man when she took off with him. She was supposed to be your best friend, for God's sake. You had the dress, the cake, the presents, the honeymoon booked ...'

'All right, all right, don't rub it in,' Rhiannon laughed. 'You'll start giving me nightmares. And I'm not saying I wouldn't like to poke her in the eye with a sharp stick if I ever saw her again because I would. But really, when it comes right down to it, she's just not important any more.'

'So you won't be inviting her to the wedding?' Lizzy grinned.

'Very droll,' Rhiannon smiled sweetly.

'And what about your dad? Are you inviting him?'

'I don't know,' Rhiannon sighed. 'Oliver thinks I should, but to be honest, I don't think he'd be terribly interested. I hardly ever see him now and he's never really forgiven me for the fiasco of the last time, which he's still convinced was my fault. So much for parental support, eh? Anyway, if I did invite him I'd have to invite that dreadful little tart he's married to and the very thought of her in her white high heels, black tights and broad West Country accent with those screaming little brats hanging on to her shoulder straps is making me go hot and cold already. Whatever my father saw in her I'll never know, except what does any fifty-year-old fool see in a twenty-year-old pair of tits?'

'Makes you wonder what she ever saw in him, really, doesn't it?' Lizzy remarked. 'Without wishing to be rude, of course.'

'Rumour has it that because I went to a private school she assumed he had a pile of money stashed away. I imagine she's found out by now that it was the insurance from my mother's death that financed my education. Anyway, a call came in for you earlier that I just know you're going to be thrilled about.'

Rhiannon's eyes were sparkling with mischief and Lizzy's heart leapt into her throat at the prospect of the call coming from Andy. In fact it had to be from Andy, because there was no one else she'd be thrilled to hear from and Rhiannon knew it. 'Oh, who was it?' she asked, flipping open the cover of a bridal magazine in an effort to appear casual. 'You know, you'd look fantastic in something like this,' she said, turning the magazine for Rhiannon to see. It was pathetic, she knew, but suddenly she didn't want Rhiannon to answer because if the call hadn't been from Andy she didn't want to know. She wanted to stay high on the hope, if only for a few more moments, because today had been one of the worst of her life since Richard died and she didn't think she could keep this mask of normalcy in place much longer, especially not if she had to deal with the crushing disappointment of finding out that Andy still hadn't been in touch.

'Have you seen the price?' Rhiannon said, as they gazed down at the breath-taking Ungaro creation on the page.

'What is money when you're in love?' Lizzy responded airily. 'And really, you'd look absolutely gorgeous in a dress like that. You're tall enough and curvaceous enough.' This was crazy and she knew it. She was using flattery now to try and soften Rhiannon into giving her the response she wanted. 'So who was the call from?' she said abruptly.

'Oh yes.' Rhiannon grinned. 'Sharon the fruitcake Spicer.'

Lizzy's eyebrows went up as turning over another page she heard herself say, 'Oh God, not her again.' Inwardly she was falling apart. The sharp sting of tears blinded her eyes; the desperation in her heart stifled her breath. Why was this happening? Why did it matter so much when it shouldn't matter at all? Had she really reached such a point of loneliness that she could allow herself to behave like this?

'I'm afraid so,' Rhiannon said, still looking at the magazine as they flicked idly through.

Taking a breath, Lizzy forced a smile to her lips. 'I wonder what she wants this time,' she said, suddenly remembering that Sharon Spicer had once told her she was a Samaritan. Dear God, Lizzy, no, she gasped inwardly. Don't even think about it. The woman's insane.

'Why don't you call her and find out?' Rhiannon teased.

Lizzy laughed, then groaned. 'Sharon Spicer is just about the last person I need in my life right now,' she said. Then glancing at her watch she added, 'What time are we off for that drink? I need to make a couple of calls first. And did anyone make notes of the planning meeting? I'd like to see them when they're ready.'

'Speak to Jolene,' Rhiannon answered. 'And maybe you could scribble down your own ideas so I can take a look at them.'

'Or maybe', Lizzy suggested, 'we could discuss them over lunch tomorrow.'

'We could,' Rhiannon answered, turning to her diary, 'except it looks like I'm already booked. Mike

Melbourne, parliamentary whip and wicked raconteur. Should be fun. Why don't you come along?'

'No, it's OK,' Lizzy said, her smile starting to falter. 'I can use the time to write my commentary for the South Africa film. Jolene tells me I have the great pleasure of editing through the night on Thursday.' Just what she needed, she was thinking, to sit there hour after hour, frame after frame, watching Andy's face, listening to his voice and feeling almost as though he were in the room with her. 'Just popping to the loo,' she said and before Rhiannon even had a chance to look up she was gone.

Minutes later she was sitting in a lavatory cubicle, her face buried in her hands, rocking herself back and forth as she let the tears flow. She was so lucky, she was telling herself forcefully. So damned lucky that they hadn't pressed charges for what she had done that morning. Just thank God the man in the car had a wife who suffered with PMT too, so he knew what it could do to a woman. He'd understood; at least he'd tried to understand and the policewoman at Chelsea had been sympathetic too. More than sympathetic for she'd given Lizzy the phone number of a doctor who specialized in hormonal stress problems and he'd agreed to interrupt his National Health rounds at Charing Cross Hospital to see Lizzy privately for an hour just after lunch.

She had some medication now. Something to soothe her nerves and calm the pains in her head. Maybe, after she'd taken the pills for a couple of days things wouldn't seem so bleak any more. Maybe she'd have her life back in perspective and stop weeping like a child or boiling over with anger and resentment. And, please God, she'd stop hating Rhiannon for being so happy and having everything a woman could ever want in her life, at a time when she, Lizzy, was so inconsolably depressed and felt as if she had nothing at all.

'Come on,' she whispered to herself, forcing her head up and wiping her face with her fingers. 'You have to pull yourself together. Things aren't so bad really.' Tears welled in her eyes again as she thought of Richard, but pushing her mind past it she took several deep, shuddering breaths and tried again. She was going for a drink with the rest of the team, then she'd been invited to dinner at Calvin's and Polly's. So this evening she wasn't going to be alone. She'd have company. She was going to be with people who cared for her and whom she cared for too. OK, it was all about celebrating Rhiannon's and Oliver's wedding plans – and the house, she mustn't forget the house – but was that really so difficult when in truth she was happy for Rhiannon? It was just hard to show it right now, that was all. But she would. She'd have herself together in a moment and then she'd be the Lizzy everyone knew and loved. The Lizzy who made them laugh, who wasn't afraid to speak her mind, who was coping so well with being on her own. She smiled sadly at her reflection. Perhaps if she said that often enough, she would wake up one morning and find it was true.

Chapter 10

'There we go,' Naomi grinned, dropping a fax on Oliver's desk, then folding her skinny arms as she watched him pick it up. 'From Rhiannon,' she told him. 'It's a list of the shopping she wants you to get on your way home. She's got to work late, then she's got a fitting for her dress at half seven, so she won't have time. She wants spaghetti, tuna fish, canned tomatoes, a couple of onions and some french bread. She also wants to know if you remembered to call the insurance company back.'

Oliver's humorous eyes were watching his secretary, waiting for her to finish. 'You forgot the PS,' he remarked, glancing back down at the fax.

Naomi's impish grin widened. 'Thought you might like to read that yourself,' she said, 'seeing as it's a bit personal, like.'

Reading it again Oliver laughed, then putting the fax to one side he said, 'Did you confirm the flight for to-morrow?'

'Yep. You're on the ten forty arriving in New York at thirteen forty.'

'And coming back?'

'Friday night. Getting into Heathrow at quarter to seven Saturday morning. Three days before you get married, so no sweat. Oh yeah, the travel agent called to say that there's no prob with the flights you wanted for your honeymoon.'

'Well, there's a relief,' he said dryly. 'Did you get me a first-class sleeper back from New York?'

Naomi pulled a face. With her dark, shaggily cropped hair, enormous hooped ear-rings, pierced nostril and layers of snake-skin patterned lycra she was, Oliver guessed, at the very peak of whatever fashion she was toting. 'They wouldn't clear it,' she said awkwardly.

Squeezing his jaw with his fingers, Oliver glanced about the room. Then bringing his eyes back to hers he forced himself to smile. 'It's OK,' he told her. 'Not a problem. I'll get it all sorted when I'm in New York. Did you have any difficulties with the honeymoon? They accepted the credit card?'

'For that, yes,' she answered. 'But I booked it last Wednesday. The first-class sleeper I only tried yesterday.'

His face tightened and for a moment it looked as though he might bang a fist on the desk. But getting himself quickly back under control, he fixed her large brown eyes with his and said, 'Pop downstairs to Bruce's and see if there's some way he can raise the funds for a first-class sleeper.'

'He's an accountant, not a magician,' she retorted.

'Very droll. And while you're down there ask him if the funds in Jersey are still safe. I need to know that there's something Straussen doesn't have his hands on.'

Naomi was on the point of returning to her own office, which doubled as a reception, when the mention of Straussen's name prompted her to turn back. 'I forgot to tell you,' she said, her face colouring, 'we had a visitor while you were out.'

Oliver's eyes narrowed.

She nodded. 'Yeah. One of *those* visitors,' she confirmed.

'What did he say?'

'Just that he was looking for you and he'd call back later. But I knew he was one of them, I can always tell.'

'And he knew I wasn't here because he watched me walk out of the building,' Oliver remarked, staring at nothing as he spoke his thoughts aloud.

'They don't scare me,' Naomi assured him, her elfin face a picture of defiance.

Oliver's eyes moved swiftly back to hers. 'They should,' he told her briskly. 'They're dangerous people and I should have known better than to leave you here alone. Except, of course, they don't want anything from you. They just wanted to let me know they're still there, as if I didn't already know.'

Naomi looked at him for some time, her big round eyes reflecting the concern she felt for the best boss she'd ever had. 'What are you going to do, Oliver?' she said, going back to his desk. 'You can't let it go on like this. It's intimidation. I know, 'cos I asked my Jerry and he told me. They're breaking the law, Oliver, and I really think you should go to the police.'

Sighing, Oliver pressed his lips together and slowly shook his head. 'It's personal, Naomi, you know that ...'

'But it's intimidation,' she insisted hotly. 'And that's against the law.'

'Yeah,' he said distractedly.

'Are you going to see the old man when you're in New York?' she asked.

He nodded. 'He's the reason I'm going. Now, let's try getting Fullerton at De Beers on the line, shall we?' he said, taking a loupe from his drawer and unfurling the black felt cloth in front of him.

'I thought you wanted me to go and see Bruce?' she reminded him.

His head came up and he stared at her thoughtfully for a moment. 'Sure, of course,' he said. 'Yeah, make that a priority.' He smiled. 'She's got expensive tastes, has my future wife and I need to know that I've got the deposit for that house in Holland Park or she's going to be a very disappointed bride.'

'Are you kidding? How could any woman be disappointed when she's getting you as her old man?' Naomi cried in mock amazement.

'You're right, it's pretty impossible,' he grinned. 'But you don't know how demanding Rhiannon is.'

Naomi's eyes twinkled. 'I reckon I got an idea,' she said, nodding towards the fax on his desk and with a jaunty lift of her eyebrows she left the room.

A few minutes later Oliver heard the main door close, telling him that she had left to go and see Bruce, his accountant, whose office was on the floor below. Ordinarily he'd have just picked up the phone and spoken to Bruce himself, but normal channels were no longer open to him now that Straussen was having his calls monitored, and the existence of his Jersey bank account was something he just couldn't afford for Straussen to get wind of, not when Straussen was playing with the rest of his funds as if he was some kind of joke juggler who couldn't control the balls.

Setting down his loupe, he got up and walked over to the window. The narrow, busy street of Hatton Garden, the centre of London's diamond trade, was, as usual, in colourful and perpetual motion. Dealers, cutters, retailers, wholesalers, secretaries, bankers, lawyers and a hundred others affiliated to the trade were weaving precarious routes through the traffic as they crossed from the bourse to the other side of the street, or disappeared in and out of the crumbling Victorian buildings. Some stopped at shop windows to browse, still others were just passing through London's answer to New York's 47th Street.

It didn't take him long to pick out the bozo who was watching him, the guy was like a Haagen-Daz fudge tub in his cream double-breasted suit, chocolate brown shirt and yellow tie. But he hadn't been sent here to conduct an anonymous stake-out; he'd been sent, as Naomi had so rightly put it, to intimidate. And it was working.

Sighing, Oliver turned back to his desk and with his hands in his pockets stared down at Rhiannon's fax. Smiling, he read the PS again and knowing she was giving him his lead for what they were going to do tonight he felt the stirrings of desire.

He took a few more calls, the third of which was from the agent who was selling his apartment in Knightsbridge. She wanted to know if he was serious about including the furniture in the price. He told her he was and heard her sigh with excitement, for such a prized collection of antiques could fetch a fortune at auction.

As he put the phone down he was looking at Rhiannon's fax again, reading the reminder for him to call the insurance company. She had no idea that the stolen furniture had been returned to his flat, he hadn't known himself until he'd called round to see if there was any mail. Of course Straussen had been behind the ridiculous theft and replacement scheme, trying yet another way to brandish him a liar and create difficulties in his relationship with Rhiannon. Naturally, there were plenty of other ways Straussen could do that, but it seemed that the old man was trying to force Oliver to back out of the relationship of his own accord. But the hell was Oliver going to do that, for apart from loving her, Rhiannon was his only surefire route out of the goddamned nightmare of the contract he had with Straussen.

Later that evening, having prepared the supper, Oliver was stretched out on one of the deeply sumptuous sofas in Rhiannon's basement flat reading that morning's edition of the *Wall Street Journal*. Being June, the night was still light, but a fine drizzle was coating the patio garden where pots and baskets and small beds of vivid geraniums and petunias clustered around the goldfish pond and rockery. Next door's cat was sitting on top of the wall, keeping his usual vigil on the temptingly fat goldfish and in his hutch beside the log pile the feisty grey rabbit they were looking after while Mrs Romney, the landlady, was in Spain for a week, was munching solemnly on the carrot slices Oliver had just fed him.

After reading a fairly depressing forecast on the South African economy, he turned over the page and began checking the performance of the various stocks and shares he had in New York. He was feeling considerably more relaxed now than he had a few hours ago, mainly because Naomi had come back with the news that everything was OK with the Jersey account. Added to that was the confirmation he had been seeking that Wei Hang, the Chinese cutter he did most of his business with in New York, had managed to rearrange his schedule so that he and Oliver could meet while Oliver was there. Wei Hang, it seemed, was keen to discuss Oliver's proposals that they expand their businesses by combining. Of course, Oliver would only be in a position to do that if he succeeded in getting Straussen off his back, but despite the unease that crept in when he thought of it he was determined, for tonight at least, to remain optimistic. He wouldn't be seeing Rhiannon again until three days before the wedding and though the mere thought of standing up there and taking those vows was making him sick with nerves, the very last thing he wanted was for her even to suspect the way he was feeling.

No, it would all be OK, he told himself, starting to smile as he thought of the way Rhiannon's mounting excitement these past few weeks had begun to infect everyone around her. It was as though everything about her, her hair, her skin, her eyes, her smile, just everything, had taken on a new zest for life, an energy and a vitality that was fuelled by the kind of happiness he would almost rather die than destroy.

Dropping his hand down to the floor beside him, he scooped up the radio phone and answered it. It was Jolene, Rhiannon's office manager, wanting to give her the latest gossip. Swinging his legs to the floor, Oliver pulled a message pad across the heavy glass and beechwood coffee table and jotted down that Richard Copeland, the current head of Channel 4 and Rhiannon's avid supporter, was on the brink of announcing his early retirement. Oliver knew how disappointed Rhiannon would be to hear that, but probably nowhere near as outraged as she was going to be to hear who was being tipped to replace him. Then remembering that Lizzy had called earlier, Oliver wrote that down too before going back to his paper. Actually Lizzy had told him not to bother with a message, that she'd see Rhiannon in the morning. She'd sounded, Oliver thought, a lot brighter than she had for a while which might have been good, had he not had the distinct impression she'd been drinking.

Hearing Rhiannon's footsteps running down the steps outside, he glanced at his watch. It was nine fifteen and not having eaten since breakfast he was starving. He imagined she would be, too, except she'd hardly been eating lately thanks to pre-wedding nerves. And, unless she'd forgotten the PS on her fax, there was every chance they wouldn't be eating for a while yet this evening.

The ring on the doorbell instead of the key in the lock told him she hadn't forgotten, and already starting to feel himself harden he got up to go and answer. As he walked along the hall past the bedroom, she rang again and raising an eyebrow at her impatience he pulled open the door to find her standing there looking as flushed and as lovely as he'd ever seen her in a white, knee-length flared skirt, tight, wide tan belt, white shirt and low-heeled tan shoes.

Though her eyes were alive with mischief her voice was perfectly steady and polite as she said, 'Mr Maguire?'

'That's me,' he responded.

'I'm from the estate agents down the road. I hope I'm

not late for our appointment.'

'Not at all,' he said, standing aside for her to pass. She must have removed her bra in the car, for he could see quite clearly that she wasn't wearing one and with a sharp pang of lust he wondered if she had already removed her panties too. 'The living-room's right through there,' he told her, closing the door and following her down the hall. He wasn't too sure yet exactly how she wanted to play this, but sometimes finding out was half the fun. 'Can I get you a drink?' he offered.

'Oh yes, white wine would be splendid,' she answered, tossing a glance back over her shoulder as she walked into the living-room. 'Gosh, this is lovely,' she declared, gazing admiringly at the large french windows that looked out over the patio garden and the warming yet fresh shades of peach, green and cream that seemed almost to flow between the sofas, the curtains, the walls and the carpet. 'I really don't think we'll have any problem selling this. How much did you say you wanted for it?'

'A hundred and fifty,' he answered, going through to the kitchen to fetch the wine. When he came back he found her sitting on a sofa with her legs crossed, her skirt riding high over her long creamy thighs and her plump rosy nipples pushing hard against the flimsy fabric of her blouse.

'Oh, thank you,' she smiled as he handed her a glass of wine. 'Tell me, have you lived here long?'

'A few years,' he answered, going to sit on the opposite sofa. 'And how about you? Have you been doing this job long?'

'Oh no,' she laughed, tossing her hair over one shoulder then running her hand over the generous swell of one breast as she pushed her blouse more firmly into her belt. 'I only started a few weeks ago, but I think I'm beginning to get the hang of it now. It's a wonderful job for meeting people. Of course you do get the naughty ones from time to time, you know, the type who're always trying to touch you up and get you to take your clothes off, but I can handle it pretty well now.'

'I'm sure you can,' Oliver remarked, hardly able to contain his laughter as he realized what she was asking him to do. And marvelling at her ability to keep a straight face he said, 'You have very lovely breasts.'

'Oh, thank you,' she said, looking down at them. Then sitting forward she put her glass on the table and got to her feet. 'Now, is it correct that you want to sell everything in the flat too? All the furniture and knick-knacks and things.'

Oliver's smile drained. She had already turned away, moving towards the circular table beside the window where she kept her silver-framed photographs and quaint porcelain pill-boxes so he was unable to see her face.

'And would the contents be included in the purchase price?' she went on, as though he had answered, 'or would they be extra?'

Still he didn't speak, unable to make himself believe that she would play this sort of game with him, yet unable to accept that this was mere coincidence.

Stooping over the table to take a closer look at the photographs she said, 'I'm sure these aren't for sale, are they? I mean, you must want to keep *some* of your memories.'

Oliver was barely breathing.

'Who are these people here?' she asked, pointing to a picture of herself, Lizzy and Jolene. 'And here, and here. Oh, do come and tell me all about them. I mean, if you don't mind,' she added, turning to look at him.

Getting slowly to his feet, he kept his eyes rooted to hers, searching for any sign of artifice or rancour. He saw only laughter and the opaque suggestion of a growing desire. But the coincidence, the innuendo, were impossible to ignore. Even so, as he moved towards her he saw the faint flicker of curiosity in her eyes, as though she was sensing his doubt. He wished to God he knew what was going on here. Had one of Straussen's people paid her a visit? Was this some kind of obscure revenge she was building up to, or was it, as it seemed, a genuine playfulness that had unwittingly stumbled upon reality and guilt?

'Do you really think I've got lovely breasts?' she asked, smiling coyly into his eyes.

'Yes,' he whispered.

She turned to look at the photographs again. 'I can take my blouse off if you like,' she offered, bringing her eyes back to his.

'I'd like that very much,' he told her softly.

Their eyes remained locked on each other's as she unfastened her buttons one at a time, then sliding the blouse from her shoulders let it fall around her hips.

'You're beautiful,' he murmured.

'Thank you,' she responded politely, but as she made to turn away again he caught her arm and pulled her back.

'No, darling,' he said gruffly. 'No more. I want *you*, not some stranger. I love you and I want you and I'm going to make love to you, but it has to be *you*.'

'Oliver, what is it?' she laughed uncertainly. 'You look so worried and afraid ...'

'I'm neither,' he lied. 'I'm just so damned crazy about you that I can't make love to another woman even if it's you who's playing her part.'

As his mouth came down hard on hers she clung to him, pulling him as close as she could, raking her fingers over his back and searching for his tongue with her own.

He was painfully erect by now, but he felt no desperate urgency to make love. He simply wanted to hold her, to touch her and feel her trembling with the power of her feelings as he already was with his. He couldn't lose her now. Dear God, he just couldn't. But he wouldn't, he told himself firmly. It would all go according to plan. If need be he'd pay with his life rather than continue under the nightmare of their control. His heart stiffened with unease, for in truth he didn't know if his bravado would stretch that far – he just hoped to God that it didn't end up being put to the test.

Two nights later Oliver was driving a rented Buick along US9, heading into Westchester County. Somewhere off to his left was the long grey expanse of the Hudson River, ahead of him, some twenty miles on, was the sprawling riverside estate of Theo Straussen.

The ten o'clock news came on the radio, leading with the latest on the President's South American tour, before moving on to the continued unrest in Bosnia. Pushing the buttons to find a music channel, he slowed behind a Texaco tanker, then pulled out into the left-hand lane. His face was drawn with exhaustion, a two- day stubble spiked his chin and his eyes felt like sandpaper. But despite the near overwhelming tiredness his mind was alert – the adrenalin pumping through his body making him edgier and more nervous than ever.

The past two days had not gone well. The meeting with his lawyers had been a disaster and still he couldn't see any way out of the net Straussen had trapped him in. Everything he owned was now in jeopardy, his business, his investments, his apartments in London and New York, even the funds he had secreted in Jersey. If he didn't do what Straussen wanted he would lose it all.

Refusing to give up hope, he focused his attention on the road ahead and on how he was going to handle the next couple of days. He was spending them at Straussen's mansion, the great Gothic monstrosity on the banks of the Hudson where the old man conducted his business, nurtured his precious family and lavished hospitality on his cronies.

On reaching Tarrytown he turned off the highway

and began winding through the deserted lamplit streets towards the outlying countryside. The moonless sky was an impenetrable ocean of darkness, no breath of air moved through the syrupy heat. He was wondering how Rhiannon would respond when he told her that their dream house was now no more than that. He wished to God he could believe she'd stand by him, but the funds she had put up as her share of the deposit had already been claimed by Straussen.

A few minutes later he was passing the towering black iron gates to the Romanov estate, telling him that he had less than eight miles to cover before reaching his destination. As he followed the Romanovs' perimeter wall, he felt strangely affected by the air of tragedy that seemed to emanate from the place. Somewhere, in behind those walls, was the house in which Max Romanov had shot and killed his wife Carolyn. As far as Oliver knew, the place was never used now and hadn't been since the night Carolyn died – though there was no outward sign of neglect, nor anything to suggest that the estate had become a Mecca for ghoulish sightseers and murder mystery fanatics who still, more than a year down the line, couldn't leave the case alone.

Pushing his fingers hard into the sockets of his eyes, Oliver dismissed Romanov from his mind. Whether or not the man had bribed his way out of justice made no difference to him. He had his own set of problems to deal with right now, problems that needed his whole attention if he was going to get through these next couple of days and come out at the end of them with something still intact.

Ten minutes later the security guard at the gates of Straussen's estate raised the barrier for Oliver to enter. As he drove towards the house Oliver's stomach was like a lead fist. Through the trees he could see the pointed arch windows of the first-floor rooms where lights from the chandeliers cast their conical glow across the gravelled forecourt below. In front of the dour grey arches of the front porch was Straussen's Rolls-Royce, his wife's Mercedes and a Chrysler Le Baron that he knew belonged to one of the sons.

As he stepped out of his own car he could hear Straussen's grandchildren squealing with laughter as they charged about the house. Looking up, he saw Reuben, Straussen's eldest son, watching from the drawing-room window. He was a short, thickset man with a hawkish nose and narrow hooded eyes. He and Oliver stared at each other, then Rachel, Straussen's wife, came to the window and seeing Oliver waved out before turning to speak to someone behind her. Seconds later the front door opened and one of Straussen's minions took Oliver's bags from the car.

'Mr Straussen's in the den,' the minion told him and waiting for Oliver to go ahead into the house he closed the door quietly behind them.

Chapter 11

'At least two of the long-term projects should be coming in during the next couple of weeks,' Rhiannon said, slotting her key into the front door and stooping to pick up her shopping as she nudged it open. 'I'm particularly interested in this scandal at the Home Office which should be ripe for exposure some time next month. There's also this problem Reece is having with the French authorities. They're obviously trying to block his programme and we're not getting much support from the Brits, so obviously we're touching a sensitive nerve somewhere. Carrie's over in San Francisco, checking out ...'

'Rhiannon, give it a rest,' Lizzy groaned, following her into the sitting-room and dumping her shopping on one of the sofas as she collapsed, straight-legged, into the other. 'We've been over this a dozen times already. The place isn't going to fall apart while you're away, if anything it'll be a relief to get back to normal after all the excitement.' She yawned loudly, then braced herself as Rhiannon rewound the tape on the answerphone.

When the single message had replayed Rhiannon hit the button to erase it, her frustration as evident in the gesture as it was in the nervousness of her eyes and bleakness of her skin. 'Tea or wine?' she said, cutting Lizzy off before she could speak. 'Say wine and I'll make it champagne.'

'Then wine it is,' Lizzy responded.

As she turned towards the kitchen Rhiannon hesitated, suddenly remembering Oliver's concern that Lizzy might be drinking too much. But, unable to think of a way to broach the subject, she continued on to the kitchen and took a bottle of Moët from the fridge.

In fact it had been her intention to have a heart to heart with Lizzy at some point while Oliver was in the States for she knew full well that Lizzy was longing to talk, but somehow, what with the wedding and the programme, time had run away with her and the opportunity for a chat had consistently refused to present itself. And now that it had, she was just too jittery to think of anything beyond the fact that Oliver should have returned from New York that morning and hadn't. He'd left a message on her machine the day before to say he wouldn't be on the flight he'd originally booked, but he'd failed to say when he would be coming and when she'd tried his apartment in Manhatten she'd got no reply, not even the answerphone.

'When are you picking up your dress?' Lizzy called out.

Rhiannon's insides contracted. 'You mean *the* dress?' she said shakily, almost too afraid to think about it. 'On Monday. What about you? Is yours ready?'

'Maria brought it round last night,' Lizzy answered, coming to stand in the doorway. 'They were thrilled, you know, she and Evetta, that we asked them to do the dresses. They put everything else on hold to make sure they were finished in time, did they tell you?'

Rhiannon smiled. 'No, but I guessed as much. I'm just sorry that we can't give them any more publicity, but honestly, I don't think I could stand the press being around, not when it's such an intimate affair.' In fact, right now, the very idea of the press getting wind of her wedding was turning her cold with dread.

'I think they were more than happy with a whole half-hour promoting their talents,' Lizzy responded sardonically. 'They're nearly as famous as the celebrities they're dressing these days. Thanks,' she added as Rhiannon passed her a glass of champagne. 'What news on your dad, by the way? Is he coming?'

'Oh God,' Rhiannon muttered, putting a hand to her head as the very thought of it lodged like a bullet in her brain. 'Yes, he is. And the bimbette.' Her face was suddenly very pale as fear twisted her heart. 'Oh Christ, Lizzy, you don't think it's going to happen again, do you?' she cried. 'He's not going to let me down just days before the wedding?'

'Don't be daft,' Lizzy laughed, squeezing her arm. 'He's just got held up, that's all. He'll be back tomorrow and then you can find yourself something else to get in a state about.'

Rhiannon's smile was weak. 'It's not like him not to call,' she said, staring down into her glass.

Lizzy looked at her, wondering which was the best tack to take. 'Was he planning on seeing Straussen in New York?' she asked, deciding to go straight for it.

Rhiannon's heart turned cold. 'Yes,' she answered, bringing her eyes back to Lizzy's. 'But don't ask me what's going on there, because I still don't really know. Whenever I bring the subject up he just tells me to stop worrying, that everything's being taken care of and that he blew it all out of proportion when we talked in South Africa, because he was angry.' Inhaling deeply, she threw back her head and took a large mouthful of champagne. Then looking at Lizzy again, she said, 'I'm sorry. I know you need to talk and I ...'

'No, *you* need to talk,' Lizzy interrupted, feeling much better than she had in weeks and realizing what a miracle cure being needed by someone you loved was for loneliness. 'Did you ever do a background check on the guy? Straussen, I mean.'

Rhiannon shook her head. 'No. It seemed, well, it

seemed disloyal somehow, and ...' She looked down at her glass.

'And you were afraid of what you might discover?' Lizzy finished bluntly.

Dully Rhiannon nodded. 'Pathetic, isn't it?' she sighed.

'Yes,' Lizzy agreed. 'And human. But you do realize, don't you, that what it means is that you don't quite trust Oliver?'

Rhiannon's eyes flashed. 'That's not what it means at all,' she snapped. 'What it means is that I didn't think it would be a particularly admirable thing to do to go behind his back. This Straussen guy is obviously not to be taken lightly and the last thing Oliver needs is me snooping around and maybe making things worse than they already are.'

'OK, OK,' Lizzy said, 'keep your hair on. Can we go and sit down? My feet are killing me after all that shopping.'

Picking up the bottle of champagne, Rhiannon followed her into the sitting-room and, clearing a space on the coffee table to prop up their feet, they flopped down at either end of one of the sofas.

Looking down at the diamond on her left hand, Rhiannon felt herself assailed by nerves again. 'By the way, did I tell you', she said, changing the subject, 'that Morgan and Sally Simpson are planning to come over in July?'

Lizzy shook her head. 'For any particular reason?' she asked.

'If there is they're not saying,' Rhiannon answered. 'Anyway, I'll worry about that when the time comes. Did Jolene tell you about Richard Copeland retiring?'

Lizzy's eyebrows arched. 'We had quite a long discussion about it on Thursday afternoon,' she reminded her.

Rhiannon tutted irritably. 'Of course,' she said. 'Sorry,

my mind's all over the place right now. Maybe we should talk about you. It'll give me something to focus on that matters, rather than driving myself insane over things that probably don't.'

Lizzy shrugged. 'What about me?' she said. 'I'm lonely. What more is there to say than that? I'll survive.'

Rhiannon's eyes sought hers and realizing what a lousy friend she'd been these past couple of months she said, 'You still miss Richard, don't you?'

Lizzy nodded, then forced herself to smile. 'Yes, but it's only to be expected,' she said brightly. 'I just wish I could get the bitterness under better control. I get so angry at times that I almost feel like killing someone. I mean, I *do* feel like killing someone.'

Rhiannon's eyes were imbued with feeling as they searched Lizzy's face. 'Have you thought about maybe getting some kind of counselling?' she suggested.

'Oh yes, I've thought about it, but what I need more than a therapist is a man in my life, someone to share things with, the way I used to with Richard. OK, maybe not the way I used to with him, each relationship is different and I shouldn't be looking to replace what I had, but I'm only human and, well ...' Her voice trailed off as she looked dejectedly down at her glass.

Rhiannon smiled. 'I imagine, if you'd heard from Andy, you'd have told me,' she said.

Lizzy sighed and let her head fall back against the sofa. 'You're right, I'd have told you,' she said. 'I just wish ...' She paused, then after taking a sip of her drink she said, 'I just wish I knew why he's not returning my calls. Better still, I wish he'd never asked me to live with him, 'cos some idiot brain cell in my head went and took it seriously.'

Rhiannon's head tilted curiously to one side. 'Are you saying you've changed your mind, that you *do* want to go and live with him?' she asked.

'Do I hell!' Lizzy retorted. 'I just wish he hadn't asked,

that's all. It was a mean thing to do, making me feel like I mattered, then forgetting about me the minute the plane took off. Still, I suppose it's shown me just how desperate I am that I'd go on mooning about a man this long after I slept with him. And I am desperate, I admit it. I hate being on my own. It's like I'm only half alive. I've got no one to talk to, no one to do things with ... Sometimes I go from Friday night right until Monday morning without speaking to a single soul and then, when I hear the sound of my own voice it makes me jump. I hate it. It's not a life, it's an existence and please don't tell me that I have to get out more and make more of an effort to meet people, because I've already tried that and it depresses me more than ever. It's not natural, it's forced. I don't want to be there and no one really wants me there because no one really wants to be bothered with single people, especially not single people of my age. I'm a misfit and I'm made to feel like one. I don't have a husband, I don't have any children, all my friends have deserted me and I'm so awash in self-pity you'd better open another bottle of champagne so I can drown myself completely. So,' she grinned, after draining her glass, 'are you sure you still want to talk about me?'

Though she laughed Rhiannon was watching her closely. 'I had no idea it was so bad,' she said.

Lizzy shrugged. 'Why should you? I didn't want to burden you, not at a time like this, and besides, what could you do? What can any of us do? Richard's gone, he isn't coming back and Andy ... Well, God only knows what Andy's doing and who the hell cares?'

'You. Obviously.'

'No. I'm just using him as an excuse to feel sorry for myself. Or, to put it another way, I'm flogging a dead horse because I don't have another one to flog.'

Rhiannon smiled. 'But if it weren't for him you wouldn't be feeling this way.'

'Wrong. If it weren't for Richard I wouldn't be feeling this way.'

Rhiannon was shaking her head. 'I'm not so sure,' she said. 'You were getting over Richard. You were pulling through. And this with Andy has really set you back. If he didn't matter, Liz, he wouldn't have had such an effect.'

'Not true. He's just the first man I slept with after Richard and I expect, given a few more weeks, I'll even have forgotten his name. Now, get the phone will you, it might be Oliver.'

Rhiannon was already reaching for it, a horrible sickening sensation returning to her stomach as inwardly she pleaded with God for it to be him. But it was Evetta, who was designing her wedding dress, letting her know that she was going to put a half-veil on the hat as well as a cloud of net around the brim, but if Rhiannon didn't like it when she came on Monday it could be changed in a matter of minutes.

After replacing the receiver, Rhiannon stood staring out at the garden. The churn of panic inside her was starting to break through her resolve as the dreadful nightmare of the last time she'd come so close to getting married assaulted her in wave after relentless wave of remembered pain and humiliation. The presents that had to go back. The calls to cancel the church, the cars, the cake and the flowers. The dress that would never be worn. The rings that would never leave their boxes. The sympathy, the shock, the sniggers, the stares and the unbearable desolation. She had never felt more alone in her life than she had during that time. Her best friend had run off with the bridegroom and her father had blamed her. Surely to God Oliver wouldn't put her through that again?

'No, of course he won't,' Lizzy laughed. 'The man is crazy about you, anyone can see that, and the wedding's going to go ahead despite all the rubbish you're telling yourself right now.'

Though it gave her a momentary lift to hear it, Rhiannon sighed as she wandered back to the sofa and sat down. 'So where is he?' she groaned. 'Why doesn't he call? He must know that I'm half frantic by now. I mean, it's only three days until we get married, for Christ's sake, and he goes and does a disappearing act on me.' Her eyes came up to Lizzy's. 'Do you think I should go over to New York to look for him?'

'No, I don't,' Lizzy laughed. 'You'll just end up passing each other mid-ocean. He'll call, Rhiannon. Better still, he'll probably walk in that door any minute and surprise you.'

'If he does I'll knock his damned block off,' Rhiannon said churlishly. 'Oh, for Christ's sake, let's change the subject. I can't stand this. I'm just going to drive myself insane. Did you ever ring that woman Sharon Spicer back?'

Lizzy's head jerked up in surprise. 'Whatever made you think of her?' she said. Then without waiting for an answer, 'No, I did not call her back and, fingers crossed, garlic round the door and crucifixes wielded, she seems to have given up calling me. What are you doing now?'

'Trying his number in New York again,' Rhiannon answered, jabbing at the buttons. After twenty or more rings she slammed down the receiver. 'Well, that's that then,' she said briskly. 'He could have come up with something a bit more original than walking out on me at the eleventh hour, since that's already been done, but ...'

'Oh shut up,' Lizzy told her, pouring more champagne into her glass. 'Why don't you do something useful like unpacking the shopping?'

'What's the point?' Rhiannon snapped. 'A girl who isn't going on honeymoon doesn't need a trousseau, does she?'

'But a girl who *is* going on honeymoon does,' Lizzy retorted. 'So, let's have a look at what you bought?

What's the temperature like in Marrakesh at this time of year? How did you find out, by the way?'

'The tickets were delivered here the other morning.'

Lizzy nodded, then slanting a cautious look in Rhiannon's direction she said, 'Why Marrakesh? It's horrible. You'll hate it.'

'How can I if I'm not going?' Rhiannon responded irritably.

'Was it your choice, or Oliver's?' Lizzy asked.

'I mentioned once that it was somewhere I'd like to go,' Rhiannon answered with exaggerated patience. 'And since we can only take five days it probably seemed a good idea.'

'You're staying at La Mamounia, I take it.'

'Yes, we are. At least, we're supposed to be. Let's go out. Let's go over to PJ's. There's bound to be someone there we know and I feel like getting seriously drunk and disorderly in a public place.'

'What if Oliver calls and wants you to go and pick him up from the airport?'

Temper sparked in Rhiannon's eyes. 'You're not seriously suggesting I sit around here waiting for him, are you?' she replied bitingly.

'He might be in some kind of trouble,' Lizzy said tentatively and immediately winced as Rhiannon clasped her hands to her head and started to rant.

'Don't say that!' she cried. 'I'm going out of my mind here. He *is* in trouble and we both know it. But what kind of trouble? Has someone hurt him? Shall I call the police? They'll just think what everyone else will think, that he's got cold feet and gone into hiding rather than face me. And maybe that's what he has done. But what if ... Oh Christ, what am I talking about? What's all this fucking jibberish that's coming out of my mouth? I'm losing it, Lizzy. I'm falling apart ...'

'No, you're not,' Lizzy smiled, putting her arms around her. 'You're behaving the same way anyone would if they were in your position. But he'll be back in time, Rhiannon. You just wait and see.'

But by Sunday evening there was still no word and Rhiannon's dread that he had walked out on her was only surpassed by the fear that something terrible had happened to him. Lizzy had gone home to pick up some clothes and was back now to lend moral support and try to bring some common sense to the madness. But as the hours ticked by even she was running out of excuses and the comfort she offered was starting to sound hollow even to her ears.

Looking up from the commentary she was writing as the sitting-room door burst open, she laid down her pen and watched Rhiannon as, swathed in thick white towels, she started to pace the room. 'When do you think I should call the register office?' she demanded. 'I mean, I have to let them know that the wedding's off. Do you think I should call first thing in the morning?' Each word tightened the ache in her heart as disbelief and panic flashed wildly in her eyes.

'You don't have to call that soon,' Lizzy responded. 'He still might ...'

'What about my engagement ring?' Rhiannon cut in. 'It's worth a fortune. Do you think I should give it back? What shall I do with it? How the hell can I give it back when I don't even know where he is? OK, OK,' she said, holding up her hands as a by now familiar look stole into Lizzy's eyes. 'I'm calming down. I'm not over-reacting any more. My name is Rhiannon Edwardes. I'm twenty-nine years old. I live in Kensington. And I've been stood up twice at the altar.'

Despite herself Lizzy laughed and to her relief Rhiannon managed a smile too. But it was only fleeting as she curled into a corner of the sofa and stared concentratedly at nothing while winding her finger round a loose thread in the towel. 'I can't go and pick my dress up in the morning,' she whispered finally. 'I just can't.'

Lizzy pressed her lips together and looked away. Then returning her eyes to Rhiannon she said, 'Look, if it comes to it I'll handle everything for you. You won't have to go anywhere or call anyone. But it's not going to come to that.'

Rhiannon's face was so pale that even her freckles seemed to have faded under the strain. Her eyes were dark and heavy and, swamped in towels as she was, she appeared almost to have shrunk. 'What am I going to tell my father?' she said brokenly.

Lizzy looked at her, watching helplessly as a single tear rolled down her cheek.

'I never thought he'd do this to me,' Rhiannon said, her voice thick with pain. 'I thought I was insecure about the way he felt about me, but I realize now that I wasn't. I truly believed he loved me.' She tilted her head down to look at her lap. 'I really did believe it.'

'He does love you,' Lizzy said softly.

Rhiannon shook her head, then covering her face with her hands she finally gave in to the terrible desperation inside her and wept as though her heart would break.

Randy Theakston walked across the sitting-room of her elegant two-storey brownstone on New York's Upper West side and handed Theo Straussen a Scotch. His heavies had remained in the car and without their bulk dwarfing him Straussen appeared slightly larger than normal. He was seated on a brown leather Chesterfield and as his deep-set eyes wandered the curious collection of art on the walls Randy carried her vodka across to a wing-backed armchair.

'Maguire's on his way back to London,' Straussen informed her, in his smooth, gravelly voice.

Randy nodded. She allowed a few seconds to pass then said, 'Are you planning on turning up at his wedding?'

Straussen chuckled. 'Maguire's having nightmares about it,' he answered.

'He told you that?' Randy asked, surprised.

'He didn't have to. The man would have to be some kind of moron if he wasn't.'

Randy's lips pursed as her head went down. 'I've got to tell you, Mr Straussen', she said eventually, 'that I'm not entirely comfortable with this.'

Straussen was unperturbed. 'You've been paid, Randy,' he reminded her. 'You did a good job, now as far as you're concerned it's over. So don't you go losing any sleep over what might or might not happen from here.'

Randy's eyes moved away and settled on a spiky green fern in the hearth. Outside, the sound of running footsteps echoed down the street, while somewhere in the distance the wail of a car alarm provided the neighbourhood with a persistent wake-up call. 'It's Rhiannon Edwardes that concerns me,' she said finally.

Straussen smiled. 'I thought it might be,' he commented.

Randy's eyes narrowed. Then with an impatient sigh she put her glass down and leaned forward in her chair. 'Let me speak to her,' she said.

Straussen's expression was pained. 'That's not a good idea, Randy,' he told her.

'But innocent people are going to end up getting hurt,' Randy protested.

'That's the way of the world,' Straussen sighed. 'And try looking at it this way: if Maguire had done to you what he's doing to me, wouldn't you want to fuck him over?'

'Of course I would, but it's *how* you're doing it that's bothering me.'

Straussen shook his head and sighed. 'All I'm doing, Randy,' he said, 'is sticking to the agreement.'

Andy was sprawled across an old leather sofa in Perlatonga's covered lounge, his hands stuffed deep into the pockets of his khaki shorts, watching the rain bounce a foot in the air as it slammed into the ground. The sky overhead was a bulbous mass of angry, purple cloud and the incessant noise of the storm was like a full-throttle hose hitting a wall. Across the way, in the clubroom-cum-shop a few of the guests were watching videos of bush life, while the hardier souls were out there with their rangers literally soaking it all up.

Doug had just flown back that morning after five days in Jo'burg, bringing the accountant and a new ranger with him, while Willem the camp administrator had, a few minutes ago, ambled off with a flea in his ear for bothering Andy with things that Andy didn't want to be bothered about. He had more pressing matters on his mind right now, like Sheila, the Perlatonga lioness. She was sick and Doug wanted to call in a couple of vets from the Kruger Park. Andy did too, but it wasn't professional to get involved with the animals like this. They'd already interfered once, if they did it again they could be putting the lioness's life at risk in the future by not leaving her to fend for herself now. Trouble was, they were both pretty attached to the old girl and neither of them wanted to see her suffer.

'Here, thought you looked in need.'

Andy looked up as Nanette, one of the camp's hostesses, put a steaming mug of coffee and a plate of ginger biscuits on the table next to him.

'Willem said you almost bit his head off,' she remarked, raising her voice to make herself heard over the violent hiss of the storm, 'so I'm going to scoot now before you try the same with me. But I thought you should know we just had a radio call from Chris. He spotted Sheila a few minutes ago and she was up and walking.'

Andy's eyes widened. 'Cubs with her?' he asked.

Nanette nodded, then turned as the kitchen door slammed behind Doug who was coming towards them with his own coffee and a handful of mail.

'Hear the news about Sheila?' he said, sinking into the

armchair adjacent to Andy as Nanette sprinted off across the camp through the rain.

'Yeah,' Andy nodded, watching her go. Then picking up his coffee he said, 'We'll go out and take a look for ourselves this afternoon. How was Jo'burg? Leandra still at you to go and shack up in the big city?'

'A girl never gives up till she's got what she wants,' Doug responded, sliding a postcard out of the mail and holding it out to his brother.

Andy's face was expressionless as he looked at it, then glancing at Doug he took it and turned it over to see who it was from, even though he already knew. 'So what's her news?' he said, flicking it on to the cushion beside him. 'You must have read it.'

Doug lifted his stalker boots on to the table and took a mouthful of coffee. 'She's wondering why you haven't written back to her, or returned her calls,' he answered. 'No big deal, she says, she's just wondering, that's all.'

Andy looked at him, obviously expecting him to say more, but Doug merely popped a biscuit in his mouth.

When he looked up again Andy was still watching him and starting to grin, Doug said, 'Are you going to answer this time?'

'What's there to say?'

Doug shrugged. 'Maybe you could tell her about Catherina.'

'Why would I want to do that?'

'Just a thought. Where is the gorgeous creature, by the way? I haven't seen her since I got back.'

'Last time I saw her she was moving her things into our place,' Andy responded.

Doug's eyebrows arched, but as he started to respond he saw Catherina herself threading a path through the dining area towards them and stopped to watch her, as entranced now as he had been the first time he'd seen her. With her thick, glossy black hair, long brown legs and dark Italian eyes she exuded more sex appeal than a Hollywood siren and more style than a catwalk preen-queen.

Able to tell by the look on his brother's face that she was on her way, Andy turned to watch her too, his face softening as she looked at him and started to smile.

'All finished?' he said, surreptitiously sliding Lizzy's postcard in between the cushions.

'All finished,' she confirmed, going straight to Doug to welcome him back. 'We missed you,' she told him, stooping to kiss him on either cheek and appearing totally oblivious to the effect her very generous display of cleavage was having on him.

'I missed you too,' he responded, causing Andy to choke back a laugh at the strangled tone of his voice.

'Did anyone tell you about Sheila?' she asked, sitting down beside Andy and stretching her superb legs out alongside his.

'Yes,' he answered, allowing his eyes to roam the soft, dusky skin right up to the hem of her shorts. 'Good news, eh? We're going out to take a look after lunch. Want to come?'

'Oh, yes, I'd love to,' she beamed, tossing her hair over one shoulder. Then quite suddenly she was back on her feet. 'My goodness, I almost forget,' she cried. 'I promise Willem I help him for an hour before lunch. He is teaching me so much, you know,' and before either of them could respond she was running off across the camp, taking their slavish eyes with her.

'You know who she puts me in mind of?' Doug said. 'Oliver Maguire's woman, Rhiannon. Not the looks, the body.'

Andy nodded. 'Yeah, I know what you mean. Darker skin, but all legs and tits. I wonder how that's working out.'

'Didn't Lizzy mention anything in any of her letters?' Doug said, starting to sift through the mail.

'Don't ask me,' Andy snapped, getting to his feet, 'I don't read them,' and leaving the postcard where it was he stalked off into the rain.

Chapter 12

As Oliver spoke the words to make her his wife, Rhiannon's heart was faltering under the weight of emotion. She watched as he slid the dainty gold band on to her finger, then lifting her eyes back to his she had to bite her lips to stop herself laughing and sobbing as he gazed down at her in a way that seemed to shut out the rest of the room. His face was pale from lack of sleep and like any other bridegroom he appeared slightly nervous, but there was no mistaking the feeling in his words, nor the profound love in his eyes.

Vaguely Rhiannon wondered if he was aware of what either of them was saying; of course he would know they were exchanging marriage vows, but if his longing to hold her was as pressing as hers to hold him then the registrar's closing words would be like a fading echo around the strength of their need.

Behind them the dozen or so guests watched with dreamy and in some cases tearful smiles as the registrar invited them to sign, then Oliver pulled Rhiannon into his arms and bowing his head beneath the rim of her hat covered her lips in a long and tender embrace.

'Me next, pa-leeze,' Jolene muttered, pinching the corners of his lipsticked mouth with thumb and forefinger.

The others laughed as Lizzy nudged him and laughing too, Rhiannon and Oliver broke apart.

'Congratulations,' Lizzy smiled, hugging them.

'Thank you,' Rhiannon whispered, still dazed by the ceremony as well as the kiss and feeling Oliver's arm circle her waist she turned to look up at him.

'You are just divine!' Jolene declared, elbowing his way forward and pouting his lips invitingly towards Oliver.

Oliver's eyebrows went up, then with a quick wink at Rhiannon, he leaned forward to kiss Jolene in exactly the way he went on to embrace all the other guests – on both cheeks.

The next half-hour passed in something of a blur. Rhiannon wanted so desperately to savour every moment of the day, but it all felt so hazy that only odd snatches were penetrating her mind. She looked more radiant, more beautiful than she ever had in her life. Her ivory silk dress with its high gold-brocaded neck and dramatically cut-away shoulders clung to the contours of her body, accentuating the fullness of her bust, the roundness of her hips and the tantalizing length of her thighs, before flaring at the knee to fall in loose folds to her ankles. Her wide-brimmed hat was pleated in the same ivory silk and seemed almost to float in an abundant sea of fine white gauze. She stood on the steps of Chelsea Town Hall beside Oliver, seemingly oblivious to passers-by and the slowly crawling traffic of the King's Road, as they laughingly posed for photographs and Oliver's fingers tightened possessively around hers.

'Don't let's hang around,' he murmured in her ear.

Laughing, she raised her face to his.

'Perfect! Just perfect!' everyone cried. 'Hold it like that.'

'Don't tell me you're hungry,' she teased.

Treating her to an outrageously suggestive look, he led her down the steps and around the corner to the waiting car.

'It's right here,' she told him, as he glanced up and

down the street as though searching for it, and sliding into the back seat she waited for him to get in after her.

Knowing where they were headed, the chauffeur eased the Mercedes away from the kerb towards the dense traffic of the King's Road. Some of the guests were still grouped at the corner, looking extremely chic in the sunshine with their brightly coloured hats and expensively tailored suits. Some of the *Check It Out* team pretended to hitch a lift as the Mercedes passed, while Jolene, resplendent in electric pink, strutted into the road to halt the traffic for them to pull out.

'You look so beautiful,' Oliver whispered as they turned in the direction of Sloane Square.

Rhiannon smiled and let her eyes rest on his mouth as though asking for a kiss. But he merely gazed at her, feeling an incredible desire pass through him.

'So, Mr Maguire,' she said huskily.

He smiled, but instead of addressing her the same way he took her hand in his and turned to look out of the back window.

'Darling, are you all right?' she asked, half turning to see what on earth he could be looking at. 'You seem so on edge.'

He laughed and pressed her fingers to his lips. 'I am,' he confessed. 'I guess I'm still pinching myself that I got to be this lucky.'

She was watching him closely, but knew that the strain in his face probably had more to do with the fact that, thanks to a heavy weekend and pre-wedding nerves, he'd hardly slept all night, than it had with anything more sinister. Plus he was still upset that he had been unable to finalize things with Straussen. He hadn't had time to tell her much about that yet, but she guessed he would over the next few days.

'I think I should warn you about my father and the bimbette now,' she said, pulling a face. 'They're extremely likely to get drunk and embarrass us all, as if she hasn't enough already with that hideous white suit and British Homes Stores hat.'

Oliver grinned. 'I can't say I noticed,' he responded. 'But your father seems OK.'

'He is, when he wants to be,' she answered as they both swung round to see what all the beeping was about behind them. It was Lizzy and Jolene in Lizzy's Beetle with three others from the team squashed into the back seat. Giving them a wave and returning the hundreds of kisses being blown at them, Rhiannon looked up at Oliver to find that he had broken out in a sweat.

'Are you sure you're OK?' she said, taking a handkerchief from his pocket and dabbing his face. 'You're not coming down with something, are you?'

'I don't think so,' he answered, loosening his tie.

When they arrived at the Ritz their table was ready, set out in a private dining-room which was furnished with all the inherent elegance the hotel was famous for. Smartly uniformed waiters were there to offer champagne and canapés while the *maître d'* made sure all the guests were shown straight through. Rhiannon's father and his young wife were the last to arrive, having taken a wrong turn at Hyde Park Corner. When they walked in the others were all laughing at something Christian, the best man, had said during a quick unofficial toast while Naomi, Oliver's secretary, scowled at Oliver in an effort to will his eyes to hers.

With a quick shake of his head, as though telling her that now was not the time, Oliver turned to welcome his new father-in-law.

'Here, this is a bit of all right, innit?' Moira, Rhiannon's stepmother, declared before Oliver could speak.

Unable to stop herself Rhiannon cringed, knowing that she would never be able to think of the brash and busty twenty-four-year-old blonde with her thick West Country accent and bursting seams as any kind of relative of hers.

'Yeah, looks like we're in for a good bit of grub here,' Rhiannon's father replied in his equally broad West Country accent, while rubbing his hands gleefully together. 'Got a hole in my belly that's making it think me throat's been cut,' he added, grinning at the others in full expectation of their laughter. With his wiry grey hair, drinker's nose and tobacco-stained teeth it wasn't hard to work out that he was not the parent Rhiannon resembled.

'Champagne, Mr Edwardes?' Oliver said, bringing George Edwardes's attention to the waiter who was hovering at his elbow.

'George! Call me George, son,' George boomed, slapping Oliver on the back. 'And yeah, I'll take a drop of the fizzy stuff. What about you, Moira? Are you going to have some?'

''Course,' she giggled. 'When have you ever known me turn down champagne?'

'When have I ever known you to turn down a drink, full stop,' George guffawed, turning again to the others and winking like a holiday camp compère.

'I don't believe this,' Rhiannon muttered in Lizzy's ear. 'We haven't even sat down yet. And stop laughing, will you, it'll only encourage them.'

'I'd forgotten Oliver was meeting them for the first time,' Lizzy whispered behind her champagne glass. 'Oh God, it's such a treat. Look at him, he's completely out of his depth and you, you should see your face, it's a right picture, it is.' She concluded in such an hilarious West Country voice that Rhiannon couldn't help but laugh.

'It's terrible to be ashamed of your parents, I know,' she confessed, 'but wouldn't you be, if you were me? Oh my God, what's he doing now? No, he's not going to make a speech! Lizzy stop him. Do something! Dad! No, we're all about to ...'

'Button it up there, girl,' George interrupted. 'I just

wants to say a few words 'fore we d'sit down. Go and stand with your new wife there, boy,' he instructed Oliver. 'That's right, yeah, put your arm round her. Look good together, don't they?' he demanded of the others, who were clearly as bemused as Rhiannon had dreaded they would be.

Oliver gave her a comforting squeeze, then his eyes shot to the door as a waiter came in with the hors d'oeuvres. Rhiannon gestured for the waiter to continue, hoping that the laying down of the first course would keep her father's speech short and her embarrassment to a degree marginally below heatstroke.

'Well, I just want to say', George began, motioning for the champagne waiter to refill his glass to the brim, 'that I'm very happy you could all come here today.' He paused. 'Especially Oliver.'

As Rhiannon's eyes closed she felt Lizzy and Jolene shake with laughter beside her.

'I expect you all know what happened the last time,' he went on, 'but we don't want to dwell on that now, do we; we'll just be thankful that Oliver turned up, eh?'

The dawning discomfort in the room didn't even dent the broadness of his smile. 'So,' he continued after a mercifully silent slurp of champagne. 'Our Rhiannon might be full of airs and graces now that she's a big-time producer, but that don't carry no weight with me. She's still my daughter and always will be. Not that I'm not proud of her, mind you. And her mother would be too, if her mother was here to see her today. She was the apple of her mother's eye, she was, and it was thanks to her mother that she got that fancy Welsh name of hers and the fancy education too, because I'm just a humble milkman – proud of it, mind you – but we milkmen don't earn the kind of brass it takes to send our kids to schools like our Rhiannon went to. We paid for that out of her mother's insurance, according to her mother's wishes.' He sighed and shook his head. 'And I just thank God that her poor mother didn't live to see what happened the last time our Rhiannon tried to get married, 'cos she'd have turned in her grave with shame.'

Apparently blissfully unaware of the reaction to his remarks he pressed on unashamedly, "Course we don't see all that much of each other now. Our Rhiannon's too busy and I got meself a new family to look after these days. Two boys we got, five and three. Little buggers, the pair of 'em. Staying with their gran today. She's as good as gold with 'em. What?' He looked down at Moira who had just nudged him.

'They don't want to hear about that,' she hissed, blushing as she glanced towards the mesmerized ensemble.

'No? No, well, like I was saying, we haven't been all that close these past few years, me and our Rhiannon, but I'm still her father and I haven't forgotten that. And now you're married there's no reason for you not to come home a bit more often, my girl. No one's talking about you any more and all the neighbours are dying to meet the bloke you're finally getting married to ...'

'And I'm looking forward to meeting them too,' Oliver interrupted. 'And rest assured, we'll be visiting as often as we can.' His smile was full of charm. 'Thank you very much for your speech and for making the journey up to London today,' he went on. 'Rhiannon and I both deeply appreciate it and we both hope you're going to enjoy your lunch. Now, I guess we're all getting a bit peckish, so if everyone would like to take a seat?'

'I haven't quite finished yet, son,' George Edwardes bristled.

Oliver's expression was mild as he turned to look at him, but it was clear to everyone present, if not to George, that he wasn't going to tolerate any more snipes at Rhiannon about what had happened in the past. 'I'm sorry,' he said politely.

Disgruntled and thrown off track Edwardes drained

his glass, then stuck it out to be refilled. 'I just wanted to say', he grunted, 'that I wish you and Rhiannon every happiness in your married life and that I hope you intend to look after her a bit better than I did.'

Oliver was about to respond to this surprisingly touching admission when Edwardes cut him off.

'Like I said before, at least you managed to turn up,' he grinned, 'which has to be a good start if nothing else.'

'To Mr and Mrs Maguire,' Lizzy cried, raising her glass.

'Mr and Mrs Maguire,' everyone chorused.

'Priceless, the man's simply priceless,' Jolene muttered to Lizzy. 'Tell me, does he know anything about me?' he added, fluttering his inch-long eyelashes.

'Like what?' Lizzy replied.

Jolene bared his teeth in a wicked smile. 'Like gender,' he said.

Lizzy laughed. 'I doubt it,' she said.

'Sublime,' Jolene murmured, and with an outlandish wiggle of his hips he sauntered over to where George Edwardes had just sat down at the table and plonked himself in the next chair.

Three hours later, leaving her father deeply infatuated with the most exotic creature he had ever encountered and her stepmother sagging indecorously in her chair, Rhiannon followed Oliver to the door where they both turned back to make their final farewells.

Throughout the lunch, despite the good time everyone else seemed to be having, Oliver's tension had almost reached breaking point. That Rhiannon's father could have caused her the embarrassment he had in his speech and then to compound matters by becoming so drunk, had made him so angry that it had been all he could do to stop himself physically assaulting the man. And that Jolene had managed to work his hand along the old boy's thigh and on to his crotch wasn't something

Oliver found particularly funny even though the bastard deserved it. He doubted Rhiannon had spotted it, though he knew for a fact that everyone else around the table had and it wasn't something Oliver was in the least bit pleased about happening at his wedding. Except maybe he should be thankful for small mercies, since a whole lot more could have gone wrong than a few offended sensibilities and a duplicitous fondle.

He was in danger now of his fear controlling him rather than him controlling it. That he and Rhiannon had managed to get this far through the day without any sign of Straussen or his henchmen was, Oliver knew, a Straussen-designed miracle intended to serve just the purpose it had – to intensify terror. Never strike when it's expected could be Theo Straussen's motto. Probably was, for all Oliver knew.

Rhiannon had no knowledge of the danger they were both now facing, it certainly wasn't something Oliver was prepared to make her a wedding gift of. Besides, he could be wrong. It could be that Theo Straussen and his thugs were still in New York and had no intention of joining the party. It could also be that somewhere in the world three-carat diamonds grew on three-foot trees.

'Thank God that's over,' Rhiannon muttered as they walked out of the Ritz and into the blazing sunshine that was baking Piccadilly.

Oliver turned to look at her, his eyes dancing with humour that she should have made such a remark about their wedding day.

'He's a nightmare,' Rhiannon grumbled as their Mercedes drew up outside the hotel. 'Either that, or I'm a snob.'

'A bit of both, I reckon,' Oliver teased, holding the car door open for her to get in first. 'Back to Olympia as fast as you can,' he told the driver, glancing at his watch as he slammed the door closed. 'Providing the traffic's not too bad we should have about an hour before we leave for the airport,' he said to Rhiannon, trying to will the dread from his mind of what they might find when they returned to the flat.

'I can't imagine how we're going to fill it,' Rhiannon remarked drily. 'Incidently, I should come clean here, I know where we're going. The tickets turned up at the flat last Friday while you were in New York.'

Frowning, he said, 'What tickets?'

'The air tickets, for our honeymoon,' she laughed.

'But how can they have turned up at the flat when they're in my briefcase? I had them sent to the office over a week ago.'

Rhiannon's curiosity mingled with her laughter. 'So we're not going to Marrakesh?' she said.

His frown deepened as he shook his head incredulously. 'Well, as a matter of fact, we are. But I don't understand about these other tickets. They were in our names, I take it? I mean, we haven't been sent someone else's by mistake?'

'No, they were definitely in our names.'

'Can I use the phone?' Oliver said, leaning towards the driver.

'Sure.' The driver passed the mobile over and accelerated through an amber light at the Knightsbridge junction with Brompton Road and Sloane Street. By the time they were passing the Albert Hall, Oliver had finished his call.

'Well?' Rhiannon prompted.

He shrugged. 'It seems there was a mistake at the travel agent's,' he answered. 'For some reason our tickets – the ones I have in my briefcase – got cancelled, then when they realized what they'd done they called the office to warn me and Naomi told them to send the reissued ones to the flat.'

'You don't seem happy with that explanation,' Rhiannon said warily.

Again he shrugged. 'No, I'm happy with it,' he

replied, 'I just hope, after all the credit card business and everything else that's been going on, that we're not going to turn up at the airport and find the reissued tickets have been cancelled too.'

'To be honest,' Rhiannon said, linking her fingers through his, 'I don't really care where we spend our honeymoon as long as we spend it together.'

To her relief the smile returned to his face. 'To be honest, neither do I,' he said, squeezing her hand.

Twenty minutes later Rhiannon was reaching up to unpin her hat as Oliver followed her into the cramped and untidy bedroom of her basement flat. The unmade bed, half-packed suitcases and yards of strewn tissue paper that had protected her dress and hat were just as she'd left it, allowing them no room to make love, as they were both extremely eager to do.

'Let's go into the sitting-room,' he suggested, kissing the back of her neck as she tossed her hat on the bed.

'Mmm, OK,' she murmured leaning back against him. 'But undress me here.'

'With pleasure,' he smiled, and unfastening the hooks and eyes at the back of her collar he carefully lowered the zip.

As she stepped out of the dress he shrugged off his tailcoat and unbuttoned his waistcoat. 'Oh Christ, just look at you,' he groaned as she turned to face him in a transparent ivory body and gold high-heeled shoes.

'I love you,' she whispered, walking into his arms and unfastening his cravat as he kissed her.

'I love you too,' he said, sucking her lips between his as he tugged off his waistcoat and threw it on the bed. It was quickly followed by his starched, wing-tipped shirt and pin-striped trousers until, like her, he was completely naked. She was still in his arms, running her hands all over his body as he pressed his erection against her and pushed his tongue deep into her mouth.

Still holding each other, they walked into the sitting-room and laying her down on a sofa he began to make love to her. They were so lost in each other that neither of them noticed the giant bouquet of flowers in a cut-glass vase on the coffee table beside them, so neither of them knew that someone had entered the apartment while they were out, to leave the traditional token of congratulations on a wedding day. Not even when their passion was spent, as they lay on the floor waiting for their laboured breath to subside and the roses and carnations bowed over them, did they notice their gift.

In fact, an hour later, when Oliver carried their luggage out to the waiting Mercedes the flowers had still gone unnoticed – so too had the card that came with them.

Chapter 13

Despite its twentieth-century lustre and sophistication the magnificent Mamounia Hotel, in the heart of the exotically strange and entrancing town of Marrakesh, could easily belong to a bygone era. With their embroidered red waistcoats, voluminous white breeches and the ubiquitous fez on their heads, the attendants might have stepped straight from the harems and inner sanctums of a Suleiman palace. And the vast marble pillars, shiny mosaic floors, expert marquetry and decorous indoor fountains turned the whole place into a breathtaking alchemy of Andalusian, Moroccan and art-deco splendour.

The *Au Baldaquin* suite, where Rhiannon and Oliver had spent the past twenty-four hours rolling around the taffeta-draped four-poster bed and listening to the dreamy sounds carrying on the breeze from the string quartet playing beside the pool, was *le dernier cri* in romance. Rose and peach pastel silks fell in opulent pleats over the pale linen walls and wide muslin-draped french windows opened out on to a large ornately carved mosaic balcony. An abundance of luscious white flowers had been placed around the suite and the exquisite Carrera marble bathroom basked in the subtle glow of muted ivory light.

Squinting against the dazzling sun as she stepped out on to the balcony, Rhiannon slipped on her sun-glasses to gaze down at the glittering blue pool with its island of palms and surrounding forest of lemon-and-white-striped parasols. The air was perfumed with flowers; the sky was a perfect blue. Behind her Oliver stirred in his sleep and glancing back to see if he would wake, she twisted her hair from her neck and clipped it on the top of her head. Then smiling ruefully to herself, she wandered to the slender orange-beaded balustrades and let her eyes roam the vibrant colours and dense green foliage of the gardens and the shimmering silhouette of the Atlas mountains on the horizon.

The gastric affliction that had struck Oliver in the early hours was showing no sign of letting up and Rhiannon was undecided whether or not to call in a doctor. If he was still feverish and unable to keep anything down by the end of the day she guessed she would have to, despite the fact that he was insisting she didn't.

Removing her bikini top, she massaged a lavish amount of cream into her faintly bronzing skin and settled down on one of the loungers to read. Every now and again she glanced at the narrow gold band on her left hand and felt her heart jump. It seemed incredible, yet she now knew the power of that gold band, for it made her feel so much closer to Oliver, so much more a part of his life than she had before, which was a wonderful discovery when she hadn't been able to imagine them any closer than they already were.

In sickness and in health, she thought wryly to herself, as Oliver groaned and tossed and turned in the air-conditioned room behind her. Her heart went out to him in his misery and pain, for of all times to be stricken with the Moroccan version of Montezuma's revenge a honeymoon had to be the most unfortunate.

At four o'clock, when he still hadn't woken, she decided to go down for a swim. The string quartet was playing a mellowing medley of Twenties tunes at the far end of the pool, as she wound her way through the randomly placed sun loungers where the stupendously rich were tanning their sun-shrivelled bodies and the ever-hopefuls were glistening in oil. The haunting chant of the muezzin began warbling from the town's minarets and smiling wryly to herself she realized that it was easy, in this safely cocooned paradise, to forget that beyond the high dusky-pink walls enclosing the hotel there was a whole other world. A world teeming with culturally disparate people whose flowing gallabiyahs and carelessly wound turbans fluttered through the packed and pungent lanes of the souks in a ceaseless current of colour and noise.

Pausing as a pool attendant rolled a parasol past her, she felt suddenly inexplicably uncomfortable and began to wish that she'd brought a robe or sarong with her. As it was she wore only a bikini with a hotel towel draped over one shoulder. It was unusual for her to feel self-concious, but for some reason, as she approached the edge of the pool and dropped her towel on an empty lounger, she felt oddly disturbed by the scrutiny of her fellow bathers. It seemed furtive, almost voyeuristic, as though she and they were at opposite ends of a peep show. She glanced up and it was as though an invisible magnet suddenly tugged a hundred pairs of eyes in the opposite direction.

Frowning curiously and wondering why she should feel so absurdly conspicuous, she was about to turn back when she noticed that one man had continued to stare at her. Not only that, he was astonishingly brazen in his admiration and obviously not in the least bit embarrassed to be discovered. He was sitting half a dozen or so loungers away, his elbows resting on his knees, the dark hair on his chest and arms clinging damply to his skin and a large nugget of gold dangling from a chain around his neck.

He had to be Italian or French, Rhiannon decided as she averted her eyes, for only the Latins stared so frankly and lecherously at a woman and expected to be esteemed for it. Except he hadn't looked particularly lecherous, just friendly, she thought, and she was vaguely sorry that she'd been so horribly English in the way she had so abruptly turned away. But to glance back now would only encourage him and that she most certainly didn't want to do. So, with the sun blazing relentlessly down on her, she stepped up to the edge of the pool, raised her arms above her head and made a perfect dive into the deep refreshingly cool water.

It was, of course, a totally insane thing to do and why she hadn't realized it sooner would forever be a mystery to her, for against the force of the water her microscopic bikini quite simply didn't stand a chance. It was only as the bottom tangled itself around her knees that she realized what had happened and as she went into an underwater wrestling routine to try dragging it back up over her legs, while attempting to keep herself from either sinking or surfacing, she could only watch in dismay as the strapless top drifted blithely out of reach.

Within seconds she was desperate for air so clutching her bikini bottom tightly she allowed herself to rise swiftly through the water when, to her horror, she felt something snap. A hip clasp had broken, meaning that her bikini bottom was now all but useless.

As she broke the surface, filling her lungs with air, the warmth of the sun was as nothing compared to the heat of her embarrassment. Keeping her eyes closed and trying to persuade herself that no one had noticed, she began a pathetic one-handed doggy paddle towards the edge of the pool. Oliver was never going to let her live this down, though she wished to God he were there now, for at least then she'd have someone to go in search of her top while she held on to the final shreds of her modesty.

There were only a handful of swimmers in the pool, none of whom appeared to be aware of her predicament.

She was at the edge now, but the water was still too deep for her to touch the bottom, so she had no choice but to cling on to the tiled lip of the pool with one hand, while with the other she held her bikini bottom together. Having no idea how many people were watching and definitely not wanting to know, she began working her way towards the corner ladder. When she got there, with any luck she might be able to signal to someone to bring her towel to the steps. But of course no one was looking and everyone was deaf. She glanced helplessly up at the balcony to their suite, but there was no sign of Oliver and the man who'd been staring at her just now had transferred his interest to a book.

Faced with no alternative, she climbed awkwardly up the steps still pinning the two sides of her bikini bottom together with one hand while using the other to haul herself from the water. Her breasts, which were unquestionably ample anyway, felt enormous as she walked around the corner of the pool, past her admirer, and over to where she had left her towel. At least she thought she had left it there, but though her shoes and sun-glasses were still on the lounger the towel had vanished.

Groaning inwardly and torn between laughing and screaming, she slipped on her shoes and tried not to think about walking through the hotel bar, across reception to the lift and riding up to the second floor where no doubt an army of housekeeping staff would be waiting with well-trained averted eyes to wish her a good afternoon. This was worse than the nightmare of being found naked in Sainsbury's.

'Excuse, me. May I be of assistance?'

Rhiannon swung round to find her admirer standing behind her, a vaguely humorous smile in his eyes as he held up a towel.

'Oh, yes, thank you,' she said, forcing herself not to snatch it. 'I don't know what happened to mine. I know

I left it here ...'

'The pool guy probably took it,' he told her, smiling at her in a way that made her feel as self-conscious as it did appreciated. Though his voice was heavily accented, his English was perfect and Rhiannon was again struck by the friendliness of his smile.

'Yes, I guess so,' she said, wrapping the towel tightly around her. Then laughing she added, 'I feel such a fool. Thanks for coming to my rescue.'

'You're welcome,' he smiled. 'Happy to oblige,' and raising a hand in farewell he returned to his lounger and lay back down with his book.

It was quite some time after Rhiannon had disappeared inside that he picked up the phone beside him. When he finally made the connection he spoke into it quietly and sparingly. 'Maguire's sick,' he said.

'How sick?'

'Nothing terminal.'

'The girl?'

'I've just met her.'

'Where is she now?'

'Gone back to her room.'

'Keep an eye on her. If Maguire's sick she might go out alone. Did either of the Straussens arrive yet?'

'Yes, first thing this morning.'

There was a pause, then the voice at the other end said, '*Cosecha, amigo.*' Harvest time, my friend, and the line went dead.

'*Votre mari, il est malade*?' the guide asked Rhiannon, turning in the front seat of the taxi to look back at her.

'*Oui,*' she responded. '*Malheureusement.*'

'What goes wrong with him?'

'Tummy,' she answered, patting her own.

The guide nodded gravely, then turned to the driver and began issuing a string of unintelligible commands as they swept out of La Mamounia's drive. The driver merely nodded his head and smiled affably while steering his taxi off the main road and into a warren of cluttered streets. Clouds of dust billowed up from the caked earth as they passed, while tired and worn-looking donkeys trotted in front of the car, their eyes as forlorn as the dusky-faced children who sat carelessly on the roadside. Beggars riddled with flies crouched in doorways, their gnarled hands cupped for coins, their dark, leathery faces reflecting the years of poverty and pain.

As the taxi pressed on through the crowds heading for Djemma el Fna – the centre of the medina – Rhiannon gazed out of the window, both fascinated and appalled, as she watched the women in their shapeless gallabiyahs and variety of head-coverings going about their business. The heat was blistering, beating down on the russet walls of the town as though to set them alight. Wood carvings, silver jewellery, sizzling food, squawking livestock and a hundred other sights and smells spilled over the roadsides, while giant storks nested on the rooftops and the vibrant green of giant palms contrasted starkly with the arid streets and striking blue of the sky.

As she took it all in she wished Oliver were there to experience it too. She'd left him propped up in bed, a single fresh sheet covering him, a stack of newspapers and magazines within easy reach and the doctor's number imprinted on his memory just in case.

He'd insisted he was feeling much better today and had almost come along, but at the last minute a sudden dizzy spell had persuaded him that his first jaunt out had better wait a while yet. 'But don't be gone too long,' he had told her. 'And do as I said, get the concierge to find you a guide.'

Their parting kiss had been so lingering and provocative that she'd very nearly stayed, but seeing how pale he was and realizing that, though he might like to think otherwise, he was probably still not capable of much more than the thought, she had left. The concierge had eventually come up with Mohammed, a veritable giant of a man with a wide, gentle face and seven teeth – one for every day of the week, he had glibly informed her.

As they came to a halt in the midst of the teeming, seething crowds of Djemma el Fna, Rhiannon zipped up her belt-bag and strapped her camera securely across her body. Stepping out of the car, she looked around in amazement. The heat and the noise were incredible, as thousands upon thousands of people in bright, flowing gallabiyahs and brocaded headwear wove a path through the overladen stalls, passing by snake-charmers who were piping tunes for their reptiles; water-vendors who were jangling their bells and tourists who were wielding their cameras. Steam wafted from numerous kebab and couscous stalls, multi-coloured carpets hung from windows and walls, false-teeth sellers beckoned potential clients and monkeys hopped on to unsuspecting shoulders. There were endless bowls of snails and seafood, row upon row of dried sheep- and snake-skins, giant rocks of salt, whole families whizzing by on mopeds, a constant beat of drums ... The diversity and splendour were indescribable, the atmosphere was like nothing she had ever experienced.

'Hey!' she cried as a monkey landed on her back and encircled her neck with its arms.

'Photo, ma'am. Photo,' the owner nodded eagerly, while tugging at her camera.

'I take,' Mohammed butted in, thrusting the monkey man aside and unhooking Rhiannon's camera. 'Give him five dirhams,' he said when the picture was taken.

Rhiannon obliged, taking the coins from her pocket as she handed the monkey back.

'You take drink, ma'am,' a water-carrier insisted. 'Hot day. You take drink.'

'You need guide, ma'am? I good guide.'

'You want carpet, ma'am? Come with me, I give you

good price.'

Laughing and covering her ears, Rhiannon turned to Mohammed.

'You go! All go,' he shouted, shooing them away with his hands. 'You follow me, ma'am. You stay with me. Don't get lost. Souk is big place. Very crowded. You stay with me.'

In the heaving, pressing mass of humanity that churned through the souk it was almost impossible not to get lost, but somehow, as they wound their way through the sprawling network of lanes, Rhiannon managed to keep Mohammed in sight. Or, more accurately, he seemed to sense when she had been swallowed up by the crowd, or accosted by an exuberant salesman and came back to find her.

She had rarely seen such a riot of colour or known such an amalgam of smells. All around her, from the frayed bamboo ceilings, down to the straw-littered ground, there hung yard upon yard of gaily dyed thread, glittering gold slippers, hand-tooled leather bags, crimson gallabiyahs, copper pans, saffron-coloured scarves, gold, silver, turquoise and amber jewellery and sack upon bulging sack of herbs and spices in flavours and quantities that defied imagination. And the noise was tumultuous.

By the time they entered a dark, sour-smelling stairwell at the heart of the souk, Rhiannon had no idea where they were.

'You meet my cousin,' Mohammed told her, as she rounded a bend in the staircase ahead of him. 'He good man. Honest man. He sell you carpet if you want one. Not if you don't. He give you very good price because you friend.'

As he spoke, both he and Rhiannon were turning to look back down the stairs to where a woman in a blue gallabiyah was coming in through the door. Seeing them watching her, the woman bowed her head shyly and hesitated, waiting for them to move on, as though politeness forbade her to continue until they did.

Minutes later Rhiannon was flopping into a sumptuously cushioned couch in a room that contained mountains of rugs in every colour and size imaginable. Mohammed's cousin, Rashid, was pouring mint tea from an ornate silver service and asking if she preferred kelim carpets, very new carpets or very special, very genuine antique carpets. Taking the gilt-edged glass of tea, Rhiannon looked around. Through the beaded curtain, in the next room, three teenage girls sat at a giant loom, weaving and knotting with their finely skilled hands, while small wiry men hefted and folded the rugs they had recently laid out for other buyers.

'I come back in half an hour,' Mohammed told her. 'My cousin look after you. He make you good price.'

'Just don't forget me,' Rhiannon responded, turning her face towards the whirling table-top fan beside her. 'I'll never find my way out of here without you and I'll never be able to carry everything on my own.'

No sooner had she spoken than all her packages were laden on to one of Rashid's young assistants who was instantly despatched to the Mamounia Hotel.

'Now you are free to buy more,' Mohammed grinned as the boy vanished down the stairs.

'The carpet we ship,' Rashid assured her. 'Or maybe, like Cleopatra, we roll you up and deliver you to your husband in it.'

Rhiannon's eyebrows arched at the unexpected humour; it was a response that seemed to delight both Rashid and Mohammed as, giggling like schoolboys, they bade each other farewell and Mohammed took himself off.

Half an hour later Rhiannon was still mulling over her decision. Rashid's workers looked tired and bored and the teenage girls at the loom had long since disappeared. Rashid himself was seated on a short three-legged stool beside the couch, maintaining a limitless spiel and mint tea. Ending up choosing something she didn't really want, simply because it was impossible to say no to this man, Rhiannon handed over her credit card and waited while he went off downstairs.

A while later she glanced at her watch. Rashid's workers had left the unfolded rugs where they were and disappeared along with their boss. The looms in the next room had been abandoned a while ago and it was some time since she'd heard other tourists passing through. The cacophonous bustle of the souk outside was incessant, though muted by the windowless walls and deep insulation of the densely piled rugs. A musky incense was burning in a clay pot beside her and the discarded tea glasses sat cold and smeary on the small glass table.

Frowning, she looked at her watch again, then getting up from the couch she fixed her visor back on her head and pulling aside the beaded curtain wandered across the deserted workshop to the stairs. She hadn't noticed the thick steel door on her way up, probably because it had been open then. Now it was closed, sealing the only exit to the stairs.

Her heart gave a twist of unease. Why on earth would the door be closed? Surely they hadn't gone home and forgotten about her.

There was no handle on the door, no way at all of moving it. She looked around the room with its silent shadows, high slit windows and abandoned loom. The beaded curtain swayed in a current of air from the fan. A thin spiral of smoke rose from an incense stick on a shelf beside her. Her only companions were the shapeless piles of rugs, clustered around the walls. Everything seemed suddenly odd in a way she was finding very hard to define.

Turning back to the door, she was about to call out when the single overhead bulb went off, plunging the room into darkness. A quick fear pulsed in her heart and reaching out to search for a switch, her hand hit the incense pot, sending it crashing to the floor. She looked down at the red glow, then hurriedly extinguished it with her foot. Her hand was on her heart, as though to smother the unease. Her eyes were adjusting to the darkness, but there was nothing to see, nothing to hear.

'Rashid!' she called. 'Rashid! Are you there?'

She spun round. The door was moving. The solid bulk of steel was inching slowly towards her. She rushed to it, thrusting her hands into the gap and pulling.

'Oh thank God,' she gasped as a man stepped into the room. 'I thought I was going to be here ...' She stopped as another man came in behind him.

Rhiannon stared at them, her eyes wide with confusion as she instinctively backed away. 'What is it?' she said. 'What do you want? I don't have any money.'

The first man moved towards her, reaching for her. Her heart thudded with terror as she raised her arms to defend herself. 'I told you,' she cried, 'I don't have any money. Rashid took my ...' She gasped as her arms were wrenched behind her, almost snapping the bones. Then a fist smashed into her face, bringing the blood spurting from her mouth and nose. Pain and terror rendered her speechless, as the grip on her arms tightened and her head was jerked back by her hair. Then her head was thrust suddenly forward as her legs were kicked out from under her. The grip on her arms stopped her falling, the pain was worse than anything she'd ever known.

'Please,' she sobbed. 'Just tell me what you want.'

Her head was yanked back and she saw a woman standing in the shadows.

'Please,' she whispered, tears and blood mingling on her face. The woman stared through the slit in her veil, then lowering her eyes she turned and left the room.

Rhiannon didn't even see the blow coming. All she

knew was the terrible blinding pain as it exploded through her head and the slump of her body to the ground as she was swamped by darkness.

When the knock came on the door, Oliver was dozing. An open magazine was slipping from his lap and a CNN report from Somalia was playing quietly on the TV. Down by the pool the string quartet had finished for the day and early evening cocktails were being served in Le Bar du Soleil.

Unsure what the tapping was, Oliver inhaled deeply and blinked open his eyes. The double doors to the bedroom were open giving him a clear view of the sitting-room, and hearing a key turn in the lock and the call of 'room service', he quickly pulled the sheet back over his legs.

'Come in, carry on,' he called out to the room attendant, who was still at the far end of the suite's passageway, waiting for permission to enter.

As the door clicked closed Oliver turned off the TV and wrapping the sheet around him, hauled himself up from the bed. He was still faintly light-headed and his limbs felt as though they'd gone three rounds with Tyson, but there was no doubt he was on the mend. 'The towels need changing,' he said, as the room attendant appeared in the sitting-room, 'and if you'll just give me a couple of minutes I'll ... Oh, Jesus Christ,' he murmured as Theo Straussen, his two sons and a pair of thick-necked heavies filed into the suite.

'Oliver,' Theo Straussen said, holding out his hands.

Oliver's eyes moved from one saturnine face to the next. Fear was growling in his gut as his heart rate accelerated and his skin broke into an icy sweat. Instinctively his hand clenched the sheet more securely in front of him as his panicked thoughts stripped the blood from his face and caused a vein to throb in his neck.

'Oliver,' Straussen repeated. His expression was

mournful and vaguely incredulous. 'What did you think you were doing, son?'

Oliver's throat was too constricted to answer.

'Why did you do it?' Straussen said, shaking his head as though he couldn't make himself believe that Oliver would treat him this way. 'I told you at the weekend that our contract stood firm. I thought you heard me, son. I thought you were paying attention.' He sighed and put a despairing hand to his head.

Several seconds ticked by until, looking up, Straussen said, 'I'm not going to go into the details of our agreement, 'cos we did that at the weekend. I just want you to tell me what you thought was going to happen when you double-crossed me like this? I mean, did you think I was going to let you keep all I gave you? Did you think I was going to let you walk away from this, like your end of the deal didn't need fulfilling? I gave you everything, Oliver. I made you what you are today. But you know that. You remember when we sat down and drew up the deal ... Diamonds were what you wanted, so diamonds were what you got. Then later, London was what you wanted, so London was what you got. What more could I have given you?'

Anything Oliver might have wanted to say was silenced by the dread of the response it would provoke.

Straussen made a gesture towards his sons, who turned to the closets and began removing Rhiannon's clothes. Oliver watched them, a terrible panic driving the fear in his chest.

'I don't like having to do these things, Oliver,' Straussen said, 'but you leave me no choice. I own you, son. I bought you and you got to abide by that.'

Oliver's eyes fell away.

'She's here,' Straussen told him, after a pause. 'Marcia's right here in Marrakesh. I brought her with me to remind you.'

'Oh God,' Oliver groaned, his face turning whiter than

ever. 'Theo, I tried to tell you,' he said pleadingly, 'at the weekend, I tried to tell you ...'

'I heard what you told me, son,' Straussen cut in, 'but it seems you just didn't hear me. I stuck to my side of the bargain, Oliver, now you got to stick to yours.'

'But I can't do that,' Oliver cried. 'Not now. It's just not possible.'

Straussen had him fixed with his sharp old man's eyes. 'Oh, but it is,' he said smoothly.

Oliver's stomach churned with a fresh onslaught of fear, for he knew only too well what Straussen meant. 'For God's sake, Theo,' he breathed, 'Rhiannon knows nothing about this.'

Straussen looked at him incredulously. 'I didn't imagine for one minute she did,' he replied. 'But it's a bit late to be concerned about her now, wouldn't you say?'

Oliver was silent as putting his hands in his pockets Straussen walked over to the window. 'Tell me,' he said, following the laborious path of a camel on the far side of the city walls, 'what would you do if you were in my position and someone had done something like this to a person you loved?' He turned back, his green eyes meeting Oliver's in an ominously tragic gaze.

It was a trap Oliver wasn't going to fall into, for he knew it would be as good as signing his own death warrant. Except they wouldn't kill him, not while Marcia was still on the planet. What they might do to Rhiannon, though, was something that was whipping the heat of fear in his heart.

'Yeah, I guess you'd do the same as me,' Straussen responded to the silence. 'And who could blame you? But I want to tell you, Oliver, that I have tried to understand you. I know my girl's no beauty, I know it's hard for a woman like her to satisfy a man like you, but to do what you've done to her, Oliver ... To go right ahead with your craziness and marry another woman, like my girl don't exist no more ... Now that I just can't understand. You see, the world don't change its shape 'cos you're uncomfortable with the one it's got. And deals don't just disappear because they don't suit you no more. You got to face up to reality here, son. Closing your eyes don't mean the rest of the world can't see you. And getting yourself a wife don't turn my girl into some clause in a contract that's too minor to count.

'Now, I know and you know that you didn't really believe you'd get away with this. You been committed to Marcia for three years, and three years is a long time to be telling a woman you're gonna marry her and doing nothing about it. So we're not going to let that continue. She's a good girl, she cares about you, and she was prepared to wait until you said the time was right – and this is what you do to her. It wasn't clever, son, not clever at all. And think about how that poor wife of yours is gonna feel when she finds out about all this. 'Cos she's gonna have to know, Oliver. You realize that, don't you? She's got to be told why you can't stay married to her.'

'Theo, you can't do that,' Oliver said, a note of desperation creeping into his voice.

'Oliver, this is me you're talking to,' Straussen reminded him. 'I can do it.' He paused. 'Or, I can take back everything I've given you,' he said. 'So you see, I'm a reasonable man. I'm giving you a choice. Your wife or your life.'

Oliver looked at him; sweat was pouring down his face as denial raged through his mind.

Straussen watched him, waiting for him to speak; his expression was a mask of incalculable patience.

'My engagement to Marcia is a farce,' Oliver suddenly blurted. 'She knows that, the whole damned world knows that. And you said,' he went on, pointing a furious finger at Straussen, 'you said, when I agreed to the deal, that you would turn a blind eye to my affairs. You said I was free to ...'

'An affair isn't the same as getting married, boy,'

Straussen interrupted.

'And turning a blind eye isn't the same as fucking around with my money, stealing my car, raiding my flat or removing fifty-thousand-dollar diamonds from my briefcase.'

Straussen's eyebrows showed his interest. 'That ring didn't belong to you, son,' he reminded him. 'It belonged to me. You were just taking delivery.'

'Which is exactly what I did. But then you got someone to lift it from my briefcase and plant it in Rhiannon's bag. So what was I supposed to tell her when she found it? That it wasn't for her?'

Straussen's amusement was registering in his eyes. 'Fifty thousand dollars is a lot of money, Oliver,' he said. 'Most people would have found an excuse.'

'I've paid for that ring,' Oliver raged.

'You did?' Straussen said, obviously surprised as he looked to his sons for confirmation.

'What you've taken from me in the past six weeks amounts at least to the value of that ring,' Oliver blustered. 'So yes, I've paid.'

Straussen nodded thoughtfully. 'I'm a fair man,' he said, 'and I got to admit that you might have a point there. Yeah, I reckon you could be right. The ring I bought for you to give my girl is now on another woman's finger. So, we could either remove the ring – and the finger – or we could, as you say, accept that the ring is paid for.' He took a few moments to think it over. 'You know,' he said in the end, 'I've got a bit of a problem with my girl getting second-hand goods, so you might have struck lucky here, Oliver. Your woman might just get to keep that ring. Yeah,' he nodded, seeming pleased with his quick decision, 'I think we can look on the ring as a kind of compensation for all the heartbreak you're gonna bring her.'

'Jesus Christ, Theo!' Oliver yelled in frustration. 'You can't play with people's lives like this!'

'Oliver, quit telling me what I can and can't do,' Straussen said. 'We got a contract between us, a legally binding contract, that says you got to marry my daughter or you're obliged to surrender everything you own, everything I gave you, back to me.'

'I can't marry, Marcia,' Oliver replied desperately. 'Why do you think I've dragged it out all this time? She repulses me, Theo. She makes my skin crawl. Do you really want your daughter to be married to someone who feels like that about her?'

Straussen was nodding, the corners of his mouth were pulled down and his eyebrows were raised as he appeared to mull over everything Oliver had said. When finally he spoke he said, 'You know, I'm going to do something here, Oliver, that is generally against my nature. I'm going to let you get away with those ugly things you just said about my girl. I'm going to let you get away with them because I understand you're troubled and you're not really thinking about what you're saying. But when you took those marriage vows two days ago you knew exactly what you were saying, and an insult like that, well now, it can't be overlooked, son – it just can't.'

As the five of them stood there, like a rare family portrait, Oliver's eyes shifted from one to the other, knowing what was coming and that he was powerless to stop it. For one incredible moment he thought he had found salvation in a genuine housekeeping call, but the knock on the door produced only a whispered message, then whoever it was went away.

Oliver was still standing beside the bed, the sheet draped in front of him, the terror of what was to come finally surpassing the insanity that had made him think he could get away with it.

Theo Straussen was listening intently as the message was relayed to him by his eldest son. His moss-green eyes were rooted in space as he nodded, pursed his lips, then nodded again. Finally Reuben stood back, spoke quietly to his brother, then returned his attention to Oliver.

Straussen took a breath to speak, then creasing his brow he drew a hand over his mouth as though so saddened by what he was about to say that he was finding it hard to speak. 'Oliver,' he said finally. 'Oliver, my son. I wish to God you'd never put me in this position. It gives me no pleasure to do this, boy, no pleasure at all. But remember, it was you who loaded the gun, you who put my finger on the trigger and now ...'

As his voice trailed off Oliver's eyes darted frantically between the five impassive faces. It was as though he was watching the mourners at his own funeral.

'That was a message from Jordan,' Straussen went on. 'You remember, Joe? Sure you remember Joe. Well that message was from him. I'm sorry, son, I'm sorry to the bottom of my heart to tell you this, but your new wife ...'

Oliver's eyes were bulging with terror, his heart was a furnace of denial.

Straussen glanced at one of the heavies, then returning his eyes to Oliver he said, 'Did you ever hear of Fulbert's revenge?' he asked pleasantly.

Oliver merely looked at him.

'Fulbert,' Straussen prompted. 'French guy, had a niece by the name of Héloïse. Back in the twelfth century.'

Though Oliver could hear the words, none of them was penetrating the horror of what might have happened to Rhiannon.

Straussen stood aside for one of his men to step forward.

Suddenly Oliver's eyes dilated. Fulbert. Fulbert, the uncle who had avenged the breach of his trust, the abuse of his favour and the honour of his beloved niece by having a man castrated.

Oliver's face turned yellow as he took a step back,

pressing a hand to his groin. There was no knife in sight, but he didn't doubt its existence, nor did he doubt Straussen's deadliness of intent. His heart rate slowed, then suddenly picked up, crashing against his ribs in utter panic as he sank to the floor and watched the men come.

'It was her fault, Theo,' he sobbed wretchedly. 'She asked me to marry her ... You can't blame me. It was her fault.'

Chapter 14

The day's second call to prayer was beginning to wail through the minarets as two heavily robed men came out of a deserted mosque on the far edge of town. In the mid-day heat the surrounding rose-coloured walls and turrets seemed to undulate like a mirage and the golden waves of sand dunes ebbed lazily away, melting into the far horizon.

As the men looked up and down the street the only witness to their presence was a solitary stork nesting at the corner of a nearby roof. A car came out of a side-road and pulled to a stop in front of them. As they got in, a woman turned from the front seat to watch them. Her face was grey and sweat oozed from the open pores on her cheeks. For a moment it looked as though she might speak, but seeming to decide better of it, she returned her gaze to the mosque. The driver watched her, waiting as her pale, close-set eyes travelled the ancient walls, fixing for a moment on the narrow arched windows of an upper storey, before falling to the scuffed and broken mosaics of an empty courtyard. Her profile was lit by the midday sun; her coarse mousy hair was tugged into a tightly knotted plait and the copious soft down on her top lip glistened with beads of perspiration.

When she'd finished she turned to look straight ahead and stayed that way until the car drew up outside the Mamounia Hotel.

Maintaining their silence, they rode an elevator to the second floor where Joe Jordan, the larger of the two men, led the way to the honeymoon suite. All Marcia had wanted was to take a look at the woman, which she had done yesterday at the carpet shop; then to see where they were holding her, which she had just now when the driver had taken her to collect Jordan and Taylor from the mosque.

Someone, Marcia thought it was probably her brothers, had gone to the mosque last night to talk to the woman. Marcia wondered how she was feeling now. She didn't think her brothers would have harmed the woman, but really there was no telling and not wanting to think about it, she blanked it from her mind and walked past Jordan through the door of the suite into her father's embrace.

As he hugged his daughter, Straussen's affection was clear in his eyes, for this ugly duckling that had never made it to a swan was every bit as precious to him as the rest of his children. Or maybe, as though to make up for her homeliness, he loved her just that little bit more.

'Did you see the place?' he asked, holding her face between his hands and smiling indulgently into her eyes.

Marcia nodded and returned his gaze with her habitual uncertainty. Then, seeming to sense what he wanted, she broke into a smile. It was almost a travesty, for Marcia's fear of the dentist had prevented Theo from spending a small fortune to rectify the cruelty of nature.

'Where is he?' she asked, turning to look around the room. There was no sign at all of the business that had been conducted there yesterday; the chairs were in place, the curtains were perfectly draped and every vase brimmed over with vibrant white flowers. The bed was made, the cushions were plumped and in the bathroom the towels and toiletries were neatly displayed.

'I'll take you to him,' Straussen answered, walking over to the closets. As he pulled open the doors he turned back to look at her, wanting to witness her pleasure when she saw her own clothes hanging beside Oliver's. 'We're going to do things a bit different,' he said, glancing at Jordan and Taylor and winking. 'We're going to give Oliver his honeymoon, but you, Marcia, are gonna be the bride. We'll get the details of the wedding fixed up just as soon as we get back to New York, but there's no point wasting a honeymoon while it's right here on offer, now is there?'

As the men chuckled Marcia blinked, then laughed too.

'Good idea, hey?' Straussen smiled, beckoning to his sons to come in as one of them put his head round the door. 'The honeymoon before the wedding.'

'Hi, Marce,' Reuben said, greeting his sister with a brotherly kiss. 'How did it go at the mosque?'

'All I did was take a look,' Marcia replied.

Reuben looked surprised. 'You didn't go inside?' he said, going to help himself to a beer at the mini-bar while his younger brother embraced Marcia. 'Didn't you want to meet her?'

'No,' she answered. 'There wasn't time.'

Reuben looked at his father.

'Where's Oliver?' Marcia said. 'I'd like to see him now.'

'He's right along the hall,' Straussen answered.

'Still sleeping,' Reuben added.

Marcia looked from one to the other.

'Oren's going over to the mosque later,' her father told her, referring to her younger brother. 'Joe and Taylor're going with him and I think you should go along too.'

'Me?' Marcia said in surprise.

Straussen nodded and smiled, then speaking to Oren he said, 'I take it you won't be needing me.'

Oren shook his head. 'No, we can handle it,' he answered.

Straussen's approval was expressed in a warm grasp

of his son's shoulder, for both Oren and Reuben knew how upset their father was by all this – in fact, he couldn't stomach it any more than he could a man who squealed and blubbered the way his future son-in-law had the night before. OK, the guy thought he was going to lose his dick, so you'd expect him to be a bit upset, but the way Maguire had carried on just wasn't dignified in a man. Whatever Marcia saw in him he would never know – what *any* woman saw in him, come to that, was a god-damned mystery to Straussen. Oh sure, he was a good-looking guy who could turn on the charm like few others Straussen knew, but when it came to things that mattered the man almost deserved to be parted from his chum for being such a god-damned coward and liar. But Marcia was devoted to the son-of-a-bitch, had wanted him from the minute she'd set eyes on him, which was how Straussen had come to strike up the deal with Maguire that had promised his daughter a husband and Maguire a very elevated place in the diamond world. And now, despite what the bastard had done, Marcia had made Theo promise not to hurt him too much, which was god-damned lucky for Maguire, 'cos if Straussen had had his way the man would be propping up freeways in a dozen different States. As it was, he was going to be a bit sore for a while, though the broken nose would mend and not many of the bruises would show. However, it wasn't over yet. No, they still had a way to go, 'cos the woman had to be made to understand that it was in her own best interests to let Maguire go. And that little bit of persuasion was something Straussen was happy to leave in the capable hands of his sons.

Through a crack in the warped wooden shutters Rhiannon could see the remains of what had once been a fountain. It appeared to be at the centre of some kind of ancient courtyard, but the mosaics were so faded and cracked that there was little trace now of the intricate patterns they had once made. From the angle she was looking at she guessed she was on a second or third floor, but of what kind of building or where was impossible to tell. The silence was like an empty pocket where only trapped and weary insects buzzed listlessly in the heat, easy prey for the occasional bird that swooped from nowhere to feast.

The sunlight was so dazzling that she could only look for a few seconds before having to turn her eyes away and wait for the blade of white light to subside. Her jaw still throbbed from the blows she'd received and her head was pounding so hard that any quick movement brought a pain that almost rent her in two. Her mouth was dry, her clothes were stained with blood and sweat and her throat was raw from the futile cries for help she had shouted through the night. The rest of her body ached and shook, but no amount of physical suffering could be as bad as what she was feeling inside.

Returning to the untidy pile of straw in the corner, she sank down into it and hugged her knees to her chest. Sweat trickled unchecked over her face, while the heat sucked all the air from the room. She sat staring at nothing, the matted strands of her hair fluttering in the draft of her breath.

Hour after hour ticked by until the bands of light seeping through the shutters turned to faint ribbons of colour. Her need for water was increasing, along with the growing fear that she had been left there to die.

Her head rolled back and a single tear trickled down her face. Then her eyes closed as the pain expanded through her heart. Maybe the worst part of this was not understanding why he had never told her. Squeezing her eyes tightly closed she reminded herself that it didn't matter why. All that mattered was that they got through this. They loved each other, they were married now and if Oliver ended up losing everything, then so be it. She would stand by him, they would rebuild his life together.

A silent sob shuddered through her and biting her lips to stop herself crying she covered her face with her hands. Just please God he was still going to have a life to rebuild.

As confusion and despair merged with the pain inside her she heard a car engine purr to a halt outside. Immediately her eyes drew focus. It was the first time in hours that a vehicle had come this close. Fear and hope began to thud in her chest as pulling herself painfully to her feet she went to press an eye to the slit in the shutters. She could see no more than she had before, a strip of deserted courtyard, bathed now in a rosy twilight glow.

As she turned from the window her face was taut with dread. Would they let her go, or were they planning some other means of getting her out of Oliver's life?

The sound of footsteps scuffed on a distant staircase as she slid down the wall and stared at the door. Her heart was beating so fast she was finding it hard to breathe; the pain in her limbs throbbed and ached and weakened her strength. She had no way of knowing how to deal with this, for never in her life had she come across people who behaved like this.

Every muscle in her body suddenly jarred as something crashed into the door. Unable to stop herself she started to shake. There was another crash, then another. Someone was levering off the cross beams they had hammered into place that morning. Rhiannon's fingers dug into her palms, an icy sweat was coating her skin. Suddenly the door burst open and her heart felt as though it was being torn from her chest.

There were four of them, three men and a woman. Rhiannon stiffened with shock as her eyes fixed on the woman. For one blinding instant pity soared through her, then suddenly it was as though she was dying inside. Oliver was standing on the threshold. His face was as chalk white as the walls, his eyes were glazed with pain and his face was even more bruised and battered than her own.

Her heart was pounding, then she started as her suitcase hit the floor, clothes spilling from the sides, an airline ticket taped to the top. Everyone was talking, shouting, moving about the room, but all Rhiannon could do was look at Oliver, and wonder why his eyes were refusing to meet hers.

'Oliver,' she heard herself whisper.

He seemed to flinch, but as the man, Oren, turned to look at him, his eyes remained as empty as the gulf starting to open in her heart.

'Oliver!' she cried.

For a moment it seemed as though he might respond, but then Oren was standing between them.

'OK,' Oren said, nodding to the other men.

Rhiannon turned and her eyes rounded in terror as one of the men pulled a commando knife from the belt of his jeans. Her mind was in sudden uproar. She opened her mouth to scream, but no sound came out. One of them grabbed her by the hair and yanked back her head, while the other drew the knife, in one clean slice, right across her throat. The wound was superficial but the terror sank right through to her soul. Then her eyes bulged and her chest began to heave as the knife moved to her waist.

'Are you watching this, Maguire?' Oren sneered. 'Do you see what happens when you don't stick to a bargain?'

Oliver's head remained drooped to one side until Oren walked over to him and yanked his face up.

'You were supposed to marry *her*, you dumbfuck,' he spat, jerking his thumb towards Marcia. 'Remember? You signed. You took your share, now you got to deliver.' He turned back to the scene on the floor and gave a brief nod of his head. 'Open her up, Joe,' he said. 'Let him take one last look before he makes up his mind.'

'No!' Rhiannon screamed, as in three quick strikes the knife ripped open her clothes. 'Oliver! For God's sake, stop them!' she cried, trying to fight them off. 'Don't let them do this. Oh God, no!' she sobbed as they pinned her arms above her head and jerked her legs apart. 'Please, no.'

'You got to choose here, Oliver,' Oren grinned. 'You give everything back you took from my father and it could be that you get to keep the girl. Or maybe,' he said, 'she don't mean that much.'

'For Christ's sake, Oren,' Oliver hissed. 'Let her go.'

'You got to choose, Oliver,' Oren said. 'Remember? Your wife or your life.'

Everyone was looking at Oliver, waiting for him to speak. Rhiannon's horror at his continuing silence was so great that it eclipsed even her fear.

'OK,' Oren said, turning back to Rhiannon, 'seems we got our answer from him. Now we need one from you. But first I got to tell you that nothing's gonna happen to you just so long as you tell me that you want an annulment from this jerk. Have you got that?'

Rhiannon looked at him.

'Is that a yes?' he said. 'You want an annulment?'

Rhiannon's eyes moved to Oliver.

'Oren, just let her go,' Oliver whispered.

'You shut the fuck up,' Oren snapped. 'It's her I'm talking to. Now,' he said, turning back to Rhiannon, 'these guys here, they're about ready to fuck you, but I can stop them doing that, if you just give me the word.'

'No! Let them fuck her!' Marcia suddenly shrieked.

The room went quiet as everyone turned to her in amazement.

Marcia stood against the wall, her hands clenched at her sides, her eyes gleaming with excitement.

Oren shrugged and looked at Jordan. 'You heard the woman,' he said.

'Oh God, no!' Rhiannon gasped as Jordan began

unzipping his fly. 'Please no.' She looked up at Marcia. 'Please,' she begged. 'Don't make them do this.'

But Marcia wasn't listening.

Rhiannon tried to struggle, but she was no match for the men holding her. She could feel their hands clamping round her wrists and ankles, their breath on her face, their bodies closing in on her.

'Oliver! Help me! Please!' she cried. Her entire body was juddering with terror, tears streamed from her eyes and blood trickled from her neck. She was dragged away from the wall and laid spread-eagled across the floor. She could feel their hands on her breasts, brutal fingers clenching her nipples and again she tried to kick out. But it was no good. They were too strong for her, too quick in their responses. They were going to rape her and there was nothing she could do to stop them. And Oliver was just going to stand there and let it happen.

Knowing that once it was over she would want only to die, she closed her eyes and willed her mind to leave her body. It was the only way she was going to be able to endure what was about to happen.

It was a while before she realized that no one was moving, that a voice, a stranger's voice, was barking out orders and that somewhere in the distance people were running. Barely aware of what was happening her head rolled to one side, as the pressure of weight left her body. Then someone was beside her, covering her with the tattered remains of her clothes. She felt a hand on her arm, a hand that was both gentle and firm as it carefully eased her to her feet.

The room was full of people, but her eyes were barely able to focus. Dimly she was aware of being led past them, of Marcia shrieking and struggling to break free of the man holding her. The other men were perfectly still. Oliver's head was bowed. She was taken from the room, then lifted into someone's arms and carried along a shadowed passageway, down a broken staircase and put into a waiting car.

It was a long time later, as they approached the lights of another town, that Rhiannon finally remembered where she had seen her rescuer before.

'Beside the pool,' she whispered. 'You gave me your towel.'

Smiling, he cast her a quick glance, then returned his eyes to the road.

Rhiannon looked at him, her dry, aching eyes sweeping over his profile. 'Who are you?' she asked, her voice as raw and broken as her lips.

Again he smiled and arching an eyebrow he said, 'Let's just say I'm a friend.'

As the chief stewardess moved past him, leaving a perfumed trail of L'Eau d'Issey in her wake, Max Romanov got up from his seat and made his way to the bathroom. They were, by now, just over half-way to Seattle where the monthly group executive meeting was being held at the First Avenue offices. Production heads, financial and legal officers, marketing directors; in fact all the chief operating officers of the Romanov organization around the country were flying in for the meeting, as they did every month, though the location always varied. Ellis Zamoyski, Max's personal CFO and close friend, was on the Romanov jet with him, his attention at that moment wholly engrossed in a set of new proposals for pension agreements that were displayed on the computer screen in front of him.

As Max retook his seat he asked the stewardess for more coffee and was just unfolding the *Wall Street Journal* when his telephone rang. Taking it from his inside pocket, he leaned across Zamoyski to point out something on the screen, then turning the phone on he took a call from Maurice Remmick, his chief legal officer and godfather to his children.

'I thought you'd want to know,' Remmick said. 'A call

just came in from Ramon. He found the girl. She's with him now.'

'Is she OK?' Max asked.

'I think so.'

Max nodded. 'Where are they?'

'Still in Morocco. Ramon's putting her on a plane back to London in a couple of days.'

'OK. Do you have any details?'

'Not many,' Maurice answered. 'Seems it was an eleventh-hour recovery and not surprisingly the girl wants to know who Ramon is. He's asking what he should tell her.'

'Whatever he likes,' Max responded with an ironic raise of his eyebrows, 'just so long as my name doesn't get mentioned.'

'I reckoned that's what you'd say,' Maurice chuckled. 'So, did you get a chance to look over the distribution deal that came up from Atlanta?'

'Did you look at your E-mail this morning?' Max replied drily.

'Not yet,' Maurice confessed.

'You got my answers there,' Max told him. 'Is Ula with you?'

'No. She's got some dental appointment downtown somewhere. She'll be here in a couple of hours. Do you want me to have her call you?'

'No. Just get her to fax Galina's schedule over to Ron Phedra's office. Tell her to use the private number, I'll pick it up there. I can hear the kids in the background, put them on, will you?'

'Daddy!' Aleks cried a couple of seconds later, leaving Max in no doubt that his son was spraying cookie crumbs all over the desk.

Laughing, he said, 'What are you doing in my study? Didn't we make you one of your own last week?'

'Yes, but Uncle Maurice won't use my telephone,' Aleks grumbled.

Since Aleks's phone was the very latest in Fisher Price technology Max reckoned Maurice could be forgiven. 'So, you're helping Uncle Maurice run things, are you?' he said.

'Yep.'

'And I don't suppose you're getting in the way at all?'

'No,' Aleks responded earnestly.

Max grinned. 'Well, don't let me interrupt any further,' he said. 'Put Marina on.'

'I have to go to school now, Daddy,' Marina said bossily when she came on the line. 'Mrs Clay is waiting.'

'OK, honey. Did you remember to invite your friends round for your birthday party next week?'

'I don't have any friends,' she retorted.

Even though he knew it wasn't true, the words cut through Max's heart. 'Sure you have friends, honey,' he said gently. 'You got Kathy and Lydia and Savanna ...'

'I hate them,' she said.

'Then you don't deserve to have friends.'

'Well, I have got friends, so!'

Smiling, Max said, 'You're an impossible little minx at times, Marina, but I love you.'

'You're impossible too,' she retorted.

'But you love me?'

'Only sometimes.'

'OK. I guess that'll have to do.'

'I love Mommy all the time,' she said angrily.

Max took a breath, let it go, then said, 'I know, sweetheart. And she loves you all the time too.'

There was quiet at the other end of the line and in his mind's eye Max could see the bottom lip coming forward and starting to tremble. 'I want you to come home, Daddy,' she said tearfully.

'I'll be back tonight, honey,' he told her.

'But what if I'm sleeping? That'll mean I won't have seen you *all* day.'

'If you're sleeping I'll come and carry you into my bed

then I'll be the first person you see tomorrow. How about that?'

She sniffed.

'OK?'

'OK,' she said grudgingly. Then, 'Will Mommy be there too?'

Max's eyes closed as his daughter's pain and confusion sealed themselves around his heart. 'No, honey,' he said softly. 'You know she won't be there.'

'It's my fault, isn't it, Daddy?' she suddenly blurted. 'It's my fault she's dead.'

Oh my God, he groaned inwardly. This was the first time anything like this had happened in months, so why did it have to happen now, on the god-damned phone? 'No, honey,' he said instilling as much firmness and gentleness into his voice as he could. 'It's nobody's fault. It was an accident.'

Marina was silent.

'Are you still there, sweetheart?'

'Yes.'

'Go and find Mrs Clay and tell her I said you could stop by McDonald's on the way home from school.'

'Do you mean it?' Marina said breathlessly. 'You never let me have McDonald's.'

'That's not true. I just don't let you have as many as you'd like.'

After clicking off the line, he pushed the telephone back into his pocket and sat staring thoughtfully past Ellis out of the window.

'Marina?' Ellis said.

'Mmm,' Max nodded. 'I'm going to have to talk to her counsellor again. I think maybe she needs some extra help.'

'Maybe she needs a new mommy.'

Max's eyebrows flickered. 'You mean, Galina,' he said.

Ellis choked back a laugh. 'Well, I can't think of anyone else I would mean,' he responded.

Max laughed and turned back to his paper.

'I heard you mention the Straussens,' Ellis said. 'Did Ramon find the girl?'

'Yep. Seems he did.'

'And?'

'And nothing. She's all in one piece. Ramon's putting her on a plane back to London and I guess if she never sees Maguire again in her life it'll still be too soon.'

'So what do you care?'

Max frowned. 'Who said I did?'

'Then why d'you get involved?'

'For Galina's sake.'

'Oh yes, of course, I was forgetting,' Ellis replied and with a brief shake of his head he returned to his computer.

Chapter 15

The summer had passed much more quickly than Rhiannon would ever have expected. Gone already were the long, balmy evenings; the nights were drawing in and the heat was fading, along with her wounds. That night in Morocco was something that rarely, if ever, got mentioned now; she'd put it behind her, was moving on with her life.

Right now, her small Kensington garden was alive with laughter as champagne flowed and something by Janet Jackson blared out of the CD. The pond's goldfish shied under a lily-pad, next-door's cat had vanished and, locked in its cage, Mrs Romney's rabbit munched curiously on a dock leaf while watching the interminable ebb and flow of glittering, vibrating bodies as they writhed and twisted and threw themselves about to the music. Everyone who was anyone in the world of journalistic television was there. Not necessarily those at the top, but those with wit and style, originality and flair; the movers and shakers, writers and producers who made it all happen.

Inside the apartment, cards, flowers, ribbons, bows, unopened and opened gifts spilled from tables, sofas, chairs and walls, even the bed. The delicious pop of champagne corks rang almost constantly from the kitchen, the whoosh and fizz of the bubbles making everyone shriek and laugh and thrust their glasses out for more. The table of catered food looked like a battlefield strewn with streamers and limp balloons; the floor was littered with discarded high-heeled shoes and crushed paper hats.

At the midst of it all was Rhiannon. Everyone danced around her, clapping to the beat, stamping their feet and whooping as she twirled. The *Check It Out* team showered her with glitter that clung to her skin and sparkled in her hair. She looked radiant. So alive, so full of energy and exuberance that it was almost impossible to believe that this wild and riotous party was being held to mark her departure from *Check It Out*.

Cheering and clapping her hands over her head, Lizzy bumped her hips against Rhiannon's as James Brown took over the CD. Jolene moved in, an exotic triumph in a sheath of red and gold sequins; Martin followed suit as Carrie and Rohan romped and gyrated, pulling everyone into the mêlée, while a couple of ITN guys emptied Moët over Rhiannon's and Lizzy's heads.

At the edge of the garden, trying desperately not to feel out of place as they jigged about awkwardly to the beat, were Morgan and Sally Simpson – the proprietors of *Check It Out* who were taking over the running of the programme starting next Monday. Firing Rhiannon had been one of the hardest things either of them had ever done, especially after all she had been through.

'I feel such a heel,' Sally said to her husband as they watched Rhiannon and Lizzy tilting their faces to catch the champagne.

'What!' he shouted.

'I said I feel a heel,' she repeated. 'Do you think she's doing this on purpose? I mean to make us feel bad?'

'If she is, it's working,' he responded, desperately wishing they hadn't come, but knowing there was no way they could have avoided it.

Sally's sun-weathered face hardened for a moment, then turning to look at Rhiannon again she felt her heart give a twist of guilt. 'She's not that malicious,' she said grudgingly. 'At least, she never used to be.'

'It's not our fault,' Morgan reminded her firmly. Though, in truth, they both knew how bored they had become with the lotus-eating life in the Caribbean and how they'd been dying to get their hands on the programme for months. But after all she had done there was no way they could ask Rhiannon to step aside, especially when, apart from money, they had contributed next to nothing since the programme's conception. For a while they had toyed with the idea of asking Rhiannon to share the exec-producership, but then Mervyn Mansfield had been appointed commissioning editor for Channel 4's news and features and the problem – at least from the Simpsons' point of view – had been solved.

Looking at Rhiannon now, Sally felt the ache of disloyalty and a fierce almost murderous hatred of Mansfield. To her, he would forever be the focus of blame, even though in her heart she knew that neither she nor Morgan had fought hard enough for Rhiannon to stay – in any capacity. But how could they when Mansfield's ultimatum had been unequivocal: either Rhiannon went or *Check It Out* was off the air. Under any other circumstances it might have been interesting to try calling his bluff, for axing a ratings-puller like *Check It Out* would be plain crazy. But since Mansfield's grudge against Rhiannon was as deep as it was personal, the Simpsons had seen no point in antagonizing him unnecessarily, not at this stage of his editorship, anyway. So they had taken a deep breath, put a tight rein on their consciences and extracted Rhiannon's resignation.

That had been over six weeks ago. Since, the entire team had resigned in a show of solidarity – it was Rhiannon who had talked them into staying. And on the face of it, since there had been no indication to the contrary, it appeared that Lizzy was going to stay too. Morgan was convinced of it, but Sally wasn't so sure.

They were very close, Rhiannon and Lizzy, and after all that Rhiannon had been through Sally couldn't see Lizzy letting Rhiannon face anything alone, not yet, anyway, because three months was no time at all to get over the kind of trauma Rhiannon had suffered. In fact, her throat still bore a faint purplish mark from the knife that had cut her, which was probably nothing compared to the devastation she was still carrying in her heart; a devastation she never spoke of to anyone, with the probable exception of Lizzy.

Knowing Sally and Morgan were watching them, Lizzy shimmied back to back with Rhiannon and treated her new bosses to a dazzling smile. Actually, she'd have liked nothing better than to punch out their lights, but this was the way Rhiannon wanted it, so this was the way it had to be: no bitterness, no recriminations, no reprisals.

As the record ended Rhiannon flopped breathlessly into Lizzy's arms, whereupon they both toppled drunkenly into the fountain. Actually neither had had as much to drink as their behaviour suggested, though Rhiannon appeared much closer to letting go tonight than she had throughout all the long, painful summer days since her return from Marrakesh. Lizzy just hoped that it wasn't hysteria fuelling the exuberance, for she, more than anyone, knew how utterly broken Rhiannon was by the prospect of no longer being a part of *Check It Out*. The very real closeness of the team had played such a vital part in seeing her through the past three months that Lizzy could hardly envisage her coping without it.

In fact, no one but Lizzy knew how bad it had really been, for only Lizzy knew how Oliver had been prepared to stand by and let two men rape Rhiannon right in front of him; and only Lizzy knew that all the money Oliver had borrowed from Rhiannon had never been repaid. Worse, and in Lizzy's book totally indefensible, was that on four separate occasions now Oliver had called Rhiannon and pleaded with her to see him. How the bastard had the nerve Lizzy would never know, any more than she would ever begin to understand what had made him go so far, only to back down when he had. She guessed that maybe that was the worst part for Rhiannon, finding out that she hadn't meant as much to him as she'd thought.

The party raved on towards dawn and by six even the diehards had gone, leaving Rhiannon and Lizzy alone with the chaos. A lot had happened during the past ten hours, enough to keep them laughing and gossiping for another hour or so, until exhaustion finally defeated them and they fell asleep on the sofas.

Rhiannon was the first to wake, around midday, when the merciless rays of an Indian summer sun beamed like lasers into her eyes. Groaning, she reached out for a cushion and covered her face.

'Oh fuck,' Lizzy grumbled.

Several seconds ticked by before Rhiannon lifted a corner of her cushion and peered across the room at Lizzy. Though it hurt there was no way she could stop the splutter of laughter when she saw the paper plate Lizzy had used to ward off the sun sticking to her face in gooey blobs of cream.

'Please, don't,' Lizzy implored, sliding the plate off her face and letting it drop to the floor.

'Buck's fizz?' Rhiannon offered maliciously.

'Oh God!' Lizzy groaned.

'Bellini? Pimm's? Scotch on the rocks?'

Lizzy opened one eye. 'What did I ever do to you?' she demanded weakly.

Grinning, Rhiannon lifted herself carefully up from the sofa and attempted to straighten her dress. Failing, she tugged it over her head, hooked up the straps of her camisole and padded into the kitchen. She'd lost several kilos these past few months and the freckles on her body seemed somehow to have paled with her confidence.

Finding the kettle beneath a pile of streamers and plates, she filled it and hunted around for a couple of mugs. Her movements became quick and precise, as the devastation of her life started suddenly rising within her. But she kept on moving, making the coffee, humming tunefully through the pain and fear while willing herself away from the despair. It was hard, so hard that it was almost impossible to make herself believe she would never be going back to the office again. For her it was over, while for the others it carried on. Her eyes closed, her breath for the moment was locked. It was like losing a child. Not as bad, of course, nothing could be as bad as that, but it felt as bad – it felt as though her precious only child had been taken away and installed in the arbitrary care of strangers. No one had the right to do that, the programme was hers, it was she who had conceived it; she who had nurtured it through to its launch; who had named it, shaped it, set it back on its feet when it stumbled and swelled with pride when it roared. How could they take it away from her now? *How could they*?

'Hey, how are you doing out here?' Lizzy said gently.

Rhiannon let her breath go. 'Fine,' she said, sweeping back her hair. 'Just fine.' She forced a smile. 'I'll survive, even though sometimes it feels like I won't.'

'I know,' Lizzy said, wanting to wrap her arms around her, but knowing that was the surest way to make her break down. Maybe letting go wouldn't be such a bad idea, though, except she had many times these past few months, enough times to know that tears were only a release, never a cure.

'So,' Rhiannon said cheerfully, 'I think we can safely say the party was a success, don't you?'

'Unequivocally,' Lizzy agreed, knowing already how it would be written up in the papers. Rhiannon was popular and everyone knew that Mervyn Mansfield's petty envy was behind her departure, meaning that outrageous innuendo and blood-letting parodies were going to find their way into certain diary columns now that the news of it was out. But no matter how loyal her colleagues, nor how shamed they might make Mansfield feel, for Rhiannon the inevitability of going public with her enforced resignation just meant more hurt and humiliation on top of what she had already suffered when the news of her annulment had leaked out.

'Did you talk to Morgan and Sally at all?' Rhiannon asked, pouring boiling water on to the crystals of instant coffee.

'No, but I smiled a lot,' Lizzy answered.

Rhiannon, in the midst of a yawn, lost it in a laugh. 'Did anyone talk to them?' she wondered.

'The rabbit looked interested for a while,' Lizzy responded, gazing despondently out at the garden. 'What are we going to do about all this mess?' she groaned. 'I don't think I can face it.'

'Oh, it won't take long once I get started,' Rhiannon assured her, carrying two cups of coffee into the sitting-room.

'Well, I'm hardly going to let you do it on your own, am I?' Lizzy retorted, flopping back on to the sofa and unwinding a soggy streamer from around her toes.

'Aren't you?' Rhiannon looked at her, waiting for their eyes to connect. The subtext that had crept into their banter had brought a by now familiar discomfort to Lizzy's eyes.

For days, weeks, ever since she had known she was leaving *Check It Out*, Rhiannon had waited for Lizzy to say she was leaving too, that together, with the skills and contacts they had, they would start a new programme and eventually poach their own team away from Morgan and Sally. To be fair, at the beginning Lizzy had suggested exactly that, but still dazed from the blow, Rhiannon had insisted that Lizzy stay where she was, that the last thing she wanted after all the work they had put in was for the programme to lose its identity which, if Lizzy left too, it almost certainly would.

Now, Rhiannon wasn't at all sure that was what she wanted; in fact, in her heart she knew it wasn't, for though there were times when the programme felt like the most important thing in the world, there were others when she just wanted to smash it apart or erase it as if it had never happened. If it hadn't she might never have met Oliver and she and Lizzy might never have grown so close as to make Lizzy's silence now as bewildering and hurtful as Oliver's betrayal.

Why, Rhiannon wondered, as she sipped her coffee. Why was she afraid to ask Lizzy what was going through her mind? They had never held back on each other before, so why now? Or was this just the start? Was this the way it was going to be? Drifting further and further apart as their lives took different paths and their goals became shared by somebody else. Fear and misery were constricting her throat. It was too much to bear. She couldn't lose Lizzy too, she just couldn't. Without Lizzy she'd never pull through. Yet she could already feel the distance creeping between them, as though Lizzy were being drawn inexorably away, disappearing into a world that was spinning out of reach.

'Have you thought any more about Mavis Lindsay's offer?' Lizzy said. As the words left her lips she could almost feel the dread they had inflicted and wished to God she could take them back. More than that, she wished she could tell Rhiannon what she was planning to do, for that was what Rhiannon was waiting to hear – that her best friend wasn't going to walk out on her too. But Lizzy couldn't do that. She wished to God she could, but if she did she would be giving Rhiannon hope where, for the moment at least, Lizzy believed there to be none.

'Uh, no, not really,' Rhiannon answered hoarsely. 'Well, a bit.'

Lizzy could see how utterly lost and afraid she was,

despite the valiant effort to hide it and the words were forming on her lips to tell Rhiannon her own plans. But still she held back – now wasn't the time. She wondered if there would ever be a time and could have wept at the way fate was dragging them apart. But life had to move on, change had to take place and courage, on both their parts, had to be found. It wasn't that Lizzy was planning to stay with *Check It Out*, because she wasn't, but her future didn't lie with Rhiannon either, no matter how desperately she wished it did. And one of these days, when she judged the time to be right, she would tell Rhiannon what she was going to do – by which time, hopefully, she would be able to explain why she was doing it, because right now she wasn't sure she understood it herself.

'Do you think you can work for someone else? I mean, after all this time of being your own boss?' Lizzy asked, going over old ground, but knowing that it helped Rhiannon to discuss it.

'Mavis is worried about that too,' Rhiannon answered. ' "As you know, sweetie, there can only be one executive producer," ' she said, mimicking Mavis's Scottish accent to perfection, ' "but I'm quite prepared to give you a chance to go back to producing if you're prepared to take it." '

Lizzy's face was a picture of distaste. 'The woman lends a whole new meaning to rock brain of the universe,' she muttered, referring to the music quiz that Mavis produced, 'but at least she's letting you know how you'd stand.'

'True,' Rhiannon agreed. 'And I'm thinking about it.' She sighed. 'Actually, my financial situation being what it is, I'll probably have to take it, since it's the only offer I've had that starts virtually straight away.'

Lizzy's face tightened, but to start berating Oliver now was going to get them nowhere.

Rhiannon's eyes moved to the floor as her heart

twisted with disappointment. It was crazy and she knew it, but she longed to talk about him, to hear his name spoken and be allowed to remember how it had been between them before it had all fallen apart. But nobody liked to mention his name these days, not even Lizzy and the way she, Rhiannon, was trying to blot out the pain by casting her mind back to the spring, to the time when they were so much in love was, she knew, a cowardly retreat from the future. So pulling herself together she took another sip of coffee and said, 'By the way, did I tell you I had a letter from Galina Casimir?'

Lizzy's eyes widened in surprise. 'No, you didn't,' she said, her mind racing ahead in an effort to figure out what this could mean. 'When?' she asked. 'What did she say?'

'It arrived yesterday morning. I forgot about it in the build-up to the party. She's invited me to her wedding.'

Lizzy's mouth fell open at the staggering audacity and unbelievable timing of such an unexpected invitation. 'How can she do that?' she finally cried. 'I mean, how can she write to you now, out of the blue, as though running off with the man you were going to marry was about as major as running off with a cold, and invite you to her bloody wedding? Doesn't she realize what she did? Doesn't she know what's just happened to you? No, no, all right she probably doesn't, but nevertheless ...'

Rhiannon's smile was weak. 'She's marrying Max Romanov,' she said.

Again Lizzy's eyes dilated as she realized she'd temporarily forgotten who Galina Casimir was involved with. Then suddenly she started to laugh. 'Well, it should be quite a wedding,' she said. 'The man's richer than God and she's more beautiful than ever should be allowed. Will you go?'

'I don't know. I haven't really given it much thought.'

'If it's the money ...' Lizzy began tentatively.

'She sent me a ticket,' Rhiannon said wryly. 'First

class, open return.'

'Wow!' Lizzy commented. 'She really wants you to be there.'

'It seems that way.'

'I wonder why.'

'Didn't you know? Always the bridesmaid ...' Rhiannon responded, failing to keep the bitterness from her voice. 'If I go, this'll be my third time.'

'She's asking you to be her bridesmaid?' Lizzy said incredulously.

'Maid of honour,' Rhiannon corrected.

'The woman's got more front than Blackpool.'

Rhiannon laughed.

'Is this the first time she's been in touch since she took off with Phillip?' Lizzy asked after a pause.

'Yes,' Rhiannon nodded.

'Amazing,' Lizzy murmured. 'What else does she say? Anything about Romanov?'

'Just that she's marrying him,' Rhiannon answered.

'Mmm,' Lizzy grunted. 'Nothing about how he got off a murder charge, I suppose?'

Rhiannon arched an eyebrow. 'You know, it's funny that,' she replied, 'she didn't mention it at all and you'd have thought she would, wouldn't you? I mean, it's the kind of thing a person would normally mention in passing, how her fiancé managed to get away with murder.'

'What do they call it?' Lizzy said. 'There's a name for wife murder, isn't there?'

'Uxoricide,' Rhiannon answered.

'Yuk!' Lizzy grimaced. 'Sounds like something you put down the lav.' Then getting up from the sofa she said, 'I'm going to get more coffee. Want some?'

'Mmm,' Rhiannon nodded, passing over her cup.

A couple of minutes later Lizzy was back. 'So,' she said, curling her legs under her as she sat down again, 'you're going to meet the infamous Max Romanov. Remind me what he does again.'

'He's into publishing.'

'That's right. In a pretty big way, as I recall. Aren't they girlie magazines that he produces?'

'I think he publishes journals and magazines on just about every subject you can think of,' Rhiannon answered.

'Mmm, well, it should be an experience, meeting the man himself – I mean, if you do decide to go. Would you like to go?' she ventured. 'Do you think it would give you any problems seeing Galina after all this time?'

'I don't know,' Rhiannon answered. 'I don't think so. In fact, in a way, I'd quite like to see her. I can't really explain it, but when I got the letter it felt ... Well, it was weird. I mean, I was just thinking about her the day before and then there she was, or there the letter was, lying on the doormat. Actually, I've been thinking about her a lot lately, I suppose because of what happened with Oliver ... Well, obviously because of that ...' Her voice trailed off and for a while she seemed lost in thought. Then staring down at her cup, she said, 'Tell me, do you believe in destiny?'

Lizzy's eyes flickered in surprise. 'Yes, I suppose I do,' she answered. 'Why?'

Rhiannon looked at her. 'You mean you don't believe that we can control our lives?' she said.

'In certain ways, yes, but if we had full control, well, we'd none of us ever die, would we?' Lizzy replied.

Rhiannon pulled down the corners of her mouth. 'No, I don't suppose we would,' she remarked pensively. 'And none of us would ever be ill, we'd never get hurt; we'd all be rich, beautiful, talented, happy and gloriously content.'

Lizzy looked at her in surprise. 'Are you saying you think destiny is responsible for all the bad things that happen?' she said.

'No, I just don't think destiny can be denied. Take my own case, for example. I obviously wasn't destined to be married to Oliver and by making it happen I just ended up hurting myself. I believe that's what happens when you try to force destiny. I wanted to be married, I wanted to prove to the world and to my father that someone loved me enough to go through with it and look where it got me.' She paused for a moment, then seeming suddenly to lose patience, she said, 'Oh, what the hell do I know. It's just what I keep telling myself, that destiny has set me another course and that's why all this is happening now, to free me up for whatever life has in store next.'

Lizzy looked impressed. 'Now that I like the sound of,' she said. 'Providing it's good, of course.'

Rhiannon laughed. 'The one thing you can guarantee,' she responded, 'is that there are no guarantees.'

'So we should never trust anyone or anything?' Lizzy challenged.

The light suddenly died in Rhiannon's eyes as she turned to gaze at the garden. 'I'm hardly the person to ask that question,' she said, feeling her heart tighten at how terribly wrong she had been in her unquestioning trust of everything that had mattered so much in her life.

'I'm sorry,' Lizzy said gently. 'I wasn't thinking.'

A minute or more ticked by silently.

'Oliver called again,' Rhiannon said finally. Her voice was flat and toneless, her eyes remained unfocused on the garden.

'When?'

'The day before yesterday.'

'What did he want?'

'To see me. He's here, in London.'

Inwardly Lizzy swore. 'And Marcia?' she said tightly.

Rhiannon shrugged. 'I suppose she's in New York.' She sighed heavily, then sucked in her lips as though to stop herself speaking. 'He says he hates her,' she said in the end. 'He can't stand to be near her, and if you saw her ...'

'It doesn't matter what she looks like,' Lizzy responded, 'he married her.'

'I know.'

'So what did you say when he asked to see you?'

'I said no, the same as I always do.' Her eyes came back to Lizzy's. 'But it's hard,' she said. 'So damned hard. I know that sounds crazy after all that happened, but it's the truth. Or is it? Oh God, I don't know. It's like I just can't get past it. I try to, but every time I think I'm getting somewhere something happens, like a letter arrives for him, or a film comes on the TV that we saw together, or I hear about someone buying a house, or a carpet turns up from Marrakesh. Can you believe that? The carpet actually turned up? I never saw my credit card again, but the carpet I've got. And the bill. Did I tell you that? I've got the bill for the hotel. It was sent here, to me. No mention of Oliver's name on it anywhere. Miss Rhiannon Edwardes, it said, *Miss* Rhiannon *Edwardes*. So tell me why don't I hate him? Why, now I know that he never existed, that the man I loved was just a figment of my imagination, can't I stop loving him? He pretended to be everything I wanted ... He *was* everything I wanted and I'm finding it almost impossible to tell him no, I don't want to see him, because I *do* want to see him. I want none of this ever to have happened. I want him to be the man I thought he was, the man I'm still in love with, the man I thought I married.

'So tell me, Lizzy, why does life dish out this shit? You try to be good to people, you try to be fair and you hope you'll get the same back. But you don't. All you get is smacked in the face, kicked in the teeth – your mother dying when you're just a kid; your father rejecting you; your best friend running off with your bridegroom; your husband dumping you to marry someone else, and the programme you created being snatched out of your hands – and a silence between you and me that I just don't understand and I don't know if I can bear any more. So believing or not believing in destiny doesn't matter a fuck, because whatever you believe, whatever pathetic philosophy you choose to comfort yourself with, it still hurts like fucking hell and if this was all meant to be then you can bloody well keep it.'

The tears were barely visible in the paleness of her face, but the anger and torment glittered darkly in her eyes and tightened her mouth in a way that drew the pain deep into Lizzy's heart. 'I'm sorry,' Lizzy whispered. 'I'm really sorry. It's just that ... Oh God, Rhiannon, I don't want to hold back on you. God knows, it's the last thing I want. And believe me, if I knew how to tell you ...'

'Just tell me!' Rhiannon demanded. 'Just say the words. I feel like the whole damned world is shutting me out and I'm starting to panic, Lizzy. *I'm starting to panic.*'

'I'm going to South Africa,' Lizzy blurted out. 'I'm going to live with Andy.'

Rhiannon's face froze as the words hit her heart like stones. 'When?' she whispered. Then shaking her head, 'Why have you never mentioned this before? I thought ... I thought he wasn't answering your letters ...'

'He's not. I haven't spoken to him since we were there in February.'

Rhiannon's face was white, her eyes wide with confusion. 'Then I don't understand,' she said. 'How can you be going to live with him if you haven't even spoken to him?'

'He asked me once if I would, so now I'm going to spend some time with him and if it works out I'll stay,' Lizzy told her.

Rhiannon's mind was spinning. 'Does he know?' she asked after a pause. 'Is he expecting you?'

'No. I'm going to surprise him.'

'Oh my God!' Rhiannon cried. 'Lizzy, no! You can't do that. It's insane ...'

'I know,' Lizzy interrupted. 'But it's the way I'm

going to do it.'

'But what if he's found someone else? Surely you ...'

'If he has, then I'll know we were never meant to be, won't I?' Lizzy responded, cutting her off.

Rhiannon put a hand to her head and eased her fingers into her hair. 'I don't believe this is happening,' she said through her teeth. 'I just don't believe you'd do something like this.'

'It's why I didn't want to tell you,' Lizzy protested weakly. 'I don't want you to think I'm walking out on you now when ...'

'I'm not talking about me, I'm talking about you,' Rhiannon shouted. 'Where the hell's your pride? You spend one night with the man *and* his brother – let's not forget his brother! – they both screw the ass off you, then neither of them ever contacts you again and now *you* are going to surprise them by turning up on their doorstep. You do remember which twin he was, I take it? I mean you might get them confused, after all it was dark ...'

'Rhiannon stop it!' Lizzy snapped.

Rhiannon's eyes were flashing with rage. 'He was the first man you slept with after Richard died,' she yelled, 'and there hasn't been anyone since, so now you think you're in love and you're going to throw your life away playing Jane to his Tarzan. Well, take it from me, a couple of screws does not a marriage make!'

Lizzy glared at her. 'Perhaps you'd like to tell me what does a marriage make,' she shot back, 'since you seem to be the expert around here.'

Rhiannon flushed and was on the point of biting out another bitter response when she suddenly turned away. Her heart was still thudding with temper and her hand was clenched tightly on the arm of the sofa, but for the moment she said nothing. Her thoughts were in such chaos that she didn't know what she wanted to say anyway. She was aware, however, of a tightness in her chest, or was it in her head, that was bringing back the misgivings she had experienced the day they had left Perlatonga. She couldn't remember exactly what they were now, except she'd had a feeling that one day they would return. And the feeling, she suddenly remembered, hadn't been a good one, as though some inner sense was trying to warn her to stay away. She looked at Lizzy and felt the coldness of anger start to leave her.

'I'm sorry,' Lizzy whispered. 'I shouldn't have said that. It was totally uncalled for and I apologize.'

Rhiannon took a breath, started to speak and found nothing came out. 'No, I'm sorry,' she finally managed. 'I shouldn't have reacted like that, I shouldn't have said those things ... It was just the shock, I suppose.' She focused her eyes intently on Lizzy's. 'Have you thought this through?' she said. 'I mean, obviously you have, but ... Well, I thought you were adamant that the bush wasn't for you, that you couldn't bear to live anywhere but London ...'

'I thought I was too,' Lizzy said, 'but now I'm not so sure. I still think about him all the time, I still write to him even though I've stopped sending the letters. I keep imagining what my life would be like down there, how fulfilled I might be, or bored, or happy, or excited, or cut off ... I try all the scenarios and I keep coming back to the same thing, that I have to give it a go. That destiny, or fate, call it what you will, brought us together for a reason and I have to find out what that reason is. I could be wrong, obviously I could. It might just be the cravings of a sexually deprived forty-year-old that are driving me, but my instincts are telling me that it's more.'

Rhiannon was quiet as she thought about her own instincts and wondered whether she should voice them. 'I have to ask this,' she said in the end. 'How can you be so sure he still wants you when he's never called or written or even acknowledged the copy of the programme we sent him?'

'I can't,' Lizzy answered dolefully. 'Nor can I explain the way I feel, I just feel it. OK, I'm probably going to make a total idiot of myself by turning up on him, but I know I'm going to do it. I don't know when, I just know I will.'

'Won't you even call him when you get to Johannesburg?'

'I hadn't planned to. Hell, I haven't planned anything yet. I just know that I'm going to go. I'll drop the bombshell on Sally and Morgan, on Monday, then ...' she shrugged, 'we'll wait and see. I'll go when I feel the time is right.'

Rhiannon nodded, but it was clear that she was still finding this news hard to adjust to. 'There's never been anything stopping him getting in touch with you,' she pointed out.

'I know. And if he wanted me to be a part of his life he'd let me know. At least you'd think he would. But he isn't letting me know, probably because he doesn't want me, doesn't even think about me.'

'I'm sure he does,' Rhiannon protested. 'But if that's what you think then I just don't understand why you're doing this.'

Neither do I. I told you, I can't explain it. And maybe when the time comes I will call him beforehand and tell him I'm on my way. I just don't know. All I know right now is that I'm not staying with *Check It Out*. Who knows, maybe it's time to set the bird free and see whether it flies or falls without us. I know we hadn't ever planned to do that, but it seems that life has another agenda for us now, and doing what it has to you, it's made me see that we were in danger of becoming satisfied, even smug, with the success we've had and lazy about trying anything new. So perhaps it's time we did. We've both spent the best part of our lives in television and maybe we'll spend the rest of them there too, but right now we've got some time out and it could be that someone somewhere is trying to tell us something.'

Rhiannon smiled. 'Obviously you think they are, or you wouldn't be going to South Africa.'

Lizzy's eyebrows went up as she shrugged. 'We'll see. I think the important thing is that we both move forward.'

Rhiannon instantly felt herself shrink from the prospect. Then with a wry smile, she said, 'Subtle, but I'm getting the message.'

Lizzy smiled too. 'Seeing Oliver isn't going to change anything,' she said softly, 'and you know it. It's just going to cause you more pain and confuse you to the point that you might never let go.' Her eyes were imbued with feeling as she went on. 'Believe me, I know what you're going through. I know what it's like to suddenly run out of road and go over a cliff you had no idea was there.' She gave a mirthless laugh. 'It's hell on earth having your dreams ripped apart and your life suddenly change course on you and if I knew the best way of handling it, believe me, I'd have told you three months ago. But what I can tell you is that I won't be going anywhere until you're ready to grasp the nettle and take the new path that's been set for you. And whatever that path is, I can tell you now it's got sod-all to do with a music quiz.'

Despite the tears in her eyes Rhiannon laughed. 'I need the money,' she pointed out. 'And the contract's only until March.'

'Starting when?'

'The middle of October.'

Lizzy nodded. 'When's Galina's wedding?' she asked.

Rhiannon frowned. 'Uh, October I think. I don't remember the exact date.'

Lizzy sucked her lips thoughtfully between her teeth, while keeping her eyes fixed on Rhiannon's. 'Why don't you go?' she said finally. 'Getting away from here for a while might do you good. OK, I know a wedding is going to be pretty hard to take at this point in your life, especially Galina's, but think of it this way: at least you're getting to see life taking its revenge for what she did to you.'

'How?' Rhiannon said, screwing up her nose.

'Would you want to marry someone who'd killed his wife and got away with it?' Lizzy responded.

Rhiannon chuckled. 'Point taken,' she said.

'And considering how publicity shy the man is,' Lizzy went on, 'if you managed to get yourself some kind of scoop, well, just think what an interview with Max Romanov would do for your career – both sides of the Atlantic.'

Rhiannon was shaking her head and laughing. 'You're incorrigible,' she said.

'But I'm right.'

'You're also crazy if you think he's going to confess to me, on camera, that, actually, by the way, his wife's death was murder.'

'He doesn't have to, we all know it was and we're all fascinated to know how he managed to turn it into a mishap half-way through the preliminary hearings. But I don't suppose we ever will,' she added ruefully. 'No, all you have to do is get him to chat about himself, or Galina, or his companies, his house, his kids – does he have kids? Yes, I thought he did. Get him to talk about being a single parent. Better still, get him to talk about what he's done to help his kids deal with their mother's death.'

Rhiannon's face was in her hands as she laughed. 'You're unstoppable,' she said. 'And who was it saying just now that it's time for a change from TV?'

'I only said it might be,' Lizzy retorted. 'And for an interview like that I'd make a comeback. Except you'd be better at it than me, it's more your kind of thing.'

'Don't let's get carried away,' Rhiannon said. 'To begin with he'd never agree to it, even if I had the nerve to ask, which I wouldn't. And to end with I haven't even decided if I'm going.'

Lizzy's eyes narrowed. 'I thought you said just now that you'd like to see Galina again,' she said.

Rhiannon grimaced. 'I'm curious,' she said.

'Well she's pretty big-time famous now,' Lizzy pointed out. 'What's the name of the make-up again? Conspiracy, isn't it? I bet she'd give you an interview. Actually, if you could get them both together for an interview you'd have every network on the planet knocking at your door. You know, the more I think about this, the more convinced I am you have to go to that wedding. I imagine it's a strictly private affair. Well, it has to be, because it hasn't hit the news at all, at least not that I've heard.'

'Very strictly private,' Rhiannon confirmed. 'Galina has specifically requested that I keep it to myself until such time as Max decides to go public with it – which will very probably be after the ceremony.'

'Well, there you go,' Lizzy laughed. 'You're getting this handed to you on a plate. You get them to let *you* break the news of their wedding and then you run their interviews. No network in the world is going to turn you down, especially not if you've got your wits about you and just happen to be shooting a little home movie of the nuptials as they happen. Crikey, Rhiannon, it might not be worth losing your own husband and programme over, but there again it just might.'

'What!'

'Destiny,' Lizzy reminded her. 'It could just be that this is meant to put you on the map in a way that *Check It Out* never could.'

'Just a minute,' Rhiannon cried, 'how come I've suddenly acquired Olympean-style ambitions while you, who're sitting here plotting it all out, are off to the bush? Maybe I just want a quiet life with a few animals about the place too.'

Lizzy grinned. 'There's always Doug,' she said.

Rhiannon cocked an eyebrow, then leaning forward to put her cup on the table she said, 'Reading between the lines here, I think you're trying to persuade me to go to the wedding so that you can go to South Africa at the same time. Am I right?'

'Guilty,' Lizzy confessed. 'It only occurred to me a few minutes ago that it could work out that way and I don't see any reason yet why it shouldn't. Do you?'

Rhainnon looked at her. 'No,' she said quietly. 'No, I suppose not.'

They sat in silence for several minutes.

'What's she like?' Lizzy said eventually. 'Galina, I mean. What's she like as a person?'

Rhiannon inhaled deeply as she thought. 'Well, she may have changed by now,' she said, 'but the way I remember her ...' She smiled with sudden surprise, 'Actually the way I remember her best is when we were at school. Boy, was she a handful – and weird. She used to frighten the other kids half to death with the stories she told and I have to admit I was afraid of her myself until I got to know her. We had to share a room in one of the school annexes and no one, but no one, wanted to be out there at the far end of the hockey pitch in the dead of night with Galina Casimir for company. Some girls even got their parents to write letters claiming that Galina gave their daughters nightmares, which was true, she did, me included. But my dad wasn't interested in little girls' tantrums so no letter got written to the headmistress to save me from a fate worse than death. Which of course it wasn't, but I remember I hardly slept a wink all that summer holiday I was so dreading going back to school.'

Lizzy was smiling curiously 'What was so frightening about her?' she said.

Rhiannon sighed. 'I don't suppose it was so much her as her grandmother,' she answered. 'I've often wondered since if any of what she told us was true. I know some of it was, like her grandmother being a Russian countess who fled the country, I think some time just before or during the Second World War.' She thought about that for a moment, then sure she was right, she went on, 'You know, with all the things that have been coming out of Russia these past few years I'd say that most, if not all, of Galina's stories were probably true. They were told to her by her grandmother, though why on earth anyone would tell a child such terrible things I'll never know.

'I met the old lady once. She was very tall and very serene-looking, an unmistakable aristocrat, and nothing like I'd imagined she'd be. I was expecting a witch, of course. A witch who ate little children for breakfast, because that was what Galina told us she did.' Rhiannon smiled softly, then after a beat continued. 'I only spoke to her a few times,' she said. 'She was always kind, though in a remote, almost other worldly kind of way. I guess it was all that happened to her during the Stalin years that made her the way she was, and, considering some of the things that went on during that time, I imagine she would be considered fortunate to have come out with even a part of her sanity, no matter how damaged it might be.'

'Do you mean she was mad?'

'Not mad, no. Just not like anyone else I knew.'

'Do you have any idea what did happen to her?' Lizzy asked.

Rhiannon inhaled thoughtfully. 'I believe', she said, 'that she was held prisoner by the NKVD – an earlier incarnation of the KGB – for something like ten or maybe even twelve years. Before that, she was hiding her family in a ghetto somewhere in St Petersburg, or Leningrad as it was known then, keeping them starving and filthy and half demented with lice so that they would blend in with the other kids and not come to the attention of the police. But then one of the neighbours was arrested and the next thing they knew the NKVD was swarming all over the tenement and the Countess's children were taken. Two of them, the younger boy and girl – the girl being Galina's mother – were sent to a camp, though the Countess didn't find that out until many years later, and Vladimir, the eldest son, who tried to defend his mother, was never seen or heard of again.'

'Oh my God,' Lizzy murmured.

'The Countess was taken to the Lubyanka,' Rhiannon continued, 'thrown into a cell that stank of sweat and blood and vomit and God only knows what else, with God knows how many other people, half of whom were already dead or dying. There was a collection once a day, apparently, when the bodies were hauled out and burned, or whatever they did to them, and those who were still alive were either taken somewhere to be tortured for information they didn't have or didn't even exist. Or if they were already tortured beyond coherence they were left, literally, to rot to death. They were rarely given any food, maybe the leftovers from an officer's table or the occasional bucket of offal. No one ever knew where the scraps came from and I guess they were so hungry they didn't stop to ask.

'From what I recall she was in the Lubyanka, or at least one Soviet prison or another, for ten or more years, before some kind of underground group found her and managed to get her out.'

'Where was her husband in all this?' Lizzy asked.

'As far as I know he was around right up until the time of the arrests,' Rhiannon answered. 'But he wasn't at home when the NKVD came and I imagine he didn't even know where his family were taken. According to Galina he was killed during the Battle of Stalingrad.'

'God, there's no happy ending here, is there?' Lizzy complained.

'No one had a happy ending in Soviet Russia,' Rhiannon responded, 'you know that.'

Lizzy nodded and lowered her eyes as though shamed by the levity of her comment. 'So,' she said, 'an underground movement got the Countess out. What then?'

'I don't know all the details,' Rhiannon said, stifling a yawn. 'At least, I can't remember them now. I just know that she ended up in London and that being who she was she had several well-placed connections who eventually managed to track down her daughter. Her other son had apparently died in Kolyma, a Siberian prison camp, when he was eight.'

'How old was he when they took him away?'

'Six or seven, I think. Anyway, they found the-daughter somewhere in Georgia. She was five years old when she was taken from her mother, she was twenty-five when she saw her again. During her time in Kolyma she was repeatedly tortured – even as a child – as well as being sent out in sub-zero temperatures with next to no clothes to help pile wood or shovel snow. The details of those twenty years were always vague in Galina's mind, mainly because no one ever really got to hear them. Her mother couldn't speak, you see. The trauma had robbed her of the power of speech. She wrote some things down, but apparently she didn't like to be reminded of those times and who could blame her? It seems she wasn't beyond romance though, because a couple of years after being rescued by her mother she met and fell in love with an Englishman whose name, as far as I know, was never divulged, which very probably means he was married. Anyway, there's little doubt that whoever he was, he was Galina's father, but after Galina's mother died of TB when Galina was five the Countess took over Galina's upbringing and as far as I know the father's never been heard of again.'

'And Galina's never tried to find him?'

'Not that I know of. She never seemed particularly interested, to be honest.'

'That's unusual.'

Rhiannon shrugged. 'Not if you know Galina,' she said.

Lizzy mulled that over for a moment, then by way of a prompt for Rhiannon to continue she said, 'So her grandmother brought her up?'

Rhiannon nodded. 'I don't think they ever had any money. Everything was grace and favour. The Countess, right up until she died, continued to work at getting people out of Russia and I think those who went on to make their fortunes, or managed to get their fortunes out too, always made sure that she and Galina were taken care of.'

'She sounds a remarkable old woman.'

'Mmm,' Rhiannon responded. 'She was. But her scars never healed. Well, scars like that don't, do they?'

Again they fell into silence until Rhiannon said, 'It feels strange talking about Galina after all this time. I mean, once, she was so much a part of my life that it was natural to think about her. But now, it feels a bit like rediscovering something precious from your childhood and finding out that actually it's quite different to the way you remembered it.' Rhiannon seemed surprised at her reflection. 'You know, I don't think I'd ever considered her unhappy before, but she must have been, the way all the other girls tormented and made fun of her.'

'Why did they make fun of her?' Lizzy said.

Rhiannon pursed her lips thoughtfully. 'Retaliation, I suppose. She would frighten us all by telling us what gruesome things her grandmother would do to us if we didn't leave her alone, so, being kids, we used to dare each other to annoy her.'

Lizzy nodded. 'So how old were you when you two started sharing a room?' she asked.

'Thirteen, going on fourteen. Galina was fourteen the day term started, I remember. She turned up in her chauffeur-driven car, the wicked grandmother nowhere in sight, thank God, walked into the room we were sharing and burst into tears. I always was a soft touch when it came to tears and finding out that it was her birthday and that everyone, including her grandmother, had forgotten, was too much for a thirteen-year-old to bear. I had to make it up to her somehow and looking back I think I went on making up for that forgotten birthday the entire time I knew her.' Rhiannon sighed and shook her head. 'She really knew how to exploit a kindness, but at the same time there was no one kinder than her. She'd think nothing of giving you her last chocolate, her last pair of tights, even her last fifty pence. Just God help you if you ever got in her way, because if Galina wanted Galina got and she didn't care how she went about getting it. She was jealous of everybody and everything, she hated the world; in fact, looking back on it, she was probably one of the most self-centred people I've ever met.

'I'll never forget the day I got back to our room and found all my underwear cut up into pieces. God, what a mess she'd made. And do you know why? Because my bust was bigger than hers. Crazy, I know, but that's the way she was. She was sleeping with boys by then, so that kind of thing mattered to her a lot more than it did to me.' Rhiannon smiled sadly. 'It's quite tragic when you look back on it, but at the time we all used to think she was frightfully grown-up and sophisticated the way she used to sneak out at night and go on dates. She always claimed that she had sex with two or even three boys at a time, but whether or not it was true I've no idea. I know it didn't take her long to graduate to men though, because I saw a couple of them coming to pick her up in their cars. They used to cut up a bit rough sometimes too, but that never stopped her going, never even seemed to bother her, actually. I don't know, she was such a set of paradoxes – as selfish as she was generous; as spiteful as she was loyal; as arrogant as she was shy; and now, with hindsight, probably more screwed-up and lonely than anyone else I've ever known. Had she been less beautiful she'd probably never have got away with half the things she got away with, she might even have received the proper care and attention she so obviously needed, but she was so breath-takingly lovely that I don't think anyone ever really saw beyond it.'

'Beauty's impediments,' Lizzy remarked quietly.

Rhiannon pursed the corners of her mouth. 'She was the most spoiled child I knew and the most ignored. Her grandmother knew people all over the world, particularly in the States, and each holiday Galina would be shipped off to one or other of them, given everything a teenager could ever dream of and more, then transported back to spend the last few days with Granny before restarting school. She adored her grandmother and hated her. She was terrified of her, but used to cry for her at night and watch the post every day for letters bearing the old lady's scrawl. When the Countess died Galina went to pieces. She was in her twenties by then, twenty-two or twenty-three, I think. On the day of the funeral I found her shut up in the old lady's bedroom, all the curtains pulled so it was dark in the room and the old lady's clothes draped all over the furniture. Galina was hugging them, holding them up to her face so she could smell them, and sobbing into them as though they could give her the comfort she craved. She'd been there for almost a week by the time I found her, so by then she was starving and filthy and half-demented with grief.'

'Poor thing,' Lizzy said. 'And there was no other family?'

'Not that I know of. There were plenty of friends, but Galina barely knew them. There was one old man though, who came over from the States for the funeral. She seemed quite close to him, but she never introduced us and when I asked who he was she just said something about her grandmother having helped him once. No, on the whole, she had no one, no family, no friends, except me of course, though that was the first time I'd seen her in three, maybe four years. She went off to the States when she was eighteen, to Los Angeles I think. I can't be sure, because she never stayed in touch and she only ever came back that once, when her grandmother died.'

'And again just before you and Phillip were due to get married,' Lizzy reminded her.

Rhiannon smiled wryly. 'That was a long time later,' she said. 'She told me that she'd inherited a lot of money since we'd last seen each other, I think she said it was from the old man who'd come to her grandmother's funeral. Whether or not it was true I have no idea. She told so many lies, you just never knew with Galina.'

Lizzy grimaced and shifted position. 'Well, whether she inherited a fortune or not, she's certainly about to marry one, so I don't suppose she'll begrudge her tights in the future either.'

Rhiannon smiled. 'You know, five years doesn't seem so long, yet in other ways it feels like a lifetime. She could have changed beyond all recognition in that time, or she could be exactly the same.'

'I'll put my money on her being the same,' Lizzy said. 'Not many of us change that much. Though, on second thoughts, with all that loot coming her way she might be an even bigger nightmare than she already was.'

'Nightmare?' Rhiannon frowned.

'Well she doesn't exactly strike me as the answer to a good night's sleep,' Lizzy responded.

Rhiannon wrinkled up her nose. 'Maybe she's not,' she said. 'But as difficult as she can be, she's totally and utterly adorable too.'

'I'll take your word for it,' Lizzy replied. 'Just let me know if you decide to go over there and I'll book my ticket to Jo'burg.'

Rhiannon's mouth dried. The little trip down memory lane was over and here, at the end of it, was the harshness of reality. 'I honestly think you should call him before you go,' she said. 'Apart from anything else, why waste the money?'

Lizzy's eyes narrowed. 'Thanks for the vote of confidence,' she remarked.

Rhiannon laughed. 'I'm sorry. I didn't mean it like that. It's just come as a bit of a shock to find out that you still feel the way you do about him, or that you'd lay yourself on the line like that. It doesn't seem to make any sense. But then, nothing much does these days. Where are you going?'

'To get a bin liner,' Lizzy answered. 'I'm going to start cleaning up this mess.'

Rhiannon blinked. 'What did I say?' she called out as Lizzy disappeared into the kitchen.

'Nothing. I just think we should start clearing up.'

Getting to her feet, Rhiannon followed her to the kitchen. 'Are you sure I didn't offend you?' she said.

'Positive,' Lizzy laughed. 'Don't be so sensitive. Now, where are the bin liners?'

'Under the sink. Do you know who I was thinking of last night?' she went on after a pause.

'Who?'

'Ramon. You know, the guy who turned up out of the blue in Marrakesh.'

'Oh yes,' Lizzy said, her interest immediately perking up. 'Have you heard from him or something?'

'No. Not a word. I still don't have a clue who he is.'

Lizzy grinned. 'You know, you could be *Check It Out*'s answer to Lois Lane,' she said. 'Did he have his underpants on over his trousers?'

'Very droll,' Rhiannon commented, refraining from reminding her that she was no longer *Check It Out*'s answer to anything.

'But he was a bit of a super hero,' Lizzy protested. 'And, from what you say, a bit of a looker too.'

'He was OK,' Rhiannon responded. 'Not really my type though. Too ... How do I put it? He was too

Mediterranean. I find Mediterranean men slightly effeminate, don't you? All hairy chests and handbags.'

Laughing, Lizzy said, 'I know what you mean, but there's obviously more to Ramon than a hirsute bod and a Hermès bag, wouldn't you say?'

'Mmm, yes I would,' Rhiannon agreed. 'And you know what's really bothering me, what I would really like to know, is how he managed to find me? Or, come to that, why he was even looking, because believe me, if you'd seen that mosque, you'd know it wasn't the kind of place someone just happened to be strolling past.'

'So,' Lizzy said, 'what are you saying?'

'What I'm saying', Rhiannon answered, 'is that I think I'm going to make it my business to find out who he is, if for no other reason than to thank him.'

Chapter 16

'Go on,' Max said, replacing his mobile phone on the dash while using his other hand to spin the car out on to the Pacific Coast Highway.

Galina's lovely blue eyes sparkled with laughter as she recalled what she'd been telling him before the telephone had interrupted her. 'OK. So there I was, doing my PR bit,' she continued, folding out her sun-visor to block the glowing radiance of the sunset, 'trying to get the punters to sign up for a make-over, when this voice suddenly booms out over the crowd, "y'all keeping the girl too thin now. Yessirree, she sho' looks unnerfed to me." She was a huge great mama, with a chest like a pillow and a smile that was so white you expected it to ping. She was fifty-seven, she told me, and her skin, which she made me touch, was, to quote her, softer than liquorice. She didn't need no conspiracy to keep her looking young, she said. But I needed one of her special fruit cakes to fill me out, so I just had to run along now and get myself together to go back to her place for a tea fit for the Queen of England.'

Max was smiling. 'Where was this?' he said.

'Some department store in Memphis,' Galina answered with a dismissive wave of her hand. 'Or maybe it was Baton Rouge. They're all beginning to blend into one now.'

Max glanced at her and as their eyes met she started

to laugh.

'So, you went back to this old mammy's place for cake?' he said, lacing her fingers through his.

'Yeah. Why not?' Galina responded. 'She was cute. I liked her and she was serious about me being too thin. I mean, she was genuinely concerned, I could see that, so I gave the Svengalis the slip and went off to do my own thing for a while.'

Laughing, Max glanced in the rear-view mirror and pressing his foot down hard, pulled out to overtake a convoy of U-Hauls as they climbed the hill towards Malibu.

Delighted with his laughter, Galina raised his hand to her lips and kissed it. Her lovely face was glowing, her short, dazzlingly blonde hair contrasted with her olive skin like a sunlit mist around a bronze. The fact that she had caused a full-scale panic in the Conspiracy camp with her two-and-a-half-hour truancy was a matter of great amusement to her, now that Max found it funny too. Dealing with all the frayed nerves and angry relief when she'd returned in one piece hadn't been quite so much fun though. Even less fun was being torn off a strip by Maribeth Courtini, Primaire's West Coast President, who had leapt on the first plane out of LA to join in the search. Galina could understand that Maribeth would be angry about the wasted journey, but had she not apologized for her outburst the instant it was over, Galina might very well have walked out on her contract, for she certainly did not appreciate being spoken to like that, especially not in front of other people. Fortunately, though, Maribeth had remembered, just in the nick of time, that Max Romanov had yet to be told how Galina had managed to slip her security net. From the outset his instructions had been explicit: when travelling away from Los Angeles Galina was to be watched twenty-four hours a day, either by a Primaire representative or a security guard, preferably both. On top of that, all her telephone calls were to be monitored, both those she made and those she received, and reported back to Max. Maribeth was one of the few people who appreciated why the security around Galina had to be so tight and had she been able to tell the others then this unfortunate lapse might never have occurred. As it was, someone had relaxed their vigil somewhere and for that heads would roll. It was the only way to make sure it never happened again.

Smiling contentedly to herself, Galina now turned to look out at the million-dollar luxury estates they were passing as they drove towards home. The best part of the entire escapade was that she'd lied through her teeth about where she'd been and no one, not even Max, had managed to find out. In fact, the whole thing had been so easy to pull off that she was tempted to try it again. She'd be careful not to push her luck, though, for the only reason Max hadn't found out the truth this time, she was sure, was because he was so preoccupied with Marina. In fact Galina had been surprised when he'd come to collect her from Maribeth's Brentwood condo himself just now, when he could easily have sent someone else; though, after three weeks away, she'd have been sorely disappointed if he hadn't shown up himself. But she'd have understood, for Marina was becoming a very real concern to them both lately and despite Galina's pleasure at seeing him walk in the door earlier she was sorry now that she had made him leave his daughter.

It seemed that Max was about to speak when his telephone rang again.

'At least you know it's not me,' Galina quipped, wondering whether her constant calls when they were apart irritated him. If they did he never gave any sign of it, but Max was a master at disguising his feelings, as those who knew him well were only too aware. And even if he did mind, Galina knew she'd continue to call anyway, for just the idea of going more than a few hours without speaking to him was intolerable.

By the time he finished his call they were turning into the Romanov estate. The palm and maple lined avenue was dappled with sunlight and shade as the dark Mercedes saloon glided smoothly towards the house and Galina rested her head on Max's shoulder.

'Did someone bring some things over from my apartment?' she asked.

'Yes,' he answered. 'Enough for a couple of nights, if you want to stay that long.'

Galina chuckled. 'I'll be staying for good soon,' she reminded him, stretching out her left hand and admiring the discreet marquise-cut sapphire he had given her the day they had settled on a wedding date.

'You can stay for good now,' he told her, kissing the top of her head as he brought the car to a standstill in front of the house.

'Do you want me to?' she asked, turning to look up into his eyes.

'You know I do.'

'But nothing would change when we got married if I moved in with you now,' she objected.

He shrugged. 'We'll do it whichever way you want,' he said.

Her eyes remained on his for some time as she wondered what he was really thinking, if he really meant what he was saying. 'Can we make love tonight?' she said huskily.

Though it was fleeting, she felt his resistance as though it were a sharp slap in the face and drawing away she made to get out of the car.

'Honey,' he said, taking her arm and pulling her back. 'Galina, listen to me,' he said as she tried to snatch her arm away. 'I've told Marina she can sleep with us tonight. She's looking forward to seeing you. She'll be waiting up for you.'

Galina's head fell forward as she struggled to contain

her resentment and remind herself that Marina was just a child. 'Are you sure you're not using her as an excuse?' she said through her teeth.

'Hey, come on,' he protested. 'She needs help. You know that.'

'And I need you,' she cried, turning to look at him and glaring fiercely into his eyes.

'I know,' he said. 'But right now we've got think of Marina.'

'And when we get married? Will we still have to think about her then?' She slapped a hand impatiently on the dash. 'What the hell am I saying? Of course we'll have to think about her then. But tell me, Max, is she going to be sleeping with us every night for the rest of our lives? Will we ever get any time for ourselves?'

'Of course we will.'

Her eyes were still simmering with temper. 'And when we get this time, will we make love?' she challenged.

His eyes held resolutely to hers as deep down inside he fought the revulsion. 'If we do, we do it my way,' he told her quietly.

Galina's jaw stiffened as her perfect nostrils flared and her blue eyes turned to ice. 'You hate me, don't you?' she declared.

'I love you, Galina. You know that.'

'Then make love to me, god-damnit!'

Again he looked at her and allowed seconds to pass before he spoke. 'Where did you go in Memphis?' he asked softly.

Galina started, but recovered herself quickly. 'I told you,' she replied, 'I went to have ...'

'Cut the bullshit,' he interrupted. 'I want to know where you were.'

'Having tea with an old lady,' she seethed. 'If you don't believe me ...'

'I want to believe you, but you tell so many god-damned lies ...'

'Well this time I'm not lying. I went to have tea with an old lady who gave me some cake. And I don't know why you're attacking me when you're the one whose picture was in the paper going into some restaurant in Brooklyn with Luigi Avellino who everyone knows is a mobster. So maybe you'd like to explain that?'

To her surprise, after a moment's hostile silence, he started to laugh. 'OK, you want to know, I'll tell you,' he said. 'I'm considering getting into the prostitution racket and I thought Avellino could give me some pointers.'

Galina's face was tight with fury, but as he finished her mouth started to tremble with laughter. 'You're a terrible liar,' she told him, knowing that the Mafia's control of magazine distribution meant that he frequently did business with them.

'Only when I want to be,' he responded. 'So, are you going to come inside or are we going to sit here all night?'

'Where're the children?' she asked.

'Waiting for you in the den. Marina's put all your cuttings in a book and the TV ads on to one tape. She's dying to show you.'

Galina's face softened. 'Did she do all that for me?' she said.

'Sure she did. She loves you, honey. We all do. You've just got to learn to love yourself.'

'I know,' she responded, her eyes moving sightlessly towards the house. 'Do you think I ever will?' she asked solemnly. 'I mean, after everything I've done.' Then without waiting for him to answer she said, 'At least I don't have murder on my conscience; I don't think I could live with that.'

Max's face was inscrutable as he watched her for a while, then said, 'We have to make up our minds whether we're going to hold the ceremony in the house or the garden.'

Galina's dazzling eyes came up to his. 'I'll marry you anywhere,' she said hoarsely, 'just so long as I marry you.'

Ula, Max's personal assistant, pushed the print key on her computer, shot up from her desk and grabbed the phone. Next to her, at his own desk, Maurice Remmick, Max's lawyer, was engaged in a rapid exchange with the New York broker about an article Susan Posner – The Poisoner – had published in that morning's *LA Times* alleging that Max had been involved in some kind of insider trading when he'd purchased a whole whack of Primaire stock just prior to the announcement of Galina's contract. Ellis Zamoyski, Max's finance director and Ula's live-in lover, was engrossed in the preparation of a new take-over bid that Max was going to present to the board the following week.

They were, all three of them, in the spacious, west-facing study of Max's Malibu home, where their own desks were grouped around Max's, giving only Ellis a straight-on view of the ocean. The room was a basic rectangle, with cool, whitewashed walls, a neutral ceramic floor and a low, flat ceiling. On the walls was an impressive collection of black lacquer-framed photographs, mostly of Stephen Richardson's metaphysical connections between disparate objects. The few pieces of occasional furniture scattered about the room were each of a fascinating and unique design, like the post-modernist pyramid table in bleached eucalyptus wood and air-brushed glass, or the priceless figurative sculptures imported from Spain, or the baffling cubist chairs that Max's dealer had picked up at a Paris auction. The vast sliding windows on the west side of the room led out on to a marble-tiled courtyard and on the east to sloping acres of diligently tended garden. The island of four desks just off-centre of the room, where the latest computer technology jostled for supremacy over landline telephones and Ula's precious Rolodex, was the very hub of Romanov Enterprises; those who presently occupied it were the absolute mainstay of Max Romanov's life.

Ula paused for a moment, allowing herself to feel the welcome touch of a sea breeze as it drifted languidly across the room. Her short, inky black hair was finger-combed back from her face and the colour in her cheeks was making her look as fraught as she was feeling. It was the middle of the day, it was hot, the air-con had packed up an hour ago and her head was aching fit to burst. On top of the day's normal workload, which was considerable, calls were coming in from all over, requesting confirmation of the rumours that Max and Galina were getting married. Thousands upon thousands of dollars were being offered by newspapers and TV for exclusives on the wedding, while caterers, florists, photographers, dressmakers, printers, musicians, entertainers, hoteliers, clairvoyants, even the clergy, were all offering their services *gratuit* just for the chance to be associated with the 'wedding of the year'. Ula's response was the same every time: she knew nothing about a wedding and hoped they all had a nice day.

Picking up the invitation list that had just rolled off the printer, she gave it a quick look over, then tucking it into her wedding file she sent the electronic version to Max's E-mail address. Right now he was in Washington attending a publishers' convention; later today he was taking the company jet to Baltimore where Galina was shooting a commercial. Tomorrow the two of them would fly back to LA, then the countdown would begin.

Ula glanced at her calendar. Eleven days to go. All fifty of the invitations had now been accepted, though Rhiannon, Galina's friend, had yet to confirm that she could fly over from London four days earlier than originally planned – in other words a full week before the wedding. Quickly calculating the time difference between LA and London, Ula spun her Rolodex, then punched Rhiannon's number into the phone. After three rings the answering machine picked up. Ula left a message asking Rhiannon to get back to her about the change of flight so she could make arrangements to have her collected from the airport. Also, Galina was wondering whether Rhiannon would like to stay at the house in Malibu or at Galina's apartment in Marina del Rey. Maybe Rhiannon would like to get back to her, Ula, about that too, so she could get things set up.

After replacing the receiver, Ula keyed in her E-mail and found a message from Lauren, Max's PA in New York. Someone from *People* magazine had managed to obtain the exact time and date of the wedding. Did Ula think Max would like to make a change?

No, Ula didn't think so, but she'd check with Max first.

'It was bound to get out,' Maurice said, when Ula told him. 'And you know as well as I do that even if Max wanted to make a change Galina would never stand for it. She called earlier, by the way, wanting to know what time Max was getting into Baltimore tonight.'

'Yeah, she called me too,' Ellis said, glancing up from his monitor. 'Max got his phone turned off or something?'

'He's at a convention,' Ula reminded him.

'Oh, sure,' Ellis said, returning to his screen. 'What news on the insider trading?' he asked Maurice.

'Don Pink wants to issue a statement first thing tomorrow,' Maurice replied, referring to Max's New York broker. 'He's getting one drawn up now for Max's approval. My guess is Max'll take a run past it. They can't prove anything and you know how he feels about getting involved in anything that'll put his name in lights.'

'Oh shit, that reminds me,' Ellis said, making quantum leaps in thought connection, 'Galina's friend, Rhiannon, called first thing. She's arriving Saturday. I wrote the details down somewhere,' he added, searching the paperwork on his desk.

'I just left a message on her machine asking for this,' Ula said, snatching the Post-It out of his hand. 'Did you stop by the vet's this morning, like I asked?'

'Sure I did,' Ellis responded, obviously pleased to have got something right.

'So?' Ula prompted. 'How's the cat?'

'Oh, yeah,' Ellis said. 'Yeah, he's doing fine. We can pick him up on our way back through. He said to say he mee-owses you,' he added with a wink at Maurice.

'God, you're so anal sometimes,' Ula responded. 'Don't you think he's anal, Maurice?'

'Count me out of this one,' Maurice said, reaching for his phone. Ula's snipes at Ellis were what passed as domestic harmony between those two and like all their other friends, Maurice knew better than to get involved. 'Maurice E. Remmick,' he said into the phone as Mrs Clay, the children's nanny, walked in with a loaded tray.

'E?' Ula said, looking at Ellis.

Ellis shrugged and was about to turn his attention to lunch when he heard Maurice say: 'Sure. How you doing, Denton? Long time no hear.'

'Is that Denton Fairfax? From Jackson?' Ellis butted in. 'Tell him I'm still waiting on those figures he promised. He should have had them here ...'

Maurice held up his hand for Ellis to stop. 'No, there's just me, Ellis and Ula,' he said. 'Max is in Washington, but I can always reach him if it's urgent.'

'Yeah, I'd say it's urgent,' Fairfax responded. He was the CEO for the Tennessee, Alabama and Louisiana based publications of Romanov Enterprises. 'I got some pictures here,' he said, 'and I'm telling you now, they ain't the kind of pictures you're going to be happy to see. You know Brian Sealon?'

'The editor of *Southern Belle*?' Maurice replied, referring to one of the three adult magazines that was owned by Romanov.

'That's him,' Fairfax responded. 'Good guy. Knows what he's doing. The pictures were delivered to him this morning and he brought them straight to me. So, is there something going on over there that you guys aren't telling the cops about?'

Maurice frowned. 'I'm not following you, Denton,' he said.

'I'm talking about the girlfriend, Galina Casimir,' Fairfax explained. 'Do you know where she is right now?'

'Sure, she's with the Conspiracy people in Baltimore. I just talked to her five minutes ago.'

Fairfax paused. 'OK,' he said, 'so this isn't about what I thought it was about. But I got to tell you, Maurice, it still isn't looking good. These shots I got here, well ...'

'I take it they're of Galina,' Maurice said, shooting a look at Ellis and Ula.

'Yes, that's who they're of. And if there's no kidnapping going down, then all I can say ... Hell, I don't know what to say, and once you see this stuff you'll know what I mean.'

'Put him on the speaker,' Ellis said as the door closed behind Mrs Clay.

Maurice punched the button and Fairfax's voice came into the room. '... they're going to cost Max a packet to keep out of the press,' he said.

'Exactly what are the shots of?' Maurice asked, his eyes rooted to Ellis's.

Fairfax gave a mirthless laugh. 'I don't know if I care to describe them,' he answered.

'Oh Christ,' Ula muttered. 'Who took them? Do you know?'

'These aren't the kind of shots you leave your card with, Ula,' Fairfax responded. He was quiet for a moment, then said, 'You know, I can't make head nor tail of this. I mean, in some she looks just about terrified out of her mind. She's all squeezed up in a corner and you'd think, looking at her, that some kind of psycho was coming at her. I mean, we're talking real terror here. Yet there's this other one I'm looking at where ... Well, hell, she looks like she's giving it away for free.'

Ula looked at Maurice and Ellis. 'How many shots are there?' she asked.

'A dozen or more. Ten by eight colour.'

'Is she easily recognizable?'

'Even with an eight-inch cock in her mouth there's no mistaking it's her,' Fairfax said crudely.

Maurice winced. 'Have you got any idea where the negatives are?' he asked.

'Not yet. Brian's working on it now.'

'Brian?' Ellis mouthed.

'The editor,' Maurice reminded him. 'Who else knows about this?' he asked.

'As far as I know, just me, Brian and the dude who delivered the shots.'

'Did he tell you the price tag?' Ellis wanted to know.

'Not yet. But you can bet your life one's on the way. Do you want a couple of samples down the wire? It might give you some idea how much you should expect to pay.'

A few minutes later Maurice was holding half a dozen photographs of Galina. Whoever the guy with her was he'd been careful not to show his face, but when it came to exposing other parts of his anatomy he'd been nowhere near so discreet. It would appear that Fairfax had spared them the shot of oral sex, but the explicit angles of a cowering and terrified Galina with tears pouring down her cheeks and pleas for mercy contorting her face were more than any of them wanted to see. The violation she had suffered was total, the pain and terror seemed almost to animate the shots.

Fairfax's voice came over the speaker. 'You still there?'

'Yeah, we're still here,' Maurice answered, turning the

last couple of shots round for the others to look at. They were the ones that had confused Fairfax, for Galina was laughing and, like he'd said, appeared to be a willing, if not controlling, participant in the sexual act she was engaged in. They came as no surprise to Ellis, Ula and Maurice, though.

'I'd like to get this sorted before Max gets ahold of it,' Maurice said. 'Is there any chance?'

'Depends on the guy with the negs,' Fairfax answered. 'Like I said, Brian's working on finding out who he is. I'll let you know as soon as I hear anything worth telling.'

As the line went dead Ellis looked at the last couple of pictures again and could do nothing to stop the twinge in his groin. He wondered if they were having the same effect on Maurice and Fairfax. He'd lay money they were, for surely no red-blooded man could look at a picture of a woman as wanton as that, with a penis half-inserted inside her, and not wish it were his.

Throwing them on the desk, he sat down and buried his face in his hands. Ula picked them up, looked them over slowly, then said, 'So it seems Max was right about Memphis.'

Ellis lifted his head. 'You know what I'm thinking?' he said, 'I'm thinking we're gonna have to get hold of those negatives before the seller takes them to Primaire.'

'If he hasn't already,' Maurice said.

They were all quiet for a moment until looking at Ula Maurice said, 'Didn't anyone see who she went off with down there in that Memphis store?'

Ula shook her head. 'Not that Maribeth could find out. One minute she was there, the next she was gone. No one remembers seeing her go, which is pretty damned weird if you ask me, considering she's the star attraction. You'd think everyone would be watching her, wouldn't you?'

Ellis's thoughts were clearly travelling in another direction. 'Did we check out that guy of a few years ago?'

he said. 'The one it turned out she stole from her best friend.'

'Yeah, we checked him out right at the start,' Maurice answered. 'He's clear. Living in Oklahoma with some night-club singer now.'

'So, what do we do?' Ula said after a pause.

Maurice and Ellis looked at her.

'Well, there's no way we're gonna be able to keep this from Max,' she said, 'so do we wait for him to come back, or do we get him on the phone now and make his day?'

It was Maurice who answered. 'Let's wait and see what Fairfax gets back with.'

Three hours later Denton Fairfax had vanished. According to *Southern Belle*'s editor, Brian Sealon, Fairfax now had the negs, but how he had managed to pay for them or even locate them was a mystery to all. All Sealon knew was that one minute he, Sealon, was on the case, trying to track down the negs and the next Fairfax was saying he had them in his hand and would be back in the office the next day. Where he was planning to be until then was anyone's guess.

Maurice was extremely nervous. So was Ellis. If Fairfax had the negatives they didn't understand why he hadn't called to say so. Nor did they understand why the recovery had necessitated a trip out of the office that was going to last the rest of the day. So what the hell was the man doing and why wasn't he keeping in touch the way he had been told? Surely to God he wasn't pulling some kind of double-bluff, not when he was a personal friend of Max's. But holding that kind of key to that kind of bank could do strange things to a man.

At that moment Ula was talking to Galina, assuring her again that Max would get to Baltimore on schedule. Ellis was on the line to Boston where another of Romanov's adult publications was located, checking out that no one had been in touch there trying to sell some unusual goods. Maurice was speaking to Brian Sealon who had just called to let them know that there was a rumour going down in Jackson that Max Romanov was about to be arrested for some kind of insider trading.

'Hell, where do you guys get your information?' Maurice was grumbling. 'The Poisoner's got nothing to substantiate her story, 'cos it just didn't happen. I'm telling you, as his lawyer, it didn't happen. And if there was an arrest going down I'd know about it. So what's new on Fairfax? Did you locate him yet?'

'Put me on to Dag Vasser,' Ellis barked into the phone as he made the connection with another of Romanov's adult magazines.

'Galina, you're being a pain in the proverbial,' Ula told her bluntly. 'I got other things to do here than keep taking calls from you with the same darned questions. Shit, it's your wedding I'm trying to organize, so give me a break will you.'

'Tell him it's Ellis Zamoyski and it's urgent,' Ellis said.

'Hey, Galina, you nearly made me laugh,' Ula cried.

'Dag? Zamoyski. Yeah, I'm doing fine. So tell me, did anything unusual show up on your desk today? Something you don't normally get that you might want to tell me about?'

'OK,' Maurice said to Sealon. 'Keep in touch,' and he banged the phone down.

'Yeah, it is pretty hectic here,' Ula told Galina. 'Mainly thanks to you, sugar.'

Maurice's and Ula's eyes met as Maurice began pressing out Max's mobile number. It was still disconnected.

Ellis was trying to break into Dag Vasser's diatribe on just what kind of shit had turned up on Vasser's desk that day, that was no different from any other day, but did Ellis have any idea how many sickos there were out there? 'Yeah, I get your point,' Ellis sympathized. 'Yeah, sure. Dag, listen ... For Christ's sake man, give me a break here, will you? We got an emergency on our hands and I need you ...'

'I don't know how the news got out about your wedding,' Ula protested. 'We're not even certain it has yet. It's just a suspicion. Yeah, sure that's what all the noise is about. What else would it be about? I don't know. You tell me.'

Maurice keyed his phone pad to take an incoming call. 'Maurice Remmick,' he answered.

'What happened to the E?' Ula demanded in a quick aside.

'I hear what you're saying, Dag,' Ellis said, 'but I'm just not in a position to tell you any more than that. That's right, yeah. We got word a few hours ago. It could just be some whacko on a whim, but we can't be too careful. The stuff he claims to have is pretty sensitive and Max isn't gonna want it made public, not under any circumstances. I don't know why the guy might contact you, chances are he won't. But I want you to put all your key people on alert and if anything comes their way ... Trust me, they'll know. Yeah, that's right, then you call us here in LA.'

'OK, honey,' Ula smiled. 'I'll tell him if I speak to him first. Aleks and Marina send their love, by the way. I know I told you that earlier, but they said to tell you every time you called. OK, OK, so I forgot a couple of times.'

As Ula and Ellis hung up their calls, they were both on the point of taking fresh ones when Maurice signalled for them to stop.

'Sure, I really appreciate you letting me know this, Ed,' he was saying to the president of Romanov Enterprises in New York. 'No, I don't know the ins and outs of it yet, but believe me it'll be sorted by the end of the day. Do they have the numbers here? Just Ula's. OK. If there's any more news you know how to get ahold of me. I'll be over there just as soon as I can.'

'What was all that about?' Ellis asked as Maurice rang off.

'The FBI are trying to track down Max over this insider trading,' Maurice answered, his face looking haggard as his mind raced in a thousand different directions. 'That was Ed Sherwin on the line. A Federal Agent just contacted him and Ed's given him Ula's number.'

Ula's eyes dropped to the flashing lights in front of her.

'Why not yours?' Ellis said. 'You're his lawyer.'

'Sherwin wanted to warn me first,' Maurice answered, looking at his watch. 'I'm going over to New York to put the brakes on this before it gets out of hand. I'll keep trying Max. If either of you guys speaks to him first have him call me right away.'

'What do we tell him about Denton Fairfax and what's going on in Jackson?' Ula asked.

'You'll just have to give it to him straight,' Maurice told her as he started packing up his briefcase. 'He's a big boy. He can handle it.'

Ula looked at the phone lights again. 'Oh, hi, Max,' she said, faking a call. 'How you doing? Oh yeah, things this end are just great. The date of your wedding has leaked out. Galina's got herself photographed with some guy's dick and the FBI want to question you about the Primaire stock deal. I'm out of here,' she said, getting to her feet. 'Ellis, you can answer the phones.'

Ellis looked at Maurice. 'What do you want me to tell the Feds when they call?' he asked.

'The truth. That Max isn't contactable right now and his lawyer is *en route* to New York. Take his number and tell him you'll get a message to me to have me call him as soon as I arrive in the city.'

Ellis nodded. 'And Fairfax?'

'You're on your own with that one,' Maurice replied, heaving his briefcase off the desk. 'I don't know what the guy's about and none of us will until he decides to get in touch.'

By seven that evening Ula and Ellis had fielded over a

hundred calls, most of them wanting to know if it was true that Max was going to be charged with insider trading. Pleading surprise and ignorance, they moved from one call to the next, both fervently hoping that it would be the other who picked up on Max. Maurice was in the air now, due to arrive in New York some time around ten, where the FBI were waiting on his call. There was still no word from Fairfax and Galina was at a hotel just outside Baltimore wanting to know why Max hadn't showed up yet.

'Wouldn't we all like to know,' Ellis grunted as he clicked off the line from Galina. 'We still got him on auto-call-back?' he asked Ula as she dropped the receiver and flopped back in her chair.

'Yep,' she replied, running her hands over her face. 'What about the cat?' she said, suddenly bringing her head up. 'Someone's got to go collect the cat.'

'I'll call and say we'll come by tomorrow,' Ellis yawned, reaching for the phone. 'Or why don't you go ask Leo if he'll do it now?' he said, referring to the ageing household manager.

'Yeah, I'll do that. I'll look in on the kids while I'm at it too. I just wish the hell Max would ring. Did you see Marina's face just now when I told her we couldn't get through to him?'

Ellis nodded sombrely. 'I asked Galina to call her, that should keep her happy for a while. Ask Cook if there's any more of that pasta she brought in earlier, will you?'

Ula treated his waistline to a disdainful look and was just heading out of the door when she heard him say, 'At last! We've been trying to get ahold of you since noon.'

Immediately Ula turned back and went to sit on the edge of her desk as Ellis put the call on the speaker.

'Where have you been, man?' Ellis demanded. 'All hell's been breaking loose here ...'

'Did you speak to Galina?' Max's voice came into the room, cutting him off.

'Sure. She's in Baltimore wanting to know where the hell you are.'

'Is she OK?'

Ellis's eyes flicked to Ula. 'Mad as hell,' he answered, 'but yeah, I guess she's OK.' He paused. 'We got a bit of a problem though, Max. Well, actually, it's a hell of a problem. Denton Fairfax called earlier ...'

'I know,' Max interrupted. 'I'm in Memphis now. Denton's right here with me.'

Ula and Ellis stared at each other. 'Denton Fairfax is with *you*?' Ellis said stupidly. 'I thought ...'

'Yeah, I know what you thought,' Max said. 'But he's right here with me and I've got the negs.'

Ula was reeling.

'Destroy the copies Denton sent you,' Max went on. 'The situation's sorted.'

'How much?' Ellis asked, ever the accountant.

'We'll talk about it when I get back,' Max answered prosaically.

'Did you manage to find out who the guy in the pictures was?' Ula asked.

'No.'

Ula looked at Ellis.

'So who did you hand the cash over to?' Ellis wanted to know.

'The photographer.'

'Didn't he tell you who the guy was?'

'He says there were two guys besides him. One was in the shots, the other just hung around watching.'

'No rogue shots of either?'

'Not that we could find.'

'Are you certain you got all the negs?'

'As certain as we can be.'

Ellis frowned. 'So what happens now? Will you put a watch on the photographer?'

'Where's Maurice?' Max asked, ignoring the question.

Ellis looked at Ula, then nodded to the speaker as

though inviting her to reply.

Glaring at him, Ula said, 'Maurice is on his way to New York, Max. We had a call from the FBI. They want to talk to you about the allegations The Poisoner ran regarding the acquisition of Primaire stock.'

'What time will Maurice get to New York?' Max wanted to know.

'In a couple of hours,' Ellis answered, gathering from the tone of Max's voice that the FBI enquiries had come as no surprise either.

'Good. OK,' Max responded. 'I'm gonna call the kids now. Ula, get on to Galina will you and tell her I'll see her back in LA tomorrow night, unless I have to go to New York.'

'She's not gonna be happy to hear that, Max,' Ula warned, while groaning inwardly at the prospect of being the messenger.

'I'm not too happy with her right now,' Max retorted sharply. 'But don't tell her that. Just tell her I got caught up in Washington and I'm having dinner with the President so I don't have time to call.'

'She won't believe that.'

'She's not supposed to.'

Flattening her lips and raising her eyebrows Ula turned to Ellis as he started to speak. But Max cut him off.

'Ramon's flying in on Friday,' he said. 'I want you there at the airport to meet him, Ellis.'

Ellis's eyes widened. 'You got it,' he replied. So Max *was* going to put a watch on the photographer. 'Where's he gonna be staying?'

'At the house,' Max answered. 'OK, I'm gonna call the kids now. If there's anything else, you know where to get hold of me.'

The following morning, as Max flew to New York and Galina returned to LA, Denton Fairfax sat in his Jackson office looking down at a copy of the *Memphis Times*. On the third page, only a few column inches from the story of Max Romanov's suspected insider trading, was a brief report of how Memphis photographer, Carl Broadhurst, had been found in his downtown studio with a bullet through his head. Broadhurst, it said, was twenty-eight, had lived in Memphis all his life and was well known in the gay community. Police had no leads at this time and were asking anyone who knew the victim or who had seen anything unusual around the location between five and seven o'clock on the afternoon of the ninth to contact them on the number below.

Two days later Ramon Kominski flew into LAX via Houston, carrying a false passport and driver's licence. Ellis was waiting in the arrivals lounge, as instructed by Max. As the two men met they shook hands warmly, then started out to the parking lot.

'How long are you staying?' Ellis asked.

Ramon's slightly crooked teeth flashed in a grin. 'That depends,' he answered in his heavily accented English.

'You know Max has been arrested?'

Ramon halted his step; the pupils of his dark-green eyes were boring into Ellis.

'For insider trading,' Ellis explained, then frowned, as Ramon visibly relaxed.

'That's Maurice's concern,' Ramon said. 'My concern is only to discover who is doing these things to Max and Galina.'

And then? Ellis was tempted to ask. But he didn't. It was none of his business and he would be better off not knowing anyway. Ramon Kominski was older now, had settled into a nice comfortable life, way up in the hills of the beautiful Pyrenean province of Avlana. But it wasn't so many years ago that he had led a ruthless and determined band of Separatists in their fight for an independent state. Killing was almost second nature to Kominski, the first and only surviving grandson of an impoverished Russian Jew and his beloved Basque wife. Terrorism was as much a part of Ramon's life as the Dow Jones was of Ellis's. It had come to him with his mother's milk. And there was nothing that Ramon Kominski wouldn't do for Max Romanov, the first and only grandson of the wealthy Russian Jew who had helped so many to escape the raging brutality of communism – Ramon's grandfather included.

When they got to the house Ula was waiting for them with the news that Max's bail hearing had been set for an hour hence. It was the first time Ula had met Ramon and she felt herself shiver at the danger and excitement he exuded. He was about the same height as Ellis, but much fitter and more solid and whilst not exactly better looking he had an air about him that was so commanding that even the clocks seemed to pause. And that voice ...

'I'm sorry,' she drooled, 'what did you say?'

Ramon's green eyes were dancing. 'I asked if I might clean up after my travel, then maybe I take a look at the wedding list,' he said.

'Here, take it with you,' Ula said, thrusting it into his chest as though she'd be equally happy to come with it.

Chuckling as he walked out of the room and Ellis grabbed Ula back, Ramon followed Leo to the guest wing. As they went, Ramon quickly scanned the list, making a mental note of the names he didn't know. It was on the second run-through that he fixed on a name near the top of the page, a name he was sure he knew, but for the moment was struggling to place. Then, suddenly remembering, the corners of his eyes creased with surprise and by the time he reached his room he was smiling quite openly.

Waiting only until Leo had left, he threw the list on the bed, stripped off his clothes, then went to stand at the open french windows where he gazed down on the breath-taking view of the ocean. So the girl from Marrakesh was going to be at the wedding, was she?

Laughing aloud, Ramon turned back into the room and, hands behind his head, sprang full length on to the bed. This was going to make life even more interesting than he'd anticipated – providing, of course, Max managed to get himself out of jail.

Chapter 17

'Rhiannon! Rhiannon!'

Rhiannon scanned the airport crowd half smiling and half frowning as she tried to locate the voice.

'Over here!' Galina called.

Rhiannon saw her, leaping up and down at the back of the crowd trying to get a glimpse through. Laughing, Rhiannon swerved her luggage cart around the slow-movers in front, then blithely let it go to catch Galina in a noisy and fervent embrace.

'I don't believe it!' Galina shrieked excitedly, totally oblivious to the attention she was attracting. 'You look fantastic.' She was holding Rhiannon at arm's length and gazing delightedly into her face. 'Oh God, you're so gorgeous,' she cried, pulling Rhiannon back into her arms. 'I've missed you so much. I can hardly believe you're here.'

'I've missed you too,' Rhiannon told her, surprised to discover it was true. 'And just look at you. You always were lovely, but you've grown so lovely now I feel positively dazzled.'

Galina's vivid blue eyes were alive with laughter as, throwing her a quick glance, she whisked the luggage cart out of the way, steered it towards the exit and out on to the walkway that ran along the front of the terminal building. 'Tell me everything,' she demanded, lowering her sun-glasses from the top of her head to shield her eyes from the sun. 'I want to know everything you've been doing since the last time we saw each other. Start with the flight. How was it? Are you exhausted? Do you want to sleep?' She laughed and letting her head fall back gave a groan of pure joy. 'God, you don't know how glad I am to see you,' she said. 'I was so afraid you wouldn't come. But then I knew you wouldn't let me down. Everything's ready for you. Everyone's dying to meet you. Have you ever been to LA before? You're going to love it. It's a crazy place, full of whackos and weirdos, but I've got to tell you, babe, if you're looking for a man to get you over that jerk you told me about, well, I'm going to make it priority number one to find you one. It won't be easy because there are a lot of gays in this town, but we'll get past them and who knows, you might fall madly, wildly, incurably in love and stay. Wouldn't that be great? You and me together again, just like old times. God, I'm so excited. I'm so glad I was here to come pick you up myself. Ula was going to come. She's Max's assistant and you're going to just love her. Everyone does. She's so disrespectful, but somehow she manages to get away with it. She lives with Ellis. Ellis is Max's accountant. And then there's Maurice, Max's lawyer. Maurice is married to Deon who's a bit of a fluff, but she's OK. Now let me see, who else is there? Oh my God, yes! The kids! Marina and Aleks. They're absolutely adorable and you're going to fall in love with them on sight. Just like they're going to fall in love with you. I've told everyone all about you ...'

'Galina, take a breath,' Rhiannon protested.

Galina laughed. 'Sorry,' she said, pulling the cart to a halt at the kerb. 'I can't help it. I'm so excited to see you. Now you just hang on here while I run across to the parking lot and get the car. I'll bring it round and that way we won't have to wait for an elevator to come free,' and treating Rhiannon to another quick squeeze, she ran over the crosswalk towards the multi-level parking lot opposite.

Watching her go, Rhiannon smiled and felt her heart warming with affection. Five years was a long time and it seemed incredible now to think that for at least three of those years she'd have cheerfully wrung Galina's neck for the heartache she had caused her. More incredible still was how faded her memory of Phillip had become, when he had once been the very centre of her world, the man she had totally believed it would be impossible to live without. She wondered if one day she would think that way about Oliver ...

Moving restlessly, she glanced down at her watch. It was a few minutes after four LA time, making it just past midnight in London. She wondered what Lizzy was doing now and felt a sudden pang of homesickness. Considering she'd only just landed, to be feeling that way now was untimely to say the least, but there it was, spreading a melancholy cloud over her heart, as though to remind her that the next two weeks, enjoyable as they might be, were going to change nothing. All that she had left behind would still be there when she got back, unsorted, unchanged and seemingly irresolvable. Closing her eyes, she let her head fall forward for a moment and suddenly too tired to stop it, she felt the fear starting to swamp her.

Looking up as someone tooted loudly on a car horn, she felt a smile pull itself from her sadness – a sleek white Mercedes with Galina behind the wheel was gliding towards her. God, it was good to be away from England; to get out of the clouds and the rain to somewhere where the sun was shining so brightly and people were so friendly and helpful and Galina was so ridiculously happy to see her.

'By the way, the answer is yes, I have been to LA before,' Rhiannon said, feeling her spirits revive as Galina helped load her luggage into the trunk of the car. 'But only for three days. So, tell me I'm going to love it.'

Galina grinned and slammed the trunk closed.

'You're going to love it,' she said obediently. Then laughing, she walked round to the driver's side and got in. 'Seriously, you *are* going to love it,' she said. 'It's a great place to visit, especially when you know people, but you do reach a point when you have to get out. Max has always based himself here, but he's away on business half the time – well, we both are now, since I've been doing this Conspiracy thing. Have you seen any of it, by the way? Has it reached England? It should have by now.'

'Are you kidding?' Rhiannon laughed. 'Every time I open a magazine or turn on the TV you're right there staring back at me.'

Evidently delighted, Galina swung the car out into the traffic and headed off towards Lincoln. Then, after several quick glances at Rhiannon, as though reassuring herself that she really was there, she said, 'I can't believe five years have gone by since we last saw each other.'

'Incredible, isn't it?' Rhiannon replied.

Galina smiled. 'Looking at you now it feels like five days,' she said. 'How on earth did we come to let so much time go by when we were always so close?'

Rhiannon's eyebrows arched. 'You don't think it might have had something to do with the little matter of you running off with Phillip, do you?' she suggested.

'Oh my God!' Galina cried, clasping a hand to her mouth. 'I'd forgotten about that.'

'Like hell you had!' Rhiannon laughed, bunching up her hair to allow the cooling breeze of the air-con to blow around her neck.

Galina laughed too. 'OK. I hadn't. But I was hoping you might have.'

Rhiannon's eyes went to the roof in disbelief. 'You haven't changed a bit,' she smiled, turning to gaze out at the passing hotels and car rental lots that lined the route out of the airport.

'Nor have you,' Galina responded, clearly taking the

remark as a compliment, which, Rhiannon conceded, it probably was.

'So,' Galina continued, pulling out to overtake a white limousine, 'tell me everything about this jerk you got yourself involved with. Did you say you married him?'

'Yes, I did. But I don't want to talk about it.'

'Why ever not?' Galina cried.

'Because it still hurts,' Rhiannon said frankly.

'Then all the more reason to talk about it,' Galina protested. 'After all, we're friends, aren't we? And who can you talk to if you can't talk to your friends?'

'All right, I'll tell you about it,' Rhiannon promised, 'but just not right now, OK?'

'OK, we'll save it till we get back to the apartment,' Galina said. Then shooting Rhiannon a mischievous look she started to laugh. 'Are you sure you want to stay in the apartment?' she said. 'You're more than welcome at the house, you know. There's acres of room and everyone's just dying to meet you.'

'So you said,' Rhiannon reminded her. 'But I wouldn't mind just relaxing on my own for a while. You know, getting my bearings and taking some time to try and get a better perspective on the unholy mess I've left behind. I lost my job a few weeks ago.'

'Oh no,' Galina groaned, 'you really have been going through it. What was the job? You were still at the BBC when I left.'

Rhiannon explained about *Check It Out*, aware of the slight dizzying effect Galina was having on her.

When she'd finished she turned to look at Galina and her eyes widened in surprise as Galina said, 'Don't give yourself too hard a time over the fear. It's absolutely natural, believe me. Those are two really big set-backs you've suffered, losing your husband, then your job, and getting past it is going to take a lot of time and a lot of courage. And though it probably doesn't feel much like it right now, you can take it from me, you've got both.'

Rhiannon continued to look at her.

Smiling, Galina reached out and squeezed her hand. Then the mischief crept back into her eyes and giving her a playful punch she said, 'Come on, you're here to have a good time and forget all that shit. And to be my maid of honour, of course.' She paused for a moment as her head went thoughtfully to one side. 'You know, I reckon I might be able to wangle a couple of days free this week. If I can, what do you say we spend them together? Just us two. We can shop and lunch and go to the gym and do all those things Hollywood people do, like get breast implants and hair extensions and lyposuction and tattoos and ... Oh my God, that reminds me, I have to go get my nails fixed before Max gets back. Did you know he'd been arrested, by the way?'

Rhiannon took a breath, then let it go in a laugh. 'Yes, I read it in the papers just before I left,' she said, realizing that she should have known better than to worry about bringing the subject up when Galina's own special line of directness gave a new meaning to tact. 'In fact, it put me in two minds about coming,' she added.

'Oh, don't worry, he's not guilty,' Galina assured her.

'It wasn't that that bothered me,' Rhiannon said, smiling at such guileless loyalty and wishing Lizzy could have been there to enjoy it too. 'It was the fact that there might have been a hold-up with the wedding. So, when is he getting back?'

'Later tonight. He'll be in a foul mood, I know it already. He hates being in jail.'

Unable to stop herself Rhiannon gave a splutter of laughter.

Galina looked at her and winked. 'Still, at least this time he was only there for a few hours,' she said. 'Last time he was there for weeks.'

'You mean when his wife was killed?' Rhiannon said.

'Yeah,' Galina responded in a deep conspiratorial voice. 'That's right. God, it was awful. We're not allowed to talk about it now. Or at least we're not supposed to. But we do, of course. I mean, how can you not?'

Rhiannon was unsure how to answer that, so she tried another question. 'Did he kill her?' she said, blinking at her own temerity.

'Mmm,' Galina nodded, glancing in her rear-view mirror as she turned left on to Fiji and headed into Marina del Rey. 'Yeah, he killed her. I thought everyone knew that.'

Rhiannon sat for a moment, slightly stunned and not at all sure where to go next. 'Then how did he get away with it?' she asked finally.

Galina's face broke into a grin. 'Even if I knew, I wouldn't be able to tell you,' she said. 'But I don't know. Actually, there was a time when people thought it was me who killed her. Did you know that?' Her expression had changed to one of piqued indignance. 'In fact,' she went on, 'I reckon some people still do think that. But I didn't. I was in hospital right here in LA when she died and the last I heard they still hadn't made a bullet that can be fired from Los Angeles and find its target in New York. At least, not one that fits a .38.'

Rhiannon laughed, but again she was at a loss. It was almost as though they were discussing some schoolgirl prank that Galina had got mixed up in rather than the murder of her fiancé's first wife. 'If you know Max did it,' she said, 'then how come you're marrying him? I mean, doesn't it bother you?'

Galina shrugged. 'Not really. Max is killing people all the time. I mean, not actually killing them himself, you understand, the way he did Carolyn. Usually he gets other people to do it. You know, gangsters and druggies and hit men and the like.'

Rhiannon could only stare at her until finally Galina winked and Rhiannon's lips pursed as she realized she'd been had. 'OK,' she said, looking out at the forest of yacht masts and American flags that were visible beyond the restaurants and apartment blocks of the marina. 'So was it an accident; or wasn't it?' she asked.

'Well, I've got to say it was, haven't I?' Galina said. 'I mean, the charges were dropped and he's about to become my husband, so it would hardly do for me to go round telling people he's a murderer, now would it?'

'But do you know?' Rhiannon persisted. 'Did he ever talk to you about it?'

'Of course he did.'

'So? What did he say?'

'That it was an accident.'

'How?'

'She was trying to shoot him, he grabbed the gun, they struggled and the gun went off. You know the scenario, you've seen it a hundred times in the movies.'

'Do you believe him?'

'Absolutely and completely.' Galina's eyes were dancing as she pulled the car to a stop outside a six-storey apartment block with white wrought-iron balconies and turquoise and white striped awnings.

Remembering the pleasure Galina took in her own perversity, Rhiannon decided to side-track for a while. 'Why were you in hospital?' she asked.

'I got mugged,' Galina answered getting out of the car. 'Pretty badly, actually,' she said across the roof. 'It took ages for the bruises to go, almost as long as the cuts. I had twenty-three stitches all told. In my back, my arms, my legs, there are a couple of scars here on my neck look. Well, you can't really see them now, but they were there. It was really bad. The doctor said I was lucky to be alive.'

'Did they ever catch who did it?' Rhiannon asked, meeting her at the back of the car.

'Not as far as I know. They never do. Lucky he didn't touch my face, eh? I wouldn't be doing what I am now if he had, that's for sure.'

'What did he take?' Rhiannon said as they began unloading the luggage.

'Nothing. I didn't have anything on me.'

'Where did it happen?'

'Not far from my old apartment in Venice. Max refused to let me go back there after. But I insisted on keeping my independence so he found an apartment here for me. It's a secure building with guards and everything to keep Max happy and it suits me fine. Everyone minds their own business. There's none of that in-your-face got-to-tell-you-my-life-story stuff, not unless you want it, anyway.'

'Do you spend much time here?' Rhiannon asked, looking up as a uniformed porter took hold of her suit-case before she could lift it.

'Mmm, about half and half,' Galina answered. 'Max wants me to give it up now we're getting married, but I'm not keen to. It's somewhere for me to come and hide out when he's in one of his vile moods. Besides, I like having my privacy, don't you?'

Rhiannon inhaled deeply as she thought about that. 'Well, yes, of course I do,' she replied. 'But isn't that part of getting married, giving up your privacy? I mean, that's one of the downsides, I know, but it has its com-pensations, or so I'm told. Besides, from what you've said I'd have thought that Max's house was big enough for you to lose yourself in if you felt the need.'

'Oh, it's big all right,' Galina chuckled, 'but it's definitely not big enough to escape from Max, not if he doesn't want you to escape, anyway. Actually the whole of LA isn't big enough to escape from Max. He's got his bloody spies out everywhere. I'm sure he bribes the people here to keep an eye on me and let him know what time I go out, what time I get back, who's with me, how long they stay.' She laughed. 'I've even suspected that he gets them to check my laundry.'

Rhiannon screwed up her face. 'Why would he do that?' she said.

'Because', Galina answered, nodding at the doorman

as they walked into the cool marble lobby and over to the elevator, 'he's always trying to find out if I'm sleeping with anyone else.'

Rhiannon's lip curled in distaste. 'And he gets them to check your laundry to find out?' she said.

Galina laughed and shrugged. 'I don't know,' she answered, pushing the button. 'He might.'

'How on earth do you stand it?' Rhiannon said, 'having your every move monitored like that?'

'I love it,' Galina grinned. 'It proves how much he loves me and how he can't stand the idea of me screwing another man.'

Rhiannon looked at her as the lift rose to the third floor and Galina, obviously enjoying herself immensely, gazed innocently ahead. 'So do you?' Rhiannon asked as the lift doors slid open. 'Screw other men?'

Galina laughed. 'Of course!' she cried. 'Whenever I get the chance,' and sailing out into the grey-carpeted corridor, she took out her keys and made an abrupt right turn to the end apartment.

'*Et voilà*!' she cried, throwing open the door and walking into a wonderfully sunlit living-room whose vast, double sliding windows opened on to a white mosaic veranda overlooking the marina. 'This is home,' she declared, grinning at Rhiannon's obvious admiration of the sumptuous white sofas, glass-topped tables, huge white feather fans and deep-piled white carpet. The art on the walls and untidy stack of magazines on a coffee table provided the only colour in the room and the terrace, for even the garden furniture was padded with thick, spongy white mattresses.

'And these', Galina pronounced, directing Rhiannon towards an enormous vase of white lilies which were set on the counter top that divided the kitchen from the living-room, 'are especially for you. I bought them myself this morning.'

Rhiannon was smiling, touched by the childish note of

pride in Galina's voice, for of course, she had no way of knowing that lilies would evoke such painful memories of the honeymoon suite in Marrakesh. Quickly pushing them aside, Rhiannon stooped to sniff the scent of the flowers, then turning to Galina she said, 'They're lovely. Thank you.'

'You're welcome,' Galina smiled back, her deep-blue eyes reflecting the emotion that had caught gently in her voice. The rays of dazzling sunlight slanting in through the window made her hair seem whiter than ever and her flawless skin shone like burnished gold. She had never, Rhiannon thought, looked more lovely.

Galina glanced at her watch. 'Oh crikey! Look at the time!' she cried. 'My nail appointment's at five, so I'll have to dash. There'll be plenty of time to gossip over the next couple of days. Pierre will be right up with your luggage. Here,' she added, digging into her purse and bringing out a five-dollar bill. 'Give him this. You'll be OK, won't you? Everything's been taken care of. Ula even rented a car for you. Pierre will show you where it's parked. And Ula's left a note somewhere, I think, or she said she did. It's probably next to the bed. The main bedroom's right through there.' She was pointing at a closed smoked-glass door. 'There'll be a list of telephone numbers somewhere too, I'm sure. Mine and Ula's and Max's and the main one for the house. I think Ula stuck some maps in the car. There's food in the fridge and Ralph's, the supermarket, is just up on Lincoln – which is the road coming in from the airport. There's a stack of take-out joints and delivery services and bistros and restaurants and singles bars around the area, and a gym downstairs in the building and a pool and jacuzzi. All the residents here get together on a Sunday morning to say hi and swap divorce and therapy stories. I'm serious,' she laughed when Rhiannon pulled a face. 'One to be avoided. Anyway, I've got to run. Are you sure you'll be all right here? Just call if you need anything. Actually, I might be back later if Max is being too vile. If not, you'll get to meet him some time tomorrow. It'll be an experience, I promise you. Anyway, I'm out of here. Make yourself at home, feel free to use the phone and anything you can't get to work, just call down to the lobby for help.' And treating Rhiannon to a quick kiss on either cheek she was gone.

Feeling as though she had just been released from a tornado, Rhiannon stood still for a moment, blinking and trying to catch up with her thoughts. She wasn't too sure what she'd expected when she arrived, but it certainly wasn't to have been abandoned so soon. However, she had been and to stand there feeling sorry for herself about it wasn't going to change it. So, turning to the window, she released the catch and slid it open.

Stepping from the air-conditioned apartment, the heat hit her like a fire. She drew back, then slipping off her jacket walked over to the glass-and-filigree balustrade to gaze down at the marina. She was trying so hard not to think of Oliver, but right at that moment her longing for him was impossible to master. She didn't want to be here alone. She didn't want to be here at all. All she wanted was to turn back the clock, to find herself marooned in a time before the pain had begun, a time when her life wasn't ruled by fear, a time when she still believed in her dreams.

Starting as Pierre called out that he had left her luggage in the bedroom, she turned quickly back into the apartment to tip him. She was too late, the front door was already closing behind him and the telephone was ringing.

'Hi, Rhiannon?' a stranger's voice called cheerily down the line before Rhiannon had a chance to say hello.

'Yes, it's Rhiannon,' she answered.

'Hi, it's Ula, Max's assistant. Welcome to Los Angeles.'

'Thank you,' Rhiannon smiled.

'Everything OK for you?' Ula asked. 'Galina pick you up OK?'

'Yes, everything's great,' Rhiannon assured her, wandering into the bedroom and feeling a pleasing lift in her heart when she saw how inviting it was, with its huge white wooden bed, mountainous cushions and plush white drapes.

'Galina just called from her car and told me she'd abandoned you,' Ula said. 'So I thought I'd call and check you were OK. I'd come over if Max weren't due back in a couple of hours, but ...'

'It's all right,' Rhiannon interrupted, smiling. 'I'm fine.'

'Well you just call if you need anything, do you hear? I've left all our numbers there. You'll find them next to the phone. Do you like the apartment? Cool, isn't it? You should be comfortable there, but if you want to change your mind and come stay at the house, just let me know.'

'I will, thanks,' Rhiannon said. 'Just one thing before you go, is it safe to go out alone at night around here?'

Ula paused. 'No, not really,' she answered. 'I mean, it should be, but I wouldn't take the chance if I were you, not after dark. Unless you're going in the car of course. I got you a Chevvie Cabriolet, by the way. Drive around with the doors locked at night and don't head down to the beach, it can be a real dangerous place when it gets dark. If you want to eat out tonight then try the Café del Rey on Admiralty. You'll need to take the car, but parking's no problem. Do you have any dollars? I left you some. They're in a drawer next to the bed.'

'Is there anything you haven't thought of?' Rhiannon laughed.

'I hope not,' Ula replied. 'I'll have Max and Galina on my case if there is. Anyway, I got a few calls coming in here, so I'll catch you tomorrow, OK? Sleep well and remember, call if you need anything,' and the line went dead.

Walking back into the living-room, Rhiannon replaced the radio phone on its base and looked down at the list of numbers Ula had left. With the note were a fold-up street map of Los Angeles and the keys to the Chevvie. Rhiannon picked them up, turned them over in her hand and stared sightlessly down at the map. Then hearing Ula's voice echoing in her ears, she dropped the keys and went to deadlock the front door. She was probably over-reacting, as common sense told her that nothing was likely to happen to her in a block as secure as this one, but as she turned to gaze around the beautifully benign room she could feel an inexplicable unease working its way into her heart. Her eyes darted into the corners, seeking out heaven only knew what. She was very still and tense. It was as though she was expecting some kind of menace to emerge from the shadows, which was crazy she knew, but the longer she stood there the more convinced she became that something, somewhere, wasn't right.

It was a while before it occurred to her that she was allowing journey fatigue to play tricks on her mind and quickly pulling herself together she went into the bedroom to begin her unpacking. Later, she told herself firmly, she would follow Ula's suggestion and drive to the Café del Rey for dinner – and maybe, if she was awake early enough in the morning, she would begin her day the California way and go for a run along Venice Beach.

It was just after three in the morning when Rhiannon was torn from a particularly unpleasant and disjointed dream by the sound of the phone. It took her several seconds to orientate herself, then sliding across the bed she fumbled with the light and picked up the receiver.

'Galina?' a voice at the other end said.

'Mmm?' Rhiannon responded, still struggling to bring herself round.

'Did I wake you? You're gonna be glad I did.'

'I'm sorry,' Rhiannon croaked, 'this isn't Galina. Can I give her a message?'

There was silence at the end of the line, then the echo of the receiver being replaced on the hook.

Clicking off her end, Rhiannon pulled her hand back under the sheet and lay staring at nothing. Outside, the night was as still as the moonlit objects around her, and the air seemed to breathe in the shadows. The blood was throbbing thickly through her veins; for no reason she could fathom the call had unnerved her. But then the effects of the sleeping pill she had taken pulled her back into a saturnine dreamscape and the next thing she knew it was morning and the telephone was ringing again.

'Hi! I didn't wake you, did I?' Lizzy cried. 'What time is it over there?'

Rhiannon blinked open her eyes and looked at the clock. 'Ten past eight,' she mumbled, pulling herself up from the bed and noticing she had left the lamp on all night. 'And yes, you did wake me.'

'Haven't you got the hang of jet lag yet?' Lizzy laughed. 'You were supposed to be up about four. Anyway, how's it going so far? More to the point, how's Galina?'

Rhiannon smiled. 'Galina's great,' she answered. 'She hasn't changed a bit. Well, she has. She's crazier than ever, a bit more grown-up, just as naive, twice as beautiful, totally unfazeable and ... Oh, I don't know, I didn't see her for long, but it's already doing me good to be here. At least I think it is.'

'Any sign of Max yet? Or is he still in jail?'

Laughing, Rhiannon tucked the receiver between her ear and her shoulder and getting up from the bed walked out to the kitchen. 'As far as I know he got back last night,' she answered. 'She told me he killed his wife, by the way.'

'What, you mean, she told you it wasn't an accident?'

Lizzy said incredulously.

'No, she said it was an accident, but she said it in such a way that you knew she was lying.'

'No kidding?' Then laughing Lizzy said, 'You didn't waste much time, did you? Have you mentioned anything about an interview yet?'

'Give me a break,' Rhiannon protested. 'I only got here last night.'

'But do you think there's a chance?'

Rhiannon shrugged. 'It's hard to tell without having met Max. I mean, if it were left up to Galina I could almost guarantee she'd give me an interview. Not about Max, obviously, but she'd happily talk about herself and what life's like as a supermodel. I suppose that's what she is, do you? A supermodel? Anyway, without being modest about this, she'd do it if for no other reason than to help get my career back on the road.'

'The very least she owes you,' Lizzy retorted. 'So, when do you get to visit Babylon?'

With it being so early in the morning it took Rhiannon's brain a moment to switch, then understanding, she started to grin. 'Today, I think,' she answered. Then suddenly, out of nowhere, she remembered the phone call that had woken her in the middle of the night. She was on the point of mentioning it to Lizzy when she realized that really there was nothing to tell. So leaving it, she said, 'Have you called Andy yet?'

'Oh God, don't,' Lizzy shivered. 'I've been on and off the loo all day trying to pluck up the courage.'

'But you *are* going to call him before you go?'

'Yes. Now let's change the subject. Did you talk to Galina about videoing the wedding?'

'No, not yet.'

'But you will.'

'Yes. When I feel the time is right.'

'Well don't leave it too late,' Lizzy warned.

'You're much better at this than I am,' Rhiannon

groaned, opening the blinds to let the sun stream in.

'Are you kidding? You were the one who took all of ten minutes to get her to tell you Max did it. Now all you have to find out is whose palms he greased, or what favours he called in to help him get away with it and you'll make such a name for yourself you'll probably go down in history.'

'It was an accident,' Rhiannon reminded her.

Lizzy snorted in disbelief. 'That's what they always say,' she responded.

'Well, even if it wasn't,' Rhiannon said, 'the LAPD, or no, it happened in New York, didn't it? The NYPD didn't seem able to prove it was deliberate, or premeditated or whatever they were after, so I don't reckon much to my chances, do you?'

'As a matter of fact, I do. The NYPD aren't best chums with Galina. You are. And call me old-fashioned, but I reckon best chums tell each other a whole lot more than they're likely to tell a cop.'

Rhiannon was about to disagree when she suddenly saw that Lizzy might have a point. 'Especially', she said, her mind racing on ahead, 'if the police never questioned her.'

'What do you mean? They had to question her. I mean, how could they not?'

'At the time of the shooting Galina was in hospital right here in LA,' Rhiannon informed her. 'Meaning that after the police verified her whereabouts they probably never spoke to her again. I mean, she could hardly be a witness, could she, when she was the other side of the States all tucked up in a hospital bed?'

'I suppose not. But they must have asked her at some point if Max had ever pillow-talked about killing his wife.'

Laughing, Rhiannon said, 'Maybe they did ask her, and maybe Galina lied.'

'What was she in hospital for?' Lizzy asked.

'She was mugged.'

Lizzy was quiet for a moment. 'Seems like it was a bad night for the women in Max Romanov's life,' she commented. 'One gets herself shot, the other gets herself mugged.'

'Mmm, I was thinking the same thing myself,' Rhiannon responded. 'But if I'm going to find out what really happened I'll need to take it in stages. First, I'll try Galina out with the idea of an interview, just her. Like I said, she's almost bound to go for it, because, loyalty aside, the Conspiracy people will grab the free publicity with both hands – providing I can get a slot for it of course.'

'You shouldn't have any problem there,' Lizzy assured her.

'No, probably not. Anyway, then I'll see how Galina takes to the idea of me videoing the wedding. There's no question that she'll have to get Max's agreement, if not outright permission, on that, and my guess is the best I can hope for is that he'll give the go-ahead providing it's only for my private use. If that turns out to be the case, I'll have to see how moral I'm feeling when it comes to the crunch – or, more to the point, how broke. The jackpot, of course, would be if he agreed to the wedding being shot and gave a joint interview with Galina in which he allowed me to ask questions about his first wife's death. If I got that I'd start believing in pots at the end of rainbows and lamps where genies hang out. Still, at this stage anything is possible and temporarily misplaced optimism would be a much more constructive way, I think, of describing my pessimism.'

Lizzy chuckled. 'I'll take a bet with you now', she said, 'that you'll win him over. With Galina on your side I don't see how you can fail.'

'I wish I had your faith,' Rhiannon replied. 'And I hope you realize that if I do succeed, then the NYPD notwithstanding, I'll have got what virtually every other journalist, chat show host, novelist, biographer and amateur detective in the entire United States has been after ever since the charges were dropped.'

For a moment even Lizzy was daunted. 'Then all I can say is, Rule Britannia,' she responded finally.

'There's a bleep coming down the line,' Rhiannon laughed, 'which I imagine means someone is trying to get through, so I'd better ring off.'

'OK. Call me if you've got any news.'

'Same your end,' Rhiannon replied. 'And call Andy now!' She rang off before Lizzy could protest and took a call from Ula asking if she could be ready by ten when Ula would come by to drive her over to Malibu.

At five minutes to ten Rhiannon was standing in front of the mirror wanting to rip an Armani dress apart at the seams for it looked more like a pile of old ironing than it did a stylishly-cut shift dress that should be perfect for a day out at a Malibu mansion. Just what the hell did someone wear when visiting that kind of place? More to the point, how did one dress for a first meeting with one of America's leading business tycoons who, apart from everything else about him, was on the point of marrying her old school friend? And what the hell difference did it make what she wore? She didn't imagine for one minute that he was agonizing over his wardrobe in the hope of impressing her. And who wanted to impress him anyway? He was just another man. A multi-millionaire and possibly, probably, a murderer, it was true, but nevertheless just a man.

It was only now, as her mind buzzed about in such an idiotic turmoil while clothes piled up fast on the bed and the clock ticked past ten, that she realized how incredibly nervous she was at the prospect of meeting Max Romanov.

She was on the point of trying to psych herself back to calm when the doorman called up to announce Ula's arrival. Deciding the Armani dress would just have to do, Rhiannon scooped up her bag and keys, gave herself one last quick check in the mirror, then locking up behind her ran down the stairs to the lobby. Seeing her uncertainty, the doorman pointed outside to where a tall, willowy brunette with transluscent white skin, crimson cheeks and lively blue eyes was standing beside a black Toyota and looking eagerly towards the door as Rhiannon came out.

'We've all been hearing so much about you,' she said, holding Rhiannon's hand between both of hers as she shook it. 'Hell, I feel like I know you already. Did you sleep well? Still a touch jet-lagged, I guess.'

'Actually, I think I'm fine,' Rhiannon smiled, wincing at the faint echo of an American accent that had found its way into her voice. 'Nervous, but fine.'

'Nervous?' Ula said in surprise. 'Not about meeting Max, surely? He's a pussy-cat.'

Rhiannon's left eyebrow formed a cycnical arch, making Ula laugh.

'I swear it,' she said, pulling open the passenger door for Rhiannon to get in. 'We'll take my car. Someone will run you back later. And believe me when I tell you Max is a sweetheart. He's sure looking forward to meeting you.'

Not entirely believing that, Rhiannon waited for Ula to slip into the driver's seat, then fastening her belt she said, 'Where's Galina?'

'Oh, didn't I tell you on the phone?' Ula said, frowning at her forgetfulness as she started up the engine. 'She and Max had to go see the rabbi this morning. They should be home by the time we get there,' she added pulling out on to Via Marina. 'Max just flew in from New York last night, as I expect you know, so he and the guys will probably go straight into conference when he gets back from the rabbi's. The guys being Maurice and Ellis who Galina probably already told you about? She did? Good. Anyway, I expect you read the papers so you'll know Max is facing insider trading charges which has put him in a real good mood, let me tell you, 'cos Max just loves being charged with crimes he didn't commit. I take it you know this isn't the first time it's happened.' There was a wry lilt to her voice that made Rhiannon laugh and almost tempted her to try drawing Ula out, but on hasty reflection she decided she'd be wiser to leave it until she knew her a little better.

A few minutes later they were cruising along Ocean Boulevard heading towards the Pacific Coast Highway which would take them out to Malibu. Ula continued chattering about Max and his children and Galina and Ellis and the cat, Snoop, who had recently been spayed. Rhiannon listened and laughed and gazed out at the spectacular views over Santa Monica Bay and the mountains that swelled into the sea fog and wondered idly if she could ever bring herself to live in LA. Just the one brief visit she had made a couple of years ago had been enough to show her how everything was on such an impossible scale here that saturation point was merely the start line. The entire town, from what she recalled, was like a giant movie screen where endless cameos of life and death, horror and love, eccentricity and innovation combined to create the great magical dream of Hollywood. It was an energizing, terrifying and wholly unreal place to visit – and to live there, Rhiannon imagined, would probably be very much the same.

The journey to Malibu seemed much shorter than she had expected it to be, for in no time at all Ula was turning off the Highway and winding along the bluff towards the edge of the cliffs.

'Not far now,' she said, slowing up to let a speeding Volkswagen pass before she made a left turn into a shady winding road that led them past some of the grandest-looking estates Rhiannon had ever seen. It was at the end of that road that Ula paused, while a security guard activated the two vast black iron gates in front of him and waved them through.

Rhiannon looked about her, drinking in the glorious blue of the sea and sky that provided the backdrop to the towering palms that lined the drive. Up ahead she could see the outer walls of the house and the closer they drew the more nervous she could feel herself becoming. It was rare for her to feel inadequate or out of her depth, but she was certainly feeling that way now and right at that moment she wasn't holding out much hope that an actual meeting with Max Romanov was going to improve her condition. The surprising thing was that until that morning she'd never really given him much thought before, not on a personal level anyway. He was simply the man at the head of a publishing empire, or at the centre of a murder scandal, or whom Galina was going to marry. Whereas now, quite unexpectedly, he was turning into some kind of icon whom she had no idea whether she should fear or revere.

'Hey, why so gloomy?' Ula teased as she circled the car around the forecourt fountain. 'We're all on your side, you know.'

Rhiannon's head came round. 'I wasn't aware there were any sides,' she said.

Ula laughed. 'Lighten up, will you,' she said. 'It was a joke. I told you, Max is a great guy. You'll see. He'll be real polite in welcoming you to his home. He'll tell you how honoured he is that you came all the way over from England. He'll show you round, tell you something about the history of the place. He'll invite you to stay if you get lonely at the apartment. He'll make sure you've got his private number and tell you to call if there's anything you need. He'll introduce you to the kids .... Shit, I don't know what he'll do, but take it from me, it's not going to make a bit of difference what else is going down in his life, he's going to make you feel more welcome than you've felt in a long time. I know, because I've seen him in action a lot of times, and he's got a real knack for tuning out the bad and turning on the charm.'

Rhiannon stepped out of the car and looked up at the beautiful colonnaded façade of the Italian-style villa with its pure white walls, multi-levelled red-tiled roofs and exquisite domes. She could hear the sound of children shrieking and splashing about in a pool. The sun was so bright that the vibrant colours of the flowers climbing the walls and filling the beds seemed to shimmer and slip into each other like running paint on a page.

'Where is everyone?' Ula said to an old man who was coming out of the front door to greet them. 'Rhiannon, this is Leo,' she continued without waiting for an answer. 'He's worked for Max's family since before Max was born. He's a bit deaf now, so you have to speak up.'

Feeling a little as though she was moving through a dream, Rhiannon shook the old man's hand and followed Ula into the enormous entrance hall, where twin cantilever staircases rose from each side of the room and circled round to meet at a Venetian-style balcony that overhung an enchantingly simple indoor fountain at the centre of the hall.

Rhiannon broke into a smile. 'I don't think I've ever seen anything so lovely,' she murmured, allowing her eyes to follow the dramatic sweep of the walls right up to the skylights, then back down to where the twin landings of the upper floor stretched around the semicircle like giant arms ready to embrace.

'I'm glad you think so.'

At the sound of a male voice Rhiannon swung round and felt her mouth turn dry as Max Romanov walked across the hall towards her. He was taller than she'd expected and much darker. He was also, with his glowering black eyes, thick, heavy brows, prominent nose and generous mouth, one of the most attractive men she'd ever encountered.

'Welcome,' he said, holding out his hand. There was no pleasure in his eyes, not even the hint of a smile on his lips.

Rhiannon struggled to find her voice, but the shock of his brusqueness after all Ula had said was suddenly compounded by the sight of the man walking into the hall behind him.

Following the direction of her eyes, Max turned round and was on the point of introducing him when he suddenly swore under his breath. Rhiannon's eyes darted between the two men as Ramon moved towards her, so unfazed by the moment that he might almost have been expecting it.

Raising her fingers to his lips he said, 'It would appear, oh, lovely senorita, that we are destined to meet again.'

To her amazement, considering the terrible memories this man should evoke, never mind the shock of actually seeing him again – and of all places here – Rhiannon found herself responding to the humorous light in his eyes. He lowered her hand and the whiteness of his smile in his dark, craggy face almost made her laugh as she was reminded of something Lizzy had once said about an old crooner they had just filmed. 'He's the kind of bloke that tangoes his way straight to your libido, then promptly drops you on the first back flip.'

It wasn't hard to see that Ramon was exactly that kind of man, but right now, for the second time in her life he was the most welcome sight Rhiannon could imagine. For as he stood there smiling at her with all the warmth of a Mediterranean sun, she could feel the coldness of Max's presence like a chill Siberian winter gathering on a close horizon.

Chapter 18

'I like to think', Rhiannon said, 'that coincidences happen for a reason, or that maybe they aren't coincidences at all.' Smiling the challenge, she glanced over at Ramon, then returning her eyes to the spectacular view of the ocean as they ambled down the hillside towards the private beach below, she said, 'Or is that too Celestine?'

Eyebrows raised, Ramon moved a blade of grass from one corner of his mouth to the other and dug his hands deeper into the pockets of his shorts. His dark, leathery skin was glistening in the heat, a glimmer of mischief was playing about his eyes. A few minutes ago she had tried to thank him for what he had done in Marrakesh, but he had gently brushed her words aside, as though telling her that his role was something she should not trouble herself with remembering. Which didn't mean, she had realized, that he was trying to diminish what had happened; it was simply concern that his presence might be causing her some distress.

It had, initially, but the awkward and startled moments of her arrival had happened several hours ago now, when Galina's excited rush into the hall couldn't have been more timely. Clapping her hands with delight that Rhiannon and Max had already met and appearing not to notice the tension, she had proceeded to make the introductions, telling Rhiannon that Ramon was an old friend of Max's family and that Max was in a foul mood because his lawyer, Maurice, whom Rhiannon would meet at lunch, hadn't yet managed to get the charges against him dropped. Then kissing Max briefly on the mouth, she had narrowed her eyes at the blackness of his temper, told him to call the rabbi to apologize for his rudeness that morning, then had promptly taken Rhiannon off for a tour of the house.

Rhiannon hadn't seen Max since, not even at lunch when she had met Ellis and Maurice and Maurice's wife, Deon. Max's children had sat either side of Galina at one end of the table, demanding her attention and apparently delighting her with just about everything they said or did. In fact, had she been their natural mother she couldn't have been more doting, nor more attentive to their discipline and manners. At the same time she managed to keep up with the conversation going on around her and looked so impossibly lovely and happy, sitting in the dappled shade of the bougainvillaea-draped gazebo, that Rhiannon couldn't remember ever having seen such a picture of perfection.

Ramon had put in a second appearance some twenty minutes ago when he had found her and Galina sitting with their feet dangling in the pool as they discussed arrangements for the wedding. When he'd invited them to join him for a stroll down to the beach Galina had started out with them, then suddenly remembering something she needed to discuss with Max, she had gone back to the house. That was when Rhiannon had tried to thank Ramon for Marrakesh and she appeared to be getting no further now with the mysterious coincidence of them both being there, than she had with her apology.

'OK,' she said, when he still didn't answer, 'let's try this another way. How does it come about that I know Galina and you know Max and that we should find ourselves guests at their wedding only a matter of months after you rescued me from what might very well have proved a fate worse than death? Would you call it coincidence or would you call it something else?'

His eyes crinkled at the corners as he gazed out to sea. 'You are assuming I am here for the wedding,' he responded.

'Would you be here for any other reason?' she countered.

He shrugged. 'Maybe not.'

She was left thinking that maybe he was, but deciding there were already enough avenues to pursue without going down that particular one, she said, 'I'm sure Galina told me, but remind me, how do you know Max?'

Contrary to her expectation, there was no hesitation in his reply. 'Our families go back a long way,' he told her. 'We are both descended from Russian Jews. To us that means something.'

'And the Straussens?' she said, hoping to catch him off-guard.

'The Straussens?' he repeated, apparently unfazed.

'I'm sure you know who they are,' she said affably.

He smiled. 'They are not of Russian descent.'

'But you do know them?'

'Of course.'

She waited, hoping that some kind of an explanation would follow, but his silence was as relaxed as the heat-hazed mountains and apparently as impenetrable.

'Have you ever discussed what happened in Marrakesh with Max?' she said, surprising herself with the abruptness of the question when the possibility that he actually might have had only just occurred to her.

'No,' Ramon answered. 'We've never discussed it.'

The tone of his voice caused Rhiannon's eyes to widen. 'But he knows what happened?' she said, turning to look at him.

'Yes.'

'How?'

Ramon took a moment to consider his reply. 'He was

concerned for you,' he said finally.

Rhiannon frowned. 'That doesn't answer my question,' she said. 'And why would Max Romanov be concerned for me when he doesn't even know me? More to the point, how did he know that there was any need for concern?'

Ramon was smiling. 'You must ask Max,' he said. 'I am not sure he will tell you, but it is him you must ask.'

For a moment Rhiannon looked annoyed, then rolling her eyes she said, 'You know I won't do that.'

Ramon laughed. 'Don't tell me you are afraid of him? He is a difficult man, it is true, but he loves his children.'

It was Rhiannon's turn to laugh. Then deciding to change the subject she said, 'Will you be staying in LA long?'

'A few weeks, maybe,' he answered. 'And you?'

'Just two weeks.'

'You must get back for your work?' he said.

'Mmm,' she answered, moving her eyes off down the beach to where the rocks spilled out into the sea. London suddenly seemed a very long way away, but even at this distance the future still felt bleak. 'Maybe we could meet up later in the week,' she suggested, forcing a brightness into her voice. 'We could be tourists together.'

'It would be my pleasure,' he told her. 'But I am afraid that I will be leaving Los Angeles in the morning to attend to some business in the south. Naturally, I shall be back before the wedding. Maybe we can spend some time together next week. Will you still be here?'

'Yes.'

'And you are staying where? Not at the house, I see.'

'No, at Galina's apartment.'

He nodded, pushing his bottom lip forward.

'So, what kind of business are you in?' she asked. 'I mean, when you're not rescuing damsels in distress.'

'That is my speciality,' he said.

Rhiannon's smile widened. 'Do you have a cape?' she

asked. 'Do you change your clothes in telephone kiosks and walk up walls? Or do you have a fetish for flying mammals?'

Laughing he said, 'I gave up the gimmicks some years ago. They're not dignified in an old man. Now, all I have is a weakness for beautiful women.'

'And a knack for avoiding questions,' she added, enjoying the compliment. 'But I don't give up so easily.'

'Then I shall enjoy being pursued,' he smiled, glancing back up the hill. 'As we are being now.'

Rhiannon turned to see Galina and Max strolling after them, their arms draped loosely around each other's shoulders, a murmured exchange as they approached causing them both to smile. It was like watching summer and winter, one of them so golden and fair, the other so dark and forbidding, yet as they laughed their beauty made Rhiannon's heart tighten – though whether it was entirely admiration was hard to say, when the prospect of another meeting with Max was putting an uncomfortable edge on her nerves.

'I hope we aren't interrupting anything,' Galina said, her eyes dancing merrily as they moved back and forth between Ramon and Rhiannon.

'As a matter of fact you are,' Ramon told her, turning to wink at Rhiannon. 'But things can always be resumed at a later date,' he added.

Rhiannon smiled, then her eyebrows went up as Max held out his hand to shake hers. 'I'd like to apologize for my rudeness earlier,' he said, 'and welcome you to LA.'

As Rhiannon lifted her hand she could feel herself being drawn into the arresting power of his eyes. He wasn't, she was thinking, quite as good-looking as she'd initially thought. Or maybe he was. She smiled again, then almost started at the response of her body as their hands touched. Her eyes were still on his and she could see that he wasn't unaware of the effect he was having.

'First the rabbi, now me,' she said, colouring as she

cast a quick glance at Galina.

A small frown creased Max's brow.

'Max spends half his life apologizing,' Galina told her.

Rhiannon's eyes moved back to Max's and she felt her heartbeat start to slow as he laughed. Then realizing she was still holding his hand, she let go so abruptly that she embarrassed herself and brought an expression to his eyes that she would prefer not to have seen. But if he was mocking her and thinking her as ridiculous as she suddenly felt, she was going to do nothing to disillusion him, for she knew instinctively that the further down that road she went the more ridiculous she would inevitably become.

Beside them, Galina was tucking an arm through Ramon's and laughing at something he was saying, while her free hand reached behind her for Max's.

Taking it, he tightened his fingers round hers and, nodding almost imperceptibly to Ramon, he said, 'Darling, walk Ramon back to the house, will you? I want to have a chat with Rhiannon and Ula's got a couple of things she wants Ramon to take a look at.'

'Of course,' Galina said, beaming at Rhiannon. 'You two get to know each other and make sure you come back liking each other, do you hear me? It's important to me that you do and don't you go giving her the third degree, Max. What she does and who she sees is her own business, OK?' Her face was tilted towards his, their lips very close.

He kissed her briefly and Rhiannon felt more colour stain her cheeks as his eyes came up to hers.

'Don't take any nonsense from him,' Galina told her. 'He's a bully and today he's in a bad mood, despite the apologies. Of course, it's my fault. Everything's always my fault – except *I*', she continued, turning back to Max, 'wasn't the one who tipped The Poisoner off about the Primaire shares.'

Max winced as Ramon laughed, then pulling her into

his arms Max gazed down into Galina's face. 'Get the hell out of here,' he whispered, 'and leave me to deal with your friend.'

'My friend and *our* bridesmaid,' she reminded him, taking Ramon's hand as she started to turn away. 'So don't go frightening her away. I'm serious, Max, don't be horrible to her. She's the only friend I have and I want to keep her.'

As they walked away Max watched them for a while, then turned to look at Rhiannon. Once again Rhiannon felt herself respond to the disturbing penetration of his eyes.

'It's easier to walk on the sand if you take your shoes off,' he told her, slipping his bare feet out of the black leather loafers he was wearing and leaving them where they were.

As she kicked her own shoes off Rhiannon watched him stroll on ahead and found herself tracing the solid shape of his calves, the coarse black hair that covered his dark skin, the muscular outline of his buttocks and thighs beneath the neutral-coloured shorts and the width of his shoulders and strength of his arms beneath the plain white polo shirt. His whole physique emanated a power and fitness that most men would envy, but even that paled beside the uncompromising force of his eyes and his indisputable air of authority and control.

'I imagine', he said, as she caught up with him, 'that you're figuring from Galina's remark that I'm guilty as recently charged.' The roar of the ocean as it rolled on to the shore backed his words, yet the noise in no way diminished the deep resonance of his voice – nor did the wind fail to convey the note of irritation he obviously felt at being forced to address the matter.

In fact Rhiannon wondered why he was bothering when what she thought, or believed, was surely of no consequence to him.

'How are you settling in to the apartment?' he asked,

apparently unconcerned by her failure to respond.

Surprised by the sudden change of subject and reluctant to let go of the first, Rhiannon said, 'Very well, thank you. Why were you charged if you're not guilty?'

His eyebrows went up, but she didn't miss the contempt as he turned aside to look at the sea. 'The last I heard, a man was innocent until proven guilty, or did the system change in the UK?' he said, turning back.

Rhiannon flushed. 'No,' she answered. 'It's still the same. But what I was meaning was, surely a man in your position doesn't get as far as being charged with a crime unless ...' Turning cold as she suddenly realized what she was about to say she immediately changed course, '... someone set him up for it,' she finished lamely.

'Or unless he committed the crime,' he said, letting her know that she had in no way fooled him.

'Or unless he committed the crime,' she repeated tersely.

'If I'm guilty,' he said, 'then I guess they'll be able to prove it.'

'If you're guilty,' she responded, 'then hopefully this time justice will be served.' She could feel the blood burning in her cheeks as he turned to look at her. Brazening it out, she lifted her eyes to his and saw, to her surprise, that she had amused him. Irritated, she said, 'In case you hadn't noticed, we're getting off to a very bad start here, so for Galina's sake if nothing else, perhaps we should start again. But before we do I think you should know that I couldn't give a flying fig whether you're guilty or not – of either crime!'

He kept on walking, pushing his feet into the sand and letting his hair whip about his face as Rhiannon struggled to keep up. Suddenly feeling a fool for trying, she stopped and turned towards the water's edge. He was disturbing her in so many ways that it was a relief to have just this short distance between them, if only to prove to herself that she had the strength to defy the determination in his stride that seemed to pull her along with him.

From the corner of her eye she watched him move on down the beach and felt a depressing heaviness creep into her heart. Recognizing it for the loneliness it was, she closed her eyes and waited for it to subside. Then staring down at her feet she watched the waves frothing around her toes and tried not to think. Nothing about today had been easy and she suddenly felt exhausted. There was too much subtext, too little straight talking and, at least where Max was concerned, a confusing lack of courtesy. Even at lunch, when everything, at least on the surface, had appeared normal she had felt a strangeness in the air that had seemed to put a bewildering distance between her and those around her. It was a little like watching life in a mirror; it all looked perfectly real, was extremely easy to see and believe in, but in truth it was nothing more than a reflection, an impossible tableau to touch. At the time she'd put the peculiarity of her feelings down to a lingering jet lag, but then there had been Ramon's reticence and now this, with Max ...

Realizing he was coming back towards her, she kept her head down, unwilling to admit that he intimidated her, but knowing it to be true. She felt swamped by his intellect and wrong-footed by his sudden changes in mood. His hostility bemused her and his derision offended her. It made her head throb trying to think of suitable ripostes when all she wanted, all she'd prepared herself for, was a straightforward first-time conversation with the man her friend was about to marry. Instead, what she had ... She shook her head slowly. What did she have? She wished she knew. Whatever it was, it was proving a very long way from the Californian welcome she had expected, or the relaxing break from London she had so badly needed.

When he was standing just a few feet away she lifted her head and gazed out at the burgeoning rose of a sunset. She took a breath to speak, then realizing she didn't know what to say, she simply let it go. She was so aware of him being there and wondered why his proximity was filling her with such sadness and futility. Was that the way he was feeling? Was he somehow managing to project the emotions in his heart into hers? It was crazy even to think it, especially when she barely knew him, but crazier still was the way they were standing there now, a painful distance between them as though they had injured each other deeply and were both too afraid to touch the open wound.

How much more fanciful was she going to get today, she wondered, as sighing, she started to turn towards him. When her eyes reached his face she found he was staring out to sea and appeared so absorbed in his thoughts that he might well have forgotten she was there. Then, as though recalling her presence, he lowered his eyes to hers. 'Do you still see Maguire?' he asked.

Rhiannon blinked as her heart somersaulted and somewhere inside she started to shake. 'No,' she said softly.

He nodded and looked back to the horizon.

'Ramon said I should ask you ...' she began, then taking another breath she forced herself to continue. 'I'm trying to work out how everyone links up here,' she said. 'Do you know Oliver?'

'No,' he answered. Then returning his eyes to hers, he said, 'I know the Straussens. I knew about the deal Maguire had with the old man ...' His mouth pursed at the corners. 'No one expected him to go as far as to marry you.'

'I wish someone had stopped it,' she said.

His nostrils flared slightly as he lowered his eyes and she looked at the thick, luxuriant crescents of his lashes. She seemed so very aware of everything about him, yet she couldn't be sure of the effect any of it was having. It was as though she had lost touch with her senses as she tried to follow the twists and turns of his moods.

'How did you know about it?' she asked.

Turning to look at her he said, 'Galina wanted you at the wedding, so I had some people look into who you were and what you do.'

Surprised by his frankness, she slanted her eyes down the beach, giving herself some time to think. 'Are you nervous of all journalists?' she asked finally. 'Or just those that threaten to get close?'

'More nervous of those who *try* to get close.'

'I was invited,' she reminded him.

His smile didn't waver, but his dark eyes were suddenly hard.

Don't speak, Rhiannon, she was telling herself. *Just hold out with the silence and force him to explain.*

'Galina and I will be leaving for honeymoon on Saturday,' he said. 'I hope we won't be seeing you again after that.'

Rhiannon's eyes dilated as the shock of his words hit her like a slap in the face, but before she could respond he continued.

'Galina told you I killed my wife,' he said, coolly dealing another blow. 'She couldn't, or didn't, tell you how I got away with it, but I'll tell you this: if you're stupid enough to think you stand even the smallest chance of getting either her or me to talk about what happened in front of a camera then you've got serious problems with your ego. Let me make myself plainer, take your eye for the main chance somewhere else, Miss Producer, because no matter what you think Galina owes you, you're sure as hell not going to find it through me.'

Rhiannon stared at him, hardly able to believe what she was hearing, too stunned even to take a breath.

'There's no jackpot in my house,' he went on ruthlessly, 'no pots at the end of rainbows or lamps where genies hang out.'

Rhiannon's mouth fell open as her own words echoed

back at her.

'Your intention to abuse my hospitality to the extent of selling my private life to the highest bidder', he continued, 'is about as low as your profession gets. You'd never pull it off, but the fact you were prepared to try makes you cheap and unworthy and I don't want cheap, unworthy people in my house. So take your sweet talk, Miss Producer, take your camera and your aspirations of fame and go check out someone else's life, because ours isn't for sale.'

Despite the fury that had leapt into her eyes, Rhiannon was reeling with shame. She had never, in all her life, been spoken to like that, nor had her motives ever been so brutally exposed for their hypocrisy. He made to turn away, but grabbing him by the arm she pulled him back to face her. 'Does Galina know you listen in to her calls?' she challenged furiously.

'Ask her,' he responded, his black eyes burning with anger.

'Be assured I will,' she responded cuttingly. 'And don't *ever* speak to me again the way you just did. OK, I'll admit my intentions weren't entirely altruistic when I decided to come here and yes, I would have used you and Galina to restart my career if I could. But it wasn't the only reason I came and if I'd known how much it would upset you I'd never even have considered it. And that's as far as I go defending myself, because from where I'm standing you're just about the last person on earth who should be taking apart someone else's morals.'

'Have you finished?' he asked tightly.

Realizing her hand was still on his arm she removed it, but her eyes were still blazing into his as the wind tossed her hair around her face and behind her the ocean roared on to the rocks. 'I should be able to go back to London tonight,' she told him. 'If not, there's bound to be a flight in the morning.'

His eyes narrowed with contempt. 'If there was an honest motive behind your coming here then I presume it was to give Galina the support she needs.'

'She doesn't need any support,' Rhiannon replied scathingly.

His eyebrows shot up, but it was a second or two before he responded. 'She's protected,' he said. 'And she's loved – a great deal. But she doesn't have a friend she can call her own. I dominate her life, everything she is and does is because of me. She needs something, someone, of her own. And she's chosen you.'

'Obviously against your wishes.'

'No, I approved of you, after I'd had you checked out. Seems I misjudged you. You're typical of someone in your profession. Mendacious and conceited enough to think you can get away with it.'

Rhiannon stared at him in disbelief. 'You can't seriously expect me to stay here now,' she said. 'Not after saying something like that.'

'I'm not expecting you to do anything. I'm just letting you know that as long as you intend to try uncovering something that's not there to be uncovered you're not welcome in my house.'

'So what am I supposed to do now? Persuade you my motives have suddenly become honourable and beg you to give me a second chance?'

Despite the sarcasm in her voice he looked at her expectantly.

She laughed. 'In your dreams,' she snapped. 'I'm on the next flight out of here.'

He shrugged and turning away, walked back to where he'd left his shoes.

Rhiannon stood for some time watching him, feeling the water wash around her ankles as the sea breeze lifted the hair from her shoulders and an onslaught of emotions swirled around her heart. The strangest thing was that despite how definite she had sounded, she had no intention of leaving and she was pretty sure he knew it. Odder still was that she had never felt so offended or insulted in her life, nor quite so elated. It was as though she had been tossed around in a storm, sliding over the decks of an unnavigable boat, knowing that any moment she could find herself overboard and that to show any sign of weakness would bring an irreversible defeat. But somehow she'd managed to hang on, to pull herself repeatedly back from the brink and meet the challenge head on. OK, she hadn't come through completely intact, but her pride would soon mend and her wits would resharpen. For the moment, though, she was happy to stand there alone and allow the calming roar of the waves to erase the anger from her thoughts and the vastness of the mountains to dwarf the misgivings in her heart.

A while later, tugging her hair away from her face and holding it behind her head, she went to retrieve her shoes and climbed back up to the house. Galina was waiting, eager to know how she'd got along with Max. Rhiannon wondered where Max was, as smiling and laughing she provided Galina with the reassurance she seemed to crave, while Ula stood quietly to one side and watched.

Something really wasn't right there, Rhiannon was thinking to herself as Ellis and Ula drove her back to the apartment later. In fact, a sixth sense was telling her that something was horribly wrong. At this stage it was impossible to tell what, but Max's paranoia about journalists, coupled with Galina's perplexing behaviour and everyone else's concerted efforts to appear happy and relaxed, when they were obviously anything but, was evidence enough that something was being hidden. Well, of course, the whole world knew what it was, but there was more, she was certain of it and a telephone call to Susan Posner, with whom she had the briefest of acquaintances, might just prove informative. But before that she must call Lizzy, who, presumably, would be in South Africa by now.

The light was starting to fade as Lizzy climbed aboard the twelve-seater plane at Skukuza airport. There were seven others flying out to Perlatonga that night, a party of three elderly Dutch couples and Rayna, a breathy, lash-batting blonde from Sydney, who'd read about the Reserve in the *Queensland Gazette* and had decided to treat herself to a visit to celebrate her thirtieth birthday. She was hoping, she'd confided to Lizzy during the three-hour wait they'd had while a fault in the plane's engine was rectified, to land herself a ranger, or better still, one of the gorgeous Morrison brothers who apparently owned the Reserve and were both, so she'd read in the *Gazette*, Australian, straight and unattached.

The far horizon was a molten mass of colour, turning the rolling acres of bush into a dense and shadowy wilderness as the plane rose smoothly from the runway. Wanting very much to avoid Rayna for the rest of the journey, Lizzy had slipped into a single seat on the port side of the cabin where she sat gazing down at the diminishing coconut-thatch umbrellas that were sprouting like mushrooms around the front of the airport building. She was, by now, in such a turmoil of nerves that whole minutes were passing without her seeing or hearing or even registering what was happening around her. Her stomach was in perpetual freefall, her heart was thudding and her mind, when it functioned, kept freezing in disbelief that she had come so far. What she was going to say when she saw him, how she was going to explain why she was there, or what the hell she was going to do if there was nowhere for her to stay, she couldn't even bring herself to consider. She was in a state of total inertia, incapable of thinking ahead, powerless to turn back, yet totally and brutally aware of her madness.

When at last they landed, her fellow passengers began

fussing excitedly as they prepared to disembark. Rayna's head popped up from behind her seat; her mascara was smudged, but she'd touched up her lipstick and folded her silky hair decorously over one shoulder. Meeting Lizzy's eyes she smiled; Lizzy smiled back, then glanced at the pilot as she wondered if he had radioed ahead to let them know he had an extra passenger on board. It was almost certain that he would have, but had he told them her name? Elizabeth Fortnum. Would Andy realize that was her? Would he be waiting when she stepped out of the plane?

The plane's door was heaved open and the loud chirping and rasping of an African night swamped the cabin, turning Lizzy's heart over as it swathed her in memories. A warm, scented breeze fluttered her hair as she stepped out into the darkness and tried not to feel as though she was stepping into a void.

'Hey, Lizzy!'

Hearing her own name she blinked, then focusing on the man at the bottom of the steps her heart began to pound. 'Doug!' she cried, running down the steps to greet him.

Laughing, he caught her in his arms and spun her round. 'I thought it was you when they radioed through,' he said, 'but the Elizabeth threw me. So, how are you? It's great to see you.'

Soundly relieved and encouraged by how genuinely pleased he appeared, Lizzy laughed and hugged him back. 'It's great to see you too,' she told him. 'It's OK, is it? Me arriving unannounced like this? There's somewhere for me to stay?'

'Are you kidding? There's always somewhere for you,' he assured her. He was grinning all over his face as he held her hands in his and gazed at her incredulously. 'Shit, I can't believe it,' he said. 'I just can't believe it. You're actually here.'

'I'm actually here,' she repeated, laughing as he seized

her again and hugged her as though he had never been so happy to see someone in his life. 'How long are you staying?' he asked, as he let her go.

Lizzy's heart skipped a beat. This was Doug, she reminded herself, not Andy. And if Doug knew she was here, then surely Andy must too. So where was he? 'I'm not sure,' she answered. 'It depends ...'

'Hell, it doesn't matter,' he interrupted. 'It's just good to see you. Can't wait to see Andy's face,' and with a laugh that sharpened her unease he turned to the other ranger and started giving orders.

To Lizzy's frustration he allocated Rayna a space in his own jeep, while the Dutch group were loaded aboard the other and driven off down the airstrip. Minutes later they were bumping along after them, Rayna ensconced between Lizzy and Doug in the front seat, the pilot stretched out on one of the bench seats behind. They stopped several times, once to look at a family of hyenas feasting on the carcass of an impala and twice to listen to the distant roar of a lion. The stops were mainly for Rayna's benefit, but Rayna was more interested to know how Lizzy and Doug knew each other, why Lizzy hadn't mentioned it before, where Doug came from in Australia and whether or not it was true they served a cocktail called a screaming orgasm. Lizzy winced, but had to remind herself that she too had once made use of that cocktail in much the same way. Suddenly she turned cold. Would the same happen to Rayna tonight as had happened to her on her first night? Both brothers. Rayna was slinky and gorgeous and so obviously available that the possibility was too high to dismiss and if the way Doug was already responding to her was anything to go by, the seduction had been clinched on the booking form.

Seeing the lights of the camp up ahead, Lizzy crooked an ironic eyebrow as she rehearsed how she was going to cover her nerves and humiliation when she got there.

She now knew, because Doug had just told Rayna, that Andy had been out on a drive when the plane came in and had no idea yet that Lizzy had been on it.

'Heck, is this going to be a surprise for the bloke,' Doug grinned, glancing over at Lizzy.

'A nice one, I hope,' Lizzy responded.

The radio squawked over his reply and before she could ask him to repeat it they were pulling up under the trees in front of the camp.

The next few minutes passed in a daze as staff and guests milled around the reception, sorting the luggage, checking in and arranging dinner. Lizzy watched them, feeling like a ghost at the wrong seance, while trying to will herself into some kind of action. A receptionist was talking to her, telling her that she had chalet number six and that one of the guards would take her and her luggage over, but Lizzy was barely registering the words.

She didn't see the brunette at first, her hair was so black that it was lost in the darkness as she walked across the camp, but as the two of them walked into the light of reception Lizzy felt a cold paralysis stealing through her body. Andy's arm was draped possessively around the girl's shoulders, hers was curled around his waist.

Lizzy's cheeks flared with colour as her heart twisted with shame. Quickly averting her eyes, she could only wonder why the hell Doug hadn't warned her. How warped did a man's sense of humour get that he could greet someone the way he had greeted her, whilst knowing what she was about to walk into?

Reluctantly her eyes moved back across the reception. The three Dutch couples were about to depart with their escorts and Doug was introducing Rayna to Andy and the brunette. Andy's arm was no longer round the brunette, but as he listened to whatever Rayna was saying he looked down at the brunette and smiled. He was besotted, anyone could see that and Lizzy just wanted to die. She started to move, then her heart stood still as his eyes suddenly found her and at first confusion, then astonishment, then total disbelief registered on his face.

Forcing a smile to her lips, she walked boldly towards him, holding out her hand ready to shake his. 'Hi,' she said. 'How are you?'

His bronzed, handsome face was still frozen in shock as, barely aware of what he was doing, he took the hand she was offering and shook it. 'Great,' he answered, staring at her as though she were some kind of apparition. 'Just great.' Then appearing to collect himself a little, he added, 'How are you? What are you doing here?'

She shrugged and threw a quick glance at Doug whose grin was painfully wide. 'I was just passing,' she said with a casual wave of her hand.

Andy turned to Doug, obviously about to ask what he knew about this, when the brunette nudged him, reminding him she was there too. But Andy seemed not to notice as his eyes returned to Lizzy's.

'Hi,' Lizzy said, holding a hand out to the brunette. 'I'm Lizzy.'

The girl's eyebrows instantly shot up. 'I'm very pleased to meet you, Lizzy,' she said with a careful glance at Andy.

'This is Catherina,' Doug jumped in. 'Our stepsister.'

Lizzy felt herself start to sway as the suddenness of relief loosened the tension in her limbs. 'It's lovely to meet you,' she smiled. 'Are you living here, or just visiting?'

'I'm just coming to the end of a four-month stint,' she answered. 'I'm starting Uni the week after next.' Her gorgeous face suddenly lit up. 'You know, I've heard so much about you, but I never thought I was going to get to meet you.'

Lizzy's eyes went instantly to Andy's. 'What have you

been hearing?' she asked.

'It's OK,' Andy said, putting a hand over his sister's mouth. 'I'll tell her myself. How long are you staying?' he asked Lizzy.

Lizzy shrugged. 'I'm not sure,' she answered, feeling a knot of emotion starting to gather in her throat. *It was going to be all right. He was pleased to see her. Wasn't he*?

Dimly she was aware of Doug leading Catherina away as those left in reception disappeared behind bamboo screens or melted into the darkness. Andy's blue eyes were fixed on hers, the incredulity starting to give way to laughter.

'I was beginning to give up hope,' he said softly.

Lizzy's head went to one side as she frowned.

'I thought you'd never come,' he whispered and lifting her chin with his fingers he pulled her towards him and covered her mouth with his.

By the time he let her go Lizzy's eyes were shining with tears. 'Why did you never write or answer my calls?' she asked, her voice catching on the emotion lodged in her throat.

'I didn't want you as a friend,' he answered. His eyes were looking far into hers as his fingers sank into her hair. 'Why did you come?'

Biting her lips in an effort not to laugh or cry, she said, 'I'm not sure. I mean ...' She took a breath and rolling her eyes, she said, 'Because I wanted to find out how I would feel when I saw you again.'

His eyes darkened as brushing his thumb gently over her lips, he said, 'Do you know the answer to that yet?'

She nodded and as his mouth found hers again she clung to him, pressing herself to him and feeling him respond to the need quickening inside her.

'We've got a lot to talk about,' he whispered, holding her face up to his, 'but right now I think we've got other things to attend to.'

Chapter 19

'Where have you been?' Rhiannon demanded, sinking into the downy white cushions of Galina's sofa and nestling the phone into her shoulder. 'I've been trying to get hold of you for days.'

'We've been making up for lost time,' Lizzy responded drolly. 'What do you think we've been doing?'

Despite the slight catch in her heart at the prospect of what this could mean, Rhiannon's eyes were simmering with laughter. 'You mean it's worked out?' she said.

'Mmm, I think you could say that,' Lizzy replied.

'Well?' Rhiannon prompted. 'Details please.'

Lizzy's sigh was one of perfectly feigned boredom. 'Darling, it was moonlight and madness from the moment I arrived.'

Rhiannon laughed. 'Did he know you were coming?' she said. 'You did tell him, didn't you?'

'No. I just walked into the camp, into his arms, then into his bed. We emerged about an hour ago, when I got all your messages.'

'Wow! You mean you've been making love for five days?'

'More or less. We talked a bit too. He claims he always knew I'd come, which I don't believe for a minute, because even I didn't know I would until I got here. But you know what men are like – they have to say these things, it puts starch in their egos. The truth is, he's been pining for me all this time, but had too much pride to tell me or ask me to come. He says he asked once and that was enough. The next move had to come from me, which it did and now we're planning babies.'

'You're not serious!'

Lizzy laughed. 'I am. Well, we've talked about it, anyway. I'm not getting any younger, remember, and we'd both like kids so we've given up the contraception and we're at it morning, noon and night. But that's enough about me, tell me about you. What have you been up to? How's it going over there?'

'OK,' Rhiannon answered, aware of how fast her heart was suddenly beating. 'But getting back to you. Are you serious, Lizzy? I mean, I know you, you love to wind me up, so tell me the truth, are you really intending to ... stay there?'

Lizzy's hesitation was only momentary, but it was enough to tell Rhiannon that there really was no joke, Lizzy and Andy were going to try and make a go of this. Rhiannon's eyes moved to the tangerine sky outside, where the sun was descending into the shimmering blue Pacific. The sense of loss she was already feeling was pulling at her heart and the prospect of returning to London was suddenly unbearable.

Lizzy laughed awkwardly. 'God only knows how this sort of life is going to suit me,' she said, 'but, hell, what have I got to lose?'

'Nothing, I suppose,' Rhiannon answered, getting up to go and pour herself some wine. 'And if you feel it's the right thing to do ...' She stopped, then pushing herself on, she said, 'Don't tell me I'm going to get to play maid of honour twice in the same year I was nearly a bride.'

Lizzy's wince was almost audible. 'I wouldn't do that to you,' she replied soberly. Then, 'No, we have no plans to get married. Actually, we haven't even spoken about it. Now come on,' she prompted, 'tell me what's been going on over there. When's the wedding? This Saturday, isn't it?'

Rhiannon inhaled deeply. 'That's right,' she said, unplugging the cork from an already open bottle of chardonnay and filling a glass. 'And everything's totally last minute. I only had a fitting for my dress yesterday, but apparently the woman's a genius and will have it ready by the day.'

'What's it like?'

'Ivory silk, very plain. Actually, it's beautiful. So's Galina's. I'll take photographs.'

'Speaking of which,' Lizzy pounced, 'how are you getting on with the idea of a video, or doing an interview?'

'Oh God,' Rhiannon groaned, closing her eyes as she sank back down on the sofa. 'Don't remind me. I had the most terrible show-down with Max over all that, he virtually ordered me out of his house. God, it was awful.'

'What do you mean? What happened?'

'What happened is that he has Galina's phone tapped, the phone that I'm on now, so you and I were revealed in all our scheming glory last time we spoke. He even quoted back at me some of the things I said.'

'No!' Lizzy gasped. 'What did we say? Or no, I don't want to think about it. Is someone listening in now?'

'I'm told not,' Rhiannon answered. 'Ula, Max's assistant, left a message on the voice mail to tell me, and I quote, "to please feel free to use the telephone whenever you like, it's in normal working order now."'

'Get out of here,' Lizzy laughed. 'What kind of guy is he, for God's sake? Or more to the point, what's Galina up to that needs *checking out*?'

Rhiannon smiled at the familiarity of the phrase. 'God knows,' she answered. 'She says she sleeps with other men, but heaven only knows if it's true. I know I wouldn't if I had someone like Max.'

'It could be true,' Lizzy suggested. 'After all, why else would he be having her calls listened in to? What are they like together? Do they seem close?'

'Very,' Rhiannon answered, then started to frown. 'I mean, they do, but ... Well, something doesn't feel right. Don't ask me to explain, because I can't. It's just a gut feeling I have that all is not as it should be around here.'

'Have you mentioned it to Galina?'

'I haven't had the chance. She was going to try and work it so we could spend some time together before the wedding, but she seems to have forgotten about it now. She went to Chicago on Monday on some Conspiracy assignment and doesn't come back until late tomorrow. She called me on Sunday, the day after I had the bust-up with Max, but she didn't mention it, so obviously he hadn't either.'

'I see,' Lizzy muttered. 'Tell me some more about him. I mean, I take it he didn't shout at you the entire time you were there.'

'Almost,' Rhiannon mumbled, feeling the heat of her embarrassment returning as she saw, and almost felt, the anger she had seen in his eyes that day on the beach. But it wasn't only embarrassment. Her heart faltered and she held her breath, waiting for the feeling to pass. It was incredible, irrational even, but there was no denying the intensity of the attraction she felt for Max Romanov and had been feeling virtually since the moment she'd met him. Of course she hadn't recognized it as that at first, but now she did she was finding it almost impossible to stop thinking about him in ways that aroused her so much she sometimes wondered if she was losing her mind.

Trying to push it aside now and summoning all the objectivity she could muster, she said, 'I think he's an extremely wealthy man who's very used to ordering people around and getting his own way. He's got ... a very definite air about him, not arrogance exactly, more ... Well, more confidence, I suppose. Actually, he's quite sinister in a way. Is sinister the word I'm looking for?'

she said, cocking her head to one side as she tried to stay in tune with what she was saying. 'Maybe not. I don't know. He's got this way of looking at you that makes you feel like the emperor who's just been told the truth about his new clothes. Do you know what I mean? He sees right through you, strips you bare of everything, but manages to keep a wall around himself that makes you feel that even if you touched him you'd be no closer to him than if you were the other side of the globe.' She was struggling to think of more, something that wouldn't alert Lizzy to the way she was feeling, but would tell her how powerful yet remote he was, how unbelievably attractive and disturbing he was, how just the conjured image of his naked body could turn her bones to jelly.

Then, quite suddenly, her mind switched to Ramon and slapping a hand to her head she cried, 'My God, I didn't tell you who else was there, did I? Oh Lizzy, you're not going to believe this, but Ramon, the guy who rescued me in Marrakesh, is staying at the Romanov villa. At least, he was, he's flown off somewhere now for a couple of days, but can you imagine the shock I got when I saw him? He's here for the wedding too, at least I think he is. He was a bit vague about that. Anyway, apparently he's an old friend of Max's, the Russian-Jewish connection, and get ahold of this, it was Max, so Ramon tells me and Max didn't deny it, who was responsible for Ramon being in Marrakesh when he was. I mean that Ramon was there for a specific purpose, namely to get me out of trouble should I fall into it, and Max was the one who organized it.'

'You're kidding me,' Lizzy responded in amazement. 'But how did Max know?'

'He'd been having me checked out,' Rhiannon answered. 'As a friend of Galina's, *and* a journalist, I apparently had to be vetted, so obviously he discovered that I was seeing Oliver, and because of Oliver's connection to the Straussens he guessed there was a chance I might end up in some kind of trouble, so he sent someone in, enter Ramon, to keep an eye on it all.'

'I don't believe it!' Lizzy cried. 'Is the man some kind of control freak, or something? And why would he care what happened to you? I mean, to go to all that trouble when he doesn't even know you.'

'But Galina knows me and as Galina's friend I qualify for his protection. Or that's the way I read it,' Rhiannon replied. 'More or less, anyway.'

'So where did you say Ramon was now?'

'I'm not sure. He said something about having some business to attend to in the South, but I imagine he'll be back by the weekend.'

'And Max? Where's he?'

Rhiannon's heart turned over. 'As far as I know he's here in LA,' she answered. 'I haven't seen or spoken to him since Saturday when he made me feel ... like something nasty the sea had washed up. God, if you'd heard the way he spoke to me, Lizzy. I'm not going to repeat it because I don't think I could survive the shame a second time round. Anyway, what it left me in no doubt of was that he loathes journalists with an almost pathological frenzy and Susan Posner's up there at the top of his list. Do you remember her? She did some background stuff for us on some actor a couple of years ago?'

'Vaguely,' Lizzy answered.

'Well, for whatever reason she's very definitely Max Romanov's *bête noire*, so naturally I tried calling her to find out why. She's in Seattle at the moment, back tomorrow I'm told, so hopefully she'll return my call.'

'What do you expect to find out?'

Rhiannon shrugged. 'I'm not sure really. Anyway, getting back to Galina, I'd forgotten how odd she can be at times. I mean, I probably didn't notice it too much before; you don't when you grow up with someone, do you? I mean, they're just the way they are and you accept them for that. But when you haven't seen someone for a while their quirks and foibles and eccentricities become much more noticeable. At least hers seem to have. It's either that, or she's getting worse.'

'What do you mean, worse?' Lizzy said.

'I don't know. Worse in the sense that you never seem able to pin her down. She makes me think of a dandelion, floating around without a care in the world, looking drop-dead beautiful and ecstatically happy with her life, but if you gave her one quick puff she'd break into a thousand pieces. Except, like I said, she seems really happy, so I don't understand what's making me say that. Max obviously adores her and she loves being ruled by him, or so she says, and her relationship with his kids is quite wonderful to see. Add to that her new-found fame and fortune and you've got ... Well, I don't know what you've got, but it certainly isn't what you'd expect. Something's going on behind the scenes somewhere, I'm sure of it and what's more, I get the distinct impression that everyone in that house knows what it is and are all, to one degree or another, involved in keeping it covered up.'

'And you think Susan Posner might know what it is?'

Rhiannon shrugged. 'She might.'

'What's your guess? I mean, you must have some kind of theory on it by now.'

Rhiannon was shaking her head. 'That's the strange thing, I don't. I mean, there's nothing to put your finger on. Nothing at all that you could pin it to and say that's what they're doing, or that's what the problem might be. Their performances are flawless, yet somehow you know they're acting.'

'Well, it all sounds very intriguing to me. A bit Stephen King-ish in fact. You'll have to let me know what you find out from Susan. Anyway, what about LA? What do you think of the place itself?'

Rhiannon smiled, as a pleasing lift coasted around her heart. 'Actually, I love it,' she answered. 'Obviously, I haven't seen much of it yet, but the buzz you get here, Liz, is like, well it's like a drug. The adrenalin really gets going around these people. They're electrifying. They're all about showbiz and you just can't help being swept along by it. I mean, it's terrible really, because you lose your perspective on the outside world totally, at least I have. It's like everything happens here, so who the hell needs the rest of the world? Their lives are movies, their nourishment is megabucks and their fantasies are a daily reality. It's fascinating, seductive and so unbelievably stimulating that the thought of returning to London is too depressing for words. Especially now you're not going to be there. Sorry, I didn't mean that,' she said hastily. 'I'm not trying to make you feel guilty, I'm just saying that I don't feel like there's much of a reason to go back.'

'It's OK, I understand,' Lizzy smiled. 'So why don't you stay?'

Rhiannon laughed. 'Believe it or not, I've been thinking about it. The trouble is I don't think there's much chance of me getting a green card.'

'You never know unless you try,' Lizzy responded. 'What would you do if you did get one?'

Rhiannon sighed. 'God knows. The kind of TV I do is mainly New York and Washington based. Here it's more mini-series and movies. And it's hot! It's been over a hundred degrees today. What's it like there?'

Lizzy said, 'Hot, but not that hot. Did you find out where Max and Galina are going on their honeymoon, by the way?'

'Not yet, no. Honestly, I've hardly spoken to anyone about the wedding. In fact I'm beginning to wonder if it isn't all some kind of hoax. Well, I guess we'll find out on Saturday.' She looked up as someone knocked on the door. 'That's odd,' she said, frowning. 'No one's supposed to be able to get up here without coming through security.'

'What? What are you talking about?'

'Someone's at the door,' Rhiannon explained, getting to her feet. The unsettling feeling she'd had the first night she'd arrived was suddenly stealing over her again.

'It's probably a security guard,' Lizzy told her, seeming to sense her unease. 'Go and see who it is and if you don't come back straight away I'll panic.'

'So helpful,' Rhiannon said in a whisper, as whoever it was knocked again. Then telling Lizzy not to go away, she dropped the receiver on the sofa and went to put her eye to the security scan. When she saw who was in the hall outside her heart leapt to her throat and taking a quick step back she pushed a hand to her mouth as the rest of her started to shake. Then taking a deep breath and willing herself to remain calm, she picked up the keys, slid them into the lock and pulled the door open.

Max's eyebrows were raised, his dark eyes were both knowing and curious as he looked at her, as though, she thought, he had guessed what confusion his arrival would cause.

'Hi,' she smiled.

'I hope I'm not disturbing you,' he said. 'I tried calling from the car, but the line was busy.'

'Uh, yes,' Rhiannon said, stepping aside to allow him to pass. 'I was speaking to ... a friend. If you'll excuse me a moment I'll just finish the call.'

Waving her towards the phone, he went to stand at the window and looked out at the dusk-shrouded marina.

Watching him as he slipped his hands into his trouser pockets, Rhiannon could feel the breath locking in her lungs. Then quickly picking up the phone, she put it to her ear.

'Rhiannon? Are you there?' Lizzy was calling.

'Yes, I'm here,' Rhiannon answered, turning away from Max.

'Who was it?' Lizzy asked. 'I heard voices. Have they gone now?'

'No,' Rhiannon said. 'I have to go,' she added, barely able to hear herself through the thudding of her heart.

'Don't you dare go now,' Lizzy cried. 'You sound very peculiar. Who is it, Rhiannon? Who's there with you?'

Rhiannon glanced back over her shoulder. Max was still standing at the window, gazing out at the yachts in the harbour.

'Rhiannon?'

'I have to go,' Rhiannon repeated. 'Everything's OK. It's only Max.' Strangely, as soon as she said the words she seemed to relax and smiling as he turned to look at her, she told Lizzy she'd speak to her again soon and ended the call.

Putting the phone down, she turned to face him. The apartment was very quiet and no sound drifted through from outside. There was no antagonism now, Rhiannon realized as they looked at each other, quite the reverse in fact, for his dark eyes were softening as his mouth curved at the corner, and in response she felt the smile fade from her lips. The desire burning between her legs was like nothing she had ever known before and had it not been happening to her she would never have believed it possible just to look at a man and feel the way she was feeling now. Quickly she averted her eyes, but her cheeks were already stained with colour.

'I owe you an apology,' he said.

Rhiannon nodded and made herself look at him again. What is it about him, she was asking herself. Why is he doing this to me? Does he even know he's doing it?

'The way I spoke to you on Saturday was inexcusable,' he said. 'But I hope not unforgivable.'

Rhiannon's eyes searched his face. She was aware of the way her nipples had hardened, making themselves visible through the T-shirt she was wearing, and wondered if he had noticed them too. For some reason she wasn't embarrassed and as he smiled she felt herself smiling too.

'It was unforgivable,' she told him. 'But then so too were my intentions.'

His head went to one side as he looked at her and this time she knew he had noticed her breasts.

Touch them, she was silently imploring, *please, just touch them*.

He lifted his hand and looking down she saw that he was waiting to shake. Again her cheeks flooded with colour as, attempting to disguise her confusion with a laugh, she took his hand.

'Shall we make a fresh start?' he said.

'Of course.' She turned and waved a hand towards the drinks. 'Can I get you something?' she offered, amazed at how steady her voice sounded when she was in such turmoil.

He nodded. 'Sure. I'll take a Scotch. Did you speak to Galina today?' he asked as she turned away.

'No. Did you?'

'Sure. She calls pretty regularly. Every couple of hours if she can.'

Rhiannon's surprise showed as she looked back at him.

He smiled. 'It's a habit we fell into a long time ago,' he explained. 'She likes to know what I'm doing, I like to know what she's doing.'

'Water?' Rhiannon said, pouring a generous measure of Scotch into a tumbler as she tried to adjust to the good humour and easy-going manner that were making him an entirely different man from the one she had met on Saturday.

'I'll take it neat,' he answered. Then going to sit on the armchair facing the sofa, he stretched his long legs out in front of him and crossed them at the ankles. 'So what have you been doing with yourself?' he asked as she handed him his drink and, feeling slightly more in control of herself now, returned to the sofa.

'Catching up with a few friends,' she said. 'Getting myself acquainted with the city and the car. Thank you for organizing the car, by the way, but I really must insist on paying for the rental myself.'

'You must?' he said, arching an eyebrow.

Rhiannon laughed. 'I must,' she repeated, knowing instinctively that he wasn't going to argue, but that she'd never end up paying for it anyway.

'Does the apartment suit you?' he said.

She nodded and looked around. 'It's a beautiful apartment,' she said.

Sucking in his bottom lip, he nodded and flicked his eyes towards the window. 'You know you'd be welcome at the house,' he said, looking back at her. 'I hope that was made clear to you.'

'It was by some,' Rhiannon answered, her voice loaded with irony.

He grinned and laughing, Rhiannon felt herself responding to him again. Then remembering what Ula had said about the way he could turn on the charm, she felt herself deflate.

'I get the impression something's bothering you,' he said.

Rhiannon's heart hammered as the blood left her face. Dear God, was he really reading her mind?

'Is it Maguire?' he said.

Rhiannon stared at him, then laughing through her surprise she said, 'No.'

'Then what?' he said.

She was still smiling. 'Why do you think something's bothering me?' she asked.

'You're on edge,' he told her. 'Anyone can see that. Are you sure you're comfortable here?'

Rhiannon frowned. 'Shouldn't I be?' she countered.

He looked at her for some time, then finally he said, 'I don't like Galina being here and, to be frank, I don't like you being here either.'

Rhiannon's laugh was unsteady. 'Why on earth not?' she said. 'There's plenty of security downstairs. Assuming that's what's concerning you.'

'Do you feel safe here?' he asked.

She hesitated, then seeing no point in lying she said, 'As a matter of fact, no. At least, not all the time. I can't quite explain it, but it's like ...' She looked at him, already embarrassed about what she was going to say. 'It's like somebody died here,' she said. 'Or something horrible happened.'

Again he sucked in his lips as he thought about her answer. Then taking another sip of Scotch he said, 'I'm not aware that anyone ever died here.' He was staring down into his glass and allowed several seconds to elapse before continuing. 'Galina uses the apartment to get away from me,' he said. 'Or so she says.'

'Does that upset you?'

'No. What upsets me is what she does here.'

Rhiannon stared at him, at a loss what to say next.

'She entertains other men here,' he said.

Rhiannon took a breath. 'If you know that then why do you allow it to continue?' she said.

He smiled, then sitting forward to put his glass on the table, he said, 'Can I take you to dinner? I could use some company and ...' He shrugged. 'I could just use some company.'

Surprised and touched that he should confess to anything even remotely approaching a weakness, she said, with a calm that amazed and impressed her, 'I'll have to cancel my other arrangements first, if you don't mind waiting.'

Half an hour later they were seated at a window table in a far corner of the chic and spacious Café del Rey, a mile or so down the road from Galina's apartment. It was populated, as usual, by LA's young executives with their smart striped shirts, Armani jeans and mobile phones.

Max's eyes were on Rhiannon as she dealt with the muted excitement and curiosity their arrival had evoked.

'Do you mind all this attention?' she asked, meeting a few unabashed stares and finding herself the first to look away.

'Yes,' he answered.

She looked at him. 'But there's nothing you can do about it?'

He shook his head, then seemed suddenly concerned. 'Does it bother you?' he said. 'Would you rather go some place else?'

'Is there anywhere you wouldn't be recognized?' she asked, not without irony. When he didn't respond she said, 'No, let's stay here. They'll get fed up in a minute.'

Looking up at the waitress as she began to hover with her notepad he winked at Rhiannon, then nodded for her to start reciting her spiel.

'Hi, my name is Cindy, and I am your server tonight,' she began, her pretty, girlish face singing hospitality as she focused her entire attention on Max. 'Paul, our assistant manager, will be over directly to tell you about the specials we have tonight and if there's anything on the menu you would like explained I'll be happy to help out.'

Max glanced at Rhiannon, whose eyes were reflecting the amusement in his. 'OK, Cindy, bring us a bottle of chardonnay,' he said, still looking at Rhiannon. Then turning to Cindy he said, 'I don't know what you have here ... A Château St Jean?' He pronounced 'Jean' the French way, then realizing that the waitress hadn't understood he tried saying it like the woman's name and got an immediate response.

'Is it a Californian wine?' Rhiannon laughed as the waitress left.

'Yep.' Reaching out for the pack of matches that was triangled on the corner of the table, he lit the candles between them. Rhiannon watched the movement of his hands, then lowered her eyes as she felt the scrutiny of those at nearby tables.

'So, do you like Los Angeles?' he said, tossing the matches into an ashtray. 'What you've seen of it so far.'

'Yes, actually I do,' she answered.

'You sound surprised,' he commented. 'Didn't you expect to?'

'No, I don't think I did,' she said truthfully. 'At least, not so quickly. But everything's always heightened when you're on a short trip like this. Everyone wants to see you, catch up on the news at home, show off what their new lives are like ... You know what I mean, I'm sure. What about you? Do you like it here?'

Sitting back as Cindy turned up with the wine, he inhaled deeply and said, 'For me this is home, so I guess I never really think about whether I like it or not.'

Waiting until he had tasted the wine she said, 'I imagine you know a lot of people here.'

He nodded, signalled Cindy to pour and said, 'Probably more than I'd like to know.' His eyes creased at the corners as he smiled. 'Or maybe it's the other way round. I don't seem to have too many friends these days.'

Rhiannon's eyes followed Cindy as, in her tight black pants and white shirt, she wiggled towards another table. 'Do you feel let down by that?' she said, turning back to Max.

He pondered her question for a moment. 'No, I don't think so,' he answered. 'By the time Carolyn died I'd about had it with the life-style we were leading, so it was no loss when all our so-called friends found other parties to go to and other sources to tap for "the next big project".'

Rhiannon's eyebrows rose. 'Does that mean you were once into financing movies?' she said.

He smiled and picked up his wine. 'Sure,' he

answered. 'I still am, but I let Maurice and Ellis handle things these days. Shall we drink a toast?' he suggested.

Rhiannon picked up her glass.

'Let's drink to you,' he said, his eyes resting wholly on hers. 'Welcome to Los Angeles.'

'Thank you,' she smiled, touching her glass to his and hoping beyond hope that the hundred ways in which she wanted him weren't reflected in her eyes.

The assistant manager arrived then and proceeded to describe the house specials. Rhiannon listened attentively and couldn't remember a thing when he'd finished. Without even glancing at the menu Max handed it back and ordered the blackened swordfish. Looking quickly down the list in front of her, Rhiannon hit on the spinach fettucini with smoked salmon and passed her menu over too. She wasn't in the slightest bit hungry, but the wine was making her light-headed.

'You know, you intrigue me,' she said, resting her chin on her hand and daring to look him in the eye.

He laughed and leaning slightly towards her as he indicated the other diners, he said, 'If you were to ask any of them, I think you'd find that you are generating far more interest than I am right now.'

'Because I'm with you,' she pointed out.

'Which puts me at a distinct advantage over them,' he said. 'Because I can find out exactly who you are just by asking.'

'You already know who I am,' she reminded him, not unaware of how very adeptly he had managed to steer the subject away from himself.

He grinned. 'I thought you English were big on subtext,' he teased.

'Generally we are,' she responded, 'but I'm never too sure with Americans.'

Laughing again, he took a sip of wine and held her eyes. 'They tell me you produce a pretty good show back in London,' he said.

'I used to,' she corrected. 'I was ousted just before coming here.'

His surprise seemed genuine, so too did his concern. Then nodding he said, 'That explains a few things I heard in your phone call. Do you think you'll have any trouble finding a new job?'

She shrugged. 'I might. I've got a music quiz to go back to, but it's not really my thing. To tell you the truth, I'd like to find something here. Oh, God, what do I sound like?' she groaned, feeling suddenly self-conscious and trying to cover it with a laugh. 'The whole world wants to make it big in LA, so what makes me so different? Nothing, is the answer. The trouble is, when you're here it actually seems possible. But it's just a dream because I don't have a work permit, nor do I stand much chance of getting one.'

'Have you tried?' he asked.

She shook her head. 'I wouldn't know where to start.'

'Then I'll have Ula put you in touch with a couple of immigration lawyers. Speak to them, you never know, it might not be as difficult as you think.'

She smiled her surprise. 'Thank you,' she said.

For a moment he looked as though he was about to say more, then appearing to change his mind, he looked down at where his fingers were resting on the stem of his glass.

Rhiannon's eyes moved over his face, following the long sweep of his lashes, the Slavic flare of his nostrils, the harshness of his jaw, the fullness of his mouth. She wanted him so badly that she could almost feel the pressure of his lips on hers, the touch of his breath on her skin, the weight of his body, the invading hardness of his cock ... Stopping herself, she turned to her reflection in the window and forced herself to think of Lizzy.

Several minutes passed until finally Rhiannon said, 'Did I say something to offend you?'

He looked up, but his expression was unreadable as

the candlelight flickered in his eyes and he started to smile. 'I'm sorry,' he said, 'I was …'

'Hi, how are you doing here?' Cindy gushed, plucking their wine bottle from the bucket beside the table. 'Can I get you folks anything?'

Max's irritation was palpable and Cindy's cheeks paled as she struggled to understand what she had done wrong.

Easing the bottle from her hand, Rhiannon thanked her, told her she could go, then topping up their glasses herself she returned the bottle to the ice. When she looked at him again Max was laughing.

'You're pretty terrifying, you know,' she told him.

'I don't seem to terrify you.'

She thought about that for a moment. 'Do you want to terrify me?' she asked.

'No.'

'You did when I first met you.'

'Shall I apologize again?'

She shook her head. 'No need.' Then in a pensive voice she said, 'I wonder if you terrify Galina. I must make a point of asking her.'

He gave a shout of laughter. 'I don't know anyone in this world who frightens Galina,' he said. 'In fact, I swear she's incapable of fear.'

Rhiannon smiled. 'You may well be right,' she said. Then after a pause, 'I was wondering, was yours one of the families she used to stay with during school holidays all those years ago?'

He nodded. 'My grandfather had something of a passion for her grandmother,' he said. 'But the old lady rarely came with her, which was a great disappointment to him.' He smiled. 'It would make the old guy happy to know that Galina and I are getting married,' he said. 'I think it would put things straight for him.'

'Is that why you're marrying her?' Rhiannon said, managing to make it sound like the most natural question in the world when in truth she couldn't quite believe she'd said it.

He looked at her, assessing her, then slanting his eyes towards the window he stared out at the darkness for a while. 'I'm marrying Galina because I love her,' he said, bringing his eyes back to hers.

Rhiannon blushed as her heart turned over and she quickly looked away. 'I'm sorry,' she whispered. 'It was unforgivably rude of me to suggest otherwise.'

Their food was set down in front of them and picking up her fork Rhiannon began to twist the fettucini. Max drank some more wine, then lifting his cutlery he started on the fish.

They ate in a silence that was so awful that it was all Rhiannon could do to stop herself apologizing again, which she would have had she not wanted just to forget it had happened. She was trying desperately to think of something to say, anything that might get them over this terrible impasse, but she couldn't get her mind to function beyond the glaring belief that he was lying; that he didn't love Galina at all. Or maybe it was just what she wanted to believe.

'Do you ever see Maguire now?' he asked, breaking the silence at last.

'You asked me that the other day,' she reminded him. 'The answer is no.'

He nodded and putting down his fork he picked up his wine again. 'Did you love him very much?' he asked.

Feeling the knot in her stomach tightening, Rhiannon nodded. 'Yes. Enough to consider going back to him,' she said.

Max's eyes widened. 'After what he did?'

Rhiannon's eyes dropped to the table. 'I won't do it,' she said, 'but I've thought about it. I mean, when something like that happens ... Well, it's so hard to deal with that sometimes it's easier to pretend that it didn't happen at all. And Oliver's nothing if not a master of pretence. Or should I call it self-delusion? Whatever, it was an experience I'd prefer never to have had, and one that I think will make it very hard for me to trust anyone again.'

Max nodded thoughtfully, then said, 'Were you faithful to him?'

Surprised by the question Rhiannon said, 'From the day we met.' Then remembering Galina's other men she looked down at her plate again. 'Are you faithful to Galina?' she ventured after a while.

He laughed. 'Yes, I'm faithful to Galina,' he said.

'But she sleeps with other men.'

'I'm afraid so.'

'Why? If she loves you.'

'Does she love me?'

'She says she does,' Rhiannon whispered, feeling horribly out of her depth.

He smiled, then sighing he said, 'The biggest problem Galina and I have is that she loves me. If she didn't this would all be so much easier.'

Rhiannon frowned. 'I'm not sure I follow,' she said.

He was silent for a while, then looking up he said, 'It means a lot to her, you being here, you know?'

'Then I'm glad I came,' Rhiannon said.

His eyebrows flickered, then setting down his knife and fork he picked up the wine bottle and emptied it into their glasses.

Rhiannon's plate was still half full, but she could eat no more. She was so tense that her neck and shoulders were aching and her hands were almost rigid. He was one of the hardest men to be with she had ever come across, yet there was nowhere else on God's earth she'd rather be.

'I'm going to be honest with you, Max,' she said, after their plates had been cleared, 'I get the distinct impression that something is wrong in yours and Galina's lives. Please don't think I'm asking what it is, I'm just saying that ...' She felt herself start to colour as she suddenly realized what she was saying. 'Well, if you need someone to talk to,' she went on lamely, wishing desperately that she had never started.

'Thank you,' he smiled. His eyes were gently searching her face as he waited for her embarrassment to pass. 'I'm not saying you're right about there being something wrong,' he went on when she looked at him again, 'but if you are, then I'm going to ask you for Galina's sake, for all our sakes, not to try to find out what it is. Just be a friend to her, is all I ask, because she needs all the friends she can get.'

As he spoke Rhiannon felt her heart tightening, for there was no question in her mind now that he did love Galina, that he loved her perhaps more than he could bear.

Then surprising her again he said, 'Would you like to walk on the beach?'

Rhiannon smiled. 'I thought it was dangerous at night,' she said.

His eyes were dancing. 'I think we should be OK,' he said drolly.

It was just after ten when they left the restaurant, just after midnight when they finally returned to Galina's apartment. As Rhiannon slid the key in the lock she was laughing and breathless and still, despite the short drive back, slightly flushed from the sea air. It had been an incredible two hours spent paddling in the waves, shouting above the roar of the ocean and digging their toes into the sand as they sat talking and watching the moonlight ripple over the sea. It had been another Max entirely that she had encountered then, a Max who was as light-hearted and humorous as he was candid and relaxed. He'd spoken a lot about his children, making her laugh with the dry, self-mocking tones of his pride and telling her without actually saying it how very deeply he loved them. He'd told her about Carolyn, his wife, how they'd met, how unsatisfactory the marriage had been, yet how very hard they had both tried to make it work. He'd said nothing about the way she'd died and Rhiannon hadn't asked. She'd simply listened as he'd opened up to her in a way she had the feeling was rare for him. And she had done the same, telling him things about herself and her family, her hopes and her fears that until now she had barely known herself. As serious as some of their subjects were, they'd found plenty to laugh about too and even now, as Rhiannon pushed open the door and switched on the lights, she could feel her heart tripping on the laughter she knew was in his eyes.

He was such a paradox, she was thinking to herself as she dropped the keys on a table and watched him walk into the kitchen to put on some coffee. His moods changed so swiftly and each one, when it came, felt as irrevocable as the next. He was exhausting, yet exhilarating and so breath-takingly perceptive that now they were no longer in the protective shadows of moonlight she didn't dare to look at him directly for fear he might read her thoughts.

'Do you take it white or black?' he said, setting two coffee cups on their saucers.

'White, but there isn't any cream,' she answered, curling into the corner of the sofa and resting her chin on one hand as she watched him. Beneath the black polo shirt and beige cotton trousers he was wearing she could see the solid outline of his body, but not wanting to torment herself any more she let her eyelids drop.

Looking up and seeing her eyes closed he smiled. 'You tired?' he asked. 'Maybe I should go. It's pretty late.'

'No! No,' she said, almost tripping over herself in her haste. 'I'm fine, I was just thinking, that's all.'

His eyes held hers and her cheeks flamed as she prayed desperately that he hadn't picked up on her thoughts.

'So?' he prompted, carrying the coffee around the kitchen bar and setting it down on the table in front of her. 'You going to share whatever it was you were thinking? It looked pretty good.'

Rhiannon swallowed hard and tried to push herself past the note of intimacy that had crept into his voice. She was imagining it and she knew it, but still she was responding to it. 'I was just thinking about this Saturday,' she said, picking up her coffee as he relaxed into the facing chair. What astonishing perversity of mind had suddenly launched her into the very last subject on earth she wanted to discuss right now she would never know.

'You mean the wedding?' he said.

She nodded, then tilting her head curiously to one side she said, 'You know, I've started to think that it's all a hoax, that there's not actually a wedding this weekend at all.'

He laughed. 'Why on earth would you think that?' he said.

She shrugged. 'I don't know. I suppose because there don't seem to be many arrangements going on and no one seems to talk about it – at least not very much.'

'Believe me,' he said, 'were you over at the house you'd be talking about nothing else and the only thing you'd be in any doubt about is whether the ceremony's taking place in the house or the garden. Galina can't make up her mind and as of this afternoon she's refusing to discuss it.'

Rhiannon gave a laugh of surprise. 'But it's her wedding,' she protested. 'How can she not discuss it?'

His dark eyes showed only humour as he said, 'Galina can do pretty much anything when she puts her mind to it.'

Rhiannon looked at him and knew that were her mind not so clouded by the way she felt about him, she would probably be handling this much better. As it was, she barely knew what she was saying until the words had left her lips. 'Are you looking forward to Saturday?' she asked, twisting her own knife.

He grinned and leaning forward put his cup back on the table. 'That's a hard one,' he said. 'I guess I'll be glad when it's over.'

'Have you made any plans for a honeymoon?'

His eyebrows went up and his eyes were suddenly fixed so very intently on hers that Rhiannon felt herself starting to blush.

In the end he got to his feet. 'Time I was going,' he said.

Rhiannon stood too and walked to the door ahead of him. 'Thank you,' she said, turning to face him. 'I really enjoyed the evening.'

His expression was unreadable as he looked down at her, but there was an intensity about his eyes that was turning her weak with longing and she knew she had never been so close to begging a man to stay. 'I'm glad we've become friends,' she said softly.

Long minutes ticked by. Rhiannon could feel her breasts rising and falling as her breath shortened and her heartbeat thumped. Her eyes remained rooted to his as sharp, insistent pangs of lust buried themselves deeply inside her and the need to touch him grew to a point she couldn't bear.

At last he moved and as his hand covered her breast her lips parted and her knees almost gave way. His eyes held hers with a power that was almost as sensuous as the caress and as his fingers tightened on her aching nipple she groaned aloud.

He watched her, never taking his eyes from her face as his hand moved over her breasts. She looked back at him, telling him with her eyes that he could do anything he pleased, anything at all.

He leaned forward, covering her mouth with his and pushing his tongue deep inside. Then letting her go, he gazed down at her again while taking the hem of her T-shirt and pulling it over her head. She could feel herself trembling as his hand travelled over the flimsy lace of her bra and unable to wait she reached behind her and unfastened the clasp.

As she bared herself to him he looked down at her, brushing the backs of his fingers over her hard, protruding nipples, stooping to suck them into his mouth, then lifting his head to look down into her face again.

'I want you to fuck me,' she whispered.

His eyes seemed to flash as his jaw hardened and before she knew what was happening she was in his arms and he was kissing her with an urgency she had never felt in a man before. Within seconds their clothes were on the floor and she was falling to her knees to take him in her mouth.

He held her head as she sucked him, twisting her hair in his hands and pushing himself deep into her throat. Leaning over her, he ran his hands over her buttocks, then pushed a finger inside her. Crying out she fell against him, clinging to him as the sensation tore through her body. Then suddenly he pulled her to her feet, shoved her against the door and drove his fingers deep inside her as his tongue entered her mouth. She could hear herself moaning as she melted against the pressure of his fingers, then he was lifting her up, wrapping her legs around his waist and penetrating her fast. She cried out again, her voice echoing in his throat as he pumped himself into her with short, hard strokes. His lips were still on hers, their tongues were entwined, his hands were squeezing her buttocks and his penis was forcing her past all limits of sensation.

'Oh my God,' she murmured, her head falling back against the door as he pulled his mouth from hers and began to increase the length and speed of his strokes. Her head spun from side to side, her fingers dug into his shoulders and her back arched as she pushed her breasts to his mouth. She had never made love like this before, had never begged anyone to fuck her the way she was begging him now. She was so dazed by lust that she barely knew what was happening as he carried her to the table, his penis still buried inside her, his mouth still brutally claiming hers. But she knew it when he turned her over and penetrated her from behind, she knew it too when he stretched her arms out across the table, then circled her waist with his hands and rammed himself into her with such force that the exploding pulses of her orgasm gripped his penis as savagely as her hands gripped the table. It was as though her entire body was convulsing with the power of a release that refused to complete. She was sobbing, sinking her teeth into her arm and gasping for breath as he pushed himself into her, again and again and again. Then he was lifting her up, pressing her head back on his shoulder and burying his tongue in her mouth. His hands were holding her breasts, pulling her nipples and moving to the join in her legs. With his fingers and his mouth and the savagery of his pounding hips he drew her orgasm out to the point where she could no longer stand. She sank back against him and holding her as he exploded inside her, he stroked her and kissed her and pressed her to him until he was spent.

Then, lifting her in his arms, he carried her through to the bedroom and laid her down on the bed. Her hair was tangled around her face, her chest was still heaving as her body shuddered and glistened in the moonlight. For a moment he stood looking down at her, watching her eyelids flutter and her breasts rise and fall. Then gently brushing the hair from her face, he lay down beside her and wrapped her tightly in his arms.

They lay quietly together listening to the sound of each other's breath and the steadying rhythm of their hearts. She was aware that he hadn't spoken at all, yet his body, his kisses, his caresses and his passion were saying more than she dared hope was true. She turned her face into his neck and felt his lips graze her forehead as his arms tightened around her. The scent of him stole into her senses, quickening her heart as the gentle strength of his embrace engulfed her.

Minute after minute ticked by until finally she felt herself drifting into sleep. Dimly she was aware of him turning her in his arms so that her back was against his chest and his legs were supporting hers. Sliding her hand into his, she drew his fingers to her mouth and kissed them. She slept then, so deeply that when she woke in the early hours he was already inside her. She hadn't felt the penetration, but the feeling of him now, so big and solid inside her, tore a response through her body that was almost a pain. She lay quietly, her breath starting to shorten as her nipples responded to the tender quest of his fingers and the rest of her came alive to his touch. He turned her face to his and kissed her mouth, then easing himself out of her he turned her round and pulled her on top of him. Taking him back into the depths of her as she knelt over him, she looked down into his face in the growing dawn light. Slowly she began to ride him. His eyes were in shadow, but she knew they were on hers. His lips were pale, his jaw was stained with the inky darkness of stubble. His hands stroked her breasts and she began to move faster. His thumb penetrated the join in her legs and her head fell back as she gasped. His hips were rising to meet the downward thrust of hers, his hands were touching her all over. Her breasts swung and bounced and she cried out as he squeezed her nipples hard. It was driving her crazy, pushing her closer and closer to the edge as her nipples felt they might burst with the incredible response to what he was doing.

And then she was there, flying, falling, soaring to the very root of every sensation in her body. 'Max!' she screamed. 'Oh God, Max.'

Quickly he pulled her into his arms, pressing her to

him as his mouth found hers and his hands held her.

'Max, I can't bear it,' she sobbed as he laid her on her back. 'Oh God, help me,' she cried as her orgasm broke through her threshold of endurance.

But he continued to move in and out of her, slamming in hard with each thrust of his climax. She clung to him, twisting her fingers in his hair and listening to herself sob. She had never known anything like this. Nothing in her life had ever felt so strong. Nothing had ever pushed her to the limits she had reached that night, nothing and no one had ever even come close.

Her breath was still ragged as he kissed her again, tenderly and brutally, commandingly and comfortingly. The length of his body was pressed to hers, his breath was in her lungs, his penis still inside her. She had never dreamt she would feel part of another human being, but that was the way she felt now. It was as though he was consuming her, drawing her into him, even as he pushed himself into her.

She wished he would speak, yet she dreaded he would. She longed to know how this was affecting him too, yet she was terrified to hear it. In two days he was marrying Galina, in whose bed they were now lying, their bodies not only entwined, but still joined. She wanted him to grow hard again, to keep himself there, to fill her so full of himself she could no longer think.

It was a long time before he finally lifted himself up from the bed, by then they were back in the position they'd slept in. Rhiannon feigned sleep. She was too afraid to look at him, too desperate for him to stay to be able to watch him go. Inside she was crying out for him to speak, but she knew he wouldn't.

Early morning sunlight was filtering through the blinds as the front door closed behind him. Rhiannon lay where she was, her throat aching with tears as her heart thudded with confusion and pain and the certain knowledge that something inside her had changed completely.

She had no idea what, all she knew was that her emotions were so raw that even as she wept she was feeling a joy she'd never felt before. She turned her face to the pillow and despite the intensity of all they had shared, she wondered if he had been using her as some kind of payback to Galina. He'd made love to her here, in Galina's bed, in the very bed where Galina entertained her other lovers. So had she been used? Was she some kind of pawn in a bitter and twisted game between two people who loved as much as they hated?

She wondered if she would ever know the answer to that, if she would ever share another night like that with him again. She felt suddenly drained and tired to the point of exhaustion. Yet there was an impatience growing inside her, a longing, a craving, an insatiable hunger for so much more of him that she felt swamped by her own need. What had he done to her? How could she ever make love with another man now?

Hugging the pillow more tightly to her face, she tried to empty her mind. She must try to sleep, for she was too tired to think clearly now, too dazed to detach herself from the overpowering effect of the night. She was aware of the tears on her cheeks and of the way her heart was already contracting with the fear of what lay ahead. She thought of Galina and the wedding, and felt an indescribable pain slide across her heart.

Downstairs Max was waiting for the doorman to bring his car round. His face was pale and drawn, his eyes were unfocused and heavy with fatigue. As the Mercedes came to a stop at the centre of the forecourt he walked forward, rubbing a hand over his chin, then pushing it on through his hair.

From a window opposite a telescopic lens was capturing his every move, telling its own story of a tired man emerging from his girlfriend's apartment at sunrise, having just spent the night with an unknown woman –

the same woman he'd been with at the Café del Rey the night before, just prior to a romantic stroll on the beach. The café and beach shots were already in print, had hit the newstands a couple of hours ago, which Max would find out the minute he got home, maybe even sooner if he stopped along the way.

Chapter 20

'Surprise!' Galina shouted, kicking the front door closed behind her and dropping her Vuitton bags on the floor. 'Surprise, surprise,' she laughed, running into the bedroom and throwing herself on top of Rhiannon. 'We're going to Vegas!' she cried, hugging Rhiannon tightly and rolling her across the bed. 'We're going to *Vegas*!'

'Galina, let me breathe,' Rhiannon laughed, trying to untangle herself.

'We're going to *Vegas*!' Galina repeated elatedly, sitting back on her heels, her beautifully fresh face alive with laughter and mischief as she gazed down at Rhiannon. 'God, you should see yourself,' she grinned. 'It must have been a hell of a night.'

Rhiannon's heart froze as the guilt swamped her and without thinking she quickly averted her eyes.

But Galina didn't seem to notice. 'Max and I are getting married in Vegas!' she declared. 'Isn't it exciting? It's all arranged. We're flying out there on Saturday morning. Max and I will go get our licence as soon as we get there, then we'll meet up with the rest of you at the Love Heart Chapel, or whatever it's called, and we'll have the wedding of the year right there on the Strip in Vegas.'

Rhiannon was staring at her in disbelief. But it was a joke, of course it was a joke, she just couldn't get a grip on it yet, that was all. Without thinking she turned to look at the clock and dimly registered that it was past midday.

'So, what do you think?' Galina urged. 'Brilliant, isn't it? You said you wanted to go to Vegas and now you're going.'

Rhiannon blinked and looked at her again. 'I said I wanted to go to Vegas?' she echoed, wondering if she was dreaming this.

'You know you did,' Galina laughed. 'You said it the other day. You said it would be good to get to Vegas while you were here. Well, now you will. I've arranged it.'

Rhiannon's disbelief was going beyond dimensions she could handle. 'It was just a throw-away, Galina,' she muttered. 'I didn't mean it. I mean, I did, but not for one minute did I expect you to go and get married there.' She took a breath. 'But you're kidding me, aren't you? You're not serious, I know you're not ...'

'I am!' Galina cried, laughing and throwing out her arms. 'I'm deadly serious. It's a great idea. It'll be such a scream and after the wedding we can hit the casinos and break every bank in town.'

Rhiannon blinked several times. The awful realization that Galina probably did mean what she was saying was dawning on her at last. 'What does Max say?' she asked, feeling slightly breathless.

'He thinks it's a great idea,' Galina laughed. 'Everyone does.' She bounced off the bed and headed for the kitchen. 'Coffee?' she called back over her shoulder. 'Silly question. Of course you want coffee. Are you planning on getting up today? No problem if you're not, I was just wondering. I'll bring the papers to you in bed if you like. I think you should see them. The shots of you are fantastic. And of Max. Was he good, by the way?' She giggled. 'Did he blow your mind? I want all the details.'

Rhiannon's eyes were wide, her insides felt as though they were being crushed. She must be dreaming, she had to be, either that or she was losing her mind.

'I hope you don't think he's going to run off with you before the wedding,' Galina went on chattily as she spooned fresh coffee into the filter. 'I mean, it would serve me right for what I did to you, I know, but it won't happen, so *please* don't get your hopes up 'cos I couldn't bear it if you got hurt. Max is absolutely crazy about me, you see, he'll do anything for me, even sleep with my best friend to cheer her up. Did it cheer you up, darling?'

Rhiannon was reeling. Her fingers were digging into the bed as though trying to steady the world. The shock of Galina's words was tearing at her, the horror that she might be hearing the truth was so great she was unable to move.

'Well, I have to be honest here,' Galina went on, flicking the power switch and unhooking clean cups from the rack, 'I didn't actually ask him to sleep with you. I was going to,' she assured Rhiannon hastily, 'because I thought you might like it, but he obviously read the situation perfectly, the way he always does, and decided to indulge me, the way he always does. *So*, did you like it? Was he the best you've ever had? I'll bet he was.'

All Rhiannon could do was look at her. This couldn't be happening. This conversation wasn't taking place. There was simply no way she could be lying here in Galina's bed still bruised from Max's love-making and being cheerily asked by Galina if he was the best lover she'd ever had *and* being expected to reply.

To her immeasurable relief the telephone rang. It was Ula calling her with the name and number of an immigration lawyer. Rhiannon jotted the information down, thanked Ula and rang off. Then burying her head in her arms, she squeezed herself tightly as though to shield herself from any more.

'Shall I run you a bath?' Galina offered, breezing past into the bathroom.

Rhiannon didn't answer, she merely watched as

Galina stooped over the wide, oval-shaped bath and spun the brass taps. Then picking up a bowl of expensive salts, she began sprinkling them liberally into the cascading water. All the time she was singing, humming happily under her breath, just like any woman in love.

'How did the trip to Chicago go?' Rhiannon asked, trying to bring some normalcy to the situation as, dispensing with modesty, she threw back the duvet and slid to the edge of the bed. As she stood she could feel the stiffness in her muscles and a quick memory of him inside her shot a bolt of lust right through her.

'Oh, yes, it was great,' Galina answered, putting the bath salts back on a shelf and starting to undress.

Rhiannon watched her, her discomfort increasing with every garment Galina discarded. 'Uh, I'll take a shower, shall I?' Rhiannon said, indicating the frosted-glass cubicle beside the bath as Galina stepped out of her underwear and turned to look at herself in the mirror.

'Oh no!' Galina protested, wetting her finger, then smoothing it over her eyebrows. 'I thought we could take a bath together, the way we used to at school. I'll wash your back, you wash mine and you can tell me everything Max did to you last night.'

Rhiannon's face was pale. 'Galina, I really don't think ...'

'You've got wonderful breasts,' Galina interrupted, looking at Rhiannon's reflection in the mirror. 'I hope Max told you that. They're so ... big! And your waist and hips are so slim. You've got a perfect figure, you know. Women in this town pay fortunes to look like you. I know!' she suddenly cried, clapping her hands in excitement. 'Where's your camera? Let's put it on auto and take a picture of the two of us together in the nude!'

Rhiannon's mouth fell open. 'What on earth for?' she said.

'For Max, of course,' Galina laughed. 'Think what a treat it would be for him to be able to peek into his wallet any time he liked and ...'

'Galina, stop this!' Rhiannon snapped. 'This is crazy and you know it!'

'How is it crazy?' Galina laughed. 'Don't you want him to have a picture of you in the nude?'

'No!'

Galina's eyes were sparkling. Then shrugging, she said, 'OK, suit yourself. It was just a thought,' and leaning over the bath she began mixing the water with both hands.

'Come on, get in,' she said, reaching behind her for Rhiannon's hand.

'Galina, I don't really ...'

'Come on,' Galina insisted, waving a hand through the air to clear the steam. 'I'll put the jacuzzi on so you can relax back and enjoy yourself,' and grabbing Rhiannon's hand, she pulled her over to the bath.

'Galina, we're not schoolgirls any more,' Rhiannon protested as Galina stepped into the water.

'We can always pretend,' Galina twinkled. 'Come on, you take the comfy end, I'll take the taps. And don't worry, I'm not going to come on to you, I'm not that way inclined.'

Feeling like she was moving into a space, a time even, that was totally apart from reality, Rhiannon stepped into the bath and sank slowly into the steaming perfumed water.

'That's it,' Galina smiled, kneeling down in front of her and watching her through the mist. 'Does it feel good?'

Rhiannon nodded. It did, and the gentle vibration of the jacuzzi soon began to ease the tension from her limbs. At the other end Galina stretched out her legs and lay back too, resting her head on a folded towel and tucking her hands beneath her to stop them floating to the surface.

Neither of them spoke for some time as they relaxed

with their eyes closed, inhaling the soothing aroma of the salts and listening to the muted burr of the jacuzzi as it gently massaged their bodies.

'Isn't this wonderful?' Galina murmured after a while.

'Mmm,' Rhiannon responded.

Galina's eyes opened and she started to smile. 'Why don't I bathe you while you tell me about Max,' she suggested.

Immediately Rhiannon tensed, though her eyes remained closed. 'I don't want to talk about Max,' she said. 'I'm not going to deny what happened, but for God's sake, Galina, I can't talk about it, at least not to you.' By now her eyes were open and she could see the beatific smile on Galina's lips.

'OK,' Galina said softly. 'I understand. Just let me bathe you and we'll forget about Max. Come on, turn around, let me do your back.'

Wondering why on earth she was going along with this, Rhiannon lifted herself up and turned around. Behind her Galina rubbed soap into a sponge, then began gently stroking her back. Rhiannon's head fell forward as the wonderful soothing sensations coasted through her. Galina's fingers moved to her neck and massaged it as she continued to rub the sponge over her shoulders. Then letting the sponge go, Galina took up the massage with both hands, easing herself in closer to Rhiannon and letting her legs slip around Rhiannon's hips.

There was no denying the intimacy, nor the eroticism of the situation, yet Rhiannon wasn't uncomfortable with it, not even when Galina pulled her head back on to her shoulder and began to stroke her face.

'Shall I wash your hair?' Galina offered.

Rhiannon nodded, then sat forward as Galina reached for the shampoo, before moving back to the taps and pulling Rhiannon's shoulders down until her hair was submerged in the water. Using her hands, she scooped more water over Rhiannon's face and neck, then squeezing shampoo from the bottle, she raised her knees so that Rhiannon could rest her back against them and began to soap Rhiannon's long auburn hair.

Minutes later Rhiannon's eyes closed as Galina eased her head beneath the water again to wash away the soap. Holding her breath, Rhiannon waited for Galina to finish, feeling the long tangled strands of her hair winding around Galina's fingers. It was a while before she sensed Galina's hand on her face, holding her beneath the surface. A quick fear bit into her chest. She attempted to lift her herself up and felt Galina resist. She spun her head to one side, then took in air as Galina's hand fell away.

'Do you remember those stories I used to tell about my grandmother?' Galina asked as she settled Rhiannon back against her knees and began to soap her hair again.

Rhiannon's eyes were wide as she stared at the shower and wondered if she had imagined the pressure of Galina's hand.

'Yes,' she answered vaguely. 'Yes, I remember.'

Galina smiled. 'Gosh, it all seems such a long time ago now, doesn't it?' she said, her hands massaging Rhiannon's head in small circular movements. Then she was gently drawing her back under the water.

Rhiannon wanted to resist, but for some reason she couldn't. There was nothing to be afraid of, she was telling herself. Galina didn't mean her any harm. This was just the way it used to be at school, Galina washing her hair, then her washing Galina's. There had never been anything sexual in it, nor menacing. So why was she afraid now?

The water closed over her face and Rhiannon's heart contracted as Galina's hands circled her throat. Trying not to panic, Rhiannon pulled herself up, but her hair was trapped beneath Galina's leg. Her eyes flew open, but she could see nothing in the milky translucence of the water. Then Galina's hands seemed to float away, leaving her free to rise.

'Me now,' Galina said, passing Rhiannon the shampoo.

Turning to face her, Rhiannon took the shampoo and watched Galina's eyes move over her breasts.

'Did he touch them?' Galina whispered.

Rhiannon's heart stood still.

Galina smiled. 'Of course he did,' she said and turning around she arched her back until her head was in the water.

'I know you don't want to talk about Max,' she said as she sat up again and Rhiannon poured shampoo on to her hair, 'so I will say only this: for your own sake, don't let him touch you again. If you do, then please believe me, Rhiannon, you won't be the only one who will regret it.'

Rhiannon was silent. There was nothing she could say, especially when she had no idea whether what she had just heard was a straightforward threat or a genuine warning. She looked up as the telephone started to ring and unhooking the receiver on the wall beside her Galina answered it.

'No, this isn't Rhiannon,' she said, turning in the water so she could see Rhiannon's face, 'but she's right here, I'll pass you over.'

Rhiannon looked at her and knew instinctively that this wasn't a call she was going to welcome.

'It's Susan Posner returning your call,' Galina smiled.

Max's eyes were on Ula as she closed the study door behind her and crossed the room to join them. Ramon was there, having just flown in from Memphis, so too were Maurice and Ellis. White sunlight was filtering through the blinds, spilling over the island of desks where, for the moment, their computer terminals lay idle. Outside, the gardeners were strimming the lawns while the pool man dragged his nets through the crystalline water.

Though Max was still watching her as she sat on a sofa Ula could tell that his thoughts were elsewhere. A full day and night had passed since he'd slept with Rhiannon, a time during which Galina had returned from Chicago and the charges of insider trading had been dropped. What Max thought of any of it was known only to him, for he'd spoken to no one with, Ula thought, the possible exception of Galina. And how Galina was reacting to the fact that he'd spent the night with her best friend only days before their wedding was something Ula had yet to find out. Just as the press had yet to learn exactly whom Max had paid off this time to get the charges against him dropped.

Ula's eyes came to rest on Maurice who was sitting in a club chair, an ankle resting on one knee as he sipped his coffee. He was watching Ellis jotting down a number he was being given by someone at the other end of the phone.

When Ellis had finished Max glanced at Ramon.

Ramon started to speak. Ula watched him, as entranced by his accent as she was by what he was saying.

'With regard to the murder of the photographer,' he began, 'the Memphis police are looking for a smartly dressed man in his early forties. They have no particular leads, but it is their belief that the man is not from Memphis.'

'I thought they were following some kind of gangland theory,' Ula said.

'They are,' Ramon confirmed. 'Which doesn't rule out the smartly dressed man.'

'Do they have any idea at this stage *why* the photographer might have been killed?' Maurice said.

'If you are asking do they know anything about the photographs of Galina, then the answer is no, they do not,' Ramon answered frankly.

Max's eyes moved to the window and remained there as Ula said, 'And what about your own enquiries, Ramon? Did you find out anything new?'

'At this stage all I can say is that should it ever get out that there were any photographs of Galina, Max will become an immediate suspect in the murder.'

All eyes went to Max as he said, 'Is there any evidence to say that I was in Memphis that day?'

'Not that anyone has located so far,' Ramon said. 'But you were in Memphis that day, so the evidence is there to be found, should anyone decide to go looking.'

'Is anyone likely to do that?' Ellis asked.

'Anything is possible,' Ramon answered.

'So the bottom line', Ula said, 'is that you haven't managed to find out who did kill the photographer?'

Ramon's eyes went to Max. 'No,' he said.

A short silence followed, then Maurice said, 'But if we do manage to find out who killed the guy then presumably we're going to find out who's giving Galina her cover.'

Ramon looked at him long and hard. 'That is my belief, yes,' he responded. Then returning his gaze to Max he said, 'I have seen the photographs, the beatings are becoming more brutal.'

They all looked up as Max got to his feet and walked to the window. 'I presume', he said when finally he turned round, 'that without a lead to whoever killed the photographer the chances of a connection being made to Galina are remote.'

Ramon nodded. 'But reality has to be faced. If this man, whoever he is, wants to put you in the frame for murder, then there is every chance he will succeed. You were in Memphis at the time the crime was committed, it was your girlfriend who was photographed and beaten and at least one of the descriptions of our mystery man who was seen at the studio around the time of the killing fits you perfectly.'

Max smiled. 'Of course,' he said.

Ula watched him closely, aware that her heart was slowing as he continued.

'And let's not forget the attempted blackmail,' he said. 'Only hours after the man shows up at *Southern Belle*'s offices demanding a fortune he's found shot through the head.'

'Which means,' Ramon said, 'this is a very clever frame-up.'

'Or', Max responded, 'that I did it.'

Ula looked at Maurice and Ellis whose faces were as pale as her own. Then returning her gaze to Max, she said, 'Where is Galina now?'

'At the apartment with Rhiannon,' he answered. 'They're joining us here in the morning to fly down to Vegas.'

Considering the fact that Max's and Rhiannon's night together had been splashed all over the press, Ula was amazed that Galina could bring herself even to speak to Rhiannon now, never mind share an apartment with her. And the very idea that Rhiannon was still going to stand as Galina's supporter would, at least to some, seem even more bizarre than Galina's stunning choice of venue. But Ula was used to Galina's outrageous last-minute ideas, just as she was used to the way Max indulged them. The rest of the world would probably think he was crazy for going along with it, for anyone less likely to be found getting married in Vegas was hard to imagine. But Max only ever overruled Galina on things that mattered and to him, Ula knew, the location of where they got married couldn't have mattered less.

Chapter 21

Galina was in infectiously high spirits as the Romanov company jet began to circle Las Vegas airport preparing to land. Having had no problem catching her excitement, the children were chattering incessantly while clambering from Max's lap to Galina's and even venturing elsewhere in the plane to make new friends. At least Aleks did, Marina seemed to prefer her daddy's lap or quizzing Galina about anything from her favourite things to why she, Marina, couldn't have her ears pierced. They were cute children, Rhiannon thought as she watched them, surprisingly unspoilt considering their father's wealth, though like most kids she imagined they could be a handful at times. They had inherited Max's dark colouring and Slavic looks, though Rhiannon guessed the blue eyes must have come from their mother.

Apart from Max's inner circle, Rhiannon knew no one else on board, though she'd been introduced to them all before leaving LA. They were mainly, she'd gathered, Romanov's most senior executives who'd flown in from various parts of the country to attend the wedding. There were also two of Conspiracy's make-up artists, a couple of dressers and a hair stylist who had come along to assist Rhiannon and Galina. What any of them made of this last minute re-route to Vegas Rhiannon had no idea, but it was clear from the brief conversation they'd had during the flight that Maribeth Courtini, the head of Primaire's operations on the West Coast, was as stunned by the sudden change in plan as Rhiannon. But the decision was Galina's and if appearances were anything to go by Max was perfectly happy to go along with it.

Seeing him for the first time since they had spent the night together had been even more difficult than Rhiannon had expected. They'd met at the airport just before boarding the plane. All eyes had been on them, watching and waiting to see how they would respond to each other now, just two days after their betrayal of Galina had been publicly revealed. Rhiannon had taken her lead from Max, greeting him warmly but politely, as though they had never exchanged more than a formal hello in their lives. Her embarrassment had been excruciating as she'd wished herself anywhere in the world rather than where she was, and though the expression on his face told her nothing, she was sure he must feel the same way. There was a moment, just a fleeting second, when their eyes connected, but then he was letting go of her hand and turning away to greet more guests. Forcing herself to continue up the steps of the plane, Rhiannon had fallen in beside Ramon, taking his arm and smiling, while feeling herself breaking apart inside. How could he appear so cool and unmoved by what they had shared, when they both knew that it went far beyond the mere act of making love? But if that were true, why hadn't he called her since? Why had he made no attempt to see her? Because, she reminded herself harshly, today he's marrying someone else and you were just what the rest of the world thinks you were, a one-night stand that wasn't as discreet as it should have been.

Glancing across to where he was sitting beside Galina now, Rhiannon's heart turned over. He seemed so relaxed, so content with his life and amused by his children. And the way he was behaving towards Galina could leave no one in any doubt of how very much he loved her. But Rhiannon could feel herself fighting it, telling herself it was only an act. She wondered if Galina had told him about the call from Susan Posner. It would account for his coolness towards her, his refusal to look at her. But she had shaken Susan off, told her that she was going back to London much earlier than she'd expected so wouldn't be free after all. Galina had heard her say that, but what had Galina told Max?

The temperature was over a hundred degrees as the wedding party descended the steps of the plane and walked the short distance to a fleet of limousines that was waiting to transport them to the hotel. Rhiannon travelled with Maribeth, Ramon, Ellis and Ula. She was overwhelmed by the sheer number of people moving about the streets. It was as if half of America with its vests, tattoos, quivering, sun-burned flesh, crew cuts and winner's smiles, was oozing in and out of the towering, flashy hotels that rose like great vulgar phoenixes from the burning dust of the streets.

As the others talked and laughed, pointing out the vast Mississippi steamboat with its thousands of twinkling lights and hooting funnel, the Egyptian pyramid and sphinxes, the pirate ship where some kind of mutiny was currently being staged, Rhiannon could only wonder at what she was doing there. She gave no outward sign of her distress, but she desperately needed to speak to Lizzy, to try to get some kind of balance on the way she was feeling, for left alone with it like this she was driving herself insane.

But what could she say? Lizzy, I've fallen head over heels in love with Max Romanov. I've never in my life felt like this about a man before. I never even knew it was possible to feel this way. I only have to think about him and I'm wet. I only have to look at him and my heart feels as though it's going to collapse under the sheer weight of emotion. Is this love, Lizzy? Or is it just lust? Please Lizzy tell me, make me understand what is happening to me.

'Oh my, will you take a look at this?' Maribeth laughed as their limousine swept into the driveway of the Mirage Hotel. 'This must be the waterfall that erupts into a volcano at night,' she said, as they all turned to look at the glistening lake in front of the hotel where a mountain of water was gushing over the edge of a cliff.

'Are you serious?' Ula cried. 'A volcano? This I've got to see. Ellis, you're sitting on my skirt,' she complained, tugging it out from under him. 'Did you remember to bring the ring, by the way?'

'Ramon's the best man,' Ellis interrupted. 'Ask him if he's got the ring.'

'Do you have the ring?' Ula demanded.

Ramon's eyes were brimming with laughter. 'Max has the ring,' he told her.

'Oh God!' Ula gasped, suddenly spinning round in her seat to look out of the rear window. 'Did they remember to go to City Hall to get their licence? They were supposed to do it as soon as we arrived.'

'Ula, shut up,' Ellis grumbled, starting to climb out of the car as the chauffeur came back to open the door and a swarm of jockeys and porters descended.

As Rhiannon followed the others into the hotel foyer she felt her mouth fall open in amazement. She had never seen so many people in a hotel lobby, nor so many gaming machines in one place. There were thousands of them, row upon row of shiny, blinking, number-rolling, wheel-spinning slot-machines stretching as far as the eye could see, which had to be at least a quarter of a mile. And the noise! The hoot and whistle, bleeps and sirens and constant cascade of tumbling coins was like an endless musical score playing backwards on a fairground organ. More amazing still was the vast aquarium of sharks that was set to one side of reception and the tropical forest of imported and plastic palms that lined the route to the elevators, passing through the heart of the gaming area with all its bars and restaurants, change booths and raffle prizes and where batallions of new and seasoned gamblers were trying their luck at anything from roulette to craps to common-or-garden bingo. As they walked through, Rhiannon noticed signposts directing them to the white tigers, the dolphins or the boxing arena where a heavyweight, all-star match was taking place that very night. It seemed that there was nothing this hotel couldn't cater for.

They were whisked straight up to the penthouse floor where an exclusive check-in service was laid on for VIP guests. Ula dealt with it, while Rhiannon was shown to a suite which compared easily in size with the entire cul-de-sac she'd grown up in. She was given a welcome glass of champagne to sip while the room attendant demonstrated how the room responded to various switches and buttons.

Apart from the gimmickry, the suite was tastefully furnished with French-style antiques and marble floors. The vast double bed was draped in pale brocade and the ceiling above was mirrored. Smiling to herself, Rhiannon was on the point of entering the bathroom when the main door opened and Galina came bounding in with her entourage of make-up artists, dressers and hair stylist.

'Hi!' she gushed, signalling to the porter to bring in the luggage. 'Isn't this wonderful?' she cried, throwing out her arms and spinning around. 'Do we have an apartment each? I specifically told Ula that we must have an apartment each.'

'The second apartment is through here, ma'am,' the porter told her, passing through the wet bar and pushing open a door the other side.

'OK, that'll do me,' Galina responded after taking a look. 'You have the bigger one, Rhiannon.'

'Don't be ridiculous,' Rhiannon cried. 'It's your day, you take the big one.'

'No, I insist that you take it. No arguments now, not today. Besides, I'll only be here for a couple of hours so you might as well make yourself at home right away. Max is next door with the kids, but the kids are moving in with Mrs Clay later on in the day so that we can have the place to ourselves. Everyone's staying until Monday, by the way, so we can lose our fortunes tonight and win them back again tomorrow. I just can't wait to get started, can you? Do you play blackjack? I just *love* blackjack. It was all I could do to make myself walk past it just now. Actually, Max dragged me past, but he's promised we can play tonight.'

From the frown that had settled on her face it was clear that she wasn't paying much attention to what she was saying. 'You know, I really think we should have Marina in here, don't you?' she said. 'After all, she is a bridesmaid and she might like to get ready with us. What am I saying, of course she'd like to get ready with us. Belinda, go fetch her, will you? And tell Aleks he can come too if he likes.'

Belinda was back in a few minutes with a message from Max reminding Galina that it was her day so she was to let him sort out the children and they would meet her at the chapel in a couple of hours.

The time passed swiftly as the Conspiracy team went busily and humorously about their work, keeping Galina and Rhiannon entertained with their Hollywood gossip and lightning repartee. Cornelius, the hair stylist, who was some kind of quick-fingered magician as well as the other half of a riotous double-act with Mimi, tried several different looks with Rhiannon's hair, before finally settling on a kind of loose French roll that suited her so well that she couldn't stop herself wondering what Max would think when he saw her. Dismissing the thought quickly, she laughed at something Mimi was saying, but there was no denying that the closer the clock crept to three the more tense she was becoming. She could see that Galina was too, as she snapped at Belinda, apologized, then turned helplessly to Rhiannon as though asking what she should do next.

'It's OK,' Rhiannon smiled slipping an arm around her and turning her to the mirror. 'The dress looks beautiful. You look beautiful. Max is going to be so proud.' As her heart faltered on the words, Galina's eyes met hers in the mirror.

'Thank you,' Galina whispered.

Rhiannon smiled again, then took a step back to clear Galina's reflection. The ivory silk dress, with its low-cut shoulders, simple lace panels and long, flowing skirts, was exquisite. The jewels sewn into the bodice glinted and shimmered in the sunlight and the flowers in her lovely blonde hair lent her a quality that was almost ethereal. She looked, Rhiannon thought, more beautiful, yet somehow more fragile, than she had ever seen her. Her blue eyes were wide with apprehension, her full, sensuous lips seemed to tremble with fear.

'You look lovely,' Rhiannon whispered.

Galina's eyes fell to the floor as two spots of colour rose in her cheeks. 'Thank you,' she said again. Then turning to Rhiannon, she touched her fingers lightly to Rhiannon's wrist and said, 'So do you.' Her eyes swept down over Rhiannon's ivory silk dress. 'Max will think so too,' she said softly.

Rhiannon felt the warmth drain from her smile as her heart folded around the words and sensing the discomfort of the others in the room she said, 'It's time we were going.'

By the time she and Galina arrived at the chapel everyone else was there, gathered on the small square of lawn outside the door. The roar of the traffic and incessant swirl of dust kicking up in its wake seemed part of another world beside the cosy tranquillity of the chapel which, with its glossy white walls, quaint arched windows and slender little steeple, was a bijou version of picture book perfection. It sat like a gleaming little jewel between two flagrantly impervious tower blocks and in front of a tawdry, tired-looking shopping mall. Above the chapel, straddling it on great iron legs, was a flashing neon sign advertising its twenty-four-hour-a-day service.

As they stepped from the back of the limousine a hot, dry desert wind rustled Galina's dress and loosened several strands of Rhiannon's hair. Marina, in a miniature version of Galina's gown, ran to Galina and took her hand. Aleks, in his smart tailcoat and red bow tie, was right behind his sister, clamouring for the other hand. Rhiannon took Galina's flowers so she could attend to the children and unable to stop herself, looked across to where Max was standing with Ramon and Maurice.

He was wearing a black tuxedo and looked so tall and handsome and incongruous in this setting that Rhiannon could only wonder again why he had agreed to it. He was watching Galina as she walked hesitantly towards him, glancing at him shyly as she waited for his approval. His eyes were inscrutable, the set of his jaw seemed harsh and almost impatient. Yet, as she reached him and tilted her face to look at him, he gazed long into her eyes, before lowering his mouth and touching it lightly to hers.

Feeling someone's hand slide into hers, Rhiannon turned to find Ramon standing beside her. 'Don't worry,' he whispered through his smile, 'it will soon be over.'

Rhiannon's eyes dilated, then unable to stop herself she said, 'Why is he allowing her to do this? It's so awful, Ramon. It's so tacky.'

'It's what Galina wanted,' Ramon answered, gesturing for her to go forward as Max and Galina walked into the chapel.

The organ was playing as the guests filed in and Max and Ramon walked ahead to the altar, while Galina waited with Rhiannon and Marina at the back. It didn't take long for everyone to settle and as the organist changed tune Galina, Rhiannon and Marina started down the aisle.

Rhiannon watched and listened and struggled to make herself believe it was happening. It was so phoney and schmaltzy and hideously tasteless that it almost made her want to laugh. The minister was a Dolly Parton look-alike with long, feathery lashes, gleaming red lips and an impressive pale-pink wig. The end of each pew was lavishly trimmed with huge pink net bows and pink carnations. The altar was pink, so was the bible, so was the organist. Rhiannon had never seen so much pink, it was like being inside a blancmange.

Yet, as ghastly as it all was, there was no escaping the reality of the vows as first Galina, then Max repeated them and then, quite suddenly, before anyone could reach for their hankies they were being pronounced man and wife.

The rest of the day passed in a whirl as they were driven back to the hotel, shown to a private dining-room and served champagne and lobster. The excitement was running high as toasts were made, more and more corks were popped and Galina sat beside Max so flushed and happy that it was impossible not to feel happy for her. For his part Max appeared much more relaxed than he had at the chapel, but the way he was continuing to avoid Rhiannon was affecting her deeply. He had looked at her only once since the ceremony and Rhiannon had almost wished he hadn't, for he had let her see that his need of her was every bit as intense as hers was of him.

At seven he and Galina disappeared to put the children to bed, but everyone knew that Mrs Clay was there to do that. Not knowing what else to do and unable to face being alone in her room, Rhiannon joined the others at the tables. She gambled and lost, gambled some more and lost again. At one point she caught a glimpse of herself in a mirror and felt almost afraid of the person looking back. Her eyes were feverishly bright, her lips were pale and random tendrils of hair were cascading about her face and neck as though she had just run through a storm. Then quite suddenly she felt reckless and crazy and so sexually alive that it was as though her entire body was burning up in the heat of it. She was drunk and she knew it, but she didn't care.

It was almost midnight when Ramon steered her away from the amorous attentions of an oil-rich Texan and led her towards the lobby.

'Where are we going?' she murmured as he opened the rear door of a limousine and gestured for her to get in.

'Where do you think?' he countered, sliding in after her.

She thought, then shaking her head she said, 'No, I give up. I don't have a clue.'

Ramon smiled, then signalling to the driver that they were ready to leave, he concentrated his gaze on the road ahead.

'Are you rescuing me?' Rhiannon hiccuped as they turned off the Strip and headed towards the desert.

He laughed. 'Possibly,' he answered.

She was silent then and a few minutes later her head fell back against the seat. She gazed up at the ceiling and willed the tears to sink back into her eyes. She wanted to be drunk, she wanted to blot out the pain, the whole god-damned meanness of the fate that was doing this to her, but the journey was sobering her and she couldn't stop thinking about Max, or Max and Galina and what they were doing now. Biting her lips, she turned to look out of the window. All she could see was the ghostly image of her reflection. Gone were the glaring neon signs, gone was the interminable flow of traffic. There was only desert, endless miles of inky black desert

Taking a breath, she pushed a hand into her hair and tried to connect with her thoughts. Nothing seemed real any more, everything had lost its sense of normalcy, purpose and direction. It was insane that she should have allowed herself to become so affected by one night with a man, but she had and now she didn't know how to control it. She wanted him so badly she couldn't think of anything else. He was there in her mind, in her heart, in her body and soul and she couldn't let him go. But she would have to. She must force herself.

'We're here,' Ramon said a few minutes later.

Rhiannon's eyes opened and she looked around. But there was nothing to see in the darkness, except the headlights of another car.

'Thank you,' she murmured as the chauffeur opened the door for her to get out.

The warm wind assailed her, blowing her hair about her face and drying the tears on her cheeks. She turned to watch Ramon as he walked around the car to join her, then suddenly her heart stood still.

'Oh my God,' she breathed as she saw Max coming towards her.

They stood together in the moonlight holding each other tightly as Ramon and the chauffeur drove away. The strength of his arms was steadying her, but the confusion in her heart was making her cling to him all the harder, until gently easing her away he looked down into her eyes, before pressing his mouth to hers.

'Are you OK?' he said.

'Yes,' she whispered, tilting her head back to look at him. 'Just tell me what's happening, why you're here. Oh God, I can't believe you're here.'

Taking her face in his hands, he gazed down at her again. 'Susan Posner?' he said, his eyes watching her closely.

'Oh God,' she groaned. 'It was nothing. I swear to you, it was nothing. I was going to see her, but after we ... After the other night ...'

'It's OK,' he said, pulling her back to him. Her lips

parted and their tongues entwined, as he pressed her body hard against his.

When finally he let her go she laughed shakily and turned to look into the night. 'There must be a hundred things I should say now,' she whispered, feeling her cheeks start to burn, 'but all I can think of, all I want ...' Feeling him tense she brought her eyes back to his. 'I want you to make love to me,' she said. 'I want you to do all the things to me you did the other night and more.' Her head fell forward on to his chest as she choked back a laugh. 'God, what must you think of me,' she murmured. 'This is your honeymoon night and you're here with me and I don't know why and I ...' She stopped as he lifted her face back to his and gazed long into her eyes.

Her heart was thumping as he reached behind her to unzip her dress, then letting it fall to the sand he peeled away the fine lace body and pushed it down over her legs. The feel of the breeze on her skin was as erotic as the caress of his eyes and as he drew her against him she could feel herself melting in the consuming heat of her need.

Their love-making was every bit as erotic and passionate as before, as he turned her away from him and slipped his fingers down to the join in her legs. Then keeping his hand there he leaned her over the car and entered her from behind. With his other hand he turned her mouth to his and kissed her so deeply, so hungrily and commandingly that her lips trembled under the force of his need. He was so hard and uncompromising in the way he held her that the sensations coursing through her were more savage than the thrust of his hips. When she came he could feel the convulsions racking her as his fingers and his penis took her deeper and deeper into the sensations, until his own climax broke under the persistent pressure of hers.

When at last the tension began to leave their bodies

and their breathing slowed he turned her in his arms and gazed down into her eyes. It was impossible to tell what he was thinking, but the fact that he was there, holding her in his arms as the dying tremors of their love-making receded, was enough. Her heart pounded against his as she looked back at him and no words made it to her lips.

'Where are we going?' she asked, when a few minutes later they got into the car and started to drive away from Las Vegas.

Any wild notion she might have had that they were about to run off together was crushed by his response. 'Not far,' he said.

Rhiannon looked out at the night and wondered if she was dreaming. She didn't know what to say. He seemed strangely remote, yet so dominatingly there. It was as though he was resisting her, yet the very fact that he was with her, that he had made love to her the way he had, holding her so close, keeping his mouth almost constantly on hers, told her that he wanted her as much as she wanted him. Her eyes closed as she willed her instincts to guide her. 'What about Galina?' she heard herself ask.

'Galina's in a private gaming room playing blackjack,' he answered. 'She'll be there most of the night.'

Rhiannon nodded. There was no emotion in his voice; it was impossible to tell what he was thinking. Then, barely connecting with the fact that she was asking it, she said, 'Does she know you're with me?'

His eyebrows rose in a quick expression of humour. 'Not yet,' he said, 'but she'll probably guess.'

Rhiannon looked down at her hands as a thousand thoughts chased about her head trying to find something to hold on to.

A few minutes later they were entering a huge, well-tended estate where artfully lit sculptures of lions, fauns, satyrs and cherubs sat among the imported palms that lined the drive. At the end of the drive was an exquisite French-style château whose reflection shimmered in the moonlit lake before it.

'Is this yours?' she asked, knowing instinctively that it wasn't.

'No. It belongs to someone I know.'

'Is anybody at home?' she asked as they came to a stop at the foot of a beautifully crafted stone staircase that led up to the château.

'I'm told not,' he answered.

Rhiannon got out of the car and waited for him to join her. When he did she looked up into his face, wishing she knew what to say. She got the feeling that he regretted coming, that he almost resented her for putting him in this position, though it was one he had engendered himself. She attempted a smile as his eyes alighted briefly on hers, then her heart turned over as he drew her into his arms and dropped his head against hers.

'Max, what is going on?' she said, pulling back to look at him. 'Please explain this to me. I need to know what's happening here.'

'You know what's happening,' he said softly.

'No. I need you to tell me. You're the one who got married today. You're the one who had Ramon drive me out here, so tell me, Max, what is this all about?'

Lifting his head, he turned to gaze down at the moonlit lake, then pulled her more tightly into his arms.

'Max, please,' she said. 'I've never felt with anyone the way I feel with you. I can't think about anything but you, so don't do this to me. Just tell me how it is that I can feel this way when I've only known you a week and as far as I can remember you've never even called me by my name.'

As he looked down at her she could see the struggle he was having with himself and wished there were something she could do to ease it. But until he told her what was in his mind she had no way of reaching him. Then, seeming to sense the anguish he was causing her, his eyes softened. 'Rhiannon,' he whispered, lifting a hand to her face.

Her eyes fluttered and her heart expanded as the warmth of his tone settled around it.

'I think I love you, Rhiannon,' he whispered.

As he turned away and fixed his eyes back on the water Rhiannon could feel her heart and her throat tightening with all the emotions that were gathering inside her.

'Were you anyone else,' he said finally, 'I'd never be able to tell you this. It's only because of your history with Galina, because you knew her as a child ...' He stopped, looked at her, then took a deep and obviously troubled breath.

'There's something wrong with her, isn't there?' Rhiannon whispered.

'Yes,' he answered.

Rhiannon was silent, until finally realizing that she would have to help him some more, she said, 'So what is it? What's so wrong with her that you had to marry her?' She hadn't meant to sound so cynical or bitter, it had just come out that way and now that it had there was no taking it back.

He smiled distantly. 'I didn't *have* to marry her,' he said. 'I married her because ... Well, I married her for a lot of reasons, but it's true, if I'd known I was going to feel this way about you ...' He stopped and looked down her. 'We just met last Saturday,' he said softly, 'we made love on Wednesday and I've hardly been able to stop thinking about you since. But you have to understand, I couldn't turn my whole life, *her* whole life, upside down when we, you and I, don't even know each other.'

Rhiannon's eyes were unfocused as she lowered them to the water. 'Then what are you doing here?' she asked, her voice dropping to a whisper.

'I'm here', he said, 'because we need to talk. We both know that something's happening between us, but I want you to understand why we can't take it any further than it's already gone.'

'I don't recall asking for it to go any further,' she said defensively.

'OK, then maybe it's just me who wants that,' he replied.

Rhiannon's heart melted. 'No, I want it too,' she sighed. Her eyes came up to his. 'Did you make love to her before you came here tonight?' she asked, hating herself for it, but unable to stop herself.

Sighing deeply, he pressed his fingers into his eyes, then said, 'I haven't made love to Galina more than three times in my life and none of those times has been in the past three years.'

Rhiannon looked at him, her brow creased with confusion even as her heart rose with joy. But as she started to speak he put his fingers over her lips.

'I'm going to trust you now,' he said, 'in a way I never thought I'd trust anyone, especially not someone in your profession. But I'm going to do it because you need to know this and because I need to tell you. You're right about Galina, there is something wrong with her. It's not physical, it's psychological. It comes from the things her grandmother told her as a child and put in its simplest form it means she suffers from a transference of guilt. There's no actual name for the disorder, but there is a recognition of her symptoms that puts her at a high-risk level of suicide.'

Rhiannon's heart gave an unsteady beat. She knew Galina of old, knew only too well how easily she manipulated and lied and twisted people around her fingers. 'Is that why you married her?' she said. 'To stop her killing herself?'

His eyes came to hers and he smiled. 'I could find other ways to stop her killing herself than marrying her,' he said.

Embarrassed, Rhiannon looked away. 'So what are her symptoms?' she said quietly.

His eyes moved out to the darkness and she heard him swallow as he said, 'Maybe now isn't the time to go into it all, maybe it's enough just to say that she has taken on the burden of the old Countess's suffering and lives it as though it were her own. She's obsessed by the violence and believes that the only way she can atone for what happened to her grandmother is to suffer the same way. She has no sense of right or wrong about this, nor of self-worth or self-preservation. She does it because she believes she has to and because in a perverse, tragic kind of way it makes her feel good. It's why I have her telephone monitored and why she's followed or watched when she's not with me, so that I can try to protect her from herself. I don't always succeed, but I try. It's more than anyone else would do for her, more than she would ever do for herself.'

He took another breath and let it out slowly. 'The real problem now', he said, 'is that she has someone helping her, someone who doesn't give a damn what happens to her, but who sure as hell gives a damn what it's doing to me. He's using her to get to me in ways it would make you sick to hear. He helps her find the crazies who live out their warped and sadistic fantasies on a woman who can't help the way she is. He exploits her weakness, pays them to abuse her, then sends her back to me. I've even received photographs, most recently from Memphis, which turned up on the desk of one of my editors. The curious thing about that was why the pictures were taken to one of my magazines, when it was obvious they'd never find their way to print. Blackmail is the easy answer, but there has never been any demand for money. And now I know there won't be, because the motive isn't money.'

He stopped so abruptly that Rhiannon's eyes widened

in surprise. 'How do you know?' she asked. 'How can you be so certain?'

'Because', he answered, 'Ramon's managed to find out who paid the photographer to take the shots, then deliver them to *Southern Belle*, and it's very definitely not money that this guy wants.' He pulled a hand angrily across his face and stared hard into the night. 'The photographer's dead now,' he said. 'He was killed a couple of hours after he delivered the photographs to *Southern Belle*. And the guy who was in the photographs with Galina? Well, I guess like most guys with his kind of tendencies, he'd rather not have them made public, so he doesn't pose any threat.'

'So who's behind it?' Rhiannon asked.

Max's eyes briefly met hers, then he lowered them to the lake. 'Maurice,' he answered.

'Maurice? Your lawyer, Maurice?' she murmured in amazement.

He nodded. 'My lawyer Maurice. He's using Galina in a way that makes me want to kill him just to think of it, and he's just paid for a guy to be shot and very successfully made it look like it was me who did the shooting.'

Rhiannon's eyes moved anxiously over his face. 'But why?' she said. 'Why is he doing it?'

He took a moment to get his anger back in check, then looking at her he said, 'I guess you could say that it's his way of paying me back for Carolyn's death. He was in love with my wife from the day I married her and remains in love with her to this day. The ironic part of it is that she never loved him. Oh, I think they may have had an affair somewhere along the line, Carolyn and I were always having affairs, but we always knew about them and neither of us ever tried to hide it. Sometimes we discussed them, other times we even shared them. It was a promiscuous marriage, to say the least, but that's not to say we didn't ever get jealous of the other's partners, because we did and Carolyn could get pretty noisy about it at times, like threatening to divorce me, take the children away and never let me see them again, that kind of thing. But it was always said in the heat of the moment and by the next day it would be forgotten. At least by us it was, what we had no idea of was the way Maurice was taking it all to heart and starting to see himself as her avenger.

'Of course it was her death that really triggered him and looking back, I can only blame myself for not having seen it all sooner. He believes I shot her because of Galina. He believes that I wanted her out of the way so that I could marry Galina and keep my children. I can understand why he would have thought that, but he's wrong. Galina and I never had an affair, though not even Carolyn believed that. She hated Galina, she wanted her out of our lives and most especially out of the children's lives. Marina's been crazy about Galina almost since she was born and Carolyn was jealous of their closeness. But Galina had nowhere else to go. Her grandmother was dead and I was the nearest thing she had to family. So to have turned my back on her then would have been an act I'd never have been able to live with. Besides, I didn't want her to go. I cared about her and I still do. She's a victim of what happened in Russia's dark years as sure as if she had been there herself. And there are many more like her. Ramon and I and several others we know do what we can to help, but Galina is *my* responsibility and it's not one I want to be rid of as if she were nothing more than a statistic in history. She was the centre of my grandfather's world, and now she's the centre of Marina's and Aleks's too. She's so much a part of my life, of all our lives ...' He paused, then after a breath continued, 'No one's ever really understood her, but as far as it's possible I do. I know what she is and isn't capable of and I know that Carolyn's fear that she might harm the children, considering how she suffered herself as a child, was unfounded. Galina would never hurt my children, not only because she loves me and them more than anything else in the world, but because Galina simply doesn't have it in her to hurt anyone, except herself.'

Rhiannon was watching him closely. His unfocused eyes stared into the darkness and the distant tone of his voice made it sound as though he didn't know whether he believed what he was saying or not. A fleeting memory of the way Galina had held her head beneath the water flashed through Rhiannon's mind, then she was thinking about Carolyn and understanding why she would have been so afraid for her children. But Max knew what he was doing and if there was one thing Rhiannon could be sure about it was that he would never put his children at risk.

He started speaking again. 'My grandfather always wanted Galina and me to marry,' he said, 'and Galina always believed we would. I guess I thought we would too. I thought that maybe the older she got the less I would think of her as a sister and start thinking of her as a woman. But it never really happened. And then I met Carolyn, Carolyn got pregnant and we married. The psychiatrist thinks it was my marriage that finally ended what little self-control or self-worth Galina had and started her off on this course of masochism and self-destruction she's now on.' His eyes came back to Rhiannon's and he looked at her for a moment before saying, 'Which means I'm partly to blame. No, listen,' he said as she made to interrupt. 'I'm going to tell you something now that you probably never knew, never even dreamed of. Galina running off with the man you were going to marry was very likely a result of me marrying Carolyn. She had suffered a loss, so someone close to her had to suffer one too. It took several years for her to find a way of doing it, but she found it with you. She needed to prove to herself that she had the power to break a heart the way I broke hers. Of course, once she'd got the guy to run off with her she didn't want him any more, so they split up, he moved to Oklahoma I hear, and she returned to LA. The first I knew about her being back was when I got a call from Cedar Sinai telling me she'd been admitted. She'd been gang-raped the night before, which resulted in a hysterectomy.'

'Oh my God,' Rhiannon breathed, reeling with the shock of his bluntness.

They were both quiet until Rhiannon said, 'Is there *nothing* anyone can do to help her?'

He shook his head. 'They say not. It's too inbred in her now, she's gone too far and besides she won't accept any help. She hasn't seen the psychiatrist in over a year and if I try to make her she simply goes out after and gets herself beaten half to death. It's as though she's using it as a way of punishing me for making her do something she doesn't want to do.' He sighed heavily and rested his head on one hand. 'It's a god-damned nightmare,' he said. 'I care about her, I want to protect her and I want her to stay a part of our lives, but ...' His voice trailed off as though he really didn't know what he wanted any more.

'She has regular health checks,' he continued after a while. 'I insist on that and she doesn't put up too much of a fight. She knows about AIDS, obviously, but knowing about it and understanding what it could do to her still doesn't stop her. We thought, Maribeth and I, that landing the Conspiracy contract might act as some kind of deterrent, that the fear of disgrace, should it ever get out what she was doing, might just stop her from doing it.' He laughed drily. 'Naive, to say the least,' he said, 'but by then I'd exhausted all other means of distraction or moral persuasion and I couldn't help wondering, if she had something of her own, a career that would put her name and face in lights and give her the recognition and adoration she craved, if it might just be the cure we'd all been looking for. Not that I was going to let Maribeth or Lanny Harman, Primaire's chairman, go into it blind. They had to be told about her promiscuity, which they were, and in the end they decided to take the risk. I pay for the security that surrounds her and, should anything ever go wrong, should the Conspiracy range fail because of something Galina does, I have signed an agreement to make full financial reparation.'

Though Rhiannon didn't comment she was well aware of how enormous a sum that would be and could only marvel at how far he was prepared to go to try and give Galina a life.

'But it won't fail,' he went on. 'To that degree Galina knows exactly what she's doing and though she likes to tease and alarm the people around her, she won't put anything into jeopardy because she knows how much it matters to them all.' He smiled. 'It's just a shame she doesn't care as much about herself as she does for others. If she did, we could be looking at a whole different scenario here.'

As their eyes met, Rhiannon lifted a hand to his face. 'So what you're really saying', she whispered, 'is that you married her out of pity.'

His mouth moved to one side as he considered what she'd said. 'You're right, I do pity her,' he said finally, 'but it's not the only reason I married her. I married her because it was what everyone wanted, including me. We're used to each other, we know each other so well. There was no reason not to marry her – and all I've told you tonight is what's wrong with her, but there's a whole lot that is right with her too. Though I guess', he went on softly, 'that I'm never going to feel like this about her.'

Rhiannon's eyes were still on his and as he looked at her in the moonlight she could feel the power of his emotions stealing into her heart. 'What are you going to do about Maurice?' she asked after he kissed her.

He inhaled deeply, then letting it go he said, 'I still haven't come to a decision on that.'

'Does he know you know?'

'Not yet. He will though, when the time is right. Ramon and I staged a meeting with him, Ula and Ellis the other day and I have to hand it to the guy, he plays a pretty cool game. He's got it all worked out, right down to getting me accused of insider trading so that when I walked away from the charges it looked like I'd bought my way out of it – again. What's more, he manages to make it look as though it was him and his loyal expertise that got me off. Max Romanov, the guy who killed his wife and got away with it, now gets away with a serious financial indiscretion too because he can afford to buy the right people. God only knows what he's got stashed up his sleeve for the future, but he's going to find out soon enough that he shot his strategy to pieces the day he ordered that photographer killed.'

'How?' Rhiannon asked.

'A man is dead,' he said soberly. 'That is something, unlike the rest of it, that has to be addressed and soon. Ramon is ready to go to the police with what we know, which is enough to put Maurice behind bars for a good long while.'

'When will Ramon go?'

'As soon as I give the word.'

Rhiannon nodded, then resisting the urge to reach out for his hand, she said, 'I want to ask what's stopping you, but I think I already know the answer. He's got something on you, hasn't he? Something to do with Carolyn's death?'

His failure to answer was answer enough and her heart turned over at the distant look that came into his eyes.

'Whatever answer I give you now', he said finally, 'will not be a truthful one. So, please, don't ask any more.'

'Are you afraid to trust me?' she said.

'Not now, tonight,' he responded. 'But in a month,

maybe a year, I'll be afraid to trust you then.' He looked down into her face, then putting his hands on her shoulders he smiled through the pain in his eyes. 'The two nights we've spent together have been two of the most precious I can remember,' he said, 'but there's nowhere for us to go now that isn't going to lead to misery and heart-break ... No, don't!' he said as she tried to pull away. 'There's no point trying to fight it. Galina's my wife now and that's the way it's going to stay. You can survive without me, she can't.'

Rhiannon's eyes were closed, her brows were drawn against the pain of his words. 'I don't want to believe this is happening,' she whispered.

'Listen,' he said firmly. 'I know what you've been through, I know how much Maguire hurt you and the last thing I want is to add to that pain. But that's what I'll end up doing if we try to pretend there's any future in this. It would be the easiest thing in the world for me to tell you I want you to stay; that I want you to be a part of my life so that we can see if what we have is as special as it feels right now. But do you hear what I'm saying? Do you understand what that means? It means I'm asking you to be my mistress. So tell me, is that what you want? That we live a life of deception? That I turn you into a woman who's got no real place in my life, who has to come second always to my wife ... ?'

'Then why don't you get her some proper help?' Rhiannon cried, breaking away from him. 'Why did you have to marry her, for Christ's sake?'

'I thought I'd just explained that,' he said.

'But you don't even make love! What kind of marriage is that?'

'It's not going to stay that way,' he answered.

Rhiannon's eyes closed as the jealousy seared through her.

'Hey, come on,' he said, 'what do you want, that I go back there and tell her it's over?'

'Yes, why don't you? I had it done to me!'

He watched her as she turned away again, then sliding a hand into her hair he said, 'Look, what happened, happened. I don't regret any of it, but I couldn't call everything off because I'd just had what amounted to the best fuck I'd ever had. And maybe that's all there is here, Rhiannon, maybe we're just getting this out of proportion ...'

'You bastard!' she yelled, rounding on him ready to strike.

Catching her hand, he pulled her to him and held her so tightly she couldn't move. 'Listen to me,' he growled, 'right now I never want to make love to another woman in my life except you. But we've both got to face the fact that it's not going to happen that way. The way it's going to happen is we are going to say goodbye to each other here and never see each other alone again.'

'Don't say that!' she cried. 'Stop making decisions as though I have no part in them.'

'Just go back to London and forget ...'

'For Christ's sake, Max!' she seethed. 'I have no life in London. There's nothing there for me now. Everything I want is here, right here, looking at me now. No! Don't shake your head that way!' she cried, stamping her foot as she spun away from him in anger.

He waited a moment, then laying a hand on her shoulder he said, 'Rhiannon, I'd give anything in the world for it not to be like this, but you have to understand that I can only give what's in my world. I can't give what's in Galina's, or in my children's. I can't wreck their lives for the sake of my own. You're strong and they're not. They need me, you only want me. You'll get through this. In time you'll forget and move on to someone else. Someone who is free to love you and give you everything you deserve. I wish to God that man were me, but it's not. So please don't make this any harder than it already is.'

Her back was still turned as his arms closed around her again. Tears ran down her cheeks as she struggled hard to overcome the pain and denial that were racing through her. She gazed out at the horizon. The early dawn sky was like honey melting over the desert, the warmth was like a balm before the coldness set in.

'Let go of me now, Max,' she said finally.

'Rhiannon ...'

'No,' she interrupted. 'You've told me what you brought me here to tell me, now please, let me go.'

His hands didn't release her immediately, but when finally they did it was as though he was letting her fall apart. 'I'll call Ramon and have him come pick you up,' he said.

Rhiannon nodded and continued to gaze out at the dawn. Anger and confusion mingled painfully in her heart and filled her throat with sadness. So that was it. Once again, life had offered her so much with one hand, only to slap her in the face with the other. Would she ever find the courage to trust again? Would she ever stop wanting this man who, even as she looked at him now, could turn her heart inside out with longing?

Clicking off the line to Ramon, Max threw the phone back onto the car seat and walked slowly towards her. 'He's on his way,' he said.

Rhiannon's eyes darkened with pain as she turned abruptly away.

'Hey, come on, don't let's say goodbye like this,' he said softly.

'Why not?' she choked. 'What difference does it make? No! Don't touch me. We go no further, remember?' She spun round to face him. 'You know, you're right,' she said bitterly, 'we weren't any more than a good fuck and there are plenty more of them to be had in this life. And to be honest with you, Max, you really didn't need to take the time to explain anything tonight, because to me it couldn't have mattered less.'

Ignoring the hurt in his eyes, she walked past him and around to the other side of the pond. Sitting down on the walled edge, she wrapped her arms around herself as though to tell him not to come close again, then fighting back the tears she counted the minutes to Ramon's arrival.

Six days later Max was lying on his bed at the Malibu mansion staring sightlessly up at the ceiling as he held Galina in his arms. The curtains were open, allowing the moonlight to cover their bodies in a soft, silvery glow. Galina's head was resting on his shoulder, she had one arm wrapped tightly about his neck and one leg over his two. As she sobbed and shivered, he absently stroked her hair and felt her tears falling on to his chest. He was wearing his undershorts now, but he'd put them on only a few minutes ago. Galina was naked, but that wasn't the way she had come to him. Her clothes lay scattered about the room, torn and bloody, like discarded remnants of her dignity.

Hearing her swallow, he tightened his hold on her and kissed the top of her head. She turned her face into his chest and he held her as she continued to cry. Minute after minute ticked by, until eventually she lifted her head and rolled on to her back. He put a hand out for hers and taking it she bunched it under her chin.

Her nose was still blocked with tears and her throat sounded raw and constricted as she said, 'Did you tell her about Carolyn?'

'No.'

Galina's eyes moved back to the middle distance. 'Thank you,' she said.

'Why are you thanking me?'

'For everything you've done for me.'

Max was silent.

'You don't have to do it, you know.'

'Let's not talk about it any more,' he said as she sat up

and turned to face him. Taking his hand, she placed it over her breast. For a while she kept his hand covered as if, without the support of hers, his would fall away. Then replacing his hand on his chest, she turned to sit on the edge of the bed.

She looked so vulnerable in the moonlight, so child-like and defenceless, that without thinking he began to stroke her back. She let him for a while, then getting to her feet she walked towards the door. When she reached it she stopped and he could hear the breath labouring in her chest as she tried not to sob.

Before she could get out of the door he was there, behind her, pulling her back into his arms. 'I'm sorry,' he said, 'I'm sorry, I'm sorry.'

'I've told you before, it doesn't matter,' she said as he led her back to the bed.

'But it does,' he whispered.

Her eyes moved uncertainly between his. 'What are you going to do?' she asked.

He smiled and touching his fingers to her cheek he said, 'Start loving you the way I should?'

Laughing and sobbing, she put her arms around his neck and hugged him. 'Do you think you can?' she said.

He looked around at the small dark piles of her clothing and running his hands down over her waist he felt her flinch as he touched a bruise. 'Yes,' he said, holding her to him, 'just as long as we do it my way.'

Chapter 22

Being back in London was like returning home before the welcome party was ready. Not that Rhiannon had been expecting a party, but coming back early to no commitments, no messages, virtually no mail and no Lizzy was like waking up to a void in time, a pause in life's process, a kind of twilight zone in passing. On the other hand it meant that the facing of harsh and depressing realities, like the looming horror of the music quiz and a day-to-day existence without Lizzy and *Check It Out*, could remain on hold for a while, giving her the chance to deal with the frozen chaos inside her.

There had been no one to meet her at Heathrow, so she'd taken a taxi in from the airport, travelling slowly through the drizzling, cloying rain to Kensington where the street lamps were flickering in the early evening gloom and the sound of running feet splashed through the puddled streets. She'd felt so remote as she'd tried to make some sense of her life, of why all this was happening to her.

Though Lizzy was the one Rhiannon wanted to see, it gave her something of a lift to receive so many calls from other friends as they gradually discovered she was back. She went out a lot, occasionally to shop or to meet up with a friend, but mainly to walk. She spent hours roaming around London, drinking in the familiarity of the city she had long thought of as home, watching the speeding, angry traffic, gazing up at the neutral sky and feeling the rain plaster itself softly to her face. She'd never taken the time really to look at London before and wasn't entirely sure why she was doing it now, except it felt like a ritual that had to be gone through. There was a kind of peacefulness in her observation, a comfort to be drawn from the anonymity of the crowds. Whilst walking, watching, listening and assimilating, she could remove herself from the centre of her own world and become absorbed in things that, should she choose, need never touch her.

How she felt deep down inside differed from day to day, but in the bleakest, most panic-filled moments, when loneliness billowed out of the darkness like a huge, smothering black shadow, she used her love of London to remind herself she was safe. There was nowhere else in the world she wanted to be, even though, in her heart, she knew she no longer belonged. Or was it simply that she didn't want to belong? That she couldn't find the spirit to pick up the threads of her life and sew them into a future she so desperately didn't want?

Perhaps if Max were to call, she'd be handling this better. She hadn't expected him to call, except now that he hadn't she realized she'd been desperately hoping he would. She relived the two nights they had spent together over and over in her mind, taking comfort from the words he had spoken and hurting herself with the terrible need to hear more. The longing for him was so raw in her heart that it moved through her body like a soldering seal of pain. It held her together, but it was destroying her too. She had only to envisage his face to feel herself falling apart, had only to remember his touch to know that she couldn't bear never to feel it again. Putting this distance between them had only heightened the despair and intensified the need. She had hoped that coming back to England would help her to gain a better perspective on her feelings, even a mistrust of her instincts, that would ultimately enable her to put it behind her. Instead she felt more confused and disorientated than ever; more desperate to be with him and more terrified she never would be. Sometimes the urgency was so consuming that no amount of tears, no pleading with God or pacing the floor, could soothe it. She felt trapped inside her emotions; imprisoned by a need that could never be fulfilled.

She remembered how impossible she had found it to let go of Oliver, so was she doing the same now with Max? Was she allowing herself to become obsessed with a man she barely even knew? She didn't know why she would do that, but obsessions, by the very nature of what they were, didn't stand up to reason. Nor did they take account of the dispassionate analysis she forced herself through to try to make herself accept that it simply wasn't possible to love someone this much when, in every way but one, he was little more than a stranger.

But he didn't feel like a stranger. What he felt like was a connection with herself, an understanding of her own existence. She loved him in a way she had never loved before and would never love again. She knew that as certainly as she knew that she would never, no matter how hard she tried, be able to put her feelings into words simple enough for anyone who hadn't experienced this kind of love to understand.

But she tried. Two weeks after they had said goodbye, she tried to voice her thoughts and her feelings aloud in the desperate hope that the confusion and the pain would somehow dilute in the telling.

Jolene was quiet for some time after she told him, his soft brown eyes gazing at nothing as he held his wineglass against his chin and considered her dilemma. His dark, handsome features shimmered like liquid in the candlelight, his cropped, frizzy hair made a hazy outline to his head, while his hooped ear-rings swayed from the several holes in his ears. He was wearing Armani jeans, black high-heeled ankle boots and a silver polo neck sweater – the long, silvery blonde wig he generally wore was spilling from the bag at his feet. Missing Lizzy the way she was, it hadn't been hard for her to open up to Jolene, in fact it had been all too easy. Whether it had been wise, though, she was starting to doubt, for she had never confided in him like this before.

At last his eyes came up to hers and taking a deep, troubled breath, he said, 'You're right, it is hard to understand the way you're feeling when you hardly know the man, so you're going to have to ask yourself, Rhiannon, is it really him you want, or is it just a payback for Galina and what she did to you?'

Rhiannon's head drew back in surprise. 'Have I ever struck you as being that petty before?' she bit back.

Jolene held up a hand. 'No,' he said, 'but that doesn't mean you aren't capable of it; we all are. She stole the man you were going to marry, ergo, it would be perfectly understandable if you wanted to do the same to her.'

'You can't honestly believe that all I'm feeling now is cheated of revenge?' she cried.

Jolene's eyebrows went up. 'As a matter of fact, no, I don't think that's all you're feeling,' he confessed, 'but I had to ask and frankly, it would be a hell of a lot easier on you if that was all, because if what you're telling me is true, then what's going on inside you now is nothing short of hell.'

His words cut deep into her heart. Her gaunt freckled face showed her suffering, her eyes were lost in dark shadows and her normally lively hair was twisted into a single careless plait. In the past she'd always believed she had the strength to get through anything, that somehow she could face whatever life threw at her, deal with it and move on, but these past few months had proved how shamingly wrong she had been. She no longer knew in which direction she should move, or how to go about picking up the pieces of her life, for the trauma of what had happened with Oliver, the loss of her job and now the consuming need she felt for Max, were all undermining her courage and confidence in a way that was frightening her even more than she was prepared to admit. Yet she knew in her heart that were it not for Max she would be coping; that were it not for the persistent feeling inside her that she must wait, that it wasn't all over for them yet, she wouldn't be allowing her life to remain on hold like this.

As her eyes came back to Jolene's she at last registered the unspoken message in what he had just said and feeling the pull on her conscience she said, 'You sound as though you've been there.'

He nodded and rolling his glass along his jaw he said, 'Yeah, I've been there. It's a long story, one I'll save for another day, but I know what it's like to feel the way you're feeling now and I can't put it into words either. All I know is it's the best and the worst feeling I've ever had in my life.'

Rhiannon swallowed and waited for the pain to ease in her heart. 'Do you ever see him now?' she asked.

Jolene shook his head. 'Never,' he answered. 'He's married, got a couple of kids, good job, public figure, all the usual crap.' He sighed, then after taking a sip of wine he said, 'Am I allowed to ask, if Mr Romanov feels the same way about you as you do about him, then why did he marry someone else?'

'He had his reasons,' Rhiannon answered.

Jolene eyed her carefully. 'Do you believe those reasons?' he said.

Rhiannon nodded. Then looking down at her glass she said, 'At least I believed them when he told me; I'm not so sure now. I mean, I suppose it's hard to make myself believe anything right now.'

'Especially that any straight man in his right mind could resist a babe like Galina Casimir?'

Rhiannon smiled weakly. 'He spent his honeymoon

night with me,' she reminded him.

Jolene nodded. 'Which makes him the prize bastard of all time,' he pronounced flatly.

Rhiannon's eyes widened.

'Well, how would you feel if he did it to you?'

Rhiannon was silent.

'Look,' Jolene said gently, 'if the man's capable of doing something like that, if he can stand up there and swear before God and Dolly Parton to love, honour and screw for the rest of his life a woman who's more beautiful than sin, while you're standing there watching him and big-time available, then you're going to have to face it, Rhiannon, he doesn't feel the same way about you as you do about him. I know he said he did, but most guys don't find things like that hard to say. And I know you're not going to want to hear this, but you don't have to look any further than your own fuck-up of a marriage, if you can call it a marriage, to know how capable a man is of lying, or at least avoiding the truth.'

'I thought you said you knew how I felt,' Rhiannon responded, trying to keep the edge from her voice.

'I know how *you* feel, yeah. What I don't know is how *he* feels. And to be frank, with a track record like his I'm staggered that you allowed yourself to be alone with him, never mind screwed by him. I mean, the guy *killed* someone, Rhiannon.'

'Oh, for God's sake!' Rhiannon cried, jumping to her feet. 'I expected more of you, Jolene. I ...'

'No!' Jolene snapped. 'What you expected was me to tell you that it's all going to be all right, that it'll work out in the end, that of course he loves you, not the creature he married ... Well, I can't do that, Rhiannon. He's the one who has to do that. I can only go on what I know about the man from the press and what you just told me. And none of it looks good. What's more, if she were here, I know Lizzy would say the same. You haven't had nearly enough time to get over Oliver, in fact as far as I was aware, just before you went to LA you were thinking about going back to him. That alone should show you what a poor judge you are when it comes to men. The bastard practically bigamized you, or whatever the word is, and you consider going back to him! And now, less than a month later, you're telling me you're in love with the man whose wedding you just went to, a man who, by your own admission, screwed you the night of his honeymoon, then very neatly saw to it that you disappeared from the country so's not to cause him any awkwardness later.'

'It wasn't like that,' Rhiannon protested. 'You're twisting it into something it wasn't ...'

'Am I? Or are you?' Jolene cut in. 'I know you hate me for saying all this, but I'm voicing your own worst fears and you know it. So face up to them, Rhiannon! It's the only way you're going to deal with this and get on with your life. You might be right, he might love you more than any other woman in existence, this might be tearing him apart even more than it is you, but based on what you've told me so far I've got to tell you that I've got a big question mark over that.'

Rhiannon's back was turned, her arms were folded as she stared out at the lamplit garden. She couldn't imagine now what had persuaded her to confide in Jolene when she should have realized before that it just wasn't possible for him to understand what she was telling him. She wasn't a part of his world and he wasn't a part of hers, not in this sense anyway, and she felt now that her confidence had been a betrayal of Max, that somehow she was allowing Jolene to come between them and she wanted it to stop.

'All this stuff about him in the press,' Jolene went on, 'it's got to come from somewhere, Rhiannon. You know that. They don't make these things up. OK, they might misunderstand or misconstrue, but they don't manufacture, especially not where a man like Max Romanov is concerned. So you've got to ask yourself why he never takes the press on, why he's never sued anyone for libel, or got injunctions slapped on stories he must know are about to make headlines. They say he bought his way out of a murder charge and now out of an insider-dealing charge. What next, Rhiannon? Or what more? What more is there that we don't even know about this man?'

Rhiannon was thinking of Maurice and all Max had told her. She was thinking of Susan Posner and wondering if she had been a fool not to meet her. She was thinking of Galina and the confusion of her mind. She was thinking of Max and how eagerly she had believed everything he had told her. She thought of his children and how much he loved them. She thought of the hours he had spent with Galina before coming to her in the desert. She thought of the way he had put his hand on her breast that first night; the way he had kissed her, made love to her and held her. She wondered about the things he hadn't wanted to tell her; then she heard everything Jolene was saying and wished to God that Jolene would leave.

'I know you want to believe in this,' Jolene said. 'I wanted to believe in it when it happened to me too. And there are things you can believe, like what a great screw it was, like how special it made you feel at the time, like something as powerful as that doesn't happen to everyone, 'cos it doesn't. It's unique in your life, you've never felt it before and you'll never feel it again. But it belongs to that time, those hours or days you spent together, and that's right where it's got to stay. He told you that, just like my guy told me. It didn't stop me hoping, though, it didn't stop me telling myself that it was bound to work out in the end, because something as strong as that couldn't be for nothing. But it doesn't work out, because it can't. He's married, he's got kids, he's got commitments, he's got a whole damned history in which you don't feature at all – and believe you me, Rhiannon, he's not going to give any of it up for you, whether he loves you or not.'

'I know,' she whispered. 'He told me he wouldn't.'

'Then believe him.'

'I'm trying.'

Jolene got to his feet and went to pour them both more wine.

'This won't go any further than these four walls, will it, Jo?' Rhiannon said as he handed her a glass.

'On my honour, no,' Jolene answered, his lashes casting spiky shadows over his cheeks as he blinked. 'And I'm sorry if some of the things I said hurt you, but I wish to God someone had done the same for me when I needed it. Three years I wasted believing he would come back to me, that somehow things would work out, partly because my so-called friends assured me it would and partly because I just couldn't make myself accept that life would let me feel so much for one man and then snatch it away. But it would, and it did.'

'It seems to have worked for Lizzy,' Rhiannon said, her lips stiffening as she tried to hold back the tears.

'Lizzy's a different story,' Jolene answered. 'Andy's got no other ties. He's free to love her and she's free to love him.' He shrugged. 'I guess one of these days you'll meet someone who's free to love you.'

'It won't be the same.'

'Of course it won't. It'll be a compromise. Life is always a compromise. Lizzy's giving up London to be with Andy; you'll give up your dreams of Max to be with whoever.'

Rhiannon's heart twisted inside her and she turned away quickly before Jolene saw the tears fill her eyes. 'It makes me so angry,' she said a few moments later.

'Life is meant to make you angry,' Jolene laughed. 'Its whole fucking *raison d'être* is to piss you off.'

Laughing too, Rhiannon said, 'I meant, *I* make me angry. I feel so pathetic, moping about here trying to get a focus on my life and failing to think about anything but him. I pretend I'm thinking about other things, but I never really am. I keep having conversations with him in my head and it's driving me nuts. I'm supposed to be starting that bloody music quiz on Monday and all I can think about is smashing Mavis Whatsit in the face for being the only one to offer me a job when I always thought I'd have job offers coming out of my ears, should I ever find myself in this position, which I never dreamt I would.'

'Oh, tell Mavis Whatsit to go fuck herself,' Jolene snorted and with a typical Jolene flop of the wrist he wiggled back to the sofa and sank into it. 'You don't *need* her,' he said when he realized Rhiannon was watching him and drawing a semicircle with his chin, he turned to look the other way as he elaborately crossed his legs, then let his eyes slide back to hers.

Rhiannon was watching him carefully. 'What are you saying, Jolene?' she asked. This was a Jolene she knew, a Jolene who liked to beat about the bush with his gossip and huff on his nails while his audience tried to second-guess him.

'I'm just saying, you don't *need* her,' he repeated.

'Then what do I need?'

He nodded, then pursing his lips thoughtfully he said, 'What you need is to tell her to go fuck herself, before she tells you.'

Rhiannon's heart turned over. 'Are you saying that she's withdrawing her job offer?' she said.

'What I'm saying is she's got no job to offer.'

Rhiannon's head dropped into her hand. 'Jolene, I'm sorry,' she said, 'but I'm just not up for this. You're going to have to come to the point.'

Jolene tutted. 'Her show's being axed,' he said. 'She'll find out tomorrow.'

Rhiannon's eyes were round as she lifted her head and looked at Jolene. 'Are you sure?' she said, fighting back the panic. She had to have this job, she just had to. Not only for the overdraft, but for something to focus her mind on before she lost it completely. 'Who told you?'

Jolene grinned. 'My lips,' he whispered, sealing them with a finger. 'But it's a fact. Mavis Lindsay and her moozak for morons are strangers in the night.'

'Oh, Jesus Christ,' Rhiannon murmured, looking distractedly about her. She went to sit on the edge of a chair, put her glass on the table and placed her hands on her knees. She looked about to spring up again, but remained where she was as her mind raced along the empty roads ahead and her heart twisted with fear. 'What's happening to me, Jo?' she whispered. 'I feel like someone's put a curse on me. First Oliver, then my job, then Max, now my job again. How much more can go wrong?'

Jolene shrugged. 'You've got a roof over your head,' he reminded her. ''Course, you won't have that much longer if you can't pay the rent,' he added pensively.

Rhiannon's eyes flashed as she threw him a look, then picking up her wine she began pacing the floor. 'I've got to find a job, Jo,' she said. 'Why can't I find a job? I'm more qualified than most of those jerks out there will ever be, so why can't I find a bloody job?'

'Because you're a threat,' Jolene responded. 'You've had your own programme, a really successful one too, so no one wants you coming in stealing their thunder, do they? Or showing them up for what talentless shitheads they are. Besides, what the hell are you doing pissing about trying to find a job? You're not an employee, you're an employer. You're the ideas person, the one who makes the heart beat.'

'I'm also the one who needs to earn some money,' Rhiannon retorted. 'And fielding fresh ideas about the place doesn't ease an immediate problem with the cash-flow. Besides which, maybe you'd like to tell me just where I'm supposed to be getting these ideas from?'

Jolene pulled a face. 'You've never been short of them before,' he reminded her. 'What's so different now?'

'I was never having a confidence crisis before,' she snapped.

'There you are!' he declared with a flourish of his hands. 'An idea! You can do a series on mid-life crises.'

'I didn't say mid-life,' she retorted. 'I said confidence.'

'Same thing, isn't it?'

Rhiannon eyed him nastily, then despite herself she laughed.

Jolene's eyes widened with approval. 'You look like hell,' he told her, 'but the smile helps. Anyway, confidence, mid-life, call it what you want, separate them if you like, you're the expert, not me. But if you're asking me I reckon it would make a damned good series. I mean, everyone experiences some kind of crisis at some point in their lives, don't they?'

Rhiannon's eyes were steady as she looked at him. 'Yes,' she said. 'Yes, they do.'

'So why not focus in on them?'

Rhiannon's expression was starting to turn to one of outright suspicion. 'I've had this conversation before,' she said, struggling to remember when and who with.

Jolene grinned.

'Well come on,' she prompted, 'enlighten me.'

'You had it with Morgan and Sally Simpson on February the twenty-sixth 1992,' he informed her.

Rhiannon blinked.

'Lizzy was there too,' he continued, 'and I took the minutes.'

Rhiannon was shaking her head in amazement. 'You're something else, do you know that?' she laughed. 'It was one of the many meetings we had when we were trying to come up with an idea for a series, before we finally hit on *Check It Out*.'

'Well done,' he congratulated her. 'And *In Focus* very nearly won.'

'That's right,' she said, as it all came flooding back to her. *'Health In Focus. Scandal In Focus. Divorce In Focus. Europe In Focus. Jobs In Focus.'* She went on, reeling off more and more of the ideas she remembered being bandied about during that long-ago meeting. Then her eyes rounded. 'And *Crises In Focus*,' she said. 'We discussed a separate six-part series for that, didn't we? Mid-life was one. Infertility was another. Loneliness. Sexuality. Confidence. And death.'

'Bingo!' Jolene grinned. 'So what are you waiting for?'

Rhiannon sat down. Her eyes were half-bright, half-concentrated with excitement, her pulses were racing. This was just what she needed, the challenge of getting something new off the ground, of channelling her energy into something constructive and absorbing, something that, if it worked, would help rebuild her confidence and take her mind off Max. A quick panic suddenly struck at her heart. The thought of moving forward without him, of focusing her life on something that had nothing to do with him, felt so disloyal that the temptation to abandon the idea right now was almost overwhelming. But she couldn't allow herself to do that. No matter how much it hurt, she had to force herself to let go and get on with her life. She remembered what Jolene had said, that it had been three years before he had stopped hoping and believing, and here she was, just two weeks after it had happened to her, being presented with a way through that, if nothing else, would at least help keep her sane.

'Do you have the minutes of that meeting?' she said, looking at Jolene.

His eyebrows arched. 'Thought you'd never ask,' he smirked and whisking them out of his bag he dropped them on the coffee table between them. 'Oh, and just to get you even more fired up,' he said, 'Merv "the Machete" Mansfield has recently axed just about everything in sight, with the exception of *Check It Out*. Meaning that your baby has been allocated another six slots a year and Merv is overseeing the new title sequence himself.'

'Bastard!' Rhiannon spat.

Jolene grinned. 'We start transmission next Thursday, by the way. The first programme's on *Policing the Internet*.'

Rhiannon's mouth tightened.

'Everything we've got in the schedule so far has come from either you or Lizzy, or was approved by you when you were there,' he told her. 'That's not to say no fresh ideas are coming forward; you chose the team, you know they're more than capable. Trouble is, Morgan and Sally aren't. I mean, those guys couldn't make a decision if it came in a Fisher Price start-up pack. They've lost it, Rhiannon. They were good once, but they can't hack it any more.'

'Are you expecting me to do something?' Rhiannon said bitterly.

'There's nothing you can do. Merv the Machete'd rather axe the programme than see you back on it. The trouble is Homer and Marge are killing it anyway, and by the time Old Merv catches on to the fact it'll probably be too late.'

'Homer and Marge?' Rhiannon said.

'Morgan and Sally. The Simpsons. Oh, never mind, you clearly aren't tuned into Satellite,' Jolene said.

Admitting her failing Rhiannon said, 'So who have they got fronting the programme?'

'They've exhumed somebody from the old *Panorama* days to get them through the first few programmes,' Jolene answered. 'In the meantime they're auditioning like mad and scaring themselves witless. They don't know what the audience wants today and Lizzy's a hard, if not impossible, act to follow. The rest of the team are still taking a crack at it, the way they always did, but Lizzy was the one who fused it all together, as you know, and the fuckwits are trying to find someone just like her.'

'They'll never do that,' Rhiannon commented. 'They'd do better to go for someone totally different. Anyway, it's no longer my concern.' She paused as the truth of that hit her and wondered if a time would ever come when she could utter those words and mean them. 'What I need to concentrate on now', she continued, 'is getting a workable structure together for *In Focus,* then deciding who to approach with it.' She sighed. 'The problem is, how am I going to live meanwhile?'

'I thought Homer and Marge gave you squillions when they paid you off.'

Rhiannon's eyebrows arched. 'Not quite,' she replied. 'And Oliver left me with quite a lot of unpaid bills.'

Jolene's expression told what he thought of that. 'Can't you get some development money from somewhere?' he suggested.

'Maybe, but it takes time and I'm broke right now. No, what I need is a way of earning money that will enable me to develop a new programme – and ...' Her eyes suddenly opened wide and she looked excitedly at Jolene. '... I might just have come up with the solution,' she said.

Jolene's head jerked back in amazement. 'Do the government know about you?' he muttered.

Rhiannon laughed. 'Tell me,' she said, 'how do you think Homer and Marge would respond if I very discreetly offered my services as a consultant?'

'Are you kidding? Very discreetly, they'd probably bite your hand off.'

'Float it past them tomorrow,' she said. 'Don't tell them it was my idea. Make it look like yours, that way they'll be coming to me, rather than me to them, and I'll be able to negotiate a higher fee.'

'Ruthless,' Jolene grinned, rubbing his hands.

There was a good deal more colour in Rhiannon's cheeks by the time she walked Jolene to the door and considerably less fear in her heart. At last she was starting to see her way through, she was taking up the reins of her life and setting it back on track with the same spirit and energy that had always driven her before.

'You feel like a divine visitation,' she told Jolene as he kissed her goodbye.

'If you're pregnant it's nothing to do with me,' he cried.

She laughed. 'You know, I was losing it before you came here tonight. I was going under, I'm sure of it. Things don't look quite so bleak now.'

'You're not the type to go under, sweetie,' he told her. 'It's the coward's way out and whatever else you are, you sure ain't no coward.'

Her answering smile was shakier than she'd have liked. Being brave when someone was there and pushing her on was one thing, the prospect of now being left alone with the desperation in her heart and the pressing needs of her body was another altogether. But she had *In Focus* to think about now, she must remember that and throw herself into it completely.

'Oh, by the way, I almost forgot,' Jolene said, as Rhiannon opened the front door and they both looked out at the dank, moonless night. 'Lucy Goldblum has been trying to get hold of you.'

'Lucy Goldblum who used to be with Thames?'

'The very same. She didn't say what it was about, but you should give her a call. Anyway, got to run. Things to do, places to go and all that. I'll be in touch.'

As Rhiannon wandered back into the sitting-room she was smiling and frowning. Lucy Goldblum was someone she knew very well and both liked and admired, for Lucy's success with the programmes she'd produced for Thames was probably even greater than Rhiannon's had been with *Check It Out*. And maybe, Rhiannon was thinking to herself, Lucy wanted to offer her a job. Oh God, it would be so wonderful if that were the case. It would be the answer to all her prayers right now, for not only would it bring some much-needed money in, but Lucy's would be the very desk she'd want to put her programme ideas on, once they were in working order.

Turning off the lights behind her, she pushed open the bedroom door and stood for a while in the blue-grey light pooling in from the lamp-post outside. Already she could feel her heart twisting with the need to see him and sinking down on the bed, she covered her face with her hands. This had to stop, and it had to stop now. She had to learn to let go and get on with her life. She had something to look forward to now, something that would focus her mind and take her further and further away from him until he was no more than a fading silhouette on the horizon. OK, it might hurt like hell to think that way, but she had to face it, he was already in the past and it was up to her now to make herself move forward into the future.

In her Culver City apartment Susan Posner's face was taut with concentration as she listened to the voice at the other end of the phone. Her pencil was poised over her notepad, her eyes were focused on the few crucial words she'd already written down. In front of her the cursor on her computer screen flashed its impatience to continue. She'd been mid-way through a stinging attack on the Six-Chix, a team of top-heavy, talentless old tarts who were embarrassing themselves nightly in various Hollywood venues, when the telephone had rung. The Six-Chix were now clean forgotten, along with an exposé of a crooked theatrical agent, as Susan Posner listened intently to everything her caller was telling her.

That she was commonly known as The Poisoner didn't bother her in the slightest. She was more widely read than most in her field, mainly because people loved to read about a'' the shit in other people's lives. And the way Susan Posner delivered the shit was compulsive reading. She wasn't afraid to tell things as they were, or at least as she saw them, and if there were people out there who couldn't hack it, that was just too bad. She never lied, she was just a creative broker of the truth when it suited. She felt passionately about women's rights, wrote about them extensively and had, in her way, improved the lot of many more of her sex than most knew about. She trusted very few people, suspected everyone of ulterior and unworthy motives, particularly the do-gooders of the world, and had made it her mission in life to 'out' the closet corrupters and fraudsters. As a result, she had won herself more enemies than friends, but gradually people were beginning to realize that if there was a wrong that needed righting, an offence that needed uncovering, or a hypocrisy that needed exposing, then Susan Posner would grasp the nettle with both hands and hold on in there until justice was seen to be done.

Her call was coming to an end. She'd made several more notes in the last couple of minutes and now she waited for the line to go dead, before throwing the receiver across her desk and letting go a jubilant whoop of triumph.

'Don't tell me. The Pulitzer,' Celia, her room-mate, commented, letting her glasses slide down her nose as she looked up from the giant Websters she had balanced on one knee.

Susan grinned. 'Don't rule it out,' she answered. 'No, that was an occasional but very reliable contact I have in London, informing me that Max Ramonov spent his honeymoon night with, wait for this, not the blushing bride, Galina Casimir, but Rhiannon the-woman-he-spent-the-night-with-two-days-before-his-wedding Edwardes.'

Celia removed her glasses.

Susan laughed and springing up from her desk walked across to the coffee machine they kept on the window-ledge.

'How does this person know?' Celia asked.

Susan's eyes were shining. 'Because Rhiannon Edwardes just told him,' she declared.

Celia looked sceptical. 'Do you believe that?' she said.

Susan nodded. 'Sure I believe it. This guy's never let me down before and he's got a real close relationship with Rhiannon.'

Celia was chewing the stem of her glasses, her thin, serious face tilted into the sunlight streaming through the windows. 'So, can you use it?' she said as Susan handed her a coffee.

'You bet I can use it,' Susan confirmed. 'I've just got to work out the best way.' She shook her head slowly. 'What a bastard, huh? Screwing another woman the very night he gets married. Except it's exactly the kind of thing Romanov would do.' Her eyes were glittering, her hands clenched tightly on her cup.

'You sure do have it in for that guy, don't you?' Celia remarked.

'The son-of-a-bitch murdered his wife and got away with it,' Susan retorted, her lip curling with loathing.

'So you keep saying. But how do you know that for sure?' Celia challenged.

'I know,' Susan answered. 'And I'll tell you something else I know. Galina Casimir's got a serious mental problem that forces her to go out and get herself beaten and screwed by anyone willing to do it. At least, that's the story Romanov's putting out. The truth is, Romanov's doing it himself.'

All traces of humour had vanished from Celia's face.

'Sick, eh?' Susan said.

Celia's eyes moved across the cluttered surfaces of the room until they came to rest on an old, liberally autographed plaster cast of Susan's leg. 'Look, I'm with you on the fact that he probably killed his wife,' she said, turning back to Susan, 'but this stuff with Galina ... I mean, I'm not saying he wouldn't do it, maybe he would, but ...'

'Not would, *did* and continues to do,' Susan corrected. She sank down in the badly sprung armchair between the two sash windows and took a thoughtful sip of her coffee. 'I wonder what he's about with Rhiannon Edwardes,' she said, almost to herself.

She was quiet after that as she mulled over in her mind everything she knew. Since Maurice Remmick, Romanov's personal lawyer, had started feeding her information on Romanov she had been steadily building a profile of the man that, apart from all the other problems it was going to cause him, was eventually, and this time conclusively, going to nail the bastard for the murder of his first wife Carolyn.

There was a time when Susan had been convinced that Galina Casimir had pulled the trigger on that dark December night, but she knew better now. Galina had been in a hospital right here in LA getting herself stitched up after a particularly nasty mugging, or so the records said. Susan had her own theories on how Galina had come by her injuries and they had nothing to do with a mugging. Susan also had her theories on how Max Romanov had, at least so far, managed to get away with murder; her problem was getting them confirmed. But she would and when she did she was going to see that bastard go down for every god-damned crime he had ever committed – along with all those other motherfuckers who were shielding him.

Chapter 23

Ula was alone in the spacious study of the Malibu mansion. The bright California sun was streaming in through the plate-glass windows and for once the sky, stretching out to the horizon, was a perfectly clear blue. Ula's delicate face was creased in concentration as she gazed sightlessly out at the view and tried to get to the root of what had been bothering her for a while now. It was bugging Ellis too, for they had discussed it several times and neither of them had yet come up with an answer to what might be causing the coolness that had suddenly developed between Maurice and Max. For no reason she could fathom, Ula felt sure it had something to do with Galina and for once Ellis agreed with her. Not that he had any theories on what it might be either, but since Galina had moved permanently into the house there had been no cosy soirées that had included Maurice and Deon and Ula had noticed that any invitations Maurice and Deon had extended had been refused. Whether Maurice was feeling the chill was hard to say. He gave no outward sign of it, but he wasn't a stupid man and he had to be aware by now that Max had started talking regularly with Kurt Kovar in New York – an attorney who had been recommended, Ula had recently discovered, by the ubiquitous Ramon Kominski.

So what was it all about, Ula wondered, getting to her feet and wandering over to the window. Folding her arms, she stood staring out at the gardens. She was tempted to ask Galina, because Galina was the easiest and most disarmingly honest person imaginable when it suited her. The trouble was she could also be the most evasive and untruthful when it didn't – and she and Max seemed so close these days that Ula sensed that even if she did pluck up the courage to ask she would draw a blank. To approach Max was out of the question, for he never welcomed anyone prying into his personal affairs, and to ask Maurice somehow didn't feel right. Which in itself was peculiar, for none of them had ever had any secrets from each other before, nor had there ever been any reticence in confronting an issue if any of them considered there to be one. And there was one, Ula was certain of that; she just wished she knew what the hell it was.

She looked round as Max's personal line started to ring and going to answer it, she flipped on her computer screen intending to get back to work.

'Hello, can I help you?' she said into the receiver.

There was no immediate reply and Ula was on the point of repeating her greeting when the line went dead.

Shrugging, she put the phone down again. Not such an unusual occurence, people often didn't speak when they got wrong numbers, though Ula had the distinct impression that had Max answered the phone whoever it was would have spoken. Which meant that the mystery caller, who'd made the connection a couple of times lately, wasn't prepared to speak to anyone but Max.

Going to pour herself a coffee, Ula wandered out of the study, through the family room and into the atrium. From there she could see Max and Galina playing with the kids in the pool. She watched for a while, then turned soberly back to the study. The picture of domestic bliss was a convincing one, but no matter how hard Ula tried she couldn't buy it – what was more, she knew why she couldn't.

Sitting back down at her desk, she cupped her coffee in both hands and began to chew her lip. She'd seen them, Max and Rhiannon, the morning after the wedding. She'd been up all night gambling and having decided to go and get some air before taking herself off to bed, she had wandered out into the sultry dawn heat and headed off towards Caesar's Palace, where more weary and disillusioned gamblers were emerging from their own spectacular defeats. It was when she had returned to the Mirage that she had seen Max, standing outside the hotel with Ramon, obviously engaged in some kind of angry exchange. Then Rhiannon had appeared with her bags. Max had instantly gone to her and when she'd tried to turn away he'd pulled her into his arms. Then lifting her face up to his, he had spoken softly to her in a way that could leave no one watching in any doubt of their intimacy.

Unnoticed, Ula had continued to observe them as they got into a black saloon car and Max spoke briefly to Ramon before pulling away. As they drove past her, Ula could see how pale and strained their faces were. Then suddenly Ula had panicked, had even started after them, for in those few brief moments she had been afraid they were going away together. But Ramon had stopped her and told her that Max was simply taking Rhiannon to the airport and after that it would all be over.

It seemed that Ramon was right for, as far as Ula was aware, there had been no contact between Max and Rhiannon since that day. Furthermore, Max and Galina appeared so very much in love and were so obviously sharing a bed at last that Ula just couldn't think why she should be so worried. The trouble was she couldn't get that morning in Vegas out of her head, nor could she help wondering if the caller who wouldn't speak to her was Rhiannon. She was inclined to think it was, though whether Rhiannon had actually spoken to Max, Ula had no idea. What she did know, however, was how very used Max was to getting what he wanted and what lengths he was prepared to go to to get it. She had only to consider the circumstances surrounding Carolyn's death to realize just how powerful and resourceful her boss really was. But in his shoes, with his money and influence, Ula had to ask herself, wouldn't she have done the same thing? The answer was yes, she would have, for no one, when faced with an alternative, would choose to spend twenty-five or more years in prison.

Ula's eyes suddenly flew open as the Memphis photographer came unbidden to her mind. Her heart started racing and she felt sick inside. She'd almost rather die than be thinking what she was thinking now, but it seemed there was no way she could stop herself, for there was so much about all that that still didn't add up. She looked across at Maurice's desk and asked herself if maybe Maurice knew more than he was telling and if it was what he knew that was at the root of his foundering relationship with Max. Should she broach the subject with Maurice, she wondered? Should she get Ellis to? Or should she keep her thoughts to herself and pray to God that it would all just go away?

'So how's it going with Lucy Goldblum?' Lizzy asked, as she and Rhiannon pressed their way through the Harrods Christmas shoppers into the Egyptian Hall.

'Not bad,' Rhiannon answered, pausing at a cluttered table and hooking her shopping on to one arm to reach out for a pill-box engraved with hieroglyphs. 'Still early days, though, and her current contract with Thames doesn't finish until the end of the month, but in principle we think we can work together. What about this for my stepmother?' she added, showing the pill-box to Lizzy.

'Will she know what it is?' Lizzy asked.

'No.'

'Then get it. Have you pitched the *In Focus* idea anywhere else, besides Lucy?'

'Mmm, I've talked to a couple of people,' Rhiannon answered, counting out the change in her purse and handing it and the pill-box to an assistant. 'I've got a meeting with someone in the City next week to try to raise some money there, but I don't hold out much hope, no one's parting with any cash right now.'

'How much do you need for a pilot?' Lizzy asked as they merged back into the seething mass of shoppers and headed towards fashion jewellery.

'Twenty thousand. Twenty-five would be more realistic, but I can call in a few favours.'

They were parted for a few moments as the crowd proved impossible to penetrate and Rhiannon was swept sideways by an onward surge from the Food Hall. Grabbing her, Lizzy yanked her back and pressed a path through to Butler and Wilson.

'So, you really think you're cut out for a life in the bush?' Rhiannon said, changing the subject as she spun a laden carousel of ear-rings.

Lizzy's eyes rolled as they moved on to the next counter. 'It's incredible, I know,' she said, 'but I've spent the past two months up to my eyes in rhino shit and cat spit, dealing with know-it-all tourists and celebrity conservationists and it just gets better all the time. I mean, obviously it's because Andy's there, but I really am starting to love it. It's so different from anything I've ever had in my life before, and I just can't get enough of all the things he's teaching me about the animals and getting involved in the day-to- day running of the camp. There's so much to do, you wouldn't believe it, especially now Doug's spending less time there.'

'Is he?' Rhiannon said. 'You never mentioned that before.'

'Didn't I? Well, he is, which is why he was so thrilled when I turned up, because he didn't want to leave Andy in the lurch, but he does want to spend more time in Jo'burg with his girlfriend. She runs a local radio station there and Doug's keen to go back to university and ... Well, I guess it's all working out.'

Rhiannon looked impressed. 'It certainly sounds like it,' she commented. Then smiling as she moved on around the display cases she said, 'I'm so glad you're here, you know. I've missed you.'

Lizzy watched her as she picked up a bracelet, laid it on her wrist, then put it back again. Rhiannon was looking so pale and had lost so much weight since Lizzy had last seen her that it was obvious she had been a great deal more affected by what had happened with Max than Lizzy had realized. And with everything else that was going wrong in her life ... Lizzy's heart went out to her, for she remembered how afraid and alone she had felt all those months ago when she had been struggling so hard to keep her own life together. She recalled all too clearly the way she had shut Rhiannon out and tried to deal with things alone, the way Rhiannon was doing now. Except there was something different about Rhiannon, something that was baffling Lizzy as much as it was concerning her, for it wasn't like Rhiannon to hold back on her and it very definitely felt as though she was now.

'Aren't you going to ask about Sharon Spicer?' Rhiannon prompted as they moved on towards the escalators.

'Oh God, I forgot about her,' Lizzy cried. 'Did you meet her?'

Rhiannon laughed. 'I did and you're a genius,' she said. 'The woman's a born presenter. I've seen her at least half a dozen times since you suggested her and she can't wait to audition. In fact, she's so excited she's even offered to put in some money – providing we take her on, of course.'

Lizzy's eyebrows went up. Then laughing she said, 'She's a real whacko, but she could very well end up doing for people in crisis what Barbara Woodhouse did for dogs. Is she still a Samaritan?'

'I don't know, I didn't ask. I thought they weren't supposed to tell you anyway.'

'They're not. She only told me because she was trying to persuade me to become one myself. She thought I had what it took.'

'Remind me how you know her?'

'She lectured in psychology when I was at Birmingham,' Lizzy laughed. 'I'm telling you, the woman is loaded to the brim with talents you'd never expect her to have. She's a concert violinist, did she tell you that?'

'No,' Rhiannon grinned.

Lizzy was shaking her head in fondness. 'She can drive you nuts at times, but she's got one of the kindest hearts I've ever come across and a totally brilliant mind. She's Magnus Pike in a skirt. And she's got time for people like you just wouldn't believe. Have you camera-tested her yet?'

'We're doing it Friday. Jolene's managed to get us a studio down at Teddington for a morning for a third of what it would normally cost.'

'Well done, Jolene,' Lizzy commented, her tone reminding Rhiannon what she thought of the way Rhiannon had confided her relationship with Max in, of all people, the office gossip.

'Did I tell you, by the way,' Rhiannon said, as some twenty minutes later they wandered on to the platform at Knightsbridge station, 'that I had a Christmas card from Galina?'

Lizzy's eyes rounded as she turned to look at Rhiannon – this was the first time she'd mentioned Galina's or Max's names since Lizzy had arrived, and for some unimaginable reason Lizzy hadn't been able to find a way into the subject herself. 'No,' she said, 'you didn't tell me.'

'Oh, well, it arrived the other day,' Rhiannon told her,

following her on to the train. 'She put a note in with it telling me that she's coming over to London in February – Conspiracy are launching some new fragrance apparently – so she'll be doing a whistle-stop tour of Europe before Max flies over to join her and take her on a belated honeymoon somewhere in the Swiss Alps. Gstaad, I think she said. Anyway, she says she realizes what a busy schedule I've probably got, but if we can work out something between us, she'd love to see me for a coffee, or even a lunch, while she's here.'

Lizzy took a breath, gave herself a moment to assess all that, then said, 'So are you going to see her?'

Rhiannon shook her head. 'No.' She looked down at her shopping as someone squeezed past, trying to get further down the train. 'Have you got many more presents to get?' she asked, turning back to Lizzy.

Lizzy blinked at the sudden change of subject. 'Only a couple,' she answered. 'How about you?'

'The same,' Rhiannon answered.

Lizzy watched her for a moment, waiting for a crack to appear in the demeanour, but Rhiannon only widened her eyes and started to laugh.

Realizing she was going to get no further, Lizzy struggled to bring her wrist up to look at her watch. 'Andy's supposed to be calling me at six,' she said, 'and my sister's expecting me at seven, so I guess that means I should go straight home. Damn it, I was hoping to come back to yours for a quick drink. What are you doing this evening?'

'Probably writing a script for Sharon's camera test,' Rhiannon replied.

'I could come over tomorrow,' Lizzy offered, as though trying to make up for a disappointment she wasn't even sure she'd sensed.

'Why don't you give me a call in the morning,' Rhiannon said. 'I'm not sure what I'm doing yet.'

Lizzy looked at her, trying not to be hurt, then nodding she said, 'OK. I'll do that.'

Still smiling, Rhiannon lifted her gaze to the Underground map above them. Lizzy looked away and tried to imagine how she would feel if she were in Rhiannon's shoes, what might be going through her mind now, so that she could at least try to get a handle on what was going on here. In the end she decided she just had to come right out and ask. 'Is there something you're not telling me?' she demanded.

Rhiannon looked slightly startled. 'Like what?' she said curiously.

'I don't know,' Lizzy answered. 'That's just the way it seems. Like you know something and you aren't telling me.'

Rhiannon shrugged. 'No,' she said, 'I don't know anything – at least nothing that I'm keeping back from you.'

'It's to do with Max, isn't it?' Lizzy challenged.

Rhiannon didn't even flinch. 'What's to do with Max?' she said.

'You've heard from him.'

'No, I haven't,' Rhiannon said. 'What makes you say that?'

'Because you haven't mentioned him once since I got here.'

Rhiannon frowned. 'I'm not sure I follow the logic of that,' she said. 'But this is my stop. Call me tomorrow, OK?'

As the doors hissed closed and the train pulled out of the station Rhiannon ran up the steps, slotted her ticket through the machine and hurried out on to the Earls Court Road. It was getting dark now and the temperature was near freezing. She walked quickly, eager to get home before the cold seeped through to her bones.

The traffic on the Cromwell Road was at a standstill as she weaved her way through and headed in the direction of Olympia. She was on the point of turning into the street where she lived, when she suddenly registered the sound of someone walking behind her. It was a sound, she realized, that had been with her for some time, and her heart gave a sharp twist of unease as the footsteps seemed to quicken with her own. She started to run, then suddenly turned. The presence of another human being bearing down so purposefully and violently upon her was so shocking that her mind seemed to freeze. A cold, hard grip closed around her wrist. Disbelief and terror gripped her, turning her legs weak. She gasped as a bruising pain thudded into her back and she was thrown against a wall. Instinctively she clung to her bags, her teeth gritted with rage and determination to hold on. But the sudden wrench on her wrists was so brutal that she was dragged to her knees and putting out her hands to save herself she let the bags go.

As her assailant disappeared into the night she knelt where she was, struggling for breath and shuddering with shock as her heart pounded with fear. No one came by as, finally, she managed to haul herself unsteadily to her feet then continue on towards home. All she'd had in her purse was a couple of pound coins. Her credit card had been seized in Waitrose the day before and her front-door keys were in her coat pocket.

Letting herself into the flat, she closed and locked the door behind her and tried to remember if anything in her bag had contained her address. Then, realizing she was shaking, she went to pour herself a large, stiff drink.

As she gulped it her heart continued to pound. She took several deep, steadying breaths, then went to look in the mirror. Her face looked bloodless and haunted. She turned away and swallowed some more whisky. Lizzy was right, she was holding back, but not about Max. Dear God, if only it were about Max.

Snapping that off before it went any further she picked up the phone to call the police. They wouldn't really be interested, she knew that, but it was her duty to report the mugging.

Replacing the phone a few minutes later, she thought about what had happened and felt a great surge of fury sweep through her. She caught it just in time and smothered it. Feeling angry with the world would be very satisfying in its way, but it was about as productive as shooting with an empty camera, for it wasn't going to change the fact that Morgan and Sally Simpson had turned down Jolene's suggestion that she be appointed a consultant for *Check It Out*; nor was it going to conjure a nice fat commission for *In Focus*. Much less was it going to pay the rent. Without the telephone she'd be sunk, but the chances of her raising enough money to pay the bill right now were about as likely as being able to raise the dead. It was hard to imagine how she had managed to get herself into such a financial mess, but with the huge credit card bills Oliver had left her with, which included three and a half thousand pounds for their honeymoon in Marrakesh, not to mention the hire of his wedding outfit and lunch at the Ritz, she could feel almost physically sick just thinking about it.

Of course, if Lizzy knew how critical things were she'd insist on coming to the rescue. But Rhiannon didn't want loans or charity, what she wanted was to get out of this mess on her own. Feeling suddenly swamped, she sank into a chair and downed the last of the whisky. Life hadn't been kind to her this year, and right now she wanted nothing more than to howl with self-pity and rage against the world. Frustration and fear were pushing her towards the edge, but she couldn't let go. She couldn't allow herself to go under. What she must do was find a way through it. In fact she had found a way.

Her blood turned hot, then instantly cold and feeling dizzy she put a hand to her head. Just thank God her handbag hadn't been snatched the day before. If it had there would have been a fifty-thousand-dollar diamond ring inside. As it was, the ring was safe in a drawer in her bedroom, ready to be sold on Monday. The price she had been offered was less than half its value, so it wouldn't clear all her debts, but it would certainly come close The only reason she hadn't sold it before was because the peculiar circumstances surrounding the way Oliver had given it to her made her doubt that the ring was really hers. In fact ever since she'd decided to sell it she had been daily expecting someone to come calling for it. But if they did that was just too bad, because after Monday she would no longer have it. Her heart started to thud again and closing her eyes she began thanking God over and over for the good fortune that had allowed her to be mugged today, rather than yesterday.

Chapter 24

Christmas came and went. Rhiannon spent it with Sharon Spicer among the fat fake-holly sprigs and paper-chain trimmings that Sharon had used to decorate her apartment. Outside the wind kicked up a storm along the Finchley Road, while in the cosy warmth of the cluttered flat they ate roast duck, pulled crackers and talked about life. Sharon was a kind and curious woman whose eccentricities were as entertaining as her anecdotes and whose commitment to *In Focus* was more heartening than most other things in Rhiannon's life right now.

It was past midnight when Rhiannon got home that night to find a message from Lizzy on the machine. The sound of Lizzy's voice made her cry – something she hadn't allowed herself to do in weeks. But it was Christmas and she missed Lizzy so much, and was so afraid of not being able to turn her life around, that she still hadn't found the courage to tell anyone of the trouble she was in. But it was getting better, she reminded herself firmly. She had sold the ring now and though it hadn't cleared her overdraft entirely, nor put any cash in her purse, the bank had at least agreed to return her credit cards.

As the weeks passed and *In Focus* gradually began to take shape Rhiannon's confidence started to rekindle. Lucy Goldblum was on board now, working full time on the project along with Rhiannon and Sharon and at the end of January the three of them became directors of Unlimited Focus, the company they had set up to umbrella the programme – and any other they might make. Money wasn't exactly rolling in, but they managed to get enough together for a pilot and Sharon's and Lucy's personal investments were helping finance the ongoing research. Then an unexpected windfall came Rhiannon's way, when a City bank pledged a twenty-thousand-pound development fund. Sharon treated them all to champagne that night, before taking off to sit her stint as a Samaritan.

Despite her kindness and inherent concern for others it was easy to see how lonely Sharon was, though she worked hard at hiding it with her boundless energy and enthusiasm for life. But she never mentioned a friend and no one, as far as Rhiannon knew, ever called her or invited her out. But all that started to change as Rhiannon made a point of introducing her around and there was soon little doubt in anyone's mind that once Sharon hit the screens she was going to become an overnight sensation. And with the British propensity for fads and trends, she would very likely become the role model for anything from hormone replacement to hang-gliding – she might even, Lucy remarked, get asked to host the lottery!

'The trouble is we just can't get anyone to commit totally,' Rhiannon grumbled to Lizzy one morning on the phone. 'Everyone loves her. They love the pilot too. They're all agreed on its potential, but no one will part with any money.'

'But that doesn't make any sense,' Lizzy protested. 'If they love it, why won't they support it?'

'Because the positions of power are currently peopled by peevish little men with grudges, like Mervyn Mansfield, or intellectual eunuchs who are too busy politicking and festivalling to spare a thought for making programmes. Plus the fact that no one's actually got any money. It'll change, of course, but we could have a way to go before the hiatus is over.'

'Is anyone else having the same problems?' Lizzy asked.

'Just about everyone I talk to. That doesn't mean nothing's getting through, what it means is that unless you go to the broadcasters with at least seventy per cent of the budget already supplied by other sources they don't want to know.'

'Do you have anything at all?' Lizzy asked.

'About forty per cent,' Rhiannon answered. 'And more promises of tabloid publicity and talk-show slots than a kiss'n'tell queen could dream of. Still, I guess it means that as soon as we get the green light we'll be ready to go without any delays, which is an improvement on the situation we were in when we started *Check It Out*, as you will no doubt recall.'

'How's Lucy working out?'

'Just great. In fact, once we do get things underway I'm considering pulling back and letting her run the show. She and Sharon have bonded, as they say, and I've got several more ideas I'd like to concentrate on when I've got the time.'

'Sounds good,' Lizzy commented. 'Maybe things are starting to look up.'

'I hope so,' Rhiannon responded. 'Anyway, enough about me. What gets you on the phone so early in the morning?'

'It's ten o'clock here,' Lizzy reminded her. 'We've all been up since four thirty.'

'So don't tell me, you and Andy are about to go back to bed,' Rhiannon groaned. 'Take notes, will you, then ring me back and remind me what it's like.'

'Oh come on, it hasn't been that long,' Lizzy laughed.

'It feels like it,' Rhiannon replied.

'Any news from the other side of the Atlantic?'

'No. Nothing,' Rhiannon answered, her heart and her stomach abruptly flying into disarray. Galina had arrived in the country the day before and just knowing she was so close was affecting Rhiannon badly. Not that she had any intention of contacting her, it was simply that the proximity wasn't one that Rhiannon was coping with very well.

'How do you feel about all that now?' Lizzy asked.

'Oh God, I'm so busy I hardly ever think about it,' Rhiannon lied. 'Now what about you? How are things with you?'

There was a pause at the other end of the line that halted Rhiannon in the process of flicking through her mail and brought a sudden trepidation to her heart. 'Lizzy? Are you still there?' she said.

'Yes, I'm still here,' Lizzy laughed. 'Andy just ... Well, you don't want to know what he did, suffice it to say I couldn't speak for a moment. Anyway, the reason I'm calling, apart from to find out how you are, of course, is to tell you that ... Well, to ask you really, if you can spare the time to come over some time in the next couple of weeks. There's a reason I'm asking, which is that I have something to tell you and I want you to be here when I tell you.'

Rhiannon started to smile. Obviously Lizzy was pregnant, but she wasn't going to spoil the telling by guessing. 'I'll look at my calendar,' she said, 'but I'm pretty sure I can make it.'

'Are you serious?' Lizzy cried excitedly. 'Just like that! You're going to come. I thought I'd be on the line for hours trying to persuade you.'

'But you know what a push-over I am,' Rhiannon teased. 'And I miss you. I want to see you and I'd love to see Andy again and the thought of a holiday right now, in the middle of the most depressing month of the year, is a very welcome one. Actually, come to think of it, it was this time last year that we were over there, wasn't it?'

'That's right,' Lizzy answered. 'So, what will you do, call me back with your flight times? Or would you like me to book it from this end?'

Again Rhiannon smiled. 'No need,' she said. 'I'll call you back when I've arranged it. It can't be for another ten days or so, though, I've got a couple of meetings arranged that I've been waiting weeks for so I'll come once they're out of the way.'

'OK. Whenever you can,' Lizzy said.

Replacing the receiver, Rhiannon continued sifting through her mail searching for anything that looked marginally less aggressive than a bill. Finding nothing, she tossed the whole lot back on the table and went into the kitchen to pour herself another coffee. She was feeling annoyingly restless and indecisive this morning and speaking to Lizzy had done nothing to improve it – if anything, she felt worse now than she had before Lizzy called. It couldn't be anything to do with Galina, for she had absolutely no intention of going along to Selfridges later in the day where Galina was presenting the UK launch of Conspiracy's new perfume, so there was no reason to be getting worked up over that. No, it was Lizzy being pregnant that was upsetting her. Well, perhaps upsetting wasn't quite the right word, but she couldn't think of a better one so that one would have to do.

Actually, now she came to think of it, she was thrilled for Lizzy. OK, it meant that Lizzy really wouldn't be coming back, but she'd known that anyway, so she could hardly claim to be disappointed by it at this late stage. In fact, the more she thought about it the more excited she felt at the prospect of going back to Perlatonga and seeing Andy and Doug and sharing in the celebrations. So why was she pacing up and down like a caged animal with her heart leaping about all over the place and her route to the bathroom becoming ever more frequent?

Well obviously it was to do with Galina, she finally

admitted as she boarded the tube into the West End. She might just as well own up to it, because denying it was only making her worse. She was dreading that Galina would call and that she would end up agreeing to see her. On the other hand she couldn't stand the thought of Galina not calling, which was ludicrous when she had no desire to see her and nothing to say even if she did. So why was her mind going over and over a script that neither of them was ever going to play out, nor stick to should they happen to meet? Why was she trying to imagine what Galina's reaction would be if she saw her, when all she had to do was get off the train at Bond Street, cross the road and go and find out. There would be hundreds of people in Selfridges today, all there to see Galina in the flesh and get a free sample of the Conspiracy perfume. She could just pop in and say hello, wish her well, then leave. But why would she do that? What was the point when she really didn't want Galina figuring in her life any more? Well, it wasn't so much that she didn't want Galina, it was that Galina obviously couldn't come without Max and Rhiannon only had to think about Max to know how unwise it would be for her to see him again. But he wasn't going to be there, was he? Galina had specifically said that he wouldn't be arriving until the end of her tour, so what was the harm in going to say hello to Galina? The harm, she told herself firmly, was that the only reason she was even considering it was because in some perverse way it would bring her closer to Max. So no, she wasn't going to go and that was final. She had a busy morning ahead of her, an important lunch and more than enough going on in her life to keep her mind out of danger zones and engrossed in things that mattered.

She was already off the train and half-way across Oxford Street when, to her horror, she realized that she had got off at Bond Street and was now heading in the direction of Selfridges. Then she relaxed as she remembered that she was on her way to St Christopher's Place, which was close to Selfridges, where she was meeting up with Morgan and Sally Simpson in the café below the *Check It Out* office. She knew what the meeting was going to be about; the ratings were slipping, they still didn't have a presenter and the programme ideas that she and Lizzy had left behind were starting to run out. So they were going to ask her, as blithely as if they hadn't turned her down before, whether she would consider acting as a consultant. At least, according to Jolene they were, and Jolene was almost never wrong.

Rhiannon had spent some time thinking about what her response would be when they asked and she was still torn between telling them to go straight to hell and making them beg. She guessed she'd probably opt for the latter, since, apart from still needing the money, she was quite taken with the idea of having two programmes to sort out rather than one. Of course, her dealings with *Check It Out* would have to be confidential or Merv the Machete would start sulking and smash up the game. But the secrecy didn't matter, it would out in the end anyway and Rhiannon had a lot more confidence in *Check It Out*'s durability than she did in Merv's. In other words, according to Jolene, Merv's days were already numbered. So it could be, depending on who was appointed in Merv's place – and rumour had it that it would be Felix Rolfe – that Rhiannon would find herself not only the chief producer of *Check It Out* again, but Series and Executive Producer of *In Focus*. The power was already going to her head.

Smiling to herself, she pushed open the door of Selfridges and sailed on towards the cosmetic counters. It was only when she found herself hampered by the crowd that she realized how, caught up in her daydreams, she had allowed her feet to carry her to the very place she had no desire to be. She instantly froze and felt herself flush hot with nerves. Pressing a cold hand to her cheek, she looked frantically around her. Galina was nowhere in sight, nor was the Conspiracy display, so she could get out now before anyone spotted her.

But she didn't. Instead she allowed the crowd to carry her forward until she was forced out to one side and left standing somewhere between gloves and cosmetics. She could see part of the Conspiracy display stand now and the subtle fragrance of the perfume drifted agreeably in the air. She glanced to one side and caught a reflection of herself in a mirror. Her long red hair tumbled down her back and framed her wind-blown cheeks like autumn leaves. Her skin, as always, was pale, but the cold had raised a colour beneath her freckles and her lips were red and moist.

She turned back to the display stand and felt her heart tighten as a gap opened in the crowd. She could see Galina now, her snow-blonde hair, her delicate olive skin and gently slanting blue eyes. She was wearing the Conspiracy colours, a lilac short-jacketed suit with a white silk top, and her tall, slender figure was moving with the grace of a woman who had been born to elegance and style. She was laughing and chatting so naturally and informally with the public that Rhiannon could only admire the ease with which she charmed them. She was so very beautiful and so radiantly happy that it would be impossible not to be enchanted by her, and the confidence she exuded was so recognizable that Rhiannon felt her heart contract. Galina was a woman who loved and knew she was loved in return.

Rhiannon bowed her head, then forcing herself to smile, looked up again. This was hurting a great deal more than she'd have imagined, for seeing Galina was telling her more clearly than anything how very far she was from getting over Max and putting what had happened behind her. She still wanted him so badly that it turned her weak just to think of it. She felt so bound by her feelings that she feared they were never going to let her go.

She started to turn away, then for no particular reason turned back for one last look. Later she would ask herself, if she had carried on walking away would things have turned out differently? Could all that followed have been avoided? Would she be living now with a guilt so terrible it was threatening to destroy the rest of her life? But that was later. Now, as she and Max looked at each other through the crowd, their eyes drawn instinctively to each other's, all she knew was that the emotions pulling through her with such incisive purity – the need, the love, the want, the incredible power of everything he was evoking inside her – were all there for him too.

Galina stood on tiptoe and kissed him while his eyes remained on Rhiannon. He had obviously just arrived and the unexpected bonus of his appearance was causing a ripple of interest to spread through the crowd. The press had all gone, so there were no flashlights or shouted enquiries, there was only the intrigue of the shoppers and Galina's obvious pleasure at seeing him.

No gesture was made, no glimmer of recognition, not even of surprise. He merely looked at Rhiannon, holding her eyes in wordless affinity. In those seconds Rhiannon's heart stopped beating, her mind ceased to function and the world around her blurred into obscurity. Then he looked away and she was released.

She turned and walked out of the store. She went to her meeting with Morgan and Sally, agreed to consider their offer of a consultancy, then took a taxi to her lunch with a prospective sponsor, before descending into the Underground station at Piccadilly and waiting for the train to take her home.

Hour after hour passed with her barely noticing. She scanned the recent issues of *Newsweek* and *Time* magazines; replayed a couple of videotaped programmes that had interested her; made notes for her next meeting with Lucy and dealt with the the several telephone calls she needed to make. Late in the afternoon she changed into a short-waisted cream sweater and an over-the-knee rust-coloured skirt. Then, after lighting the fire, she went to put on some music.

She was utterly calm, yet the moment the doorbell sounded her heart rose to her throat and she felt so nervous she was almost afraid to answer.

Her stockinged feet made no sound as she walked along the hall to open the door and when she saw him her heart folded so painfully around the emotion that she could find no words.

He pulled her into his arms, holding her silently, burying his face in her hair and closing his eyes at the onslaught of need that claimed him.

'Are you OK?' he whispered, pressing her closer.

'Yes,' she answered.

He lifted his head and gazed long into her eyes, then very slowly he started to smile. 'You knew I'd come?' he said.

She nodded. 'When I saw you today, yes, I knew.'

His eyes darkened. 'Do I get to pass the door?' he asked.

Laughing, she stepped back inside and closed the door behind him. Then taking his hand, she led him through to the sitting-room. He seemed so big in the cramped, cosy surroundings, but not out of place. Turning back into his arms, she linked her hands behind his neck and looked up at him again.

'How long can you stay?' she asked.

'Three days,' he answered.

Her eyes widened with surprise, then laughing she said, 'I can't believe this. I had no idea you'd be there today. Galina said you weren't coming until the end of her tour.'

'Originally I wasn't, but our plans changed. Galina's flying to Paris tonight,' he said. 'Tomorrow she'll be in Edinburgh, Thursday she'll be in Manchester.'

'Will you stay here?'

He nodded. 'God, you look so good,' he breathed, sweeping her face with his eyes.

'So do you,' she said, feeling herself brinking on tears again. 'I forgot what you looked like. I couldn't remember your face. I tried calling you, but I could never summon up the courage to speak.' She laughed. 'I felt such a fool. Did you guess it was me?'

He nodded.

'Oh God, what am I crying for?' she said. 'I had myself so together just now. Can I get you something? A drink? I have Scotch ...'

'No, don't go,' he whispered and lowering his mouth to hers he kissed her with a depth and a tenderness that seemed to unravel her entire soul. His lips and his tongue were hungry, but not demanding, his hands held her close and his body told her the strength of his need. When he looked at her again she was breathless and flushed with the heat of her own longing.

'Are you going to take off your coat?' she asked shakily.

He laughed. 'I guess it would make this easier,' he said, shrugging it off. Then putting his fingers under her chin he tilted her face up to his and kissed her softly and lingeringly on the mouth. 'Are you sure this is OK?' he whispered.

'I'm sure.'

Bringing her mouth back to his, he kissed her again as she slipped her hands between them and felt his hardness. She lowered his fly and he helped her release him, then groaned into her open mouth as she circled his erection with her hand and squeezed it hard. Then jerking her in tighter to him, he kissed her harder and more intimately than ever.

Keeping him encircled in one hand, she reached down and lifted the hem of her skirt. She'd left off her underwear, knowing that once she was in his arms she would be unable to wait. All she wore were cream self-gartered stockings.

'Oh Christ,' he murmured, smoothing his hands over her buttocks.

As they sank to the floor she pulled her sweater over her head to reveal her naked breasts. He took each one in his mouth, sucking hard on her nipples as she opened her legs wide and lifted her knees. As their bodies came slowly together they gazed long into each other's eyes, knowing and understanding that this was the way it was meant to be. He smiled, then his eyes fluttered closed as she contracted her muscles around him. Then laughing softly he drew back and pushed deeply into her again.

'I love you,' she said, touching his face with her fingers.

'I love you too,' he said, turning his mouth to her fingers and kissing them. 'I want you to tell me how it's been for you,' he said, 'whether you think about me and want me the way I think about and want you. I want to make love to you and look at you and wonder why I feel the way I do about you and why, when it causes me so much pain, I don't want it ever to change.'

'It won't ever change,' she told him softly.

He kissed her again and began moving his body against hers, filling her full of himself as his tongue entered her mouth and his hands clasped her tightly to him.

'I want to feel your skin on mine,' she whispered.

Lifting himself up he eased himself gently out of her and began stripping off his clothes. She wriggled out of her skirt, tossed it aside, then lay watching him, her eyes reflecting the humour in his as he laughed at her abandon.

His body was firm and solid, powerfully erect and commanding. He knelt beween her thighs and watched her watching him. Using his fingers, he traced the freckles on her skin, moving them over her breasts and nipples, down over her tummy and into the golden hair between her legs. Her breath caught as he touched her, then raising her hips with his hands, he lowered his mouth and began to tease her with his tongue.

Her head moved from side to side as the sensations turned her weak with desire. Her fingers moved into his hair and a cry of release burst from her throat as within seconds she came. Lowering her hips back to the floor, he lay over her and rolling her on top of him he bunched her hair in his hands and brought her mouth harshly to his. They kissed for a long and deeply sensuous time until the need of her body was soaring to a pitch again and raising herself on her arms she gazed down into his face. She started to smile, but feeling the power of him pressing against her and the seriousness starting to cloud his eyes, her smile was swallowed into a sudden and overpowering love.

'Put me inside you. Put me in now!' he said urgently.

Obediently she opened her legs and took him deep inside her. He rolled her on to her back and as her feet locked behind him he began to jerk himself into her with short, rapid strokes.

'I love you,' he whispered, his voice ragged with emotion. 'Rhiannon. Oh, Christ, Rhiannon!' he gasped as she reached beneath their bodies and gently pressed his balls against her. His mouth came crushing down on hers and his rhythm suddenly changed as the seed began erupting from him in long exquisite bursts. He slid his hands beneath her and brought her even closer, continuing the motion of his hips. The base of his penis was rubbing her clitoris and already he could feel her climax starting to break. Her fingers dug into his back, her legs gripped him hard as her entire body turned rigid.

'Max,' she cried. 'Oh God, Max.'

'Let go,' he whispered. 'Just let it go.'

He could feel her closing around him, so tightly that every pulse of her orgasm shuddered through him as it exploded inside her. Her heart was thudding hard into his, her breath was shredded by moans of continuing release. He kissed her again and again, then looked down at her, waiting for her eyes to open. Their bodies were still joined, their skin clung damply to each other's.

When finally her eyelids flickered open she gazed up at him and watched him as looked down at her. Neither of them smiled and neither spoke. They simply looked at each other until he put his open mouth over hers and kissed her again.

'Are we going to stay like this for the next three days?' she asked a long time later. They were lying side by side on the floor now, her head resting on his shoulder, their legs comfortably entwined. The only light came from the sleepily flaming logs in the hearth, which cast a warm, flickering glow over their naked bodies and seemed to seal them from the wintry night outside.

Smiling, he raised the arm that was covering his eyes and used it to pull her closer. 'Do you want to stay like this for three days?' he said.

She thought about that for a moment. 'It's tempting,' she said.

Laughing, he kissed the tip of her nose, then getting to his feet he began hunting around for his clothes. 'I've got a bag in the car,' he said, pulling on his undershorts. 'I'll go get it.' He stopped then and looked down at her lying there in the firelight. 'You look so beautiful,' he murmured.

Smiling, she lifted a hand and linked her fingers through his. Then drawing herself up to her knees, she lowered his shorts and took him deep into her mouth.

'Are you just planning on leaving it like that?' he said, when letting it go she looked up at him.

'I thought I would,' she replied. 'That way there's more chance of you coming back.'

Taking her by the elbows, he raised her to her feet and linked his hands behind her. 'Do you think there's a chance I wouldn't?' he said seriously.

Putting her head to one side, she said, 'No.'

'Then tell me what you do think.'

'I think', she said, 'that I'm going to love having you here for three days.'

His gaze moved from her eyes to her mouth and back again. 'I never knew it could feel like this,' he whispered.

She smiled and let her eyes linger on his lips before lifting them back to his. 'What about Galina?' she said softly.

He sighed and dropped his forehead against hers. 'I'll go get that bag,' he said.

'So that's how it stands,' he said a couple of hours later. 'We don't make love often, but it does happen and when it does it's OK. Nothing like the way it is for us, but it stops the marriage from being a total sham and as a family it's brought us closer together. That's not to say we don't have our problems, every family does, but on the whole we're working things through.'

'And the violence?' Rhiannon said. 'The self-abuse and all the other things she used to do?'

'So far so good,' he said. 'There's only been one what you might call relapse ...' He stopped and as his eyes met Rhiannon's she could see how much he disliked putting Galina's problems into words. 'It affected her pretty badly,' he said. 'I guess it frightened her to think that even though she had what she always wanted she still had a way to go before she was cured.'

'What brought it on?' Rhiannon asked. 'Do you know?'

He shook his head. 'I'm not sure. She's worried about Marina, I think it might have had something to do with that. If she can't figure something out, or if she can't make something work, she feels she's got to punish herself.'

'Why does she worry about Marina?'

He sighed deeply and looked down at their joined hands. 'Marina's had her problems ever since Carolyn died,' he said. 'She's in counselling, but it's taking some time and lately she's been finding it hard. Galina worries about that. She thinks it's her fault, that she's not trying hard enough. The trouble is, the harder she tries the further she seems to be pushing Marina away. And that's a tough call for Galina when she's always been the centre of Marina's world.'

'And what about Maurice?' Rhiannon said. 'Have you managed to sort that yet?'

'I don't know if that one will ever be sorted,' he answered. 'He still tries making moves on Galina, but so far she's resisting.'

'Why on earth don't you confront him?' Rhiannon said.

'Because I can't. No, you know why I can't, so don't let's go down that road.'

Leaning her head against the back of the sofa, Rhiannon looked at his dark, handsome face and though she could see the strength, she could see the terrible strain and anxiety too. 'Where is all this going to go?' she whispered.

His eyes opened in surprise. 'Do you mean you and me?' he said.

'You and me, yes. But Maurice and Galina. These things don't just go away, Max. If he's got something on you and you don't deal with it, it's going to stay that way for ever.'

'You're not telling me anything I don't already know,' he sighed.

'Then do something about it.'

'I told you, I can't,' he responded and put his fingers on her lips as she started to protest again. 'Just leave it,' he said softly. 'I promise it won't be an issue for ever, but there's nothing I can do right now.'

Holding his fingers to her mouth she kissed them,

then leaning forward, she kissed him on the lips. 'I care about you,' she said.

He smiled. 'That's good to hear.'

They kissed again, their lips gently exploring each other's as their fingers entwined. When at last she pulled away she saw a teasing light dancing in his eyes. 'Do you care enough to feed me?' he said.

Laughing, she kissed him again and got up from the sofa. 'There's a choice of pasta or Chinese take-away,' she offered.

'Pasta,' he said, glancing over his shoulder as the telephone started to ring. 'Shall I make a start while you get that?'

Rhiannon grinned her surprise. 'Yes, why not?' she said and picking up the receiver she watched him walk barefoot into the kitchen, tightening the belt of his black towelling robe as he went. When he'd come back from the car they'd made love once more, then after taking a shower had decided not to bother dressing again that night.

'Hi, Rhiannon Edwardes,' she said into the phone.

'Hi. How are you doing sweetie?' Jolene sang.

'I'm doing just fine,' Rhiannon replied, mimicking his tone. 'How are you?'

'Pretty good. And have I got news for you?'

Carrying the phone to the kitchen, Rhiannon leaned against the doorjamb to watch Max rummaging around in the cupboards. 'Give it to me in three straight sentences,' she said, nestling the receiver on her shoulder.

Jolene chuckled. 'Guess who's in town?' he said.

Rhiannon's stomach tightened even as she started to smile. 'Who?' she said, knowing already what his answer would be.

'A certain US publisher,' he answered. 'He flew in this morning.'

'Is that right?' Rhiannon smiled as Max turned to

look at her.

'Are we going for a tomato or a cheese sauce?' he asked, filling a saucepan with water.

'Tomato and tuna,' she answered. 'You'll find the tomatoes in the bottom of the fridge.'

'What?' Jolene said. 'Who are you talking to?'

'Not you,' Rhiannon answered. 'So, go on with your news.'

'That's it,' Jolene said. 'He flew in this morning.'

'That's not news,' Rhiannon told him, 'that's history.'

She waited, then started to laugh as Jolene said, '*Oh-mi-God*, he's there now.'

''Bye, Jolene,' she said, 'nice talking to you,' and pressing down the aerial she clicked off the line. 'Where does Galina think you are now?' she said to Max, taking a packet of dried pasta shells from the cupboard and tearing it open.

'At the apartment in Belgravia,' he answered.

Rhiannon looked at him with eyebrows raised. 'I didn't know you had an apartment in London,' she said.

'There's a lot', he said, kissing her, 'you don't know about me and too damned much I don't know about you. What's your schedule over the next couple of days?'

'Changeable,' she answered. 'At least some of it is. There are a couple of things I will have to go out for, though. I suppose going out together is out of the question?'

'Probably,' he said, starting to chop the tomatoes.

'So what do you intend to do for the next three days?'

'I've got plenty to do,' he said, 'but with the phone and computer right here, I don't need to leave the apartment much.'

'What about if Galina calls?'

'She'll call the mobile. It doesn't tell her where I am.'

Rhiannon looked troubled by that.

'She doesn't call as often as she used to,' he said, 'and if I could organize it any other way, I would, but I can't.'

Seeing that she still looked concerned, he put down the knife and pulled her into his arms. 'Believe me, I hate the deceit as much as you do,' he said. 'More than you do, because you're worth more than this, a whole lot more which is why I'm not going to ask you to come live in LA.'

'Does that mean you were planning to?' she asked, lifting her arms around his neck.

'I'd be lying if I said I didn't think about it.'

Her eyes narrowed with laughter. 'The answer's no,' she said, 'but ask me anyway.'

'Will you come live in LA?' he said.

'You mean will I give up everything for you?'

'That's why I wouldn't ask,' he replied. 'I can't ask you to do something I'm not prepared to do myself.'

She sighed, pulled a face and said, 'Shall we leave this where it is and move on to something else?'

Kissing her, he said, 'I think we should. Tell me what you've been doing these past few months. Are you working now?'

As they cooked and set the table and opened a bottle of chianti she told him about *In Focus* and Sharon and the frustration of not being able to raise enough finance as well as dealing with people she knew to be either inebriated or inept. Sensing he was about to offer her the money, she side-stepped it before he had the chance and moved on to Merv the Machete, *Check It Out*'s falling ratings and the offer of a consultancy she had received that day. He wanted to know everything from how she had managed to upset Merv the Machete to how she was presenting her *In Focus* package. He threw out several suggestions and ideas, both for presentation and content, and she couldn't help but notice and appreciate the way he was taking such genuine interest in her life.

They were sitting at the table and half-way through their meal by the time he got round to the subject of Oliver, but though he was pleased to hear that she'd sold the diamond to help her over the bad spell, the fact that her account remained overdrawn wasn't something he was going to tolerate, no matter how loudly she protested.

'If you'll just listen,' he said, raising his voice above hers, 'I'm not offering you the money. What I'm saying is that Theo Straussen should make good on those debts.'

'No, Oliver Maguire should,' she responded, 'but since his father-in-law controls him I don't see that ever happening.'

'My point exactly. So let Straussen take care of it. I'll speak to him tomorrow. Now, no more arguments, subject closed.'

'You don't have to do that,' she said, 'I can manage.'

'Do you enjoy bailing this guy out?' he challenged.

'No, of course I don't.'

'Then get him off your back. Hey!' he barked, when she made to protest again. 'Let me do this for you.'

Smiling as she realized how ungracious she was being, though still not ready to give in entirely, she said, 'I'll think about it.'

'God save me from independent women,' he muttered.

'Deliverance in three days, not before,' she responded and putting down her fork, she poured more wine into their glasses.

'Are you going to finish that?' he said, when she proceeded to hold her glass in her hands and stare at him across the table.

She looked down at her plate. 'Why?'

'Because if you're not, I will,' he said.

Rhiannon nodded thoughtfully. Then putting down her glass she leaned back in her chair and said, 'Would you have come if you hadn't seen me in the store today?'

She could see the candlelight reflected in his eyes as he looked back at her. 'No,' he answered.

'You wouldn't have?' she said, more upset by that

than she wanted to show.

'I had no intention of complicating your life,' he replied.

'But when you saw me you changed your mind?'

He picked up his wine and stared down at the dark ruby liquid. 'I still don't want to complicate your life,' he said, looking at her again. 'I don't know what happens after this. I can't make any promises and I can't ask you to make any either. But I think we both know that it won't be the last time we see each other.'

Rhiannon's eyes dropped to the plate in front of her, then picking it up she carried it around the table. 'Maybe now isn't the time to talk about the future,' she said, putting the plate down and waiting as he moved his chair back to make room for her to sit on his lap. 'Shall I feed you?' she whispered, sitting astride him.

'Yes,' he answered, his eyes falling to her breasts as she pulled open her robe.

She turned, picked up his fork and filled it with food. Then twisting back she put the fork in his mouth and tried not to respond to the way his fingers were brushing over her nipples.

'More wine?' she offered.

He nodded and as she turned to pick up his glass he lowered his head and drew a nipple deep into his mouth. When he had finished she gave him the wine and let him drink as she deftly unbelted his robe. He looked down as she took his penis in her hand and began to move it up and down. Then his eyes came back to hers as she manoeuvred herself to take him inside her. As she sank on to him he slid his hands under her robe and peeled it away from her body.

'More food?' she murmured tremulously as, using both hands, he caressed her breasts.

He nodded and she turned to pick up the fork.

She fed him until the last mouthful had gone, then pushing everything to one side, he picked her up and laid her across the table. He was still inside her, his hands were holding her hips, his eyes were drinking in the loveliness of her hair and skin in the candlelight.

He moved gently in and out of her, then taking her hands, he held them to where their bodies were joined and said, 'I've never wanted to do so much with one woman in my life.' He tried to smile, but there was no humour in his eyes or his voice as he said, 'I feel as though you're my life.'

Chapter 25

The following morning they woke late and lay in each other's arms laughing and teasing each other and ignoring the time on the bedside clock, as outside the sounds of people going to work disturbed the still, frosty morning. In the end Rhiannon was the first to get up and slipping into a track suit and pair of sneakers jogged to the end of the road to pick up the papers and some milk.

By the time she got back Max was in the kitchen slotting bread into the toaster and attempting to work out the coffee machine. The curtains were open and unexpected sunlight was spilling on to the carpets in the sitting-room and thawing the frost around the window-panes.

'So what's on the agenda today?' he asked, after kissing her hello and letting her get on with the coffee. 'Do you have to go out?'

'Not until this afternoon,' she answered, glancing over her shoulder as he filled a bowl with steaming water to begin the washing up from the night before. 'I'm seeing my partner, Lucy, for an hour before she goes off skiing. Why don't you leave that, we'll do it after breakfast.'

'Are you sure?' he said.

'Just go and sit down with the papers,' she smiled. 'I'll bring your breakfast in when it's ready. How do you take your coffee?'

He laughed, amused by the idea that their intimacy had reached unprecedented limits on one level, but hadn't yet attained the cream-or-sugar-in-coffee stage on another.

Treating him to a dangerous look, she reached up to take a couple of mugs from a cupboard, then relaxed back against him as he slipped his arms around her. 'Did you get the *Wall Street Journal*?' he murmured, kissing her neck.

'The European edition,' she murmured back. 'It's on the table. Did anyone ring while I was out?' she called after him as he disappeared into the sitting-room.

'No,' he lied, not seeing the point in telling her that Galina had called him. It hadn't been a particularly long conversation, but he was thankful, nevertheless, that Galina had chosen the few minutes that Rhiannon was out to let him know how much she was missing him. The ease with which he had assured her he felt the same wasn't something he was proud of and he certainly wouldn't want to do it with Rhiannon there.

Sifting through the papers, he decided to postpone the *Journal* and take a look through the London *Times*. His concentration wasn't all he would have liked it to be – with Rhiannon so close at hand and the simple domesticity they were sharing giving him so much pleasure it was hard to think of much else. He smiled to himself and turned the page. He'd never dreamt he would find it so easy to blot out the rest of his life when his responsibilities, both personal and professional, were usually so paramount and consuming. Yet here he was, not caring too much about anything beyond this woman and this apartment and perfectly happy to pretend that it could go on for ever. What did concern him, though, was what it was going to do to Rhiannon when he left, for though he didn't doubt her strength or ability to cope, he simply couldn't bear the idea of hurting her.

Looking up as she came into the room, he felt the

great power of his feelings lock around his heart. They barely knew each other, but they were so easy with each other, so certain in their belief in the other's love, that it was hard to accept that it was a relationship with nowhere to go.

'There's an article here about some city in the north of England,' he told her as she handed him a coffee and put a plate of toast on the table in front of him. 'It's put itself up for sale.'

'Up for sale?' she repeated, licking her fingers.

'So it says here,' he replied, taking a sip of coffee, then putting down his cup. 'So far they've had interest from Japan, the United States and France.'

'I don't believe it!' she cried. 'That would make a fantastic programme.'

Riffling back through the pages, he found the story, folded the paper in half, then picked up his coffee as she sat on the arm of the sofa beside him to read over his shoulder. He read it again too, then leaning forward to pick up some toast he passed her a slice and turned over the page so they could finish the article.

'It's perfect for *Check It Out*,' she said, sipping her coffee. 'I'll get one of the researchers on to it right away. Anything else?'

'Nothing that leapt out at me,' he answered, ripping the city purchase story out of the paper and putting it on the table. 'And get the terms of your consultancy sorted before you start giving them the benefit.' He looked up at her, then started to laugh. 'OK, I'm sorry,' he said. 'You do it your way.'

'I will,' she smiled, kissing the top of his head, 'but I like it when you get tough. It makes me feel cared for.'

'Don't doubt it,' he remarked, turning back to the paper.

They read together quietly for a while, munching their toast and drinking their coffee until Rhiannon went to get the pot to freshen their cups. As she retook her position on the edge of the sofa, Max absently put an arm over her legs and continued his study of the financial pages, while she picked up the *Guardian*. The radio was playing softly in the background and the warmth from the radiators was causing the windows to steam. Rhiannon glanced up as the mail dropped through the front door, but engrossed in the story she was reading she ignored it.

'Do you know something?' Max said, putting the paper aside and resting his head back on the sofa.

'What's that?' she asked, still reading.

He waited until, realizing he hadn't continued, she turned to look at him. He smiled. 'This is a first for me,' he said, gazing up at her.

She looked puzzled and his smile widened.

'Hell, this is the first time I've been in love,' he laughed. 'I've cared for people, I've cared a hell of a lot for them, even loved them, I guess, but feeling the way I do about you I know now that I've never actually been in love. Isn't that something?'

Rhiannon's eyes were steeped in laughter and surprise as her heart embraced his words. Uncrossing her legs, she started to lean over to kiss him when, to her utter amazement, she fell off the edge of the sofa and hit the floor with a thud.

'Did you push me?' she demanded as he exploded into laughter. 'You did, didn't you?' she said, sitting up and trying, not very successfully, to glare at him.

'The hell I did,' he laughed.

'Then how did I end up down here?'

'It beats me,' he said, laughing even harder as he realized she'd taken her coffee with her and dumped it all over herself.

She continued to glare at him. Then only just managing to keep a straight face, she said, 'You know, that's what they call going off the deep end for a man.'

He burst out laughing again and reaching for her,

pulled her up to her knees. 'It is?' he said. 'I thought it was you making a regular English charlie of yourself.'

Her eyes narrowed. 'Very funny,' she remarked. 'Look at me, I'm drenched. It's even in my hair.'

He shook his head and tried not to laugh any more.

'You were saying,' she said, 'before you pushed me over the edge.'

'Not guilty,' he said, holding up his hands. 'But I was saying, don't you think it's something that ...' Unable to stop himself he burst out laughing again. 'Hell, I'm sorry,' he said, 'but I don't reckon I can go anywhere with what I was saying now without seeing you disappear over the side of the couch.'

Laughing too, she said, 'If I'm never going to live this down I guess the only thing I can do now is go and take a shower. Are you coming?'

'You bet,' he replied, and putting down his paper, he scooped her up in his arms and carried her noisily through to the bedroom.

At about the same time, which made it close to midnight in LA, Susan Posner was leaving yet another message on Terry Marlowe's answerphone in London. Marlowe was a paparazzo she'd hired many times in the past to pick up the European end of a story, and if she could trust anyone with this assignment it was him. Since Jolene Jackson had called to tip her off that Max Romanov was with Rhiannon Edwardes, Susan had left half a dozen or more messages on Marlowe's machine, knowing, because she'd checked, that he was in London; but having no other number for him than the one she was calling, she was calling it every hour on the hour.

This time she was just about through reinforcing her urgency when there was a click on the line and Marlowe came on in person. 'Pozzer,' he said in his broad south London accent. 'What's all the commotion?'

'I've got something for you,' she answered crisply.

'Drop whatever else is on your schedule and get yourself round to the address I'm about to give you.'

'How much we talking, Poz?' he drawled.

'The usual, plus half,' she declared with no hesitation.

'Double plus half,' he responded.

'It's a deal. Got a pen?'

'OK, so who am I looking for here?' he said, when he'd taken down the address.

'Max Romanov,' she answered.

Marlowe took a moment to crank up his memory. 'The publisher guy?' he said.

'That's him.'

'The guy who married the babe with the Russian name a couple of months back?'

'Galina Casimir,' Susan provided. 'That's him. I want as many shots as you can get of him going in or out of the address I gave you and if you can get any of him and the woman he's staying with there, you'll earn yourself a bonus.'

'I take it the woman's not Mrs Romanov,' he yawned.

'Correct. Her name's Rhiannon Edwardes.'

'Never heard of her. Who is she?'

'A TV producer who doubled for Mrs Romanov the night of Mrs Romanov's wedding.'

'Kinky. Is there a time frame on this?'

'Just get back to me the minute you've got something,' she said and after giving him a handful of numbers he could reach her at she started calling the London tabloid editors to begin negotiations for exclusivity.

As she talked, she nestled the telephone on her shoulder and not for the first time since she'd received them began going through the photographs Maurice Remmick had appropriated from Romanov's personal files. The ones of Rhiannon were of her with another man and had, so Remmick claimed, been taken in South Africa some time last year. Apparently Romanov had paid someone to get the shots and had kept them in his private collection ever since. As they stood they were unusable for their explicitness precluded their going to print in anything other than a soft-porn publication, but doctored up a little they'd do fine for a tabloid. The problem Susan was really having was with the shots Remmick had given her of Galina, for this kind of abuse was so sick that Susan wasn't at all comfortable with the idea of any woman having to suffer the distress of their exposure. But fortunately, in this instance, exposure wasn't what she intended – at least certainly not in their entirety. No, what she intended was to let the world know what a perverted son-of-a-bitch Galina was married to, while doing what she could to protect Galina from the ignominy of having her torment made public. The fact that Romanov was also a killer was something, for the moment, that Susan was going to rest easy on, for she now knew how, on that dark December night, Max Romanov had premeditatedly and cold-bloodedly killed the mother of his children and then proceeded to get away with it. That anyone could twist the facts to save himself the way Romanov had was so way off the scale of human decency that even Susan had a problem believing it. It made sense, though, it all added up, right down to how long it had taken Romanov to change the scenario from murder to mishap. The only problem she was having was proving it.

In a way Susan was sorry for what this exposure was going to do to Rhiannon, but she wasn't going to lose too much sleep over that when Rhiannon was far tougher than most, could easily withstand the public disgrace and live to fight another day. Besides which, she was sleeping with her best friend's husband, for God's sake, a sin in Susan's eyes, that didn't afford her too many privileges anyway. Susan just hoped that Marlowe would come up with something in the next twenty-four hours, though, because she wanted the story of Romanov's adulterous affair across every British paper she could name before he and his wife vanished into the remote mountains of Switzerland.

Much later that evening, after Max had spoken to his children in LA and Ed Sherwin, Romanov's president, in New York, he made one last call to Ula, then tossing the phone aside, stretched his legs out on to the coffee table and put his head on Rhiannon's shoulder. She was watching a bad situation comedy and nursing a half-finished glass of white wine.

'All done?' she said, resting her head on his.

'All done,' he confirmed.

'Any more to eat?'

He shook his head. 'No, that was plenty,' he said, referring to the Chinese she had picked up on the way back from her meeting with Lucy. 'Mmm, that feels good,' he murmured as she shifted herself round and began to massage his shoulders. He lifted an arm and looked at his watch. 'Do you realize we've gone a full seven hours without making love?' he said.

'Are you going into withdrawal?' she asked anxiously.

Laughing, he tweaked her nose, then closing his eyes he relinquished himself to the pleasing motions of her hands. 'Tell me some more about your father,' he said after a while. 'I think I kind of like the guy from what you've told me so far.'

'Don't mock,' she scolded, cuffing him round the ear.

'Who's mocking?' he protested. 'He sounds a pretty regular sort of guy to me.'

'Why don't you tell me about your grandfather instead?' she countered.

Though his eyes were closed his eyebrows went up. 'OK. What do you want to know?' he said.

'Anything. Tell me how he came over from Russia. Where was he from in Russia?'

'Moscow. The Arbat.'

'So he was a peasant?'

'Correct.' He tilted his head back to look up at her. 'Why don't we take a walk while I tell you this?' he suggested. 'I could do with the air – and the exercise.'

'Great idea,' she said, pulling her legs out from under him.

A few minutes later, wrapped up warmly in scarves and big coats, he followed her up the steps into the street, before hugging her arm against him as she slipped a hand into his pocket. As they walked, she listened with total absorption to his grandfather's story, barely noticing where they were going as she learned about the fiery passion of a fearless young idealist whose politics and poetry had rung from every café in the Arbat and whose eventual disillusionment and fear for his life had led him to the world's greatest bastion of capitalism.

They discussed at length the current situation in Russia and the former USSR and though Max was obviously impressed by the extent of her knowledge, there were still several issues he felt compelled to put her right on. She was intrigued to discover that he was deeply involved in the immigration and resettling of many *émigrés* from his grandfather's homeland, finding them homes and employment and helping them trace their relatives. Ramon and several others were similarly involved in Europe, he told her, which was how he had first come to meet Ramon.

By the time they returned home the subject had changed to their teenage years and she was laughing at his wild exaggeration of a young boy's – his – first experience with a woman.

'I don't believe she was sixty,' she declared, pushing open the front door and peeling her scarf from her face.

'I didn't say sixty!' he cried. 'I said sixteen.'

Laughing again, she said, 'And how old were you?'

'Twenty-eight,' he answered.

Hitting him with her scarf, she hung up her coat and

went through to the sitting-room. 'No calls,' she said, checking the answerphone, then gave a quirky sort of smile as, at that very instant, his mobile started to ring.

It was where he had left it, tucked between the cushions on the sofa. She turned to look up at him and seeing the expression on her face he drew her into his arms. 'I'll take it in the bedroom,' he said softly.

She nodded and smiling as he kissed her, she turned to the kitchen. If it was Galina, as she strongly suspected it would be, she really didn't want to eavesdrop so she was going to put as great a distance between them as the apartment allowed.

Closing the bedroom door behind him, Max keyed in the call and put the phone to his ear. 'Max Romanov,' he said.

'Max, it's Ramon. I don't want to know where you are or what you're doing, I just want you to know that I've had Remmick on the line trying to find out the address you're going to be at in Switzerland.'

'What did you tell him?' Max asked.

'I asked him why he wanted to know.'

'And?'

'He says he's got some important documents he needs to fly out to you some time in the next couple of weeks.'

'So why was he asking you where I'd be?'

'I don't know. Maybe he just had a hunch I might know.'

'What did you tell him?'

'That I'd get back to him.'

Max inhaled deeply. 'OK,' he said, 'leave it with me,' and pushing a button to end the call he quickly dialled Maurice's home number in Malibu.

'Is he there, Deon?' he asked when Remmick's wife answered.

'He just popped out, Max. Can I give him a message, or shall I have him call you?'

'Have him call Ula to let her know what documents

he's got that need flying over to Switzerland,' he said.

'OK, I'll do that,' Deon said, sounding as though she was writing the message down. 'Anything else?'

Her tone was so ingratiating that it was evident to Max that not only was she aware of her husband's fall from favour, she was frightened by it. Well let her stay that way; a little spousal pressure wouldn't do Remmick any harm right now and Max had more pressing matters to concern him than the fears of Deon Remmick.

'Galina, hi honey,' he said into the phone a few minutes later. 'Did Maurice try to get ahold of you today?'

'No,' she answered from her hotel suite in Edinburgh. 'Not that I know of, anyway. Why?'

'Apparently he's trying to find out where we're staying in Switzerland.'

'Oh God,' Galina muttered. 'Why does he want to know?'

'It's not worth going into that,' Max told her. 'Just make sure, if he does manage to get hold of you, that you don't tell him where we'll be.'

'Don't worry, I won't. I tried to call you earlier to tell you to fly up here, but your line was busy.'

'I was probably talking to the kids,' he said, mentally side-stepping the relief he felt at not having to give an excuse for not going. 'Did you call them yet today?'

'I was just about to,' she answered. 'How is it going for you down there in London? Have you pulled off the deal with the Venhausen guys yet?'

'Still working on it,' he answered. 'When do you get back?'

'The day after tomorrow. We arrive at Heathrow around midday. Will you be there to meet me?'

'No,' he answered, thinking of Rhiannon and how hard it was going to be to leave her. 'But I'll try to meet you at the apartment for lunch.'

'OK. Are you all right? You sound kind of funny.'

'Just tired, I guess.'

'And missing me?'

'Of course missing you.'

'Do you love me?'

'You know I do.'

'Then say it.'

'I love you,' he said, a hand pressed to his forehead as he forced the words from his lips. Why hadn't he thought about this, why hadn't he realized that being here with Rhiannon and loving her so much would build a resentment towards Galina that was very likely only going to get worse?

'Are you going to ask how things are going?' she said.

'Sure,' he responded.

She kept him on the line for almost half an hour, filling him in on every detail of her day as he listened patiently, making all the right comments in all the right places and thought constantly of Rhiannon and how he wanted nothing more than to get back to her. But he didn't even attempt to hurry Galina, partly because he didn't want to hurt her by seeming uninterested, but mainly because he didn't want her calling him back during the night to seek reassurance when it dawned on her that he had brought their call to an early end.

'Hi,' Rhiannon said, looking up from the book she was reading when eventually he joined her in the sitting-room. 'Everything OK?'

He nodded, then coming to a stop in front of her he said, 'I'm sorry. I didn't think it would go on that long ...'

'Don't,' she cut in gently. 'We know what we're into here, so don't let's complicate things even further by feeling we have to apologize to each other.'

Taking her hands in his, he pulled her to her feet and circled her in his arms. 'I wish I could tell you that we'll work something out,' he said gruffly, 'but right now I don't know what the hell to tell you, because I just don't know where the hell we're heading.'

'It's OK,' she said, seeing the torment in his eyes. 'I don't need any promises. All I need is to know that you care.'

Smiling at the understatement, he hugged her tightly and said, 'I do a hell of a lot more than care, Rhiannon Edwardes. And one of these days you're going to get to find out just how much more.'

The following day was both busy and domestic, as Rhiannon took herself off to the garden centre early in the morning and Max went to meet Ed Sherwin who'd flown in on the red-eye from New York. After dropping bags of soil and seedlings at the flat, Rhiannon quickly showered and changed, then took a taxi to Mayfair where she was lunching with some executives from Kodak who were interested in sponsoring the programme.

When she returned, mid-way through the afternoon, it was to find Max in the cluttered walled garden, rooting out weeds from the rockery and clearing some of the winter debris. He'd already unblocked the fountain, she noticed, and seeing her come in was keen to know where she wanted the seedlings.

Laughing, she threw her arms around him, kissed him long and hard, then went off to retrieve her gardening clothes from the laundry. They worked for an hour or so, passing the trowel and fork between them while they talked about Max's meeting with Venhausen and Venhausen's offer to administer Romanov's UK and German holdings.

'I've got a couple of things in my briefcase I'd like you to take a look at,' he told her, wrapping his freezing hands around the steaming mug of cocoa she was handing him.

'Oh?' she said in surprise.

He smiled and for the first time she saw an awkwardness come into his expression that was so at odds with the confidence she was used to that she could only blink in amazement. 'I'm not saying you have to act on anything,' he said. 'You don't even have to take a look if you don't want to. I just thought it might help, that was all.'

'I'm becoming more intrigued by the minute,' she said, her eyes dancing with humour as they attempted to arrest his. 'What is it?' she laughed. 'What do you have in the briefcase?'

He took a deep breath, looked at her, then laughed at his own unease. 'I've just put together a couple of ways you could go about raising money for the programme,' he said. 'No, don't interrupt! Like I said, you don't have to act on it, you can do everything your way and forget I ever mentioned anything if that's what you want. I just think you should know that interest in what you're doing doesn't necessarily need to stop at the shores of the UK. If you're a sound investment, and I think you are, there are plenty of sources to be tapped on mainland Europe and in the States. There's also Australia, South Africa, Canada and Asia. I've put together a list of banks and corporations you can try and a kind of guide how to deal with these people – like the facts and figures and forecast planning they will expect to see up front before you go see them, then what you will need to take when you do go. I'll give you a letter of reference if you want one, but it could be that you feel I'm already intruding too far and are getting ready to tell me to back off and mind my own business. I won't be ...'

'Max,' she said, taking a step towards him and lifting her face to his. 'Just kiss me, will you?'

Looking down into her eyes as he kissed her, he felt a great knot of emotion binding itself round his heart. 'Do you want to see it?' he asked, when they broke apart. 'Well, you can take a look later. It doesn't have to be now.'

'I want to see it,' she said, laughing. 'Of course I want to see it, I don't understand why you think I wouldn't.'

He shrugged and flattening his lips, he looked off towards the edge of the garden. 'I guess', he said, 'I don't want you to think that I'm trying to take over your life. I swear I'm not offering you any money myself, all I'm doing is putting you in touch with people who might.'

'Do you think I'd turn your money down?' she said.

He nodded. 'Yeah, I think you would.'

She frowned and chewed her lips as she thought about that. 'You could be right,' she said, 'I might.'

Though he was hurt by her answer he couldn't help admiring the honesty and integrity behind it. Then laughing self-consciously he said, 'This is another first for me, having to consider a woman's independence before I go crashing in with help that just might not be welcome. I mean, I deal with women in positions of power all the time, on a professional level, but never on a personal level, at least not this personal, and it feels kind of ... Well, I don't know how it feels, I guess I just need to get used to it.'

'Oh, Max,' she said, her eyes brimming with laughter.

'Oh, Rhiannon,' he mimicked, tilting her chin and running his thumb along her lower lip.

'I had no idea I made you so nervous,' she teased.

'Terrified,' he told her, his breath mingling with hers in the cold air. 'Terrified of feeling this way and terrified of losing you.'

'Don't,' she murmured, pulling her lower lip between her teeth as her heart turned over. They had less than a day left now and despite how certain they'd both felt at the outset that they would see each other again, now the time for him to leave was drawing close the certainty was starting to wane.

'I'll go run a bath,' he whispered, kissing the cold red tip of her nose.

When he'd gone Rhiannon sat on the edge of the rockery and nursed her cocoa on one knee. They had poured so much into these past couple of days, but it wasn't nearly enough to satisfy a need that only grew with each fulfilment. Sucking in her breath, she looked at the fountain he had repaired and smiled weakly. Somehow she would have to find a way of continuing without him, but it was going to be like taking the warmth from a smile, or the belief from a hope. The smile and the hope could exist, but without the warmth and the belief they meant nothing. It was going to be hard, so very hard, but she wasn't going to think about it now. Why spoil what little time they had left? They loved each other, they were both secure in that love and who could say, maybe something would work itself out so that they could be together. She grimaced as the truth of what she was hoping for eddied guiltily around her heart, for the only way they could be together was if something were to happen to Galina.

Getting to her feet, she carried their cups into the kitchen, then went to find him in the bathroom. He was standing beside the bath, a ghostly figure in the billowing clouds of steam. His hands were buried in his pockets, his face was deep in thought. Seeing her come in he reached out an arm and drew her to him.

They stood quietly together, waiting for the bath to fill, then taking off his clothes he stepped into the water and lay down. When Rhiannon was undressed she got in after him, sitting between his legs and leaning back against him. He washed her and caressed her and held her and whispered things in her ear that made her laugh and love him even more.

'Let's do something special this evening,' he said when, much later, they were lying together on the bed.

Rhiannon's eyes widened. 'Like what?' she said.

'Well,' he said, looking up to the ceiling as though searching for inspiration, 'we could ... fly over to Paris and find ourselves a discreet little restaurant on the Left Bank and a hotel that knows how not to recognize its clientele.'

Rhiannon was laughing in amazement. 'Are you serious?' she said, propping herself up on one elbow and looking down at him.

'Very,' he said. 'The Romanov jet is here. We can go and come back again without anyone ever knowing we've gone.'

The idea of being in a place where no one else in the world knew them to be, of being so private and exclusive to each other and so removed from reality made her heart throb with the pure want of it. She looked down at him, her eyes shining with emotion as she tried to think of the words to tell him how much she loved him. In the end she gave up and simply said, 'I'll go and find my passport.'

They flew back into London late the following morning to a temperature that hadn't risen above freezing, and a sky that was laden with snow. As Max drove the rented BMW back towards Kensington, Rhiannon turned on the radio to listen to the news. Blizzards in certain parts of the country had already caused four road deaths that morning and British Rail was in its usual poor-weather chaos.

'We should have stayed in Paris,' Max smiled, reaching out for her hand.

Rhiannon smiled too, but her heart was as burdened with dread as the sky was with snow. In less than twenty minutes they would arrive at her flat and not long after that he would leave.

'When are you going to Switzerland?' she asked, attempting to put some lightness into her voice.

'Sunday. Galina's got a few commitments here in London, but by Sunday she'll be through.'

Rhiannon nodded and turned her eyes to the passing trees that were rigid with frost and the parked cars that were still frozen over after the night's subzero temperatures.

'I'm going to talk to her,' Max said.

Rhiannon turned to look at him, surprise causing her heart to jump. 'Do you mean about us?' she said hoarsely.

He nodded.

'But I thought ...'

'Rhiannon, this is crazy,' he interrupted. 'We should be together and you know it. Just these past three days have shown us how right we are for each other, on every level, and I want us to have the chance to find out where it's going, if we really can live together, build a life together and share a family and future like other people in love. God knows we've got enough stacked against us, with all your commitments here in London and mine in the States, but we can work those through if Galina would just ...' He stopped and Rhiannon felt the guilt that had silenced him move through her too.

'What are you going to say?' she asked.

'I don't know. I—,' He took a breath, then sighed and shook his head. 'I don't know.'

Several minutes ticked by until Rhiannon, on the point of speaking again, suddenly became aware of what the radio DJ was saying. Her insides froze and her eyes were wide with shock as she turned them to Max. His face was already pale, the tension in his jaw visible.

'So,' the DJ cried chirpily, 'the hunt is on. They left Rhiannon Edwardes's Kensington flat late yesterday afternoon in a black, seven-series BMW and haven't been seen since.' He chuckled. 'Think I'd do the same if someone told me my affair was about to hit the press and my Mrs was on her way – *and with a Mrs like Galina Casimir what's the man thinking of*? Still, we've only got to think of Camilla Parker Bowles and Paula Yates to be reminded that it's not always beauty who wins the beast. Anyway, what we want to know – or what the great British tabloids want to know – is where are they now? Have they eloped? Are they just hiding from the happy snappers or are they waiting for the lovely Galina to fly into London later this morning to tell her what good friends they've become? Stay tuned, fellow gourmands of gossip, we'll be back with more after this break.'

Rhiannon reached out and turned off the radio. Max kept his eyes on the road ahead. Uppermost in both their minds now was the fact that thanks to the 'great British tabloids' Galina would already know. It was a hell of a way to find out, a public betrayal that no one, least of all Galina, deserved. Rhiannon tried to imagine what it would be like to pick up a newspaper just a few short months after your wedding and discover, along with the rest of the world, that your husband loved someone else. Her stomach clenched with nerves. The story wouldn't be told like that, of course, there would be no mention of love; it would be put across in as seedy and salacious a manner as possible, with every cliché, innuendo and *double entendre* the hacks could muster and with a complete disregard for the pain they were causing the innocent.

'I'll have to be there when she flies in,' Max said. 'The press'll be all over your apartment, is there somewhere I can drop you?'

'Don't worry about me,' Rhiannon answered, her heart thudding with misery and anger that they were being forced to part like this. 'Just drop me at the next lights. I'll take a cab from there.'

'Where will you go?' he said, throwing her an anxious glance.

'I've got the keys to Lizzy's house. I'll go there.' She could see from the look in his eyes that he was having an even harder time about the way they were going to say goodbye than she was, but there was nothing they could do – the papers were on the newsstands, the deceit and duplicity were out and despite how badly it hurt, Rhiannon had to concede that right now Galina's need was the greater.

'Just here will be fine,' she said, as they reached a set of red lights. She was barely able to get the words past the swelling misery in her heart, but gathering up her bag, she pushed open the car door, then turned briefly back to him. 'Don't get out,' she said. 'I'll get my coat and bag from the back, then just drive on. I love you.'

'I'll call you,' he said as she pressed her lips to his.

She smiled, touched his cheek, then getting out of the car, went round to the boot, took out her things and slammed it closed. She knew, as he merged back into the traffic, that he was watching her in the mirror, but turning away quickly she started to search the traffic for the yellow light of a taxi. One came almost immediately and giving the driver Lizzy's address she climbed into the rear seat and sat with her forehead resting in one hand until the journey was over. It wasn't so much a fear of being recognized that was causing her to hide her face, it was more a need to hide the tears of frustration and despair.

Lizzy's small terraced house off Chiswick High Road was cold and unwelcoming – at least it seemed that way until Rhiannon found the heating controls and threw off the dust sheets. After lighting the gas fire she went to search out some coffee, then thought better of putting on the TV. She'd been to this house so many times over the years that it was like a second home, but never once had she imagined finding herself here alone and in such a state of anxiety and distress. She looked around at the weathered pine surfaces, the copper pans hanging from an overhead rack, the garlic and dried chillies and Sainsbury's pots of herbs. She must call Lizzy and tell her she was there, but first she had to find someone who would bring her the papers and some things from her flat.

Since Sharon had gone off skiing with Lucy, Rhiannon picked up the phone and called the *Check It Out* office. Jolene wasn't there, but Carrie, one of the senior researchers, needed no persuading to help out.

'You're not going to like what you see,' Carrie warned her an hour later when she dropped a newspaper on the kitchen table. 'It's only in the *Mail* so far, obviously they got the exclusive, but you can be sure it'll be all over the rest of the tabloids by this time tomorrow.'

'How nice, something to look forward to,' Rhiannon responded bitterly. The time she had spent waiting had been terrible as she'd paced the floor, trying to bring herself under control and accept that this nightmare was happening. It was almost too shocking to absorb, that one minute they could be driving along talking about how much they loved each other and the next she was on the street hailing a cab. Her head was reeling, her heart in turmoil. He didn't know Lizzy's number so he couldn't call and though she was struggling to ignore it she had a horrible and unsuppressible feeling that this exposé had put an end to their relationship more surely and more swiftly than if one of them had died, for the damage it would almost certainly have caused Galina wasn't something Max would ever be able to walk away from now.

Realizing that Carrie was watching her, she finished stirring the coffee and handed her a cup.

'We didn't have any idea,' Rhiannon told her. 'The first we knew of it was just over an hour ago when we were driving along in the car. We'd just come back from Paris.'

Carrie nodded and tucked the frizzy sweep of her chestnut hair behind one ear. Her face was small and mouselike, with cute pointy features and big sapphire eyes that were watching Rhiannon with genuine concern. 'I think you should know', she said, 'that Jolene tipped off Susan Posner.'

Rhiannon's eyes closed as her heart turned over. 'Susan Posner,' she repeated. 'I'd guessed Jolene, but Susan Posner never entered my mind.'

'Well, hers is the byline,' Carrie said.

Rhiannon glanced at the paper, then quickly averted her eyes. 'What does she say?' she asked.

Carrie grimaced. 'In a nutshell, she's saying that Max Romanov has been abusing Galina for years, that he's a sick man who needs help desperately, that his friends have known for years that he isn't in full control of himself and that they are no longer prepared to stand by and watch him destroy Galina the way he did his first wife, Carolyn. In short, the man's a monster who should be locked away for the rest of his natural, which there's every chance he will be once the new evidence that has come into Ms Posner's possession regarding the death of his first wife is handed over to the District Attorney.'

Rhiannon looked haggard as her eyes drifted back to the paper and her heart churned with the pain of what he must be suffering now. 'If you knew him,' she said to Carrie, turning the newspaper to look at a profile shot of her and Max laughing into each other's eyes. It was too close to be able to tell where it had been taken, but she guessed it had happened when she'd run up the steps after him yesterday morning because he'd forgotten his phone. Neither of them had ever dreamt, as he'd pulled her into his arms and given her one last kiss before getting into the car, that a photographer was tracking them with a telephoto lens. But then, the subjects of such shots weren't supposed to know, were they?

'If you knew him,' she repeated, 'you'd know that he's incapable of everything she's accusing him of.'

Carrie sucked in her cheeks and though she tried to meet Rhiannon's eyes she didn't quite make it.

Rhiannon turned away and went to stand at the back door, where the stained-glass window was clouded with condensation. Lifting a finger, she wiped a ragged pattern in the moisture and looked through a blue pane at the damp and lifeless garden outside. She wondered if Galina's plane had landed on time – if it had, she and

Max would be together somewhere now, somewhere where he could shield her from this hideous intrusion in their lives. But escaping the spotlight of the press would do nothing to repair the damage that had already been done, nor would it lessen the repercussions as they continued to tear mercilessly through their lives. For her, Rhiannon, it wouldn't be so bad, but for Max it seemed the nightmare was only going to get worse.

'Does she say what the new evidence is?' Rhiannon asked.

'No,' Carrie answered. 'She's openly accused the New York Police Department of a cover-up though, so I guess she must feel she's on pretty solid ground with whatever she does have.'

'Have you heard anything on the news about Galina this morning?' Rhiannon asked after a while.

'Only that the rest of her tour has been cancelled.'

'As quickly as that?' Rhiannon said, turning round in surprise.

Carrie shrugged. 'That's what I heard.'

Rhiannon felt suddenly sick as she wondered if, apart from everything else it was going to cost him, their three days together were going to be responsible for invoking the clause in Galina's contract that made him liable for the multi-million-dollar Conspiracy campaign.

'Did you remember my address book?' she asked Carrie. 'I'd better call Lizzy and tell her I'm here.'

'It's in the box with the computer,' Carrie answered. 'You were right not to go back there, incidentally, they've got the place staked out, no doubt awaiting your return, and I had the devil's own job getting them off my tail when I left. Made me feel like Princess Di.'

Rhiannon gave no response to the feeble attempt at humour. She wanted Carrie to go now. She didn't want her here any more, because she didn't want to sit in the same room as someone who believed Max would do a single one of the things The Poisoner had accused him of, never mind murder.

'If there's anything else I can do, just give me a call,' Carrie said, as Rhiannon opened the front door for her to leave.

'Thank you,' Rhiannon replied, smiling politely. 'There is one thing, actually: you can tell Jolene not to bother calling me again. We have no more to say to each other.'

Carrie nodded and looked down at the floor. 'I'm amazed you trusted him, Rhiannon,' she said.

'Frankly, so am I,' Rhiannon retorted. 'But then it's at times like this that you find out how very few people you can trust.'

Carrie blushed. 'Look, I don't know the man like you do,' she said defensively. 'All I know is what I saw, and if he's responsible for making Galina look the way she does in some of those photos ...'

Rhiannon's face had turned white. 'Look at me, Carrie,' she seethed. 'Go on, look at me. Do you see any bruises? Do you see any cuts or scratches? Any injuries at all? Would you like me to take my clothes off so you can be absolutely sure I'm not covering anything up? All he's ever done to Galina is protect her ...'

'Rhiannon, all I'm saying is The Poisoner's case is a pretty convincing one,' Carrie cut in. 'But if you tell me he didn't do it, that he's no abuser of women ...' She stopped, inhaled deeply then said, 'I think you'd better go and read it for yourself.'

By the time Rhiannon finished reading her only hope was that Susan Posner was in hiding somewhere, because if Max didn't kill her for this, then she, Rhiannon, would. As any journalist knew, the positioning of facts was crucial to the message you wanted to get across, and the way Susan Posner had positioned her facts had turned her article into as masterful a hatchet job as Rhiannon had ever read in her life.

The pictures of Galina were horrible. The bruising on her face and welts on certain parts of her body rendered her almost unrecognizable. They were spread across the centre pages and made all the more terrible by the contrasting colour shot of how she appeared for Conspiracy.

Rhiannon felt sick to her stomach as she read about how Max had dominated Galina's life since she was a child, how he had used her early infatuation to introduce her to the sadistic horrors and mental cruelty that had now become almost a part of their daily routine; and how he had visited the same kind of torment on countless other women, including his deceased wife, Carolyn. Galina, it said, had agreed to become his second wife because she was too terrified to say no, and to show his contempt for her he had forced her to undergo a tacky and degrading ceremony in a Strip chapel in Las Vegas – before abandoning her on their honeymoon night to spend it with his latest mistress, Rhiannon Edwardes. It was also reported how, just before the wedding, he had spent the night with Rhiannon at Galina's own apartment in the Marina del Rey area of Los Angeles.

'With friends like Rhiannon ...' Susan Posner had scathingly remarked, before going on to report on Rhiannon's own failed marriage in the middle of last year and the man who had spurned Rhiannon some years before that in favour of her old school friend, Galina Casimir.

The suspicious circumstances surrounding Carolyn's death and the aborted trial that followed were dealt with in a separate window, along with the claim that a massive police and State Department cover-up had prevented justice from being done at the time of the killing. But new evidence just come to light would, Posner was confident, ensure that the guilty were finally brought to task.

Also in a story of its own was the mysterious death of a Memphis photographer who, only hours before his murder, had approached one of Max Romanov's magazines with a possible blackmail threat concerning some explicit shots of Galina. As far as was known no money had ever changed hands, nor were any photographs or negatives ever recovered from the photographer's studio. But it was known that Max Romanov had made an unscheduled visit to Memphis that day, Posner concluded.

Pushing the paper away, Rhiannon put her head in her hands and wept out of sheer fury. Never had she known a story to be so manipulated, misrepresented or misconstrued – and to have someone she loved at the centre of it was too terrible to bear. Not for a single minute did she doubt Max, all she knew was an insufferable and overwhelming impotence at being unable to do anything to help him. She felt bitterly ashamed of her profession that it could harbour in its ranks someone like Susan Posner, who had twisted everything so disastrously out of proportion and was now using it to destroy people's lives.

Later in the day she called Lucy and Sharon at their hotel in Chamonix to tell them what had happened. 'I'll call Lizzy in a minute,' she said, 'and see if it's OK to go to South Africa sooner rather than later. I'm sure it will be, but I need to get into my flat before I can go and God only knows when that will be.'

'Not a problem,' Lucy told her. 'Just hold on there and I'll give you the number for a couple of detectives who owe me a favour. Yes, here it is. Are you ready? Their names are Harrington and Farre, both sergeants. Explain who you are, that you're a friend of mine and that you would like some assistance in returning to your address. They'll work something out for you.'

'Lucy, what would I do without you?' Rhiannon choked as she laughed.

'I know, I'm priceless,' Lucy replied. 'Call me as soon as you know what's happening and where you're going to be,' and with that she rang off.

The next two days were a nightmare for Rhiannon as she watched the terrible revelations appear one after the other in the British, and now, too, the American papers. In comparison to what they were doing to Max she was getting off lightly, though her annulled marriage never failed to get a mention, nor did the fact that Galina had once stolen the man she was about to marry. The implications were that she was a wronged and bitter woman who didn't give a damn about anyone, least of all her best friend whose earlier transgression was now being paid back in spades. Poor, beautiful Galina who had been betrayed and deceived by the two people she loved most in the world. Shots of Rhiannon and Max in the garden of her flat, on the beach in Marina del Rey, walking in Kensington and even carrying out the rubbish, were splashed all over the papers. She guessed she just had to be thankful that no one had managed to hide a lens in her bedroom.

She wondered what it all was doing to Max, if he was reading any of it even, and if he was, whether he was planning to take action. She imagined that this time he would have to, for the libel was far too serious to be ignored, and since Susan Posner hadn't yet responded to the NYPD's request that she hand over any new evidence she might have, her case was losing ground by the day. On the other hand, too many people who claimed to know Max were divulging appallingly intimate details of his life – details Rhiannon knew on the whole to be true, for they were of a time when Carolyn and promiscuity were very much alive and a part of his life.

Much like the rest of the world, Rhiannon wondered where Max and Galina were. There had been no statements from either of them, nor from their lawyers – nor could anyone discover where they had gone following their reunion at Heathrow. All anyone knew was that the rented BMW had been returned to Avis and the Romanov jet had been sent back to LA with only the pilot and his staff on board. The publicists for Primaire were hotly denying rumours that Galina's contract was now under review and insisting that they had no idea where Max and Galina Romanov were to be found.

It was as if they had vanished from the face of the earth and despite how cut off and lonely that made Rhiannon feel, she felt angry too that Galina hadn't spoken out in Max's defence, when she, of all people, knew what terrible lies were being told about him. She guessed that Galina was either in too much distress to handle it, or that Max had forbidden it. But surely to God he must see that this time the accusations really couldn't be ignored.

By Sunday morning things seemed to have calmed down a little, as their story gave way to yet another royal scandal and the two detective friends of Lucy's escorted Rhiannon back to her flat. There was no sign of any paparazzi as they entered the street in an unmarked police car, nor as Rhiannon got out of the car and quickly descended the steps to her front door. It was such a relief to be back among her own things that she was strongly tempted to weep; instead she went briskly into the bedroom and began packing for South Africa. She wasn't leaving for a few days yet, but she needed to keep busy and throwing summer clothes into a suitcase, when a winter hell was unfolding around her, felt good.

What didn't feel so good was discovering the things Max had left behind. They were painful reminders of how perfect everything had seemed before Susan Posner and the tabloid press had driven a stake through the heart of something they knew nothing about. It wasn't that Rhiannon believed that what she and Max were doing was right – how could it be when it was adulterous, deceitful and in many ways unforgivable? But when they loved each other as much as they did and when

Galina was as fragile and needy as she was, what else were she and Max supposed to do? Max had given Galina his name, his children, his entire life, for God's sake, so who could begrudge him a few short days with the woman he loved? He was a man after all, a human being with needs and passions and even doubts and insecurities of his own. He just couldn't be further from the monster they were portraying in the press – the multi-millionaire business tycoon who abused his privilege and power as ruthlessly as they claimed he abused women. He was like any other man in his position, tough and forthright in matters of business and infinitely vulnerable to vicious attacks when it came to matters of his personal life. He was also a tender and considerate lover who had never made a single gesture of violence towards her, unless the urgency and passion that often overtook him at crucial moments in their lovemaking could be described as that. Were it left to Rhiannon, she would describe them in a very different way, but like Max, she wasn't going to get her say, for she knew that anything she said in public now would only be misquoted or misconstrued.

Sitting down heavily on the bed, she was on the point of picking up the phone to call Lizzy when she suddenly stopped. Someone was ringing the doorbell. Shocked, she sat where she was, trying to imagine who it could be and not quite daring to look out in case it was someone from the press and they spotted her.

A minute or two ticked by. The bell rang again, making her heart leap and planting the wild, impossible hope that it could be Max. But of course that was madness.

As though whoever it was might detect her movements, she got stealthily up from the bed and took the few short steps to the window. The lace was copiously embroidered and fell in thick concealing folds around the bay. Careful not to move them, she leaned forward and looked towards the front door. When she saw who was standing there her mouth turned dry and her heart started pounding. It was the very last person on earth she had expected to see.

Moving from the curtain, she took a deep, steadying breath, then, as the doorbell sounded for a third time, she went to answer it.

Galina's taut and anxious face showed clearly how much she had suffered these past few days – her eyes were circled in a bruising darkness, her skin was blotchy and pale, and faint but cruel lines that Rhiannon had never noticed before were closing in around her mouth.

'I hope you don't mind,' she said hesitantly.

Rhiannon's voice was still muted by surprise.

'I – I hoped we could talk,' Galina said.

Rhiannon looked at her and could see just how deep her pain ran. 'You'd better come in,' she said, stepping back to clear the way.

Galina attempted a smile and thanking her, followed her into the sitting-room.

'Can I get you something?' Rhiannon offered, aware of how uncertain she felt.

'A glass of water will be fine,' Galina answered.

As Rhiannon went through to the kitchen Galina took a moment to look around, noticing Max's computer and gloves on the table, but she said nothing as she perched nervously on the edge of one of the sofas and waited for Rhiannon to come back with the drinks.

As Rhiannon handed her a glass, Galina laughed self-consciously. 'I feel like we've been here before,' she said, 'you know, you sleeping with Max and me finding out.' Her eyes came up to Rhiannon's. 'It feels a bit different this time though,' she said brokenly.

Unable to hold her gaze, Rhiannon looked down at her drink. 'I'm sorry,' she said. 'I don't know what else to say, except I'm sorry. I never meant to hurt you, neither of us did ...'

Galina's voice was trembling as she said, 'He loves you very much, you know. He told me that. He said he wasn't going to lie about it.' Her face crumpled and she struggled to keep her lips together as though to hold back the sobs. 'I almost wish he had,' she whispered hoarsely. 'He said he loves me too, but in a different way. He'd leave me if he could ...' She took several breaths to try and steady herself. 'But he can't. I told him he must, if he feels that way about you and you feel the same for him, then I told him he must forget about me. But he won't and I don't know how to make him.'

Rhiannon looked at her helplessly. Was she really asking how she could force Max to let her go? Was she expecting Rhiannon to tell her how to do that? Rhiannon's heart twisted as, suddenly losing her grip, Galina broke down and cried, pressing her fingers to her lips as they trembled and stuttered and looking at Rhiannon as though she might know how to make her stop.

'I'm sorry,' she sobbed. 'I know you don't want me here ... Max doesn't know, he'll be furious if he finds out. Oh God, Rhiannon, help me, please. I don't know who else to turn to. No one else cares.'

Rhiannon's heart was thudding; she just wished to God she knew what to say.

'I know Max cares,' Galina went on, her voice high-pitched and stretched with emotion. 'He's the only one who really knows what it's like for me and I don't know what will happen to me without him.' She sniffed, caught her breath and wiped the back of her hand over her cheeks. 'You know, the real reason I came here today,' she said, 'what I really ...' She stopped, as the sobs stole her voice. 'I came here to beg you not to take him away,' she said finally, 'but I know that's wrong. I have to let him go if that's what he wants. I just don't know how to. I'm so afraid of being on my own, of trying to cope without him. I love him so much and things have been so good for us since we got married … Please don't think I'm blaming you, it's not your fault that he feels the way he does about you …' She broke off again as her breath was sucked into another vacuum of despair. 'Please don't take him away,' she gasped. 'I'll do anything, give you anything … I've got money, you can have it all …'

'Galina, don't,' Rhiannon pleaded.

'But I will!' Galina insisted. 'I don't care how much it is, I can find the money …'

'Galina, stop it! I don't want your money. It's not about money.'

'I know, I know,' she sobbed, driving her fingers harshly through her hair. 'I just don't know what else to offer you in his place.'

'There's nothing you can offer me in his place,' Rhiannon said, 'because nothing can take his place – in my life or in yours. Surely you understand that.'

'Yes, of course I do, but I can't bear to think of you with nothing. I know how I would feel if it were me … But you're strong, Rhiannon, and you don't hate yourself the way I do. Coming here this morning I just wanted to throw myself under a car, or get someone to beat me until I couldn't feel any more. It helps, you know, to be beaten and kicked and punched …'

'Galina, stop it!' Rhiannon said. 'You don't have to go through this any more. He married you. He loves you and cares for you and he won't let any harm come to you.'

'But what about you?' Galina implored. 'How can I stop him loving you? Why should he stop loving you when you're so much better than me? If I were him I'd love you too …'

'I'm not listening to this!' Rhiannon cut in. 'I know how hard all this is for you, I understand what you're going through, but you've got to start believing in yourself Galina …'

'But what is there to believe in?' she cried. 'I'm not worth anything. I'm no one. I'm just a face.'

Rhiannon forced herself not to respond, knowing that to continue down this road would only encourage her self-pity and unleash even more hysteria.

Realizing that Rhiannon had fallen silent, Galina looked at her warily. 'I'm just a face,' she repeated, as though prodding a balloon to see if this time it would pop.

'Are you?' Rhiannon said, her eyes suddenly hardening.

Galina nodded.

Rhiannon nodded too.

Galina stared at her meekly. 'You understand?' she whispered. 'You know that I'm just a face?'

Rhiannon held up a hand. 'Those are your words, Galina, not mine.'

Galina's eyes were wide. 'Max hates me,' she said. 'He despises me and I don't blame him.'

Rhiannon sucked in her breath. 'I'm not getting into this,' she said.

'I'd do all those horrible things to me if I were him,' Galina whispered. 'It's what I deserve.'

Rhiannon's blood started to turn cold. 'Don't do this,' she said. 'Just stop, now.'

'He tells me it's ...'

Rhiannon sprang to her feet. 'I said stop!' she shouted. 'I don't want to hear it. You're a liar, Galina. You've always been a liar, ever since I've known you, but this time you're going too far. Max loves you, he cares for you, he's doing everything he can to protect you, so for God's sake can't you show him some loyalty in return? All those things they've written about him, you know they're not true, so why the hell don't you stand up and say so? Why are you letting him go through this? What's he ever done to you except give you a life?'

Galina blinked, then putting her glass on the table she

said, 'I'm sorry. I shouldn't have come.'

'Why did you?' Rhiannon challenged. 'What did you really hope to achieve, besides making me promise not to take Max?'

Galina's breath shuddered as she inhaled. 'I thought – I hoped,' she began.

'You hoped what?' Rhiannon prompted.

Galina's head dropped. 'I hoped that I would be able to make you understand,' she said quietly.

'Understand what?'

'Why I can't let you come between me and Max. You see, it would be terrible for you if you did.'

Rhiannon's anger was quickening again. 'What do you mean?' she snapped.

Galina shook her head. 'Just what I said,' she answered.

Rhiannon turned away, folded her arms and tried to stop herself shaking. 'Where is he now?' she asked.

'We're staying with some friends of his,' Galina answered. 'Some Russian friends.'

'Until when?'

'We're flying to Switzerland late this afternoon. It's a honeymoon,' she added lamely.

Rhiannon turned to her in surprise. 'You're still going?' she said.

Galina nodded. 'All the arrangements have been made, so Max says we should just carry on like nothing has happened.'

'Like nothing has happened?' Rhiannon echoed incredulously.

Galina shrugged. 'That's what he said.'

'I take it you have seen the papers?' Rhiannon said.

Galina nodded. 'Yes, we've seen them.'

Rhiannon stared at her, then at a loss what to say next, she leaned forward and picked up her water.

'The children are flying out to join us,' Galina said. 'Max thinks it will do us all good to get away for a while, somewhere the press won't find us. So I don't suppose it's really a honeymoon after all.'

Rhiannon could feel herself relaxing – the concern for his children sounded much more like the man she knew. 'But you're skiing,' she said. 'There's nothing very private about a ski resort. They'll be sure to find you.'

'You could be right. Let's just hope not, mm?'

Rhiannon's eyebrows flickered and taking a sip of water, she allowed a silence to pass as she tried to gather her thoughts.

In the end Galina was the first to speak. 'I'm trying to protect you, Rhiannon,' she said softly.

Rhiannon's head came up, her eyes were bright with anger.

For a moment Galina seemed cowed, but swallowing hard she pushed herself on. 'This isn't easy for me,' she said, 'and in many ways I only have myself to blame. I should never have allowed him to talk me into doing all those things, but I was so young at the time and I adored him so much. He filled my life with all the things I'd never had before; laughter and ... a kind of magic, I suppose. I would have done anything for him ... I did do anything. I still do,' she added softly.

Rhiannon was shaking her head. 'You're lying, Galina,' she said. 'I know you're lying.'

Galina fixed her with wide, tormented eyes. 'It's all true, what they've written about him,' she said. 'Every word is true.'

'No!' Rhiannon cried, slamming her glass back on the table. 'None of it's true, not a single damned word, and why the hell aren't you out there defending him is what I want to know, instead of sitting there trying to tell ...'

'Rhiannon, listen to me,' Galina cut in. 'Why do you think he hasn't spoken out himself? Or brought any law suits? I'll tell you why, because you can't sue someone for libel when they're telling the truth.'

'Galina, stop this,' Rhiannon seethed. 'Just stop your lies and go.'

Galina inhaled deeply and shaking her head sadly, she said, 'I wish I was lying. I wish he never did the things to me that he does ...'

'For God's sake, you told me yourself that you'd barely slept with him before you were married!' Rhiannon yelled.

Galina's eyes darted to one side, then drawing her lips between her teeth she turned pitying eyes back to Rhiannon. 'There's so much you don't know,' she sighed.

'Then tell me,' Rhiannon challenged.

Galina looked at her for a moment, then lowering her eyes she shook her head. 'No,' she said. 'There's no point. You've already made up your mind that I'm lying and believe me, no one knows better than I how blind love can be.'

'Tell me!' Rhiannon demanded.

'I've already tried,' Galina reminded her. 'You don't want to hear it.'

'Because you're lying!' Rhiannon insisted. 'He isn't capable of even half of what they're accusing him of and you of all people know it. So why are you doing this? Why are you trying to tell me that he's systematically beaten and abused you for years when what he's really done is everything he could to protect you from yourself?'

Galina smiled. Her eyes were still imbued with pity. 'I don't blame you for being so taken in by him,' she said. 'He has a way with him when he wants that could charm any woman. I love that side of him too. I love every side of him.'

'Then why the hell are you doing this to him?'

'I'm not doing anything to him. All I'm doing is trying to make you understand that he's not the man you think he is.'

Rhiannon's head dropped into her hands as she struggled to control the mounting fury inside her. It was several seconds before she had herself sufficently in control to speak again. 'This is such an unbelievably cruel way of trying to keep him, Galina,' she said through her teeth. 'He doesn't deserve this and I'm not going to listen to any damned more of it. I want you to leave now. I want you to get out of my home and out of my life for good. You're not my responsibility, Galina. I only wish to God you weren't Max's either. But he thinks you are and for as long as he thinks you are, you have nothing to fear from me. But let me tell you this, if I ever hear you utter as much as one single word publicly of what you've tried to tell me here today, I will come after you, Galina, and when I do, make no mistake about this, I'll use the very knife you stabbed him in the back with to cut out your god-damned lying tongue. Do you hear me? Do we have that straight, Galina? I know you've got problems, that you can't always help what you do, but I'm not going let you get away with any more of these lies.'

Galina rose to her feet. Her eyes were shining with tears, her face was stained with ragged patches of colour. 'I'm sorry,' she whispered. 'I wish I knew how to make you believe me, but I don't.'

'What difference does it make when I'm never going to see him again?' Rhiannon demanded harshly. 'Why do I have to know anything when it's all over for me and him? Tell me, Galina. Why?'

Galina lowered her head. 'I just thought you should,' she answered weakly.

Rhiannon walked ahead of her to the front door, then pulling it open she said, 'What you thought, Galina, was that you would come here today and do whatever it took to make sure I'd never do anything to try to take Max away. Well, you know now that I won't, but let me put you right about one thing, Galina, because I think it's important for you to know this – it isn't you who's standing between me and Max, it's Max's conscience – because Max is a decent man who won't take his own happiness at someone else's expense. Particularly not someone who's as dependent on him as you claim to be. But I'm not Max. I can see through you, Galina, and frankly I don't give a damn what happens to you, not after what you've tried to pull here today – and were it not for how much more pain it would cause him, you'd better believe I'd take him away from you right now.'

A tear rolled from Galina's eye and trickled down her face, as pulling her coat tightly around her, she walked past Rhiannon and started up the steps to the street. When she reached the top she paused as the door closed behind her. Then wiping her fingers across her cheeks, she took a long Cher-style wig and sun-glasses from her bag, put them on and began walking towards the end of the street. She'd achieved exactly what she'd come here to achieve.

Chapter 26

Four days later, a twelve-seater Cessna with a party of Belgians, a couple of gay Swedes and Rhiannon on board, was coming in to land on the rugged makeshift airstrip at Perlatonga. They'd left the Kruger Park's airport at Skukuza just under an hour before, when the sun had been at its height and the vast, crowded expanse of the bush at its most spectacular.

Looking down on it all had made Rhiannon's heart swell and the relief she felt at being there at last was so great it was causing her eyes to sting.

She'd done a lot of crying since Galina had left on Sunday, hours and hours of it, as she'd agonized with herself over whether she had been unnecessarily cruel, whether she should have taken the time to listen and maybe in some way try to help her, rather than dismiss everything she had to say and throw her out the way she had. It wasn't that she was in any way doubting her conviction that Galina was lying, it was simply that she felt ashamed of the way she had refused to deal with Galina's pain.

On Monday a chauffeur had turned up to collect the things Max had left behind. Though Rhiannon hadn't asked, she'd waited hopefully for a message, but there was none. She had felt so let down by that, that anger had overcome her grief for a while and she was almost prepared to believe that Galina was right, he wasn't the man she thought he was. But the anger soon died and she realized that to send her messages now would only perpetuate the pain and longing, when in their hearts they both knew it was over.

'I just wish I could make myself accept that,' she sighed to Lizzy when they were alone in her chalet later. 'I keep trying to see into the future, you know, trying to get a feel, an intuition if you like, of what might happen.' Her lips pursed in a self-mocking grimace. 'I know, crazy!' she said and sighing heavily, she pushed the pillows up higher behind her and hugged her knees to her chest. 'Don't let's talk about him any more,' she said. 'I'm driving myself crazy enough thinking about him.'

Lizzy's bronzed, anxious face was shrouded in the dusk light spilling in through the open door. Her tousled blonde hair was speckled with sawdust and her khaki uniform was crumpled and muddy. She looked, Rhiannon thought, even more at home here than Rhiannon had expected.

'You know what I think?' Lizzy said. 'I think you should stop trying to second-guess the future and concentrate on the here and now. If it's going to happen for you two, it will, and no amount of self-inflicted misery because God won't let you in on His secrets is going to change it. OK, I know, that's easy to say when I'm not the one going through it, but can you tell me I'm wrong?'

Rhiannon smiled and reaching out for Lizzy's hand she said, 'You look lovely, you know. I just can't tell you how wonderful it is to see you.'

Laughing, Lizzy drew her into her arms. 'You don't have to, I know,' she said. 'I'm just sorry you had to go through all that, with the press and everything, without me being there.'

'Mmm, a real baptism of fire,' Rhiannon grimaced. 'Getting through without Lizzy!' She laughed. 'Still, one crisis down, God knows how many more to go, but I'll get through and if the going gets really tough I'll do what I've done now – get out and come here.'

'You do that,' Lizzy told her. 'Now I'm going to leave you to get ready for dinner. Remember, one of the boys will come to fetch you to lead the way through to the boma. Don't venture out alone after dark – if you need anything ...'

'Shine the flashlight until someone spots it and comes to the rescue,' Rhiannon finished with her.

'I wish all my students were such quick studies,' Lizzy laughed.

'Before you go, what's a boma?' Rhiannon said.

'The barbecue area. We've got Mozambique prawns and fresh Kingklip or Ostrich steak on the menu tonight. And Doug found this fantastic new wine when he was over in Cape Town a few weeks ago, so we'll have a bit of a celebration.'

Rhiannon grinned. 'Can't wait,' she said.

After kissing her on the cheek, Lizzy padded across the deck and began to thread her way through ferns and shrubs that were already bristling with turbulent night sound.

Rhiannon stood at the door for a while, listening to the cries of the wild as they screeched and echoed through the rapidly fading light. Overhead the sky was paling and darkness crept through the trees like errant mischief. She inhaled deeply, remembering the mixed scent of aniseed and dung and thinking of how much her life had changed in a year. It just went to show, she thought to herself as she recalled how in love she had been with Oliver, that no matter how secure and right something might feel at the time, you should never take it for granted, because just like Lizzy said, God had His secrets and He wasn't sharing them with anyone.

'... and so, we'd be very honoured', Andy declared, his unruly blond hair and handsomely tanned face glowing in the firelight as he held his glass high, 'if you, Rhiannon, and you, Doug, would be godparents to the little sprog.'

'The what!' Lizzy exploded.

'The little chap,' Andy immediately amended in his best British accent.

'He thinks it's a boy,' Lizzy informed Rhiannon, 'and I haven't had the heart to disillusion him yet.'

'On behalf of Rhiannon and myself, we accept,' Doug announced, clambering to his feet as the handful of rangers who had joined them for dinner applauded. 'And may I propose a toast to my brother?' His eyes focused gleamingly on Andy's. 'Good on yer, mate!' he grinned and knocking his glass against Andy's, he signalled for everyone else to join in.

'All this manly felicitation, it's making me quite giddy,' Lizzy declared, fanning herself.

Laughing, Rhiannon raised her glass too. 'Good on yer, mate,' she echoed, banging her glass against Lizzy's. 'When's it due?'

'Some time in August, which means it'll probably be a Leo and if it's anything like its father it's going back.'

'And if it's anything like its mother it'll have wings and a halo and it'll strum a little harp like ...'

'Enough,' Lizzy cried, stuffing a handful of grapes in his mouth. 'Private joke. Don't anyone ask.'

'Who does this remind you of?' Andy said to Doug, speaking through the grapes.

'Can you believe this?' Lizzy demanded of Rhiannon. 'We can't even announce we're having a baby without descending into vulgarity. And to think I've agreed to marry it.'

Andy's eyes opened wide. 'That's the first ...' He spat out the grapes, 'I've heard of it,' he finished.

'And the last,' Lizzy told him. 'Doug, we need more wine.'

'Are you supposed to be drinking?' Andy demanded.

'Are you supposed to be alive?' she responded.

'Oh God, stop,' Rhiannon groaned, holding her sides she was laughing so hard.

'Can I kiss you?' Andy said, sitting down and putting his arms around Lizzy.

'If it'll stop you talking,' she replied as Doug refilled their glasses.

'Hey, come on, break it up you two,' Doug commanded. 'The next thing you know she'll be pregnant.'

'Want to dance, Rhiannon?' Andy offered as the band changed rhythm and a few well-oiled guests started shimmying around the campfire.

'You bet,' Rhiannon replied, leaping to her feet.

'Teach her the bushman's shuffle,' Doug called after them.

'The what?' Rhiannon shouted above the drums.

'The bushman's shuffle,' Andy repeated, and with a whoop and a twirl he began shaking his arms and legs about in such an hysterically uncoordinated manner that all Rhiannon – and the rest of the camp – could do, was laugh.

Doug then took it upon himself to inform everyone present about the baby and within minutes the night had erupted into a wildly enjoyable party.

'Is it always like this?' Rhiannon asked Lizzy during a moment's pause from the dance floor.

'Not always this riotous,' Lizzy replied, 'but the man's insane and you just have to humour him.'

Laughing, Rhiannon looked across to where Andy was attempting to jive with a porky little American woman in a cute straw hat, while Doug flaunted himself rashly around the gay Swedes.

'You know, Max would love this,' Rhiannon smiled. 'Life is so serious for him and it would be so good for him to let his hair down and go for it like this.'

'Then the first opportunity we get, we'll introduce him to this pair of clowns,' Lizzy declared.

Rhiannon turned to look at her, eyebrows cocked. 'The first opportunity?' she repeated playfully. 'Has God been letting you in on His secrets, Lizzy Fortnum?'

Laughing, Lizzy lifted a hand to Rhiannon's face. 'I wish I could say He had,' she answered.

Rhiannon sighed. 'Let's change the subject, shall we? This is supposed to be a celebration not a commiseration. Now, where's that idiot man of yours, it's time you had a dance.'

Right on cue Andy appeared behind them and swept Lizzy into the fray. Smiling, Rhiannon watched them and seeing how wonderfully happy they were she could only wonder why she had ever had the feeling that something awful would happen if either of them ever returned to Perlatonga.

'Daddy! Watch! Watch, Daddy,' Marina cried, looking back over her shoulder to check that Max could hear.

'I'm watching, honey,' he told her, pushing his ski-goggles on to his head and squinting against the brilliant white glare of the slopes.

'OK, Aleks!' Marina called to her brother. 'Are you ready?'

'Yes,' he called back from his daring position a few yards up the slope where, behind him, an hilarious host of beginners were windmilling their arms and grabbing each other frantically in an effort to stay on their feet.

Max smiled and felt his heart tense with love as Aleks, fearless as ever in his bright-blue salopettes and matching jacket, fixed his feverish eyes on Marina, dug his poles into the snow and jettisoned himself full pelt into his sister's arms.

'Well done!' Marina shouted, hugging him. 'Did you see that, Daddy? Aleks skied on his own and I caught him.'

'Sure I saw it,' Max replied, his eyes dancing with laughter at the proud and excited looks on his children's faces. They'd been practising this little stunt for the past half-hour, while he'd sipped hot chocolate and pretended not to notice.

'I taught him how to do that,' Marina informed him proudly, skiing the few feet to where Max was sitting outside a café. Then she burst out laughing as Aleks slithered down the slope straight into his father's arms.

'Hey!' Max laughed, swinging Aleks up on to his lap and roundly kissing his cheek. It was so flushed and cold and invitingly soft that he kissed him again and bearhugged him until he protested. 'Give me five,' he said, holding up his palm.

'Yes!' Aleks cried, slapping his gloved hand into Max's. 'I'm nearly as good as Marina now, aren't I?' he said.

Marina's big eyes rose from the cup she was holding to her mouth.

'Nearly,' Max confirmed, giving her a wink, 'but not quite.'

Satisfied with that, Aleks beamed as, with an air of great importance, Marina abandoned her cup and did a quick little slalom down the hillside, just to prove how much more advanced she was than her brother. Aleks watched her, his wide blue eyes steeped in admiration.

'I can do that,' he told Max, as Marina shuffled sideways back up to the café.

'You can?' Max said, loosening Aleks's skis and dropping them to the ground beside his own.

'Yeah. I just don't want to right now.'

'Oh, OK,' Max responded.

'I'm not scared,' Aleks informed him. 'I'm like you, I'm not scared of anything.'

'Daddy's the best skier in the whole wide world,' Marina chipped in, kicking off her skis so she could perch on Max's other knee. 'Daddy skis down the black slopes, don't you, Daddy?'

'Don't be silly,' Aleks said. 'Snow's not black.'

'It's not the snow that's black,' Marina retorted haughtily, 'it's the slope. Daddy, can we ride up on the T-bar again in a minute?' she asked, watching a group of children being swept up over the hillside by the *tire-fesses*.

'Sure, honey, when Galina gets back to take care of Aleks.'

At the mention of Galina, Marina's eyes went down, her long, silky black lashes veiling her thoughts, until suddenly realizing the significance of what her father had said she looked up again in delight. 'Does that mean we can go up on our own?' she gasped excitedly. 'Just you and me?'

'Just you and me,' Max confirmed, tucking a tuft of curls back inside her hat, while wondering what he should do about this problem she was having with Galina.

'It's not black,' Aleks said, craning his neck to look up at the mountain tops. 'Show me where it's black.'

Smiling as Marina attempted to explain the colour gradations of the ski slopes, Max ordered more hot chocolate for them, then looked down the hill to see if Galina was on her way back. After snapping away furiously all morning, taking shots of the kids and Max and the breath-taking scenery around them, she'd taken the camera back to the private chalet they were renting just above the town, tucked discreetly away in a meandering cluster of snow-laden pines.

They'd arrived in Gstaad just over a week ago, having taken a flight to Geneva, then the train up through the mountains to the exclusive Alpine village. The staff Ramon had employed to look after them had been waiting at the station to greet them and transport them to the luxurious chalet. The children had flown in on the company jet just the day before and it hadn't been easy keeping his daredevil son on his feet and out of danger since.

Thanking the waiter as he delivered the hot chocolate,

Max set the children down and watched them, still chattering away, as they went off in search of the toilet. They hadn't got along this well in so long that Max could only feel dismayed at not realizing before how badly they too had needed a break from LA.

It was amazing, he thought with not a little unease as he inhaled the crisp, pine-scented air and gazed out across the spectacular white landscape, that the press hadn't caught up with them yet. It was a busy time of year for the ski resorts and as secluded and private as they were in their chalet, Max didn't imagine for one minute that they hadn't been recognized while out on the slopes. But they had two things in their favour: first, a couple of members of the British royal family were over at Klosters, providing a very convenient sidetrack; and second, it was clear to anyone who came to Gstaad often that those who frequented the exclusive resort had a healthy respect for other people's privacy and no interest at all in having their own winter breaks overrun by a marauding army of slalom-wrecking hacks who didn't know a *Geländesprung* from a Gordon's gin. Nevertheless he still lived in almost hourly dread of them turning up on his doorstep, for if they kept up what they'd started in England he would have no choice but to take action, which was the very last thing he wanted when he knew only too well what the results would be.

'Daddy?' Marina said, coming out of the café with Aleks trailing behind her.

Max looked round and noticed with concern that her face seemed suddenly strained.

'What is it, honey?' he said, putting an arm around her and grabbing Aleks by the hanging bib of his salopettes as he tottered on a patch of ice.

'I was just wondering, Daddy,' she said, bringing her dark eyes up to Max's as Max settled Aleks on his knee, 'will Rhiannon be coming to stay with us?'

Max's heart jolted and he had to take a moment to

collect himself before looking curiously into his daughter's eyes. 'Why do you ask that, honey?' he said.

Her lips trembled slightly as she said, 'I just wanted to know, that's all.'

'No, she's not coming, sweetheart,' he murmured, brushing a hand over her face. 'Why, did you want her to?'

Marina shook her head. 'No,' she answered in a whisper. Then, just like the sun making a sudden break through a cloud, she was all smiles and excitement again. 'Can we try the red slope when we go up?' she asked.

'Sure we can, if you feel up to it,' Max answered. He was longing to ask her what had prompted the question about Rhiannon, but wasn't sure if it would be wise to pursue it. She didn't appear to want to, but she had certainly been seeking reassurance on some level and loving her as completely as he did, it worried him deeply to think she might be concerned about something he knew nothing about. He tried to imagine what she might know about Rhiannon, but without asking her it was really impossible to tell, though it would be naive of him to think that she didn't have some knowledge of what was going on, or that she hadn't seen at least a couple of newspapers before leaving the States.

Watching her as she sat down in the snow to slot her feet into her skis, he tried to work out what he should do. He couldn't force what was going on in her mind out of her, but the fact that she had turned so cold on Galina these past couple of months and now with the prospect of Rhiannon joining them seeming to bother her so much, he was experiencing an unease that he knew was going to have to be dealt with.

'Marina.'

Max and Marina looked up to see Gretchen, the ten-year-old Austrian friend Marina had made the day before, standing a little shyly a few feet away.

'My mother said would you like to come and ski with us?' Gretchen asked in her impeccable, though heavily accented, English.

Max and Marina looked at each other. Marina's face had lit up; she clearly wanted to go and since Gretchen and her family had spent the afternoon with them yesterday Max saw no reason to say no.

'Hi, Gretchen,' Galina said, skiing to a halt behind the young girl. 'How are you today?'

'Oh, I am very fine, thank you,' Gretchen answered, blinking adoringly up at Galina. 'How are you, Mrs Romanov?'

'I'm very fine too,' Galina smiled. 'Have you come to ski with Marina?'

'I'm going to ski with Gretchen and her mother,' Marina replied stiffly.

Galina looked at her and pretending not to notice her tone said, 'That's nice, sweetheart. Did you ask Daddy for some money in case you need a drink while you're gone?'

Marina looked at Max. Her face was pinched with annoyance that she was being forced to do something Galina had told her to do.

'Can I go too?' Aleks asked, looking up from where he was still trying to master the buckles on his salopettes.

'No, Daddy,' Marina groaned, before Max could answer. 'He's too little and he can't ski properly yet.'

'How about coming skiing with me?' Galina offered, stooping in front of Aleks to help him with his buckles.

Aleks's eyes sparkled with pleasure, then seeming suddenly to remember something, he looked nervously at Marina, as though he was unsure how she would feel about him skiing with Galina.

It wasn't the first time Max had seen Aleks look at Marina that way when there was an issue concerning Galina, nor was it the first time that Marina had pretended not to notice. But there was little doubt that the two of them had discussed something, perhaps even come to some kind of pact concerning their secret.

'I skied all on my own just now,' Aleks was telling Galina as Max buttoned twenty Swiss francs into Marina's pocket and watched her ski happily away.

'Did you, darling?' Galina smiled, laughing and hugging him. 'You're so clever. Are you going to show me how you did it?'

Aleks needed no second bidding and was off Max's knee in a shot, attempting to jam his feet back into his skis.

As they edged their way back on to the slope Max was strongly tempted to slot his boots into his own skis and tell Galina he'd be back in an hour. In fact he wasn't entirely sure why he didn't, except his concern for Marina and her mention of Rhiannon seemed to be holding him to his chair. Had Galina and Marina spent any time alone together, Max might have suspected Galina of planting the fear in an effort to safeguard her position. But since she'd arrived, Marina had flatly refused to be alone with Galina, even for a minute, and now Max couldn't help but ask himself if Marina was feeling the same kind of fear she'd experienced the night her mother died. He hoped to God not, because if she was, all his worst nightmares were about to come true.

Feeling the tension increase in his head, he squinted his eyes towards the sun and followed the progress of a cable car as it glided into the remote spruce-covered mountain tops. Earlier, while the children were having their breakfast, he and Galina had skied the black runs together, urging themselves to greater and more reckless speeds as their skis juddered over the uneven surface and soared over precipices, to fly silently down to the next level where the sharp exhilaration of the wind rushing past suddenly picked up again as they landed. They had skied together many times over the years, it was a sport they both excelled at and loved. Carolyn had hated it, which was why she had never joined them.

Turning back to where Aleks was throwing himself happily into Galina's arms, Max could feel the pounding in his head increasing. Though his main concerns were for Marina, he could feel the choking claustrophobia of Galina's presence as though it were sucking the air from his lungs. Her behaviour since the revelation of his affair with Rhiannon and the terrible publicity that had ensued had been so out of character for Galina that he couldn't figure out a way of handling it. It was as though she had shut her mind totally to what had happened and was continuing with their marriage as though there were no lies in the foundations or cracks in the structure. She was unshakeably calm, and collected to a point that was almost religiously strange. She was making no claims either physical or emotional on Max and was so unresponsive to Marina's rejection that she might almost be oblivious to it. It was as if another woman had taken over her body, a woman who was totally at peace with herself and had no recollection or maybe even knowledge of the psychological torment and abuse that had dogged so much of her life.

It wasn't that Max had any wish for her to fall apart as a result of his and Rhiannon's affair; on the contrary, he wished to God that she were strong enough to accept it and allow him and Rhiannon to get on with their lives. As it was, she stood between them like a dazzling white winter sun that permits no one to see around or beyond it.

He sighed and pressed his fingers to his temples. He was a fool to have married her, especially when, as Rhiannon had suspected, he had done it out of guilt, pity, a misplaced sense of protection and a desire to give his children a mother they already knew and loved. But he was going to put it right now and do what Ramon and everyone else had tried to persuade him to do a long time ago.

'Snowman time,' Galina said, kicking off her skis as she sat down at the table.

Max glanced across to where Aleks was kneeling in the snow and starting to gather it into a pile. 'Want some help?' he offered.

'No,' Aleks replied. 'I can do it.'

Max smiled. 'Independence,' he said, signalling to a waiter. 'What'll you have?'

'Just a coffee,' Galina answered. *'Un crème,'* she said to the waiter.

Neither of them spoke again as they waited for the coffee to come and either watched Aleks going busily about his sculpting or made a pretence of absorbing the glorious scenery around them. Galina's frosted lips were curved in the gentle almost rapturous smile she had worn for days now, but the expression in her lavender-blue eyes was shielded by the oval black lenses of her glasses.

'Thank you,' she said to the waiter as he put a coffee in front of her.

Max watched her as she picked up the cup and put it to her lips. She was so familiar to him, so much a part of his life, an extension of his conscience, that he could hardly imagine what his life would be like without her. He smiled inwardly, as the thought alone gave him such a sense of freedom as he hadn't had in years. It surprised him not only to find he felt that way, but that the feeling should be so strong. His eyes followed her hand as she put the cup back in the saucer and he wondered how he was going to deal with his conscience when she'd gone. A horrible sinking feeling made him realize that maybe he wasn't as able to free himself from her as he liked to think.

Turning to look at him, Galina sighed rapturously, as though sensing and relishing his dilemma. 'I bet you're thinking how wonderful it would be if it were Rhiannon sitting here now instead of me,' she said.

Max's eyebrows flickered in surprise. It was the first time she had mentioned Rhiannon since the day they'd left London and the kind of remark she'd just made was a Galina he was much more familiar with than the one he'd been living with these past few days. 'No, I wasn't thinking that,' he responded mildly. 'But I could have been.'

Galina laughed and letting her head fall back, she gave a long, low murmur of content. 'Can she ski?' she said.

'I don't think so.'

'So what good would she be to you here, if she doesn't ski? No, don't tell me, as much good as I am to you anywhere else.' She lifted her head to look at him. 'Is that right?' she said.

'If you say so,' he answered.

Galina picked up her coffee and took another sip. Then setting the cup back down, she started to dig into her sleeve for a handkerchief. 'I was thinking,' she said, 'would it make things easier for you if I were just to throw myself off one of the precipices over there and never be seen again?'

'It would make it easier for me if you were to stop behaving the way you are and tell me what's behind the problem with you and Marina,' he responded.

Galina's lips pursed at the corners and he was aware of the way he had tensed as he waited for her answer. 'Marina', she said, 'has stopped wanting me in her life, because she knows that *you've* stopped wanting me. Surely you realize that.'

Max's heart turned over for more reasons than he wanted to face.

'But of course you've never really wanted me,' Galina went on, 'you just took care of me because you felt sorry for me and then you married me because you didn't know what else to do with me. And you give in to everything I want because you're terrified of doing anything to upset the children's lives any more than they've already been upset because of Carolyn's death. Am I right? Yes, of course I am. You see, I know you, Max, I know you better than you know yourself, so why are you sitting there trying to figure out how you can tell me it's over when we both know that you're never going to do it. You can't do it, Max, not because you're afraid I'll tell the world what happened the night Carolyn died; no, it's not me who'll do that, it's Maurice who'll do that, and you'd rather die than have ... Where are you going?' she demanded as he clipped his boots into his skis.

'I'm not sitting here listening to this,' he said.

Her eyebrows rose mockingly. 'Running away again, Max?' she taunted. 'That's all you've done since we've been here, you know, run away.'

Max's dark eyes were flashing with rage. 'I warned you a long time ago', he said, keeping his voice low so that Aleks wouldn't hear, 'what would happen if you *ever* tried to blackmail me. Now start believing it, Galina, because I'll go public if I have to.'

Galina shrugged, apparently unfazed by his outburst. 'What will you go public with, Max?' she said. 'The truth?'

His face was strained with loathing and anger as he glared down at her, then turning away he skied full speed down the hill, putting as much distance between them as he could before he lost control completely.

Watching him go, Galina put her thumb to her mouth and bit off a hangnail. 'The problem is, Max,' she said as if he was still there, 'you don't know the truth.'

Much later that night, when Aleks was all tucked up in bed and Galina was taking a bath, Max let himself quietly into Marina's bedroom and sat down on the edge of the bed. He was much calmer now, having spent the day working off his temper on the slopes and his only real concern now was for Marina.

Her inky black hair and freshly tanned face looked

lovely and innocent in the peachy glow of the Forever Friends nightlight she went nowhere without. It was hard to imagine, looking down at her now, that such demons as had, had found a place in her young heart, and Max's throat tightened with emotion as he felt the impotence of a father who loved so much and didn't know what to do to help.

'I'm not asleep, Daddy,' she whispered, opening her eyes to look up at him.

He smiled. 'You had me fooled,' he told her, running a hand over her face and into her hair. 'Can I get you something? A hot drink? Some milk?'

She shook her head. 'I'm OK,' she said.

'Do you want to talk?'

Shrugging, she looked away. 'If you like,' she answered after a while.

'What would you like to talk about?' he asked gently.

She shrugged again. 'Anything.'

He nodded, then taking heart, he said, 'Do you want to talk about what's making you unhappy?'

Her eyes remained fixed on the toy shelf beside her bed.

Max turned to see what she was looking at, then bringing his eyes back to her face he felt his heart turn inside out. 'What is it, honey?' he said, lifting her into his arms as two fat tears rolled down her cheeks. 'Tell me, sweetheart. What's making you unhappy?'

'I can't,' she said, her voice almost lost in a sob. 'I can't tell anyone.'

'Sure you can,' he whispered. 'I'm your daddy and you're allowed to tell daddies anything.'

Her arms tightened around his neck and she clung to him as though terrified he would let her go. 'Marina, sweetheart,' he said, swallowing hard, 'you have to tell me what's wrong. I can't make it better until you do.'

She continued to cry, sobbing into his neck and clutching his sweater in her hands.

'There, there,' he soothed, stroking her, 'I'm here and I'm not going to let anything bad happen to you.'

'Daddy, I don't want Rhiannon to come,' she choked, pressing herself even closer to him.

Max's eyes closed as the pain of her words cut deep into his heart. 'She's not coming, honey,' he told her. 'But why don't you want her to come? Don't you like her?'

Marina struggled to catch her breath. 'No, she's nice. I like her, but I don't want her to come.'

'Why not, honey? What are you afraid of?'

Every muscle in his body was tensed with the dread of her answer and he tightened his hold on her as she tried to force her way even closer to him, almost as though she would climb inside his skin if she could.

'Tell me what's wrong between you and Galina,' he said, trying another tack. 'Does any of this have something to do with Galina?'

The tension that knifed through her body was answer enough. 'But Galina loves you, honey,' he said. 'And I thought you loved Galina too.'

'No,' she said, frantically shaking her head. Then suddenly she broke down altogether. 'I want my mommy!' she gasped. 'I want my mommy to come back. Please, Daddy, make her come back.'

'Oh, Marina, Marina,' he murmured, only just managing to hold back his own tears as he hugged her tightly. 'Mommy's gone to heaven, honey,' he said. 'She can't come back.'

'But I want her to be here, Daddy.'

'I know.'

'I don't want Galina to be my mommy. I want her to go away.'

'But I thought you loved her, Marina.'

'No. She frightens me, Daddy. I want her to go away and leave us alone.'

The pain in Max's heart was almost as much for Galina as it was for Marina, for no matter what was going on between him and Galina it would break her heart to know that Marina was feeling this way. Then suddenly he realized what Marina had said and holding her back so that he could look into her face he said, 'What do you mean, she frightens you, honey?'

It was a very long time in coming and so broken apart with sobs and fear and desperate pleas for Max not to be angry that the true horror of what she was telling him took a while to reach him. When it did, it tore such an agonizing fracture through his soul that he could only be thankful that exhaustion carried her into an almost instant sleep when she had finished, thereby rescuing him from the need to respond right away. He laid her gently back on the pillow and stared down at her for a long, long time. The love and the pain and the horror were a greater force than he had ever had to deal with in his life. It was twisting his heart with such agony and guilt as he knew already could never be healed. Carolyn had tried so many times to warn him and he, fool that he was, had never listened.

Outside on the landing he stopped and turned to the window. The night was blue-grey and silvery white. Giant snowflakes floated through the darkness, blowing randomly in the wind and vanishing in a crystalline carpet of ice. The trees, burdened with snow, loomed in the darkness like fairy-tale monsters. Max's heart flipped as he thought of the phantoms that had haunted his daughter's life, of all the fear and suffering he could have spared her, if only he'd known.

Hearing Galina singing in the bedroom, he turned and walked away, descending the stairs swiftly and going to pour himself a drink. His hands were trembling; the desire to kill her was stronger than any other emotion he had experienced that night. Minutes ticked by, then snatching up the phone he dialled Ramon's number. 'I want her out of my life,' he said in a voice that shook with anger and pain. 'I want her out now.'

Chapter 27

Rhiannon and Lizzy were sitting quietly on the side of a hillock gazing down at the indolent comings and goings at Perlatonga's waterhole. A pair of Marabou storks were drinking now, while a few feet away a bad-tempered bush pig fussed and fidgeted around her brood as they tumbled about in the mud. On the opposite bank a tired old hippopotamus lay dozing in the late afternoon sun, apparently untroubled by the screeching gaggle of baboons somersaulting through the trees nearby.

'It's not hard to see why you love it here,' Rhiannon said, following the graceful flight of a cormorant as it rose from an overhanging branch. 'It's so peaceful and fascinating – I can't imagine ever getting tired of watching it all.'

Lizzy smiled. 'I know,' she sighed, leaning back on her elbows, 'all this and Andy too. What more could a girl want?' Her eyes came round to Rhiannon's. 'Sorry,' she said. 'That wasn't very tactful.'

Rhiannon's eyebrows went up and looking past Lizzy to where the Safari Suite was nestled in the small enclave of its own garden she said, 'It's OK. I'm not expecting you to fake misery just to please me. And anyway, it wouldn't please me.'

Knowing where Rhiannon was looking, Lizzy said, 'Do you ever hear from Oliver now?'

Rhiannon grimaced. 'No,' she answered. Then sighing, she shook her head, as though slightly baffled by the extraordinariness of being where she was and talking about Oliver that way when the last time she was here it had been such a very different story. 'Strange, isn't it,' she said, 'how things turn out? I mean, I can't even remember what it was like making love with Oliver now – in fact, the very thought of it turns me cold.'

Lizzy turned back to the waterhole and watched the fiery reflection of the sun playing over the surface. She wondered if Rhiannon was deliberately avoiding the subject of what had been on the news last night, or whether she genuinely didn't yet know. Actually, there was a very good chance Rhiannon didn't know, for there were only two TVs in the camp and she certainly hadn't been at the house with Lizzy when Lizzy had heard what had happened in Gstaad, and as far as Lizzy knew she hadn't been in the guest shop either, where the other TV was located. The trouble was, if she didn't know, Lizzy was going to have to tell her and right now she was completely at a loss how to put it. Deciding to leave it for the moment she said, 'I keep forgetting to ask, but are you sure you don't mind about not staying at the house? I just thought you'd be more comfortable in a chalet, what with the decorators making such a mess ...'

'Of course I don't mind,' Rhiannon assured her. 'I just hope you haven't turned anyone away because you're full up.'

Lizzy grimaced. 'I wouldn't have minded turning that bloody English couple away,' she retorted, referring to a couple from Slough who had spent the past three days trying to work out where they had seen Rhiannon before. Fortunately they'd left now and a new batch of guests were due to arrive at any time. 'Still, I suppose we just have to be grateful they had Alzheimers,' she continued, 'or we could be dealing with a bunch of human baboons right now rather than sitting here watching the real thing.'

Leaning back too, Rhiannon said, 'Do you ever get any newspapers out here? I haven't seen one since I arrived.'

Lizzy's heart skipped a beat. 'Sometimes Doug or someone brings a couple in from Jo'burg, when they remember,' she answered, 'but they're usually a week out of date by the time they get here.'

'Don't you miss hearing the news?' Rhiannon asked. 'I mean, don't you want to know what's going on in the world?'

Almost certain now that Rhiannon didn't know, Lizzy said, 'We get CNN if you're feeling in need of a fix. And Sky News.'

Rhiannon looked up to where the Cessna air-taxi was starting its descent towards the runway. 'I have to confess I do miss the outside world,' she said, 'but the idea that I've only got a few days left here is too depressing for words.'

'What will you do when you get back?' Lizzy asked.

'Carry on where I left off, I suppose. It's not going to be easy because the temptation to ring Max is growing every day and to be honest I don't know how much longer I can hold out. I know it probably wouldn't be the right thing to do, but I just can't make myself accept that this is it, that there can't be any more.' As she spoke her heart was churning with the longing that all but consumed her and feeling the pain starting to swell, she turned her head away to allow the tears a moment to recede. 'It's just getting harder,' she said, her voice barely more than a whisper.

Lizzy's eyes were squinting against the sun as she tried to steel herself to break the news that she knew was going to shatter Rhiannon's heart. She glanced over at Rhiannon and seeing how very close to the edge she was, Lizzy searched her mind desperately for as gentle a way of doing this as she could muster. 'Has it ever occurred to you', she began hesitantly, 'that some of the stuff they wrote about Max ... Well, that there might be an element of truth in some of it? I mean, from what you told me, it was pretty strong and ... Well, I can't see Susan Posner or anyone else going to press without being sure of their facts – not in a case like this.'

Rhiannon's face was cold with anger as turning to look at Lizzy she said, 'I don't believe this! Are you saying that you *do* believe it? That you actually think he's a monster and a pervert who killed his first wife and cheats on his second ... Is that what you're trying to tell me?'

Lizzy sighed. 'No, that's not what I'm trying to say,' she answered. 'I'm just asking you to be honest with yourself ...'

'Let's drop this now, before one of us ends up saying something we'll regret,' Rhiannon interrupted tightly.

Lizzy sat forward and hugged her knees to her chest. She wasn't handling this at all well and she still hadn't managed to get to the point. 'There's a wildebeest,' she said lamely, as a cautious young gnu wandered out of the shelter of the trees, its tail switching the flies on its back and its snout down ready for water.

Her face still pinched with anger and her heart thudding with misery, Rhiannon sat up to take a look. Several minutes ticked by as the wildebeest drank its fill, then wandered away. A while later the hippo sank luxuriously into the water and floated out to the middle. 'He didn't do any of that to Galina,' Rhiannon said in a whisper. 'I swear to you, Lizzy, it just isn't in him to do something like that. I'm not trying to make out he's some kind of saint, because he's not, but he's not a monster either. And before you say anything else, think how you would feel if I were doubting Andy this way.'

'But Andy hasn't been written about in the press the way Max has,' Lizzy protested, 'and I'm only thinking of you. My God, Rhiannon, you wouldn't be the first woman to be taken in by a man, to be so blinded by her feelings that she can't ...' She stopped as she realized what she was saying.

'I was taken in by Oliver,' Rhiannon said brittlely, 'so why not Max too? That's what you're thinking, isn't it? I made a fool of myself once and now I'm doing it again. Poor, stupid Rhiannon, she can't see a liar, a cheat, a wife-batterer or a murderer even when the rest of the world is yelling "behind you". Well, OK, I made a mistake with Oliver and I'll be the first to admit it, but I'm telling you now that I'm not wrong about Max. He's never done anything to Galina except care for her. He stood by her when no one else would; he got her the help she needed and he still tries to get her help even though she rejects it. He married her for God's sake, he's given her his children, his name, he's sacrificed his entire fucking life for her and you're sitting there trying to tell me that he did all those things that sick, warped woman wrote about him. Well, I don't want to hear it, Lizzy, not from you, least of all from you. Nothing's going to change the way I feel about him, I love him, I want him and I know I might never have him. That's enough to be dealing with without my best friend believing all the crap they're saying about him just because I made a mistake in the past. He's never laid a single damned finger on Galina except in affection and ...'

'She's disappeared, Rhiannon,' Lizzy interrupted softly. 'They don't know where she is.'

Rhiannon's breath froze in her lungs as her heart pounded with the fear she might have heard right. Then suddenly she was seized with an overwhelming urge to be with him, to get away from Lizzy, from all those who doubted him and lock herself in the safety of his arms.

'I heard it on the news last night,' Lizzy said, turning to look at her. Seeing how ashen Rhiannon's face had become, she reached out for her hand, but Rhiannon pulled it away.

'What do you mean, they don't know where she is?' she whispered brokenly.

'Just that,' Lizzy answered. 'Apparently she went off-piste a couple of days ago and she hasn't been seen since. They've had all the rescue services out looking for her, but so far there's no sign of her.'

'And Max? What are they saying about Max?'

'According to the news he's out there looking for her too. The brief shot I saw of him showed him getting out of a search-and-rescue helicopter and into a police car.'

Rhiannon's eyes widened with terror. 'You mean he was being arrested?' she cried.

'I don't think so. That's not what they said.' She paused and when Rhiannon said no more she went on quietly, 'They've more or less given up hope of finding her alive now. She's been missing for too long in temperatures that are too low to survive in.'

'Oh God,' Rhiannon murmured, her throat so tight she could barely speak.

'There are two theories at the moment,' Lizzy said, 'suicide and murder. You won't need me to tell you which is the favourite.'

Rhiannon looked out across the wild bushy plains to where the sun was glowing red on the horizon. 'I have to speak to him,' she said softly. 'I have to go to him, Lizzy.'

'Why don't we wait to see what they say on the news tonight?' Lizzy responded. 'You never know, they might have found her, she might have turned up somewhere safe and well and it's all blown over by now.'

But Galina hadn't turned up and though no body had either the authorities in control of the search had decided that there was no more to be gained by continuing, so pending any new information they had called off the search. Max Romanov and another man, so far unnamed, were currently helping police with their enquiries at police headquarters in Geneva. 'The police are keen to stress the fact that no arrests have been made,' the reporter said from his overcrowded spot at the foot of one of the ski slopes in Gstaad, 'and none are expected tonight. The children are reported to have been flown back to the States and Max Romanov is expected to follow some time in the next day or two. We'll keep you informed of events as they unfold. In the meantime, back to you in the studio in London.'

Walking through the decorators' debris of ladders and canvas sheeting, Andy handed Rhiannon a drink and turned to look at the small black-and-white TV screen that was perched on the edge of an untiled work surface. The programme had moved on to other news stories now, so picking up the remote control he flicked off the TV.

'I've got to tell you, I'm with Rhiannon,' he said, glancing at Lizzy. 'He's not going to finish her off now, when the ink's hardly dry on the paper after all that fuss in London, and when half the world knows his motive. He'd have to be crazy.'

Lizzy turned to look at Rhiannon. 'What do you want to do?' she said softly.

Rhiannon's eyes moved uncertainly about the room. 'I don't know,' she said hoarsely. 'I mean, I want to go to him, but how will it look if I do?'

Lizzy glanced at Andy.

'I'm going to be honest with you, mate,' Andy said, putting a hand on Rhiannon's shoulder, 'it wouldn't look good if you did turn up, 'cos like I just said, as far as the rest of the world's concerned, you're his motive. If you take my advice you'll stay put for a couple of days. Try to reach him by phone if you like, he'll tell you the best thing to do.'

Rhiannon nodded. 'You're right,' she said, her voice echoing through the terrible numbness inside her. Then pressing her fingers to her mouth, she said, 'I know he'll handle this, that somehow he'll get through it, but I wish to God I could be there with him if only to let him know that there's someone on this godforsaken planet who doesn't believe he did it.'

Susan Posner's fingers lay idle on the computer keyboard. She was gazing blindly out of her hotel-room window to where the glorious sunlit slopes of Gstaad sparkled like sequinned mantles from the heavens. She'd never been to Switzerland before and she was beginning to wish now that she'd never come, for as beautiful as it was, the two pieces of information that had just reached her were overshadowing everything.

For the moment she was too stunned to properly assimilate the meaning of what she had heard, though whatever it was she knew, because of the way her heart was thudding, that it wasn't good. The first piece of news was that a body had been found in a ravine some ten miles east of Gstaad; the second was that Max Romanov and Ramon Kominski were flying back to LA some time in the next couple of hours.

As the minutes ticked by and the relevance of the information and its disturbing reality settled in layers of dread around her heart, she tried to make herself look at what was was bothering her the most: the fact that there was now a body, or that Max Romanov looked like he was going to get away with it again? She couldn't believe it, or more to the point, she didn't want to believe it, for if Galina was being hauled from a gully in the cliffs while the murdering bastard who had done it was on his way home, then all her efforts had been in vain.

Dropping her head in her hands, she tried again to make some sense of what was happening and what she was feeling. God knew, she had done everything in her power to prevent this murder; she'd exposed his affair with Rhiannon, she'd published photographs of the violence he systematically perpetrated on Galina and she'd warned him, publicly, that there was new and incriminating evidence regarding the murder of his first wife. She'd stuck her neck right on the line for this one, for the evidence Maurice Remmick had given her had been based wholly on hearsay. But it had all added up, it had made so much god-damned sense that she could only wonder why she hadn't seen it before. And when put together with Remmick's sworn statement that he would stand by the information he had given her in a court of law, she reckoned he had to be pretty sure of his ground. So Susan didn't see any cause for sleeplessness there; what she was having a real hard time with, though, was her own inbuilt sense of knowing when something wasn't right – and something wasn't right here, she just knew it.

She considered the arrogance it would take for Romanov to believe that he could get away with it again, when he had to know that the world's press still had him in their sights. Her heart took a sickening dive as she looked down at the box files beside her that contained so many details of his life. It just didn't make any sense that he'd have done it now, when she, personally, had splattered his motive all over the press and when she'd warned him, all but told him, that he wouldn't get away with it twice. Yet he'd gone ahead and done it anyway – and goddamnit, it looked like he was going to get away with it again too. She blinked, looked down at her keyboard and tried to bolster her indignation with more conviction. It wasn't working, though; in fact the whole god-damned business was unnerving her in a way it never had before.

Hearing a commotion downstairs in the car-park, she got up and walked over to the window. By the time she'd arrived in Gstaad all the village hotels had been full, so she and the other late-comers had checked in to the luxurious Grand Chalet a few minutes away which offered one of the best views and best restaurants in Switzerland. Several news crews had set up their satellite and cable links from there and as the flurry of activity down below increased, Susan picked up her room key and forced herself to go and find out what had happened.

Common sense was telling her that the TV guys were responding to the news that a body had been found and Romanov was on his way back to the States, but she had to be sure. If there were any further developments, she needed to know before she filed her story across to the *LA Times*. It wasn't until she reached the outside door that she realized how badly she was shaking. Trying to ignore it, she pushed her way through the tangle of steel cases and tripods to an NBC stringer whom she'd met a couple of times before.

'What's going down?' she shouted above the din.

Glancing up from where he was scribbling something on a pad, the reporter said, 'Romanov's just left police HQ. They say he's on his way back to LA.'

Susan stared at him, then realizing that was precisely what she'd expected to hear, she felt herself start to relax. 'And the body?' she said. 'Any news on the body?'

He frowned. Then suddenly enlightened he tapped his pencil against the page and proceeded to give her the very answer she now realized she had been dreading the most. As he spoke, telling her that it had been the body of a Belgian woman who had gone missing the day before, Susan felt the world starting to tilt. She turned as someone called her name, telling her there was someone on the line from the States. It was the airline office clerk she'd contacted the day before, checking on flight and passenger information for the day Carolyn Romanov had died.

When finally the call was over Susan knew that her earlier hunch had paid off. But instead of the euphoria she generally felt at such moments, she simply stood where she was, staring blankly into the horror of it all. Fear began to slide through her as chillingly as the rivers that ran through the hills. Then panic seized her as though to force her to her knees, as the nightmare that had been gathering focus fast since Galina had vanished began turning into a reality she never wanted to face. She'd got it wrong about Max Romanov.

Night had chased them across an entire ocean and continent and was now finally catching them as the engines of the Romanov jet were thrown into reverse on a private runway just north of Malibu. Minutes later, Max and Ramon disembarked the aircraft and got into a waiting limousine. Both men looked haunted with fatigue, though they'd slept fitfully during the flight and had showered and changed before arriving in LA.

Max had spoken to Ula and Ellis just prior to landing. His instructions had been short and to the point. He wanted Maurice at the house when he arrived and the children out. If Maurice showed any signs of resistance they knew whom to call.

Whether Maurice had needed any persuasion was impossible to tell as Max and Ramon walked into the family sitting-room at the Malibu mansion. He was standing with his back to the flaming log fire, his thumbs hooked casually on to the pockets of his golfing slacks and the arrogant smile of a man who knew he'd won curving his long expressive mouth. Ellis and Ula were on one of the couches that flanked the hearth, but though both got up as Max came in, neither even attempted a greeting as Ramon closed the door and Max's presence in the room filled the air with danger.

'Where is she?' he demanded. He was staring at Maurice. His face was as white as the marble floors, his eyes as deadly as the fists clenched at his sides.

Maurice's wiry eyebrows went skywards as he gave a snort of incredulous laughter. 'You're asking me?' he sneered. 'It was you she was with out there, it was you ...'

'Where *is she*?' Max cut in. He hadn't taken a single step forward, but the menace in his voice caused

Maurice to flinch.

Ula watched them and prayed silently to God that she wasn't about to witness something she was going to live the rest of her life trying to forget.

Ellis, obviously stunned by what was happening, was the first to break the silence. 'Maurice, if you know where she is, for God's sake speak out, man.'

Again Maurice's eyebrows flew up in disbelief. 'You're asking the wrong guy, Ellis,' he cried. 'If you want to know where she is ask that maniac there!' He was pointing at Ramon, his pale eyes steeped in the challenge as his fleshy upper lip quivered with anger. Not by even so much as the flicker of a muscle did Ramon respond.

Ula looked at Ramon. His eyes were like glittering fragments of stone, his jaw was set in a hard, merciless line, his hands were linked loosely in front of him. Though he lacked Max's physical stature, the power in his solid, well-trained body was far meaner and readier to unleash than Max's would ever be. Or maybe Ula was wrong about that, maybe she was wrong about everything.

Her heart was thudding with fear. There was little doubt in her mind that something terrible was going to happen in this room. No one moved, but it was as though a predatory ritual was unfolding around her. She wondered if Maurice realized what danger he was in, that with Ramon there the threads of his life were fraying by the second.

'Maurice, you've got to know that you're not going to get away with this,' Max told him. 'You're insane if you ever thought you could. Now just tell me where she is.'

Maurice's head tilted to one side as he fixed Max with his colourless eyes. 'Max, I've been right here in LA these past two weeks,' he said silkily, 'so how the hell would I know where she is?'

'For Christ's sake, give it up, man!' Max yelled. 'It's

over, can't you see that? You're going to jail. You're finished, through, dead. So just tell me what you've done with her?'

Maurice's smile widened and to Ula's astonishment he started to applaud. 'Great show, Max,' he said. 'Yeah, great show. You could have me convinced too, if I didn't know what a fucking bastard you really are.'

Max's nostrils flared, but his voice remained low as he said, 'It'd give me a lot of pleasure to break your neck, Maurice, and you better believe I will unless you tell me right now what you've done with her – or what you paid some deranged son-of-a-bitch to do for you.'

There was such violence in Max's voice that Ula felt her breath freeze. She wished to God she knew what was going on here, whom she should believe and who was really baiting whom. She looked at Max and felt her heart strain with a terrible emotion. She'd never doubted him before all this and she hated herself for doubting him now, but no matter how hard she tried she couldn't understand why Ramon had been there in Gstaad when Galina had disappeared.

Ellis's loyalties, it seemed, were much less torn as he attempted to avert a showdown by walking into the middle of the room and saying, 'Look, let's try to keep this in perspective, shall we? It's not the first time she's disappeared like this and all of us in this room know that there's every chance she'll show up ...'

'Don't kid yourself, Ellis!' Maurice interjected scathingly.

'Just shut it,' Ellis barked. 'You know and I know that she's been o.d.ing on abuse for years and all that crap about Max being behind it is just that, *crap*. And I got to tell you, Maurice, if I find out you're in some way involved in this, so help me God, I'll kill you myself.' Ula stared at him in amazement as he went on, almost without breath, 'What Galina does to herself, or pays other people to do ...'

'OK, Ellis,' Max cut in.

'No! Let me finish,' Ellis seethed, still glaring at Maurice. 'If you're out to frame Max for a murder he didn't commit, which is what this is starting to look like, or if you've got Galina hidden away somewhere beaten half to death ...'

'I've been right here in LA!' Maurice yelled. 'Jesus Christ, I've seen you practically every day.'

'But you spoke to her on the phone, Maurice,' Ula reminded him, her heart starting to race. 'You spoke to her three days ago on the phone right here in this house. I know, because I heard you.'

Maurice's face had paled, but he wasn't backing down. 'Yeah, I spoke to her,' he shouted, 'I spoke to her and heard how terrified out of her mind she was. He'd told her it was over! He'd said he didn't want her any more, that she was out of his life, that as far as he was concerned she was dead. And the next thing I hear is they're looking for her body. So you tell me, what am I supposed to think now? That *I* went over there and pushed her off a fucking mountain? Give me a break, will you?'

'You were arranging something with her, Maurice,' Ula said, the sound of her own voice make her feel light-headed and out of sync with her surroundings. 'You told her, you said, "Yeah, I'll do it, the ticket shouldn't be a problem, but you'll get recognized ..."' She was thinking hard, trying to recall what else she had overheard, but Maurice's anger crashed in on her thoughts.

'I was telling her I'd help get her out of there,' he yelled. 'She knew *he*', he jabbed a finger towards Ramon, 'was on his way and she wanted out before he turned up. So I said I'd do what I could.'

Max turned to Ramon, spoke quietly for a moment, then turned back to Maurice as Ramon left the room.

Maurice's eyes darted between Max and the closing door. 'Where's he going?' he snapped.

'To call the police,' Max answered, taking the whisky Ellis was handing him.

'What the hell for?' Maurice demanded angrily.

Max looked at him. 'It could be, Maurice,' he said, 'that you're holding her hostage somewhere, or that you've had the human decency to get her hospitalized for whatever injuries she might have. I hope to God that is the case, because if it's not and she is dead, then you better know now that you'll go down for her murder as sure as you're going down for the photographer in Memphis.'

'What!' Maurice hissed. 'Are you out of your mind? I was nowhere near Memphis when that photographer ...'

'You arranged it, Maurice. We've got the proof and Ramon's about to give it to the police. The game's up for your friend Susan Posner too, she'll never work again, not in this town or any other. Kurt Kovar in New York is about ready to serve her with enough writs to make history. Now if I were you I'd start talking about what you've done with Galina.'

'I'm telling you, I don't know where she is!' Maurice cried. 'She called me, yes, but all she said was that Ramon was on his way and that she had to get out of there before something happened. She said you were real mad at her, madder than you'd ever been and she was afraid to stay.' He turned to Ula and Ellis. 'That's what she said!' he shouted. 'She said he was mad at her and she was afraid. OK, she was always saying things like that, but so was Carolyn and look what happened to her. And we've only got his word for who really shot Carolyn ...'

'Jesus Christ, Maurice,' Ula screamed, 'do you think he'd lie about something like that?'

'He'd lie about anything if he thought it would save his skin,' Maurice raged. 'He's lying now and you just can't see it. Galina was scared, I'm telling you, more scared than I've ever heard her and she wanted my help.

So I said I'd send someone over, but by the time he got there they were already out looking for her body. And that's the truth! I swear it, Ellis, that's the god-damned truth.' He swung back round to Max, his eyes suddenly bulging with fury. 'And if you think I'm taking the rap for any god-damned murder, then you better start preparing that kid of yours, because if anyone's guilty of murder round here ...'

Ula gasped as Max crossed the room quicker than she could blink and gripping Maurice's throat slammed him so hard against the wall that Maurice's eyes rolled back in their sockets and blood started to pour from his nose. 'If there was the slightest chance I'd get away with it I'd kill you right now, you mother-fucking son-of-a-bitch,' Max seethed. His eyes were glinting like blades, his mouth was a thin, vicious line of malice. 'Did you *know*?' he hissed, shaking Maurice so hard that the blood flowed even faster. 'Tell me, did you know about Galina? Because if you did you're not going to live long enough to ...'

'Max, let him go,' Ellis said, trying to break Max's grip. 'He's not worth it. Let the cops deal with it.'

Time ticked by as Max's grip tightened and his eyes burned with a fury that surpassed even his pain. In front of him Maurice was taking huge gulping sobs of air that barely made it past his throat. Max glared at him. This man was using what he knew, the confidences, the devastating truth that, as his lawyer and his friend, Max had trusted him with, to manipulate and destroy all their lives. He didn't want money, he had no need of money, he just wanted revenge for the fact that Carolyn had died not wanting him. It was sick, so god-damned sick the man deserved to die.

'Max,' Ellis said quietly.

At last Max turned away and pushing a hand into his hair he tightened his eyes. 'What a god-damned mess,' he growled, as Ellis struggled Maurice into a chair. He looked up at Ula. 'How many times did Carolyn warn me?' he said bitterly. 'How many times did she tell me, "Max, one day you're gonna find out just how dangerous that woman is." You heard her say it, Ula. Everyone heard her say it, but none of us listened. *I* never listened and look what happened? Marina, at seven years of age, takes a gun and blows her mother's brains out.' His eyes closed at the unspeakable horror of it. 'Except she didn't,' he added, almost inaudibly. 'Galina did.'

Ula was staring at him. 'Galina?' she whispered. 'You mean ...' She stopped, unable to grasp this. Then pressing her hands to her cheeks she said, 'But we've thought ... All this time, we've thought ...'

'That Marina did it,' Max finished for her. 'I know,' and the anger in his eyes was greater than Ula had ever seen.

'How do you know?' Ula whispered after a while. 'Who told you it was Galina?'

Max looked at her. 'Marina told me,' he said. 'She told me four nights ago – the night before Galina disappeared.'

Ula took a moment, then said, 'And Ramon? What was Ramon doing there?'

'He'd come to get Galina,' Max answered. 'I told him to come get her, because I didn't want her near Marina any more. God-damnit, I couldn't allow her near Marina, not when I knew ...'

'But what was he going to do with her?'

'Bring her back here, to LA, and force her to get the treatment she should have had a long time ago.'

Ula glanced at Ellis. 'How did Marina come to tell you?' she said. 'I mean, why hasn't she ever said anything before?'

'Because I didn't damn well give her a chance,' Max raged. 'I walked in, saw the body, found the gun ... I never dreamt Galina was there. I thought, like everyone else, that she was here in LA. Marina was the only one who knew she wasn't. And because I found the gun with Marina, because I'd heard the things she'd said to her mother just hours before ...' He stopped, swallowed hard, then pushed himself on. 'Do you know what made her tell me now?' he said harshly. 'What it was that forced her to break the secret Galina had made her keep?' His voice was steeped in bitterness, his face ravaged with pain. 'She broke it because she was terrified that Galina was going to do the same to Rhiannon as she'd done to Carolyn. And Marina, in her poor, confused mind, thought she'd be blamed for it, the way she had ... Jesus Christ Almighty!' he seethed. 'Why did I never realize ... ? She was a baby for Christ's sake! She couldn't have done it!'

'Sssh,' Ula said, reaching for his hands.

Turning away Max said, 'That's why I told Ramon he had to get Galina the hell out of our lives now. I couldn't have her around Marina a minute longer. I wanted to kill her. I wanted to choke the god-damned life out of her.

'She left the house a couple of hours after Ramon got there,' he went on, 'and that was the last any of us saw of her. One of the maids said she saw her going off in her ski gear, and someone at one of the bars saw her using the phone. I guess she was talking to Maurice, but whether he saw this as another way of framing me for murder or whether he's hiding her away somewhere I guess we're going to have to let the police find out.'

Ula inhaled deeply and glanced over at Ellis.

Ellis was staring blankly at the carpet between his feet. There were still so many unanswered questions, but for the moment no one seemed to know where to start.

Then suddenly Max's eyes returned to Ula's. 'Oh Christ,' he murmured, putting a hand to his head. 'Rhiannon. I've got to get ahold of Rhiannon and tell her what's happened before anyone starts accusing her ...' He stopped suddenly and as he swung round to look at her again Ula's blood ran cold.

'What is it?' she said. 'Max, why are you looking at me like that?'

'Rhiannon,' he said, almost to himself. His eyes suddenly snapped into focus. 'Jesus Christ, Rhiannon,' and snatching the phone from Ellis's shirt pocket he began dialling Rhiannon's number in London.

It took almost half an hour to track down the number of Perlatonga. By then Max's face was whiter than ever as starting to dial, he fought back a terrible premonition that it was already too late.

Chapter 28

A single beam of light jittered about the path, hunting the darkness as it led the way through a tangled forest of branches. The raucous twitter and whooping cries of the bush swallowed the muted crunch of footsteps, while the faint sibillance of breath grazed the night with a featherlike touch. Not far away, just the other side of the trees, the chatter of voices could be heard as the camp guards milled around the fire and picked through left-over food. Above, dazzling formations of stars blinked down from the impenetrable darkness of the sky, while hidden watchful eyes gazed from the thickening shadows.

Rhiannon gasped as something fluttered past her face. Elmore put out a hand to steady her, then chuckling, walked on towards her chalet. Keeping close, Rhiannon watched the flashlight dance like a wand through the trees. She was later going to bed than usual, one of the game-ranger's rifles had gone missing and Andy had wanted all the chalets searched before anyone retired for the night. Nothing had turned up, so now Elmore was escorting Rhiannon along the winding shrub-covered path to her cabin.

When they reached it she turned to wish him good-night.

'You make sho' you lock up good now, ma'am,' he warned her, training the flashlight on the door. 'We don' want no lions comin' and eatin' you in the night.'

'Thank you for the comforting thought, Elmore,' Rhiannon murmured sweetly.

Laughing, he put his head down and lumbered back into the night, leaving her standing on the chalet deck watching the bobbing beam of light until it disappeared from sight.

Tiredness was coming over her in waves as she turned to push open the door. Closing it behind her, she looked across the small vaulted room to where the mosquito nets fell in soft welcoming folds over the bed and the old-fashioned lamps nestled at the heart of their golden auras. A decanter of fresh water and a glass had been placed on the nightstand. Next to the decanter was a neat pile of books she had brought from London, all of which had yet to be opened.

Trailing a hand over the back of the newly sprung armchair where an untidy pile of clothes tumbled towards the floor, she walked to the foot of the bed and sat down. Above her a three-bladed fan creaked and whirred, stirring the empty air and fluttering the pages of a discarded magazine.

Lowering her head to her hands, she massaged her temples and inhaled the delicate scent of pot-pourri. The longing she felt for Max was so strong all of a sudden, it was almost as if he was there in the room with her. She wished to God he were, for it pained her deeply to think of how he must be suffering now, and to know that there was nothing she could do.

Becoming aware of her surroundings again, she listened to the noise outside. She felt cocooned in a shell of silence as the incessant chatter, whines and yowls of the night swelled around the walls of the chalet. Sudden screeches and protracted howls sprang from the chirruping torrent of sound, while the silent stalk of beasts and slither of quietly hissing snakes melded with the night.

The scent of pot-pourri seemed to be stronger. She

looked over to the chest of drawers. The dry crimson roses were spilling from their ceramic bowl and rocking in the teasing draft of the fan. Rhiannon watched for a moment, feeling the strange tension of the night as it whickered and rasped and seemed to close in around her. She wondered what had happened to the gun. Its disappearance had unnerved her; she wanted to know where it was.

She looked up at the mirror and was about to stand when her heart gave a sudden lurch. She spun round, her eyes bulging as horror surged through her. Someone had hung a rope from the rafters of her room.

'Oh my God!' she choked, backing away from it. 'Jesus Christ!' Her mind was racing so fast she couldn't think what to do. It was horrible. So menacing and portentous. Who would have done it? What sick mind had draped a noose from the ceiling of her room? Then a sudden madness tore at her heart as someone touched her shoulder.

She swung round, fear lashing through her like a knife. Her scream was stifled by her own fist as she saw a woman standing there. 'Galina?' she gasped.

'Who do you think?' Galina replied, reaching up to peel the wig from her head. Underneath, her hair was flat and colourless and clinging to her skull like a damaged skin.

Rhiannon tried to breathe. A thousand thoughts were crashing through her head; just one emerged from the chaos, turning her weak with fear. The rifle. Galina had the rifle. But there was no sign of it. Galina's hands were empty.

Rhiannon forced herself to breathe. She had to get a grip, but she was shaking so hard in the aftermath of shock she could barely stand. 'What are you doing here?' she said finally.

Galina laughed. 'What an amazingly stupid question,' she commented.

Rhiannon looked at her. 'How did you get here?' she demanded.

'By plane,' Galina answered. 'How else would I get here? No one realized who I was, of course, not even when they checked me in.'

Rhiannon's eyes dropped to the discarded wig and a great surge of anger rushed through her. 'Don't you know everyone's looking for you?' she cried, her voice shaking with emotion. 'For Christ's sake, Galina, they think Max ...'

'They think Max what?' Galina said coldly. 'That he killed me?' Her lips curled in an arrogant smile.

Rhiannon's heart was still thumping, her face was drawn in confusion. 'What happened?' she said. 'Why have you come here?'

Galina's eyebrows flickered. 'I thought you would have worked that out for yourself by now,' she said. She glanced up at the noose and a slow fear bit deep into Rhiannon's heart.

'Distraught after being jilted by her lover, Max Romanov,' Galina said, 'Rhiannon Edwardes tragically takes her own life.'

Rhiannon stared at her. No one knew Galina was here, no one even knew she was alive, so it would be the easiest thing in the world for her to kill Rhiannon and leave without anyone ever even suspecting she'd been here.

'Friends say', Galina went on, 'that having being jilted twice before, Rhiannon could no longer face the pressures life was putting her under ... She lost her job just a few months ago ...'

'You'll never get away with it,' Rhiannon whispered. 'You'll never make me do it.'

Galina's eyes were steady as they looked back her.

'For God's sake!' Rhiannon cried. 'Don't you think Max will know, when you suddenly come back from the dead, don't you think he'll realize ...' Her hands trembled as she dragged them through her hair. She had to make a run for the door. She had to get out of here ...

'There was a time when I could make you do anything,' Galina reminded her smoothly.

Rhiannon's eyes moved back to her.

'Do you remember that?' Galina said. 'I could make you laugh, I could make you cry, I could make you feel things ...'

'I was a child, Galina. Things have changed since then.'

Galina smiled. 'Haven't they?' she remarked drily. 'But Marina's a child.'

Rhiannon's heart stopped beating. 'What do you mean?' she whispered, feeling her face turn numb.

Galina's stare was glassy, her mind clearly elsewhere. 'Marina was younger and more malleable even than you,' she said softly. 'And so good at keeping secrets.'

'Oh God,' Rhiannon murmured. 'Tell me I'm dreaming. Please, tell me this isn't happening.'

Galina laughed. 'That would be nice, wouldn't it?' she said, 'if we could all just open our eyes and find out we were dreaming.'

'What did you do to Marina?' Rhiannon said. 'What did you make her do?'

Still smiling, Galina sauntered towards the mirror.

Rhiannon glanced at the door. She had a clear path now, but both she and Galina knew that she wasn't going anywhere until Galina had explained those remarks about Marina.

'It must be nice having a best friend,' Galina commented, picking up Rhiannon's hairbrush and turning it over in her hand.

'*What* have you done to Marina?' Rhiannon demanded.

'Especially when the best friend lives in a place like this,' Galina continued, pulling the brush through her hair.

'Galina! Put the fucking brush down and tell me about Marina,' Rhiannon yelled.

Galina smirked at her in the mirror, then turning to face her, she folded her arms and leaned against the chest. 'They say she killed her mother,' she said.

Rhiannon's heart missed a beat. 'What do you mean?'

'What I said, they think she did it.'

Rhiannon's face was ashen. Minute after minute ticked by as she and Galina stared at each other in the dim golden light. It explained so much. Why Max would never discuss his wife's death; why the charges had been dropped; why he was allowing Maurice to do what he was doing. Her head was spinning, but through the chaos she could already see the terrifying truth. 'But she didn't, did she?' she whispered. 'You did.'

Galina's eyes widened and deep down inside Rhiannon felt sick. The horror of the lie was so great that even though she'd guessed it she still couldn't make herself believe it. The pain, the fear, the torment, the unbelievable guilt that both Max and his daughter had suffered, because of this woman's staggering ability to manipulate, to grab everything she wanted for herself ...

'How?' she said. 'I thought you were in Los Angeles when it happened ...'

'I was,' Galina answered. 'And I wasn't. I mean, I was in LA in the morning, then I decided, on the spur of the moment, to fly over to New York and surprise Max. I did that sometimes, just turned up without warning.' She grinned. 'Carolyn hated it. Anyway, I got there some time around seven. No one heard me come in, it would have been difficult when they were making so much noise. God, were they making a noise. Yelling and screaming at each other like they were going to tear each other to pieces. I don't think I've ever heard a mother and daughter fight like that. You'd never believe a seven-year-old could hold her own so well, but of course, she's Max's daughter and she was fighting for someone she loved – and that someone was me. Max was trying to break it up, but Carolyn just went right on screaming at Marina, telling her she had to stay away from me, that she was going to stop me coming to the house, that I was a selfish, crazy bitch and that Max was going to have to choose between her and me ... The woman was hysterical. So was Marina. She told her mother she hated her. She accused her of always taking away the things she loved, but she wasn't going to let her take me away. She said she was going to leave with me, that she would never come back ... She even hit her mother, banging her little fists into Carolyn and telling her she wished she were dead. Max grabbed her away and carried her into the bathroom to try and calm her down. God, she was in a state. So was Carolyn. I thought about going in to try and break it up myself at one point, but obviously I would only have made it worse. So I went to my room and waited for the dust to settle.

'Obviously things were much more serious than I'd realized. I always knew Carolyn hated me and was jealous of me, but hearing her say it, hearing her throw the ultimatum at Max, telling him he had to choose between me and her when Marina was so distressed ... Well, I knew there was every chance Max would take Carolyn's side. No matter how responsible he felt for me, Marina was his daughter and Carolyn was Marina's mother. Meaning that no matter what his feelings were for the rest of us, there was never any question that Marina would come first. And Marina was Carolyn's flesh and blood. The trouble was, I didn't have anywhere else to go. Max and Marina were my life. They were my family. Max would have married me if Carolyn hadn't come along and got herself pregnant; he would have married me and Marina would have been mine. So you see, really, by rights, they *were* mine. They didn't belong to Carolyn. She'd stolen them from me and now she was trying to make Max get rid of me. Well, I couldn't let her do that. I had to defend myself, fight for what was mine, and the only way I could do that was to get rid of her. If I hadn't she'd have won, she'd have ended up taking everything that was mine and I would have had nothing. She left me no choice. So when Max went out a couple of hours later, I waited until Carolyn was asleep, then I went to her room, took the gun from her bedside drawer and shot her through the head.'

Rhiannon was staring at her, frozen in the horror of what she was hearing. There was no emotion attached to it, no recognition that what she had done might have been in any way wrong.

'What about Marina?' Rhiannon said. 'How did you ... ?' She stopped, unable to make herself put into words the hideousness of what she was about to say.

Galina shrugged. 'That was easy,' she said. 'I just took the gun into Marina's bedroom, put it into her hands while she was asleep and left it there. The only problem was, she woke up. But she was so sleepy: the fight with her mother had exhausted her. I spoke to her for a while. I explained everything to her, how I had seen what she did to her mother, that Carolyn had deserved it and that everything would be all right. I told her she was too young to go to prison and that Daddy and I would still love her, it wouldn't make any difference. I explained that I wasn't really in New York, that I was in LA, but like an angel I was talking to her in a dream, because I knew what she had done and I wanted her to know that it would be all right. Then I made her promise that she would never tell anyone I could speak to her in her sleep that way, that it would be our secret, just us two. And she never did tell, or maybe she was so sleepy she just didn't remember. Who knows? All I know is that when Max came back and found Carolyn shot through the head and the gun in Marina's bed he did the craziest thing you could think of and wiped the gun clean of Marina's prints and smothered it in his own. Then he called the police.'

Rhiannon's heart was aching as she tried to imagine the horror and desperation that had driven him to try and protect his daughter by taking the blame upon himself. 'And what about you?' she said. 'I thought there were records to say you were in LA.'

'There are. Because I was. I took the next flight back, got myself over to Venice and found a couple of guys in a night-club there who enjoyed the same kind of sport as I enjoy. I was hospitalized at two in the morning, got myself twenty-three stitches and no one ever thought to check the airlines, or what time I had wandered into the night-club. Someone did think to ask the concierge in my building if he'd seen me that day, though, and he said he had. I don't know why he said that, I guess he just thought he did.'

Rhiannon put a hand to her head. It was all so horrible and crazy and tragically irreversible that she didn't know what to say. All she could think about was Max and how terrible this must all have been for him. 'So why were the charges dropped against Max?' she said finally.

'Because I went to see Judge Zamokhov,' Galina answered, 'and told him it was Marina who had killed Carolyn. The judge was an old friend of Max's grandfather. I knew he'd listen to me and I knew he'd understand why Max had done what he had, you know, to protect his little girl. So the judge spoke in the right people's ears and the charges', she flicked her fingers, 'simply vanished.' She laughed. 'Max was furious when he found out. He didn't want anyone to know about Marina, not even someone like the judge. But then I made him realize that if I hadn't spoken out he'd have ended up in prison, or worse, and what good would he be to Marina then? So you see, it all worked out perfectly in the end.'

Rhiannon's breathing was shallow. She was so stunned by what she was hearing she could hardly make herself believe it. There was still no real emotion in Galina's voice, no remorse or guilt, just a benign matter-of-factness that she had achieved exactly what she'd set out to achieve – and that it had all been so simple that it was very probably preordained.

'So how did Max find out the truth?' Rhiannon said after a while.

Galina's head went to one side. 'How do you think?' she said. 'Marina told him. It seems she did remember me talking to her that night after all. She also remembers making the promise never to tell. And she kept that promise all this time. She never even discussed it with me. Remarkable, don't you think? Admirable, even. But then, children are the best keepers of secrets, providing you tell them in the right way.' Her eyes were shining with a sly kind of humour. 'I could always make you keep a secret,' she said.

Rhiannon looked at her and for the first time in years she felt the strange hypnotic kind of power that Galina had had over her as a child starting to steal back into her heart. But she wasn't going to let it happen. She was an adult now and those terrible confidences she had kept as a child were going to remain buried for ever. It would serve no purpose to remember them now, nor would allowing herself to recall how, just a few short months ago, Galina had managed to persuade her to get into a bath-tub, as if she had still been thirteen years old.

Galina smiled. 'I expect you're wondering what made Marina break her promise, aren't you?' she said. 'I know I would be, if I were you.' Her eyes narrowed and she laughed again. 'It was you,' she said. 'You were the one who forced her to reveal our secret, because you were the one who was threatening to take my place in her daddy's life.' She chuckled and shook her head as though marvelling at the way things had turned out. 'Obviously, in that funny little mind of hers, she'd managed to work a lot of things out, like the fact that it wasn't her who had killed her mommy. That it was me, because I'd been there that night and had made her promise never to tell. She's bright, she could work those kind of things out; her problem was she didn't know what to do about it. So, I guess like most kids, she tried to pretend it wasn't happening, that it would all go away providing she didn't think about it. But then you came along and she got scared. She thought that if her daddy chose you and not me, I'd end up doing the same to you as I had to her mommy and try to make her take the blame for that too.'

Rhiannon's heart churned to think of such pain and fear in a little girl's heart. God only knew what damage it had done, or how much, in the years to come, she would suffer for all this. Her eyes moved back to Galina. There was nothing she could say, no words to express what she was feeling inside. She had always known that Galina would go to almost any lengths to get what she wanted, but that she could have done this to an innocent child, a child who had loved and trusted her so much, a child whom she claimed to love too, was an act of such despicable cruelty that it went beyond any words Rhiannon could find.

'I know what you're thinking,' Galina said.

Rhiannon waited.

'You're thinking that I should be forced to own up to what I did. That's what Max said. He wants me to confess and get help. He won't stand by me, though. He told me that. He said he doesn't want me in his life any more. He says we're through, that he never wants to see me again.' She swallowed hard, then forced a laugh through it. 'I suppose he thinks that'll leave the way clear for you,' she said.

Smiling, she pushed herself away from the chest and walked back across the room. 'He's wrong about that though,' she said, her face only inches from Rhiannon's as she passed, 'because it's not going to happen.'

Rhiannon's heart was starting to pound. Her eyes were drawn to where the wig lay tangled on the floor, then a sharp fear stabbed at her heart as the missing gun suddenly flashed in her mind again. Her eyes flew back to Galina and the smile on Galina's lips turned her blood to ice.

They continued to look at each other, their eyes seeming to fence in the darkness as Galina's gleamed a challenge that in the end Rhiannon was forced to meet.

'You're not sick,' Rhiannon whispered. 'All those stories you told about being disturbed by your grandmother, about taking on the guilt yourself, feeling that you have to suffer the way she suffered ... They're just an excuse, aren't they? You do what you do because you enjoy it.'

Galina's smile widened.

Rhiannon watched her, feeling the disgust sink right into her soul. 'And Maurice,' she said, 'Maurice finds the men for you.'

Galina's eyebrows lifted as her jaw went to one side. She didn't admit it, but she didn't have to – Rhiannon knew it was the truth.

'No, you're not sick,' Rhiannon said, 'at least not in the way you want everyone to believe. You're worse, much worse.' Her lips were tight with revulsion. 'I'd never have believed that anyone could fool Max,' she said, 'but you managed it, didn't you? God, how you managed it. You turned yourself into a victim, knowing that was the surest way to get to him. You knew how much he cared about what happened to his family, to your family, to all the people who suffered during those terrible years and the lasting effects on the generations that have followed. You knew that and you used it, twisted it, exploited it ...' Her eyes closed as her heart flooded with pain. 'And what you did to his daughter ...' she whispered. 'Dear God, Galina, your manipulation, your selfishness ...' She stopped and took a breath. 'I just thank God they've ended up costing you so much. But however much, it'll never be enough to make up for what you've done to Marina.'

Galina laughed and Rhiannon looked at her in mute disgust.

'Where's the gun?' Rhiannon asked.

Galina seemed surprised, then impressed.

'It's in here somewhere,' Rhiannon said.

Galina's expression turned to one of delight. 'How do you know that?' she said.

'It would be the only way you could force me to put that rope around my neck,' Rhiannon answered.

Galina wrinkled her nose, as if trying to make up her mind what her next move in the game should be. 'You know, I lied about the rope,' she said in the end. 'I let you think it was for you, but it's not. It's for me.'

Rhiannon's eyes widened as her heart slowed on the terrible realization of what Galina was intending. It was strange how easily she could read her now, when she'd never been able to before. Everything was planned out and as though Galina had explained it all in words Rhiannon could see how very simple it was. She was going to kill them both.

Rhiannon started to speak, then stopped. Galina was reaching into the shadows behind her, her eyes still fixed on Rhiannon's.

As she brought the gun out Galina's eyes were shining with humour. The single barrel was pointing at the ceiling, the butt plate was resting in the crook of her arm, her fingers circled the trigger guard.

Rhiannon's heart was thudding like a fist. Her chest was on fire, a blinding panic swept through her head. Galina moved towards her, edging her back around the bed, pushing her away from the door.

'You know, I wasn't sure I would do this,' Galina said, a faint echo of surprise in her voice. 'When I stole it, I didn't know if I would use it.'

Rhiannon's eyes widened in horror as the barrel of the rifle came down to her face. She was only three feet away, there was no chance of Galina missing and no way she could get to the door. Strange colours clouded her eyes. She tried to speak, but her voice wouldn't come. A thousand images crowded her mind. Carolyn dead. Marina with the gun. Galina whispering to a child. Max holding the gun. Galina's finger hooking the trigger. Rhiannon's heart pounded through her ears, deafening her, swallowing her into a void of terror. Her throat closed over. She was against the wall. She couldn't move. There was nowhere to go.

Then suddenly Galina's eyes dropped to the gun and without thinking Rhiannon lunged. Galina screamed. Her finger tightened on the trigger and the gun exploded. Rhiannon flew back against the wall as Galina was thrown into the chair. The gun clattered to the floor and the dying echoes of the explosion reverberated around the room.

Long minutes ticked by; the ceaseless chorus outside continued. The room remained deathly still.

The only sound Galina could hear was that of her own heart as she struggled to her feet and crept to the edge of the bed. For a moment she was confused as she realized she could see the outside – there was a hole in the wall as big as her fist. Then she looked down at Rhiannon.

Rhiannon's body lay sprawled on the floor; the nightstand was on top of her, broken glass and sodden books all around her and the dark mass of her blood was staining the wall.

Galina knelt down beside her and lifting the nightstand out of the way, pulled the hair from Rhiannon's face. She fumbled for a pulse, pressing her fingers to Rhiannon's neck, searching her wrist. Then noticing the blood pooling on the floor beneath her, she let her go and stood up.

Somewhere in the distance she could hear a telephone

ringing. The sounds of the wild drowned it as the beckoning cry of hyenas spiralled through her heart. She looked down at Rhiannon's tangled, lifeless body. Then lifting her head, she looked around as though she might find someone standing in the shadows. She smiled vaguely to herself, then going to the door, she put out her hand and turned the key.

Still dazed with shock and tiredness, Lizzy was finding it hard to come to terms with what had happened through the night. She shuddered to think how long Rhiannon might have lain there had Max not called when he had, for the sound of a single gunshot in the bush at night might only have alerted them to poachers, or to a guard heading off an intruder. Certainly none of them would have thought of Rhiannon, because none of them had known that Galina was in the camp, and even if they had, they would never have dreamt that the gunshot had meant what it had.

Andy was already yelling for Doug even before he'd put the phone down on Max. Ordering Lizzy to stay where she was, he and Doug had raced through the camp to find Rhiannon lying in a pool of her own blood and an empty noose hanging over the bed. What had looked like blood spattering the wall behind Rhiannon had turned out to be the contents of the decanter, and finding a faint flicker of a pulse in her wrist, Andy had carried her swiftly back to the house, while Doug and Elmore had gone in search of Galina.

By then the other guests were coming out of their chalets, wanting to know what all the fuss was about. One of the rangers tried to calm them, while Andy bathed and stitched the gash in Rhiannon's head that had knocked her unconscious and Lizzy worked on stemming the flow of blood from the bullet wound that had mercifully and miraculously only grazed her shoulder. If it had entered her body there was no way in the world she'd be alive now, for the bullets in those guns were designed to stop elephants.

Doug and Elmore had returned in the early hours with Galina. Whether she had been attempting to escape, or whether it had been some grotesque kind of suicide mission, Lizzy guessed none of them would ever know. All they did know was that of all the beasts that could have killed her, it was a snake that had in the end claimed her.

Now Lizzy was sitting with Rhiannon, watching her as she slept. God only knew what kind of nightmare she'd been through in the lead-up to what had happened, and Lizzy could only feel relieved that Max was on his way, for probably only he could deal with this now.

Hearing a landrover pull up outside, she let herself quietly out of the room and went to see who it was.

'How is she?' Andy asked, climbing down from the jeep, his unshaven face gaunt with fatigue.

'OK, I think,' Lizzy answered. 'Why don't you come inside now and let me make you a drink?'

'How are you?' he said, putting a hand on her belly as they walked into the house.

'I'm fine,' she answered. 'Don't worry about me.'

'But I do,' he said softly.

Lizzy smiled and turned into his arms. 'What's all this going to mean?' she asked.

He stared past her for a while, his eyes focusing on nothing in the paint-splattered decorator's yard of a kitchen. Then slowly he started to shake his head. 'I don't know,' he answered. 'It could be that the publicity will draw in more people than we can handle, but it's the kind of people that bothers me.'

Lizzy lifted her head and looked into his eyes. 'Where's Galina now?' she asked.

'In Rhiannon's chalet. There's a guard on the door to stop all those fucking ghouls out there trying to get one for the album.'

Putting a hand on his cheek, Lizzy turned him to look at her and as his eyes rested on hers he gave a rueful smile.

'Sorry,' he said, dropping his forehead against hers. 'I know getting mad about it isn't going to help.'

'Did you speak to Max again?' Lizzy said.

He nodded. 'He should be here any time.'

Rhiannon was looking up at Max's face, tracing every line, every crease and shadow and feeling her heart stir under the weight of love. His dark, penetrating eyes, with their thick black lashes, were watching her; his brows, his long aristocratic nose, his wide pale-lipped mouth and his unshaven jaw all showed signs of the stress he was under. He smiled and trying to smile too, she said, 'They told me you'd be here when I woke up.'

'Did you believe them?' he whispered.

'I don't know. I think I only came round for a few minutes.'

'You did,' he confirmed. His eyes moved anxiously over her face. 'How do you feel?' he asked.

She considered it for a moment. 'OK, I think. My head aches, my shoulder's numb, but OK.' She paused and feeling her heart contract, she said, 'Galina told me about Marina.'

He swallowed hard, then nodded. 'She's going to be fine,' he said. 'We've got some work to do, but we'll get there.' His eyes closed and he took a moment before speaking again. 'I never wanted to believe she did it,' he said, 'but the evidence was there ... When I got back that night ... I saw the gun. I heard the things she'd said to her mother, but I still didn't want to believe she did it. So I didn't let myself believe. We never discussed it. I just told her it would be all right and then I did what I thought, what seemed like the only thing I could do.' Sighing, he shook his head. 'You make a lot of mistakes at a time like that,' he said. 'The shock ... You just can't think straight. She was so young ... I couldn't let her go through it. So I made a decision and by the time I realized ... it was too late to turn back.' He smiled grimly. 'If you knew the things I've been thinking all this time,' he went on. 'I knew I'd handled it all wrong, but I didn't know what to do to put it right. I was scared out of my mind that maybe she'd had some kind of black-out, something that might come over her again. I didn't want anyone to know what she'd done, I didn't want her to go through that. But then I didn't know if Aleks was safe ... Christ, I didn't know if any of us was ...' He shook his head and his face darkened with anger. 'I should have listened to Carolyn. She tried to warn me, I should ...'

'Sssh,' Rhiannon said, putting a finger over his lips. 'Blaming yourself isn't going to change anything now. We have to look forward and find the best way to repair it. Marina loves you, and you and your love is all she needs to get her through this.' She paused for a moment, then said, 'How do you think she'll take what's happened to Galina?'

Max shook his head. 'I don't know,' he answered. 'She's pretty much cut herself off from Galina lately, but there's no knowing how this is going to affect her.' His eyes were concentrated on hers as though somehow, through her, he could find the answers. It was odd, he was thinking to himself, how never before in his adult life had he felt the need to share so much of himself, or to trust and to love as he did now.

'Did you know about the violence?' Rhiannon asked. 'How Galina used her grandmother as an excuse and a way to make you feel sorry for her?'

'Yes, I knew,' he answered, 'but it was a lie we'd all lived with so long that I guess it just felt like the truth. There are plenty of people around like her, who get pleasure out of pain, I just wanted to make sure she didn't go too far. Which she did a couple of times, but on the whole it never got too out of hand. And Maurice? Well, Maurice just saw it as another way of complicating my life, so he took it. They both knew about Marina ...' His breath caught and he moved his eyes back to Rhiannon's.

Rhiannon smiled. 'There was nothing to know,' she reminded him.

He smiled too and the relief in his eyes turned Rhiannon's heart over.

'So are you saying that Galina *was* blackmailing you?' she said.

He shook his head. 'No. I made sure it never came to that. It wasn't something I wanted to live with, so I made it clear before I married her that if she ever made a single threat of blackmail she'd be out of my life faster than she could pack her bags.'

Rhiannon was shaking her head. 'Then I don't understand why you married her?' she said.

He smiled. 'Neither do I, now,' he said. 'But I guess there were a lot of reasons. Like, it was what Marina and Aleks wanted; it was something my grandfather and her grandmother had always worked towards, something that just seemed to be in the natural order of things. And', he shrugged, 'I really did care about her. Despite everything I knew about her, the violence and the lies, I cared about her. She was on her own. She didn't have anyone else and she'd been a part of my life for almost as long as I could remember. This is sounding like it was something I really thought about, but it wasn't. She was there, the kids were there and it just seemed like the natural thing to do. And by the time you came into my life things had gone too far to turn back. All the arrangements were made, the kids were happy, Galina was happy ... I just didn't see that I could pull out.'

Rhiannon's eyes were locked to his as he gazed down at her and brushed his fingers over her cheek. 'Lie down with me,' she whispered. 'I want to feel you next to me.'

They lay together for a long time, talking about everything that had happened and holding each other, until hearing a landrover rev up outside, Rhiannon glanced over to the window. 'I wonder what's happening out there?' she said.

'I guess I'd better go find out,' he said. 'Get some more sleep, I'll be back in a while.'

As Max walked outside Ellis and Ramon were coming across the camp towards him.

'The coroner, or whatever they call him in these parts, is still with her,' Ellis said. 'She'll be taken over to the plane when he's finished. The cops want to speak to you.'

Max's eyes moved to the direction of the chalet where Galina's body was undergoing a preliminary autopsy. Then, as Andy came to join them, he said, 'I won't be giving any statements to the press, so what you say, how you handle this, is up to you. My guess is the biggest headache, initially anyway, is going to be dealing with the sightseers when they get to hear that this is where Galina Casimir lost her life.'

'We can handle that,' Andy told him. 'What I need to know is whether it's going down as an accident or a suicide.'

Max sighed, as the implications of both crowded his mind. 'Could you live with an accident?' he asked. 'Would it hurt the camp?'

'Probably more than a suicide would,' Andy answered frankly.

'Then I'll talk to the coroner.'

'When do you want to leave?' Ellis asked.

Max turned to look at him. 'As soon as we can,' he answered. 'Before tonight.'

Ellis's surprise showed. 'What about Rhiannon?' he asked. 'Is she OK to travel?'

'Rhiannon's not coming,' Max answered.

*

When he returned to the house, after speaking to the police, Rhiannon was lying just as she had been when he'd left her, her pale, tired face looking up at him from the pillows.

'Hi, how are you feeling now?' he asked, sitting down beside her and lifting her hands into his.

'I slept for a while,' she answered. 'I'm more worried about you, though. You should be with Marina.'

He nodded. Then lowering his mouth to hers, he kissed her gently. 'We'll get through this,' he whispered. 'You know that, don't you? It's just going to take a while.'

'I can wait,' she answered.

'We'll stay in touch,' he said, 'but let's try not to let the press get ahold of it.'

She gave a splutter of laughter. 'But the whole world knows about us, Max,' she protested.

'And very soon the whole world is going to know that Galina died here, at Perlatonga, with only you and your closest friends to say that it happened the way it did.'

'And a coroner,' Rhiannon reminded him.

Max's smile was sardonic. 'It won't be the first time I'll have been accused of paying someone off,' he stated.

Rhiannon's face paled. 'Oh God, I hadn't thought of it like that,' she murmured.

'It might not happen that way,' he said. 'I just want you to be prepared in case it does. Besides, I've got to think of Marina. She already knows you're in my life, but she's going to need some time adjusting to everything else, before she can take on something as important as a new mom.'

Rhiannon's eyes widened. 'Was that a proposal?' she said.

He smiled and kissed her again. 'Not yet,' he said. 'We've still got a way to go before we get there.'

'But we will get there?' she prompted, feeling

suddenly more nervous than she'd care to admit.

'We'll get there,' he promised. 'But I want you to get on with your life, and don't put anything on hold for me, because I don't have any idea how long all this is going to take.'

Chapter 29

It was seven months later, almost a year to the day that Max and Rhiannon had first met, that Rhiannon was getting ready to launch the *In Focus* series and Lizzy, a ten-week-old baby boy sleeping in a crib at her side, was helping to send out invitations to the screening. Not realizing what he was setting himself up for, Andy had grumbled continuously throughout the morning about how bored he was stuffing envelopes, so had now been dragged off to the Tower of London by Sharon to get himself 'inspired, fired and altogether wired'. His face upon departure had kept Rhiannon and Lizzy chuckling for hours after.

On the floor below the *In Focus* office the *Check It Out* team were preparing for a new season of programmes with Rhys Callaghan as their producer and Fergus McCavey, a zany, stupendously knowledgeable and quirkily good-looking Oxford drop-out, as their presenter. Morgan and Sally Simpson had returned to early retirement only days after Mervyn Mansfield had been axed as commissioning editor back in May, and Austin Wicklow, an unknown entity from a northern independent channel, had been appointed in Mansfield's place. Wicklow had had no problem at all in accepting Rhiannon as executive producer of *Check It Out*, nor with commissioning her new series, *In Focus*.

Though Rhiannon was maintaining overall control of

both programmes, Lucy had taken charge of *In Focus* on a day-to-day basis, while Rhys Callaghan was doing the same for *Check It Out*. Rhiannon's office, for the time being, was in the new suite they had taken over for the *In Focus* series, but having so many more projects in the developing stages now, she was operating more and more from home so as not to interfere with, or indeed be sidetracked by, the work going on around her.

Today, however, they were all in the office as Austin Wicklow had contacted Rhiannon yesterday to inform her that he wanted the first episode of *In Focus* to be ready for transmission at the end of September, rather than the third week of November. As luck would have it, the first programme needed only to be dubbed, but it had left them with next to no time to organize promotions, publicity, screenings and all the other hundred and one things that had to be done before the launch of a new series. Added to that was the problem of getting the follow-up episodes in the can ready for their transmissions, though Lucy was on it and Sharon was all set to begin shooting six days a week for the next five weeks – starting tomorrow.

Lizzy and Andy were in London visiting Lizzy's family and showing off Dominic – or Nick, as Andy preferred to call him. It was easy enough for them to extend their stay, with Doug running things back at Perlatonga, so they would definitely be there for the launch. But with such short notice to all the reviewers and diarists Rhiannon was feeling anxious about how many would be able to make it.

'Are you kidding? No one's going to miss this launch,' Lizzy cried. 'Not only is it a new Rhiannon Edwardes brainchild, it's the official début of the nation's favourite whacko.'

Laughing, Rhiannon said, 'Does Sharon know that's what you call her?' she said.

'I expect so,' Lizzy answered. 'Did you see her on the

Late Show last night, by the way? She was hysterical.'

'Wasn't she?' Rhiannon chuckled, frowning as she tried to recognize the name on the envelope she'd just sealed. 'And guess what, she's in *Hello* next week, *chez-elle* at her new warehouse in Wapping. I didn't have the heart to tell her that warehouses were a bit passé these days, she's so proud of it.'

Lizzy was laughing. 'And what about you? What features are they running on you?'

'Nothing on me,' Rhiannon answered. 'I've turned it all down.'

'But you're your own best publicity,' Lizzy protested.

'I've seen enough of myself in the papers for one lifetime,' Rhiannon responded. 'You weren't here six months ago when it was all going on. It was hell, let me tell you, and I have no desire to court that sort of attention again.'

'It's hardly the same,' Lizzy objected. 'This is the launch of a new programme – that was ...' She screwed up her nose. 'What would you call that?' she said.

'As near as you can get to an accusation of murder without it actually being one,' Rhiannon provided, glancing up as an explosion of laughter erupted in the researcher's office outside. 'Plus harassment in its grossest form. No, I'll consider doing a couple of interviews on the night, but other than that, my doors are very firmly closed.'

Lizzy sucked in her bottom lip and looked as though she was going to say more, but instead leaned over to check on Nick. 'What about Max?' she said casually. 'Are you going to invite him to the launch?'

Despite the way Rhiannon's heart fluttered she laughed. 'Are you kidding?' she said. 'I mean I'd love to, but he'd never come to something like that, not with all those journos around.'

'Have you asked him?'

'No, of course I haven't.'

Their eyes met across the leather-topped desk and knowing exactly what was going on in Lizzy's mind, Rhiannon said, 'This isn't something you can push, Lizzy. Marina's got to come first and ...'

'I'm not suggesting you push it,' Lizzy interrupted. 'I'm just suggesting you invite him. That's all.'

Rhiannon sighed and pursing her lips, started to shake her head. 'If I could, I would,' she said. 'But he hasn't called me in over two weeks.' She looked at Lizzy, knowing that to no one else in the world would she show how worried she was about that.

'Have you tried calling him?' Lizzy said.

'Of course I have. He's never there and he hasn't returned any of my messages either.'

Lizzy frowned as she thought. 'How are things going with Marina?' she asked. 'Does he ever talk about it?'

Rhiannon nodded. 'Yes, we talk about it quite a bit and I'd say from what he tells me that she's coming along just fine. She talks quite openly with the counsellors about what happened now, she doesn't appear to be blocking anything, but she still gets upset and afraid and the visit to the house in New York, you know, where it all happened, was pretty traumatic from what he told me.'

'I should think it was,' Lizzy commented. 'When did that happen?'

'A couple of months ago. Max was really nervous about it. Right up to the last minute he was going to call it off, but then, I don't know, something must have persuaded him it was the right thing to do, so they went. She was OK while they were there, he said, it was after that it really seemed to hit her.'

Lizzy inhaled deeply. 'I guess she has to go through it, though, in order to come out the other side. How was she the last time you spoke to him?'

'Calmer, he said. She'd had a good report at school, which he was particularly pleased about.'

'But no news since?'

'Not from him. Ula says things are improving all the time – which they must be for Max to be away as much as he is.' She shook her head. 'I just don't understand the silence,' she said. 'It doesn't make any sense.' Then closing her eyes tightly, she pressed her fingers into the sockets and said, 'Tell me, how did I manage to fall in love with a man who lives an entire ocean and continent away, whose life is as complicated as a medieval mystery and as deeply entrenched in the United States as mine is in England? And while you're at it, perhaps you wouldn't mind telling me how the hell we're going to resolve it? I mean, who's going to give up what? Or maybe we're destined to live apart for the rest of our lives, with just the occasional telephone call and postcard to keep it all going. Or maybe he's realized how impossible it all is and he's working on breaking us up gently.' She gave a short, angry laugh. 'Breaking us up,' she said, 'that's a joke when I haven't even seen him since March.'

'Mmm,' Lizzy remarked. 'Do you hear that, you little fiend?' she said looking at her son whose wide blue eyes were staring up at her. 'She hasn't seen him since March. He hasn't called her in two weeks and she thinks it's probably all over. You're a man, you tell us, is she drawing the right conclusion?'

In reply, Nick emitted a prize-winning burp and waved his arms about in prideful joy.

'Just like his father,' Lizzy commented, scooping him up and starting to unbutton her shirt.

With her chin resting on her hand Rhiannon watched as Lizzy fed a hugely distended nipple into his mouth. 'Does it hurt?' she said.

'What, this?' Lizzy said in surprise. 'Not really.'

'What about the birth?'

Lizzy's eyebrows rose in a manner Rhiannon knew so well that she burst out laughing. God, how she missed those looks!

'Was Andy there?' she asked.

'Was he there?' Lizzy echoed. 'He was on the bed with me screaming for God. Of course, it could have had something to do with the fact that I was squeezing his balls at the time. I mean, if I was going through it I didn't see why he shouldn't too.'

Laughing, Rhiannon watched the baby for a while longer, then leaning back in her chair, she said, 'You know, I was just thinking the other day that if Max and I do make it, if by some miracle we manage to work out a way of being together, then how are we going to bring the children to you and Andy for holidays when Perlatonga has all the associations it has now?'

Lizzy looked at her in exasperation. 'Rhiannon, why don't you try worrying about traffic jams in time-travel?' she suggested.

Rhiannon screwed up her nose in confusion.

'Why are you giving yourself a hard time over that now,' Lizzy said, 'when you've got a whole stack of other things to sort out between you before you even get close to dealing with that?'

Rhiannon grimaced. 'You're right,' she said. A few seconds ticked by. 'Do I remember you telling me you destroyed the chalet?' she said.

Lizzy nodded. 'Yes, we did,' she answered.

'Do you still have people coming just to see where it all happened?' Rhiannon asked.

'Not so often now, thank God. Anyway, let's get off this subject shall we? I want to hear about George.'

Rhiannon blinked. 'George? My father, George?' she responded. 'I'm afraid Sharon's the one you'll have to ask about George. All I know is the bimbo's gone, he's sold his milk round and he's starting back to school the week after next.'

Lizzy's eyes rounded. 'Are you serious?' she laughed. 'I didn't know about the school bit. What's he studying?'

'Egyptology. The man doesn't know a pyramid from a pint of gold top, but apparently he wants to find out. What's more, he and Sharon have booked themselves on a cruise down the Nile for some time next spring. *And* they want me to go with them.'

'With Sharon and George!' Lizzy cried. 'Oh go, Rhiannon. Please, please go. It's the only way we'll get to find out what they're like together.'

'You go,' Rhiannon retorted.

'Believe me, if I could I would,' Lizzy vowed. 'So now, remind me what happened to Moira and the kids.'

'Moira and the kids are living with a twenty-year-old disc-jockey from Bedminster Down,' Rhiannon answered. 'That's how this whole thing got started between George and Sharon. He rang me up when Moira left him – the first time he'd spoken to me in months, I might add – and he still hasn't forgiven me for getting myself in the papers again, because of course I do it deliberately to annoy him! Anyway, he rang me up in a dreadful state, so I went down to see him. Sharon happened to call me while I was there, he answered, the two of them got talking and the next thing you know Sharon the Samaritan was in her little pope-mobile beetling down the M4 to the rescue.'

'Oh God, this is wonderful!' Lizzy gasped, holding her sides laughing. 'So how often do you see George these days?'

'Much too often,' Rhiannon responded. 'Just thank God I don't have a second bedroom or I swear he'd move in. Sharon, of course, has suggested that we all move into her place. Can you imagine it, me living with those two? And *he*, traitor and fraud that he is, thinks it's a good idea, because I obviously need keeping an eye on so I don't get up to any more daft business that'll get me face in the papers.'

Rhiannon could give such a perfect imitation of her father's West Country accent that Lizzy was breathless with laughter. 'What did he say about the last time?' she asked. 'You know, about Max and everything?' She braced herself. 'It's going to be priceless, I know it.'

Rhiannon laughed. 'Actually you're wrong, because it was so obviously beyond his milkman's rhetoric that it rendered him speechless. Which is a let-down to you, I know, but was a God-sent mercy to me.'

'Is he coming to the launch?'

Rhiannon shuddered. 'I'm not thinking about it,' she answered. 'Sharon invited him and I can hardly turn round and say no, can I? After all, he is my father. And I just know that this is God's way of punishing me for all my sins, because the man will do something to show me up, he always does. But I'm not thinking about it, because however bad I imagine it to be, it's bound to turn out a thousand times worse.'

Six days later Max was walking into his office in New York, having just left a Group Planning Meeting where he'd spent most of the morning. Sitting at his desk, he quickly checked through his E-mail, dealt with a couple of things that couldn't wait, then doing a swift calculation of the time difference, he picked up the phone to call Rhiannon. It would be seven thirty in London, so there was a chance she might have left the office by now, which as it turned out she had, so ringing off he dialled the number of her apartment. She answered on the fourth ring.

'Hi,' he said, sitting back in his chair and propping his feet on the desk.

'Max?'

'Were you expecting someone else?' he smiled.

'No. But I was expecting you three weeks ago. Did you get my messages?'

'Sure I did.'

'So why didn't you call back?'

'Well, I've been kind of busy and ...' He paused,

'Well, I've been working on something that's kept me pretty tied up these past few weeks.'

There were several beats of silence before she said, 'Then please don't untie yourself for me,' and the line went dead.

At the other end Rhiannon was shaking with anger. He'd call back, she knew that, but she was damned if she was going to answer just because it suited him to speak to her now. Tied up, indeed! She'd show him tied up and wrenching the phone line out of the wall, she went to run herself a bath.

She was just about to start undressing when she realized that with the line disconnected she wouldn't have the satisfaction of knowing he was trying to get through. So, padding back through to the sitting-room, she replugged the phone and switched on the answering machine.

It was eleven o'clock by the time he finally called back and because he'd made her wait so long, she stubbornly refused to pick up as she sat, pressed into a corner of the sofa, listening to his message.

'Hi,' he said, 'I guess you're probably there, but you're too mad at me to pick up right now. I don't blame you, but I'll explain everything when I see you. I just wanted to say that I've heard the launch of your programme's been brought forward, that you're doing it on Thursday and well, I was wondering if there was an invitation going spare ...'

Rhiannon snatched up the phone. 'Would you say that again?' she said. 'That last bit. I'm not sure I heard right.'

'Sure,' he said, the smile audible in his voice. 'I was asking if I could come to the party.'

Rhiannon's disbelief was fluttering in her heart. 'You mean here, in London?' she said.

'Well, that is where it's happening, isn't it?' he said,

sounding confused.

'Yes, that's where it's happening,' she confirmed, still not entirely sure she believed this.

'I can be there by Thursday afternoon,' he said. 'I know it's going to be a busy time for you, but can you meet me at the flat?'

'I can meet you at the airport if you like,' she offered, thinking what an insufferable push-over she was and not really caring.

'No, it's OK. I've got some business to see to beforehand. I should be able to get to the flat around four, though. How does that suit?'

'I'll be here,' she said. 'But Max, you do realize that the party is going to be full of reporters, don't you?'

'I sure hope it is,' he responded. 'It's not going to be much of a launch if it's not.'

'Max!' she cried. 'What aren't you telling me?'

'That I love you?' he guessed. 'Yeah, I should have told you that before. I love you, Rhiannon. I'm goddamned crazy about you and I've missed you more than I'll ever be able to tell you ... How about I save the rest until I see you?'

Rhiannon was laughing. 'I don't know what to say,' she told him. 'I haven't seen you in seven months, I don't hear from you for three weeks and now suddenly you're going to be here.'

'You could always tell me you love me too,' he said.

'You know I do.'

'It's still good to hear.'

'OK, I love you,' she said. 'And I miss you too.' She paused. 'Especially right now.'

She heard him chuckle and felt an answering heat starting to spread right the way through her. 'Are you in the office?' she asked.

'Yes, but the door's closed.'

She hesitated, strangely embarrassed to go on. 'Shall we save it for Thursday?' she said.

'OK,' he answered, his voice as intimate as the desire pulsing between them. 'Will you do me a favour?' he said.

'What's that?'

As he told her she started to laugh. 'If I do that,' she said, 'we'll never get to the party. Or maybe that's the idea.'

He laughed. 'No, we'll be going to the party,' he said. 'There's just a few things we've got to catch up on first.'

He arrived ten minutes early with a bunch of red roses and a bottle of vintage champagne. Rhiannon led him through to the sitting-room, put the flowers in water while he opened the bottle, then touched her glass to his before drinking. She wore nothing except a pair of high-heeled shoes. It was the favour he'd asked for and one she had no problem granting.

They made love for over an hour, unable to get enough of each other, doing everything they could to make up for lost time and by the time they went back for a second glass of champagne Rhiannon felt bruised, almost satiated and very deeply loved.

Laughing at the way she was looking at him, Max cupped her face gently in his hand and brought her reddened and tender mouth back to his. 'You're beautiful,' he told her softly, 'and I don't want to live another minute without you in my life. In fact I don't intend to live another minute without you in my life. We've just got to sort out how we're going to work it.'

Rhiannon's eyebrows went up. 'Why do I get the impression,' she said, sitting down on the sofa and curling her legs under her, 'that you already know the answer to that?' She was wearing a dressing-gown now, knowing that if she didn't they really wouldn't get to the party. His luggage remained in the boot of the car so he was still naked except for the towel wrapped around his waist.

'I wish I did,' he told her, taking a sip of champagne. 'All I know is that things are working out our end. Marina asks about you a lot, she knows I'm here and she's feeling OK about it. But there's only so far you can go asking the permission of a nine-year-old and as far as Marina and I are concerned we reckon I've gone that distance. She understands that I love you and that I want you to be a part of our lives and she says she's willing to give it a go if you are.'

Rhiannon gave a splutter of laughter. 'She said that?' she choked, wiping the spilt champagne from her lips.

'Her words exactly,' he confirmed. 'Were it left to me I'd probably put it a different way.'

Rhiannon thought about that, then eyeing him steadily she issued the challenge. 'Which way would you put it?' she said.

'Well,' he said, 'before I start committing myself here, I want to know what your plans are.'

'Plans?'

He looked at his watch. 'In just over an hour you're going to be launching a new programme,' he reminded her.

Rhiannon leapt up. 'Just over an hour!' she cried.

'And there's *Check It Out* too,' he continued. 'And did I hear something about a new channel?'

Rhiannon gaped at him. 'You know about that?' she gasped. 'How do you know about that?'

He grinned. 'Because I got a call from one of the backers asking me if I thought you were a good risk,' he told her.

Rhiannon was so stunned she couldn't speak. She hadn't told anyone about this, not even Lizzy, for the offer of running her own satellite TV channel had only come two weeks ago and she still didn't quite know what to make of it. Then suddenly her eyebrows came down. 'What did you tell them?' she asked suspiciously.

'I said I thought you were a great risk,' he laughed.

She continued to frown. 'What does that mean, exactly?' she said. 'A great risk.'

'What I said', he told her, 'is that I'd put every cent I owned behind you.'

'And of course the man had read his newspapers and knew you were biased,' she said, her hands on her hips.

'He may have thought that,' Max conceded with a shrug, 'but why ask me if he already knew what I was going to say?'

Rhiannon was still eyeing him warily. 'I'll get back to you on that one,' she said.

'I'll keep the line free,' he told her, 'but if you're thinking I'm anything to do with the consortium that's starting up this channel you're wrong. The first I heard of it was when I got a call from Hans Sverhardt, the Swiss banker who's putting up some of the money.'

Rhiannon's eyes narrowed.

'I swear I've got nothing to do with it,' Max cried, holding up his hands in innocence. 'I just got asked for a reference.'

'It's OK, I believe you,' she said.

'So why are you looking at me that way?'

'Because', she said, sitting on his lap and putting her arms around him, 'I've never met anyone more able to control my career, yet more at pains not to – even though it would make his life a whole lot easier if he did.'

He laughed. 'Ah, but only in the short term,' he said, before kissing her very intimately for a very long time. 'And I want you long term, Rhiannon,' he said. 'Very long term. So the decisions have to be yours as well as mine.'

Rhiannon's eyes were on his and so full of love it made him laugh. 'I was thinking,' she said, looking at his lips, 'there might be a way ...' She stopped, as taking her by the shoulders he pushed her back to take a good clear look at her.

'You've been thinking about us?' he said with a mock

incredulity that she quickly realized wasn't quite so mock. 'Are you telling me you might have a solution as to how we can spend our lives together?'

Rhiannon looked at him, knowing that there was more to this yet not sure what or how.

He laughed. 'I wasn't in touch for a while,' he said, 'because I hoped it would concentrate both our minds on finding a solution. I've come up with one, I just hope to God it's the same as yours.'

Rhiannon started to grin. 'You first,' she said.

He shook his head. 'No, you first. It has to be you, because if I'm wrong about this I don't want to have to own up to everything I've done towards making it happen.'

'Oh God, Max,' she laughed. 'I love you so much.'

'I know that,' he said, holding her off as she tried to hug him. 'Will you just tell me what you want.'

'OK,' she said. 'New York. I want to live in New York.'

His eyes closed and his head fell back against the chair. 'Thank God for that,' he murmured.

'What?' she laughed. 'You knew I was going to say New York?'

'Let's just say I hoped you would,' he confessed.

'You're amazing,' she said, shaking her head and laughing.

'Yeah, I guess so,' he agreed. 'So, you reckon New York will work for you?'

She nodded. 'I don't see why not,' she answered. 'I did as you said, I got on with my life, didn't put anything on hold for you, but I have made myself reasonably dispensable here in London and if I take the satellite job, New York will be an obvious base. Plus, I'd enjoy the challenge. Now, what about you? Will it work for you too?'

'Sure it'll work for me.'

'What about the children?'

'I think it'll work for them too. I've sold the house where everything happened and Marina's been helping get a whole lot of other houses lined up ready for you to look at. That's why I wasn't in touch, because I couldn't trust myself not to tell you and the last thing I wanted was for you to think I was pushing you. So that's why I say thank God you said New York, because I've spent the last three weeks ... I'm going to start repeating myself here and I don't think we've got time for it.'

'I've got all the time in the world for this,' Rhiannon told him happily.

Laughing, he put his fingers under her chin and brought her mouth to his.

'Oh God,' she groaned, her head falling back as he let her go. 'It's all too perfect. Something's going to go wrong. If not today, then next week, next month, next year.'

'That's what I like, a woman who looks on the bright side,' he commented. 'It really works for me, that.'

'I'm serious,' she cried. 'Something *will* go wrong, because something always does.'

'Then we'll work our way through it,' he replied.

'I wish we could just stop the world and stay exactly as we are now,' she sighed.

'But I promised George we'd be at the party,' he said.

Rhiannon's smile fled. 'Who?'

'George. Your father,' he answered.

Rhiannon stared at him in disbelief. 'George? My father?' she repeated.

'Now don't get mad,' he said, already pinning her arms to her sides, 'but you've got to understand, I've never asked anyone to marry me before, which I know sounds strange coming from someone who's been married twice already, but it's a fact. So I thought, as this was the first time, I'd do it the right way. Well, the old-fashioned way is I guess how you'd describe it.'

'Oh God, I don't believe this,' Rhiannon groaned.

'Please tell me this is a nightmare. You've met him, haven't you?'

He nodded and just the look on his face caused Rhiannon's embarrassment to start at her toes. 'I met him just before I came here,' he said.

Rhiannon didn't know whether to laugh or scream. 'Don't keep me in suspense any longer,' she said, steeling herself.

Max's eyes were alive with laughter. 'He took a while to think about it,' he said, 'then he told me that I had his blessing on the proviso that: I didn't run off with another woman a week before the wedding; that I didn't show up with any butt-ugly fiancées the week after the wedding, and that I was prepared to spend my honeymoon night with you and no one else.'

'No, please, tell me he didn't say that,' Rhiannon begged, hiding her face. 'Actually, he's not my father. I found him ...'

'That's what he said,' Max confirmed, cutting her off. 'And there was one other proviso,' he added.

'I don't know if I can bear this,' Rhiannon muttered.

'He wants us to go on a trip down the Nile with him.'

Rhiannon's face was back in her hands. 'Don't tell me you said yes,' she implored. 'Please don't tell me you said yes.'

Max lifted her face. 'Well someone's got to say yes to something,' he said, 'and I haven't heard one from you yet.'

'Yes,' she said instantly. 'Yes to everything. What's the question?'

'The question is ...'

'Shouldn't you be down on one knee?' she interrupted.

'Don't push it,' he warned.

'Can we go back to Paris for this?' she asked.

'Sure we can. What about the party?'

She was on the point of saying that they didn't need

to go, when she realized that if they didn't they were going to miss out on the big entrance she was so looking forward to.

'I can see tomorrow's headlines already,' she whispered to him an hour later as a murmur of surprise spread through the crowd and a panoply of flash bulbs popped all around them, 'Max and Rhiannon Get In Focus.'

'Paris is a great idea,' he responded, making her laugh, and shaking Andy by the hand as Lizzy embraced Rhiannon, he added, 'I think we're in very grave danger of upstaging your show.'

'You haven't met Sharon yet,' Rhiannon told him and winking at Lizzy, she turned her face up to his and laughed as the cameras went wild trying to capture the kiss.

ALSO AVAILABLE IN ARROW

A French Affair

Susan Lewis

When Natalie Moore is killed in a freak accident in France her mother – the very poised and elegant Jessica – knows instinctively there is more to it. However, Natalie's father – the glamorous, high-flying Charlie – is so paralysed by the horror of losing his daughter, that he refuses even to discuss his wife's suspicions.

In the end, when their marriage is rocked by yet another terrible shock, Jessica decides to go back to France alone in search of some answers. When she gets to the idyllic vineyard in the heart of Burgundy she soon finds a great deal more than she was expecting in a love that is totally forbidden and a truth that will almost certainly devastate her life . . .

'One of the best around' *Independent on Sunday*

'Spellbinding! . . . you just keep turning the pages, with the atmosphere growing more and more intense as the story leads to its dramatic climax' *Daily Mail*

arrow books

ALSO AVAILABLE IN ARROW

Just One More Day: A Memoir

Susan Lewis

In 1960s Bristol a family is overshadowed by tragedy . . .

While Susan, a feisty seven-year-old, is busy being brave, her mother, Eddress, is struggling for courage. Though bound by an indestructible love, their journey through a world that is darkening with tragedy is fraught with misunderstandings.

As a mother's greatest fear becomes reality, Eddress tries to deny the truth. And, faced with a wall of adult secrets, Susan creates a world that will never allow her mother to leave.

Set in a world where a fridge is a luxury, cars have starting handles, and where bingo and coupons bring in the little extras, *Just One More Day* is a deeply moving true-life account of how the spectre of death moved into Susan's family, and how hard they all tried to pretend it wasn't there.

'Susan Lewis fans know she can write compelling fiction, but not, until now, that she can write even more engrossing fact. We use the phrase honest truth too lightly: it should be reserved for books – deeply moving books – like this' Alan Coren

arrow books

ALSO AVAILABLE IN ARROW

Wicked Beauty

Susan Lewis

Tim and Rachel Hendon are riding high on an ideal marriage and growing political success. Tim is already in the Cabinet, and as they celebrate yet another election victory, they have no idea that they are on the eve of a nightmare that is going to devastate their lives.

After a high-profile murder, campaign manager Katherine Sumner has disappeared. Is she the killer? Or will the information she has on top government officials make hers the next body to turn up on the coroner's table?

Certain that Katherine is alive and in hiding, acclaimed reporter Laurie Forbes joins forces with Rachel Hendon to search out the truth behind one of the world's most secretive and dangerous organisations.

In a gripping tale of forbidden love, uncontrolled passion and the ultimate exploitation of power, *Wicked Beauty* proves there really is a crime worse than murder . . .

arrow books

ALSO AVAILABLE IN ARROW

Intimate Strangers

Susan Lewis

Investigative journalist, Laurie Forbes, is planning her wedding to Elliot Russell, when she receives a tip-off that a group of illegally smuggled women is being held somewhere in the East End of London. During her search unexpected and devastating events begin throwing her own life into chaos, so fellow journalist, Sherry MacElvoy steps in to help. Taking on undercover roles to get to the heart of the ruthless gang of human-traffickers, neither reporter can ever begin to imagine what dangers they are about to face.

Neela is one of the helpless Indian girls being held in captivity. Her fear is not only for herself, but her six-year-old niece, Shaila. A disfiguring birthmark has so far saved Neela from abuse, but she knows it is only a matter of time before she is sent for – and worse, before Shaila is taken. Her desperate bids to seek outside help are constantly thwarted, until finally she, and the women with her, agree there is only one way out . . .

'Spellbinding – you just keep turning the pages, with the atmosphere growing more and more intense as the story leads to its dramatic climax' *Daily Mail*

'Mystery and romance *par excellence*' *Sun*

arrow books